QUEEN'S GIFT

QUEEN'S GIFT

By Inglis Fletcher

Queens House

Larchmont, New York

Republished 1979 by Special Arrangement
with The Bobbs-Merrill Company, Inc.

Copyright© 1952 by The Bobbs-Merrill Company, Inc.

Library of Congress Cataloging in Publication Data

Fletcher, Inglis Clark, 1888-1969.
  Queen's gift.

  Reprint of the 1952 ed. published by Bobbs-
Merrill, Indianapolis.
  I. Title.
[PZ3.F6336Qe 1978]   [PS3511.L449]   813'.5'2   78-5778
ISBN 0-89244-005-8

QUEENS HOUSE
Larchmont, New York 10538

Manufactured in the United States of America

FOR JOCK

*And his generation.
They are the inheritors of
the noble young Americans
whose courage and determination
gave us our liberties.
Their far-seeing wisdom
gave us our Constitution,
the rock on which our republic
stands today in strength and unity.*

To the Freemen of the Town of Edenton
Gentlemen:

The distinguished honour of having been unanimously elected your Representative in the ensuing convention, without the least solicitation on my part, has made an impression on my heart which no time or circumstances can efface. My gratitude for it is inexpressible, but I am sensible will be shown in the most proper manner, by the zeal and fidelity with which it will be equally my duty and pleasure to execute this important trust. I shall have nothing to lament, but that my abilities will fall so far short of my ardent ambition to serve you. Under the conviction of my present sentiments, that the security of every thing dear to us depends on our adoption of the proposed constitution, I consider it one of the most awful subjects that was ever proposed for the consideration of a free people, and in giving it my utmost support (as I probably shall do), I shall have occasion for all the strength I can derive from the pleasing consciousness that in so doing I shall truly speak the respectable sense of my constituents. This will animate me beyond every thing in what I conceive the cause of Truth and Liberty. . . .

But I am convinced the more narrowly the constitution is examined by impartial minds, the more highly it must be approved; and from the consideration of our present critical situation, it will, perhaps, be deemed the only probable means of safety we have left.

I am, gentlemen, with the greatest respect and attachment,

Your faithful and obedient servant,

Jas. Iredell

1788

FOREWORD

THIS is the story of a village and a plantation during the years that followed Lord Cornwallis' surrender at Yorktown and of North Carolina's ratification of the Federal Constitution in 1789. The political struggle between Federalist and Antifederalist was nowhere more bitter than in North Carolina, the last state but one to approve the Constitution.

Since Edenton was the seat of the Federalists, I have chosen it as the village to represent all the villages, and Queen's Gift to represent the plantation life of the Colonial and Revolutionary periods.

Edenton was incorporated in 1722, but it flourished as a village many years before that date. Earlier it was called Queen Anne's Town, and it grew during her reign. The plantation grants dated back as far as Charles II and his eight Lords Proprietors. Edenton was once the capital of the colony and the residence of the Royal Governors, some of whom rest under flat marble tombs in the churchyard of old St. Paul's.

Since the wealth of the state was derived from agriculture, the planters who owned the productive lands along the waterways were of utmost importance. They produced the money crop, tobacco; they raised the pigs and sheep and cattle needed for food; their forests produced tar, pitch and turpentine, so vital to naval stores, for foreign trade. Their cotton crop was of growing importance to the state's economy. In addition, many planters served in the government of their state and their country.

At the time of the Revolution the Borough of Edenton had six hundred inhabitants. Of these, five men were of national importance. They play their part in this story.

For the sake of story unity the actual incidents have been compressed into the period between the two conventions assembled to consider ratification of the new Constitution—the Hillsborough Convention of 1788 and the Fayetteville Convention of 1789. Dates of historical significance have not been altered, but incidents of lesser importance are used wherever they add value to the story line. For instance, Lady Anne Stuart visited Edenton a few years earlier than the novel indicates, and Thomas Barker actually died a few months before the starting date I have selected.

To-day Edenton—old Queen Anne's Town or the Town on Queen Anne's Creek—still retains the flavor of Colonial life. The old Courthouse, Cupola House, St. Paul's Church are in daily use. The homes of many men who helped to establish our nation are still residences. In these parlous times "it gives one to think" and reflect on the sturdy independence, the courage and integrity of these men. It took patience to mould the ploughshare from the sword, to weld the ideals of liberty and freedom into a union firm enough to perpetuate the goals for which Americans had fought with such bravery and singleness of purpose.

This is the last of seven novels in the Carolina Series, which begins with the first attempted colonization by the English on Roanoke Island and ends with the state's ratification of the Constitution in 1789.

This does not mean that I shall write no more historical novels with a North Carolina background. It does mean that the characters, some of whom have appeared in several books, are making their farewells. Let us hope that each of them has played his part worthily in interpreting his period in the long-neglected history of North Carolina.

Among printed works I cordially acknowledge my indebtedness to: *Life and Correspondence of James Iredell* by Griffith J. McRee; *Colonial Records of North Carolina; James Madison: Father of the Constitution* by Irving Brant; *Ratification of the Federal Constitution in North Carolina* by Louise Irby Trenholme; and *Ante-Bellum North Carolina* by Guion Griffis Johnson. For unprinted material I am indebted to the State Historical Commission's Archives for use of the Charles Johnson collection and the Norcom papers. Also to the Hayes collection of Governor Samuel Johnston's papers; the Chowan County Courthouse records (Edenton); papers of the Revolutionary period; and the Cupola House records, cared for by the Shepard-Pruden Memorial Library in Edenton. To Mr. Blackwell P. Robinson for research on Wilie Jones of Halifax; and to Professor Hugh Lefler, Department of History, University of North Carolina, whom I consulted for sources of North Carolina history.

INGLIS FLETCHER

Bandon Plantation
Edenton, North Carolina
June 30, 1952

CONTENTS

Book One

EDENTON

Book Two

HILLSBOROUGH

Book Three
QUEEN'S GIFT

BOOK ONE

Edenton

People will never look forward to posterity
who never look back to their ancestors.

—EDMUND BURKE

The Doctor

1
DR. ARMITAGE spoke to his bay mare and by a gentle pull on the rein turned his riding-chair off the dusty Virginia Road into the heavier dust of Broad Street.

Edenton lay before his eyes, clinging close to the tawny waters of Albemarle Sound. Neatly encompassed between the meanderings of Queen Anne's Creek and the wider waters of Pembroke Creek, the village presented a beauty at sunset that was absent when the sun was at its zenith. The sky cast a golden glow over the Sound at the end of the street and the small white houses took on the same gold until there seemed no break in the sky colour except where it was interrupted by the dark mass of the trees on the opposite shore. There giant cypresses left the earth-banks and waded out into the glittering water, forming a green barrier between the golden water and the golden sky.

The doctor drank in the beauty of the sky and its water reflection. That day he had fought a valiant but losing fight against death. He was weary in body and soul. An old friend had passed away, one the county could ill afford to lose in these troublous days.

It was early July in the year of 1788, a year of turmoil and stress. Not of war, for the revolt against England had been won. Freedom was something more than a dream of brave men. What had begun at Lexington had been finished at Yorktown. Freedom from oppression was a living reality, within the grasp of men of the New World. But the fighting had not ended with the battles. It was flaming again in the land, from the north to the south, throughout all the thirteen states.

Now it was a struggle between brothers. A Constitution had been framed in Philadelphia. Its advocates said it would replace the loose league of states formed under the old Articles of Confederation with a strong and enduring union. It would secure liberty and peace, provide a strong defence and strengthen business and commerce.

But not all men were of one mind. Last September the Constitution had been sent to each state, there to be ratified or rejected. A tempest of debate had broken. Opponents denounced the new plan as a plot to rob the states of independence and impose tyranny on the plain people. They bitterly attacked its failure to provide a bill of rights. Nowhere was the strife fiercer than in North Carolina.

Dr. Armitage's mind was troubled. For the past months he had seen old friendships torn, neighbours warring with neighbours, families divided. Scurrilous articles against public men appeared in papers, in pamphlets and broadsides. Men's reputations were assailed, the lie was given to public officials. The integrity of men lately praised as heroes of a great war, nobly fought and nobly won, was challenged. All heroic behaviour was forgotten, lost in the torrent of invective, of aspersion, of accusation. Evil forces entered, blotting out the heroic days, scattering disturbance and dissension over a land struggling to rise above the ravages of war and battle.

As a surgeon the doctor had seen war at its worst. At Guilford Courthouse, at Yorktown, through the long days in the Dismal Swamp with men dying of deadly fever, he had fought to save lives for the future. Then he had believed that when the battles were won men could go back to the old patterns of living. It seemed now a vain hope, for men had changed. Something had entered them, a hardness, an unrest for which there was no surcease. Of one thing he was certain: he would not be a party to their disputes. Let the politicians wrangle. He was a man of peace. His business was to heal the sick, to bring new life into the world, to ease the last hours of those who were leaving life. But the doctor knew it would be hard to hold aloof. Conventions in eight states had ratified the Constitution. Approval by one more would put a new government into effect. News was expected at any moment from Virginia and New Hampshire. Men would talk of nothing but politics and of the meeting in Hillsborough this month when North Carolina would make her decision.

The sun was below the cathedrallike spires of trees across the Sound. Few people walked the streets. Men had gone home from work in the shops, the law offices, the forges. Thin spirals of grey smoke rose from chimneys where slaves had started the supper fires. A few men worked in their little gardens, tending rose vines, cutting flowers, or moved about the rows of carrots and rutabagas and greens of their kitchen-gardens. Children on the lawns sang "King William was King James's son" as they played an old game; their young voices rose high and sweet. Here was peace. Here was a village as it should be.

The mare quickened her pace as she turned of her own accord into the gates of Cupola House. The candles were lighted, and in the outside kitchen the slaves moved about, preparing the doctor's lonely supper.

He experienced the feeling of content that always came to him when he approached his own hearth. He had long since overcome the sadness caused by the death of his wife. When his daughter had drowned herself after her *fiancé* had been killed in the Revolution, he had met that sorrow with a philosophy born of close association with birth and death.

His body servant Crit held the door wide for the doctor. "Cook, she say 'tain't no time for no great dressin' and fixin'. She done ready to push de pan of batter bread into de oven. She say de bread falls flat if hit sits too long."

"Tell cook not to push the bread into the oven until I give the word. I want to bathe. I'm dusty as a shoat, riding twelve miles from Rockahock on dusty roads."

"Yes, sar. Dat I know. Bath all laid. First I fix a little tot of rum for your tiredness. Mr. Johnston's boy Jack done fetch us a little keg of rum from Jamaica."

The doctor sank down in a fireside chair and stretched out his long thin legs while the slave removed his dusty boots, poured a portion of rum into a glass and filled it to the brim with hot water.

"Better you drink it hot, sar. It's best for weariness."

The doctor sipped the hot mixture. The liquor was comfortingly warm to his stomach. "Give me a pipe, Crit," he said.

The slave shook his head. "Now, sar, I laid out a fresh shirt and your blue nankin small-clothes and some white hose. 'Tain't no time to set a smokin' wid water all hot in your little sittin' tub."

The doctor's tone was querulous. "I've changed my mind. I'll have my supper first, then bathe and go early to bed."

Crit paid no attention. He began to peel off the doctor's hose. "Yes, sar, Liza she fluted them little ruffles same like in Mr. Hewes's funeral shirt. It looks might' fine since she set dat hot crimpin' iron in de linen, and I done washed and combed your new tie-wig Dr. Williamson sent down from New York."

The doctor rose into a sitting position. "Crit, you rascal, speak out. What's going on to-night that I have to get into my new nankin breeches and a ruffled linen shirt? Who was here today while I was in the country?"

"Many people, sar. Some no accounts want you to fetch new babies, cure their ague; mamas bring children wid cuts and broken heads. De captain, he didn't stay long."

"The captain?"

"Yes, sar."

The doctor looked at his slave with exasperation. He well knew that he could not hurry the man, who, with his native sense of the dramatic, always waited to tell his big news until the last.

"People came from Tyrrell. Dey said ague was comin' up might' bad, sar. Mostes' everybody dey shiver and shake every third day."

"Crit, don't wait to break the news gently. Do I have to go across the Sound to-night?"

"No, sar. Dey go to Dr. Norcom when dey find you have gone out Virginia Road."

"Well, what is it then?"

From long experience with the doctor's whims Crit had learned to approach his master from the blind side when it came to relaying unpleasant news about a trip to a birthing after midnight or a journey to an outlying plantation to decide whether a slave had cholera, pox or a case of poison ivy. To-night Crit must be tactful. He poured a third toddy. Actually he was on the horns of a dilemma: an irate cook in the kitchen whose batter bread might be ruined by delay, and the doctor's wrath when he was told he would be obliged to go out.

Twice he started to speak, but decided against it. After supper would be a better time.

The doctor was relaxed and happy after the third portion of rum. He reached for his long-stemmed clay pipe that hung in a rack near the mantel.

Crit was at his elbow, assisting him to rise. "Now, master, de bath is laid. Plenty of hot soapy water like you said. Yes, sar, warm and soapy, and your pretty shirt all ready."

The doctor grinned. "You old rascal! You've got some reason for dressing me up like a fine dandy. Out with it."

"Best you eaten you supper first, sar."

"So I'll be in a good humour?"

The black man held up both his hands. "How you speak, sar! Ain't you always in good humour, sar? Jes' yesserday I told Mr. Johnston's boy Jack dat I had de goodest-humoured master in de whole of Chowan County."

The doctor did not answer. He went into his bedroom, stripped off his under-garments and stepped into the oval tin tub. Crit took up a sponge and soaped his back silently. There was a time for speech and a time for silence. The doctor wanted silence when he bathed.

Crit removed the plates, placed a decanter of Madeira in front of his master and wiped an invisible speck from a cotton-stem glass. When the doctor had poured the ruby wine a maid brought in a bowl of Staffordshire blue filled with red-cheeked peaches.

"Mistress Mary Rutledge she bring dem."

"I hope you thanked her properly. Did she leave any message?"

"Yes, sar, I did, an' no, sar, she didn't. She jes' say she hope you enjoys 'em all right."

Crit, seeing his master's humour was good, said, "Captain Meredith he say he liken you to step out to he ship. He say he got somethin' matter wid he crew. Maybe plague, maybe pox. Somethin' catchin'."

The doctor set the wine-glass on the table. "So that's your bad news. I thought there was something, the way you have been waiting on me so attentively. Where's his ship? At Joe Hewes's dock?"

"No, sar. He's ship she's ridin' out on de water by de Dram Tree."

"Damnation! I'm not going out on the bay to-night. Why, I wouldn't go for General George Washington. Not to-night. Why did you get me all rigged up in this shirt if I have to go out on the bay in that leaky boat of mine? Blast it, are you crazy?"

"Not no more'n usual, Doctor. The captain he say please to come over to

Horniblow's after your supper. He would be pleased to see you dere. Like as not he take you to he ship."

"Let him come here. Send a boy over to invite him to have a glass with me."

"Sar, 'tain't only the captain. It's some fine folk from London what come on he's ship. Ladies and gen'lem'ns dat have high-soundin' names. Dat's why I got out your beses' ruffled shirt. I knowed you don't want dose fine people with high-soundin' names to think you are country. Now do you?"

"I suppose not," the doctor grumbled as he rose from the table. "Well, what are you standing there for? Bring me my cape and my stick. The one with the gold knob."

"And your new hat from Dr. Williamson?"

"All right, all right, my new hat. I suppose I must make myself into a macaroni for these ladies and gentlemen with big names."

As Crit opened the wide front door the wind came with a rush. The candles in their tall glass protectors sputtered and went out. The doctor muttered something about the weather. Crit said, "De devil he have a big breath to-night." A small Negro boy was waiting on the stoop, holding a glass lanthorn. Its single candle made a light, but Dr. Armitage was so familiar with the way up King Street to Horniblow's Tavern that he could have walked the distance blindfold.

He pushed the door of the tavern. It opened from Stygian darkness into the warm brightness of the great room. A dozen voices welcomed him. Tavern slaves took his cloak, his three-cornered hat and his stick. At the end of the room two planters, Jimmy Blount and Lem Creecy, were seated at a small table engaged in a game of draughts. A crowd of townsfolk and planters were gathered about the billiard-table, where Nat Allen and young Vail were playing off a game. The clicking balls made a quick, merry sound, interspersed with the thuds of darts hitting the board in the far corner of the room where a game was in progress. Other groups were at tables, tankards of ale in hand, talking crops and politics. Frequent laughter came from a group of younger men who were telling rowdy tales over their brandy.

In the evenings yeomen and planters were accustomed to join townsfolk in a bit of frolicking, enjoy masculine society and discuss their crops. To-night they wanted to hear the latest political news from the Congress in New York. They wanted to discuss reports in the *State Gazette* of the Virginia convention where Madison fought for his Constitution against Patrick Henry's fiery eloquence. Each man had partisans here.

Horniblow, the tavern keeper, came out from behind the bar and made his way across the room to the doctor. The tavern keeper was a big man who had once been rotund. He had befriended the traitor Benedict Arnold when his ship came into Edenton. For a time after that he had lost weight as well as custom. But people forgot. After all, what did it matter? Arnold had long since made his way to England, where he was shunned.

Horniblow said, "Captain Meredith is in the small room behind the bar. He wants that you join him there."

Dr. Armitage found Meredith, captain of the *Devon Maid*, at a long table, a decanter of Madeira before him. Samuel Johnston, whose plantation home Hayes lay on Queen Anne's Creek, was seated across from the captain.

Meredith was talking. "The lady is travelling with her husband, Baron von Pollnitz. I was assured by the ship's agent in Bordeaux that she is the daughter of my Lord Bute. She hasn't given up her father's name. Lady Anne Stuart, she calls herself. The Baron has been Chamberlain in the Prussian Court. I cannot of my own knowledge vouch for this, but they conduct themselves as people of importance. Especially my Lady, who has a rare flashing temper and a degree of arrogance that is beyond common. They have letters to Mr. Cabarrus from a relative of his in France."

Samuel Johnston, the political leader of North Carolina, had been made Governor last year. He was a tall, solemn man of excellent features and brooding eyes. He tapped the table in front of him absently with an index finger as he spoke. "I think it will be best not to accept these people into our homes until we have consulted Stephen Cabarrus."

Meredith nodded, a twinkle in his blue eyes. "Always cautious, Sam. Always cautious." He spoke with the freedom of an old friend.

Mr. Johnston's back stiffened. "It is well to be cautious these days, Captain, with every ship that lands on our shore filled with the riff-raff of Europe."

"These folk aren't riff-raff, I do assure you, Sam. They're gentlefolk without question. Even I, a rough sailor, can see that." Meredith lifted his glass to his lips and brushed a lank lock of dark hair from his eyes. His face was red from wind and salt spray, and his eyes were set in a fine network of sun lines. His mouth was wide and cornered with good humour, though he was a strict disciplinarian on shipboard.

The doctor interrupted the talk about these strange high-born folk. "My man says you've sickness aboard your vessel, Captain."

A look of annoyance crossed the captain's face. "Aye, that I have. They've been treated by a young doctor I have aboard. Since some who are sick will disembark and be in your charge, I thought you'd best have a look at them." He pushed back the tankard and started to rise.

The doctor spoke quickly. "Wait a minute, wait a minute. Is there any one dangerously ill on board who needs immediate medication?"

"No, the doctor—he's a Scot called Moray—says not. Those who were dangerously ill have been sewed up in canvas and heaved overboard."

"As bad as that? How many?" the doctor asked.

"Four, and one of my own sailors. A sort of spotted high fever and a stricture of the lungs, a fight for breath."

"Did their bodies grow black and puff after death?"

Meredith laughed shortly. "I don't think so. We tossed them over the side mighty soon after they died. Were you thinking of plague?"

"Yes, or pox. Did you have lemons aboard?"

"Plenty. Oranges too. We docked at Cadiz after we left Bordeaux. It's not scurvy, I'm sure of that. Moray doesn't think it's plague, but he wants your opinion."

"If it isn't an emergency, I'll come out in the morning, Captain."

The captain hesitated. "I almost promised her Ladyship I'd get you out so she and her husband and their party could sleep ashore to-night."

"Any of them sick?" the doctor asked. He was disinclined to go out on the choppy waters in a small boat for the whim of an arrogant woman.

"No, but she's making an almighty row about staying on that 'stinking ship' another night." The captain looked beset and harassed.

The doctor grinned. "I'll send out a powder to put her to sleep, if you like."

"Will you, Doctor? It would please me mightily to be free of her talk."

Johnston asked the captain, "What of the husband? A nobleman, you said?"

"Yes, Baron von Pollnitz. They have two little boys with them and a young woman, Mistress Sylvia Hay. She reads with the children, a sort of governess. And Lady Anne has a maidservant."

"An entourage, no less," observed Armitage. "Sam, we must see Stephen Cabarrus to-morrow and ask questions."

"Cabarrus has gone to Halifax. There is a meeting about plans for the convention this month. He is on some committee of delegates." No one spoke for a moment. Johnston's lips tightened. "I hope Cabarrus doesn't allow himself to come under the spell of Antifederalists in Halifax. But that is hardly likely. He's convinced merchants like him need the Constitution. We'll have his vote at Hillsborough."

Captain Meredith changed the subject. "I've got a mighty fine cargo of goods for Hewes and Smith. Tell your ladies, will you? Silks and brocades from Lyons, muslins and dress lengths of calico from India. For the gentlemen French brandy and port from Lisbon." He rose from the table. "Well, Doctor, if you won't go back to the ship with me, I'll say good night, gentlemen."

The doctor said, "Wait a minute." He reached into a pocket and took out a small leather case. He opened it, selected a bottle, shook some powder into a bit of paper and twisted the ends. "Here, give this to her Ladyship in a cup of water."

The captain thrust the paper into an inner pocket. "Thanks, Doctor. Thanks. It will be a relief to be shed of her complaints. I don't care if she sleeps past the meridian to-morrow."

"I'll be aboard by ten," Dr. Armitage promised.

The captain made his way out through the crowded tap-room. His progress was slow, for he was stopped over and again to answer questions about his cargo, the state of affairs in France and Spain. Yes, he had newspapers, for six months back. Yes, he had heard that Mr. Jefferson was still in France. Yes, Europeans were deeply interested in news of America. Hundreds of young men from France, from Italy, were eager to come over to live under a new government. Surely, there were plenty of sceptics, especially the old. They thought the American idea could not succeed.

The questioners would have kept him, asking endless questions, but he held them off. "My ship will be in for a week," he said, laughing. "I'll stand on the Courthouse steps and answer questions all day long, if you like."

Horniblow accompanied him to the door. "How did you find things in London, Captain?"

"The merchants are glad enough the war is over. They felt the pinch, losing American trade. It will pleasure them to take up where the war interrupted."

Horniblow followed him onto the gallery. He dropped his voice, asked his question hesitatingly. "Did you see Arnold in London, Captain?"

Meredith's eyes were cold, speculative. "Yes," he said shortly, "I did. He's having a rough time. The British don't like traitors any more than we do, though they use them to their advantage in time of war."

Horniblow watched the sailor cross the Green until he disappeared, the lanthorn he carried bobbing up and down, shining dimly in the darkness.

Samuel Johnston filled a pipe, tamping the tobacco into the clay bowl with his thin fingers. "Meredith's a good man. He did yeoman service for our cause, running that ship of his into blockaded ports during the war. Yeoman service. Danger meant nothing to him if he could bring in a wanted cargo."

The doctor filled his pipe and lighted it with a candle. "I wonder who his passengers are. What would Bute's daughter be doing in Edenton? Or her husband either? We've got enough against Bute to hang him as high as Haman if he set foot on our shores. He was a bad influence. Being the King's friend, he always advised him——"

"Wrongly in this instance," Johnston said. "I wonder if he rests at night, he and North. . . ."

"Or the King either," Armitage added. "He lost the goose that laid the golden egg when he lost the colonies." He paused, then continued. "Sam, the farmers out Rockahock way are wondering when conditions of trade will improve. They want a fair price for the tobacco in Carolina markets, and they want to be paid in sound money."

Johnston spoke impatiently. "Tobacco! Always tobacco! Can't they wait long enough for the Constitution to be ratified? They're not alone in their complaint. Merchants and mechanics as well have felt the baneful influence of this currency. Only a strong federal government can help."

"Tobacco is their living," Armitage said mildly.

At that moment the door opened, and James Iredell and Nat Allen came in. With them was Josiah Bernard, a stranger from "out north" who had opened a printing office in Edenton. He and Allen were inseparable. The town knew him for a shrewd fellow who had lived in Boston and New York.

Iredell hung his hat on a peg, took his pipe from the rack and sat down at the table. Allen went to the door and clapped his hands loudly. When the pot-boy came he ordered ale. Iredell said he would have a bottle of Teneriffe; he understood Horniblow had a new pipe of the gentle wine.

Johnston asked, "When did you return, Jemmy? I thought you were going to Halifax and then on to Hillsborough."

"I went only as far as Halifax. The news I had there sent me back to you. Nat and Mr. Bernard, for whom he vouches, were in the outer room. I asked them to attend what I have to report." Iredell paused as a waiter entered the room. "Close the door when you leave," he said.

"Shall I hang up the 'reserved' sign, sir?" The boy looked at Samuel Johnston.

"Yes, and tell Mr. Horniblow to show Mr. Hooper to this room when he comes down."

"Yes, sir. I will, sir."

Iredell looked up in surprise. "Hooper is here?"

"He arrived an hour ago from Hillsborough. He's come to confer with you and me. It's fortunate you returned." Johnston smiled at Iredell. This man who had married Johnston's favorite sister, Hannah, was the chief strength of the Federalists in North Carolina.

"Fortunate indeed! My news will cheer a man who signed the Declaration. With your permission, gentleman, I shall not give it until he arrives."

When he stood beside the tall Johnston, James Iredell seemed almost a lad in size. In spite of his great legal knowledge, which had made him attorney general and judge, he retained a young lad's enthusiasm. He was a legal defender without peer in his state and a dispassionate judge whose one thought was to establish law and maintain order according to law. He made no hasty judgements. He was careful, deliberate in decisions, and he had the respect of all parties for his fairness. Iredell was a man of vision, one of the few who saw beyond known horizons into the distant future. The turmoil and bickering of the Congress of the states were minor things to him, for he looked past the present unrest. Every law that was passed, every act of the state assembly he examined in the light of the future. Laws of exigency carried little weight with him, for James Iredell was born an Englishman, brought up with the Englishman's respect for law. When he forswore his native land and espoused the cause of the rebellious colonists he had always in mind that the new country, a child of the old, would grow in grace, in knowledge, through its earnest and fundamental desire for liberty under law.

Even now he was defending the rights of the Tories to a proper compensation for their property which had been seized in the war. It was an unpopular defence among the unthinking and impatient folk. For Iredell it was part of his inherent belief that law should protect each and every citizen, from the lowest to the highest. He was profoundly disturbed by the contest between Federalist and Antifederalist. He was afraid that continued controversy might wreck the new state before it had time to start its growth.

The enmity of public men, Federalist and Antifederalist, was more bitter, more vocal in North Carolina than anywhere else. Iredell employed his voice and facile pen to urge the need for a strong federal system with each state fitting into the framework of the central government. In this he followed James Madison, who had guided the framing of the Constitution. Many men whose ability Iredell respected were outspoken against Madison's union of states. Wilie Jones of the neighbouring town of Halifax was as strong a leader of the Antifederalists as Samuel Johnston was of the Federalists.

All this passed through the mind of Dr. Armitage as they sipped their Madeira and their Teneriffe. He understood that no word of a political nature would be spoken until William Hooper joined them. Before they had drunk their second glass Hooper entered the room.

Hooper—the Signer, as he was called to distinguish him from his brother —was a handsome man, honest, with a nervous intensity that at times caused alarm among his friends. He had not entirely recovered from the horrible anxiety he had experienced when his wife and family were captured by the British. Armitage looked at Will Hooper now with the eye of a physician. He was too thin, too much on edge. The man has the most tragic eyes I have ever beheld in a mortal, the doctor thought. If I were his physician I'd order him to bed for a complete rest.

The men had risen as Hooper entered and they remained standing until he sat down. Samuel Johnston took the high seat at the end of the table, since he was the acknowledged leader among them. Wherever Johnston was, there was formality. He took some papers from a case and laid them on the table. Iredell took two letters from his pocket.

Dr. Armitage knocked the dottle from his pipe into the ash receiver and hung it up in the rack under his number. He said, "I'll be moving along before you gentlemen get too deep into your political discussion."

"I wish you would show more interest in state affairs, Armitage," Johnston said. "County, too, for that matter."

Armitage grinned. "I'm showing a lot of interest in the county affairs, looking after the people's health. There's a rash of birthing, as there always is after wars. Death-rate is up, and I regret to say our town has a number of young men who have learned licentiousness and show a great propensity for visiting lewd houses and brothels . . . with the usual results."

Johnston paid no heed to the last statement, but went on. "Your knowledge of the country people is greater than anyone else's, so your influence is——"

Armitage interrupted. "I think there are too many physicians who have given up the practice of medicine to become politicians."

Johnston started to reply, but James Iredell forestalled him. "I suppose you mean Dr. Williamson's leaving us for New York to sit in the Congress. I agree with you that his skill as a surgeon is great, and we all know how valuable he was as chief surgeon of the southern armies under General Greene. But, much as we need his skill as a surgeon, we need more his wisdom, his political acumen in the national scene. He served us well when he helped frame the Constitution."

Johnston spoke heavily. "We are in vastly troubled times, as deep as we were during the Revolution. Williamson is invaluable where he is. I realize that his absence leaves more work for you and Dr. Norcom, but we need you in state affairs also."

Armitage hesitated, his hat under his arm.

Iredell's eyes held those of Armitage. After a pause he said, "I know of no one who is as close to the people of the country as you are, Armitage, and your name commands respect everywhere in the state. You could render important service to the Federalists. A word from you would quiet the fears of the doubtful. You might win over reluctant ones who are playing with the idea of supporting Wilie Jones's Antifederalists. We must convince all our people of the wisdom of adopting the Constitution. The security of everything dear to us depends on it. It is imperative that we have unity in this matter. What I have to say to these gentlemen will convince you of that. Stay to hear me."

The doctor shook his head. His deep-set eyes were fixed on Iredell. "I'm outside politics, Jemmy. I did my share during the war years. My work is to look after the county's health, not its politics. I can't divide myself into two parts."

Iredell pleaded, "The freemen of Chowan trust you, Armitage, more than they trust Sam Johnston or me. Do you want North Carolina to stand alone outside the union of states? Your silence will hurt us. It will help Wilie Jones."

The doctor's mouth straightened. "Wilie Jones is a friend of mine. I have heard you praise him before these political differences arose. His side may have merit. Perhaps, as some say, we should refuse to sign until the Constitution has a bill of rights. I don't know." His voice took on an edge. "This I do know. I don't break with old friends because we have different political opinions."

James Iredell said, "Wilie Jones is an able and sincere man, though I think him tragically wrong. Let's not argue that matter now. Don't give a decision, Doctor, until you understand fully our danger. We do need you." Armitage made a movement as though to put on his hat. Iredell laid a hand on the doctor's arm. "Wait. Give me only a few minutes." He turned to the others. "I want you all to hear the letter from Hugh Williamson I found when I returned from Halifax. It gives added urgency to the other news I have." Iredell picked up one of the letters he had placed on the table and began to read. His voice was quiet, yet it held a strangely compelling quality.

"New York, 11th June '88
"Dear Sir:

"The public papers have not for many days afforded us any news. All expectation is turned toward Virginia. We take it for granted, I do at least, that North Carolina will follow Virginia in adopting or rejecting. If Virginia becomes part of the new union, then certainly we must. Any other course would expose us to the gravest dangers.

"Before he left New York in March, I heard Madison speak on this point. At a dinner which I attended, he spoke of his most earnest hope that the six states which had approved the Constitution would be joined soon by the three necessary to put its principles into effect. He was then asked whether, if nine states should approve, any state or states could hope to effect additions to or changes in the Constitution by withholding approval until they were accomplished.

"Madison's reply was so excellent and forceful in its logic that, when I arrived home, I wrote it down as I remembered it. I give it to you now. He said that the majority might with propriety say to the minority, 'It is not proper, decent or right in you to demand that we reverse what we have done. Place confidence in us as we have in one another—and then we shall freely and dispassionately consider your propositions, and endeavour to gratify your wishes; but if you do not do this, it is more reasonable that you should yield to us than we to you. You cannot exist without us—you must be a member of the union.'

"You well know that I was not always in agreement with Madison during the Philadelphia convention. With Martin, Davie, Spaight, and Blount, I sought to guard and promote the interests of North Carolina. Our hopes were sometimes defeated. Yet, in the general interest, our reservations are not important. I know that you will endorse with me Madison's sentiments as I have expressed them to you. They but emphasize our peril if a federal union is formed without us. I pray for the success of your efforts at Hillsborough.

"If the good delegates there should think it fit to submit to such services as Mr. Samuel Johnston can render, I hope he will not fail to serve as president. His wisdom enlists the confidence of all.

"I am, my dear Iredell,
"your admirer and friend,
"HUGH WILLIAMSON."

Hooper said, "Williamson puts the matter well. I confess that I came to Edenton in the hope that I might sooner hear the final result of the deliberations in Virginia. At Hillsborough I have been kept in a state of anxious ignorance. One day I am encouraged by a report that the Constitution is being embraced by a large majority. On the next I have an account that its approval is in doubt."

Iredell leaned forward. "I can relieve your anxiety, sir. I returned from Halifax because I met a special-dispatch rider who entrusted me with a message for Samuel." He passed the second letter before him to Johnston. "I think it fitting that he tell you of it."

Johnston read and rose to his feet. "Gentlemen, Virginia has approved the Constitution! There is as yet no news from the New Hampshire convention. It is believed possible that favourable action there may have preceded Virginia's. But of this we are sure: at least nine states have come into the union. I propose a toast to the new union. May God grant that North Carolina join it!"

The men rose and solemnly drank the toast. Iredell turned to Johnston. "You see, Samuel, you are called. I think you can be elected to preside over the convention. You must not refuse. Virginia's action does not make the issue sure, but it makes the cost of failure certain."

The young merchant, Nat Allen, had kept silent while his elders talked. Now he said, "Then serious trouble will break out sure as fate. The news from Virginia will win over few Antifederalists in North Carolina. They will be no less determined to defeat the Constitution. All the talk we've had before is nothing to what will come now."

Josiah Bernard emptied his glass and moved unsteadily along the table. "Watch our trade, gentlemen. Protect our trade lest we be undone by northern states."

"You're drunk, Mr. Bernard," Dr. Armitage said mildly. "Let me take you home."

"I'm not drunk, Doctor, just full of reality. No theories like the political fellows. Just tot up the ledger both sides, the winning and the losing, and where do the merchants stand then, gentlemen? Where do they stand?"

No one answered. The man might be in his cups, but he had spoken the truth. That's what they must do. Tot up the ledger.

They walked from the room, through the noise and commotion of the tavern and into the street. Hooper accompanied the others though he was staying at Tomblow's. A breeze was stirring but the night was clear.

"A beautiful evening, gentlemen," Iredell said, "but political weather is making. Mr. Hooper will want to finish our talk to-night since he's returning to Hillsborough in the morning. Sam, come along to my house. We'll sit late with the news and our plans. Nat? Dr. Armitage, surely now you see the wisdom——" He broke off as the doctor took Bernard's arm and signalled to his lanthorn-bearer.

"Thank you, Jemmy," Dr. Armitage said, "but, as you see, I have another duty." He smiled as Iredell bowed slightly and moved off with the others. Then he and Bernard started to walk slowly along King Street toward

Broad. The feeble light held by the lanthorn-bearer cast weird shadows. Bernard's tongue was loosened by the wine. "I'm a lawyer of sorts, Dr. Armitage, and a merchant of sorts, but I'm no politician, though I've listened to enough political talk to be one." He paused and fumbled tó adjust his hat. "I knew Joe Hewes in Philadelphia. Boarded in the same house. A great man he was, Joe Hewes, patriot. I well remember when he was running around among the members, begging for ships for John Paul Jones. Well, what happened to him? His patriotism killed him. Now he lies in Christ Churchyard, up in Philadelphia, an alien, far from his home—dead before his time, Doctor, as you know."

"Yes, I know, Josiah. But sometimes I think all men die at their own time."

"Sounds like Presbyterianism to me, Doctor, but I lose the point. Many a time I've heard Mr. Hewes say, 'It's a mistake for a merchant not to attend to what other merchants are doing and planning.' It seems to me that holds in politics as well. Not one of them mentioned what the opposition would do. They talked about your plans. They slipped there. Mr. Joe would have been asking, What is Wilie Jones planning? And Tim Bloodworth—what's he up to? Mark me, Doctor, the Antifederalists have a plan. Mr. Jefferson writes long letters from France, and Wilie Jones follows him like a sheep follows the bellwether."

Dr. Armitage paused at the service entrance of his house. "Perhaps you are right, Josiah. It's the old saying of the forest and the trees. Well, good night. Take the lanthorn, you've only a half block to go. Good night."

Bernard mumbled something and walked on. The doctor thought, This man has a certain wisdom.

The Village Awakes

2   LATE in the night the wind rose and there was rain. But the morning was fair. The air, rain-washed, was soft and so clear that the cypresses on the distant Tyrrell shore stood out as individual trees.

Dr. Armitage rose early. After his morning tea of yapon he went out to the little building in the garden that he used for a consulting room and surgery. Although it was not yet seven, four patients were waiting for him. The black boy who assisted in the dispensary was bottling Peru-bark mixture, and Dr. Armitage could tell at a glance that three of his patients required this remedy. Ague and chills. The late-summer flare-up was at hand, and eight out of ten patients wanted treatment for bonerack fever.

One man, a farmer whom Dr. Armitage knew slightly, lingered until the others had gone. His woman, he said, had grown a big belly while he was away in the western counties without chance to stretch himself on the bed. What was he to do? He was loath to accuse his wife of inconstancy; yet there she was, bloated out in front in a way to display her sins to the world.

The man's face was dark with anger, yet his eyes showed despair and disillusionment. "She was always a good woman," he kept repeating. "If it was war-time, I'da thought some soldier hada took her without her consent."

The doctor fingered the quill pen on the desk, taking it in and out of the sand.

"What'd you do, Doc? Sometimes I've a notion to give her seven strokes of the cat; but then my flesh cringes at such a thought."

The man loves this woman, the doctor thought. He knew little of these folks, who lived on a small farm up the Copper Neck. They were not patients of his. "What does she say?" he asked.

"Nothing. Nothing at all. She thinks I havena noticed. She's pitiful, she is. She's trying to hide herself under her ma's big India shawl. Says she's cold and got the shakes, but I think it's fear that makes her shiver when I come near her."

The doctor said, "Bring her in, Morris. Let me examine her. Mayhap she has a growth inside her that swells her up."

The man's face changed. He spoke slowly, twisting his cap in his work-worn hands. "I never thought of that, Doc, not once. Mayhap it's sinful I am, holding evil thoughts against a good woman. Thanky, sir. Thanky." He went away, walking swiftly, his head erect.

Gad, I almost hope I find a growth! the doctor thought. He put on his coat and left the dispensary for his morning walk. It was seven-thirty, and every day at this time he walked through the town from the Hewes and Smith shipyard to the Rope Walk or to the town gate at Queen Anne's Creek. The doctor loved these morning walks. They had been his habit ever since his arrival in America so many years ago. As he walked he recalled his coming to the Carolinas.

He had been young then and eager for a new career in America after a term at St. Bartholomew's Hospital in London. That he should come to Edenton had been the suggestion of Henry McCulloh, father of the Henry Eustace McCulloh who later became collector for the port of Roanoke, the name by which Edenton was once known. The younger McCulloh, as was the custom, administered his post from England, sending his young cousin James Iredell to Carolina as his deputy.

"There's only one surgeon in the whole district, and age is pushing him," Henry McCulloh had told Armitage. "Go over now and you can make your place in a new country. Your patients will be for the most part yeomen, the same sort of folk you find in your own Devon. You'll feel at home with them and with the gentry as well. There are good men there, educated men, with large plantations along the Sound. The minute it is known that you a West Country man, the county folk will flock to you."

McCulloh chuckled. "They'll pay you in produce. You'll lay in root vegetables for the winter, and barrels of salt pork and hams and bacon and tobacco. Tobacco is their money crop; the whole colony uses it for exchange. Get yourself a piece of land, if you can find one. Get a good tenant to farm it, and raise some leaf of your own. You'll find ships sailing from Virginia direct to your own Bideford, to the tobacco market there. Before you leave London I advise you to call on the North Carolina provincial agent Thomas Barker. Make arrangements to sell your leaf through him. He will see that you get top prices either at Bideford or on the Bristol market."

As he strolled Armitage recalled how foolish he had felt as he set out to arrange the sale of a crop before he had the crop or land to grow it on. But the elder McCulloh was a friend of his father and presumably an astute businessman, being a Scot. So Armitage had called on Thomas Barker to learn something more of the country to which he was going.

He found Barker in his office in Paternoster Row. A man of distinguished appearance, well dressed in the latest mode, a dark-blue coat, butter-coloured small-clothes and a purple waistcoat threaded in gold. He wore shoes of the French fashion—square toes, silver buckles and high heels painted red.

Mr. Barker complained that he had been several years away from America. He wished he could return, but he felt it his duty to remain as colonial agent as long as his country needed him. A colonial agent must be a man of integrity, preferably a solicitor with a deep knowledge of the law, who could be at ease with the highest as well as the lowest. He indicated to the young doctor that he, Barker, had all these qualifications.

Armitage had been impressed and had made a graceful speech about the Carolinas' good fortune in having so distinguished a representative. And indeed, the doctor reflected, Barker was a man of consequence. In Barker's office Samuel Johnston had acquired his knowledge of the law—the knowledge which he, in turn, had later passed along to an even more brilliant pupil, James Iredell.

After a time Barker had pulled a turnip watch from his waistcoat pocket, the seals of the fob dangling from his thin fingers. "See, it is close on to twelve. Suppose we step over to the Cheshire Cheese and have a glass of ale and one of mine host's famous rarebits."

Armitage was more than willing. He had been up since five and had had only one kipper before visiting the wards under his care at "Barts."

Thomas Barker was a good host and loved to talk about folk he knew in the Carolinas. Queen Anne's Town, as he called Edenton, furnished him with ample material for gossip. So it was from Thomas Barker that the doctor first learned of the Edenton families who were to become his patients and neighbours and friends in the years ahead. It seemed strange to remember that there had been a time when the Edenton names were unfamiliar to him. The men Barker had mentioned and men who had come to Albemarle after the doctor's arrival ran together through his mind: Iredell, Charleton, Beasley, Vail, Blount, Joseph Hewes, Parson Daniel Earle, Pollock of Balgray, the Dawsons of Eden House, Samuel Johnston of Hayes. . . .

The doctor's backward thoughts were interrupted. He had come to the Rope Walk. Already workingmen were at hand, busy with the piles of cordage. After acknowledging their friendly greeting, he turned back and retraced his steps along Water Street. At the foot of the Green he paused. The Pollock house was shuttered. The family and staff were at Balgray, where they spent most of the year. His eye fell on the red-brick Courthouse at the head of the Green, flanked by Hornblow's Tavern and the Hardys' West Indian house with double galleries. Across the Green, Josiah Collins' grounds took up the whole of the west side. The old captain had chosen the site for his town house with the same shrewdness he had shown in selecting his plantation on Lake Scuppernong across the Sound. A sea-captain's choice, directly on the shore of the little bay that curved in from the Sound and made a fine sheltered spot for the little village on Queen Anne's Creek.

Armitage lingered for a moment, looking up the Green from his position on Water Street. He thought, as he had often thought before, how well chosen was the site for the fine, dignified Courthouse, with its handsome clock-tower. Someday the village would have the funds to buy a clock. He sighed a little. The Revolution had come before the King could present the town with a clock like that he had given Hillsborough. The men of Chowan who had fought for freedom would scarcely regret the loss.

The doctor walked on to Broad Street, a fine thoroughfare—at present deep in dust—running north from the Sound. A mile from the water's edge it forked, the left road striking away northward to Suffolk in Virginia; the right angling off to cross the Yeopim and lead to the village of Hertford, from where it ran on across the Great Dismal Swamp to Norfolk in Virginia.

There was activity in the shops along Cheapside as the doctor wandered down Broad Street. The cordwainer's was already open. The shutters at the apothecary's were down, and the sun caught the great red and green bottles in the recessed windows. The butcher's and the joiner's shops were opening. The door to Mr. West's barber shop remained closed. The peruke maker kept late hours and opened later than the other tradesmen; a man of parts, he resorted on occasion to his old trade of blood-letting.

A block up the street, across King, two Negro slaves were opening the shutters at the Hewes and Smith shop. A third Negro appeared with a bucket of water and a sponge and prepared to wash the small window-panes in the store front. The doctor smiled. Robert Smith was a shrewd merchant. He knew the ladies would be more attracted to the display of newly arrived goods if the window glass sparkled.

At King Street Dr. Armitage turned left and walked its length toward the Hewes and Smith shipyard, passing his own gate next to the Hewes house, where Nat Allen had lived since Joseph Hewes's death. A sad thing that, but Joe had lived long enough to sign the Declaration and act as Secretary for Maritime Affairs; he had got the ships John Paul Jones wanted.

What a man that John Paul was, and what a thorn in the side of the British Admiralty! Armitage recalled the day he had first seen John Paul, a sorry, saddened young man walking off a ship from the West Indies, landing in Queen Anne's Town without a penny in his pocket. Joseph Hewes had befriended him then as later—taken him home, fitted him with clothes and listened to the tale of how he'd hit a sailor with a heavy bucket when his ship was in the West Indies. The young Scot had been hustled aboard another vessel sailing for Albemarle Sound before he could be tried. Hewes had always said John Paul was a man touched by destiny. And indeed it seemed that luck was with him from the day he set foot on the soil of Edenton. It was here that, through the good offices of Hewes, he was introduced to Wilie Jones of Halifax, who shared Hewes's liking for the young fugitive and gave him the protection of his name.

It was said John Paul never forgave an enemy or forgot a friend. Certain it was that he never forgot Joseph Hewes, shipbuilder, merchant and Signer of the Declaration. They were close friends to the day of Hewes's death. Now Hewes lay in an unmarked grave in Christ Churchyard in Philadelphia. This thought always saddened the doctor. Armitage was an incurable romantic. He thought Joe should lie in the burial-ground at Hayes. He had talked to Samuel Johnston about having Hewes moved from Christ Church and brought back to lie beside his love, Samuel Johnston's sister Isabella. Sam had listened to the doctor and agreed, but nothing had been done. In the war years all personal matters had been set aside to await the outcome of the death struggle.

The doctor was at Coltrane's gate now. There was no sign of awaking in that house except a thin column of smoke rising from the kitchen in the garden. The goldsmith slept late. Five minutes brought the doctor to the shipyard. Here he found abundant activity. The warehouse doors were open, and twenty or thirty Negro dockworkers stood near the ways, ready to unload Captain Meredith's *Devon Maid*.

Armitage turned and walked briskly homeward. The sun was rising above the tops of pines in the forest that surrounded the town. Flashes of light fell on the glass of windows, making them shine as though illumined by strong candlelight. The sky was cloudless. The storm that had threatened in the early morning had passed them by. The bold cape at Hatteras had caught it and turned it out to sea. That was good. Only last year a hurricane had flattened young corn and destroyed tender crops.

Smoke was rising from many kitchens now. The six hundred inhabitants of the village were making ready to breakfast, and the day had begun. Dr. Armitage paused at his gate, held the palm of his hand level with his eyes and looked toward the Sound. The *Devon Maid* swung at anchor near the Dram Tree. He turned and went up the path to his door.

Now the village was broad awake. The day had begun. A horse-drawn riding-chair drew up to Horniblow's and paused while William Hooper came out and got in. It went toward the Tyrrell Ferry.

There was more activity at the shops in Cheapside. A fishing boat had landed at the little dock at the foot of Broad Street, and the fisherman began to unload his catch into a cart. Other carts were trundling down dusty streets to the market-house. Men from outlying districts were bringing their produce into town for the Tuesday market day.

A coach was about to leave from Horniblow's. Its horn blared, and passengers pushed their way toward it through a crowd of pot-boys and hostlers who bowed and held out their hands for coins. The coachman was already on the box, holding his restless horses with a close rein. The agent for the post put in place leather bags holding mail for New Bern, Wilmington and Charleston. Samuel Johnston, bound for New Bern, was the last aboard. With a final blast of the horn, a rattle and clank of chains and a crack of the driver's whip the coach set off.

At his breakfast table Dr. Armitage heard the noise of the stage's departure. The hour was later than he had thought. When he had finished his sauce, grits, bacon and eggs he would dress and call on Captain Meredith of the *Devon Maid* to see the sick passengers and satisfy his curiosity about the grand folk from Europe.

Journey's End

3

THREE months in a small sailing vessel of indifferent accommodations had not smoothed the always uncertain temper of Baroness von Pollnitz. The close contact with the Baron's two little sons, Hans and Eitel, had bored her. Lady Anne Stuart, as she preferred to be called, did not enjoy the continual presence of children, and she was unwilling to assume responsibility for the offspring of an earlier wife. Children belonged to the nursery. At home she saw them for an hour each day while they were having their tea, and on infrequent occasions—high days and holidays—they were allowed to come downstairs for dessert, to sit quietly as well-bred children should sit, speaking only when spoken to. During the voyage this strict regime had been broken, much to her discomfiture. Last evening as the *Devon Maid* anchored in Albemarle Sound, Lady Anne had thought with relief that, once ashore, she could re-establish the children's usual routine.

The Baron, on the other hand, had been pleased to have his sons with him. Hans, the elder, a lad of almost eight, was companionable. Growing into the image of his father, he had hair so blond it was almost white. His round blue eyes were the colour of the waters of the Mediterranean, and he held his slim little body as erect as his father. "A little soldier," the Baron often said, "my little soldier"—which made the lad very proud.

Little Eitel, who was six, was as dark as Hans was fair and as turbulent as Hans was placid. He was his mother's son, with stormy brown eyes and a mass of unruly dark hair curling about his small head. At times Lady Anne showed affection for the younger child. He was a tempery lad, and she liked that. The older boy's perfect behaviour bored her.

This morning when Eitel clamoured for attention she repeated a performance long familiar to all aboard. "Take the brat to the nursery!" she shouted to the young girl she had brought on the voyage as governess for the boys. And then, remembering there was no nursery on the ill-conditioned ship on which they had taken passage, she corrected herself. "Take him to your cabin, Miss Hay. Give him candy or one of those Seville oranges. I cannot stand his yelling."

The young governess picked up the shrieking, kicking child, turning her head so he could not gouge her eyes with his strong chubby fingers, and carried him below, where his angry wails were muffled, if not quite subdued.

The young Scot, Angus Moray, watched the performance as he stood at the rail of the *Devon Maid*. He thought, as he had thought many times during the long voyage, that he had never seen another red-headed girl who controlled her temper as well as Mistress Hay. Not once had he heard her raise her voice, no matter how violent the younger child's tantrum. Not once, during their evening walks on the open deck, had she mentioned her charges. She talked only of the blue of the sea, the soft fragrance of the breeze that blew off the West Indian islands, the closeness, the brilliance of the tropic stars. Sometimes she talked with a certain restrained nostalgia of her home in North Devon—of the rugged beauty of the high cliffs that through the ages had withstood the angry pressing of the stormy Atlantic; of the wild moors covered with bracken; of ancient ruins left by strange people who had worshipped nature and held their revels in the shadows of Brown Willie and the circle stones. "Country-folk will not go near the monuments," she had told him once. "They fear the ghosts of those ancient ones; they think they are all evil. But I never feared them. Ghosts may be good as well as evil." She had had an eerie, faraway look in her eyes then. Angus thought they were the clear amber colour of the cairngorm stone so dear to the

Scotsmen, and her skin was the lovely white that sometimes goes with rich auburn hair.

Last night she had talked again of the beliefs of the Devon folk. "A little pagan we are." She laughed. "Aye, more than a little."

Angus had been a little in love with Sylvia Hay last night as the moon came up, large and golden. A little in love perhaps, but that could not be. A young surgeon starting out in a new land with no practice and a very limited amount of money must not think of love. That was a weakness he could not allow himself for ten years at least. Yet 'when he looked on the lovely maiden under the moon he felt his pulse moving rapidly, more rapidly than was normal for a man of his years.

There was a long silence between them, during which she stood close to the rail, her face turned to watch the rising moon. Strands of her glorious hair, loosened by the wind, blew across her face. Surely she was a charming creature! Perhaps the moon added to her beauty, blurring any defects and giving her a suggestion of unreality.

Angus said, "What is it that holds your attention so closely? The moon? Or do your thoughts turn homeward, Miss Hay?" As he said the words a chill went over him. Suppose she was thinking of a lover left behind in Devon.

She answered without turning. "The moon . . . how gloriously she shines down on us, just as she has shone for all the people through all the centuries!" She turned to him with a swift movement. "Do you believe she sees us? Do you believe she knows her worshippers here on this little earth?"

Bewildered by the sudden earnest tone in her voice, he remained silent.

She shrugged her shoulders. "No, of course you would not dream about the moon. You are too . . . too practical. You would be thinking of anatomy and broken bones—a good clean fracture and how you would set it."

The blood rose in his face, and colour flooded from his collar to the line of his dark hair. "What is wrong with such thinking, madam?" he asked stiffly. " 'Tis glad enough you'd be to cry out for a surgeon if you fell and broke a bone. A surgeon who thought about how to mend bones, not a fellow whose mind wandered off into moon madness."

Sylvia Hay laughed, a clear pleasant laugh of pure enjoyment. "Oh, Moray, how delightfully serious you are! Pay no mind to the foolish things I say. Lady Anne tells me I am fey at times. Perhaps I am. The moon gives me strange, wild thoughts. When I was a child I drove my little pony across the Bodmin moors as often as I could escape from the nurse and the stable-boy. I used to dream I was back in the early times when strange people came out to make sacrifice among the tall black stones."

"You *are* a witch," Moray said. He laid his hand over hers. "You will mount a wild horse and ride skyward in an instant unless I make a magic circle around you."

She turned swiftly at his words. "Ah, you *do* understand! That wasn't the speech of a practical man."

"We Scots are said to have second sight," he reminded her.

They were interrupted by Lady Anne. "Miss Hay, do go down to the children. Little Eitel is fretful. He says he won't go to sleep until you tell him a tale."

Sylvia turned from the rail. A little reluctantly, Dr. Moray thought; the idea pleased him. "I'll go at once, Lady Anne," she said.

A moment later Lady Anne was standing with Angus at the rail, her shoulder touching his. A long dark cloud drifted across the moon, cutting through its unearthly brightness. Lady Anne shivered a little, pulling her cloak about her. "I loathe the moon," she said, pressing closer to him. "It is cold—cold and menacing. I love warmth and sunshine or the dark night, but not the thin paleness of the moon."

Angus looked down at the woman beside him. She was beautiful. Her skin was flawless, her face delicately modelled and aristocratic. In the dim light her eyes, deep blue, seemed almost black. Her long hair was loose, confined with a blue riband. She looked young, but her heavy-lidded eyes held no innocence; they held slumbering passion, an invitation that set his blood pounding. This woman had arrogance; scorning subtlety, she demanded what she wanted. In her personality there was no trace of the elusive charm that was the essence of the girl who had just left him. Yet Lady Anne roused desire in him.

Her voice, as well as her eyes, held an invitation. "I have longed to talk with you alone ever since you came on the ship at Antigua, but there was always someone about. Tell me about yourself. You must know you are handsome, a man to flutter the heart of any woman. Handsome and something more. I sense depths in you to captivate, to intrigue, to make a woman long to get beyond the reserve with which you surround yourself."

Moray said nothing. Lady Anne went on, almost as though she were not addressing him but thinking aloud. "You must have known many women, but I think you would always withhold your true self." She looked up suddenly, and as the cloud passed from the moon he could see a gleam of amusement in her eyes. "Tell me, am I not speaking the truth?"

Moray laughed. "You have a vivid imagination, Lady Anne. I suspect you make a picture of a man to suit your own fancy and then you attach the picture to any one who passes."

She tossed her head. Her blond hair, perfumed and soft, brushed against his cheek. "You are rude," she said. "Men of breeding are more subtle."

He smiled down at her. "Your Ladyship is a great beauty. You are accustomed to see many admirers clustered about you. Do you in your heart admire those sycophants who kneel at your feet?"

"No!" she said abruptly. "No, I despise them. I despise weakness in men or women. I like you because your head is high and you are your own man.

I like your looks. I think I will like you even when I know you . . . more intimately."

Clouds scudding across the sky covered the moon once more, and a warm, soft darkness obscured the deck. Lady Anne faced Angus, moved swiftly against him. She lifted her face and pressed her lips against his. She kissed hungrily, with a swift intensity.

For a moment his lips were cool against hers; then he put his hands about her slim tapering waist, pressed her body against him. "No man could resist you," he whispered. "No man . . ."

A small sound came to his ears. Angus raised his head to meet the scornful eyes of Sylvia Hay. She turned abruptly and disappeared down the companionway.

Lady Anne moved away from him. "I thought I heard a step," she said, her voice low.

He drew her body close. "It was nothing," he said, "nothing."

"I heard a sound," she protested.

"The flutter of a bird's wing, a fish jumping in the water. We are quite alone." But the moment had passed. He released her.

Lady Anne ran her slim white hands across her hair. "I've been so bored," she murmured. "So frightfully bored all the voyage! Why didn't I find you earlier? Why just to-night, the last night?"

A moment later the watch passed by, swinging his lanthorn.

The Baron's voice came from the darkness of the deck-house. "My dear, 'tis long past midnight. Are you coming in?"

"Coming, coming." Lady Anne's voice was impatient. She turned to Moray. "In Edenton we will be at a place called Horniblow's Tavern, where Captain Meredith tells me accommodations are available. Call on me there to-morrow at five. I will give you tea."

Moray had recovered himself. His voice was calm. "Thank you, Lady Anne, you are very kind."

She leaned toward him. "I can be kinder," she whispered. "Much, much kinder."

He made no response. Lady Anne moved quickly away. He watched her with sombre eyes. Her walk was as lithe and sinuous as a cat's. And she is deadly, he thought grimly. What a pity the girl had appeared just at that moment! Ah, well, he had no time for serious thoughts about women in this new life that lay ahead of him.

From the darkness of the trees that lined the shore an owl hooted, flapped its great wings. A small bird gave a shrill, frightened cry, then was silent. The bark of a fox carried across the water. Lonely sounds of lapping water, sounds from predatory forest animals seeking food in the depths of the night. He thought the woman whose lips were still warm against his was as predatory, as untamed as any forest animal, but she had power in her to make a man forget his danger.

He heard the splash of oars in the water. Captain Meredith was returning to his ship from the village. The captain crossed the deck toward his cabin, talking to the first officer. "Dr. Armitage will be aboard by ten in the morning. Ask Dr. Moray to conduct him to the ailing passengers."

"Aye, sir."

Moray came out of his abstraction at the captain's words. He would be glad to meet Dr. Armitage and deliver to him the letter of introduction from the director of St. Bart's. He hoped the doctor would agree with the diagnosis he had made of the ailing passengers and seamen, and the medication. Ah, well, the journey was over! Moray felt a certain excitement and exhilaration. He was sloughing off the Old World and preparing to take on the colouration of the New. God grant that the exchange would prove successful!

In her cabin Lady Anne was stripping off her clothes, assisted by her maid Dawkins. The woman held a thin muslin night-rail in her hands and was ready to slip it over Lady Anne's head when there was a knock at the door. "Go to the door, fool," Lady Anne said sharply. "Don't stand there gaping." Dawkins dropped the night-rail on a chair and opened the door an inch.

A grimy seaman stood in the passageway. "Captain's compliments, miss. The doctor sent this for her Ladyship." He winked. "To make her sleep —as if a body needed dosing to bring sleep! You and I know better than that, eh, my girl?"

Dawkins snatched the packet from the man's fingers. "Keep your mouth to yourself, fellow, and get away with you!" She slammed the door and turned the key noisily.

Lady Anne laughed. "You were short with the messenger, my lass. Was he one of your voyage playmates?"

The woman sniffed. "Him? He's nothing but a churl who pulls the sails. He was trying to peer in on your Ladyship—that's what he was doing."

Lady Anne ran her hands over her white body. "A pretty enough sight for any man, my good Dawkins." The maid sniffed. Lady Anne walked across the room and locked the door that led to her husband's cabin. "If I'm to have a potion to put me to sleep, I'll make sure I won't have a visitor. The heat seems to make some men amorous. No, I don't want that night-rail. I'll sleep as the Lord made me."

"But, your Ladyship, some one on deck might look through the port."

"Let them look. Now get out. I'll lock the passage door after you. Don't disturb me until I call."

The woman took up the clothes which lay on the floor where Lady Anne had stepped out of them, and left the room. Lady Anne locked the door, poured the powder in a glass of port and swallowed it. Stretching herself full length on the narrow berth, she gave herself over to thoughts of the young doctor. A personable man. Except for him she had not seen a personable man since leaving London three months ago. No one with whom to hold a lively conversation, let alone play at love-making. No one but the Baron. What a clumsy fellow he was! He thought of nothing but totting up accounts and poring over ledgers. She might better have stayed with Percy; if she had, she would now be a duchess. At least there might be some excitement in being a duchess.

She wondered if her solicitors had sent her quarterly allowance to Edenton. They had promised to get it from the Duke and send it to her in care of James Iredell, Margaret Macartney's cousin.

Her thoughts went back to the handsome Moray. She had the feeling that she had not seen the last of him. She felt drowsy—the medicine was taking hold of her. Moray . . . She wondered who he was. A good Scottish name. What strength he had! What depths in his unfathomable eyes! Ruthless, too; she liked ruthless men who were difficult to subdue. She moved a little, her face half buried in the pillow, her long blond hair streaming over her curved white shoulders.

After a time she slept, lightly at first, hearing outside noises—the water lapping against the side of the ship, the short baying of dogs, an owl hooting. Land sounds entered her consciousness, with illusive suggestion of past things. Her drugged mind translated the medley of noises into the bay of fox-hounds on Yorkshire moors, an owl's weird hoot in the woods beyond the castle and the owl's hunting cry as it fell upon its prey. Witches' sounds. Yorkshire and the wild moor in the moonlight. How beautiful, how sinister! . . . After a time the light half-conscious sleep gave way to a deeper dreamless sleep in which there were no disturbing remembrances.

Mistress of Queen's Gift

4   THE mistress of Queen's Gift rode slowly toward the tobacco sheds across the fields at the verge of the Sound. Under a great oak tree she reined her horse and adjusted her brown holland riding mask. The sun was hot, although it was not yet ten o'clock. She had the dark hair and blue eyes of some far-back Irish ancestor, but her skin was white and burned readily.

When her wide straw hat was adjusted and the ribands were tied in place she did not immediately raise the rein to signal her mount. Instead she sat quietly, her hands clasped over the pommel of her hunting saddle, and watched the Negro slaves moving down the rows. As they chopped the weeds from the soil around the tobacco plants they sang as though their work was pleasurable. Out in the Sound she could see a ship riding at anchor.

Mary Rutledge, wife of Adam Rutledge, owned the Soundside plantation Queen's Gift. It had come to her through her father Hesketh Mainwairing, whose father Roger Mainwairing had owned it before him. Duke Roger he was called when he was alive, and Duke Roger he had remained long after his death. Although Mary had borne two names other than her maiden name, to the old slaves on the plantation she was still Mis' Mannerin'. The years of her marriage to William Warden—her father's choice, a man years her senior—had been blotted out, and her second marriage had been comparatively recent. Even some of her friends among the neighbouring planters and the men and women of the village called her Mary Mainwairing.

Mary's marriage to Adam Rutledge shortly after the close of the war had had the full approval of the Edenton folk, who knew of the tragic events that preceded it. Adam's first wife Sara had died after prolonged invalidism. William Warden, a Loyalist, had been hanged as a spy by General Greene's men. Adam's home across the Sound had been destroyed during the war, so it was natural that they should settle down at Queen's Gift, Mary's lovely plantation house on Albemarle Sound.

She was thinking now of her grandfather Duke Roger, whose name had never been taken from the plantation gates. He had died before Mary's birth, yet she felt she had a special and private knowledge of him that was not part of his legend in the Albemarle. He came to her mind most frequently as she knew he had appeared riding across the plantation, his tall body balanced gracefully in the saddle, his narrow, well-set head with its mass of unruly hair turning as he surveyed the land. More clearly than in his portrait she seemed to see the penetrating eyes under heavy, brooding brows, the high bridge of his nose, a firm mouth set in a stubborn jaw. He was well named Duke Roger, for he lived in a time when strong men were needed in the young colony. Men with iron in their souls.

A voice broke into her reflections. "You are watching the ship, Mistress Rutledge? It's Captain Meredith's *Devon Maid*, I'm told. Perhaps you're thinking, as I am, that it's an outrage we can't send our tobacco direct to the Bideford market on ships that sail from our own Sound. It's a costly business using Virginia ports."

Mary turned. Her husband's overseer Marcy had ridden up, a tall, lean Irishman with reddish hair, a mass of small freckles over his nose and a wide, good-humoured mouth. He had come to Adam before the Revolution, as an indentured man sent in from Antigua. Adam had realized that he was a man of education, sensible and trustworthy. Later he had freed Marcy and sent him out to Illinois to manage Adam's Illinois holdings at Cahokia. Marcy had returned earlier in the summer to put by the harvest at Queen's Gift. Adam himself had gone to the Illinois country in April and had stayed behind to build a new stone grist-mill near Cahokia, a thriving town on the Mississippi River.

Mary smiled a little wryly. "I agree with you, Marcy. We ship our fine leaf out from Virginia and send our naval stores to Charleston for export to the European markets. Both states gain in their exports while North Carolina remains low on the lists."

Marcy quieted his restless horse, patting the shining satin of its arched neck. "There should be a way to overcome the disadvantage of our outer banks."

Mary's eyes held a glint of laughter. "Perhaps we can get Parson Earle to pray for the hurricane to break through the sand-banks and give us a wide new inlet."

"No fear." Marcy spoke gloomily. "The other way round, most likely. The next storm may fill up the inlet we use." He gathered up the reins. "Do you have any errands in the village? I'm riding in to get old Booths and bring him out to trim the horses' hoofs, if he isn't too drunk. The farrier Mel Frazier won't leave his shop to do plantation work."

"What's wrong with Abraham? I thought that was his work."

"Abraham has a misery in his back. I suspect he and Eph have been down to the pocosin, brewing white liquor."

Mary shrugged her shoulders. "I've learned from Adam to look the other way. I wish they'd get rid of that still. I'd give them an extra dole of rum on Saturdays."

"They like making whisky. Doubtless it reminds them of beer-making in Africa. There's no excitement in getting in line and holding out their cups for a tot of rum."

"I suppose you are right." She changed the subject. "You might slip into Hewes and Smith's and see if the *Devon Maid* brought any holland—I want to have covers made for the drawing-room chairs. And stop at the chemist's. Chaney says the women need indigo. They want to dye the cloth they are working on in the weaving-house."

Marcy said, "I haven't heard what cargo Captain Meredith brought, but I did hear that he brought some high-born passengers in his ship. A Baron Somebody and his wife Lady Anne Stuart."

"Lady Anne Stuart?" Mary thought for a moment. "Surely she must be the one Margaret Macartney wrote about, the one who was divorced from Lord Percy before he became Duke of Northumberland. He used to call at my grandmother's place in Yorkshire. I had not heard Lady Anne was married again. She is reputed to be very haughty."

Marcy grinned. "Well, the villagers will be bending the knee to the nobility. I hear they will take up residence at Horniblow's today or tomorrow. I wager mine host will get out the red carpet."

"I must go in and call," Mary said. "I am curious to see Lady Anne and her husband." After a moment she added, "I always liked Northumberland."

Marcy trotted down the lane lined with great cedars which Duke Roger had planted.

Mary Rutledge turned her mount and rode toward the tobacco barns. The north field that bordered Albemarle Sound was the best tobacco land on Queen's Gift. Its tobacco yield for the years following the Revolution, when the English markets were again opened to Americans, brought the highest prices. On the advice of the London agent the Rutledge crop was carefully graded by slaves, and only superior leaf was sent to the English markets at Bristol and Bideford. As she rode along the field Mary noticed with satisfaction that the plants were flourishing. The rows were almost obscured by the outspread lower leaves, and clusters of white flowers crowned the tall stems.

This week the tobacco harvest had begun. The work would continue for five or six weeks. Now the lower leaves were being stripped from the plants. Small black boys drove the mule-drawn tobacco sleds along the rows. Other slaves gathered up the already yellowing leaves and piled them on the sleds, which carried them to the sheds. There the women slaves sat on benches and tied the leaves, four or five together, into hands. These hands were hung on wooden poles and goose-neck hooks to dry in the sun. A slow process, tobacco curing, for after the sun-drying the bundles must be hung in barns until time to pack them into hogsheads. Then the tobacco was shipped to Virginia ports where it was reloaded for shipment to England.

The Negroes loved working in tobacco. Every step in the cultivation and curing was a social occasion. They worked close together, singing as they worked. A leader would start a song, sometimes using a small drum to establish the rhythm. The slaves sang in unison, their voices mellow and liquid. Those newly arrived from Africa used their native tongue; the older slaves who had been in America for some years sang the words in English.

Mary reined her horse under a beech tree to listen as the Negroes began a song.

A man with a strong baritone led off:

> *"Branch off, branch off, blaze of fire!*
> *What is it? What is it?*
> The rabbits should get up for me.
> *What is it? What is it?*
> And come to my sleeping place.
> *Where is it? Where is it?*
> You have hurt me, drums.
> *What is it? What is it?*
> You have poked at me,
> At me and a girl from your home.
> *Why is it? Why is it?*
> No girls go about;

Only boys go about.
Why is it? Why is it?
Let them herd the cattle;
Otherwise the cattle breed no calves.
Some of the children cried out,
Let me poke the fire. Let me poke the fire.
Branch off! Branch off, blaze of fire!"

How easily they worked, bending gaily turbaned heads. There was grace in the movements of their dark bare arms, long sweeping movements like the sweep of oars or heavy-headed grain pressed by the wind. Strong, pagan people, far from their villages along wild rivers and wilder forests of Africa. Caught up in the lives and ways of white folk. What did they talk about in their cabins in the quarters line? The white folk whom they served, or nostalgic backward glances toward Africa? Or did they live only for the day, without regret?

Mary had often talked of these matters with Adam. Certainly a slave had no responsibility, no struggle for survival such as he would have faced in his own land, where the struggle against savage beasts and a wild, savage country was constant. Here Negroes were clothed and fed. Their food, the roofs over their heads were the master's responsibility. The day's work done, they could lie under a shade tree in the cool of the evening. They could laugh and sing without a care.

As Mary neared the tobacco sheds a new song rose, different in rhythm from the one just ended:

"Give me a little tobacco!
Give me a little tobacco!
Alas, my big feather
That I got from my brother the crow.
Give me a little tobacco
That I may float away
Into the current
On my big feather
I got from my brother the crow.

"Give me a little tobacco
That I may float away
With the current."

The Negro tobacco overlooker stepped to Mary's side and touched his sweating forehead with two fingers. He was a huge black man named Mungo. No doubt in his own country he had belonged to a warrior tribe, Zulu or Angoni. "Missie see good weed dis day. Best since Mungo come, better nor last year or year before. Master he be pleased when he come."

Mary said, "That is good news, Mungo. But there is hard work before the ship comes to our dock."

Mungo nodded. "It is good. Tobacco will be standing on de dock waiting. See how dey work." He waved his hand in the direction of the sheds. Thirty or forty women were seated on the benches, sorting the leaf and tying it firmly into hands. The acrid smell of the tobacco was not unpleasant.

Mary rode slowly back to the house. She loved the activity of the growing season, but this year she was impatient for the harvest, to have the corn cut and shocked, the tobacco made ready. It would be shipped to England this year. She hoped for a good price. With her husband Adam away, she felt a keen responsibility. She wanted to be able to report a good crop, good prices, under her stewardship.

When Mary reached the plantation house she was met by a stableboy who reported that Dr. Armitage was in the dining-room having a pastry. Mary dismounted quickly, took off her mask and shook the wrinkles from her holland riding-habit. She hooked up the skirt for walking and ran up the steps to the long gallery. In the hall she tossed her small hat and riding-crop on a settle near the door and walked down the central hall.

Mary moved with the easy grace of a woman who has been trained to walk and stand correctly. Her back was straight and erect, her arms hung close to her sides. Long since she had forgotten the fatiguing hours of training under the stern guidance of her grandmother Rhoda Mainwairing. Hours of walking back and forth among the masses of furniture in the English drawing-room, a heavy book balanced on her head. Incessant practice of sinking gracefully into a chair and spreading her wide silk skirts to show the tips of her satin slippers. And her grandmother's relentless criticism. "You can sit a horse creditably, Mary, but you can't ride a horse into the drawing-room. Move with ease, naturally. I don't want you to prance like an unbroken long-legged colt. I can forgive a woman almost anything but lack of grace or lack of repose. Keep your feet quiet, your knees together, your hands at ease in your lap. Hold your chin up—it's a good habit. Look people straight in the eye when you speak to them or they speak to you. I can't abide a sliding, shifty eye. . . ." Sometimes Mary remembered her grandmother Rhoda's careful training, but for the most part her distinguished carriage was as natural to her as breathing.

Dr. Armitage rose as she came into the room, dislodging the large white napkin he had tucked under his chin to protect his white linen stock. The butler Ebon came forward quickly to pick it up and fetch a fresh serviette.

"You look as bright as the morning, my dear. I suppose you will tell me you were up with the sun and have already ridden from one end of the plantation to the other."

Mary poured herself a cup of tea. "Not quite the whole of the place. I did watch the tobacco-stripping for a time and rode to the tobacco sheds. I like to make my rounds in the cool of the morning."

The doctor nodded. "I've been up betimes myself. Went aboard Meredith's ship to see some sick people. Some died on the voyage. A young doctor aboard wanted my word it wasn't plague. It wasn't. A food poisoning of some kind, I'd think." The doctor leaned back in his chair. "We have grand visitors in Queen Anne's Town, Mary. High-born folk, lords and ladies and such. More titles than when the French were here, waiting to join General LaFayette's army. Yea, grander even than Cosmo de' Medici, though not so good-looking by far."

"Now, Doctor, don't tease," Mary said. "Who are these fine folk, and whatever are they doing here in our quiet village?" She did not tell him she already knew. The doctor liked to be the bearer of news, and Mary did not wish to spoil his pleasure.

The doctor's eyes crinkled at the corners, and his wide mouth went into laughter. "Ah, that arouses your interest, now doesn't it, miss? You women are all astir about great folk. Even you are curious. I see it in those wide blue eyes of yours."

"Of course I'm curious. Nothing has happened in Queen Anne's Town for months. I'm bored to distraction."

The doctor took a gold toothpick from the pocket of his waistcoat and picked his teeth free of fragments of pastry, holding his napkin discreetly before his mouth the while. "Yes, they'll take rooms at Horniblow's. My Lady wants a whole floor looking out on the Sound, with the upper gallery reserved for the family's use. There's my Lord and his Lady, or should I say my Lady and her Lord? It's my guess that *she* is the strong one. Then there are two little boys, a governess—a pretty red-headed wench—and a lady's maid."

"But who? Who are these people, Doctor? Do not keep me in suspense."

The doctor drew his chair to the window where he could see the full sweep of the Sound. "I feel the need of a smoke, Mary. Then I'll go into the story. I warn you it's gossip, and you say you don't like gossip." His eyes twinkled. He loved his little joke, as Mary well knew.

"I'll fill one of Duke Roger's pipes for you. Surely that will induce you to tell me all about our visitors."

The doctor reached for the long clay pipe. "Duke Roger," he said. "A great man, your grandfather. He was cast in the heroic mould, in body and brain and in his wide humanity. We don't have men of his kind in our generation." For a moment he watched the smoke rise from his pipe. "The lady claims to be the daughter of Lord Bute."

Mary played the game out. "Oh, the Countess Percy?"

"She's divorced Percy, she tells me. She's married to this Polish Baron von Pollnitz. She prefers to be called Lady Anne Stuart for some reason."

"Of course," Mary said, "Lady Anne Stuart."

"Did you know her in England, Mary?"

"No, not really, but Percy used to call on my grandmother Rhoda. I remember talk of trouble between the two. I had heard of a separation but not of a divorce."

"There must have been one, since the lady has married again."

"What is she like?" Mary asked. "Do you find her beautiful?"

The doctor hesitated. "Her features are perfect, her figger ditto. Most men would say she was beautiful, but I don't. She's a discontented, unhappy woman. A seeking woman."

"Why, Doctor!" Mary was laughing.

Doctor Armitage paid no mind to her merriment. "The red-headed one has more beauty in her little finger."

"Who is this red-head beauty?"

"Her name is Sylvia—Sylvia . . . Hay. A fine lassie she is."

"Doctor, you are really annoying. I want to know who this beauty is, not just her name."

"By gad, I don't know! I judged from the way the little boys were hanging close to her that she is acting as their governess."

"And the Baron?"

Doctor Armitage pursed his lips. "A Pole, but of the blondest of men, with yellow hair and blue eyes. Very stiff, very correct, very military. I was told that he was once Chamberlain at the Prussian Court and also spent some time at the court of the Elector of Saxony. It is my thought that he is a most unhappy man, Mary. I feel a sympathy for him, although he would be too proud ever to ask for sympathy. And that's the lot of them, except the young doctor from Antigua who's come over to make a position for himself. Moray is his name, Angus Moray. He thinks he is going to New Bern, but I hope we can hold him here." The doctor got up and laid his empty pipe on the mantel-board. "He has good recommendation from the chief medical man of St. Bart's, and I like his looks."

The doctor called to Ebon to bring his little satchel of medicine. "Must be going now, Mary."

Mary followed him into the wide hall. "Will you stop and see Tazey on your way through the quarters line? She's getting very feeble. I'm sure she will be better if you make her a visit. She's the only one who really needs your attention. I'll see the others in the dispensary this afternoon."

Two of the younger slaves came in and began to close the shutters and darken the rooms against the heat of the day. Mary went up the wide stairs to her bedroom to take off her holland habit. She wondered why it was that linen was hot to wear as a garment but cool as a bed sheet.

Her mind turned to these new people who had just arrived in Queen Anne's Town. She was indeed curious about Lady Anne Stuart, the wilful, unpredictable Lady Anne, who had so often scandalized and delighted London society. After a day or two she would call and see for herself. After she had dressed in a cool cream-coloured muslin frock she stepped out onto the upper gallery that faced Albemarle Sound. The sun was more than half-way to its zenith. From the house the fields stretched away to the forest, little plots of land with hedges of wild honeysuckle entwined with orange trumpet flowers.

In the tobacco fields the black men were singing a chant, slow, monotonous, yet with a certain swinging rhythm:

> "There at the fig trees
> Give me a little tobacco.
> Here is a little old woman;
> Give me a little tobacco.
> Go bring punkins from the garden;
> Give me a little tobacco.
> Bring me nego berries,
> Bring me a little tobacco."

On and on the chant continued; a boy with a little drum beat out the rhythm.

Mary thought again, as she had often thought before: Here we are, living close together on this plantation, master and slave, yet alien to one another, as far away as Africa from America. "What is it they sing?" she said to one of the girls who had come to close the upstairs jalousies. "What are they singing?"

The girl stepped to the railing. For a moment they listened. "They sing about old woman who promises to give unborn child for a little tobacco. Then she kills them all by dropping nego berries in their throats. Not nice song, missie. Not a nice song," the girl repeated.

Mary shuddered and went into the darkened bedroom. Sometimes when she wakened in the night and heard the drums talking, loneliness spoke through the drum rhythm. Fear came to her then, and she longed for the time when Adam would be with her again. Home from that far-off Illinois country. The same feeling came to her now as she listened to the rich voices chanting. Wild, primitive, savage . . .

As Mary walked to the dispensary she reviewed the week ahead. She knew it would be a day or two before she could call on Lady Anne. Busy days of the usual plantation activities—visits to the weaving-house, a couple of hours in the smoke-house counting hams and sides of bacon, trying to figure whether there were enough to last until winter when the new hams would be cured and ready for use. One day each week she spent a few hours in the dispensary. This afternoon she doled out quinine for the slaves who had bonerack fever and chills; daubed salve on sores that refused to heal; administered mullen and onion syrup for coughs; sulphur and lard for the

itch. These were,the small ailments that she could handle without consulting Dr. Armitage. She had the usual amount of harmless sugar pills to
distribute to the older women who wanted the same attention as the sick.

She was always conscious that, not content with her treatment, the
majority of the slaves sought out the old conjure woman who lived in a hut
hard by the pocosin.

Twice the old woman, Mifiti by name, had effected cures by applying
mouldy earth to deep sores. When Mary talked with the doctor about this,
voicing her apprehension, he told her that the historian Lawson had recorded the same treatment sixty years before. He had seen the Indians,
who later burned him to death, go into the swamp, obtain a curious earth
mould and bind the mixture on an Indian boy's leg. The treatment, much to
Lawson's astonishment, was successful.

Today Mary asked old Elijah about his son who for weeks had been using
a crutch because of an unusually large sore on his leg.

"Him well, missie. Brought he crutch back yesterday."

"Good. Very good. I'm glad the salve cured."

A curious closed look came over Elijah's face. His eyes were without
expression. He mumbled something and went hurriedly out of the dispensary. A girl wearing a red cotton dress and a green scarf about her head
giggled. "Hush you' mouth, you!" an older woman said, dropping her voice
almost to a whisper.

But Mary heard and realized that the boy had visited the conjure woman.
She sighed a little. No matter what Parson Earle preached, no matter what
instruction the overlookers gave, they would sneak away to Mifiti's hut.
Love potions, cures, protection from evildoers could all be had from old
Mifiti, the witch woman.

Again Mary was confronted by the contrasting worlds that existed on the
plantation: the world of the white man, the world of the black and the
world of nature. At times these forces opposed one another, struggling for
supremacy. The primitive, the savage element was restless in the confines
of civilization. The alchemy of the slaves' pagan yearnings reached out and
made itself felt in their dependence on the witch woman.

Mary walked slowly along the lane from the quarters. When she came in
sight of the house she quickened her steps. Two saddle horses were tied to
the hitching rack and a coach stood in the drive.

Down the path came Chaney to meet her. "Ladies have come. Mistress
Iredell and Madam Barker. Dey's sitting on de gallery. Better you go in by
de garden. Dey's a fresh dress laid out on you' bed, and Pam's ready to
sponge you cool."

"Take a raspberry shrub, Chaney, and have one of the boys start the
ceiling fan going in the drawing-room so there'll be a little breeze."

"Breeze she blowing off de Sound, mistress. And I brang de drink directly dey come. Come, let me fix you' pretty hair. Ladies say dey come for a big gossip."

The Gossips

5 MARY RUTLEDGE found her guests seated in the yellow drawing-room. The jalousies had been drawn so that the glare of the afternoon sun was shut out. A small black boy seated on a little stool near the door pulled lazily at the cord of the ceiling fan. After long practice he had evolved an easy method of performing the task. The string was secured to his great toe. By stretching his legs to full length he could pull the string with no more effort than a wiggle of his toes. The strips of white cotton hanging from a pole near the high ceiling fluttered gently, causing a small draft of air to circulate in the darkened room.

Mary greeted her guests in turn. Mrs. Thomas Barker and Mrs. James Iredell, who had ridden out in Mrs. Barker's fine coach, wore cool muslins and wide sun-hats. Young Nellie Blair and Lucy Tredwell were in linen riding-habits. They had already discarded their masks and hats and were drinking raspberry shrub.

Hannah Iredell, a small woman with delicate features and a skin as smooth as a blush-rose, admonished her niece Nellie. "It's so unladylike to lounge in a chair, holding a glass at arm's length. You remind me of a man drinking in a tavern."

Nellie giggled. "Aunt Hannah! How do you know? I'm sure you never saw a man drinking in a tavern!"

"I've glimpsed men at their cups as I drove by the Red Lion out on Virginia Road," Hannah Iredell answered. "But no matter. Young maidens should watch their posture, standing or sitting. I can't think what the world is coming to, with all this freedom for the young."

Penelope Barker laughed. "Your Aunt Hannah makes a quick answer, Nellie. I'm sure she never stepped inside a tavern in her life."

"Uncle Jemmy says——" Nellie started.

But her aunt cut in quickly. "Your uncle spoils you."

Mrs. Barker laughed good-humouredly. "That's what women are for. My three husbands all spoiled me. I'm sure your James spoils you. I've never seen a man so in love as he is with you. And after all these years, too."

Hannah Iredell blushed, delicately embarrassed.

"It's nice to be spoiled by one's husband," Mary said, "but really I can't see that girls are different from the way they used to be. I remember how Grandmother Rhoda had me walking about with a book on my head."

"Aunt Hannah makes me do that every day," Nellie cried. " 'A straight back is a mark of beauty. Don't cross your knees. Keep your skirts spread to cover your insteps.' "

" 'Wear a mask in the sun to protect your skin,' " Lucy added. "And, 'Don't turn door-knobs—it makes your hands broad.' "

They all laughed as the girls illustrated the familiar admonitions.

"I declare I'll be glad to get a husband!" Nellie said.

"Nellie!"

The dark-eyed girl laughed. "Oh, no one will propose to me, I'm sure of that. But that handsome, charming Italian Captain de' Medici kissed my hand once. I was just a little girl then, but I vow my heart skipped a beat."

Lucy Tredwell cried her astonishment. "He never did, Nellie!"

"He did so. He tucked his three-cornered hat under his arm and he bowed from the waist like this—a most elegant bow—and his sword clanked. It was thrilling."

"You are talking too much," her aunt said. "You and Lucy had better go for a stroll in the garden."

Nellie pouted. "Just when you are going to gossip about Lady Anne Stuart and her husband."

"It's too hot to walk in our riding-habits," Lucy wailed. "Boots aren't suited for walking in the garden."

"Get along with you, and let your elders talk." Madam Barker spoke crisply.

The girls left reluctantly, with backward glances. Mary laughed.

Hannah Iredell's smile was faint. "You can laugh, but Nellie is a handful. She abounds in energy. She says the most alarming things with complete disregard of whom she is talking to. Her uncle just laughs at her."

Penelope Barker, with the ripe wisdom of a worldly woman who had had three husbands, said, "Don't worry, Hannah. She's a lovely young miss. Her crudities will wear off." She turned to Mary and launched into the purpose of the visit. "We know you haven't been to the village. We were bound to bring you the gossip about our titled visitors. There is truly the greatest excitement about them. Tongues are wagging up and down King Street, east and west, and the merchants on Broad Street can scarce attend to their affairs. Today, as you know, is market day. By nightfall all the plantation folk along the Sound will have the news, and the river-plantation folk and the people out the Virginia Road and Sandy Hill way will be speculating."

"People are flocking to Horniblow's, hoping for a glimpse of the great folk," Hannah said. "It's positively indecent the way they display such curiosity. I think it's ill-bred."

"Well, I'm curious as a crow myself," Madam Barker admitted. "The whole town is planning to entertain them. Why, already Robert Smith is saying we should have a ball in the Panel Room, a splendid affair such as the Frenchmen gave when they were here visiting Stephen Cabarrus."

Mary said, "I suppose they have letters to some one." She did not speak of her knowledge of Lady Anne and her former husband. Penelope Barker, like Dr. Armitage, enjoyed imparting information.

"I've heard her Ladyship has letters to Stephen Cabarrus from his banker uncle in Paris." Madam Barker turned to Hannah. "It's also said she has letters from your husband's cousin Miss Macartney."

"Jemmy has gone to Hillsborough with Mr. Hooper. I don't think he knew anything about these visitors. At least, he didn't mention them to me."

"Well, he didn't know. I'm sure he is as much a gossip as my Thomas. He couldn't keep a choice morsel like Lady Anne Stuart and the Baron to himself." Madam Barker held out her glass to the maid for a second serving of raspberry shrub. "I'm thinking of giving a garden-party for Lady Anne next week. You know how the English love garden-parties." Her sharp dark eyes took on a dreamy look. "Maybe in the evening—I think the moon will be at the full next week. Or perhaps a supper at sunset. I always think the garden looks too beautiful at sunset." She put the empty glass on a tray. "On second thought, I'll have an evening affair. Supper . . . dancing on the lawn . . . little paper lanthorns . . . pitch-pine knots blazing to give light. I hear there's a strolling play company in Norfolk. I can get them over to give a little play and furnish the music."

Hannah was aghast. "Why, madam, you don't even know Lady Anne. How can you give a party?"

Penelope Barker ignored the remark. "Yes, I'll write a note when I go home. I shall have the first affair for our distinguished visitors. I think it's more suitable to have the first in the village." The flicker of a smile curved the corners of her lips. "Yes, my invitations will be out before the Eden House people know they are here." She looked at Hannah. "I don't care if Penelope Dawson *is* your cousin. You're not to tell her until my invitations are out."

Madam Barker was delighted with her plan. Her dark eyes sparkled, her face grew animated. She loved to plan entertainments and took pride in her reputation for hospitality. "Let's see." She began checking on her fingers. "You'll do something for them, Mary. I'm sure Jamie Blount will want them at Mulberry Hill. Cabarrus certainly will entertain them, and your brother Sam." She did not give Hannah Iredell a chance to answer. "That's five plantation parties, and mine in town. Oh, yes, Charles Johnson will be sure to have them at Strawberry Hill."

Mary Rutledge's eyes twinkled. "Robert Smith might arrange a horse race," she suggested.

"Good. Good. And, Mary, what about a fox-hunt, either here or at River Plantation?"

"It's a little early for a hunt. The crops are still in the fields, you know."

"Botheration! I think a hunt would be so elegant. They'd be surprised at the Rutledge pack and all the planters' fine jumpers."

"Maybe Lady Anne doesn't want to be entertained or to meet the villagers."

"Nonsense! All the nobility I've met love attention." Penelope Barker rose, her grey taffeta skirts rustling. "Mary, we must go to town. I did intend to tell you about the woman in that witchcraft case on the Yeopim and talk a little about politics, but we can't spare the time now. I must see Captain Meredith. He will arrange for me to meet Lady Anne at once."

Hannah said timidly, "Perhaps Mr. Cabarrus will want to make plans."

"With his wife in France? Nonsense. Besides, he's in Halifax or Hillsborough meeting with political bigwigs." She turned to the Negro maid. "Call the young ladies, will you? Tell them we are leaving."

"I am sorry you must go so soon," Mary said. "I thought you would stay for supper. I'm sure Chaney is cooking something special for you right now."

"Sorry, Mary, but I must get home to attend to this. We must stop at Hewes and Smith to see what frivolities Captain Meredith brought from France. I hope he has some silk dress patterns. I would like a new frock—a yellow muslin perhaps." She walked swiftly out of the drawing-room, Hannah following.

Mary stepped to the gallery. The girls were already at the upping-block. They ran up to say farewell.

"I don't want to leave. Not in the least. May we come again by ourselves?" Nellie asked.

"Yes, indeed. Come out and spend the night. We'll go across the Sound to visit Eden House."

"When? When? I'm expiring to go. May we come to-morrow afternoon?"

Mary hesitated a moment. There were accounts to be done to-night. She must check the bills of lading with Marcy. "No, not to-morrow. I shall be occupied." Seeing the looks of disappointment on the uplifted faces, she said, "One day soon."

"We will be here by eleven in the morning of any day you say!" Nellie exclaimed.

The horses were led up by a stableboy. Another held the coach door open for the ladies. Madam Barker settled herself in the left-hand corner, leaving Hannah to follow. Waving white hands and calling cries of farewell, the women drove off. Mary watched their coach roll down the long tree-lined avenue to the gates of Queen's Gift.

When she re-entered the house she found the cook Chaney standing at the door of the dining-room, her arms folded over her starched white apron.

"What for dey ridin' away jes' when I planned a good supper wid spoon bread and greens and dat ham I cook yesterday?"

"Madam Barker had to go into town, Chaney."

"M-m. Dose young ladies now, dey don't want to go. Dey come fussin' round my kitchen, askin' what I cook today. Say dey hongry. I give dem milk and some little cakes. Dey expect to eat dey supper right here. How come dey go? Doan dey like our cookin'?"

Mary spoke soothingly, trying to smooth her cook's ruffled feathers. "Of course they like your cooking, but Madam was obliged to be in town."

"I heard Madam Barker talkin'. 'Tain't proper to speak about witch women. Anyway, 'twan't a witch woman, 'twas a witch man down on Yeopim Creek. 'Twas dat fellow dat goes about wid a little willow stick, bendin' it to show where water grows, fitten for a well. He's a witch man, he is."

Mary started to interrupt. Knowing Chaney was ruled by omens and portents and conjurations, she never discussed with her the strange pagan beliefs of the Negroes on the plantation.

Chaney would not be stopped. "Witch man he do more things. He done grease he boots wid dead man's tallow. Den he call up a little fellow, right smack out of de 'cosm. Not no bigger in de head dan de two thumbs of your hand. He talk wid de witch man and tell things. The devil send him. He's de devil's little man. I done see him my ownself." She turned her head and looked over her shoulder, making protective signs with her fingers.

Old Ebon, the butler, came up, walking softly in his list house slippers. "Hush you' mouth, Chaney. Makin' such talk bring evil to you. And get back to you' kitchen."

For once Chaney obeyed. She turned and fled, her heavy body moving swiftly, her head in its bright-coloured turban bowed.

Ebon turned to Mary. "Don't you list to no such mouthin's, mistress. 'Tain't truth she speakin'."

Mary said, "I know, Ebon." She went into the dining-room. All through her lonely dinner she was quiet. It disturbed her to realize that things occurred among the blacks on the plantation that she did not understand.

Ebon sensed her thought. "'Tain't no one around dese parts dat can make magic grease. No, ma'am. Not a solitary. 'Tain't no one can make deyself change to a fox or lion. Nor come in through the keyhole."

Mary laughed. "I know, Ebon. I'm not worried that the devil will appear in a cloud of smoke."

The old man set on the table the dish he had been holding. His gnarled hands were trembling. "Don't you say dat name, mistress, lessen evil come raisin' a great cloud of wind shape, shiftin' into some wild animal." He left the dining-room hurriedly. Mary noticed he was making the same signs with his fingers that Chaney had used to hold off evil.

That night Mary stayed late in Adam's office in the west wing, working on the plantation books. Tazey, the oldest woman slave at Queen's Gift, sat in the corner, knitting long stockings. Tazey nodded over her work, and at last her gay calico turban fell to the floor, showing her grey hair braided into a dozen small plaits pinned close to her head. Though she was ill and feeble, she had insisted on taking the duty of Mary's maid Pam. "If any trouble arise, dat girl don' know how to protect you. She scairt of de conjure woman, dat she is. Dat old hag Mifiti, she doan try none of she spells while I is here."

Mary had sent Pam to bed. "I don't expect any visit from Black Mifiti, but Tazey can keep watch over me." Tazey would fret if she were sent away. Mary hoped Dr. Armitage had not found her condition too serious. She dipped her quill into the ink-well and began to write an account of the day's work, referring to a paper Marcy had left with her.

July 3. Slack season. Have men in back swamp sawing trees. Twenty men on Rutledge Riding belting turpentine trees, and a few shrubbing. Ten horse carts at work hauling dirt from the bottom pasture into the west cotton patch. Tobacco stripping. Four men working in blacksmith shop. Ten in cooper shop, making staves for tobacco hogsheads. Some men repairing fences and all ox carts at work hauling compost and straw and pine needles for hogpens. Harvest broadcast beans next week.

When Mary had entered the day's report in the plantation daily ledger she glanced back over the pages. She came on an April record which Adam had written in his firm hand a few days before he left.

Planted corn in the orchard. Commenced to plant in the low field near swamp, and the boundary field. Single ploughs cutting in manure in cotton patch. Hauling compost, a troublesome task of putting all fields under compost collected during the twelve months past.

We have all tobacco planting finished early this spring. After early ploughing on harrowed land, we transplanted the tobacco plants, on hills three feet apart, directly after the first gentle rain. One of our hands planted ten rows in one day. This after the young slaves preceded the planters, dropping the plants into the prepared hills, having care not to break or bruise the tender young plants. Five days later, the weather being suitable, the young boys went down the rows, breaking the fine crust that had formed about the tobacco plants. They used a very light hoe for the work. In a week they were ready for a light plough.

The slaves made some sort of votary offering to their pagan gods at the end of the planting, which I was supposed not to see. With a strange crooning, they moved in a circle around the oldest man, who held a young plant in his hand, while others dipped their cupped hands into the water; lifting their hands above their heads, they allowed the water to trickle through their fingers slowly.

Herk told me it was their custom to ask the skies to send gentle rain to nurture the small plants and to bring a good yield. I remember reading about some such pagan custom along the Nile. Pouring libations to the gods. There must be some connection between these customs. The Indians had the spring dances and the harvest dance.

In Devon, my father said, the yeomen brought their ploughs to church around Easter-time, where they were blessed, and the rector prayed for a good yield. And this custom we follow here also. I pray for a good growth, so that there be a superfine harvest, to please my dear wife. I may not be here until the harvest is over.

N.B. Mary, please see that tobacco is hoed for four or five weeks, and any grass about the plants is pulled out by hand. We should have an excellent market this year. I have arranged to send it to my agent in Bideford, in North Devon, remember.

Plant wheat, oats and barley next year in south field, and tobacco in the land which is now being shrubbed, in the pocosin near Blount's land. Indian corn along the shore.

Mary closed the book and sat for a moment, staring down at the desk. It was as though she had talked with Adam. She prayed that he would return soon. Perhaps his deep concern over the political situation would bring him home in time for the Hillsborough convention, to which he was an elected delegate. God grant it!

She could see him sitting on the opposite side of the table, smoking his clay pipe, his long legs stretched sidewise. He would run his hands through his blond hair, pulling at an ear-lock, when he was thinking. "Oh, Adam, Adam, how lonely I am without you!" She must have spoken aloud, for Tazey stirred and raised her head. A moment later her needles began to click. She had had her small "wink."

Mary's deep-blue eyes wandered about the room and met the lively, commanding glance of her grandfather Roger Mainwairing. The portrait of Duke Roger hung above the mantel-board. The shifting light from two candles spread flickering shadows across his face. She thought the firm, wide mouth moved as though he spoke to her. She always felt close to him in this room which had been his office. Nothing was changed—the knee-hole desk, the shelf of farm books, the long counting table. The arms of the dark leather chairs had been worn smooth by his hands. She had so often imagined him in this room, talking to her, reprimanding or praising. Sometimes she forgot the features of her grandmother Rhoda, but Duke Roger seemed always alive and present at Queen's Gift. At times she could imagine she heard his voice saying to her what she knew he had believed: *Face life squarely, little Mary. Look life in the face. Hold your head high and do not countenance defeat. And hold the land always, always. Land is your safeguard. It is your very life. Nurture it, give to it, and it will give generously in return. Do not forget that land is the basis of all wealth.* She remembered that Adam had once told her almost the same thing.

She stood up beside the table, her hands busy with a strand of dark hair which had escaped from the knot at the base of her neck. Words formed on her lips as she faced the portrait. *Grandfather, I have tried to keep Queen's Gift as you would want it. Are you pleased with my stewardship?*

A small breeze fluttered the candles on the mantel. She thought the parted lips smiled. The candles flamed up and then died out.

Tazey rose quickly to her feet, letting her ball of wool fall to the floor. She spoke loudly. "Yes, master. Yes, master. You called, master?"

Mary whirled around. The old woman was facing Duke Roger, and her black eyes had a fixed look. Then, trembling, her hands shaking, she ran toward Mary. "Miss Mary! Miss Mary, the old master *he* came to me. He said, tell her I's proud of her stewardship. Dose were he very words. I swear to God. He spoke with he natural voice, jes' like he was here among us."

A sense of unreality came over Mary, as though she had only half awakened from a dream. She had heard no sound from his lips. Only this old woman. Stewardship—the word had guided her grandfather's life. It was an integral part of his belief that men held the land only in stewardship and it was theirs only as long as they gave back as much as they took from the earth.

She looked at the trembling woman. When she spoke her voice was calm. "You were dreaming, Tazey. Go to bed—it's very late."

"He said the words right into my ears, mistress," the slave said stubbornly. "Spoke right out. Liken he always do. No'm, I wasn't making no dream words."

"Go to bed," Mary said again.

"You goin' you'self?"

"No. I'll read a little."

The old woman left reluctantly. At the door she turned, hesitated, but her mistress had already put her nose into one of "dose readin' books." She closed the door softly.

Mary laid the book down as soon as the door was closed. A strange excitement enveloped her. She felt suddenly alert, sensitive to every sound —the mournful voice of the whip-poor-will, the hounds baying at the moon, the lapping of water along the shore. The fragrance of jasmine flowers on the vine that grew thick along the gallery rail was heavy on the warm night air.

There was no wind, she realized suddenly. Not a leaf quivered on the oaks or the tall tulip poplar outside the window. Why had the candles on the mantel gone out? Those on the tables and in the sconces were burning evenly. Yet the mantel candles were protected by the glass hurricane shades.

In the silence that followed she heard the thud of a horse's hoofs in the drive. She went to the gallery and looked down. In the moonlight she saw Marcy tossing his reins to a stableboy. His voice came clearly: "Give her a good rubdown, Zeb. She's hot from the ride from town. Twelve ears of corn, after she's cooled."

Marcy unstrapped his saddle-bags and took from one a square parcel. He saw Mary on the gallery and ran up the steps to where she stood. "Since you are still up, I'll leave this package with you. Captain Meredith gave it to me. He said a merchant in Antigua gave it to him."

"What is it?" Mary asked as she took the bundle from his hands.

Marcy hesitated. "Captain Meredith says it is from your grandfather. The captain sent a note with the parcel and promised to call on you and explain further."

Mary's arms closed around the parcel, pressing it close against her heart. What did it mean, coming after Tazey's revelation? She was so shaken she could not speak. After a time she forced herself to say, "Thank you, Marcy. Thank you." She turned and went into Duke Roger's counting-room.

Marcy thought, She is overcome. She must have been devoted to the old Duke Roger. He went down the stairs and walked swiftly across the garden to his rooms in the bachelors' house.

Mary laid the parcel on the table and opened the note which had been slipped under the cord.

Dear Mrs. Rutledge:

I had the package from a merchant in Antigua. He had recently found it among the effects of his long-dead predecessor and with it a yellowed note to a clerk saying that Mr. Roger Mainwaring desired a journal and box to be bound securely and mailed to Hesketh Mainwaring at Pembroke College, Oxford. He had no knowledge of why the clerk had failed in his duty and showed the package to me as a curiosity. I explained that I knew Hesketh Mainwaring's daughter and persuaded him to let me bring the parcel to you.

JAMES MEREDITH

Mary dropped the note and sat before the table, studying the canvas-wrapped package. She felt again the exaltation she had experienced earlier. Duke Roger's journal! It seemed almost as if her grandfather were reaching out his hand to her across the years. It was strange, frightening.

Not until the case clock in the hall struck midnight did she rise from her chair. Then she placed the parcel in Adam's strong-box. The journal must wait for another time. She had not the strength or courage to open it now.

Horniblow's Tavern

6 THE tall rotund host of Horniblow's sat in a stout tavern chair in his inn, directing his Negro slaves in their cleaning of the room that Lady Anne was to use as a sitting-room. Five other rooms opening on the front gallery had undergone the same wall-brushing, dusting, floor-mopping. Every stick of furniture had been moved out into the hallways. Every floor board had been polished

and waxed, every corner of the baseboard cleaned out with twisted wire. The panels, the chair rails had received the same polishing and waxing. All to please the exacting taste of Lady Anne Stuart.

Horniblow prided himself on keeping a good, clean, respectable house, but nothing suited her Ladyship. She had come ashore from the *Devon Maid* shortly after dinner-time, about one o'clock—an hour when every respectable inhabitant of the village was catching a wee nap—and insisted on seeing the rooms at once. It had taken her half an hour to select the rooms she wanted. Separate rooms for herself and the Baron. A sitting-room for herself. A room for the children, not too close to hers—she couldn't abide their cries if they wakened in the night with a belly-ache or a nightmare—and another for the governess. The maid Dawkins could be put in a back-wing room.

The beds must be changed. Lady Anne could not abide a full canopy; she liked a drapery attached to a tall head-board in the French manner, something washable. She would send over her own sheets, cases and bolster slip. If the landlord couldn't supply draperies to her liking she would have some of her own unpacked. Her meals would be served in her own sitting-room. Oh, yes—in addition to a bedroom for the children she would require a small nursery where the children and the governess could eat and the children could play. Could the landlord complete these arrangements by evening?

Horniblow met all her Ladyship's demands except the last. He could not have the rooms prepared before the following day. After some discussion Lady Anne gave way, but she must have the rooms by noon to-morrow.

Another fifteen minutes was spent in discussing or haggling over the price of the rooms. Lady Anne declared loudly that the amount Horniblow mentioned was an outrage. He was charging London prices. St. James's Park prices at that!

Horniblow was a shrewd bargainer. He gave way slowly, a shilling at a time. Lady Anne's face grew red. Her blond curls bobbed as she shook her head in violent protest, her white hands gesticulated and her voice rose until she could be heard in the common-room downstairs. Black faces appeared at the end of the passageways as hostlers, pot-boys and house-boys gathered to hear the wrangling.

"In a manner of speaking she'll outbark him." . . . "Don't you worry the master he can yell as loud. He don't care if she *is* great folk, if it's money he loses." . . . "Hist! Step back, the mistress is comin'. She'll be settlin' things."

"If you insist on this outrageous price, I'll go right on to Philadelphia!" Lady Anne cried.

"Your Ladyship will find accommodations even dearer in Philadelphia. Besides, there is an epidemic of smallpox there."

The two bargainers stood looking at each other, neither prepared to give an inch. Lady Anne was genuinely bewildered. She was accustomed to complete servility from the lower class, yet here was an innkeeper arguing with her. Horniblow's heavy jaw was set. Gentry or no gentry, he would not give way.

At this moment Ann Horniblow walked briskly down the hall. She was a pretty, fair-haired woman with candid blue eyes, younger than her husband by a dozen years. She had quiet dignity and a gentle voice. She took in the situation at a glance and chose to ignore it. With a slight curtsy to Lady Anne she said, "If your Ladyship will step this way, I will show you a room which may please you."

Glad of a chance to break the argument, Lady Anne followed the landlady down the hall. Mistress Horniblow opened the door of a corner room and stood aside for Lady Anne to enter.

It was a large room, the ceiling high-pitched with two dormers and a door giving out on the upper gallery. Through the windows the tree-lined Green was visible. Outlined by the heavy foliage of oak and elm, Albemarle Sound sparkled in the sunlight. The *Devon Maid* was visible in the little bay, anchored near the Dram Tree. White-galleried houses, green-shuttered, which gave on two sides of the Green, were set in the midst of flowering shrubs and tall green trees. The scene was one of serenity and quietude.

The room was spotless, its fluted muslin curtains freshly ironed. The mahogany bed was draped in chintz of a gay floral pattern matching the paper on the wall. There were comfortable chairs, an armoire painted apple-green, an ample dresser and washstand with pewter basin and ewer.

"The room is newly decorated, madam. In truth no one has occupied it thus far. There is a room off which can be made into a sitting-room, and a small one across the hall will do for your Ladyship's maid." Ann Horniblow smiled pleasantly. "Of course I understand that we do not have accommodations such as your Ladyship is accustomed to, but I do assure you it is as clean as lye soap and scrubbing can make it."

Lady Anne eyed the young woman. Her grey calico gown was neat, her muslin fichu and little mob-cap were snowy white. Lady Anne smiled a little. "As you say, I can't expect perfect accommodations in a small village. I dare say it is the same in England, though I never put up at an inn in a village. One always had friends in the countryside."

She moved about the room, then stood at a window overlooking the water. "This is a pleasant prospect indeed. Now if you can get that mulish husband of yours to come down in his price and quickly make suitable the other rooms we require . . . Can you do that?"

Ann Horniblow smiled. "Don't worry, your Ladyship. Everything will be arranged to your liking so that you can come over to-morrow afternoon."

Now, the next morning, all the rooms were ready save the sitting-room. Ann Horniblow had insisted on moving in her fine falling-leaf table of walnut with two rounded ends to be used for my Lady's meals. A glass cupboard that had come from her grandmother over in Tyrrell was filled with the blue Staffordshire china. A chair imported from England stood by the fire-place, and there were other comfortables for sitting. The brass fire-dogs were polished, the candlesticks gleamed. Ann wished she could have a fire blazing in the hearth and the brass tea-kettle singing on the hob, but July and fires did not agree. She must be content to order the fire-place decorated with a few round beech logs.

Horniblow was happy. He was getting more money than he had hoped for. The nobility were notoriously penurious and close bargainers. He looked at his wife, who with complacent approval was wiping an imaginary bit of dust from the fine polish of the highboy. She placed on the bureau a bowl of heartsease from her garden. The room was finished, all the bed-chambers were in order and there was a good hour to spare.

Horniblow lifted Ann's chin and placed a kiss on her brow. "You were a fine, shrewd woman, Ann, to come in yesterday just when you did. Gad! The woman was hanging on like a bulldog. I felt myself giving in to her just to keep her mouth quiet."

Ann smiled quietly. "You are an excellent bargainer, Mr. Horniblow, but one should never get oneself into a position where one has to back down. One loses dignity, giving way."

Horniblow's red face wore a puzzled expression as he watched his wife move quietly down the hall, her full calico skirts swaying. 'Tis wisdom the lass has, and her so young. . . . He smiled to himself, remembering how village tongues had wagged when he had announced his coming marriage and the sly digs at his age when he gave his dinner the night of the wedding. The village had gossiped about that, too, for he had invited only men, no women. Let the old women gossip. He was satisfied. Well satisfied. Every-thing had turned out for the best.

The work was finished. The servants had gone below-stairs. He closed the door of the sitting-room, turning the brass knob a second twirl to be sure it was locked before he went down the narrow stairs. He didn't intend anyone should enter the room until her Grandness moved in.

The bar-room downstairs was empty. He poured himself a glass of old peach brandy and drank it slowly, enjoying the flavor. He had a fine taste for good liquor, though he did not often indulge himself. He thought with some contempt how few of the village relished good wines. They were for the most part satisfied with corn whisky, raw and green. One drink and the tongue was dulled to any flavour. A lot of yokels, he thought. Ten men at the most in all the six hundred villagers knew decent liquors. Well enough for him—he could cut the corn in half and they were none the wiser. Especially the election crowds. They drank to get drunk, sodden drunk, un-aware of any pleasure to be found in drinking. Then, roistering, yelling, fighting with bare fists, too drunk to know what they did or care where they slept, they would take themselves off, reeling down the lane to the dirty, disgusting shacks along the creek where the lewd women were housed. A poor lot indeed he thought them. The tavern keeper was fastidious in his pleasures and in his vices. No black flesh for him, no green corn whisky. He poured himself a second glass and rolled the amber liquid on his tongue. Five years since he had laid the brandy by; it was well flavoured. He must set a bottle aside for Mr. Hooper when he next came to Edenton.

He clapped his hands. A Negro boy of ten or twelve came from a back room, where he had been stretched on a bench, indulging in a brief rest.

"Get a bough off the bay tree and keep flies off me while I catch me a nap." He stretched himself in a high-backed leather chair. "Keep the bough moving and your eyes on the ship out yonder. Wake me if the captain or his guests put off the ship."

"Yes, sar. I'll keep watchin' for Captain."

Horniblow stretched his silk-stockinged legs on a bench, allowing his buckled shoes to drop to the floor. "I'll skin you alive, boy, if you let a fly light on my nose."

"Yes, sar. No, sar. Won't no fly so much as touch you' face wid one little wing."

The innkeeper did not hear the boy's protestations. He was already snoring, his mouth slightly opened.

Sylvia Hay was astonished at Lady Anne's acceptance of the simple accommodations that Horniblow's Tavern had to offer. But her Ladyship made only a few minor objections. She wanted an extra chair for the sitting-room and a folding tea-table.

"'Twill do very well, Mistress Horniblow. I shall want tea served promptly at half after four each day. The children must be served in their nursery by four."

Mrs. Horniblow hesitated a moment. "Your Ladyship knows our stock of tea is very small and not too good. I will do what I can. Perhaps Mr. Smith has had a new stock by Captain Meredith's ship."

Lady Anne gave her a blank stare.

The woman smiled ingratiatingly. "Your Ladyship does not realize that during the war we drank yapon tea or a concoction made of dried raspberry leaves."

Lady Anne laughed with no sign of irritation. "Of course, I remember now. There was a tax on tea and a war. A very stupid war it was."

Mrs. Horniblow's round blue eyes met Lady Anne's squarely. "A very grim war, your Ladyship."

"Yes, yes, no doubt. No matter. I have a stock of China tea with me. Miss Hay, will you have the tea unpacked? I shall want it this afternoon." She left them and went into her bedchamber. Sylvia heard her humming a gay song.

Mistress Horniblow's eyes were unsmiling. She appeared very serene in her Quaker-grey frock with a crisp white muslin fichu folded over her full breasts. She looked at the young governess. "A very grim, devastating war it was. As for tea, fifty women of this village signed a paper never to drink tea until the tax was taken away. That was in '75, before the war began. They signed in that house." She pointed to a white story-and-a-half cottage that stood on the Green.

"A brave thing." Sylvia spoke impulsively. "A brave, brave thing!"

The landlady showed her surprise. "You think so?"

"Yes, truly. You do not know, perhaps, that there were many of us in England who did not want the American war. Many thousands of folk. Some of our leading statesmen opposed it. The Earl of Chatham and, in Parliament, Mr. Fox, Mr. Wilkes and Mr. Barré. Even Lord Cornwallis opposed the heavy taxes."

"Lord Cornwallis? Well, he must have changed his mind, miss. He burned Suffolk and Norfolk and would have burned Edenton but our armies gave him so much trouble he had to call back the troops he sent to do it."

"Lord Cornwallis was a soldier under orders from his King," Sylvia said placatingly. Mistress Horniblow withdrew without further comment.

Sylvia went to her room. The children had gone for a walk with their father. She would use the free time to write home. She tried to settle down, but found herself restless. At last she wandered to the window.

The Sound sparkled in the sunlight. Children accompanied by black nurses played on the long Green. Women dressed in sprigged calico or muslin strolled along the paths that lined the dusty streets. They wore broad hats or carried gay little sunshades. They were followed by Negro slaves whose gay turbans and brightly coloured clothes made a pleasing picture. Quite like Antigua or Nassau, Sylvia thought, save that the houses were built of white-painted wooden clapboards instead of brick or coquina, and the gardens were protected by hedges rather than walls.

She noted also the straightness of the streets that intersected to form neat little squares. She was not sure that she liked the stiffness. English village streets wandered and turned, she thought nostalgically, and the ancient houses were crowned by uneven rooftops and picturesque chimney-pots. Here there seemed to be strict order in the plan of the village, and there were no reminders of the long generations that had contributed to its growth.

It's a new land, she thought. New and planned. Even the few people she had seen were different. She thought of Mistress Horniblow, her head high; she was courteous, but there was no servility in her demeanour, no humbleness before her betters. A strange attitude, surely. Perhaps it came from a society where black slaves did the humble tasks.

People were coming and going along the streets, some on horseback. Men in knee-breeches, white stockings and buckled shoes. Countrymen.in rough holland smocks. Sylvia stepped out onto the upper gallery and gazed at the brick Courthouse, a fine dignified building with a clock-tower; it reminded her of the early Georgian architecture. Across a broad street was a building with a lesser tower, a cupola in fact. A few residences were mixed in among the shops, some double-galleried, others of one story and a half story with pierced dormer windows. The street was shaded by oak and bay trees, and wooden awnings above the shop fronts gave the passers-by additional shelter from the hot sun.

Small boats were tied up at the docks. They looked like the Cornish fishing boats, she thought. It must be dull, shut up in a village of six hundred souls, with no London to go to for the season. Heigh ho, it would not matter whether she liked Edenton or not. Sylvia was sure Lady Anne had come here only because she might gain some advantage through having letters to Mr. Iredell and Mr. Cabarrus. More and more people appeared in the streets as she watched. She realized it must be noon. The Baron and the boys were crossing the Green on their way back to the inn. She felt sorry for the Baron. He was a kind man, though too meticulous. His mind dealt in figures, and he was short on humour. He loved his sons ardently, and the little ones adored him. Often he managed to stand between them and his wife's impatience and anger. In his protectiveness, his solicitude, he was almost like a mother.

The Baron's erect, military bearing was conspicuous in these surroundings. Many of the men who were walking along the street slouched. In their ungainly walk there was none of the precision that marked the European soldier. Yet these same men had defeated Cornwallis and Tarleton and General Burgoyne. It was all incredible.

There was Dr. Moray. She recognized him although he was a full hundred yards away. He towered above the older man who walked beside him. They were talking earnestly, the older man pointing in this direction and that, spreading his arms as though to encompass the entire village. Sylvia felt her pulse quicken. This annoyed her. Last night in the heavy darkness she had thought of Moray, the memory of his nearness to her a living thing. How could he turn from her to another woman? Lady Anne, predatory, seeking always a new sensation. How could her jaded beauty draw him? But she was very beautiful in the moonlight.

She turned away to shut the sight of him from her eyes. Have you no pride, Sylvia? she asked herself. Throwing yourself into the arms of a man! It is unmaidenly. Whatever has come over you to seek out a man with such boldness?

She sat down at the chintz-covered dressing-table and began to rearrange her hair. I shall be distant when he speaks to me, she resolved. Very, very distant and remote. After all, she too was well-born. It was only that the estate had gone to a distant cousin when her father died. That was why she must be at the beck and call of a woman like Lady Anne. She was sorry now that she had not accepted Aunt Agatha's invitation to have a second London season. But perhaps something pleasant would happen to her here in America.

The children ran into the room. "It's dinner-time, Miss Hay. The table's all set up in the nursery. Come quickly. Father is going to eat with us. Lady Anne has a headache."

Sylvia smoothed her hair without another look at her image in the mirror and followed the children. What good were heavy auburn braids and amber eyes if Dr. Moray saw no beauty in them? At dinner she shut away all thought of him. When she returned to her room she met Lady Anne's woman at the door.

"Her Ladyship's orders, Miss Hay. Will you please give the children their tea this afternoon and keep them occupied until supper? Her Ladyship expects Dr. Moray for tea, and she does not wish to be disturbed."

So Lady Anne would entertain the doctor. She didn't wish to be disturbed. Doubtless she had sent her husband off on some journey. Sylvia was astonished to hear her own voice steady and unwavering in spite of the rage that stirred within her. "Will the Baron have tea with the children?"

"No, Miss Hay. The Baron will be riding out into the country to look at an estate on the Chowan River, a matter of several miles, I believe."

After the woman had departed, Sylvia went to her dressing-table and sat looking in the glass. She glanced down at her hands folded in her lap and saw that they were tightly clenched. Her white teeth closed over her full red lower lip. I *won't* like that man! I won't! He is not half so fine as Donald. I will not let him make me resent Donald's claim on me. . . . She put her head on the table and let the tears flow down her cheeks.

After a time she got up and poured some water from the ewer into the wash-basin. Time and time again she splashed the cool water over her face. She changed her frock and put on a pale-green muslin over a ruffled petticoat of white. The picture she saw in the mirror cheered her. At least I am younger than Lady Anne, she thought, and my skin is fresher, and I don't wash my hair in soda to give it colour.

She heard the children racing down the hall, and a moment later she opened the door to their impatient knocking. Eitel was breathless. "Oh, Miss Hay, our father said please excuse us from lessons. He is going to drive us out into the country. He says to dress suitably. What shall we wear?"

"Your riding-dress, I should think, Eitel. Hans, run put on your riding-breeches and your long boots." She heard them charging down the hall, opening and banging doors. Shortly after, they clattered down the stairs.

Sylvia went to the window. Four men on spirited horses came riding down the street and dismounted in front of Horniblow's. They were well-attired gentlemen such as might be seen in any village in England. One in particular caught her attention, a tall man with dark, almost black hair, queued and ribanded. His eyes were dark and brilliant. Surely he was a Latin type. Several men stepped from the piazza in front of the inn to greet him. She heard his name spoken. De' Medici. That was strange. Why would a member of that great Italian family be here in this obscure Carolina village?

She stepped through the door and walked to the edge of the upper gallery. As she leaned against the railing, looking down, the dark man glanced up and saw her. He touched his tricorne with the tip of his gloved hand, and a flashing smile came to his lips. Sylvia stepped back quickly, embarrassed to be caught staring like any serving-maid.

A moment later she heard the Baron's voice. "Well met, Signor de' Medici. It's a pleasure to see you again after all these years."

"And in such a far-off place. Let me see, Baron, the last time it was Venice, was it not?"

"Yes, Venice, at Ca' Rezzonico. I remember very well the Contessa's grand ball. And the marvellous ceiling in Lodovico's and Faustina's nuptial chamber! By Tiepolo, was it not?"

Sylvia did not hear De' Medici's answer, but a moment later she heard him say, "We must arrange a meeting to talk over old times. *A rivederci, Baron.*"

The group moved out of earshot. Stepping forward cautiously, Sylvia saw the Baron place the boys in a riding-chair, driven by a Negro coachman. A hostler brought up a bay mare. The Baron mounted and joined a tall, spare man with a lean face who was waiting for him.

In his precise, accented English the Baron said, "I trust we have not kept you waiting, Mr. Johnson. My sons are as eager as I to proceed to Parson Earle's River Plantation. I've told them of your kind offer to show me the school there."

When they had gone Sylvia stood looking at the sparkling waters of the Sound. It seemed almost a painted scene. In the street below the gallery horsemen rode by, and Negroes drove high-wheeled Devon carts filled with produce.

In front of the Courthouse a crowd was gathering. Men in the sombre dress of merchants or barristers stood on the steps and overflowed into the street. A man wearing a badge banged on the stone flagging with his staff. She could not catch all his words, but she soon realized that a land auction was in progress. One parcel of a hundred acres in fields, with two hundred acres in timber, located on Rockahock Creek and the Chowan River. Estate of one Ebenezer Parry, deceased.

The bidding was spirited, the crowd edging close to the auctioneer. She saw the dark De' Medici come out from under the gallery and mount his horse. He glanced up quickly. Sylvia shrank back against the door. She thought with satisfaction that he had looked for her.

His voice with its rich Latin accent came to her clearly. "I will ride to

Queen's Gift now. Evidently Mr. Barker has been detained. Perhaps I may
be fortunate enough to see him when I return."

Sylvia smiled slightly. If Angus Moray took Lady Anne, she also might
find a handsome escort. She moved forward and watched the lithe, strong
figure sitting the great black horse so easily. The choice might not be at all
difficult.

With the lads out of the way and Lady Anne in seclusion, dressing for
a visit from Dr. Moray, Sylvia was quite free. Later, when it was cooler,
she would walk down the shaded streets. Now she would write some letters.
She had promised Margaret Macartney she would report her impressions of
the new country. No, she would wait to write until she had met Margaret's
cousin James Iredell, who was a barrister in the village, or a judge, she had
forgotten which. There were issues of the *Gentleman's Magazine* she'd had
no time to look at on the voyage.

The afternoon went swiftly. A maid brought her tea. A very nice tea,
she had to admit, with fresh-baked bread cut in thin slices, a peach conserve and nice short-bread. The tea had the peculiar taste of gunpowder tea,
but it was hot, and the service was Chelsea china. These folk were not too
uncivilized. The Negro maid was so smiling, so anxious to please. It was
very flattering to be the object of such round-eyed curiosity. Once or twice
she thought of Lady Anne, in her pleasant sitting-room. Doubtless Dr.
Moray had come and she would be charming her latest cavalier.

After the maid had removed the tea things Sylvia put on a wide-
brimmed leghorn trimmed with roses. She tied the velvet riband streamer
under her chin and thought her green frock looked very well, even though
it was two seasons old. She pulled on her lace gloves. Her sunshade, lined in
rose, looked well with her gown and cast a pleasant glow over her face. Let
Lady Anne charm the young surgeon. There were other gentlemen who
might prove attractive on acquaintance.

As she went downstairs she caught a glimpse of the common-room. Al-
ready many gentlemen had gathered to have their ale. She met Madam
Horniblow in the lower hall that led to a side entrance giving on the
Courthouse Lane.

As she neared the ladies' parlour she heard voices. Lady Anne's woman
was saying, "Her Ladyship is not receiving today, madam."

Another voice, raised slightly, spoke imperiously. "Did you announce to
the Baroness that Madam Barker was calling?"

"Oh, madam, I could never interrupt her Ladyship when she has given
orders not to be disturbed."

"Well, I do declare!" The voice had an indignant ring. "Announce me this
moment, my good woman."

Dawkins was obdurate, but her voice was apologetic. " 'Twould be impossible, madam. Madam is having tea with a guest. I am sorry, madam."

"Very well. I will leave a message. Madam Thomas Barker will pay her respects to the Baroness von Pollnitz at eleven in the morning."

Sylvia stood aside as Madam Barker swept out with a swish of silk petticoats, followed by the fragrance of verbena. The roses on the high-held little bonnet were quivering.

The lady's maid caught sight of Sylvia. "There's a determined woman, Miss Hay. She was bound to walk right up to her Ladyship's parlour. I had to be firm."

Sylvia said, "I hope she is not offended, Dawkins. One must be diplomatic about these things."

The maid's mouth drew into a straight line. "I've just done as I was instructed, miss. I couldn't let her walk in on the mistress and the young man. Now could I?"

"I suppose not," Sylvia said and proceeded on her way. Somehow the brightness of the day had faded a little.

Sylvia Meets Adventure

7 Sylvia had only one errand—to buy a shank of wool for a piece of crewel-work she was making. The boy at the carriage block told her she had only to walk up King Street to the corner. Hewes and Smith was the name of the shop. "Ladies from all of the town will be found there at this hour. They'll be sitting in the little garden, drinking their tea and looking at the fine things that have come in Captain Meredith's ship."

She opened her sunshade and walked the half-block. As she passed a tall hedge she heard women's laughter, followed by exclamations of admiration and delight. Doubtless this hedge screened the garden where the merchant was showing his wares to the ladies of Edenton.

Around the corner on Broad Street she found the entrance to the shop. The doorway was protected by a wooden awning mounted on iron poles. A half-dozen such shops stretched north. In the block that extended from the corner to the wharves were many other shops; some dark-shuttered, others with small-paned bow-windows in which wares were displayed. Sylvia identified a chemist's shop by its red and green bottles. The barber, next below, had a sign offering the services of Mr. West, wig maker. Sylvia stood for a moment in the doorway, looking toward the docks. A number of people were moving about. Negroes were unloading a small boat, while well-costumed gentry in knee-breeches, buckled shoes and linen coats sat on benches under a shade tree and watched the proceeding. One or another would identify his merchandise, which was then carried away and placed in a cart, later to be driven to a home in the village or a near-by plantation. Saddle horses were tied to iron racks in front of shops. Small Negro boys stood at their heads, waving green branches to drive away the pestering flies and insects.

The interior of the shop was dark, so dark that for a time Sylvia couldn't make out objects in the gloom. A clerk stepped forward, a thin young man with sandy hair and pale-blue eyes, neatly dressed in a ruffled white shirt and nankin breeches. He bowed politely and asked how he could serve her. Sylvia gave him a sample of the wool. After examining it he said that to match the yarn he must undo a package of wools that had come in the *Devon Maid*. "Perhaps madam would like to step into the garden and have a dish of tea while she waits?"

Sylvia said, "No, thank you, I'll wait here."

The clerk pulled up a chair near a barred window that looked out on the garden. "Cato, bring madam a glass of raspberry shrub."

Sylvia started to decline the drink, then thought better of it. It would be ungracious to refuse the spontaneous hospitality.

A Negro, grey-haired and wrinkled, shuffled off and returned a moment later carrying a small silver tray with a crystal cup filled with a ruby-coloured mixture. As she drank Sylvia looked about the shop. The shelves were well stocked with materials—cottons and prints, taffetas, velvets and brocades, bolts of embroideries and narrow lace edging. On the opposite side were coarser cloths, hollands, nankins. On a counter were a partial set of dishes in white Queen's ware and a stack of plates of a flowered pattern, with a number of plain plates of various sizes. Beside the fine china were stacked heavy crockery, pots and pans of copper, iron pots, brass candlesticks and a quantity of pewter. In the back of the store were unopened packing boxes and crates. The space around the crates was overflowing with horse collars, bridles, saddles. Farm implements encroached on bolts of gaudy calicoes. Andirons and fenders, candle moulds, Manila ropes, fishing gear and firearms were jumbled together. The effect was one of complete confusion, and Sylvia wondered how the clerks could find anything the customers wanted.

She sipped her shrub and found it cool and delicious. A woman's voice, clear and incisive, commanded her attention. "I called at tea-time on Lady Anne, as was proper, but she was not to be disturbed."

Another voice, gentler, said, "Perhaps it was too early, Madam Barker. The English have tea at a later hour than we. Five o'clock, I think, is the hour Jemmy told me that they always drank tea."

The first voice replied, "Are you suggesting that I do not know what is customary in society, Hannah?"

"No. No, of course not, madam." The voice was conciliatory.

"You must remember, Hannah, that Mr. Barker lived eighteen years in London when he was agent for the colony."

"But you were not with him, were you?" A third voice asked the question. Sylvia thought, That woman is enjoying herself.

"No, you know I wasn't. But I've heard Mr. Barker tell of fashionable London society often enough to know. At any rate, I did the polite thing. I called and left messages. I shall return to-morrow morning."

A young girl's voice said, "I heard that the Baron had gone out to River Plantation with Mr. Charles Johnson. Perhaps they intend putting the children in Parson Earle's school."

"How do you know that?" demanded the woman Sylvia had heard addressed as Madam Barker. "It appears to me, Clothilde, you are mighty interested in gathering gossip."

"No, no, madam. It was Mrs. Horniblow who told me. She said the Baron is a very fine gentleman. Everything appeared to please him, but the lady is very exacting."

Sylvia smiled a little. Women talked about other women in the very same way, whether in London or Edenton. Of course Madam Barker was the lady Dawkins had rebuffed.

Madam Barker shut off the young girl by saying, "And who has a better right to be exacting than Lord Bute's daughter?"

"Yes, ma'am."

"At any rate, I shall give a garden-party. It is only politeness to make strangers welcome to Edenton."

Another young girl said, "Perhaps Lady Anne will give a ball. Do you remember how those young French officers invited every one to a ball in the Panel Room before any one had invited them to their homes?"

"I remember that you were horrified, Nellie. You wrote your Uncle Jemmy and told him to warn the Duke de Braille that it wasn't the custom here for strangers to give the first entertainment." Every one laughed.

The girl's voice showed her chagrin. "Oh, Aunt Hannah, how unkind to tell that story on me! I was nothing but a child when it happened. Why, it was early in the Revolution that the French noblemen were here."

Sylvia turned in her chair. Shamelessly she looked through the window so that she could see the speakers. A table set for tea was placed under a large oak tree. The tiny garden, bright with flowers, was shut off from the street by a high hedge. As the conversation went on Sylvia could fit faces to the voices. Madam Barker, whom she had glimpsed in the ladies' parlour, faced her. A slight, delicate-looking woman whom she identified as Hannah sat next; then a third woman whose face she could not see. Two young girls made up the party. She watched a man come into the garden. He was well dressed and had a thin, saturnine face to which a long nose gave character. With him came two Negroes carrying bundles of materials, which they placed on a couple of empty tables.

The girl Nellie cried, "Oh, Mr. Smith, what beautiful muslins!"

Mr. Smith, the owner of the shop, spoke to each woman in turn, bowing elegantly. "Madam Barker, Mistress Iredell, Mistress Tredwell, Miss Nellie and Miss Clothilde. It pleasures me to see you all so full of health."

Madam Barker said, "Mr. Smith, did my lilac taffetas arrive? And the Mechlin lace for Mr. Barker's coat?"

"All here, madam. I've already sent the order to your home, at Mr. Barker's request. He vows he is well pleased with the lace and the elegant broadcloth for his coat and cape. Now, ladies, I am giving you first look at the new materials—even before I fill the Eden House order or Mrs. Rutledge's."

The clerk had come up behind Sylvia. "Madam, here is your wool. A perfect match, if my eyes don't fail me."

Sylvia turned from the window. She took the hank of wool and compared it with the sample. "Thank you, it is perfect. What do I owe?"

"Two shillings, mistress."

She rummaged in her purse and laid the coins on the counter. "Thank you so much."

"Is there anything else, mistress? As you see, we have a new shipment of china and some plate, and cutlery from Sheffield. We have taffeta silk and velvet and brocades from France." He waved a thin hand toward the piles of cloth on the counter.

"Thank you, I do not need anything at the moment."

"Merchandise goes very quickly, madam. Tuesday and Saturday the country-folk come in for their trading, and on Friday the midsummer fair will begin."

She took up the parcel of wool. "I'll come in again perhaps."

The clerk started to speak, hesitated, and then, as if he had suddenly found courage, went ahead. "Perhaps you will notify Lady Anne Stuart? I knew when you came in you must be with her party. We carry the finest stock in this part of the country, quite as fine as Mr. Hogg's in Wilmington and Mr. Cout's in Norfolk. We have two excellent manteau makers in the village." The clerk held the door open, bowing politely.

The street was more crowded than before, and the heat was stifling after the pleasant coolness of the darkened store. Sylvia paused a moment, undecided whether she would continue her walk. The water at the end of the street looked so inviting that she put up her sunshade and strolled toward the wharf.

The breeze from the Sound was cooling. It blew across her cheeks, soft and balmy. At the end of Broad Street she turned, following the water. She walked past a flagpole rising above what seemed to be a parade-ground. Presently she was in a district of warehouses and fishing boats. She crossed the front of a shipyard where men were working on the hull of a ship. Beyond the shipyard were small, unpainted houses, very different from the white-painted, green-shuttered houses of the district close to Broad Street. The farther she walked, the more shabby the houses were.

She crossed a main thoroughfare—a highway, she thought, judging by the number of horsemen, waggons and carts. Beyond the highway fumes from a tannery offended her nostrils. The street had narrowed to a small path. Just ahead was an inn of sorts, a dilapidated structure with an unkempt yard and sagging verandas. She heard loud voices and the drunken laughter of men and women.

As Sylvia started to turn back, a man who had just left the inn approached her. He was unshaved, his shirt damp with perspiration, his blue denim breeches stiff with tar. He was walking unsteadily. She stepped aside on the path and looked the other way. He stopped, caught at the ruffles of her little sunshade and looked under the frills to see her face. His breath reeked of spirits. Sylvia backed against a fence, thoroughly frightened.

"Come, little miss. Come with me and I'll stand you a mug of ale."

"Thank you, no." She tried to pass, but he pressed close to her, clutching at her wrist. She pulled away.

"Oh! High and mighty, are ye? Let me tell you, I'm as good as any one. I've got money in my pocket. I tell ye I'll stand ye a mug."

Sylvia glanced about quickly. She could not pass him in the narrow path. She did not want to turn and flee.

"Come, come, don't play coy. I know your kind. You're a five-shilling girl. Well, I can pay five shillings." He made a grab at her arm.

Sylvia acted. She pushed her sunshade into his face.

The man jumped backward, cursing roundly. "You'd put my eye out with that 'brella, I'll show you."

Sylvia heard the pounding of a horse's hoofs on the hard road. A voice shouted, "Get out of the way, fellow, or I'll thrash you with my whip."

The man jumped back. "Meant no harm, sir. These girls getting too biggety, they are."

Sylvia looked up. The rider was the Latin gentleman Baron von Pollnitz had addressed as Signor de' Medici. Her face was very white as she looked up at him. "Oh, thank you. Thank you." Her voice quivered. She strove to steady it. "The man was very drunk. I was helpless to deal with him."

De' Medici had dismounted. He appeared not to notice her agitation. "Let me escort you back to your lodgings. This is not the place for a young woman to be." With a graceful motion he turned his horse and offered Sylvia his arm.

The drunken man was shouting from the veranda. A dozen men and girls stood with him.

Sylvia's face flamed. From their low-cut dresses and the way they hung onto the men, she knew what the women were. "Oh!" she breathed, walking so rapidly that she tugged De' Medici's arm.

"You are a stranger here. It is well not to walk too far from the main streets, certainly not beyond the flagpole."

Sylvia said nothing. She wanted only to get away as quickly as possible.

"Don't run. You are quite safe." He stopped, removed his three-cornered hat and made a slight bow. "May I introduce myself? I am Cosmo de' Medici, lately Captain of the First North Carolina Dragoons."

"I am Sylvia Hay. I came to Edenton only yesterday on the *Devon Maid.*"

"Ah. Then you must have met my friend Von Pollnitz. He came over on that ship."

"I am governess to the Baron's children," she answered, looking up at him. "It was silly of me to walk about without knowing where the paths would lead me."

"I am glad I happened to be riding that way." He smiled suddenly, showing his even white teeth. "I may as well confess. I had called at Horniblow's after my return from a friend's plantation. I saw you start your walk. I followed you. I think I was hoping that I might render some slight service so that I could speak to you without being considered rude. Yes? You know, I saw you earlier on the gallery at the inn."

His manner was so ingratiating, his smile so infectious, that Sylvia laughed aloud. "Thank you again. I am grateful to have so gallant a knight as a protector."

"Now you are laughing at me. You were in no danger. A little annoyance, no more." He smiled slyly. "Besides, with your little sunshade you would soon have vanquished the enemy." De' Medici slipped the bridle reins over his arm and the horse followed obediently as side by side they walked back toward the village. De' Medici talked easily about indifferent things, the village, the people who resided in it. And then, almost diffidently, he told her of his faith in this new land.

"My plantation is in Granville County, and now I am buying land near Bath, a small place south of here," he said. "I prefer it in Edenton, but no one will sell. The people here remind me of Italians; acquiring and holding land is an obsession."

"It is the same in Devon, where I live," she answered. "I know Italy well. I love Venice. We lived there for two years. My father died in Venice." She paused a moment; sadness showed in her eyes. "His last months were made beautiful because he too loved Italy."

"You will like America," he said. "Do you plan to stay long?"

"I don't know. I have no say in this. Lady Anne is changeable, and we must move when she becomes bored."

Cosmo raised his heavy eyebrows inquiringly. "Lady Anne? What of the Baron's wishes? Does he not decide?"

Sylvia hesitated. She had a natural distaste for discussing her employers, but this man's manner invited confidence.

He sensed her reluctance. "I became acquainted with the Baron some years ago. We met in Venice, where he was on some sort of mission for his government. Every one thought him a very able man."

"A gentleman," Sylvia said. "A fine father, so thoughtful of his children. In truth he is thoughtful of every one. I particularly like his kind attitude toward servants."

They had come to the wharves. He paused. "I will leave you here, Miss Hay. You see I am not really a gallant knight. I have an appointment I can no longer postpone. You will be safe now. I hope you will allow me the pleasure of calling on you. I shall ask the Baron to present me in a more formal way."

Sylvia laughed. She had a lovely, musical laugh, and her somewhat serious expression changed wonderfully. "I don't mind an unconventional introduction, Captain de' Medici. Isn't it considered romantic to be rescued in so gallant a fashion?"

De' Medici lifted her hand to his lips. "Fortune was with me today. Let us hope that an acquaintance begun in a somewhat violent atmosphere will flower under more sunny conditions."

Sylvia walked on slowly to the Green, passed the empty stocks and the ducking-stool and made her way to the inn. As she turned into the lane between Horniblow's and the Courthouse she met Dr. Moray. He lifted his hat and bowed. He hesitated as though he would stop, but Sylvia bowed slightly and walked on, her head high. She had no intention of allowing him to think he could pursue Lady Anne and turn to her as an afterthought. Indeed not! She might be occupying an inferior position, but she was not a dairymaid, to be had for the asking. Sylvia was a proud person, as stiff-necked as her ancestors the LeHays, who had come over with William the Conqueror. In truth she considered herself superior to her employer Lady Anne Stuart in ancestry and certainly in breeding. Her father's death had changed her position. His estate had gone to a distant cousin, leaving her alone with only a small income. She could have accepted the invitation to live at her childhood home near Bideford, but instead she journeyed to London and for a year lived with her Aunt Agatha.

A short season in society had satisfied her curiosity. She determined to seek a position. One of her cousin's friends spoke to the Baroness von Pollnitz, and the position of governess to the two boys was secured for Sylvia without delay. The fact that she had spent some years abroad and spoke French, Italian and German fluently was the deciding factor. The Baron told her later, "I want my sons to have diplomatic careers, and languages are important. You speak beautifully, Miss Hay."

Sylvia had told Lady Anne few details of her background. It certainly would not please her to know that Sylvia's aunt was a friend of her former husband, Northumberland. That would never do. Besides, Sylvia derived a secret pleasure from maintaining a discreet silence about her own affairs.

She enjoyed playing the part of a quiet, well-mannered young woman, a perfect governess who knew her place and kept it.

She had managed to please Lady Anne thus far. There were times when she had difficulty in controlling her temper, which in her girlhood had been considered rather short. Now, at twenty-two, she had almost mastered it. "Lose your temper and lose the argument," her father had often told her. He would be pleased if he knew how calm she could be on the surface while raging within herself.

The children had not yet returned. She went to her room and took off her clothes and bathed. She wanted to be free of the dust of the streets and lanes, but most of all she wanted to be free of the evil represented by the drunken men and the house of lewd women.

She had dressed and was tying a black velvet riband about her throat when Dawkins knocked at her door. "Her Ladyship would like you to sup with her in her sitting-room. The Baron has sent word that he and the children are staying the night at River Plantation. They will return some time to-morrow, after dinner."

"What time does Lady Anne want me?"

"Around seven, she said. She is resting now." A sly look came into the woman's black beady eyes. "She is exhausted. By the heat, she says."

Sylvia ignored the implication. "Thank you, Dawkins. I will be there promptly." She sat down at the little desk near the window. The sun was low; a little breeze stirred the leaves on the oaks at the edge of the Green. The children and their black nurses had departed. Twilight would soon lie lightly on the village—the short, quiet time before candle-lighting that she loved. A time to sit quietly, to reflect. Presently she took up the quill and began to write to her dear friend in Bristol, Margaret Macartney.

Edenton, North Carolina
July 3, 1788

Dearest Margaret:

I haven't a proper pen. You know I like the hard-nibbed ones. You will see by the above date-mark that we have arrived safely in America. Lady Anne and the Baron have found adequate accommodations for us at an inn called Horniblow's. They have not had an opportunity as yet to present their letter to your cousin Mr. Iredell. I am eager to know him.

I have not forgotten my promise to give you my impression of the place where you have so many friends. I have a sense of isolation here. I believe Norfolk, in Virginia, is the nearest city of any consideration. I have not had time really to form an opinion, but I have met several people and observed a few more. The women are surprisingly well dressed, à la mode. The men quite fine-looking, vigorous, and ride decent horses. I have seen few coaches.

Actually, the only man I have talked with is a Captain Cosmo de' Medici. Don't be too astonished when I tell you he is of the Florentine family. It appears he came over during the late Revolution, with some of the young Frenchmen who followed the Marquis de LaFayette. He has lingered on, he tells me, because he likes the ideals of this young country. Liberty, he says, is an accomplished fact. "A great and noble experiment" were his words.

Captain de' Medici looks like the paintings of that family, the olive skin, the long oval face, with very dark brilliant eyes deep-set under heavy brows. His nose is long, and his mouth wide and a little sensual. You will think I am over-awed by the representative of the great Italian family. I am not really, but we met in a peculiar way. I will not go into that now, as it is almost time for me to have supper with Lady Anne.

There was a young doctor on the ship. His name is Angus Moray. You spend so much time in Scotland, do you know anything of that family?

I can imagine you now at Bath, taking the waters. Do tell me about your summer adventures. Who is courting whom? Has Lady L—— got over her in-fatuation for the Prince? I don't want to get completely out of touch with gossip or fashions while I am here.

We are supposed to travel on to Philadelphia before long. What Lady Anne's object is, I cannot imagine. I should think that a daughter of Lord Bute would be timid about appearing publicly in this country. I'm sure Lord Bute was as unpopular during the late Revolution as Lord North.

My felicitations to your family.

With deep affection,
SYLVIA HAY

P.S. Do send me some magazines. And what are the latest novels? Is Mr. Sheridan at Bath this season? Is his wife still the toast of the young gentlemen? The pleasures we enjoyed together seem very far away to-night. Remember how we laughed at Mr. Goldsmith's comedy *She Stoops to Conquer* a few years ago? And did we not see a play called *The Mistakes of a Night* at about the same time? I really can see you at a ball in the Upper Rooms. You always make such an appearance that you throw even the stage beauties into the shadow. Do tell me the latest fashion for the hair. What frisure have you adopted?

This pen is beyond words, and I have no knife to mend it. I know if we were face to face, you would question me more closely about the people. As I say, I have met only a few, but one thing stands out, the independent attitude of all classes. There is politeness, but no servility. There seems to be only *one* class, the servants being Negro slaves.

Sylvia knocked at Lady Anne's door a few moments before seven. She found her Ladyship lying on a couch near the window, dressed in a thin white muslin wrapper. She was fanning herself wearily with a small fan made of peacock feathers with a carved ivory handle. "Come in, my dear. Did you ever feel such devastating heat in all your life? Please tie those curtains back. There seems to be a little breeze off the water."

Lady Anne got up and moved languidly about the room. Sylvia saw that she had left off her petticoats. She wondered if she had received her visitor in this costume. For some reason she did not look vulgar, bereft of the screening underskirts. Instead she looked quite Greek, like one of the figures in the Parthenon frieze which Sylvia had seen in Nicholas Revett's drawings.

After a few minutes' silence Lady Anne said, "The Baron is planning to leave the children here when we go to Philadelphia."

Sylvia's heart sank. One thing she did not want was the responsibility for the two boys while their parents were away. Something of her thoughts must have shone in her face, for Lady Anne laughed, a gay, tinkling laugh that always charmed her masculine admirers. "Don't be worried, dear Sylvia. I have no intention of leaving you here to look after two little heathens. I need you with me. I shall make you my secretary-companion instead of governess."

"But the boys?" Sylvia asked.

"We are told that there is a very good classical school in the country near here, run by the rector of St. Paul's Church, Parson Daniel Earle. The Baron has gone out to investigate. If it pleases him, he will make the arrangements today." She waved her fan back and forth. "I find myself a little handicapped, having them with me. I want to be free to go about as I please in Philadelphia. If the Baron is away, I should have a companion, to conform to the amenities. Provincials are so critical." She laughed again, as though pleased with some secret thought. "We might even go to New York together without the Baron. My man of business will be coming over from London before long. You will find Mr. Stephen Sayre a most gallant escort, a gentleman of fashion and very, very handsome."

Sylvia thought she understood why she was promoted from governess to secretary-companion, but she made a suitable remark about New York and the pleasure it would give her to visit that capital.

There was a gentle knock at the door, and a little black boy, carrying the evening meal, came into the room. A second boy, wearing discreet dark livery, set up the table, lighted the candles and announced that supper was served.

Lady Anne surveyed the table with some satisfaction. Cold meats, a rarebit in a pottery dish, fresh greens for a sallet, pickles and preserves and hot bread made from gound maize. "Not too bad," she said as she took her place at the table.

The servant asked, "Will your Ladyship have a light, dry sherry with your supper, or do you prefer ale?"

"Ale, by all means." To Sylvia she said, "These people serve very good meals. I find myself quite astonished."

After they had finished supper Lady Anne said, "You may as well begin your new tasks at once. I have a note of invitation to be answered." She waved a slim hand in the direction of the desk. "A Mrs. Thomas Barker, Penelope Barker, called and told Dawkins that she would return at eleven in the morning—an ungodly hour, but perhaps it is the village custom. Later she sent a note by her blackamoor, asking the privilege of giving a garden-party for me next week. I have inquired of the innkeeper's wife. She assures me that Madam Barker is a woman of consequence here in the village, so we may as well accept this little courtesy and meet the villagers."

Sylvia was astonished. Lady Anne was not always so gracious. Sometimes she took on the attributes of the royal Stuarts, ignoring the fact that she was a Stuart of Bute and not royal. She took up a quill and wrote the note.

Lady Anne read it with satisfaction. "Nicely worded, Sylvia. Now look in my dispatch-case. As you know, I have some introductory letters. One is to James Iredell, a connection of the Macartneys; my sister is married to Earl Macartney. Then there is one to Stephen Cabarrus of Pembroke from his uncle, the Paris banker. There is a most delightful man, so elegantly Spanish! He accommodated me when I ran short of funds on my last trip to Paris. That rascal Northumberland was behind in my payments and I found myself quite embarrassed. But Señor Cabarrus was kind. We became quite good friends." She laughed a little and held up a slim arm, showing the emerald bracelet she was wearing. "Yes, indeed, very good friends we were. He had grace and a fine appreciation. Very sensitive to the female whims and pleasures. . . . Write to the gentlemen, please. Acquaint them with our arrival and ask them to call. Word it nicely, mind you."

Sylvia sat at the desk and composed the notes, careful to write clearly and in an elegant manner.

Lady Anne was pleased with the results. "I see that we shall get along nicely, Miss Hay," she observed in her most gracious manner. Sylvia thought, She has enjoyed herself this afternoon, so her humour is good.

Lady Anne wandered to the window. "I hear that there is a young De' Medici here. I wonder what one of that family is doing in this remote place. Heigh-ho, perhaps we may find pleasure and even a little excitement. We shall see."

Nothing was said of the afternoon, nor was Angus Moray's name mentioned. For almost an hour Sylvia wrote notes and letters for Captain Meredith to take with him on his voyage to England. When Sylvia returned to her room she went to the window. The Green was quiet; the Sound flooded with moonlight. A single figure moved in the shadows beneath the trees, and the voice of the Watch cried, "Nine o'clock, a moonlight night and all's well."

Strangers in the Village

8 EARLY in the morning a large Jamaicaman came into the Sound, carrying five hundred and fifty-five puncheons of rum and thirty-eight hogsheads of sugar. Several passengers from the British Isles were aboard, including a party of English officers. Among them was Lord Charles Montague.

The coming of the ship created great excitement. In some strange way news had spread of her arrival in the Sound long before she cast anchor in the little bay. The dock and water-front were crowded with men and women to watch the unloading. The crowd increased after the pilot came ashore with word of the passengers. No one so high in rank had set foot in the village since the Duc de Braille had visited Stephen Cabarrus during the war years. Now in one week three titled visitors had arrived.

Interest was divided between the unloading of rum (some had been sold in Wilmington) and the desire to see a real lord. Word went round, through gossip of the pilot who had brought the ship in through the inlet, that his Lordship was quite friendly, although he wore foppish clothes and spoke with something of a lisp. His five companions were young officers who affected the same manner. They were not so friendly as Lord Charles; during the voyage they had stayed in their cabin, playing loo all day and half the night.

Horniblow came down to the wharf and went at once to the customs shed, where he was closeted with the ship's captain for a good fifteen minutes. A number of villagers accosted him as he came out, but he was in such haste to return to the inn that he gave only short answers. He did say that the gentlemen would remain for a few days before continuing on their way to New York. At his front door he met Madam Barker, on her way to call on Lady Anne. "What is this I hear, Horniblow? It is truly Lord Charles Montague?" she demanded.

"Yes, madam. Lord Charles himself. He brings letters to Judge Iredell from Mr. Maclaine of Wilmington."

"Indeed! I must have Mr. Barker call at once. Are there other passengers?"

"A Captain Montague, my Lord's cousin, and four other officers whose names escape me. Pardon me, madam, I must see to their accommodations at once. They will soon be ashore. Lady Anne, the Baron and now Lord Charles! Fortunately I have room, though none to spare." He was hurrying away when Madam Barker detained him.

"What are these people doing here in Edenton?"

"The pilot says they are weary of the ship and plan to travel overland to New York. Really, Madam Barker, I must go. Will you pardon me for hurrying away? It is eleven o'clock, and they will be here within the hour."

Sylvia opened the door in answer to Madam Barker's knock. "Will you come in, Mrs. Barker? Her Ladyship is at her toilet, but she will receive you shortly. I am Sylvia Hay."

Penelope Barker entered, her carriage stately, her smile pleasant and warm. Her quick dark eyes took in the sitting-room. "I see that Horniblow has made you quite comfortable. I am glad. One always hopes that visitors will have a good impression when they come to Edenton." She sat down in a straight chair near the window. Sylvia thought she must have been beautiful when she was young. Now in her middle years, she had charm and much dignity; her hair was grey, her complexion without wrinkles.

No sooner was she seated than Lady Anne called out, "Sylvia, do ask Madam Barker to come in here."

Lady Anne was seated at her dressing-table. She was dressed in a rose satin peignoir, trimmed richly with Mechlin lace, her bare feet thrust into Spanish mules of the same rose satin. Her woman was engaged in brushing her long blond hair with swift, sure strokes of a gold-backed brush.

Lady Anne held out a slim hand. "So very kind of you to call, Madam Barker. So very kind to show interest in weary travellers." She made no apology for her appearance.

Penelope Barker made no sign of surprise at being so received. She knew from novels and her husband's tales that it was quite the fashion for great ladies to receive callers, even gentlemen callers, while their elaborate *coiffures* were being built up.

She sat beside Lady Anne and made polite inquiries about the voyage across the Western Ocean, bringing in discreet mention of Mr. Barker's long residence in England and his pleasure in being at home among his own people. She mentioned also that her former husband, Craven, was a cousin of the Earl of Craven. "He, poor dear, has been dead some years now, but he loved living here—so content with the peaceful life in the colonies."

Lady Anne made no answer. She was studying her hair in a gilt mirror. "Take it down, Dawkins. It looks as though it was arranged by a blacksmith. No, don't try to fix it by pinning here and there. Start at the beginning. Stop pulling, you fool, or I'll box your ears!"

Sylvia went into the sitting-room and returned with the note she had written to Madam Barker. She laid it on the dressing-table.

Lady Anne took it up and passed it to the lady. "You are so kind to think of inviting us to a garden-party. We have written an acceptance, provided we are here at that time."

Madam Barker slipped the note into her quilted-silk reticule without opening it. She spoke with some hesitation. "I may have to change the date. Until Mr. Barker delivers the invitation to Lord Charles Montague——"

Lady Anne sat up. "Lord Charles Montague? Is he here?"

Madam Barker's face brightened. She was delighted to be the bearer of important news. "Ah, yes. Had you not heard of his arrival? He and his party came in the large Jamaicaman, out yonder in the bay. They also will be staying at the inn."

"What is he doing here, pray?" Lady Anne turned to Sylvia. "Write a note to Lord Charles and invite him to dinner with me. Send it to Horniblow to be delivered at once."

As Sylvia rose to leave the room she heard Madam Barker say, "I understand he is travelling with his cousin Captain Montague and four other gentlemen. Edenton is quite a capital, with all the distinguished visitors."

But Lady Anne was not interested in Madam Barker's comments. "Get my plaid taffeta and my shoes with the jewelled buckles." She rose from the dressing-table, tossed off her wrapper and stood tall and slim in her brocaded stays and ruffled lace petticoats. "You will have to excuse me, madam, while I finish my toilet. So nice of you to call."

Madam Penelope rose at this abrupt dismissal. "Certainly. I was on the verge of leaving." She bowed and left the room. She wanted to say something more about the garden-party but thought it beneath her dignity to pursue the matter.

As she went through the sitting-room Lady Anne called out, "Let me know when you have set a date!" Madam Barker paused, but Lady Anne's attention had passed to other matters. "Sylvia, have you completed the note to Lord Charles? Dawkins will run down and deliver it to Horniblow. I want Lord Charles to have it on the instant. And, Sylvia, will you see that a loo table is set up? You know how Lord Charles loves gaming. And, Sylvia, do consult with Mistress Horniblow about the menu. Lord Charles loves his food."

Madam Penelope went home through the Horniblows' garden, a short cut to her house. She did not want to take off her bonnet before she dispatched her blackamoor to summon Mrs. Iredell, Mrs. Tredwell and Mrs. Jones to her house immediately after dinner. She impressed speed on the little Negro. "Run as fast as you can, Scipio. Tell the ladies it is very important, very. Mrs. Iredell first."

"Yes, mistress, I tell. Come hurriedly. Yes, mistress."

She went out on the long gallery to watch the boy and see that he turned the corner that led to the Iredells'. As she turned she saw Mary Rutledge riding down Broad Street followed by a groom. Penelope ran out to the gate to hail her. Mary pulled up her horse, in front of the paling fence.

"Where are you going? Come in and have dinner with us," cried Penelope.

Mary hesitated. "I was going to Horniblow's."

"Nonsense! We are having fish, and you know how Shadrach cooks fish."

Mary dismounted, hooked up the skirt of her riding-habit. To the groom she said, "Take the horses to Horniblow's stables and give them some water. Ask them to give you something to eat and put the reckoning on my account." She followed Penelope Barker into the cool drawing-room. A maid appeared to take her riding-hat and gauntlets.

Penelope went to her room to change. "I've been making a call on Lady Anne," she announced from the stairway. "Go into the drawing-room. Midget will bring you a cool drink. I must change to something light." She laughed a little. "I was bound to make an appearance, so I put on my new taffeta. I'm laced until I can scarcely breathe. I'll tell you all about it when I come down."

Midget followed and opened the blinds a crack. Mary sat down, admiring the way Penelope had arranged the room, with light curtains and holland slip covers for the fine furniture Thomas Barker had brought from England. An inviting room, Mary thought. Three portraits decorated the room and gave it distinction. The portraits of Thomas Barker and of Haughton, Penelope's young son by her first husband, had been painted by Mr. Wallston when he was last in Edenton. Mary wished he had painted Adam, but Adam wouldn't sit—he'd had too many important things on his mind at the time. The third portrait—Penelope herself—was a triumph. The artist had caught Penelope exactly—her questioning, alert expression, her mass of hair, her dark eyes whose slanting corners gave her a strangely Oriental look.

Madam Barker interrupted Mary's study of the portraits. "You are looking at the painting of Thomas. Not so good as those of my dear son and me, do you think? I like best the one Thomas had painted in London by Sir Joshua. I never see it at Hayes that I do not wish it were mine. Thomas was too generous when he made Sam Johnston a present of it. I've often begged Sam to give it to me or sell it or even trade it for the Wallston. But he only smiles and speaks of something else. Do you find Sam difficult to pin down to yes or no? Evasive, I call him."

Mary was saved answering, for Thomas Barker entered the room hurriedly. He tossed his three-cornered hat onto a chair and mopped his forehead. He spoke quickly, in haste to impart his gossip. "Good morning, Mary. My dear, I have news for you, great news. Lord Charles . . ."

His wife did not allow him to finish the sentence. "Montague is here at Horniblow's, also his cousin and some officers."

Thomas sank into a chair. "Oh, so you have heard already. My dear, you have a nose for news. One can never tell you anything you do not already know."

Penelope laughed teasingly. "Oh, Thomas, my dear! You are disappointed. I assure you it was by the rarest chance that I came upon Horniblow when he was walking up from the wharf. Have you called on Lord Charles?"

"Called? So soon? Why, the man's boxes have only now been taken to the inn."

"I know that. But you must make him welcome. You are the only gentleman in Edenton who can discuss the London he knows."

"Even so, give the man a chance to rest."

Madam Barker persisted. "Lady Anne has already sent him a note to dine with her. You must call directly and invite him to our garden-party. Sam Johnston is not at Hayes. James Iredell and Stephen Cabarrus are in Halifax or Hillsborough, or some place in the West. You are the one man who can adequately speak for the district."

"Nonsense, Penelope. Give the man a few hours of peace."

Penelope shut her lips firmly. After a moment she said, "Dinner will be served in a moment, dearest. Since you don't like fish, I've asked Cook to roast a squab for you. Now hurry, please. Put on a fresh linen coat. Yours looks so rumpled."

When Thomas had left the room she turned to Mary. "Men can be the most irritating creatures." A twinkle came into her eyes. "I was sure Thomas would prove refractory. He always says no, at first. Digs his heels into the earth like a stubborn mule. Fortunately I foresaw that. I sent a boy over to Horniblow's with two ducklings for Lord Charles's supper, with Thomas' compliments. He will be furious, but there is nothing he can do about it."

Mary laughed. "How wise you are, Penelope. How wise, and how adroit in managing men."

"One learns in time. After all, three husbands give one practice in circumventing their whims. I suppose you never have to resort to subtleties in managing Adam."

"I don't manage Adam," Mary said. "He manages me."

Penelope tapped Mary's cheek with a finger. "Tut-tut. That remark shows complete subtlety. Come, I hear Mr. Barker on the stairs. Let us go out to the dining-room. Did I tell you that Hannah and Mrs. Tredwell and Mrs. Jones are coming over to help me plan my garden-party?"

The ladies arrived immediately after dinner, in time to drink coffee, which Madam Barker served in her new Queen's-ware cups. Lucy and Hannah came a little before Mrs. Jones, and Penelope told them immediately of Lady Anne's acceptance. Thomas excused himself—to catch a nap, he explained.

After the maid had carried away the coffee things Penelope seated herself in a straight-back chair in front of the high walnut desk. She dipped a quill in the ink-well and sat for a moment, the feather against her chin.

"I shall have four hams brought in from the Tyrrell plantation; they are prime at this time. Chickens—baked, of course. A cold fish. Shadrach makes a beautiful aspic. Too bad crabs are not in season. We will have sliced meats cold, pork and beef, a saddle of mutton. Mutton cuts so well and gives variety. It's fortunate I have plenty of conserves and pickles. A good mustard sauce for the meats, and grated horse-radish whipped in thick cream. Mutton and lamb will be a treat for our guests, who can't have had fresh meat aboard ship." She wrote the items on a long sheet of paper. "Minced pies, cheese cakes, little tarts and a sillabub. Fruit, melons and a variety of cheeses. Can you think of anything else, Hannah? You are such an excellent housekeeper."

Hannah Iredell turned her blue eyes from the window. She had been watching the crowds of villagers walking through the dusty street to view the unloading at the wharf. "You have thought of everything, Penelope. A feast fit for a king."

"And you, Mary. Can you suggest anything?"

"Only your own little tea-cakes. I can't imagine any entertainment without the Penelope Barker tea-cakes."

Madam Barker said, "I have thought of my cakes, but they attained their fame after the Tea Party at Elizabeth King's house." She paused, and a small frown of concentration appeared on her smooth forehead. "You think it would be in good taste to have any reminder of the time we signed the paper against drinking tea? Some of our guests are English, you know. Lord Charles——"

"English guests?" Mrs. Jones exclaimed. "Who?"

"Didn't I tell you? Lady Anne Stuart has accepted an invitation to the garden-party."

Hannah said, "But you mentioned Lord Charles. Will he come?"

"Certainly. I've already taken the first step to make certain of that. Lord Charles Montague and his party of five."

Mary looked at Madam Barker. She hoped she did not show the astonishment she felt. How could Penelope sit there and calmly announce that Lord Charles would be at her garden-party when as yet she had not met the man? An organizer! No wonder she had been able to draw fifty-one women of the village into a compact group to write and sign a document of protest against tea drinking, and that in spite of the ridicule of the men of the village and the country. Mary's thoughts were interrupted by a question directed to her.

"Mary, what do you think?" Penelope was saying. "Don't you think it would be a breach of decorum to call attention to the Revolution by serving the same cakes we served at the Tea Party?"

"I fancy the English visitors have had other reminders of the Revolution more potent than tea-cakes. Lord Charles fought near here." Mary spoke dryly.

Penelope looked at her in surprise. "Why, Mary Rutledge! You sound absolutely bitter."

"I'm not bitter, but I can't forget so quickly that we lost many of our men in battle."

"The war is over," Hannah said gently, "and Jemmy says we must hold no grudges. Victors must be magnanimous."

"That's all very well in theory, but Jemmy was not at the battle of Guilford Courthouse."

Mrs. Jones said, "You were, Mary. We all know that you had a dreadful experience, nursing the wounded, while all we did was to run off to Windsor to get away from Cornwallis."

"Who never got closer than Suffolk, fifty miles away," Mary said with some heat. "You didn't see young lads bleeding slowly to death while you stood by, helpless because you hadn't enough lint to stop their wounds. You didn't watch while surgeons sawed off gangrenous legs or arms, and listen to men scream in agony because you had no drugs to give them a few hours' surcease from their horrible pain." She turned to Madam Barker. "I'm sorry, Penelope. But when I hear any one talk lightly of what we went through in those eight long years of bitter struggle I'm not quite under control."

Penelope shut her mouth firmly. It was Hannah Iredell who spoke. "I don't wonder at you, Mary. You were *in* the war. We weren't. We were only in the backwash."

Mary said nothing. Mrs. Jones touched her arm gently. "We haven't forgotten, Mary, nor can we ever forget what our army suffered."

There was silence. The little French clock on the mantel ticked on, the only sound in the room. Nothing was said. In every woman's mind were thoughts of Mary, of her first husband, William Warden the Royalist, and of his death as a traitor.

Mary broke the long silence. Her voice was quiet and natural. "I would serve your little tea-cakes, Penelope. They are delicious."

Every one began to talk at once. Penelope said, "I should have awnings over the refreshment table in case of rain. Perhaps Stephen Cabarrus will lend me the one he used when he had his fête for the French officers."

"What date have you set?" some one inquired.

"The tenth. That's the full of the moon, you know."

"Notices have been posted of a political rally to be held the same day." Hannah spoke hesitantly. "Feeling about the convention is high. The crowds may be rough, and there is likely to be drinking."

"What the villagers do will not interfere with my party. All my grounds are surrounded by a fence and a high, thick hedge. People can't even see inside. I'll ask Mr. Barker to put a guard at the gates."

The talk returned to plans for the party. Soon Mary rose, saying, "I must go on. I've trading to do at Hewes and Smith's, and I must be home before dark. I'm expecting guests for supper."

Madam Barker walked with her to the door and kissed her on both cheeks. "I'll count on you to assist me, Mary. You have such a gracious manner. You make people feel at ease."

Mary, remembering the tales she had heard about Lady Anne Stuart, tried to imagine that lady ill at ease in any circumstances. But she held her tongue. She had said enough. She was not sorry. We fought for a great cause, she thought. Let people remember that our freedom was not come by readily, or without sacrifice.

She had planned to call on Lady Anne, as Dr. Armitage had suggested, but she was in no mood now for polite mouthings. Instead she went into Hewes and Smith's to look for kitchen-ware. Chaney had requested tall crocks for laying down late peaches in brandy and for salting cabbage.

The clerk who waited on Mary suggested that she look at the Carron iron stoves which had just come in. "Winter will be here before you know it, Mrs. Rutledge, and you will welcome the warmth of a fine stove." Mary examined the stove, listened to its virtues. "Set into a fire-place, it will heat one of your great rooms," the clerk assured her.

"Set it aside, Mr. Carson. I'll have a waggon in to haul it to the plantation in a few days."

"Thank you, Mrs. Rutledge. Anything in fire-dogs or fenders? We have a full stock now. Iron lanthorns, too, very nice in design."

"Nothing more, thank you, Mr. Carson."

The clerk had turned and was staring at the door. Mary followed his gaze. Two ladies were entering. A very tall, slim woman with glorious blond hair, wearing a sprigged muslin and a hat flowered with roses. Behind her a younger woman with auburn hair and a creamy skin that sometimes goes with that colour hair. The girl was more simply dressed in dove-grey with a fichu and sleeve ruffles of white lawn. Her hat was leghorn with a band of black velvet.

"Her Ladyship and Miss Hay," the young clerk whispered, clearly flustered. "I believe they are . . . yes, they *are* coming in here! If you have quite finished, Mrs. Rutledge, I will attend her Ladyship at once."

From a point of vantage among the Carron stoves Mary observed Lady Anne without herself being seen. She looks very youthful, she thought. The scandal of her divorce sits lightly on her.

The ladies stopped at the counter where taffetas and muslins were piled high. "A dress length of this, another of the rose muslin. And the yellow. I must have a yellow—it brightens my hair, don't you think, Sylvia? Lining and cotton for stitching. Fancy finding such material in this God-forsaken country!"

Mary moved across the room and into the garden. She had no wish to encounter the visitors now.

Lady Anne's voice followed her. "Who is that woman who just went into the garden? She has a look of quality."

"Mrs. Adam Rutledge," the clerk answered. "She lives at Queen's Gift, a short distance down the Sound."

"Rutledge? I thought she might have an English name I'd recognize. I know no Rutledges."

"She was a Mainwairing. Grand-daughter of Duke Roger."

"Duke Roger?" Lady Anne's voice rose.

"Oh, he wasn't a duke, really," the clerk responded. "People gave him that name."

"Fancy a planter allowing himself to be called a duke! Rather impertinent. These provincials are really incredible, don't you think, Sylvia?"

Mary let herself out the gate and crossed into Horniblow's garden. She was angered by the woman's arrogance.

Her groom was lounging in the court-yard, near the upping-block. Half a dozen hostlers were near by, watching two young Negroes throwing dice. They rose quickly and touched their caps deferentially when Mary came in sight.

Mary mounted and rode out through the archway toward the eastern gate. She had crossed Queen Anne's Creek before her usual calm was restored. She was annoyed that she had allowed herself to grow angry over a trifle. What was happening to her boasted control over her emotions? She put heel to her horse. The mare broke into a long, swinging trot. It was not until she passed through the gates of Queen's Gift that she overcame her annoyance and regained her calm. Then she laughed. To herself she said, "I'm sure I'm not the first woman Lady Anne has irritated, but for different reasons. Certainly jealousy plays no part in my dislike."

Doctor Armitage and Captain de' Medici arrived at Queen's Gift for supper before sundown. Accompanying them was a stranger whom Dr. Armitage introduced as Angus Moray, a young doctor from Blair-Athol, Scotland. He was staying at Cupola House for the moment, Armitage told Mary.

Moray brought a message from Captain Meredith saying that it would be impossible for him to come to supper, as he would be busy reloading until late. The young Scot smiled down on Mary. "The captain gave me another message, but I am reluctant to pass it to you."

Mary said, "Have no fear, sir. Captain Meredith is an old and valued friend, and I understand him and his messages." She liked the looks of the young man, his strong, sturdy face and his frank eyes.

"I am quoting, mind you, ma'am. He said to tell you that I had no such appetite as he had, so I could eat in his place without embarrassment to you."

De' Medici laughed aloud. "The captain knows full well that the table at

Queen's Gift will always serve another and yet another without damage to the larder."

"You are very welcome, Dr. Moray. I've a little Scottish blood myself. There's always a warm welcome here for another Scot." She smiled at the young man. The news that Captain Meredith would be absent was both a disappointment and a relief. Of course she was eager to know more of how he had come by Duke Roger's journal in Antigua. Yet at the same time she was curiously reluctant to think about it. She knew Duke Roger as a living presence at Queen's Gift. Would this legacy from the past bring him even closer? Or would it destroy her communion with him by bringing a fresh awareness of his death? She need not think more about it to-night. Perhaps she would not open the journal until Adam returned.

The company sat on the long gallery and watched the sun sink behind the heavy forest on the Tyrrell shores. A sight of quiet, still beauty, to bring peace to the soul. A white heron passed with lazy flight of strong wings, the long awkward legs dragging behind. An eagle dropped from the sky and took haven in a lightning-scaled pine tree at the verge of the pocosin. A bird tuned up in a near-by magnolia tree, uttering a sweet liquid trill of haunting beauty.

Moray said, "I did not know you had the nightingale."

"We call that the mocking-bird. Sometimes her song is as raucous as a jay; at other times it is the lark or the linnet." Mary pointed to the grey bird with a flash of white in its tail. "She will sing all night to-night. Sometimes I have to send some one out to shake the tree so I can get a little sleep."

"I think I could well stay awake for such a song," De' Medici observed.

Dr. Armitage got to his feet. "I think I'll walk down to the quarters and look in on Tazey. I didn't like the look of her when I saw her Tuesday."

"Don't stay too long, Doctor. Chaney is making your favourite batter bread. You know how cross she gets if the puff sinks."

"I'll stop by the kitchen on the way and make sure I have time."

De' Medici went into Mary's yellow drawing-room. A few minutes later they heard him playing softly on the harpsichord, music that seemed a part of the quiet scene in front of them. The sun was gone; the opal tints of the afterglow filled the sky and painted the water. Neither Mary nor the young Scot spoke. Each was busy with his own thoughts.

She turned to dreams of her husband, as she so often did in this quiet hour. Moray's mind was on the fascinating woman of dominating boldness with whom he had spent a glorious hour. "No regrets," she had said to him. "I trust you will not turn out to be a man with a conscience."

So the young man dreamed, and the woman, until Dr. Armitage returned and supper was announced.

While the men lingered at table over a bottle of vintage port Dr. Armitage

told them of Duke Roger, Mary Rutledge's grandfather, and of Adam Rutledge, their absent host.

De' Medici said, "I suppose you two talked of the people of the county
while I lost myself in music."

Moray looked startled. "No. No, indeed. We sat silent, listening, exactly
as though we were friends."

In the drawing-room Mary was seated at her little Queen Anne desk,
writing a letter to be delivered to Adam at Hillsborough, telling him how
deeply she missed him. She rose when Dr. Armitage came in.

"The young men are in the garden, smoking," he told her. "I'm glad to
have a moment alone with you, though I'm afraid I bring you only worry.
Tazey is very ill." He raised his hand as Mary began to speak. "I've given
her medicines to make her comfortable. There is nothing more we can do.
She has lived a very long time."

Mary sat down and looked away. Dr. Armitage seated himself and continued. "Another matter gives me much concern. You know I have not
allowed myself to become involved in politics. A neutral position becomes
increasingly difficult. Two letters came to me today. Knowing your deep
interest in the affairs of our state, I brought them with me. One is from
our admirable friend in Halifax, William R. Davie. Let me read it to you.

> "Halifax
> "Twenty-ninth June, 1788
>
> "My dear Sir:
> "I have the pleasure of acknowledging yours of the thirtieth of last month,
> with the Pennsylvania debates and the second balance of the *Federalist,* for
> which you will be pleased to accept my thanks.
> "The decision of Virginia has altered the tone of the Antifederalists here very
> much. Mr. Wilie Jones says his object will now be to get the Constitution re-
> jected in order to give weight to the proposed amendments; and talks in high
> commendation of those made by Virginia. They have reached you no doubt,
> before this time. Those that were of any consequence, by affecting the operation
> of the principles of the Constitution are, in my opinion, quite inadmissible,
> particularly the Third, and the amendment to the judiciary.
> "Yesterday I saw Mr. Lambert, of Richmond, who said Governor Randolph
> informed him the day before he left that New Hampshire had ratified the
> Constitution.
> "We will spend the Fourth of July here, in good humour, I trust, notwith-
> standing our differences in Halifax about the new government.
> "Please to have the enclosed inserted in your *Gazette,* and make my request to
> Samuel Johnston, to correct the press for us, or your printer will make an
> entirely different story of it.
> "Mr. Lamb, as chairman of a committee, in New York, which he styles
> 'Federal Committee,' has written to Mr. Jones, T. Person and Tim Bloodworth,

recommending them to stand steadfast in opposition, and enclosing a large packet of Antifederal pamphlets to each one of them.

"It is astonishing the pains these people have taken! Wilie Jones felt some mortification in finding himself in the company of Bloodworth and Person.

"Believe me, sir, your obedient servant,

"W. R. Davie."

When he had finished reading Mary took the letter from Dr. Armitage and glanced at it briefly. She said, "I regret the great differences that have arisen over the Constitution. I fear the state will be hopelessly divided just when we want unity."

"Already there have been fisticuffs, blackened eyes and broken noggins. A pistol duel or two in the western counties, I hear. Silly fools!"

Mary sat quietly, her eyes on the tips of the buckled shoes that peeped out from under the vast ruffles of her blue muslin skirt. "I begin to wonder about the strength of the Antifederalists. We hear nothing but the Federalist side. Words spoken by Sam Johnston and Jemmy. But the state as a whole is not so unified as Chowan County."

"We are not too unified here, my dear girl. I know many countrymen are doubtful about the Constitution. Many townspeople, too, are Antifederalist. Wilie Jones has support here. You will see it come out into the open before the convention at Hillsborough on the twenty-first." The doctor got up and paced the floor, his hands in his coat-tail pockets. "Yes, you'll hear plenty of dissension. I heard some this afternoon when I took Mr. Davie's enclosure to Hodge and Wills, the printers Jamie brought up from New Bern and established in Cheapside. Men are coming in there daily, wanting to have letters printed in the *Gazette*. But enough of that. Let me read the second letter. We'll hear more about this matter, too. Tories and Englishmen are renewing their efforts to get money from the state for their own properties confiscated in the war. Here's one from Jemmy Iredell's relative and benefactor McCulloh.

"Newman Street
"London
"May 5, '88

"Dear Sir:

"This is a great, noble, generous country and America (North Carolina most especially) may, must and will, from day to day, rue her separation from us. Did North Carolina deserve anything from my hands, connected as I am here, I might do her great service. Apply to the state for the debt they owe me as their agent. For shame's sake they will not refuse payment. You will not, sir, deny this service to your friend,

"H. E. McCulloh."

"What a strange, violent letter!" Mary exclaimed. "He was always so very pleasant when he was here."

"Pleasant indeed!" The doctor almost snorted. "Lived on the reputation of a greater McCulloh, with his hundred thousand acres in this state. As for paying debts to him 'for shame's sake,' he hasn't paid me my fee for delivering his bastard child! . . . I'm sorry, Mary. That just slipped out."

Mary smiled. "I've heard of such things as bastards before, Doctor."

"You women! You know too much," the doctor growled. After a moment's silence he said, "I wonder what side Adam will support at the Hillsborough convention."

Mary was aghast at the question. "Why? Why? Can you doubt that he would want us in the Federal union?"

Dr. Armitage continued his pacing, his head bowed. "They say there is much Antifederalist sentiment in the West. Many think the Constitution does not guard their rights as free men. I have heard reports from Tennessee County. He may encounter new ideas as he returns from that Illinois country. He may want changes in the Constitution."

"Only let him return and I——" Mary's reply was interrupted as Cosmo and Angus Moray returned.

Cosmo bowed before Mary and escorted her to the harpsichord. "I have been thinking of how beautifully you play Bach, *Maria mia*. It has been too long since I have heard your music. I have been hungry for it this long time. You will play for us?"

Mary smiled at him. "Of course, Cosmo. Who could refuse after such praise?"

While Mary searched through her music De' Medici addressed Dr. Moray. "You enjoy music, sir?"

"Indeed I do, very much."

"You sing perhaps, or play some instrument?"

Moray laughed. "Only the bagpipes. I'm afraid you wouldn't enjoy that."

Cosmo's eyes brightened. He spoke with enthusiasm. "Indeed I do. I am thrilled to my heart at the bagpipes, and my feet respond to the marching skirl. Let us have music one time when you have your pipes. I will sing a ballad or, better yet, one of your ancient laments."

It was nearly eleven when Dr. Armitage got up from his chair, where he had been taking cat-naps during the music. "You young folk may sit up all night, singing and making music, but I have to be up early in the morning. Mary, I've enjoyed my supper and my evening."

They all went into the hall. A black boy was dozing in a chair. He rose hurriedly and handed the guests their hats. Cosmo raised Mary's hand to his lips and said, "I have promised a young woman to take her for a ride. May I bring her here? You will be charmed with her. A beauty she is, with a mass of auburn hair."

Moray turned at De' Medici's words. Mary saw the expression on his face change from surprise to sternness. He stood motionless, his sturdy body tense. How different they are! Mary thought. Moray seems almost awkward when contrasted with the elegance and poise of the handsome Italian.

Aloud she said, "Do bring your friend. Morning rides are most pleasant. Have dinner with me. I should love to meet your auburn-haired friend."

"Miss Hay is her name. Miss Sylvia Hay, a lovely lady, most charming, with a nice wit. An unusual combination, is it not? Beauty and wit!"

"Trust Cosmo to discover beauty in women," Dr. Armitage commented. "You Latins have the instinct."

Mary smiled, but Moray said nothing. His eyes, fixed on De' Medici, were cold and hostile, as though he were measuring an adversary.

"I quite agree with you," Mary said. "Miss Hay is lovely. I glimpsed her this afternoon. She has a fresh, clear beauty. I thought she made her companion seem a little jaded."

Cosmo's laugh rang out. "Mary, you surprise me. I thought you never gossiped."

"Gossip? No, only an observation. Good night, Dr. Moray. Do come again."

The young Scot looked distressed. Mary suddenly understood the reason. Of course. He had come over on the *Devon Maid* with Lady Anne's party. That accomplished flirt had bewitched him. Poor befuddled fellow! She repeated in more cordial terms her invitation to visit Queen's Gift. He'll be needing help before long, she thought as she watched the riders' lanthorn bobbing in the darkness. Cosmo's dark, laughing face rose before her, and she recalled, too, Moray's changing expression—from antagonism at Cosmo's praise of Miss Hay to distress at her reference to Lady Anne. She knew what had happened. Lady Anne's maturity and experience had dazzled him. Yet he resented De' Medici's admiration for the auburn-haired girl.

She sighed as she took up her night candle from the stand on the stairlanding. She was weary of conflicts, great and small. Eight years of war, of violent hatreds; now more hatreds and conflicts in politics. Human beings never ceased to make problems for themselves. Was the hard-won peace to be peace in name only?

The Fair Begins

9 SYLVIA was awakened early by the squealing and creaking of cart wheels, the neighing of horses, the bleating of sheep and lowing of cattle. She rubbed her eyes. Was she still in a troubled dream of the farm in Devon where as a child she had spent her summers? But this was not a dream. When she sat up in bed she saw

that the Green was alive with people and animals. Sylvia looked at the clock on the walnut lowboy. It was a few minutes before six. She got out of bed and went to the window.

The sun just above the eastern horizon dappled the grass, and the heavy foliage of sycamore and elm and swamp maple cast long shadows on the Green. In the night, stalls divided by strips of canvas had been set up and cattle had been moved in. Farm produce was piled high on tables around the verge of the grassy plot. At the far end was a gaily striped tent with a large placard announcing that a performance of *The Miser* would be given at eight that evening.

The crowds provided a colourful sight. There were men in blue smocks and leather breeches, others in linen coats; some had dispensed with their jackets and wore white shirts with their coloured knee-breeches and buckled shoes. The women were dressed more soberly in sprigged muslins with mull fichus and mob-caps, or in grey or puce with wide straw hats. In brilliant contrast were the gaudy clothes of the Negro slaves, the women in dresses of yellow or red, bright green or indigo, with variegated handkerchiefs tied turban-wise on their heads and heavy brass rings in their ears.

An old coloured man in a high two-wheeled cart drove slowly down the street, ringing a bell. "Melons! Early melons, the bestes' yo' ever put mouth to. Melons! Nice juicy melons fo' break yo' fast. Only two pennies."

A crowd of children ran after him. He checked his mule under the shade of a red oak at the corner of the Green near the water. "Yes, sah, break yo' fast wid a nice juicy melon."

The children climbed up on the wheels and tumbled the melons about, thumbing them to get the ripest. "They're green, Uncle. Get me a ripe one."

"You jes' wait, you young gen'lemen an' ladies. I'll pick good uns. Don' yo' go squeezin' an' pinchin'. Uncle Amos will find the bestes'."

Sylvia's preoccupation with the scene before her was broken by a knock at her door. Ann Horniblow entered, followed by a Negro girl the colour of saddle leather who carried a covered tray.

"Good morning, Miss Hay," Ann said. "I heard you moving about, so I sent Promisy for your tea. What do you think of our quiet little village this morning?"

"I am amazed, Mistress Horniblow," Sylvia said. "What is happening? Is it market day?"

"It's the midsummer festival," Ann said, smiling.

"Oh, I remember some one telling me of a fair that would begin today. But all these people! Where do they come from?"

Ann joined Sylvia at the window. "The whole of Chowan County will be in Edenton today and to-morrow. There's not a bed to be had in this house or in any inn or tavern in the village. Already some visitors are pitching tents outside the town, and many more will be sleeping in their coaches or ox-carts to-night."

Together they watched as more and more newcomers joined the crowds on the Green, some driving cattle or hogs or sheep, others leading horses or seeking places to display farm produce or women's handicraft. Ann identified people from Sandy Hill Road and Rockahock in the northern part of the county, from Emperor's Landing, from the plantations along the Sound and the Yeopim River. Others, she said, had crossed the Sound from Tyrrell or journeyed from Bertie County beyond the Roanoke and Chowan rivers. And the people on the Green were only a part of the fair crowd. Others were already at the Fair Ground on Virginia Road.

"The actors are a strolling group," she explained, "and there are always strangers who appear in the town on occasions such as this to take advantage of the crowds. Jugglers, tumblers, men who perform tricks on the slack wire. And the others who come to cheat the country-folk at cards or dice or to sell raw liquor of their own making. They are the ones who cause trouble and give our fair a reputation for intemperance and licentiousness."

In addition to the activities on the Green, Ann added, there would be horse-racing at the race-course and dancing at Signor Arcaro's ballroom in Cheapside. This year a dancing-master had rented a hall and advertised that he was qualified to teach no less than thirty-one fashionable steps—Parsby's rigadoon, minuets and contra-dances for the gentry, reels, jigs and scampers for lesser folk.

"And now I'll leave you to your tea," Ann said, turning resolutely from the window. "There's work in plenty to be done today. Promisy will serve you."

The Negro girl uncovered the tray. Beside the tea-pot were a slice of cool melon and golden-brown toast in a rack.

"Are you going to the fair, Promisy?" Sylvia asked when Ann Horniblow had left them.

"Yes'm. Mistress she say I can go to-night after work do. Yes'm, I like to go. Yes'm, maybe I can see de man walking on de rope, carryin' a parasol. He sure smart fellow, balance on he toes, 'way up in de air."

Sylvia took a shilling from her purse and gave it to the girl. "Buy yourself a riband, Promisy."

The girl's eyes brightened. "Yes, ma'am. Thank you kindly. A yellow riband." Shyly she said, "May I bind it in my hair, jes' like you, mistress?"

"Of course. I'll show you how. Are the children awake?"

"No, ma'am. Dey didn't come last night. Dey stay out dere at River Plantation wid dey daddy. Dey come back today wid Mr. Charles Johnson. He son-in-law of Parson Earle."

Sylvia hadn't known the Baron planned to stay away another night. She wondered how the Negro girl knew so much about the Baron's affairs. She was beginning to suspect that the Negroes in this strange country knew everything that went on among the white folk. Knew everything and said nothing.

"Maybe de young mistress like to go for ride. Master Horniblow he say he have a nice ridin' mare all ready fo' you eff you liken to go dis mawnin'." Promisy reached into the bosom of her dress and brought out a twisted bit of paper. "De foreign gen'man gave me dis for you, mistress."

Sylvia took the note, warm from the girl's body. It was signed De' Medici. She read it with quickening breath.

The morning is beautiful. Our host tells me he has a good riding mare, suitable for a lady. Will you join me for an early morning canter? We might ride to Queen's Gift for breakfast.

"De foreign gen'man said he want know when you be ready."

Sylvia laughed gaily. The day was beginning well. She felt wonderful. "Promisy, run. Tell the foreign gentleman, yes, I shall be ready in fifteen minutes."

The girl went away smiling. The foreign gen'man was always generous. Perhaps she could buy two ribands for her hair, one yellow, one bright purple.

Sylvia dressed hurriedly in a linen habit and riding-boots. Her hair she twisted into a hard knot at her neck and confined it in a net. What luck! No children to teach. Lady Anne never visible before noon. Wonderful, wonderful day.

She found Cosmo waiting at the foot of the stairs, booted and spurred and ready to ride. He kissed her hand. "How good of you!" he said, and led her through a succession of halls to the court-yard at the rear of the inn. A hostler was waiting, holding the bridles of two horses.

De' Medici held his clasped hands for her to mount. Sylvia was arranging her skirt over the pommel when Moray emerged from the inn. He nodded curtly to De' Medici.

"You're out early, Dr. Moray," Sylvia said.

"I'm to accompany Dr. Armitage on his calls this morning." He went directly to the point. "I came to leave a note for you, but the innkeeper told me I might find you here."

"Well?"

"I would be happy to have you go to the play to-night," he said, dropping his voice so that De' Medici would not hear. "Dr. Armitage says it is the custom here for every one to attend the play given in a tent and afterward to dance in the Assembly Room in the Courthouse." He did not give her a chance to answer, but went on hurriedly. "I would be honoured to escort you, Miss Hay."

"Thank you so much, Dr. Moray. May I give you my answer later in the day after I consult Lady Anne?" She paused a moment, a little smile dimpling the corners of her mouth. "Or are you asking the Baroness also?"

Angus Moray's face flushed, his long square jaw stiffened. There was no smile in his eyes or on his lips. "I have asked no one else," he said stiffly. "May I call later to know your decision?"

"Why, certainly. We shall be home by dinner-time." She lifted the reins and turned her horse to follow De' Medici's under the archway into the dusty street. When she looked back Angus was standing quite still, watching her, his body rigid, his feet a little apart. He looks like a sturdy Scottish pine, she thought. She was a little sorry she had given him that dig about Lady Anne—but not too sorry.

She rode with Cosmo down Queen Street, passed the Rope Walk and entered a post-road that led to Hertford. After they had crossed a little covered bridge that spanned Queen Anne's Creek they came to a fork in the road. De' Medici said, "We turn right here. Queen's Gift is on the Sound. Would you care to try out your mount?"

Sylvia rode well, sat her saddle easily and had a light hand on the bridle. She looked trim and elegant—an accomplished horsewoman, De' Medici noted with satisfaction. He liked women who rode well, danced well and were feminine without being obviously feminine or flirtatious. He liked straightforwardness in women, to a degree rather unusual in a Latin. He liked the picture she made as they trotted along the aisle of cedar trees. He said, "You hunt, of course?"

"Ever since I was a child," Sylvia replied. "My father was Master of our Hunt, a rather famous hunt in Devon. We used to meet at a little Elizabethan inn near Fairy Cross—Hoop's Inn, it was."

"They have good hunting here in the autumn. Adam Rutledge is the Master of the Hunt. I believe his wife took his place when he was in the army."

"Tell me about Mrs. Rutledge. What is she like?"

"Mary? It's difficult for a man to describe one woman to another, always. Lovely is the word I would use for her. Small, dark hair, Irish blue eyes, intelligent. With Adam away she manages two plantations quite successfully."

"She sounds formidable."

"Not so. She is very kind and hospitable. Loves hunting. Lived in England in her girlhood. Adam Rutledge is her second husband. Something very tragic about her first husband, a man some years older than she."

"Tragic?"

"He was hanged as a traitor." Cosmo drew up beside her. "It almost killed Mary, I've been told. Apparently she was intensely loyal to her husband, though not to his politics. Very, very sad it was." He looked at Sylvia thoughtfully. "William Warden was a traitor to the Republic, but he would have been a hero in your eyes. He spied for Lord Cornwallis."

Sylvia answered, "There is a difference in the point of view. The Americans called Nathan Hale a hero."

De' Medici said quickly, "And you felt the same about Major Arnold."

They were silent for a time. The soft thud of the horses' hoofs, the trilling of a bird in the hedgerow became audible in the silence.

Sylvia spoke first. Her face was grave. "I think I should have been a rebel if I had lived here. My father was one Englishman who did not believe in forcing the colonies into war. Many of us agreed with the colonists' protest that taxation without representation was unjust. We Devon folk have always been an outspoken lot and independent."

They came at last to the gates of Queen's Gift. A winding drive of holly trees, alternating with cedar and a few magnolias, led them to the house. A pleasant house, Sylvia thought, the central block scarcely larger than a Devon farm cottage, and wooden instead of brick or stone. But the two wings gave an effect of space and elegance, and its setting—among these trees, with pine forests rising on one side—was superb. A small formal garden and orchards completed the picture of country serenity.

"Charming!" she said to De' Medici.

He dismounted, flung the reins to a little barefoot Negro boy and came around to help her from her horse. Grasping her tapered waist in his strong hands, he lifted her from the saddle. For a moment she was pressed against him. She looked up into dark eyes that laughed and teased. She thought briefly that he intended to press his lips against her upturned face, but he set her down on the brick terrace. She exclaimed again at the beauty of the setting.

"Our hostess is much more charming and interesting than the prospect," he said. "Shall we go in?"

Sylvia at once recognized the slight, dark-haired, blue-eyed woman as the one she had glimpsed in Hewes and Smith's.

Mary Rutledge's greeting was very cordial. "How delightful!" she said, holding Sylvia's hand in an unexpectedly firm clasp. "So good of Cosmo to bring you to Queen's Gift. You are very welcome. Come, let us go out onto the gallery. My cook Chaney insists that I have breakfast there. 'To drink down the morning air is very good,' she says, 'but to walk in the garden when there is dew on the grass will bring a strange disease.'"

Cosmo laughed. "I walked on the Green this morning. The dew sparkled on the grass." He made a sign with his fingers. "Peasants do this against the evil eye."

Sylvia looked from one to the other. "Do you believe these things?"

"No, not really," Mary answered, "but sometimes such strange things occur that one wonders."

"For instance?"

Mary glanced over her shoulder to see that no one was within hearing. "It's silly, of course, but when one is alone on a plantation surrounded by so many Negroes one accepts certain phenomena, like curings and Mankwala —as our people call it—made against enemies. A tiny clay figure pierced by thorns, left in front of a cabin or on the pillow of a Negro, indicates an evil. The person will sicken, perhaps even die."

The aged butler appeared with the breakfast, and Mary turned to him quickly. "Ebon, has Dr. Armitage arrived yet from the village?"

"No, mistress."

"My message must have reached him some time ago, and he should be here soon. Have him taken to Tazey's cabin at once." There was concern in Mary's expression as she turned back to her guests. "Tazey is one of our oldest slaves. She was on the plantation in my grandfather's time. I fear she is very ill."

There was a certain constraint in the atmosphere as they continued their meal. "Do you live here alone, Mrs. Rutledge?" Sylvia asked after a time.

"Yes. My husband is in the West, but I expect him home, I hope in time for the Hillsborough convention."

"Ah," said Cosmo, "I have been thinking that I might go to Hillsborough. Of course I could not make my appeal on the floor of the convention, but I could perhaps speak with some of the legislators and make my endeavour to win them to my side."

Mary looked inquiringly at De' Medici. "Your appeal?"

"Did you not know? I am trying to recover the money the state owes me since the Revolution. The Commissioners of Army Accounts refused to consider my claims. The scoundrels were too busy issuing false land certificates and due bills. Now I shall appeal to the General Assembly."

Mary said, "If you want the Assembly to act, wouldn't it be well to begin by talking to your friends in Edenton who have influence there?"

"Ah, Maria, how wise you are! This I determined to do when I decided to renew my claim. Mr. Charles Johnson I have tried to approach at Strawberry Hill, but Madame, his wife, says he is at River Plantation. His Excellency Governor Johnston is in New Bern, and our good friend Iredell is on his circuit."

"Of course," Mary said. "I'd forgotten Jemmy had gone to Hillsborough." A little line of concentration appeared between her straight brows. "Yes, Cosmo, I think you would do well to go to Hillsborough. At the time of the convention to vote on ratification of the Constitution many members of the legislature will be there."

De' Medici jumped to his feet, grasped Mary's hands and kissed each in turn. "Maria, good angel, I am delighted that you agree with me! You think so clearly. I will journey to Hillsborough. I will encounter five, ten, even twenty of the gentlemen of the legislature and tell them my little story. It will help, yes?" He wheeled about and bowed to Sylvia. "I am embarrassed to talk so much of my poor affairs. Only this week I thought I must try again. I need money for the land I am buying. We will speak of other things, of your difficult journey across the sea, of hunting or any of a dozen things that may interest you."

Sylvia smiled. "But I *am* interested. I am sure Mrs. Rutledge has given you excellent advice."

A slave came to the door, Chaney's Ben. "Mistress, may I speak? Doctor Armitage is down at de quarters. He says will you come. Tazey is on she way to die."

Mary excused herself and hurried away. Sylvia and De' Medici walked the length of the gallery from which the cabins of the slaves were visible. In silence they watched Mary walking swiftly toward the quarters line.

"There is a woman of character," De' Medici observed. "I have known her and her fine husband a long time. Adam I saw first at Brandywine, where there was much fighting." He paused and smiled. "You will think I talk too much of war."

"Of course not. Naturally you would be thinking of your service. But let us walk in the garden. It looks so lovely, and this wonderful Carolina sun has drawn the dangerous dew. Perhaps Mrs. Rutledge's servant would think us safe from strange diseases."

He smiled. "I think it is quite safe. I should not be happy to bring ill luck to so lovely a lady."

Mary found Dr. Armitage at Tazey's cabin at the far end of the quarters line. With him was Angus Moray. Both men had discarded their coats and rolled their shirt-sleeves up to the elbow. Armitage had a lancet in his hand. Angus held a small china bowl. A dozen or more slaves were standing near the piazza, solemn, quiet, with watchful eyes. Mary's heart sank. They always knew, these strange pagan people, when death approached.

"What can I do, Doctor?" she asked.

"Nothing, for the moment. Angus will help me. I am going to bleed her on the chance that I can drain off some of the evil."

Mary followed them into the room where Tazey lay on a reed mat on the earth floor. Two women crouched on either side, holding her talon-like hands. Half a dozen men and women stood in the shadows. In spite of the heat of the July day a small fire was burning on the hearth.

"Get them all out of here," Armitage said under his breath.

Mary turned. "Dr. Armitage will give Tazey medicine now. Step outside. I will call you when he has finished." The Negroes shuffled out reluctantly with backward glances. One of the women who had been sitting beside Tazey moved away slowly with a sullen, almost venomous glance at Armitage. Mary knew her—the conjure woman Mifiti, who lived beside the pocosin. For a moment she thought the woman would refuse to go, but finally Mifiti passed through the door and stood just beyond, her eyes fixed on the silent woman on the bed.

Mary took a position at the foot of the mat, so that she cut off the conjure woman's view of Tazey. She thought she could feel Mifiti's eyes boring into her back. Mary gazed sadly at Tazey, who looked incredibly old and feeble.

In her concern Mary caught only an occasional phrase of the muttered comments Dr. Armitage made to Angus as he worked. "Dose them with a pint of camomile tea every morning before breakfast for the ague. . . . Give them ten . . . fourteen. The old law, one organ, the liver; disease, biliary derangement; one remedy, mercury." He looked up at Angus' puzzled face. "You know what these Negroes believe? The pocosin frogs say all night long, 'Quinine, mercury. Quinine, mercury.' And the bullfrog he say, 'Calomel, calomel.'" He turned back to his work. The bright blood was flowing from Tazey's veins into the white china bowl. The old woman on the mat did not stir. She was insensible to pain.

Outside the crowd of Negroes had increased. Now they were kneeling on the ground, forming a crescent about the cabin. A woman started a song in a clear voice, not loud, gentle as a lament. The others hummed softly, a harplike sound:

> "When my blood run chilly and cold
> I got to go, I got to go.
> When my blood run chilly and cold
> I got to go 'way beyond the sun."

A man's voice took up the lament:

> "He call you by the lightnin',
> He call you by the thunder.
> He call you by the middle night cry,
> Oh, come home, come home."

Mary knelt by the mat and took Tazey's thin hand in hers. The woman's skin was as grey as the little braids wound around her head. Tazey was an Angoni, of Zulu blood, and her skin was normally the dark of polished ebony. Now it looked ashen. Tears came to Mary's eyes. As long as she could remember, Tazey had been there, a part of Queen's Gift, a part of an old life that was fast changing.

Suddenly there was movement in the gnarled hand. Mary bent closer as Tazey lifted her hand slowly to her forehead. Her lips moved. "*Moni, Capita, moni.*" Tazey only breathed the words. Then she folded her arms across her breast.

Mary understood. The words were both a greeting and a farewell. "*Capita*"—so Tazey had always addressed Duke Roger—"*moni.*"

Armitage closed the wide-open eyes and placed pennies on the eyelids. Angus Moray helped Mary to her feet; his strong hand under her elbow steadied her. She stood for a moment looking down on the small, still body of the slave. Then she walked to the door. The kneeling crowd was silent, their eyes fixed on her. She must speak to them, but what should she say? The words they had been singing came to her lips.

"Tazey has gone away beyond the sun. She has lived a long, good life. She was ready for the call."

No one moved as she walked down the steps. The two doctors followed her. As they walked away a wail broke out.

"*Eee-aye, eee-aye, aye-ee-aye-ee-aye-ee.*"

Angus glanced back. He saw the people filling their cupped hands with dust, casting it over their bodies.

"*Ayee, ayee, ayee-e-e . . .*"

At the end of the lane they met Cosmo and Sylvia. "What has happened?" De' Medici asked.

"An ancient woman has died." Mary spoke sadly.

They walked on in silence. When they reached the terrace Mary turned to Sylvia. "I am sorry to be so upset. I suppose you couldn't understand. Tazey has always been here. My grandfather made her free, gave her a few acres of land, but she would not leave. She was my slave, but she was also my friend and often my comforter. I shall miss her sorely."

De' Medici said, "We understand. I have gone through such moments myself."

Sylvia put her hand on Mary's. A few minutes later the horses were brought up. Mary asked them to stay on, but Sylvia said, "I must be at Horniblow's by dinner-time. I'm not my own mistress, you know, but may I come again soon?"

"Please do. And you, Dr. Moray. And Cosmo, good fortune in Hillsborough!"

Dr. Armitage lingered a moment. "Tazey didn't have a moment's pain. Don't grieve too much, my dear. Lie down and take a rest."

"That I can't do, Doctor. I must find Marcy. There's a funeral feast to prepare, and we must do everything to give honour to a good, faithful woman." She detained the doctor a moment after he had mounted his horse. "Did you hear what she said at the last, Doctor?"

"Some gibberish. I didn't rightly catch the words."

"I did. She said, '*Moni, Capita, moni.*' That was the way Duke Roger's slave always greeted him. 'I see you, master.'"

She turned and went up the steps to the gallery.

The doctor looked after her. He found himself wishing that Adam Rutledge would come home. Mary had been alone far too long.

De' Medici fell in with him, and Angus and Sylvia rode on ahead. Cosmo said, "You are worried about Maria? Do you think we should all ride off like this and leave her alone?"

"You speak my very thoughts. I think I will stay."

"And I also, after I tell Miss Hay." There was laughter in Cosmo's dark eyes. "I think the young surgeon will like it that way." He rode at a trot and overtook the others at the gate. "Will you take it amiss if I stay on with Dr. Armitage? There may be something we can do. I think Mrs. Rutledge feels this death quite deeply."

Sylvia spoke impulsively. "You are very kind and understanding. I wanted so much to stay with her, but my time is not my own." She looked up at him and repeated, "You are very kind."

Angus had little to say to Sylvia as they rode toward the village, but when they reached Queen Anne's Creek he reined his horse and caught her bridle. "What is wrong? You treat me as a stranger. I thought we were friends, Sylvia. On the ship——"

Sylvia raised her eyebrows. "On the ship, Dr. Moray? Surely you know the old saying about friendships at sea. People are thrown together, then separated . . . like ships in the night." She spoke carelessly, casually, a little smile on her red lips. "Were we friends? I really don't remember."

He caught her wrist. "You know we were friends. Have you forgotten so quickly a moonlight night when——"

She broke in. "Ah, you Scots, so serious, so awfully serious! Moonlight nights bewitch one. They are so elusive. Pleasant perhaps, but . . . transitory."

He frowned and spoke indignantly. "Aye, for a girl, mayhap, but a man sees no laughter in strong feeling." The blood rushed to her cheeks, but Angus did not notice. He was looking down at his strong hand clasping her wrist. "Pardon," he said. "I didn't know I was holding so heavily. Come, let us ride."

They rode in silence to the village. Not until he had helped her dismount in the court-yard of the inn did he speak again.

"The play to-night," he said abruptly. "Will you accompany me?"

"I shall have to see what Lady Anne's plans are and learn whether she will require my services this evening," Sylvia said. "If you will stop at the inn later, I will leave a message for you with Mistress Horniblow."

Moray did not answer for a moment, and then his words startled her. "He's a fine, brave man, De' Medici. He's apt with pleasantries, while I am heavy in my tongue when it comes to pretty sayings." He looked straight into her eyes. "But I will not give up."

He sprang onto his horse without waiting for Sylvia to speak. His words left her dazed with his sudden intensity . . . but happy, very happy.

The Cock-Fight

10 THE sun had reached the meridian when Sylvia reached her room at Horniblow's. She changed quickly from her linen habit to a cool flowered gown and went to the boys' chamber. The room was empty.

In the hall she found Lady Anne's woman. "Her Ladyship is still abed," Dawkins said. "The Baron and the young gentlemen will not be back before evening, perhaps noon to-morrow. The Baron has sent a note to her Ladyship by Mr. Earle's servant."

Sylvia was pleased with the news. She would have the afternoon to herself, to write letters and make entries in her journal, which she had neglected since her arrival in Edenton.

Dawkins lingered a moment. "If you will be so kind, Miss Hay, will you ask her Ladyship to give me time off to go to the fair to-morrow?" The woman simpered a little and showed some embarrassment. "Frazier, the farrier, has invited me to see the acts and attend on the races. Her Ladyship was in an uncertain humour when I fetched her morning tea. I dare not approach her."

Sylvia wondered at the request. Dawkins liked to give the impression that she had great influence over her mistress. She showed nothing of her thoughts when she said, "Certainly I will ask her. I'm sure she will not mind. You have been so faithful in your attendance all these weeks."

"Thank you, Miss Hay." Dawkins moved closer, lowering her voice. "I'm fair tired out with waiting on her. A body can do just so much and no more. When she's in a temper with the Baron——"

Sylvia interrupted. She had no wish to gossip with a servant. "I will talk to her at dinner," she said. The woman thanked her and walked quickly down the hall toward Lady Anne's sitting-room. Perhaps she is imbibing some of this New World freedom, Sylvia thought. It must be a potent draught, for Dawkins has always been the most perfect lady's maid, taking Lady Anne's smiles and ear-boxings with equal equanimity.

Sylvia pondered again the curious lack of servility in servants and lesser folk of this country. The black slaves seemed to perform their tasks with a certain dignity, and their owners treated them in a casual, friendly way. To Sylvia, accustomed to rigid distinctions of class in England, the situation was puzzling. Fancy a butler joining in the table conversation, as had Mrs. Rutledge's old Negro at breakfast! And Sylvia had not been prepared for

Mrs. Rutledge's display of feeling at the death of the old Negro woman. She sat down at her desk, unlocked her journal and began to write.

I cannot understand the relationship between master and slave in America. There is perfect courtesy on the part of the slave, yet a certain informality on the part of the master—sympathy and even affection. This is all quite different from what I had been told to expect—sullen slaves under a yoke that included barbarous treatment, cruel whippings. I must talk to some of the village people about this. . . .

She glanced out the window. The Green was filled with folk walking in and out of the booths where farm produce was displayed. Her attention focused on an old Negro with a tray hanging by a leather strap from his neck. He wandered about, crying, "Gingie-bread, gingie-bread. Who will buy my nice hot gingie bread?"

There was a knock at the door and Dawkins entered hurriedly. "Her Ladyship begs that you will dine with her and the gentlemen."

"What gentlemen, Dawkins?"

"Lord Charles Montague and two of his officers, miss. Her Ladyship says, wear something pretty."

Sylvia glanced at her gown. "This will do well enough, don't you think?"

"Indeed you look very young and fresh, if I may say so. If you wish, I could brush your hair into more elaborate curls."

Sylvia shook her head. "Thank you, no. I'll wear it as it is."

Dawkins stood off, arms akimbo, and surveyed Sylvia critically. "You are right, Miss Hay. Simplicity for your heavy red hair, that's the thing. Leave curls and puffs and fixin' for those getting on in years." She spoke the compliment grudgingly.

Sylvia laughed gaily. "Thank you, Dawkins. Youth has its advantages, it seems."

Dawkins' mouth was prim. "Yes, miss, and a woman must make good use of her youth. I don't rightly understand a young girl who doesn't want fixin' to snare the gentlemen."

Poor Dawkins, Sylvia thought. I hope for her sake she isn't going to imitate the independent manner of American servants. Lady Anne won't tolerate it.

When Sylvia entered the sitting-room she found Lady Anne engaged in a game of loo with Lord Charles and his two officers, Captain Wilkins and Lieutenant Gorrell. The men rose from the table when Lady Anne casually introduced her—"Miss Hay, my secretary." Lord Charles was a thin, sandy-haired man with an ugly face but a distinguished manner. Sylvia liked the lieutenant at once. He was stocky, with merry blue eyes and a pug nose. His square jaw gave him a certain masculine solidity. His mouth turned upward at the corners, indicating humour. The captain was set in the usual regimental mould.

Lady Anne's humour was excellent. Masculine society of her own class was the atmosphere she liked best, and she had unfolded like a garden flower under the influence of a warm sun. Besides, she was winning. She pointed to a stack of paper money which lay on the table beside her. "I won't speak of my luck, Sylvia, or it might desert me. Already I've a pile of these strange bills. Not that I think they are worth anything."

Lord Charles said ruefully, " 'Tis all we've got, my dear Anne. If you continue this winning streak, we won't be able to buy our tickets on the Philadelphia coach."

"Splendid! You can stay here and amuse me. It costs nothing to live at the tavern. We can have fun sailing—and riding too, for I've seen some excellent horses." She smiled brightly at Sylvia. "I hope you enjoyed your morning ride. Dawkins tells me you left with one escort and returned with another."

Sylvia felt anger rising within her. She hoped she wasn't blushing. Lord Charles turned his pale-blue eyes in her direction as though he were noticing her for the first time.

"Did you enjoy yourself, my dear?" Lady Anne continued. "Where did you go?"

"We rode out to Queen's Gift and had breakfast with Mrs. Rutledge."

Lady Anne turned to Lord Charles. "*We* means Cosmo de' Medici, so-called. I wonder if he is an impostor or whether he is really one of the Florentine family."

Lord Charles put down the fish counter he held in his hand. "Gad! Is De' Medici here?" He turned to Lady Anne. "I assure you, Anne, he is not an impostor. I came to know him while he was a prisoner of war. But we had met before. We came to swords' points in the fighting at Lennew's Ferry, on the Santee in South Carolina. I all but bested him in sword-play, but he disarmed me." He turned to Captain Wilkins. "You will remember De' Medici."

"Yes. The Italian imprisoned at Haddrell's Point. I always wondered why he was over here fighting."

Lady Anne was weary of the conversation. She put two ivory counters on the table. "I understand there were a number of Europeans who followed LaFayette. Why, I can't imagine."

The captain matched her counters. "Perhaps they were romantics who were bored at home and longed for adventure."

Lieutenant Gorrell swept the table with his hand and gathered in all the counters. "They might possibly have been imbued with the idea of liberty."

Lord Charles looked at him. His pale eyes were cold. "I hope you aren't becoming infected by a lot of ringing words which mean nothing."

The lieutenant returned the glance. Sylvia could read nothing in his eyes.

"Perhaps there is something in fighting for rights, Lord Charles. At least the barons thought so when they faced King John at Runnymede."

"Don't be a fool, Tony. Your father will have none of such nonsense when you get back to England."

Lady Anne interrupted. "Why bother about these things? We'll all be home before many months. It doesn't affect us."

Gorrell said, "I'm not so sure about that. It wouldn't surprise me if the whole world is affected by what has happened here."

"All this talk of liberty and equality is very boring," Lady Anne said firmly. "Let's return to the game."

The ivories clicked on the table, and the players settled down to it. Sylvia was glad Lady Anne's attention had turned. Not quite knowing what was expected of her, Sylvia took up a book of Fielding's that lay on the table.

In a short time dinner was brought in. Horniblow had sent up a bottle of exceptionally fine sherry. Toasts were drunk, and then the party turned their attention to the excellent food. When they finished Lady Anne said, "Sylvia, there are a few letters I wish written in time to go to England on the *Devon Maid*, and Captain Meredith is sailing in the morning. On the desk there is a paper on which I've noted what I want you to say. Take it to your room, please. If you want to walk in the village later, I won't need you before supper-time."

Sylvia took the scribbled notations and departed, happy to get away. Writing a few letters would take no time at all, and then she would be free. She hoped the Baron and the children would prolong their visit to the country. Her thoughts turned to the events of the morning, particularly Angus Moray's extraordinary vehemence. His parting words to her were still in her ears. Could it be that he really wanted to be friends with her? Or was he one of those men who wanted every woman to fall under his spell?

The afternoon heat had driven the crowds from the Green. Sylvia closed the shutters to darken the room from the glare and sat down at the desk. Her first note was to Angus Moray, telling him that Lady Anne would require her presence at supper at the time the play would begin. She summoned Promisy and sent the note to Mistress Horniblow with a request that it be handed to Dr. Moray when he called.

A great bumble-bee flew into the room, buzzing angrily. She slapped at it with a towel and succeeded in driving it out the window. The smell of honeysuckle from the garden was heavy. By the time Sylvia finished Lady Anne's letters she felt herself growing drowsy. She took off her gown and flung herself onto the narrow bed. The calico counterpane was cool against her moist face. For a moment she thought again of Angus Moray. Then she drifted off to sleep.

The sun was low over the water when she woke. She glanced at the little clock. A quarter after six. Lady Anne would not sup before eight.

There would be time to walk along the water as far as the flagpole and the parade-ground.

She bathed and dressed and went downstairs. The sound of men's voices and the clink of glasses greeted her as she entered the hall. Pot-boys were running back and forth, carrying pewter mugs of ale or trays of glasses. Doors opened and closed. She saw De' Medici go into one of the private rooms, followed by Dr. Armitage and two men she did not know.

A holiday crowd filled the street and the Green, wandering aimlessly, waiting for time for the evening meal. At the corner Sylvia met Mary Rutledge, who was coming out of Hewes and Smith's.

"I've just been buying some lengths of yellow silk for a shroud for Tazey," Mary said. "She always wanted to be shrouded in yellow." A little smile hovered over her red lips. "I understand that yellow is Chinese mourning. Certainly poor Tazey knew nothing about that, but she loved the colour and hoped that she could meet her God in yellow. It's the last thing I can do for my good friend."

Impulsively Sylvia said, "I think you are wonderful to be so kind and thoughtful to a slave."

"I never thought of Tazey as a slave. If ever a human being had a free soul, it was Tazey."

Sylvia felt no rebuff in the words. Instead they gave her a deeper insight into Mary Rutledge's character.

Mary handed the package to a slave who was waiting. "You can ride home, Ben. Give this to Chaney. Tell her I will not be home until late." To Sylvia she said, "The slaves will be keening and singing and eating the funeral feast to-night." She smiled slightly. "And drinking a little, I'm afraid. My overlooker will dole out an extra tot of rum to the men. Death is not sad for a woman who has lived so long. But come, enough of this. Where are you going?"

"I thought I would walk down to the parade-ground beside the windmill. The evening is so lovely."

"I'll go with you. And when we come back I'll send my card up to the Baroness."

They walked slowly down toward the bay. Water Street was almost deserted when they reached it, but to their left they could see people clustered at the foot of the Green. And behind them more people strolled up Broad Street in the direction of the Fair Ground. Mary paused to read an announcement pasted on a pole.

"ON SATURDAY, will be run four one mile heats on Fair Ground course on Virginia Road. An elegant saddle, bridle, martingale and whip will be free for any nag that never won a purse, carrying weight for age, agreeable to New-market Rules. Entrance fee, Five Dollars. The field will be furnished with best

Liquor and Provisions. The saddle will be hung up at the starting post. Main Event, Quarter Race along parallel paths. Entrance $10."

Mary said, "You must see the racing, Miss Hay. We are proud of our horses."

"Have you an entry?"

"Not for the race. I depend on my husband's judgement about racing horses. Then the boy who rides for us broke his arm a few weeks ago or I might have entered one myself."

They turned right and walked along the water to the parade-ground, which was quite deserted. Mary pointed out a bench where they could sit and watch the sunset. An old man appeared with two young boys and fired the sunset gun. The two women stood up. In silence they watched the lads haul down the flag. The boys folded it carefully and walked away, carrying the flag with them.

Mary spoke quietly. "This makes me a little sad, but it thrills me, too. It means so much to us, that flag. It's a young flag—only a little more than ten years old. But it means battles fought—some lost, some won, but always death. It means the passing of the old, and glorious promise of the new." There were tears in her eyes. "I am sorry. For the moment I forgot that you were not one of us." Sylvia felt that no reply was needed.

They walked slowly back toward the town, talking of indifferent things. At Horniblow's Mary said, "It has been so nice seeing you, Miss Hay. I do hope you will come to Queen's Gift often. I'll run in and ask Horniblow to send up my card. Perhaps to-morrow I will see you at the races." She went into the ladies' parlour.

Sylvia walked up the stairs to her room. In a short time Dawkins came to tell her that Lady Anne was supping with the Baron, but wanted Miss Hay to come in later, about nine. They would make up a party to go to the fair. The Baron, Dawkins added, had made arrangements for the boys to board at Parson Earle's school. She could pack up their boxes in the morning.

It was after midnight when Sylvia returned to her room. She undressed, but she had no desire to sleep. The evening had been exciting. On her desk she saw the little stack of letters she had written for Lady Anne. Captain Meredith was sailing in the morning, she remembered.

She sat down at her desk and began a letter to her aunt.

Dearest Aunt Agatha:

I promised I would write you and Uncle my impressions of America. Up to now I felt I had not been here long enough to be intelligent on the subject, but to-night I have a different feeling. I have been to a fair and seen hundreds of county folk and village folk joined in the merry-making. It is not unlike our

own fairs, where travelling entertainers—jugglers and clowns and wire-walkers—
entertain the crowds.

Let me begin at the beginning. Attending the fair was Lady Anne's idea. So
she made up a party of the Baron, Lord Charles Montague, his cousin Captain
Montague and myself. As the evening progressed, we found ourselves among a
curious array of people. It is the custom here for every one to attend. The gentlefolk who live on the plantations, a class by themselves; the yeomen and small
farmers; the artisans, tradesmen, white indentured men and black slaves. It makes
a heterogeneous group. There appears to be no distinction between classes of the
white folk. They mingle in a friendly way. I mention this to show you that class
distinctions have completely broken down in America. Perhaps they never existed.
I don't know. At any rate, there is a freedom here that would not be quite understood in England. I am puzzled to know how it will work out, to have the
people so completely free.

During the evening Lady Anne . . .

Sylvia paused, wondering whether she should record for Aunt Agatha
her impressions of Lady Anne at the fair. The little party had found a table
where they could be served with ale, and when Lady Anne discovered that
the wrestling was visible from where she sat she was unwilling to leave.
All evening she had watched the wrestlers—great brawny men with bulging
muscles. When the contest was most brutal Sylvia looked away, but Lady
Anne applauded and called out to the wrestlers. In spite of the Baron's
protest she invited one of them to sit at her table and have a mug of porter.
The Baron, horrified, stood stiffly behind her chair and refused to leave her
alone with the wrestler.

Sylvia, who found the scene distasteful, wandered away to watch the
dancing on a floor of canvas sprinkled with corn-meal, lighted by gay
bobbing lanthorns. Here she was joined by Dr. Armitage and Angus Moray.
Angus, solemn and meticulously polite, made no reference to her refusal
of his invitation to the play, but Dr. Armitage assured her that the performance had been wretchedly bad and she need not regret having missed it.

The old doctor announced that he and Moray were going to witness a
cock-fight near by and gallantly invited Sylvia to accompany them. Sylvia
was somewhat startled by the suggestion; she had often heard of cock-fights
at home in England, but it would not have been considered proper there
for her to attend. Armitage, seeing her hesitation, added that ladies of
quality would be present. Sylvia thought Dr. Moray seemed shocked that
she would consider attending such a spectacle. It was this, she suspected,
that influenced her to accept Dr. Armitage's offer.

They crossed the Fair Ground and entered a path that led through a pine
woods, lighted at intervals by lanthorns swinging from boughs of the trees.
Sylvia began to regret her decision as she stumbled along the rough track,
but Dr. Moray's hand closed firmly on her arm when they met an obstacle,

and the sight of other women of genteel appearance ahead of her was re-assuring.

At last they reached their destination—a huge barn which reminded Sylvia of the vast tithe barns she had seen in England. The cockpit was inside, and as they joined the crowds surrounding it Sylvia marvelled at the dramatic scene. It was material for the descriptive powers of a Fielding or a Smollett, she decided. The arena was lighted by tall staffs of burning pitch-pine—lightwood, Dr. Armitage told her it was called. The light flickered on the faces of men and women sitting around the pit, intent on a fight to the death between two beautiful, proud cocks. The birds had pointed steel gaffs on their spurs. With these instruments of torture they struck at each other, circling, waiting, lifting their wings and flying at each other to stab viciously with the cruel steel points.

Sylvia averted her eyes and looked instead at the people around her. Their faces were cruel in the torch light, reflecting a sort of ferocious pleasure as the cocks advanced, struck and, lifting their beautifully coloured wings, drew back. At each strike the crowd yelled. So must the crowds in the arenas of ancient Rome have reacted to the spectacle of lions killing one another or pitted against a single gladiator, Sylvia thought.

The heat rolled in waves. Men had divested themselves of jackets and smocks, and their shirts were damp with sweat. A heavy odour pervaded the huge barn, smelling of the dunghill and of perspiring human beings. Sylvia felt nauseated. Turning, she found that she and her escorts were hemmed in by people who had arrived after them.

In one corner there was scuffling, and voices were raised in argument. "Antifed! Antifed!" some one shouted. And, "You damned Federalist! Think you own the earth! Get out of my way!"

People turned about, trying to see into the dusky corner. "I'll bet a hundred on the Fed!" "Taken!" Sylvia heard the sound of a bare fist against a cheek. Blow followed blow. "Stand back! Make a ring. Let them fight it out by rule. Stand back!" The crowds pressed forward, knocking over seats. They forgot the fighting cocks. Here was something of greater interest, fists and bare knuckles.

Sylvia put her lips to Dr. Armitage's ear. "I must get out of here!"

"Yes, yes. We'll try for the back door. There's going to be trouble between the Federals and the Antifederals. Get her out, Moray. That way! On the other side of the pit there's a door."

The noise increased—shouting and cursing and the sound of blows. "Get a stave! Hit out! Damned Anti!"

Dr. Moray put his arm about Sylvia and led her toward the pit. Pushing and shoving with his free arm, he forced a way through the crowd and shepherded Sylvia through a door into a small shed.

Just beyond the door Sylvia stopped short. Before her stood a bulky young lad stripped to the waist. In his hand he held a dead cock whose blood-soaked feathers he stroked gently.

"Oh, what a crime!" she cried.

The boy lifted his eyes. "Yes, ma'am, 'tis a crime I ever matched my beauty to that devil!" His eyes brightened then. "But did you see he fight thet big 'un? He was heart, all fightin' heart. 'E never give way till he had his death strike."

Sylvia clutched Dr. Moray's arm. "Do something, can't you?"

"It's too late now." The lad wrapped the dead bird in his shirt. "Yes, ma'am, too late. Better you be gittin' now. The lads are fair to makin' a free-for-all in there."

Free-for-all it was. Sylvia and Moray emerged from the shed into crowds surging out of the barn's every door and window. Women picked up their skirts and ran along the path. From the barn came a great roaring of angry voices.

To Sylvia the mob sound was terrifying. She ran through the darkness, the doctor holding her arm.

As they reached the edge of the pine forest the sound diminished. Music from fiddles and banjos took the place of the angry voices, the curses and the mob roar. Lady Anne's party was nowhere to be seen on the Fair Ground, so Moray escorted Sylvia to Horniblow's.

As they reached the inn Moray spoke bitterly. "And this is your quiet, peaceful village—only a hair's-breadth from savagery!"

Sylvia couldn't see his face, but the scorn in his voice angered her. She jerked her arm from his grasp. "It's not my village!" she cried. "But I seem to remember that there have been plenty of fights in Scottish villages—aye, and with claymores and battle-axes. These men fought with bare fists, re- member."

She entered the inn and ran upstairs, wondering at her own remarks. Why had she ranged herself with those crude, bare-fisted roughs? Was her defense of them merely a result of her recurring impulse to oppose Angus Moray? . . .

Sylvia looked down at the unfinished letter to her aunt. No, a description of the evening's activities seemed scarcely calculated to reassure Aunt Agatha about her niece's journey to far-off America. After a pause Sylvia took up her pen and continued the sentence she had begun.

During the evening Lady Anne and, indeed, all of us were much amused by the fair's innocent entertainments. . . .

The Forge and the Anvil

11

As PENELOPE BARKER's preparations for her garden party went forward the village on Queen Anne's Creek reached a high pitch of anticipation. It was like the old days before the Revolution when a visitor meant a series of entertainments and a wedding like Horniblow's was celebrated with a dinner and tea-drinking at Dr. Norcom's, a supper at Mulberry Hill on the Sound and another at James Wills's and finally a fête at Queen's Gift.

Thomas Barker, unenthusiastic at first, was now engrossed in the planning. He took charge of arrangements for dancing. Carpenters and joiners were called in to build a platform in the garden, and Thomas' friend Will Beasley agreed to let his slave, old Hezekiah, bring his fiddle—the same Italian fiddle Beasley had purchased from Henry McCulloh. The Barkers' own boy Eph was good on the banjo and could call contra-dances to the queen's taste.

On Monday before the party Thomas met Mary Rutledge in Cheapside and asked her to send two of her slaves who could play African drums. Mary hesitated. She associated the drums with the slaves' pagan dances and their secret witchcraft practices. But Thomas Barker was persuasive. "You must help me, Mary. Pen wants to make the party as elegant as a garden-party at Haddon Hall or some great English estate. I think we should make it a genuine Carolina party. Our own country-dances, Negro music, a feast and a frolic are what I want. We have some notable guests coming, people of high society. Why attempt to ape European entertainments which we can never duplicate? Why not fall back on something local, something they have never seen? How I should like to get them all dancing!" His eyes lighted; he snapped his fingers and began to pat his thighs rhythmically. "Can't you see Lady Anne Stuart dancing a hoedown to old Hezekiah's fiddling and your boys' drumming?"

Mary laughed delightedly. "Thomas, you have won me completely. I'll send my best drummers with two little drums and a big one. It will be a marvel if you can induce Lady Anne to try one of our country-dances."

Thomas clasped her hand warmly. "Good! Good! Now all I need is for you to persuade Pen that it's the thing to do. You know she thinks highly of your opinion."

"I'll try, Thomas. I'm not sure I can, but I'll try my very best."

"Thank you so much, my dear. You see, Pen wanted a pantomime or a play. She wanted to have the players from the fair, but I convinced her that they were far too crude and vulgar. Now she is angry because the Norfolk company didn't come this way." He shook his head dolefully. "You know Pen; she wants only the best. She never gives a thought to pounds, shillings and pence, Mary."

Mary patted his hand. Thomas always knew the value of money. "Don't worry. I'll see what I can do."

"Then will you talk with her? Will you go up to the house now?"

"As soon as I finish my trading."

Thomas had to be content with that. He walked down the street in the direction of his law office. Although he no longer practised in the courts, he kept a room in Samuel Johnston's office. He liked to tell those who would listen that "in this very room I taught Sam Johnston all the law he knows, and now he's our Governor. And in this very room Sam Johnston taught James Iredell all the law he knows. Isn't it strange that each man has surpassed his teacher? James Iredell is the greatest of us all . . . perhaps the greatest in the land."

He would sit at his old walnut desk and look out on the Courthouse. We've had good men here, he would muse. Edward Moseley, Christopher Gale . . . Now James Iredell comes along to rise above us all. I'm an old man, but I've laid my imprint on this county and on the colony—aye, and on the state.

Mary Rutledge found Madam Barker, dressed in a thin cotton negligee, sitting in a shaded room before her escritoire.

"Come in, come in, Mary. You are an answer to prayer. I'm completing plans for the party, but I have yet to find the proper entertainment."

Mary had always found the direct approach best in dealing with Penelope. She said, "I've been talking with Thomas. He tells me his idea is to have native entertainment, something quite original and different."

Penelope's mouth closed primly. "That Thomas! He's the most irritating man. He wants old Hezekiah playing the violin and a lot of Negroes singing African songs and beating little drums, and the good Lord knows what!" She eyed Mary shrewdly. "Are you encouraging him in this folly?"

"I think the idea is good. You can't possibly have a garden-party here that will compare with what your foreign guests are accustomed to. Why not have the courage to be different?"

Penelope got up and walked about the room, a little frown forming a line between her fine dark eyes. Mary continued, "These people have never heard Negro music. It will be as thrilling to them as it always is to us. Beasley's Hezekiah is a real artist on the violin. They've never heard the banjo played as our people play it. They haven't seen our contra-dances." Mary spoke with conviction. "It's surely worth trying."

"I had wanted something more . . . formal. A little stage set up with the lilac bushes for background, but that's impossible now, and . . ." Penelope was weakening. Mary did not press the point. After a few turns up and down the drawing-room Penelope said decisively, "I'll do it. Thomas is right. Perhaps aping the Old World is nonsense. We will be the first to recognize the talents we have right here. Come, let's make plans."

It was after noon when the program was completed and on paper. Mary refused Penelope's invitation to stay for dinner. "I haven't called on Lady Anne. I'll run over to Horniblow's for a few minutes before I go home."

"Not a word to a soul, mind you," Penelope warned as she followed Mary to the door. "A part of the charm will be in the surprise."

Mary found Lady Anne in, and alone. She was seated near a window, wearing a negligee elaborately trimmed in lace; in her hand was a small peacock-feather fan with ivory sticks which she waved languidly. She looked handsome and bored.

Her acknowledgement of Mary's self-introduction and welcome to Edenton was almost rude in its casualness. "The heat is almost unendurable," she said abruptly. "How do you stand it?"

Mary said, "It is always cool at night. In the day-time I'm quite busy. I have a plantation to manage, you know."

"You sound so energetic. I've always been told that you plantation owners lived an indolent life. I pictured you spending your days sitting in a darkened room, being fanned by Negro slaves."

Mary laughed. "I'm in the saddle by six."

Lady Anne raised her brows. "Six in the morning? What a heathenish idea!" She glanced at Mary. "You manage to look cool and very elegant even in a linen riding habit. I can't believe you have been very busy. Tell me, what is a day on a plantation like?"

"If you find rising at six heathenish, I'm afraid——"

"Really, I'm interested. Tell me what you do from six o'clock on."

"Well, I ride out with the plantation overlooker to see the planting, or the cotton chopping, or to the shore if it's fishing season. Just now it's work in the tobacco fields I must see to. That occupies two or three hours. On some days I go to the dispensary and dole out medicine to the slaves, bind up small wounds, give them their Peru bark for chills and ague, dose them with calomel. Each day I plan the meals and go to the storehouse with my cook to give her supplies for the day. That brings me to dinner-time at one or two o'clock."

"I'm usually just getting up at that time." Lady Anne laughed. "You must think *me* very indolent. Just hearing of your morning activity fatigues me. Is the remainder of your day as strenuous?"

Mary smiled. "No, in the afternoon I rest, write letters, read. Around five I'm ready for visitors, or I may ride to the village or sail across the Sound to visit friends on the other shore. We have a late supper at Queen's Gift, and if people drop in we have cards or a little music. Sometimes we arrange a dance."

Lady Anne nodded. "Not too bad a life, I suppose. You must feel quite remote, with no plays, no stimulating company. But since you have not experienced drama and the opera or the pleasure of a season at one of the watering-places, you are not aware of what you are missing. Perhaps you are better off in your unexciting rural existence."

Mary was undisturbed by Lady Anne's air of patronage. "I think perhaps we are. And our life here is not very different from country life in the Midlands—in Yorkshire, let us say."

Lady Anne looked incredulous. "Yorkshire. What do you know of Yorkshire?"

"My girlhood was spent in West Riding."

Lady Anne stared at Mary. "So?" she said. "I know no Rutledges in Yorkshire."

"My name was Mainwairing. My grandmother was Rhoda Chapman."

"Rhoda Chapman! So you are Rhoda Chapman's grand-daughter. Her feats in the hunting-field are still talked about. Then you must have known my first husband."

"Not well. He came to the house during the hunting season."

"Hunting season! That was all he knew, hunting with the Quorn and shooting in Scotland. Bah! He was a great bore." She moved restlessly, opening and shutting her fan. "Still, he had his points. And you are Rhoda Chapman's grand-daughter. Do you inherit her gift with hunters?"

"She taught me all I know."

Lady Anne looked at Mary thoughtfully. "And with that background you are content to live here in the backwater. How can you stand it? What companionship have you in this little village?"

"There are many fine folk here, Lady Anne—cultivated people. I like it."

"Bah! You are retrograding then. What kind of husband have you? One that can keep you satisfied to give up the delights of London, the pleasures of our country-side?"

A smile came to Mary's lips; a small dimple appeared at the corner of her mouth. "I am quite happy here, Lady Anne. My husband and I chose to live near this tiny village." She paused; to this woman she could not say, We have found peace here—peace and serenity and good living. The woman would not understand.

Mary was relieved when Sylvia Hay's arrival interrupted the conversation. Sylvia was followed shortly by Lord Charles, and it became clear that Lady Anne had plans for the afternoon. Mary rose to take her departure. Lady Anne's protest carried little conviction and Mary excused herself by saying she must be home before sunset.

In the corridor Mary met Cosmo de' Medici, who insisted on going downstairs with her. "I'd like to escort you to Queen's Gift," he said, "but Lady

Anne has made up a table of whist, and I cannot get out of it. The woman is an inveterate gambler. A demanding woman she is! She wants to engross two or three men at a time. I've an idea the little Hay has a difficult time with her mistress' vagaries and vapours."

"Why does she stay on?" Mary said as they reached the court-yard. The hostler brought Mary's horse. She put the toe of her boot in De' Medici's cupped hands and quickly mounted.

"I fancy Sylvia has her living to think of. A nice girl, but she is bound to have a temper, with that hair. Good-bye, Maria. I will be glad when Adam returns, so you are not alone on the plantation. I worry about you."

"Don't. I'm quite accustomed to being alone. When do you leave for the west?"

"To-morrow morning. I am going to Halifax, then to Hillsborough on the seventeenth."

Mary gathered up the reins. "You'll be among Antifederalists. Be wary of Wilie Jones. He's a most persuasive and persevering gentleman."

Cosmo looked up at Mary, his dark eyes serious. He found himself wishing that he had a Maria of his own. He dismissed the thought. "Sometimes I think there is something to be said for the Antis," he said.

Mary held up a warning finger. "Don't say that aloud in Edenton. You'll have the whole town down on you."

"I'm not so sure of that. I hear rumblings of dissatisfaction. I think it will not be too easy for Mr. Samuel Johnston to get his will at Hillsborough."

Mary thought about Cosmo's words on the way home. Perhaps he was right. Dr. Armitage had convinced her that Antifederalist strength was growing. She must talk to him again, learn more of what the artisans, the shopkeepers were saying. They talked freely to him. She had been disturbed by the doctor's prophecy about Adam. Could her husband's point of view have changed since he left? Surely not; he would follow Johnston. The Federal program would be his choice, whatever arguments for Antifederalism he had heard in the West. But Adam did not blindly accept leadership. He would do his own thinking. Mary knew a moment's doubt. Strange, he had talked little of politics before he left. The letter he had sent from the Illinois country with Marcy had said only that he still hoped to take his seat at Hillsborough as a delegate from Chowan. Jemmy and Sam Johnston would count on him to vote with the Federalists. But suppose he shouldn't? She shut her mind to such a possibility. Adam was conservative, not radical like Wilie Jones and Timothy Bloodworth. Surely he would defend the Constitution. He would see that North Carolina must vote to ratify.

Twice in the night she wakened, remembering a disturbing dream in which she had heard Adam's voice saying, "We must have the people's rights protected. The Federal government must not be strengthened at the expense of the states."

The night Mary had disturbing dreams, Mel Frazier, the blacksmith and farrier, spoke to some thirty men who had met in the old barn behind his shop. A strong man with a commanding voice and the power to reason clearly, he had become a leader among village Antifederalists. He kept abreast of developments through his friend Tim Bloodworth of Wilmington. He knew groups were forming all over the state. The feeling that North Carolina should not ratify the Constitution as it stood was steadily becoming better organized. Farmers were meeting at cross-road stores. Fishermen, printers, sailors and ex-soldiers were having their say. So far they had spoken guardedly. But resentment and suspicion were growing. Antifederalists from Halifax and Wilmington had spoken at meetings in Chowan.

Men with horses and mules to be shod came to Frazier's shop and lingered to protest. Why should they trust rich men like Governor Johnston? They remembered that during the war he had said only men of learning should have a voice in making the state constitution. Didn't he plead in the courts for Tories whose land had been confiscated? He and James Iredell had fought for McCulloh as well as for Sir Nat Duckenfield and his mother Mrs. Pearson. Did that show loyalty to the state—or loyalty to their class?

To-night there were a few Federalists among the men who stood in a ring around Frazier. He was speaking now to them and to others who had not attended previous meetings in the barn. "The printer Wills talks of Dr. Williamson and his arguments for the Constitution. I know all the doctor says." The blacksmith reached out and took a pamphlet from Wills's hand. He slapped it against his leather apron, then opened it to the light of the forge and studied a page for a moment.

"Williamson thinks the government proposed would be safe from foreign invasion and domestic sedition. Mayhap he's right. But do you want to pay taxes to support an army that could steal your liberties? We've proved we can defend ourselves. He says commerce would be protected and the value of produce and land would be increased. Was he mindful of you when he wrote that, or of the rich merchants and plantation owners?"

Mel leaned forward. A small apprentice boy pumped the bellows. The forge fire leaped up, showing the farrier's rugged face in a pattern of shadows and red light which gave him a strange, almost diabolical expression. "Our friend Williamson said much the same things right here in Edenton in November of last year. I remember his exact words: 'The proposed government will protect liberty and property, cherish the good citizen and honest man.' Bah!" He spat into the fire. "The Constitution has no bill of rights. Unless we have that, we can't be sure we're protected. We're labourers, farmers, mechanics, artisans. We want law for our safety. Williamson was our delegate to the Philadelphia convention. He had to excuse what he put his name to. Yet even he told you the Constitution was far from

perfect. You all remember. If he has his doubts, why should we feel safe?"
Again he spat into the fire.

A yeoman who lived in the Yeopim district spoke. "Doctor Williamson is
a good friend to us. You know that, Mel."

"Aye, I know. He took care of me in the war in the Dismal. He sawed
off my foot, he did. I tell you, men, we can't be thinking of past favours.
We must watch carefully what our leaders are doing. Get the delegates at
Hillsborough to see our side."

West, the peruke maker, moved forward. He was a small man but out
spoken. "Your mouth runs off, Mel," he said good-humouredly. "You are
saying words put into it by your friend Bloodworth, or Tom Person of
Granville. Let us speak for ourselves, men. Chowan men speak for Chowan
men. Be we Federals or Antis, we'll not let the words of foreign counties
be put into our mouths."

The two faced each other in the red light—the great burly figure of
Frazier, the almost delicate figure of West. Both were Scots, both straightforward, both steadfast for their side.

Some one in the background raised his voice. "I wager ten shillings on
Mel Frazier. Take up your tools and fight. The hammer against the curling-
tongs!" The crowd jeered, laughed and clapped.

"West should have his say the same as Frazier." It was Wills who spoke.
A cut above the others in education, he was more tolerant. "Don't be hasty
about forming your opinions, men. Mr. Iredell's getting something set up,
down at our shop, that will answer Mel. A long piece explaining the
Constitution step by step. It'll be all printed Thursday in the *State Gazette*.
Wait and read what Iredell has to say. You know how fair he is."

A farmer named Galloway turned toward Wills. "Dare say he's fair
enough to you. You do his bidding at your shop. But a lot of us don't like his
Tory friends."

A voice came out of the darkness. "Now don't let's fight the war all over.
We've all had a bellyful of fighting."

"Wait! Listen!" Frazier shouted and then spoke sharply as the men grew
quiet. "We'll mind what Judge Jemmy has to say. But we won't delay
action. I don't ask you to be narrow, but, by God, we've won the battles and
we're going to see that they stay won!"

Wills moved up near the forge. "Yes, we've won the battles. Now we
must win a new state. We elected delegates to Hillsborough last March.
How many of you went to cast your vote?"

Only Mel Frazier answered. "I did. But does that mean I keep quiet
while Stephen Cabarrus, Charles Johnson and Lemuel Creecy speak for me?
I'm a freeman of Chowan. I'll let them know what I think."

A young man in a blue smock and homespun breeches stepped out of the
gloom. "Who represents the freemen of the town?"

The blacksmith answered, "Iredell represents the Borough of Edenton.

He's priming to fight the Antifederalists. You have Wills's word for that."

A dozen men looked at the printer. Galloway said, "Aye, Wills is for the Federalists right enough."

"The press takes no part in this. Haven't we printed letters from both sides? *Publicola* by Maclaine and Mr. Iredell's piece took the Federalist side. But you've had a chance to read Antifederalist articles. Compare the arguments."

Mel moved toward the printer and handed his pamphlet to him. "No, Wills. Many of these men can't read. But I reckon they know facts and know their own minds. Come back and read Mr. Iredell's article and welcome. You'll see——"

A man in the crowd shouted, "What about indentured men who couldn't vote? What can we do?"

"Why, raise a ruckus, that's what you can do. We'll meet here Wednesday as we agreed. Broadsides are being posted. You'll be joined by many others. Wills can read whatever Iredell has to say. There'll be men here to answer. They'll show you how you can make your will felt without a legal vote."

"That we will, Mel. That we will. We'll let the bigwigs know they can't speak for us, and that goes for Governor Johnston and his friends."

Wills had the last word. "Better find out what you want before you begin to holler so loud." As the printer spoke he moved toward the door. It was thrown open for him. In a few moments the men began to drift away. They went quietly to their homes in the village or mounted their horses and rode to their farms. They were not unreasonable men, but determined. A wind was rising from which there could be no shelter. Men were not following their leaders blindly, nor were they indifferent, leaving politics to the politicians. A new voice was being heard. It was the voice of men who had won a bitter war by broken bodies, by sacrifice, by death. A stronger voice than had yet been heard in this New World. In it was the determination and untested power of the people.

A Feast and a Frolic

12 MARY RUTLEDGE slipped on a robe, thrust her feet into Bermuda slippers and went out onto the upper gallery. It was just four o'clock. The Sound lay in the shadow of the tall pines that crowded the high bank. Little wisps of white smoke rose from the chimneys along the quarters line where cooking fires had been lighted, but no one was stirring out of doors. Mary liked this hour of the day, the quiet and the silence of the water. The country-side reminded her

of a gigantic figure waking from sleep. Presently it would stretch and turn and come into slow, reluctant life. The quiet of the night would give way to bird song, the crowing of the cock, a fox's last bark before he took to hiding in burrow or hollow log. The slow flight of a heron would show white against the dark water of the Sound.

The air was soft and cool against her face. A bird stirred in the vast tulip poplar that grew against the house. The tree's boughs scraped and tapped in the night hours as though it begged admittance. Sometimes in a soft wind the boughs tapped gently; sometimes they made an angry, insistent, demanding sound. The tree made the slaves uneasy when the wind was high. "De wind he wants inside, mistress. He wants to crowd in wid us and wrap he arms about us. 'Tis not good, de tree he grow too big now. Better you let de boys chop he down. Some day he get so angry he crash right in. Den he have death in he hands."

But Mary refused to cut the old tulip poplar. It had been a young tree when Duke Roger built the house. She would have a few boughs lopped off, she told herself, but she didn't—only tied back the limb that thrust itself between the balcony rail and filled up the end of the gutter. She liked to stand at the gallery rail, looking into the depths of the green crown of the tree. The yellow blooms were fading now; a few days more of hot July sun and they would be gone.

She heard the scuffling of bare feet on the floor. A sleepy-eyed young house slave was walking across the gallery, carrying Mary's morning tea on a small silver tray. The girl, an octoroon, pulled a table near the rail and set the tray on it. "Mis' Chaney she say what fo' you risin' so early in de mo'nin'? She say you drink dis tea and get in you' bed right away."

Mary laughed. "You tell Chaney why fo' she up so early?"

The girl placed a chair at the table. "She makin' dose little tea-cakes for Mis' Barker's frolic to-night. She done been up since cockcrow. She got all de kitchen staff up helpin' she. She's a *workin'* woman, dat Mis' Chaney." The girl shuffled off.

Mary drank her tea, but she didn't go back to bed. Instead she put on her habit and called to a boy to bring out her saddle mare Queenie. By the time she was ready the field hands were on their way to the cotton-patch, walking single file. The women carried their chopping hoes over their shoulders and sang as they walked along the rows. A little army of workers, straight-backed, square-shouldered workers accustomed since childhood to carry burdens on their heads. Mary recalled an old saying: if you carry your burdens on your head, you do not carry them on your heart.

It pleased Mary to know that her slaves did not find life at Queen's Gift disagreeable. Their day's work began at sun-up and was broken by the long rest from noon until the sun was well past the zenith at four. No one worked in the heat of the day. From four until six the slaves were in the fields again, and there might be an hour's ploughing or cultivating after supper when the twilight was long in the summer.

As usual, thought of this year's harvest brought a frown to Mary's face and a pang to her heart. Queen's Gift must make a good showing under her stewardship! If on Adam's return she could report a record crop perhaps he wouldn't talk so eagerly of the wide prairies of the Illinois country and the rich black bottom lands where the Mississippi overflowed and left fertile soil in its wake. Mary was afraid of the West, afraid of its hold on her husband. Hundreds of thousands of acres of rich virgin land there, he had told her, while here in the Albemarle it was becoming crowded. Each time he returned from the West she sensed his unrest, as though he were constantly making comparison. His first trip out the Western road, long before their marriage, had changed him. And she remembered the day he had told her he had sold most of Rutledge Riding and his Tyrrell County land. With the land he had sold the slaves who worked it. She had not asked him what money he received or what use he would make of it. She'd known without asking. More prairie land for wheat and corn. More Mississippi bottom land. More money for the stone mill he planned to build on the river.

Deliberately Mary had closed her eyes to what was happening, hoping, hoping that Queen's Gift, her plantation, would satisfy him.

Mary's mind was still on these problems as she rode along the fields on her morning round. The sun was on the waters of the Sound now. The early-morning quiet had gone, and all about her the plantation life was in motion. In a little while the sun would bring heat and discomfort, but heat would bring growth to the fields. If only Adam . . . She made an effort to put the half-formed thought out of her mind. Surely he would not abandon the lovely Albemarle country!

Yet deep in her heart she knew the war years had changed her husband. Before the Revolution his every thought had been of land, land to develop and make fertile. Plant, sow and reap, plant, sow and reap, over and over, with the changing seasons. Why had he changed? Was the change a result of the war or of the challenge of that new wide country whose rich soil had never known a plough? Was the draw of the new challenge too strong to be resisted? Was the old losing its hold? This was an old country, narrow, limited.

She seemed to see a vast land, without horizons, stretching out into the untamed West. She thought of other men who had gone away. Some had land grants along the Ohio or in Tennessee County or the part of Virginia called Kentucky—dark and menacing land where Indians lurked in the forest, giving way slowly, fighting, murdering. Dear God, was Adam caught up in the fascination of this strange, wild country to the west? What would happen when he returned? Mary was sure of one thing: she would never go to that new country.

She was trembling when she rode up the driveway to Queen's Gift. Her horse was in a lather, and Mary realized she must have been pressing the mare into more speed ever since she left the grist-mill by the pocosin.

She looked at the house with new eyes. Queen's Gift was her home. How strong and solid it stood on the bank of the Sound! The broad façade held beauty, the wings were arms outstretched to welcome her. The smooth green lawns, the trim gardens set in a semicircle of oaks and tall dark pines, the water sparkling in the sun . . . It seemed to her that the scene held all the beauty, all the rest and peace that the world could give. She could not give it up. Never, never, never!

The stableboy who had run out to take her horse looked up at her, curiosity in his black eyes. Mary realized she had spoken the words aloud: "Never, never, never!"

In the breakfast-room Mary found Chaney, who was wearing her town dress. A silk bandanna of awesome colours bound her head, and she had her golden hoops in her ears. "De boy is goin' to bring de gig so I can go to town. I'll carry dose little tea-cakes my own self, lessen dey gits crumpled. Den I'll stay to help Mis' Barker's Millie. She got a silly head. She done lose it when people comes in a crowd. Mis' Barker she say she want me to see dat de frolic goes off all right, wid no confusion. You mind?"

"Of course not," Mary said. "Do you want Ebon to go with you?"

"Yes'm, I does. And my boy Ben. We's a team, we is. We can serve a hundred, maybe two hundred head wid no mishap. Yes'm, we's a fair team."

"That you are, Aunt Chaney." The woman lingered. Mary knew there was something more on her mind.

"How come you don't say nothin' 'bout dat supper I fix for dose foreigners last night? You don't say good or no good at all 'bout my food."

"Oh, Chaney, I'm sorry. The supper was delicious. Didn't you see how much they ate? All the gentlemen had second helpings."

"Yes'm. I see 'em when I cracked de pantry do'h. But you ain't say nothin' you'self."

"I suppose I was so busy getting card tables ready and all."

"Yes'm, dose foreign gen'lemen was sure in a hurry to seat deyselves at de cyard table, an' dat Lady Anne, she was a-fixin' to get 'em dere. Her husband an' dose others. She was askin' you to play some music too, so she could slip out in de gyardin an' walk in de moonshine, hanging onto dat young doc's arm, all lovin' like."

"Yes?"

"Yes'm. She was, an' leavin' dat pretty young lady all alone wid you an' old Doc. Yes'm. 'Tain't natural, dat it wa'nt. Dat young girl, she a-nervousin' around wid no one to talk to. She wanted to be out in de moonshine, she did. Think she saw dat fine lady a-kissin' young Doc; wid her wedded husband sittin' in de house, losin' his money to dose gen'lemens."

"Nonsense, Chaney. Your imagination is running away with you."

"Swear to God, Miss Mary. I seed it wid dese eyes. Cain't fool me, you cain't. Dat lady she so grand and mighty in she talk, and holdin' her head up; she act jes' like some of our gals waitin' round tobacco barns for de boys to lead 'em off to de hedgerows and throw 'em."

"Chaney, you must not talk that way about our guest Lady Anne."

"Ain't no invited guest, she warn't. She jes' ride out here wid her gen'le-men and stay to supper, without bein' asked special. She's man-hongry, she is. Dat young doc he don't know what to do wid she but keep on a-kissin' and a-kissin'."

Mary got up from the table. "Better not talk about it in town, Chaney."

"No, ma'am. I wouldn't want townsfolk to know dere was such goin's on at Queen's Gift." Chaney marched off, her head high.

Mary sighed ruefully. Chaney didn't like to be reminded of her manners.

The old Negro woman's observation about Lady Anne had startled Mary. She was constantly aware that the slaves knew everything that went on, and Chaney in particular had an uncanny skill at placing people. If Chaney was convinced that Lady Anne was a frivolous creature who lived for men's admiration, Mary was ready to believe that her own similar impressions were accurate. And Angus Moray, though his attraction to Sylvia Hay was undoubtedly genuine, was young enough to be flattered by the attention of a worldly woman. But Mary had not observed that Sylvia showed any interest in Dr. Moray. Well, it was none of her affair, she reflected, but she could not help wondering how poor Moray would resolve his dilemma.

Mary forgot the whole thing when Marcy came in to report on the week's progress on the plantation. She questioned him anxiously, but his account of the condition of the crop was encouraging. She felt much relieved when they concluded their session. "The weather is just right for the Barkers' garden-party," she said as Marcy prepared to take his leave.

Marcy's answer was cryptic. "The weather is fair enough, but . . ." He hesitated, turning his hat in his hands. "The weather isn't everything," he said after a silence.

"What do you mean, Marcy?"

"I don't know that I should speak out, Mrs. Rutledge, but there's a heap of restlessness among the village folk—the common folk, I mean—and in the country-side too, for that matter."

"What are you talking about, Marcy?"

"Well, some folks don't like the delegates they elected last March. 'Tis said they were told only one side of this Constitution business. Men have been here from Halifax and Wilmington, holding meetings in the county. They are saying that Governor Johnston's way of thinking about how to vote isn't fair to the farmers."

"Not fair? In what way?"

"Well, it appears that many men in the state think the common folk won't be protected in their rights if the Federalists have their way and vote to ratify as the document now stands. I don't say that I agree, Mrs. Rutledge, but it's what's been said at the meetings in the village. They say that Mr. Iredell and Governor Johnston and Dr. Williamson are all for signing at Hillsborough, but others, like Mr. Wilie Jones, say *not* to sign until the new government adds amendments that give a bill of rights for the protection of the ordinary folk."

Mary was taken aback. More evidence that the farmers up-country were not content to follow the leadership of Governor Johnston or James Iredell! "That is silly," she said firmly.

Marcy continued, his face grave, his eyes unreadable. "I'm just telling you, Mrs. Rutledge, that there's a lot of talk. Notices of a political meeting have been up almost a week. Last night more broadsides were posted on the board in front of the Courthouse. The Antis aim to hold a mock election to-night. They've heard about the business in Dobbs County, where the Federalists held a second election and got their men in. They aim to vote for other delegates here, men that think away from Johnston."

"A mock election!" Mary exclaimed. "What could they accomplish? They don't understand what happened in Dobbs County. There was a riot, and the first election was never completed. Our Chowan election was legal. Their delegates couldn't be seated."

"Beg pardon, ma'am. Their leaders understand this. They only want the common folk to have a chance to show how they feel." He paused for a moment. "They plan to name Mr. Rutledge as one of their delegates. They say they don't know what he thinks about this, but they know he is fair to every one."

Mary stamped her foot in anger. "They can't, Marcy! Why, it's ridiculous! He was made a delegate in the March election. And anyway he would never vote against the best opinions of all his friends."

Marcy said nothing.

Mary's anxiety grew. "Marcy, what do you think? Do you suppose he would vote against the Federalists?"

Marcy turned his head slightly. He did not meet her eyes. He spoke slowly, as though considering his words carefully. "A man sometimes sees things differently when he gets away for a while. I wouldn't know what Mr. Adam was thinking. He doesn't say much—you know that. I wouldn't worry about Mr. Adam if I were you. What I'm thinking about is the crowd that will be in the village. You know a political meeting day is a noisy day, with drinking and all. Not so nice for Mrs. Barker's party, to have the village full of roisterers and drunken fellows whose tongues are loose and whose fists are free and itching to fight."

Mary went upstairs and instructed her maid Pam to pack her clothes for the party; Mrs. Barker had asked her to come in early to help oversee the preparations for that night. But Mary was preoccupied as she tried to select the most suitable and becoming of her gowns. Marcy's words had disturbed her deeply. She hoped nothing untoward would happen, but she was anxious. Every one knew of the presence of Lady Anne and Lord Charles in the village. Probably every one knew also that the titled visitors would be at Penelope Barker's this evening. Country-folk were suspicious of "foreigners," and some had carried a deep-seated hatred for all Englishmen even before the Revolution. And the village had not forgotten the men lost in battle against the English. If the common people were as restless as Marcy believed, they might choose to invade the Barkers' garden. Mary was glad that the Governor and Jemmy Iredell were in Edenton. If there was trouble, certainly they could handle it in some way.

But beneath her concern over possible trouble in the village was her ever-present anxiety about Adam's course at Hillsborough. Surely he would not . . . Mary felt chilled. There was a heaviness in her head and the pit of her stomach. She hoped it wasn't the fever coming on. She lay down on the bed and in a few moments she was asleep.

Directly after dinner Mary prepared to go to the village. When she came out to get into her carriage she saw Marcy walking toward the lot. An idea came to her, and she called to Marcy. He came up and helped her into the carriage.

"Marcy, I've been thinking," she said. "Perhaps it might be a good idea if you came into the village later and brought a few of our men with you."

"I had thought of that, Mrs. Rutledge. We have a couple of horses that need shoeing. The boys can drive them to a cart. At the blacksmith's we may be able to find out more of what's planned. Mel Frazier knows what's going on. In fact, he is one of the leaders."

"Mel Frazier? That surprises me, Marcy."

"Not me, Mrs. Rutledge. Frazier has been disgruntled ever since he got back from Yorktown."

"Because he lost a foot, do you think?"

"I can't say, Mrs. Rutledge. There's plenty of unrest, right across the country. Men don't want to stay put, the way they used to. Don't worry. My sturdy lads and I will be in town to-night."

Mary found the Barker house in a state of upheaval. Hannah Iredell was directing the slaves who were arranging small tables in the garden. The Hardys and the Joneses were in charge in the library. Nellie Blair and Mary Blount were decorating the drawing-room and bewailing the fact that there were so few flowers in July.

"We found some Queen Anne's lace down Yeopim Road and made a bouquet for the dining-table," Nellie said. "I wanted to put yellow trumpet-vine in here, but every one says it's poison to touch and unlucky as well. Yellow honeysuckle will have to do."

Mary Blount said, "It has a delightful perfume, and we have plenty of cabbage roses for the out-door tables."

Mary went through the house. Everywhere there was activity. House slaves were dusting, sweeping, carrying dishes to the back galleries. In the kitchen she found Madam Barker, her wide skirt pinned back, a mob-cap covering her *coiffure*. She was talking to Chaney, who evidently had taken possession of the kitchen.

"Madam, jes' you make no worry fo' you'self," Chaney was saying. "Give us space, and we'll take de kitchen. Run, make you'self pretty. I sure don't like to see you' pretty hair all covered up wid a cap dat-a-way."

Penelope laughed. "Chaney is a martinet," she said to Mary. "I suppose I do look a sight."

"I never go near the kitchen," Mary said. "They always manage in their own way."

Penelope led the way to the garden. "I want you to look at the tables, to see if they are placed most advantageously. Oh, Mary, I wonder if I was right to consent to Thomas' plan to have only Negro music. I know our English visitors will think us a crowd of heathen, little better than the Indians."

"They probably think that anyway," Mary said cheerfully. "I think the garden is lovely. And where did you get all those pines you've added to the hedge around the garden?"

"From my plantation in Tyrrell. Thomas said I was a fool, that it was like building a hedge of pounds, shillings and pence, but I don't care. And the fence will give us privacy. Thomas was horrified when I sent two pontoons across the Sound to get the trees. He wanted to let them grow. He talked about tar, pitch and turpentine, naval stores and ships' masts, but," Penelope said with satisfaction, "I had my way. I had no intention of having the whole village gaping at us while we are eating."

A slave came up to say that the Governor and Mr. Iredell were in the drawing-room. Penelope hastily unpinned her skirt and took off the mob-cap and, pulling her hair into place, hurried down the garden path. "We must not keep His Excellency waiting. What can he want, do you suppose?" Mary followed, wondering if she should tell the Governor of Marcy's apprehensions.

They found Governor Johnston in the drawing-room, standing before Thomas Barker's portrait. After he had greeted them he said, "I always think, don't you, Penelope, that my portrait of Thomas is much the best likeness?"

Penelope made a little *moue* which brought out the dimples about her mouth. Sam loved to tease her about the portrait she coveted. "Some time you will be in a generous mood, Governor, and send it to me."

The Governor smiled but shook his head. "Never. Never. Thomas had it

painted for me in London. I've selected the place where it will hang in my
new house. It shall rest in my library, a monument to the finest law-teacher
in the colonies. But I digress. I did not come to call but to deliver a message
from my wife, who is not well. She and the children will stay on at The
Hermitage until September, so she cannot come to your garden-party."

"But you are coming, surely." There was a touch of alarm in Penelope's
voice.

"If you will have me without my dear spouse."

"Of course we want you. Are you not the most distinguished citizen of
North Carolina!"

Hannah and James Iredell came into the room. His arm was about her
waist. Hannah's face was delicately flushed. She brushed a loosened curl
back into place.

James was laughing. "My wife says it is not proper for me to kiss her in
the rose arbour. I appeal to you all, whom should one kiss in the rose arbour
except one's charming wife?"

"Hush, Jemmy!"

"My dear, I have no intention of hushing. Why should I not declare before witnesses—your devoted brother, your two intimate gossips—that I am
your devoted husband and eternal lover?"

The Governor's stern face relaxed, and he smiled a little. Penelope spoke
quickly. "Jemmy, you are delightful. Every man should pledge himself daily
to his wife. Hannah, you are the most fortunate of women. I must remind
Thomas to pay me a pretty compliment now and then."

Thomas Barker came into the room at this moment. "What's this? What's
this? Pay you compliments? Madam, I compliment you each day by remaining faithful to you."

Penelope tapped him on the cheek. "So you do, my dear."

Mary glanced at Hannah, who was looking at her husband with adora-
tion. She is as deeply in love as he, she thought, but she has not the facility
to express herself. How like her brother the Governor, dignified, reserved,
remote! It is good that she married Jemmy Iredell.

Mary waited patiently throughout the exchange of pleasantries, but as
Johnston and Iredell moved toward the door she stepped forward. "Governor, Jemmy—may I see you for a moment?"

Penelope turned quickly, detecting uneasiness in Mary's voice. "Why,
Mary, what is it? Is something wrong? Have you——"

"Nothing that need concern you, Penelope." Madam Barker's problems
as a hostess would worry her sufficiently, Mary knew, without any hints of
a possible riot. "It's just that, with Adam away, I need advice sometimes,
and where could I obtain better guidance than from these gentlemen and
your Thomas?"

"But what——" Penelope began. But Hannah Iredell, tactful as always, intervened. "Penelope, let us leave Mary with her counsellors. Come, I have had two of the tables in the garden moved, and I want your approval." And Penelope found herself borne firmly away by the delicate Hannah.

The three men watched their departure with smiles. Then Johnston said, "Now, Mary, what's worrying you?"

Mary hesitated. "I hope you will not think me meddlesome," she began, "but my overseer, Marcy, has told me some things today that alarmed me considerably. I suppose you all know of the political meeting scheduled for this evening."

"The mock election?" Iredell smiled. "Yes, Mary, we have heard of it and are much interested to see what the outcome will be."

Mary stared at him. "But do you know that the farmers and villagers will be flocking together to air their Antifederalist feelings and listen to their leaders denounce the Constitution? Marcy says their purpose is to influence the Hillsborough convention to reject the Constitution. Can't something be done to halt them?"

"Mary"— James Iredell was serious now—"Mary, we have no right, legal or moral, to prevent these men from meeting together to discuss their political opinions, however misguided we believe those opinions to be. For my own part, I would not wish to prevent them. The future of this state will be decided at Hillsborough, and it is wholly proper and desirable that every resident of the state should concern himself with the decision. The opponents of the proposed Constitution are breaking no law when they assemble to criticize it. Indeed, one of the Antifederalists' complaints is that the Constitution will impose a tyranny over the common man in that it does not guarantee him just such fundamental rights as free assembly. If we attempted to interfere with this meeting to-night, we would present the Antifederalists with proof that their objection is well founded."

Iredell spoke with deep earnestness, and when he paused he glanced at Johnston as if seeking confirmation.

Johnston too was grave. "Jemmy is correct, Mary," he said. "The Antifederalists have every right to meet publicly and propound their opinions. I have less confidence than Jemmy in the political thinking of the common people, but I cannot think the convention will be swayed by demonstrations such as this mock election. The people who will assemble to hear Mel Frazier interpret the Constitution have, in the phrase of my friend Maclaine, had a slight view of one half of it over the shoulder of another person. None of our Chowan Federalists will be influenced unduly by the results of to-night's activities."

Mary sighed. "Of course you are right, Governor, and you, Jemmy. I appreciate your explanation and I'm glad I asked, for you've relieved me greatly." She paused. "There is one other aspect that has worried me. These men may go to the meeting as citizens, but . . . well, when two hundred citizens get together and start drinking they form a mob, and mobs can be dangerous. We all know there is anti-British feeling in the town and coun-try-side. Do you think the sounds of Penelope's party and the presence here of Montague and Lady Anne might . . . ?"

Thomas Barker stepped forward. "We've wondered about that also, Mary. I have spoken to the Sheriff myself. He tells me he sees no reason to expect any violence other than the inevitable fights among the men at the meeting. However, precautions will be taken in case the oratory proves in-flammatory. Now don't trouble yourself any more, but concentrate on en-joying yourself. And not a word to my Penelope, please. It would only upset her."

Mary smiled. "Thank you, Thomas . . . Jemmy . . . Sam. I'm glad you're my friends!"

When Marcy reined his horse at the blacksmith shop near Hewes's shipyard it was late in the afternoon. The farrier was at his forge, his helper beside him. In the shop behind, Marcy saw a group of men sitting back on coils of rope and upturned boxes. All the faces he saw were strange to him; probably men from near-by counties, he thought. The blacksmith greeted him with a careless nod and went on shaping red-hot iron into a shoe.

"Have my boys been in yet?" Marcy said. "I've two horses that need shoeing."

The blacksmith said, "No, they haven't come. I don't know when I can get around to them. I'm very busy today."

Marcy sat down on a bench near the door. From his position he could see any one who passed on King Street. He lighted a pipe and watched the strong skilful hands shape a shoe for the work horse behind him. Mel Frazier moved well enough, for all his wooden leg.

A lad came down the street carrying a packet of papers. Marcy recognized him as young Ambrose, a helper at Chase's printing shop. The boy avoided the open door of the smithy and went around to the back. One by one the men got up and sauntered out of Marcy's view, toward the barn. Presently the men, eight of them, reappeared, each with papers under his arm. They walked down King Street and turned the corner. Ambrose followed them, his hands empty. Marcy glanced at Frazier. His stern face expressed nothing.

Marcy finished one pipe and had begun on a second when his boys drove into the yard. They were in a high-wheeled cart, a black horse on a lead rope following.

"Sar, we are late. Dere was a dozen horses and carriages waiting to ferry across Queen Anne's Creek from the Hertford Road."

"It's all right, Cato. The blacksmith is busy, and there are two more horses to be shod before our turn comes."

The Negro helper led the newly shod horse out of the shop. The black-smith turned to Marcy. "It will be an hour before I can get to you. Why don't you come back later?" he suggested.

Marcy tapped the dottle from his pipe. "You're right. I've an errand or two. The boys will wait here. That black is mighty fractious. No one can handle her but Cato." He stopped to adjust the bridle on the black horse and spoke to Cato in a low tone. "Keep track of every stranger who comes here."

"Yes, sar. Done see a fella at de ferry. Heard him say he from Wilmington and dey was fixin' to mess up somebody to-night."

Marcy nodded and left the shop. The blacksmith watched him as he moved away, a heavy frown on his face.

At a cross-street Marcy saw two of the strangers who had been at the smithy. One had backed a gig out into the street, blocking Marcy's way. A saddle-horse was hitched a little beyond. As Marcy pulled up he could hear what the strangers were saying.

"You take the Virginia Road. Go up as far as the turn, and work back. Don't start until sundown. I'll take the east road. Greg is looking after the town fellows. They won't begin before dark," the sandy-haired one said.

"Hope they don't get too much liquor aboard," said the other man.

His companion laughed. " 'Twill make it more exciting if they do." He slapped the reins on the horse's back and drove off along Liza's Bottom toward the Virginia Road.

Marcy was about to pass by when the second man hailed him.

"Hi! You belong in these parts, mister? Do you know where the cooperage is?"

"About three or four blocks up," Marcy told him, "close to the tan yard on the opposite side of Broad Street."

"Do they make good staves?"

Marcy said he thought so. He watched the fellow ride off, a bundle of papers in his saddle-bag. There had been no opportunity for him to get hold of one of the papers without arousing suspicion. He didn't like the look of the stranger, nor did he like the inquiry about staves. A stave was a potent weapon for breaking heads.

He rode back to the smithy. Perhaps he could get hold of one of the papers there. The smith was nowhere to be seen, and Cato said he had gone off with strange gen'lemen. He had left in a hurry, saying he wouldn't be back for an hour or more to shoe the horses.

Marcy crossed the shop and went into the back room. In a wooden chest he found what he was searching for. He took one of the broadsides and closed the lid of the box, then went outside and stood near the cart while he read it.

INFORM YOURSELVES

Citizens of Chowan County!

Don't Follow the Federals Blindly

This is what a Leader of the Antifederalists has to say:
Raise your voices, Freemen of Chowan! Safeguard your
Freedom!

Say no to the Constitution without a Bill of Rights.

Fight for the Liberties you won in War.

Distrust the Philadelphia Convention.

Alexander Hamilton and James Madison are mere boys.

Franklin is an old dotard in his second childhood.

Washington is a good soldier, but ignorant of politics.

The Constitution will make you Slaves of the Wealthy!

Defeat it. See that your leaders vote against signing.

Remember your State should be supreme. Guard its
Rights.

Be at the Court House steps at 9:30 to-night to

Cast Your Vote for FREEDOM.

Marcy pocketed the paper. To Cato he said, "Stay here until I come back. Did you bring food with you?"

"Sar, we have corn-pone. If we had a penny, we could buy gingie-bread."

Marcy gave them each a coin. "I'll be back presently." He mounted his horse and rode uptown to Thomas Barker's residence. He must get the broadside to Mrs. Rutledge at once.

Mary Rutledge was in the Barkers' garden, superintending the lighting of the table candles, which had glass shades to protect them from the wind. Dusk had fallen, and the paper lanthorns festooned among the trees and shrubs gave the garden a festive look. Negro musicians had taken their places near the dancing platform, and table waiters were hurrying back and forth, placing chairs and benches. Madam Barker, dressed in a new gown of ivory taffeta over a rose petticoat trimmed with lace, had gone to the drawing-room to await the first arrivals.

Mary turned quickly as Marcy spoke her name. "Please read this," he said.

She spread the broadside on a table near a candle and read it through. Marcy told her about the strangers who were passing the leaflets through the town.

Mary remained calm. "It tells us nothing we did not know, does it, Marcy? I was wrong to be so alarmed by what you told me earlier. The Governor and Mr. Iredell know of the meeting and its purpose, and they consider it harmless."

"Beg pardon, ma'am, but do they know these out-of-town men are counting on violence of some kind?" Quickly he told her what Cato had overheard at the ferry and of the stranger seeking staves.

"Oh, Marcy, that does sound ominous," Mary said. "Thomas Barker says the Sheriff is alerted for possible trouble, but perhaps he should be told what you've heard." She hesitated. "Do you know Mr. Iredell's house?"

Marcy nodded.

"I think you could probably catch him there before he leaves for the party if you go by the back gate and run up Gaol Alley. Tell him what you know and ask him if he thinks the Sheriff should be informed."

Marcy disappeared into the darkness of the lower garden, and Mary walked slowly toward the house. She would not say anything to Thomas or Penelope, she decided.

Guests were arriving as Mary came into the house; a steady stream of people moved through the broad hall into the drawing-room and the library. Through the front door she saw Lady Anne descending from Madam Barker's coach. So Penelope had sent it for the guests after all! Thomas had ridiculed the idea. "Let them walk in through the Hewes and Smith garden," he'd said.

"I don't want my guests to sneak in the back way," Penelope had retorted. "Let them come to the front door, like civilized people."

Now Penelope was waving urgently to Mary. "Come, get in line," she called. "Over there by the window. Hurry!"

Mary stepped into the designated place next to Mary Blount and was caught up in the flurry created by the entrance of Lady Anne, escorted by her husband the Baron and Lord Charles Montague. The elegance of Lady Anne's rose lace gown and jewelled coronet dazzled the women. She walked past the receiving line with a nod and held out both hands to Penelope Barker. "So sweet of you, so thoughtful of you to arrange this evening," Mary heard her say, and then Thomas Barker led the honoured guests toward the punch-bowl in the dining-room.

Mary looked out the window. Crowds—women and children for the most part—were gathered at the gate to watch the guests arrive. She looked about anxiously for James Iredell or the Governor, but she did not see either. She shook hands, murmured greetings to twenty or thirty guests before James Iredell came in.

"Did Marcy find you?" she asked him, dropping her voice.

"Yes, just as I was leaving the house. I stayed to read the broadside. I advised him, as you did, to notify the Sheriff that some outsiders may be planning to create a disturbance. I asked him to see the Governor as well. There is nothing more to be done, Mary, so let us be cheerful and not alarm Madam's guests."

Jemmy's manner reassured Mary. He seemed perfectly calm, smiling and talking to James Blount. Josiah Collins joined the two, and after a moment all three went toward the dining-room and the punch-bowl. I worry too much, she thought. She caught sight of her face in a mirror. Frowning, too! She smiled a little, tucked a curl behind her ear and straightened the lace fichu over her yellow bodice. She wished she had worn blue. Her gown looked a little dowdy beside Lady Anne's finery. Mary had not worn her pearls because the weather was so warm. She twisted her little ivory fan. All the guests must have arrived, for the line was breaking up. Madam Barker went out of the room, and the crowd moved toward the back galleries.

Exclamations of delight came from the women as they glimpsed the garden. "It's fairyland!" . . . "How wonderful!" . . . "Trust Pen Barker to contrive something different!" . . . "There's to be dancing on the platform." . . . "Beasley's fiddler!". . . "And six banjos—what fun!"

Penelope approached Mary hurriedly. "The Governor hasn't arrived. Wait for him and bring him out to the high table, will you, Mary? I have seated him next to Lady Anne. Oh, I do hope the food is good and everything goes off without a hitch!"

"Don't worry, Penelope. I'll wait here for Sam Johnston." Madam Barker hurried off. Mary thought she looked very lovely to-night. The grey streak in her hair rather enhanced her distinction.

She watched the people finding their places at the tables. The women looked charming, she thought, and most suitably gowned. The young girls were sweet in their muslins and wide leghorn hats. "It *is* a garden-party, isn't it? Don't people always wear hats to garden-parties?" Nellie Blair had pleaded. "Mr. Gainsborough and Mr. Lawrence paint them that way." So here they were with flower-laden hats and around their necks little bands of black velvet riband. No patches. Patches were reserved for the older women.

She heard her name called. The Governor had come into the room. His usually grave face seemed even more serious than usual.

"Did Marcy find you?" she asked as he kissed her hand.

"Yes. This business sounds rather more serious than we have thought. It's well to be aware. This fellow Marcy is a good man. Very observing. I've asked him to go to the Courthouse and watch for any trouble." Observing her anxious look, he patted her arm. "Don't worry. Steps will be taken."

Thomas Barker came into the room. "We're waiting for you, Samuel. This way. You will find Lady Anne Stuart delightful."

The supper was everything that Penelope could have desired, the music of the violin was sad and wistful. Servants moved quietly, filling wine-glasses. The Governor proposed toasts to Lady Anne, to the Baron and to the entire assembly. Laughter was light and gay. A group of Negroes stood among the trees and sang nostalgic songs of a far-off land, and Mary heard Lady Anne comment, "Delightful! So unusual, such dulcet voices!"

Some young people got up to dance a merry contra-dance to the twanging of banjos and guitars. Among them, Mary noticed, was Sylvia Hay with young Dr. Moray. They were laughing at the antics of a small Negro boy, scarcely more than a baby, who had escaped from his mother and climbed to the edge of the dancing platform. The child was shuffling about, clapping his tiny hands in perfect rhythm, until his horrified mother snatched him up and carried him away.

After a time Lady Anne and the Baron joined the dancers, but soon they stopped near Sylvia and Dr. Moray and exchanged partners. Mary, watching, was reminded again of Chaney's words about Lady Anne's tricks. One of the Creecy men approached and asked if he might get Mary a glass of punch, but she refused, remembering that she had been too worried to eat much at supper.

The dances were swifter now, the beat of the music more pronounced with the addition of two drummers. The tall blond Benbury lad claimed Mary as his partner, and she found herself facing Lady Anne in a figure. Lady Anne was laughing, tossing her curls, tipping her long skirt by the reeds, showing a handsome leg. "Wonderful, wonderful!" she cried as they crossed arms. "I must take the musicians back to England. London has never heard anything like them. It is divine music!"

Suddenly the town bell rang—a sharp, alarming note. The music stopped, the dancers were still. A buzz of conversation, low-pitched but excited, rose from the guests. Mary saw James Iredell move swiftly to the gallery where the Governor stood with Josiah Collins.

The bell rang four times more, then stopped.

"What's wrong?" some one called.

Thomas Barker, who had joined the group around the Governor, came to the gallery rail. "Nothing is wrong, good people," he said, raising his voice. " 'Tis a town meeting, that's all." He signalled the musicians to resume playing.

The people on the dancing platform waited uncertainly. Above the banjos they could hear a noise of men shouting not far away. Then Nellie Blair, impatient at any interruption of her pleasure, briskly organized her immediate neighbours for a contra-dance. Lady Anne did likewise, and others followed their example.

Mary noticed, however, that several of the men left the platform and gathered in small worried groups apart from the festivities. She excused herself from her partner and walked toward the house, where Governor Johnston, Thomas Barker, Iredell and others stood on the gallery, deep in a discussion. An outcry at the foot of the garden halted her, and she turned to see Marcy just inside the back gate.

Immediately he was surrounded by eager questioners, but he scanned the garden until he spotted Samuel Johnston at the head of the gallery steps and moved toward him. The dancers paused again as Marcy passed the platform, and the music died away forlornly.

Breathless from running, Marcy approached the Governor. "Sir," he cried, "they are defaming you from the Courthouse steps. A great press of people are crowded onto the Green and there are men among them armed with barrel staves and bill-hooks. I'm afraid there will be rioting, and the Sheriff is nowhere to be found."

Johnston's answer was lost in outcries and wailing from the women. Mary saw Penelope Barker standing near by, her face a picture of distress, gazing helplessly about as her uneasy guests surged toward the house. Behind her Mary heard Lady Anne's arrogant voice: "If there's to be rioting, Karl, let us leave at once. These people are barbarians, and I don't care to be caught up in one of their mob scenes." And Lord Charles's lisping accent: "Come, Anne, this is no place for you—or me, for that matter. I've seen these Americans in action before, knocking one another about with clubs."

Another English voice spoke. Turning, Mary saw the speaker was an officer from Lord Charles's party. "There's a way through the garden," he was saying. "Miss Sylvia knows the way."

"We must first bid our hosts good-bye," the Baron said calmly.

"Don't be stupid, Karl!" his wife snapped. "I'll not be mauled by a drunken rabble for the sake of your ridiculous social gestures. Come along at once!" She picked up her skirts and swept down the garden path with Sylvia Hay, Lord Charles and the officer. The Baron followed meekly—a pathetic figure, Mary thought.

On the gallery steps Marcy was answering the questions of Johnston and Iredell as the other guests crowded around them. As Mary watched anxiously, straining to hear what they were saying, the Governor seemed to come to a decision. He descended the steps and strode with Marcy toward the gate at the foot of the garden. Iredell followed closely with Josiah Collins and Charles Johnson, and other men fell in behind.

Thomas Barker watched worriedly as they disappeared through the gate. Then, adopting his most engaging manner, he moved among his guests, trying to calm the agitation of ladies with assurance that nothing untoward would happen.

Mary, as if drawn by a magnet, moved toward the garden-gate. There was no clear thought in her mind. She did not know what she could hope to accomplish, but she felt an irresistible compulsion to seek out the scene of the disturbance and see for herself the living embodiments of the strange force that had disrupted the peaceful life of the Albemarle.

Penelope Barker caught at her arm. "Mary, where are you going? I think, don't you, it would be best if we all went into the house where Thomas can protect us? Tell those girls by the platform, will you? Oh, that this should happen to-night of all nights! What must Lady Anne think of us!" Without waiting for an answer Penelope distractedly began shepherding the guests toward the house.

Mary had scarcely heard Penelope. She slipped through the gate into the darkness beyond and walked swiftly toward the Green, guided by the sound of men shouting and the glow of torch-light against the sky.

BOOK TWO

Hillsborough

Adam Goes to the Convention

13 ADAM RUTLEDGE, accompanied by his body servant Hercules, arrived in Hillsborough July 20. After sending Herk in search of lodgings he threaded the crowded streets toward the Presbyterian Church, where the delegates would convene tomorrow.

Hillsborough was too small to accommodate those who had come to the convention. Many of the two hundred and eighty delegates had brought their wives and children. Other men from every part of the state had streamed into the little town to attend what every one knew would be a momentous event in the history of North Carolina. They had come knowing there was scant chance they could see even one session of the convention. They hoped merely to hear the reports given in the taverns and to talk to the delegates.

The crowds seemed oppressive to Adam as he rode slowly along. Though he had taken a few days' rest at the home of a friend in Abingdon, Virginia, he was very tired from his long journey out of the Illinois country. Weeks of solitude on the wilderness trails made the pushing and clamour of the streets doubly irritating. He reined his horse almost impatiently when he heard his name called, and then dismounted to greet Archibald Maclaine.

The choleric hotspur of the Federalists seemed genuinely glad to see him. "Well met, Adam Rutledge, well met! Jemmy Iredell has kept me informed of your plans. I knew you would arrive in time to help us. We need every man of good faith. Those Antifederalist rascals are working day and night at Wilie Jones's headquarters to win more delegates. Where are you stopping?"

"Nowhere at present." For all his fatigue Adam managed a smile at the way the lawyer had leaped to politics even at his greeting. "I've sent my man Herk on a canvass for lodgings."

"You won't find any. Join us at Will Hooper's. Johnston, Iredell and I are staying there, and there are others of our party. You'll be welcome even if we have to sleep three to a bed."

Adam laughed. "I'm not of a size for that kind of arrangement. Herk will find a place for me."

"As you wish." Maclaine's voice was less cordial. "At least let me tell you our plans." Adam nodded and put his hand on his friend's shoulder for a moment. Maclaine's coolness gave way to enthusiasm as he talked of Federalist hopes and strength. There was every chance that Samuel Johnston would be chosen president of the convention. Iredell would be the Federalist leader on the floor. His learning, graceful oratory and knowledge of government earned him that position. People believed in his integrity and admired his manly, generous temper. Even those who differed from him would hear and respect his opinions. Supporting Iredell would be such men as William Davie, whose political sagacity was well known, Richard Dobbs Spaight, John Steele and Stephen Cabarrus, all men of learning and position.

"It will be a hard fight and a bitter one." Maclaine's face was flushed with sudden anger. "The lies of Antifed scoundrels are given audience. You have no conception of the extremes to which they have gone! That preacher Lemuel Burkitt has circulated the rumour that the seat of Federal government will be a fortified area from which an army of fifty thousand— sometimes he says a hundred thousand—will march out to enslave the people. Think of it! And there are even more monstrous falsehoods. Believed, sir! They are believed!"

The denunciation of Antifeds had been loud enough to attract the attention of passers-by. Several men whose attitude was obviously hostile stood in a circle around Adam and Maclaine. Adam took his friend's arm and shouldered a way forward. "I'm sure you gentlemen have no wish to interrupt a private conversation," he said. He swung his horse about so that the strangers were forced to step back and then, keeping his hold on Maclaine's arm, continued their walk along the street.

The fiery Federalist seemed not to have noticed the disturbance. "I'm on my way to Hooper's now, Adam. You'll come with me?"

"Not now, sir. I must meet my slave within the hour, and I need rest badly before I consider politics." Adam shook hands with Maclaine and promised that he would be at Hooper's home for supper. Before he mounted again he watched to see that none of the men the lawyer had antagonized were following him.

Adam turned toward the inn where he had agreed to meet Herk. There was no need to go on to the church. He would be seeing Iredell and Johnston at supper and have news of Mary there. He was almost grateful for the threat of violence that had ended his talk with Maclaine. Of course his Federalist friends would take his loyalty for granted. He did not know whether he could give it. He did not know whether he would vote for or against ratification.

In April when he left Edenton for the Illinois country Adam was sure that North Carolina should approve the Constitution. Johnston and Iredell had discussed with him its spacious architecture, and he had shared this enthusiasm for the way it reconciled conflicting interests in the promise of security through enduring union. With them he had read the *Federalist* essays, and he had been impressed with Jemmy's discourses on the genius of Madison and Hamilton.

At Iredell's suggestion he took with him to Cahokia a copy of the Constitution and what information Jemmy could give him on the proceedings of the Philadelphia Convention: some letters from Hugh Williamson, a copy of the report made to Caswell by the North Carolina delegation and various newspaper accounts taken from records of the debates which delegates had made available after adjournment. "Read well, Adam," Iredell said. "Everything you learn will be of help to you—and to us—at Hillsborough."

So he sat late night after night while Herk slept near by. His respect for the Constitution grew as he followed its measured language. Men of vision ordained here a government founded on reason, justice and the general welfare. Against ancient forces of disorder they set the power of liberty under law. Adam knew the grandeur of their conception, and he had gone eagerly to his records to trace out the course of debate.

Almost immediately he had been disturbed. There was evidence here that some delegates did not intend the liberty of which the preamble spoke to be unrestricted. A newspaper reported a speech by Gouverneur Morris on the subject of future statehood for western settlements. Adam would not forget his words. "The busy haunts of men, not the remote wilderness, is the proper school of political talents. The rule of representation ought to be so fixed as to secure to the Atlantic states a prevalence of the national councils."

Adam gave thanks for the rebuttal by James Wilson that defeated the proposal. But Morris had nearly been successful. Four of the nine states with delegates in attendance voted in favour of this tyranny. He thought of the settlers near Cahokia, his friends whose industry and bravery were winning a new country. Would men who had scorned them be alert to safeguard their liberties? More study did not relieve this first anxiety. The Constitution protected the rights of property admirably, and with this Adam had no quarrel. But the rights of men?

He went back over all he had learned. The structure of government still seemed to him the best that could now be devised. Yet it was a government formed by men who were conscious first of responsibility to those who shared their station in life. The fact that this station was also his did not content Adam. It was ridiculous to suppose that those who guided the Philadelphia Convention had intended tyranny. But was tyranny possible under their plan? The question gnawed at his mind and he had reached no answer on the June morning when he rode east.

On the long ride his uncertainty grew. In every other aspect the trip was untroubled. The weather had favoured him as he rode east to Vincennes, then south through the rolling hills that led to the Falls of the Ohio. Beyond the river he kept south and east across the broad, inviting Kentucky land until at Harrodsburg he came to the trace that would take him to

Virginia. And always he felt like a man riding toward the centre of a storm. In a Harrodsburg tavern he learned that Virginia had ratified the Constitution. He had arrived at dusk and while Herk saw to the stabling of the horses he sat in the common-room, waiting for his supper to be brought in.

Across the room a huge bearded man slapped the table with his hand and lashed out at his two companions. "Abner, you know not a jot more about this business than Timothy here. Well, you'll learn, you will, now Virginia's thrown in with this union. Our eastern folk care little enough for the likes of us out here. Do you fancy foreign states'll mind your wishes better?" He rose and stood towering over the table. "What've they told you about this Constitution? You know not a line of it. No more do I. Strength, say you? I say my strength is bein' a freeman on my own land, not bound by others!" The giant raised his arms and clenched his hands. Then with a sudden, fierce motion he dug his fists against his legs and strode through the door. In a moment the other men dropped money on the table for the reckoning and followed him.

The tavern keeper confirmed what Adam had overheard concerning Virginia's action. "Aye, we're in, right enough. Learned last week. They say enough states've signed up to make a new gov'ment. Can't tell you what states they are. I could hear Luther shoutin'. He's not usually an angry man, Luther. Most folks hereabouts are mightily worried. They ain't heard much, and they don't like what they have heard. Some say there's plans to give up our rights to ship down the Mississippi. Others say the plain people'll be worse off than under a King."

Adam paid little attention to the rude fare the man set before him. The people in the western counties of his own state might well be similarly ignorant of the Constitution, equally suspicious. He thought of the words that began the preamble. *We, the people* . . . Luther's state had ratified, but the words would have no meaning for him. This man and all like him would need assurance that they were not betrayed, could not be betrayed. Adam rose without finishing his meal and walked out into the warm evening. The doubts he had formed in the Illinois country returned with new insistence. Would the fact of a new government make sure the approval of all other states? There had to be a way even now to quiet fear, allay suspicion, provide safeguards if they were needed. *We, the people of the United States* . . . The words must have meaning to all the people. He went slowly back to the tavern. The night promised little rest.

Beyond Harrodsburg the weather continued fair. Adam and Herk rode steadily on through the beautiful new country into the tumbled hills and narrow valleys that led to the great gap in the Cumberland Mountains. In every settlement men talked of Virginia's action. Some approved, but Adam found more who were distrustful. Patrick Henry was quoted like a prophet. The fire he had poured on Virginia Federalists was still blazing here. In taverns and cabins Adam heard the alarms. The new government would lean toward monarchy. Let the President get into the field with his army and no American could free his neck from the yoke. The army would salute the President as King. The militia would fight against the plain people. The rights of citizens would be destroyed. Adam distrusted Henry, but the questions men were asking gave a sharper edge to the questions he had asked himself.

He kept with the trace through the mountain gap and on to the Virginia village of Abingdon. Here in the home of John Graham, a friend to whom George Rogers Clark had introduced him, Adam hoped to get respite from the hard life of the trail and gain the view of an informed man on Virginia's troubled politics. He had a high regard for this tall, lean soldier and gentleman who had marched to Vincennes with Clark.

The gracious hospitality of Graham and his wife Jane increased Adam's longing to be with Mary at Queen's Gift. He was not entirely sorry when after a pleasant supper Jane left the men with their port and the talk turned to the convention in Richmond where Graham had been a delegate. Graham had a gift for language, and Adam got from his description a full sense of the epic quality of the contest between James Madison and Patrick Henry. From time to time his host would read aloud from his own journal of the proceedings.

The pattern was clear. Henry, with the greater power to persuade, had made his appeal to passion and fear. Madison, with the greater power to convince, had set logic and reason against the fears Henry excited. Adam waited until John Graham paused to fill their glasses. Then he said, "There's a note of satisfaction in your voice when you read Mr. Madison's arguments. I take it he had your vote."

Graham did not answer at once. He looked down at his wine and turned the glass slowly. "Mr. Madison has great powers," he said at last. "He satisfied me of the need for a strong national government and of the excellence of his plan. Yet there was another word to be said. Patrick Henry pronounced it, and Madison gave me no answer I could accept."

He turned a few pages in his journal, read silently for a moment and went on. "On an early day of the convention Henry made the longest and—his friends say—the most powerful speech of his life. It was his premise that the Philadelphia Convention was not authorized to speak for the people. The Constitution, he said, threatened the liberties of the people by usurping the rights of the state. Let me read you his words. 'The rights of conscience, trial by jury, liberty of the press, all pretensions to human rights and privileges are rendered insecure, if not lost. It is said eight states have adopted this plan. I declare that if twelve states and a half had adopted it, I would, with manly firmness and in spite of erring world, reject it!' "

Graham had read Henry's remarks without the force Henry must have given them, yet Adam was stirred. How Henry could touch the fears and hopes of men! His motives and logic might be questioned, but never his eloquence. When his friend did not continue Adam said, "You spoke earlier of Madison's answer."

Graham referred again to the journal. "He was, as always, clear and reasonable. A bill of rights proposed by Henry and old George Mason seemed to him dangerous because it tended to limit rights to those defined. At one point he said, 'I go on this great republican principle, that the people will have virtue and intelligence to select men of virtue and wisdom. I consider it reasonable to conclude that the legislators will as readily do their duty as deviate from it.' He asked for faith in men, in Congress, to amend the Constitution after ratification. I could not share his faith. I could not accept the Constitution without a bill of rights. I voted with the minority against ratification. The decision passes to your state, Adam. I will not ask your views or urge mine on you. I will pray that your decision may be easier than mine."

After a moment's silence Adam rose and put his hand on Graham's shoulder. "I think we will talk no more politics to-night. Let's have a pipe, and I'll tell you of my Illinois country."

Graham smiled as he ushered Adam out of the room, but he said little during the rest of the evening. His distress was obvious, and Adam understood it well.

After he had retired to his room Adam wrote a long letter to Mary. Graham had a friend who was leaving for Charleston in the morning and would carry it directly to Edenton. Adam found he could not express to his wife any of his concern over the decision before him. He longed to have her near, and he wrote of familiar things they both loved. To-morrow he would turn south to Hillsborough.

As Adam dismounted at the inn where he was to meet Herk, the slave came forward from the entrance. "You is stoppin' at de Star Tavern, sar. You' clothes unpack and room all ready, sar. Go right down Cedar Lane and you come on de place. My horse stabled dere now."

Adam smiled at the giant Negro. "How did you do it this time, Herk?"

"De master laughs, but de master would be angry if he had no pillow dis night. So I say to de little man from out of de North, 'Sar, last night a man die in de room to which you are goin' now. Smallpox maybe, but dey have not yet lighted de fumes of sulphur.' De man he turn very white, say he go right on to Williamsburg. He depart, carryin' he little satchel. I put master's box in de room. I give boy penny to stand by locked door till you come."

Since Herk was afoot, Adam did not mount. Many people turned to watch him as he strode down the street. Herk, who followed a step behind, was as tall as his master, with shoulders as broad and powerful. Both walked with the long, swinging stride of men who were no strangers to the narrow paths that led through the wilderness. With his erect carriage and proud bearing Adam was a man to attract attention. Young women riding by on horseback turned to watch him. Others, walking the tree-shaded street, smiled at him from under parasols held over their heads by slaves.

The common-room at the Star was smoke-filled and crowded. Men sat at tables or stood in the aisles with others from their own or neighbouring counties. Many greeted Adam warmly, for he was well and favourably known throughout the state. He saw only two men from the Albemarle, William Sheppard and Josiah Collins. Collins, who wintered at his house on the Green in Edenton, had made his plantation Somerset on Lake Scuppernong the principal meeting-place in Tyrrell County. He wielded great influence and in a measure had taken the place of Colonel Buncombe of Buncombe Hall, who had been killed in one of the early battles of the Revolution.

Collins, a strong, hearty man with an assured air, came to meet Adam and shook hands warmly. "What does this mean, Adam?" he asked. "Are you deserting Sam Johnston and Jemmy Iredell?" Adam's expression of surprise brought an explanation. "The Star is headquarters of the Anti-federalists, you know."

"I didn't know. I've only just come back from the Illinois country. My man found a room for me here." He looked down at his travelling clothes. "I haven't even had time to change and make myself presentable."

"No matter. Come over and meet my friends. They are all in the room to the left of the bar." As the two crossed the room Collins said, "Are you Federal or Anti, Adam?"

Adam hesitated. He had no intention of discussing his political thought with Collins. He thought Collins was a Federalist but knew that he had friends in both parties. "I've been out of touch so long . . ."

Collins did not allow him to finish. "No matter. No matter. Wilie Jones was asking about you this morning. He will give you an argument. He's very persuasive, you know."

They went into an adjoining room where twenty or thirty men were seated on tavern chairs placed in a semicircle. Wilie Jones and Timothy Bloodworth sat at an oak stretcher table. Behind them hung a large picture of Thomas Jefferson. In front of Bloodworth were a number of papers, an inkstand, quills and a sanding-box.

General McDowell, one of the heroes of the Revolution, was speaking Josiah Collins went forward to take a vacant chair near Elisha Battle. Adam had refused Collins' whispered invitation to go up to the front. He slipped into a chair at the back of the room, where he could observe without being observed, and found himself beside Monfort of Halifax, who greeted him with a nod.

McDowell was speaking of the people in the western counties and in the new Tennessee settlements beyond the mountains. They were Antifederal to a man, he said. Adam knew this was not entirely correct. Iredell had told him the Federalists in Sumner County were strong. But he had no doubt that many western settlers shared the fears of the men to whom he had talked in the Kentucky country.

He looked about him, recognizing William Lenoir, of King's Mountain fame, and David Caldwell, the militant parson. Near them were Samuel Spencer and Thomas Person, ardent followers of Wilie Jones, as were Alexander Mebane, Egbert Haywood and Joel Lane, who sat together across the room from Adam.

McDowell gave way to John Tipton, who said he was representing the men beyond the mountains. Tipton spoke slowly in a level uninteresting voice. Adam's attention soon wandered. He examined the two men at the speaker's table. The aristocratic elegance of Wilie Jones, his air of assurance and complete relaxation contrasted with Timothy Bloodworth's restless energy, strong, sturdy body and brooding, fanatic eyes. The Wilmington blacksmith, as Bloodworth was called, had something in him that drove him to stand in the forefront of revolutions. "No compromise" would be his watchword. He would impose his strong will to obtain results. He was an orator who held an audience by the very violence of his arguments, pounding the table, demanding to be heard.

Wilie Jones was quite different. He was persuasive, adroit, diplomatic. As he watched him quietly listening to the speaker Adam understood that for all his casual, almost indifferent air Jones was thinking ahead of the others. His was the power, but it was power behind the scene, a secret power different from that of the emotional orator. His hold over men lay in his ability to go forward or withdraw, as the occasion demanded. He was not ambitious. He had wealth, aristocratic birth and position, yet he had become convinced that the real power lay not in the few but in the many. He was a disciple and friend of Jefferson. He believed in all that was implied by the words "We, the people," and he implemented his faith not with the ringing words of a Jefferson or a Patrick Henry, but in a more devious way. He was as powerful in his own state as they were in Virginia.

Adam wondered what was going on behind those dark, mournful eyes. There was no hint of his thought in Jones's handsome face with its straight nose and chiselled lips. It was, Adam thought, a beautiful face, beautiful in the Greek concept of masculine beauty, save that the strength of his chin negated the smooth, placid brow.

Tipton had finished his tiresome oratory, and now speaker after speaker rose to say the obvious thing or to boast in florid language about the strength of the Antifederalists.

"The Federals are in woeful minority," John Macon asserted. "We will outvote them when the test comes."

A man Adam could not see raised a timid voice. "But, gentlemen, we have strong voices against us. Governor Johnston has a powerful influence. William Davie is a great orator with a vigorous following. What of Spaight,

Cabarrus, Hill, Steele, Sitgreaves? And don't forget Archibald Maclaine. He will outtalk any one in the convention."

Benjamin Williams called out, "We have most to fear from Iredell. His reply to the Virginia objections has been hard to answer."

Wilie Jones obviously did not care to hear a review of Federalist strength. He spoke a quiet word to Bloodworth, who then raised his hand to silence the discussion. "Do I hear a motion for adjournment?"

There was a moment's silence. All eyes turned to Wilie Jones. They bow to Jones's wishes without question, Adam thought. He is the real leader. He will not allow doubts to creep in. No doubts, and no question of his authority in the ranks.

Adam got up quietly to leave the room. He would learn nothing from these men who merely parroted Antifederalist arguments. Slogans would not win his vote. As he went through the door he heard Wilie Jones raise his voice. "I have no fears, gentlemen. We will have a bill of rights before North Carolina becomes a signator to Mr. Madison's Constitution."

In Adam's room Herk was laying out his master's clothes on the wide mahogany bed. "De barber he come presently. You' hair need fixin' might' bad. Most of gen'lemens dey wearin' wigs. We have no wig wid us." There was patent regret in the Negro's voice.

Adam smiled. "We'll make do with my own hair. It's more than long enough to go into a queue."

"Sar, a nice wig is good on you. Mak' you look dressed right. I press you' nankin small-clothes and you' dark coat and wash out you' silk stockin's; shine you' silver-buckled shoes, too, lak you gen'leman once more."

Adam stripped off his travelling clothes. "A good hot bath is what I want."

"Sar, bath laid in a minute."

Bathed and barbered, his blond hair dressed, queued and tied with a black riband, Adam took the three-cornered hat Herk held out to him. "I'm going to Mr. Hooper's, Herk. See to the horses. They deserve extra rations for a few days."

"Yes, sar. Want I go wid you, less'n dey be fightin' in de street?"

Adam grinned. "You keep out of fights, you rascal. Stay here. If any one inquires for me, tell them I'll be back after supper."

Herk looked disappointed, but made no protest.

Adam set out to walk to Hooper's place. He was anxious to meet his old friends and get some late news of his wife. He felt sure she had sent a letter by one of the Edenton men.

As he approached the Hooper residence he met Stephen Cabarrus coming out. The two men shook hands warmly. "You look as strong as a back-mountain man, Adam," Cabarrus exclaimed. "I declare your own wife won't recognize you. Your face is the colour of a piece of saddle leather, but I admit you look full of health. When did you get here?"

"This morning, and I feel as healthy as an Indian. In fact, I've been living like an Indian for the past six weeks, riding and walking forest trails. When did you see Mary? Is she in good health?"

Cabarrus said, "Come inside. I've a letter for you. Mary was certain you would arrive here in time for the convention, so she gave me a letter to deliver." His large dark eyes twinkled. "Mary told me of the careful study you gave the Constitution before you left. She was sure you would manage to be on the convention floor."

They went into the house. "Come up to the bedchamber. There's a special meeting going on downstairs. Davie, Maclaine and Hooper are in there." He indicated the closed door of the drawing-room. "Johnston and Iredell have not arrived yet. I call them the strategists. They are planning ways to meet Antifederalist attacks on the floor." Cabarrus opened the door to a large room in which there were two full-sized beds.

"Four of us will be bedded here," he said as he stooped to drag his dressing-box out from under the high bed. "Did you ever see such a press of people?"

"I'm not sorry to see them," Adam said. "It's heartening to know they recognize the importance of the decision."

Cabarrus took a key from his pocket. He opened the mahogany case and took out a letter sealed in four places. Mary's habit of sealing her letters so had always amused Adam. He would point out to her that if any one wanted to open a letter, four seals wouldn't deter him any more than one. And Mary would always reply with spirit that she didn't agree. A dishonest man might break one seal on an impulse, but before he broke four he would have time to think. She believed the fourth seal would be the safeguard.

Stephen took off his coat and hung it on a wall peg. He folded his brocaded waistcoat, laid it on a chair and kicked his buckled shoes under the bed. "I'll catch me a nap while you're reading. Those fellows will be wrangling in that room for another hour. I can't stand it, talking all night and all day." In his small-clothes and ruffled shirt he crawled into a bed, pulled the counterpane over him and was almost instantly asleep.

Adam broke the seals. It gave him a good home-coming feeling to see Mary's firm, even script.

My dearest husband:

I am giving this letter to Stephen Cabarrus. I have a strong feeling that you will receive it in Hillsborough. Twice recently I dreamed that I was sitting in the choir loft of old St. Matthew's and saw you on the floor of the convention. You were addressing the convention and saying that the people must be heard. I told Stephen that I had never doubted you would come.

Everything goes well here. The tobacco harvest has begun. The leaf was ready very early this year, the earliest I remember. Many planters were caught napping, without curing materials ready or shipping plans made. Some of the small farmers were in trouble because they didn't have the hands to begin stripping. But every man helped his neighbour, so that the crop won't be half lost, as was first thought. Marcy has done wonders with our crops, as you knew he would when you sent him home to help me. All promises well.

Life in the village goes on as usual. The Eden House folk are in New York. Ann Pollock is in Newport, from where she writes interesting letters about the social doings of the great folk and just enough scandal to make the letters spicy. You know Ann. She delights to tell a tale. I don't believe she falsifies, but she colours what she says in all the hues of the rainbow. Scandal about the Bizarre affair. The Randolphs must feel terrible to have such gossip brought to public notice. True or untrue, tales of an illegitimate child born to an unmarried woman are tragic.

I'll save our local gossip until you come home. The household is as healthy as can be expected at this season of the year. Politics is the main subject of talk. There are real feuds in the making. I think the feeling runs as high as it did during the war. Jemmy Iredell has promised to tell you about the disturbance here. There was a disgraceful demonstration against Sam Johnston and Jemmy.

Dear Adam, it will be wonderful to have you home again. Three months are too long to have you gone from me.

I save this till last to emphasize that I do not want it to give you concern. A fire has done some damage to our mill. I will send the corn out to Indian Creek or Rockahock. Don't worry. Come soon.

Your devoted wife,
MARY

P.S. Reports from Virginia tell of the close division and bitter feeling in the convention. I hope you and our friends may be spared that. General Washington must be sad indeed to have such quarrelling. Mr. Madison, we hear, was distressed by Patrick Henry's speeches. Mr. Jefferson has almost as much influence as though he were here. Our own great are so divided, it makes it confusing for the lesser folk. Come home, Adam. Come home to your loving wife. I have missed you so.

MARY

Adam folded the letter carefully and placed it in the breast pocket of his coat. He sat quietly, his long body relaxed in the chair, his legs stretched full length. He allowed himself to think of his wife. All the loneliness, the longing of the past months rushed over him. He missed her intolerably. During the long absence he had not had time for nostalgic dreaming. He had crowded his waking hours with work and study that wearied both mind and body. Now, so close to her, he allowed himself the luxury of thinking how much, how very much he had missed her. He never ceased to wonder that so small a person, so delicately built, could have in her so much iron. The thought often occurred to him that she had inherited Duke Roger's vigour and his ability to think calmly and clearly.

Cabarrus turned restlessly in his sleep. Adam rose to leave the room. As he passed a window he saw a man looking at the house, a lean man clad in the buckskin of a trapper. Adam paused and looked more closely. Then he turned and ran down the stairs and out onto the stoop. "Enos! Enos Dye!" he called.

The man walked quickly forward to meet Adam, his hand extended and his weather-beaten face creased in a smile. "Mr. Rutledge! I knew you'd be comin' as a delegate, and I've been lookin' for you the town over. I saw your man Herk outside the Star. He said I'd find you here." The trapper paused as if undecided about how to go on. "There's a word I have for you—and one I'd have you give me."

Adam was amazed at the concern evident in Enos' voice. In the many years of their friendship he had never known the wiry trapper to show emotion. During the war he had been invaluable in securing intelligence, and Adam had not observed that even his most dangerous assignments ever disturbed his calmness.

"Certainly, Enos," Adam said. "Some gentlemen are having a meeting inside. Can we talk here, or would you rather meet me at the Star?"

"One place's as good as another, I reckon." The trapper frowned in his effort to find words. "It's this Constitution, Mr. Rutledge. Out in the back country I've heard a sight of tales. Mostly they say the new President will be like a King. Some say we'll lose all the rights we fought for if we sign and join the other states. That's the sum of it. I walked a long ways to Hillsborough to find out the truth of that. You're a man whose word I'd have."

Adam was moved by Enos' trust. He knew suddenly that the answer he had to give his friend was also his own answer. He chose his words carefully. "I don't know that I can give you a plain answer, Enos. I've studied the Constitution carefully. I do tell you that it was not designed to take your rights away. Great men have put their hands to it. It is a good plan to make us safe and prosperous. It is not perfect. It may be that it fails to make your rights safe from the power of any man. Be sure that in the convention every line that was written in Philadelphia will be attacked and defended. Some men on both sides will act and speak for selfish or mean reasons. There will be bitterness and trickery. But there will also be men—on both sides—who will act and speak honestly, who will weigh the arguments and decide. If we believe in this kind of government, we must find our answers in the convention. I will . . ." Adam stopped, aware that Enos wanted to speak.

"Aye, Mr. Rutledge." The trapper nodded his head. "I've no skill to say it as you have. It was sorry work I made of it tryin' to tell the crowd O'Shaughnessy stirred up that they was fools. But I have it now, and I'm beholden to you."

"O'Shaughnessy? Who's O'Shaughnessy, Enos?"

"He's a mean-spirited fellow, honin' to make trouble. I've been followin' him most of three days. He talks to the plain folk, mechanics and farmers mostly. Tells 'em they ought to fight for their rights. Tells 'em they ought to march on the convention, scare the delegates into votin' against the Constitution."

Adam was instantly alert. Mob action now would be disastrous. "Has this O'Shaughnessy had any success? You spoke of talking to a crowd."

"I don't think you could rightly say his idea worked. He might try another time. I wanted to tell you I'd be watchin'. As to what I said . . ." The trapper paused, obviously reluctant to talk about himself.

Adam put his hand on Enos' arm. "If I'm to understand the danger, Enos, I have to know what happened."

"Right enough, Mr. Rutledge. It weren't much, as it turned out. Last night down on Cedar Lane—a little below the Star—this O'Shaughnessy had a crowd of simple fellows ready to stone Hooper's house. It's a thing as would bring disgrace on us all. I told 'em that. I told 'em to tell their fears to their elected delegates. A man that won't respect law, I said, can't expect law to protect him. They believed me, I reckon. Anyhow, they walked away from the gaol bird O'Shaughnessy."

Enos' words gave Adam a new conception of the man. The trapper was silent by nature. The two of them had walked mountain paths for hours without a word passing between them. Yet Enos had persuaded an uneasy crowd to disperse. Adam was ashamed to think that he had not known how well Enos understood what he fought for in the Revolution. He said, "I pray God all our public men believe as much as you do in the dignity of our laws."

Enos extended his hand again. "Mr. Rutledge, this is my country. I want it should be great—and kept great. I'll go now. If O'Shaughnessy seems to be havin' better luck, I'll come to you."

Adam stood on the stoop for a moment before entering the house. He had not left behind him the distrust and unrest, the threats of violence and disunion he had found on the western trails. It was all here, an accumulation of fear and suspicion to burden him and every other delegate.

Letters

14 HERK was at Adam's bedside at daybreak, pulling at the foot of the sheet. Adam groaned, turned over and buried his tousled head in the pillow. A few moments later Herk tried again, this time pinching his master's great toe. "Mornin' tea, master," he said. "Mornin' tea, sar. You said wake you at sun-up, sar."

Adam sat up reluctantly. "When did I tell you such nonsense?"

"Last night, sar, when I put you to bed. Don't you rec'lect? You said,

'Wake me at sun-up. I's got some readin' to do before de convention starts.' "

Adam remembered then. He stretched and lay back on the pillow, relishing the comfort of the bed after the rigours of his long journey. His thoughts wandered to his wife and Edenton and the alarming events James Iredell had described last evening.

When he re-entered Will Hooper's house after talking with Enos Dye the meeting had been breaking up. The "strategists" had greeted Adam with great warmth. Maclaine and Davie hurried away on some preconvention business, and Stephen Cabarrus, aroused from his nap, left with them. So Adam's companions at supper were Governor Johnston, Jemmy Iredell and his host Will Hooper.

By common consent the men avoided any mention of politics during the meal. But Mary's letter was much on Adam's mind, and when the food had been removed from the table and glasses and decanters of port had been placed on the shining mahogany board he asked for information.

The Governor rose at once. "Pardon me, gentlemen. I think I'll leave James to relate the story. It is not an incident I care to dwell on." He left the room in his usual stately fashion, and his host accompanied him. Adam wondered if there was any hour of the day when Johnston dropped dignity, was lively, romped with his children or his young wife. Or was he always reserved and withdrawn? He had the physiognomy of a leader, a man of importance. He thought of himself as such, and the world took him at his own valuation. Iredell, Adam reflected, was different. He had a warm, lovable personality. His learning in law surpassed Johnston's, but people forgot that when they encountered his geniality and the warmth of his smile.

Adam became aware that Iredell was looking at him now in a curious, detached way. As though reading Adam's thoughts he said, "Sam is distressed. The events at Edenton hurt him deeply, especially when they called him a damned Tory and accused him of trying to squeeze money out of our new state to pay Englishmen for land they had stolen. They attacked me too for defending Henry McCulloh's claim. They shouted that a hundred thousand acres was too much land for any one man to hold."

Adam said, "Please begin at the beginning, Jemmy. I know nothing about the riot in Edenton."

"So you don't." Iredell reviewed for Adam the Antifederalist activity in Chowan County, culminating in plans for a mock election on the night chosen by Madam Barker for her party. "Announcements of the meeting had been posted a week before, so neither Sam nor I was surprised when in the midst of the festivities in Penelope Barker's garden we heard the town bell begin to ring."

He described the confusion that followed and Marcy's arrival with word of the Sheriff's defection. "I don't think I have ever seen Sam Johnston so angry as when he learned that our craven Sheriff, knowing there was a possibility of violence, had quietly disappeared from the town. Sam had determined to ignore the meeting, but this news convinced him that he must face the crowd and do what he could to quiet them.

"Of course I went along, as did Josiah Collins, Nat Allen, Charles Johnson and several other men from the party. Marcy led us to the rear gate, across the Hewes and Smith shop's garden and Horniblow's court-yard to the head of the Green."

Iredell paused, remembering the dramatic scene that had greeted them. The Green had been a dense mass of faces, he said, brought into relief by scores of pine-knot flares held high above the heads of the people. At the top of the Courthouse steps stood Mel Frazier, the farrier. As the Governor's party approached he was addressing the assemblage in a roaring voice: "Ask them questions and demand their answers! Tell them you'll have no part of their precious Constitution until your rights are guaranteed! Let the voice of the people be heard at Hillsborough!"

Iredell smiled. "Well, Adam, we all know that Frazier has a certain shrewdness, but this sounded too well phrased and rehearsed to be entirely convincing. 'This is Wilie Jones's work,' Sam muttered to me, and I agreed, wondering whom Wilie would have provided to supplement the farrier's limited powers as an orator."

As if in answer to Iredell's unspoken question a man, he said, had emerged from the crowd and joined Frazier on the steps. He was not an Edenton man, though to Iredell he seemed somehow familiar—a brawny fellow with a pugnacious face and straggling black hair. His voice rolled out. "Men, listen to me. These are the questions we must ask at Hillsborough. . . ."

But the crowd began to boo. Many of them had been drinking, and their temper demanded action rather than political argument. "Let us march on Hillsborough now and demand our rights!" some one shouted. Another voice boomed out, "You men from Pasquotank, let's march to-night!" "Camden and Perquimans are with you!" yelled another, and voices throughout the crowd pledged the various counties to the crusade. "I'm a Tyrrell County man myself. Tyrrell will march!" . . . "Bertie County will lead the way!" . . . "Gates? Gates? What's the matter with Gates?" . . . "We'll march! On to Hillsborough!"

The crowd was getting out of hand. The stranger's voice was drowned out by the catcalling and shouting. He whispered to Mel Frazier, who raised his hand for silence, but the crowd paid no attention. "Down with the politicians! . . . Let's march! . . . No ratification until we are protected!"

"Where were you?" Adam asked Iredell at this point in his narrative. "Didn't the crowd see Johnston towering head and shoulders above the others?"

"We were in the shadow at the side of the steps. There were bushes there that concealed us," Iredell answered. He was pacing the floor now, reliving the scene. "It was then, Adam, that I saw your wife. Mary had edged her way up to Charles Johnson and was whispering to him. Johnson turned to me: 'I'm going to get the Parson. This crowd won't listen to you or the Governor.' He slipped away. I knew he was right, for Parson Earle has a way with him. It was Mary's suggestion that sent Charles after the old Parson, and a clever stroke it was, too."

Iredell stopped pacing. "That Mary of yours is a wonderful woman, Adam. I've no doubt she would have faced the mob herself, had she thought it would do any good."

Adam nodded. His heart was full of pride.

Meanwhile, Iredell continued, Mel Frazier, finding they would not listen, had sent old Negro Empie into the Courthouse to ring the bell again. A number of the most vociferous men in the crowd fell silent almost immediately, and Iredell and Johnston became aware how many strangers were present. The bell was clearly a prearranged signal.

Soon the Green was quiet enough to give Mel Frazier a chance to be heard. "Quiet, men, quiet! Listen to what our friend, the people's friend, Bill Poole has to say to you."

The lank-haired fellow beside Frazier stepped forward again, and Iredell recognized him as a man who had once been pointed out to him in Salisbury as a leader of the Alamance disturbance back in Governor Tryon's time. The crowd quieted when Poole spoke. "Guard your rights!" he shouted. "Force your delegates to represent your wishes. Ask them the questions printed in the leaflets we will pass around.

"I will mention them briefly: First and most important, there is no declaration of rights in the proposed Constitution. Second, there is too much power in the central government. Third, the people are not secured even in the benefits of the common law. Fourth, the House of Representatives is only the shadow of representation. Fifth, the Senate has all the power of altering money bills. Sixth, the judiciary of the United States is so constructed as to absorb and destroy the judiciary of the states. Seventh, the President of the United States has no constitutional council, a circumstance unknown in any safe government. He will become the tool of the Senate. Eighth, the President has unrestricted power to grant pardons for treason, a power which could be exercised to screen from punishment those whom he secretly instigated to commit crime, and his own guilt would never be discovered. Ninth, there is no declaration of any kind for preserving the freedom of the press, no provision for trial by jury in civil cases, no protection against standing armies in time of peace.

"Gentlemen, these are a few of the objections. These great defects in the Constitution will show that it should not be ratified until a bill of rights is included to ensure that 'We, the people' are protected."

The mob did not understand what the man was talking about. Some of the younger men began a chant: "March! March! March on Hillsborough!"

Johnston said to Iredell, "He's talking over their heads. 'Tis Wilie Jones's voice I hear." He pushed forward and mounted the steps, with Iredell, Collins and Allen following close behind, until he stood beside Mel Frazier and the orator. Some one in the front row cried, "The Governor! Here is Governor Johnston. Let him answer the questions." But a great clamour arose, boos and catcalls. "No! No!" they shouted. "No Johnston! No Johnston!" The words became a rhythmic chant, repeated over and over.

Again Iredell paused in his narrative. "Johnston," he said, "turned white as paper. He raised his hand for silence, but the noise only increased. He shouted, but could not make himself heard. Then some one threw an egg which missed the Governor and hit Mel Frazier. This was the signal for a shower of overripe vegetables and stale eggs. It was no local disturbance, I am convinced. The county folk, the village folk respect Samuel Johnston as a man and as a Governor. It was out-of-town people who made the demonstration."

Many of the Edenton men resented the attack on Johnston and turned on the strangers, who promptly produced their staves and billhooks and began laying about them with great enthusiasm. What followed, said Iredell, could be called only a *mêlée*.

Collins, Allen and Iredell forcibly removed the irate Governor to the shelter of the Courthouse. Mel Frazier, appalled at what was happening, followed them inside. "Please, Your Honour," he mumbled, "I didn't know this would happen. Please, sir, we will stop it. Please, sir, we meant only to argue points and choose men to speak for us at Hillsborough."

Collins turned on him. "Frazier, this is an outrage! Johnston is your elected Governor, the highest officer in the state. You've disgraced the town of Edenton!"

Iredell smiled at the memory. "Collins' contemptuous words spurred Frazier into action. He charged outside, shouting, 'I'll stop it!' But of course he could do nothing. The crowd was in a frenzy."

"What did you do?" Adam asked. "How did you get the crowd quieted?"

"We didn't," Iredell said. "They fought unchecked, and a prettier brawl you have never seen. Heads were cracked, limbs were broken. Your man Marcy was in the thick of it, and I'm sure the marks on him are still to be seen. I looked for Mary, but she had sensibly withdrawn to the safety of Horniblow's by this time. For half an hour the battle raged, while Johnston, Collins, Allen and I stayed helpless within the Courthouse. Indeed, we were prisoners, for Mel Frazier, determined to shield Johnston from harm, had locked us in. We went to the windows and found them fastened with nails which could not be withdrawn except by tools, and we had none. At last we went upstairs. Johnston had a key to the Masonic Lodge room, so we watched the scene from its windows."

From this vantage point the four men had seen men running from all directions to join the fight. From the back windows Penelope Barker's garden could be discerned—a forlorn sight. The dancing platform was deserted. The candles in many of the gay little paper lanthorns had gone out, and others were tilted crazily. Slaves ran about, piling tables and chairs to form barricades at the gates.

A shout from Josiah Collins, who was prying up one of the windows facing the Green, brought the others to his side. Collins pointed out the figure of the aged Parson Earle, who, accompanied by Charles Johnson and supported by his slave, had reached the head of the Green. In a black cassock and the full white wig he wore when conducting a service, he was an impressive figure.

The Parson climbed the Courthouse steps and faced the mob. He spoke, but the four men at the open window above him could not hear his voice over the roar of the embattled crowd.

"Ring the bell, Nat," said Governor Johnston. "We'll use their own signal to quiet them."

Nat Allen left the room and in a moment the town bell again cut through the crowd noises. Individuals in the mass of struggling men turned involuntarily to the Courthouse and paused, arrested by the sight of the old Parson, his arms raised as though he were blessing a congregation. The shouts and curses dwindled, and as the tolling of the bell ceased Parson Earle's stentorian voice rang across the Green.

"My children, listen carefully. You all know me. I have christened you, married you, buried your dead. With my prayers I have brought the Lord's comfort to you in your time of sorrow. I pray over you now. I am a man of God, committed to do His will. I am no politician. I do not profess to know the right or the wrong of the great controversy."

A man shouted derisively, "Oh, no?" But his neighbours silenced him quickly. The old Parson had the grudging attention of the crowd now.

"I do know," the Parson went on, "that the question of ratification is of paramount importance to all of us. We have regarded battles like King's Mountain and Guilford as milestones in the state's history. They are as nothing to the decision that now confronts us. The keystone of our new states is the Constitution. It must not be considered in anger; men's opinions must not be forced by cuffs and blows. This document must be considered quietly, with wisdom, with tolerance—never in anger. Most of all, you must every one consider both sides of the controversy and then . . . then ask the Lord's guidance in making your stand for or against ratification. Go home, my children. Get down on your knees. Seek wisdom. Pray that the Lord will set your feet on the right path."

He paused, and the silence of the men before him showed that his words had reached their hearts. He extended his hands. "The Lord's blessing upon you."

Iredell halted in his story. He had told it well, he knew. "It was a scene not easily forgotten, I assure you."

"But what happened?" Adam demanded. "Did the crowd disperse?"

"When the Parson finished," Iredell said, "shouts went up: 'The old Parson's right.' . . . 'Let's go home.' . . . 'Let's think it over!' Some of the strangers doggedly revived their chant of 'March, march on Hillsborough,' but it was less hearty than before. One leather-lunged Edenton man roared, 'March to the gaol with the rascals!' The crowd laughed and took it up. 'Put the strangers in gaol!'

"I turned from the window. When a mob laughs the trouble is passing. I hurried down the stairs and found the door of the Courthouse open. Charles Johnson was escorting Parson Earle toward Horniblow's. I looked up and saw our high-born visitors standing on the inn's gallery, where they had had a safe view. No doubt it pleasured them to see this outburst of discontent among the commonalty, as Lady Anne would call them."

Adam asked, "What would have happened, do you suppose, if the Parson had not quieted them?"

"I don't know, but I am certain that neither Johnston nor I would have had the least effect, even if we had been permitted to talk. As propertied men we are suspected of advocating the Constitution to protect our own interests at the expense of the common people's."

"What is the next step?" Adam asked. "How do you know there will not be future riots, other mobs protesting that the people have no voice? You were fortunate that this disturbance ended without fatalities."

Iredell nodded. "Yes, we were fortunate." He drained his glass of port. "There was no shooting, for which we were duly grateful. But before the mob settled down they paraded Broad Street, breaking windows and banging shutters. They even forced their way into Dr. Armitage's garden and pounded on his door. He met them with his slaves, an old blunderbuss and a long rifle and drove them off. Then they turned to force an entrance to Thomas Barker's. The women were in a panic, but your Marcy arrived with some followers and routed them."

Adam sat quietly without speaking. After a time he said, "Is there some way you can answer these people, reassure them that they will be protected by the Constitution?"

"I've already answered. My replies were published the next day in Edenton, addressed to the freemen of Chowan. I hope I have answered every question."

"There is strong opposition in the West," Adam observed. "I've heard the same objections that you say were put in Edenton."

Iredell turned quickly. "Surely, Adam, you don't believe in forcing a bill of rights. You are certainly not Anti."

"I'm not sure," Adam answered slowly. "I haven't heard both sides. I think I shall follow our good Parson's advice and approach the whole matter prayerfully."

James Iredell stared at Adam. The look of surprise on his face was almost laughable. Twice he started to speak. After a time he said quietly, "All our friends are Federalist, Adam. Most of the responsible statesmen also. All the colonies have ratified, save North Carolina and Rhode Island."

"But Virginia has recognized a need for a bill of rights. Mr. Mason and Patrick Henry have seen to that. Their suggested amendments will be presented to the new Congress for consideration."

A slow flush spread over Iredell's face. His hazel eyes snapped. He opened his mouth to speak, then closed it, as though determined to control his temper. "I'll not argue with you, Adam. I'm going to give you my printed answers to Mason's objections to ratification. Wait a moment."

He left the room and returned with a pamphlet and a small bundle of letters. "I've brought you some letters also, Adam. They concern some of your friends' views on the Constitution. Read them carefully before you take your stand. The letters cover a period when you were away and did not have your finger on the pulse of the state or the country."

Adam thanked him and went off, feeling that from now on he must walk carefully, think clearly.

Adam ate with relish the breakfast Herk brought. "Before you go," he said to Herk, "hand me the packet of letters you'll find in the tail pocket of my coat." He propped himself up with pillows and bolster and opened the packet. Some of the letters were marked "by post," others "by hand." He began to read.

The first, dated from Edenton on May 22, was from Iredell's brother Thomas.

My dear Brother:
Mr. Allen, this morning, read me a part of a letter he received from a gentleman of his acquaintance, who mentioned a conversation he had with General Person, the substance of which was "that *General Washington was a damned rascal, and traitor to his country, for putting his hand to such an infamous paper as the Constitution.*" Mr. Allen's correspondent desires him to have it published, and at the same time to have it inserted that any one desirous to know his name, may be informed by the printer.

T. IREDELL

On the bottom was a notation in Iredell's hand: "Received in New Bern." A postscript was dated June 4:

The actors or players approached us at Edenton as near as Windsor. I have the satisfaction to inform you that they have wheeled about to take a view of Hillsborough and its environs, to fix upon some spot to enliven and cheer the vacant hours of the Convention Heroes. Mrs. Parsons has assumed her old line of life and is head cook to Mr. Stone at Windsor.

The second letter had been written by Archibald Maclaine at Wilmington:

Dear Sir:

I had scarcely reached this spot when I had news that South Carolina had adopted the new constitution, by a majority of seventy-seven. There is a handbill in town, directing the procession which is to take place, celebrating the happy event. It is said to exceed that of Massachusetts; was ordered by the convention by a committee drawn up for that purpose. Great pains were taken in the back country to poison the minds of the people, yet it carried two to one. I know this will give you heartfelt satisfaction. Yankee Doodle, keep it up.

A. MACLAINE

A letter from Dr. Williamson was dated from New York, 7 July:

Dear Sir:

Virginia having confederated, North Carolina in opposition, should she be disposed to stand out, can only expect countenance from Rhode Island or New York. Let me state in a few words the politics of Rhode Island. You have heard of the effect of the Know Ye Law, by which every debtor is enabled to wipe off a debt by paying two shillings sixpence on the pound, for their paper is now at 8 to 1.

The people of the State have two capital objections against the new constitution: first, they think every slave should be taxed as a white man, and not represented; second, that the States should not be taxed according to the number of inhabitants, but according to the amount of produce exported from each State. I asked a leader of the Know Ye men what Rhode Island grew and exported. He answered, Nothing except a little cheese and potash. You see how reasonable a plan his would be. Maryland, Virginia and North Carolina would be delighted with it.

The politics of New York are not so villainous in their face, but not much more honourable. During the war New York agreed to give Congress power to collect the 5 percent impost. As soon as they got possession of the city they refused to let Congress have such power, because they found the selfish advantage of imposing a duty on imports for their own use. Half the goods consumed in Connecticut, three fourths in New Jersey, all goods consumed in Vermont, and no small amount of those consumed in Western Massachusetts are bought in New York and pay New York an impost of 5 percent.

I say nothing of what the good citizens of North Carolina import from New York, wherein they pay part of the New Yorkers' taxes.

'Tis easy to discover why New York does not like the new government. But this very argument must be a very good one with the citizens of North Carolina why they should like that government. Consequently, it is to be hoped North Carolina will copy neither New York, nor Rhode Island.

When Herk came back Adam laid aside the letters and got out of bed. But while Herk was shaving him and dressing his hair he continued reading.

The next he took up was one from John Swann, a member of Congress sitting in New York.

New York, July 7, '88

Dear Sir:
   I should have acknowledged your letter before this, but it arrived at the height of the small-pox. From the slow and irregular conveyance which sometimes attends letters, you may possibly hear of the decision of this State on the new Constitution before this reaches you. However, I take the liberty to mention their extreme indecision on that subject—an indecision the more astonishing since they are apprised of its ratification by ten States. The Constitution is ably supported by gentlemen of great literary merit; but the opposition, who are by no means contemptible, seem determined to dispute the ground inch by inch.
   Sir, we are in the most painful suspense for Carolina. I confess I should be most sensibly mortified were Carolina to reject the Constitution. Doubly so, when I reflect that she would have the *countenance of Rhode Island alone*. . . .

Adam paused when Herk flourished the razor under his nose, protesting, "Sar, how you think I shave when you keep a-wrigglin' all de while?"
   Adam laughed and laid the letters on the table. He understood why James Iredell had insisted on his reading them. They were intended to support Iredell's assertion that the state's most distinguished men were aligned on the side of Federalism. Iredell was confident that the letters would counter effectively the Antifederalist opinions Adam had encountered on his journey.
   Queued and coated, Adam sat down at the desk and read four more letters, paying closest attention to one William Hooper had written in Hillsborough on July 8. One paragraph in particular arrested him:

People in this Western country have become more moderate, and many who zealously opposed ratification have changed their tone. It is said that Mebane advocates it unreservedly and endeavors to make converts. The Quakers are for it, and O'Neall's brother-bullies in its favor. I have not a tittle of doubt but that our Convention will have a favorable issue. . . .

Adam sighed and put the letter down. There was only one more to be read, a brief note from Dr. Witherspoon of New Bern:

Dear Sir:
   I have read with very great pleasure your answers to the Antifederalists' objections; and surely every man who reads them must be convinced that the objections to the Constitution are without foundation.
   If we expect a constitution the principles of which *cannot* be violated, we had better, instead of amending that proposed, amend the hearts of men.
   I am afraid there will be a powerful opposition in this State; but am happy

in observing that the proportion of well-informed men on that side will be very small.

Your publication has been made, I believe very correctly by Hodge. . . .

Adam got up and walked restlessly about the room. The letters did not satisfy him. Each man had his own reasons for believing in the Federalists' purpose, but none was concerned with the cause of Adam's doubts—the very real fears of the common people who knew that the amending of men's hearts could not be accomplished overnight. He seated himself again and opened the pamphlet by Iredell which had so gratified Dr. Witherspoon. Perhaps Jemmy's habitually vigorous expression and clear-sighted analysis would offer reassurance.

Iredell began, Adam found, by dismissing the question of a declaration of rights. England's bill of rights, he maintained, was a restriction of the Crown's authority made necessary by the lack of any written constitution to specify the Crown's powers. In the proposed American Constitution a bill of rights would be superfluous.

A neat argument indeed, thought Adam. Clear, logical, smoothly phrased —typical of the working of Iredell's orderly mind. But where in the Constitution were the prohibitions that would prevent determined and unscrupulous men from encroaching upon the freedoms of religion, speech, press, assembly?

He closed the pamphlet. Further consideration of Iredell's arguments must wait. It was time for him to start for St. Matthew's Church to take his seat in the convention.

The Convention Opens

15 As ADAM passed through the common-room of the inn toward the street door he was halted by a hand on his shoulder. Turning, he saw the grinning face of Cosmo de' Medici, whom he had known since the early years of the war.

"Adam, how good it is to see you once more!" Cosmo cried as they shook hands. "Your charming wife told me you had run away again to the far, far West. Have you breakfasted? At any rate you must sit with me while I finish my meal."

The two men made a striking pair as Cosmo led Adam through the crowded common-room to his table. They were of equal height, a few inches above six feet. Both were unpowdered, and Adam's blond hair offered an arresting contrast to the Italian's dark curls. Their military experience was apparent in their erect bearing, and both moved with the smooth co-ordination of men accustomed to the saddle.

When they were seated Cosmo anticipated Adam's question by saying, "Your Maria is in the best of health and spirits. She told me she was certain you would try to be here for the convention."

Adam smiled. "She knows me, Cosmo. I think no one else really thought I'd ride all the way from the Illinois country for this."

"This question to ratify or not to ratify is too big for you to stay out of, eh? It is your Shakespeare all over again: 'To be or not to be'—a momentous decision, surely." He paused and laid his serviette on the table. "Pardon. There is Mr. Wilie Jones coming in. I've been trying to see him for three days."

Cosmo hurried across the room and engaged the Antifederalist leader in a brief conversation. When he turned away he was smiling broadly. As he made his way back to Adam he was stopped several times by friends at the various tables. The handsome Italian had endeared himself to many North Carolinians by his vigorous adherence to their cause during the war. They ranked him with LaFayette and De Fleury and the other young Frenchmen who had come to America to throw themselves into the battle for liberty.

Back at his own table, Cosmo said triumphantly, "Mr. Jones says he will vote for me and use his influence. My cause is as good as won."

Adam showed his astonishment.

"Oh, of course, you do not know my business here in Hillsborough." Cosmo explained his plan to appeal to the legislature for the return of the money he had advanced to outfit his company during the war.

"But this isn't the legislature, Cosmo. You know this is a convention to vote on the Constitution," Adam said.

"I understand. But where can I see so many members of the legislature all at one time?"

Adam laughed. "You Italians are born politicians, grasping each opportunity that comes along and turning it to your benefit."

"But yes! One must look with open eyes, realistically. Perhaps we are born a little bit Machiavellian. At least, my house has for centuries borne such a reputation." His dark eyes sparkled. "Sometimes a quite sinister reputation."

"Where are you staying, Cosmo?" Adam asked. "The town is overflowing. How did you find a room?"

"Room?" His smile flashed. "I slept last night down here in a chair. It was not too bad. It was a large chair."

Adam said, "Get your luggage and move in with me. Herk obtained me a good room upstairs. You shall have the extra bed."

"Splendid! That will be a pleasure. I confess I am too long in the legs to rest well in a chair a second night."

Adam rose. "Since I am a delegate, I must be at the church by eleven. I don't want to miss the procession. Herk will take you to my room."

"Ah, but I'm going to view the procession. It's the kind of show I wouldn't miss. I shall have a good seat in the Market House. A good friend has arranged it."

In front of St. Matthew's Church and along the road leading to it stood crowds of people, waiting to see the formal procession of convention dele gates. All types and classes were represented. Among the masses of common folk were elegant gentlemen and fashionable ladies whose complexions were protected from the warm sun by frilled parasols held by slaves. Children perched on the high brick wall or crouched on the grass by the roadside. Peddlers were hawking cool drinks, "gingie-bread" and fruit.

Adam found the Chowan delegates assembled near the church. Since the procession was forming by counties in alphabetical order their places would be close to the front of the line. Iredell and Stephen Cabarrus were already waiting. Josiah Collins, on his way to join the Tyrrell group, came up with Lemuel Creecy. Just ahead of the Chowan men were the Bertie County delegates John Johnston, Francis Pugh, Dawson, Turner and David Stone. They talked together guardedly, as though afraid their words would be wafted on the warm morning air to the ears of opponents.

A dignified man dressed in sombre dark blue passed and took his place near the head of the line. "Judge Spencer of Anson," Cabarrus whispered to Adam. "A great patriot, a soldier without compare, the Antis claim; a villain and destroyer of the state, in the opinion of the Federalists."

Adam leaned back against the trunk of a sycamore tree, watching butterflies flitting among the flowering honeysuckle, listening to the drowsy sounds of bees in the white clover. The sky was cloudless. A soft breeze stirred the leaves of the trees. At this moment, in gardens, in fields, nature was at her most lavish. On such a day these men—more than two hundred of them—must crowd into the church to fight and wrangle, raise their voices in anger and vilification. Before the pleasant day had passed, new quarrels would be piled on old, new feuds started. Surely the delegates must be as reluctant as he to give up this moment of peace and beauty.

The crowd now extended far down the street, for, besides the delegates, some members of both houses of the Assembly who had not been elected to sit here had come as advisers and onlookers. All were dressed in their best. Some were in the uniforms they had worn in the Revolutionary War, and the buff and blue stood out among the more sombre colours. But those in dark coats and buff or grey breeches brightened their costumes with elaborate brocaded waistcoats with gold or silver or jewelled buttons, lace at wrist and throat, white silk stockings and shoes with well-polished buckles of silver.

Their hats were tricorns, some with cockades, and there were a few dress

swords to be seen, although swords had not been worn much since Yorktown. Pages and aides on horseback rode up and down the line, carrying
messages or guiding the late-comers to their positions.

Charles Johnson arrived to join the Chowan group, and Iredell asked
if he had seen Governor Johnston.

"He will come at the end of the procession," Johnson said. "The order,
according to General McDowell, is for us to march to the church steps
and form a line on either side. The Governor and Council, arriving last, will
start the march into the church. Each county will fall in line behind them
as they pass. The counties at the end of the alphabet go first. We will be
among the last to enter."

Cabarrus did not approve the plan. "That will force Chowan delegates to
find seats at the back of the church," he complained.

"No matter," Iredell said. "We will be heard."

Lemuel Creecy spoke. "You will be heard, Jemmy. Johnston says if he
is elected president of the convention, it is up to you to carry the debates
against Spencer and Person."

"Aye, and against Caldwell and Bloodworth and Wilie Jones," Charles
Johnson said. "Although I doubt that Jones will speak a great deal. He
prefers to work behind the scenes."

Iredell moved restlessly. His small compact body was tense, and his hands
clasped and unclasped. He was always so before he spoke. But when he
got to his feet all nervousness left him. He turned sharply and faced Adam.
"Were the letters I gave you of any help?"

Adam felt an intense sympathy for his friend, who now carried so great
a burden. "Yes, Jemmy. I regret only that we had no real opportunity to
talk together."

"You've made up your mind?"

"I've reached some conclusions. There's not time now to tell you of them."
Iredell laid his hand on Adam's arm. "We'll have our talk."

The town clock—the same clock Governor Tryon had got from King
George III—boomed out eleven strokes. A band started to play, and the
procession moved toward the church.

The Chowan men had only a short march. Following the A's and the
B's, they began forming lines on either side of the path that led to the
church doors. The drum corps set the pace, slow and steady but not funereal
—well suited, Adam thought, to the solemnity of the occasion.

The chatter and laughter among the women clustered near the entrance
to the church grounds subsided. Their comments dropped to a murmur as
they looked down the lines and mentioned the names of men of importance:
Elisha Battle, Stephen Cabarrus, John Sitgreaves, William Grove, Thomas
Owen, Joseph Winston, John Macon, Josiah Collins, Thomas Brown.
"There is Lenoir!" a woman exclaimed in a sibilant whisper. "And James
Kenan. Isn't that Joel Lane over there by John Branch? They say they're

going to have the capitol on Lane's plantation if he can get enough votes."

"Oh, there's William Davie!" said another. "How handsome he is! Look, he and Wilie Jones are obliged to walk together in the Halifax group. They are bitter enemies, you know."

A third woman spoke out. "I think Wilie Jones is the handsomest of all. So aristocratic!"

A constable spoke to the group, and the whispers stopped.

Adam, having taken his position at one side of the path, turned to watch the advance of the other delegates. The scene was oddly moving. Trees on either side of the street cast deep shadows broken by rays of sunlight which illumined the faces of individuals in the double file of marching men. Adam was struck by the expressions of the marchers—sober, earnest, thoughtful. It was clear that these men recognized the responsibility they faced.

Now the Council of State was approaching, flanking the tall, spare figure of the Governor. Adam heard one of the women standing near whisper, "The old Roman." As Johnston advanced there was a scattering of applause which grew in volume and was sustained until the Governor had passed into the church.

Johnston looked neither to right nor left. Not a muscle moved in his face. But as his friend passed, Adam saw that his deep-set eyes were very bright, as though tears were close.

The men from Chowan entered the church among the last of the delegates. Adam found a seat in the last row. It suited him to sit with his back against the wall. The feeling it gave him, he had often told Mary, must be inherited from ancestors who, defending themselves in sword-play, had welcomed a wall as protection against attack from behind.

From his seat Adam commanded a view of the whole church. The formal mood of the procession had not yet passed. Few of the delegates were talking. Most looked straight ahead to the front of the church where the clerks of the convention were putting in order their quills and sanding-boxes. They will write history, Adam thought. We *are* history. Our actions here will influence the lives of generations to come. God grant that we may be wise and strong!

With the prayer he felt a sudden surge of confidence in the ability of the convention. This grew as he cast his vote for Johnston as president of the convention and listened to the roll-call which made his election unanimous. For Adam, to whom the formal procedures of government were familiar, there was excitement even in the preliminary business. He found a gratifying sense of order in the speedy adoption of the rules of the convention, and he approved the refusal of the committee on elections to seat any delegates from Dobbs County on the ground that neither of the two elections there was valid.

Ahead of him delegates settled down in their seats while a clerk droned on in a monotonous voice, reading the various acts and resolutions which had brought the Hillsborough convention into being. The church was growing warm and many of the men removed their coats. Some were dozing. There was a moment of complete silence as the clerk finished reading; then a restless stir and a hum of conversation as James Galloway rose to move that the Constitution be discussed clause by clause.

Adam waited confidently to hear support for Galloway's motion. Several Federalists were on their feet to second, but Wilie Jones won Johnston's recognition. He bowed slightly to the chair, then faced the delegates. The question of whether to ratify should be put immediately, Jones said. The Constitution had so long been the subject of deliberation, the members of the convention had had such ample opportunity to consider it that it would be imprudent to waste the time of the gentlemen and the funds of the state in pointless deliberation. The decision could be made now.

Shock brought Adam forward in his seat. He scarcely heard what Person was saying in support of Jones. Anger swept over him. He had come hundreds of miles to meet here in open convention with other representatives of the people. An immediate vote would be a mockery of republican government. He looked toward Iredell, who was impatiently tapping the seat in front of him with a folded paper. Would Jemmy speak out? Maclaine?

It was to be Iredell, Adam saw. He was on his feet the moment Person stopped speaking. "Mr. President! Mr. President!" Iredell's call cut across the clamour from the floor. Johnston, grave and impassive in his tall pulpit chair, recognized the delegate from Edenton. Iredell waited until the noise had subsided, then began speaking in a low-pitched voice which carried clearly over the room.

"Mr. President, I am greatly astonished at a proposal to decide immediately, without the least deliberation, a question that is perhaps the greatest that ever was submitted to any body of men. This is a subject of great consideration. The Constitution has been formed after much deliberation by honest and able men of probity and understanding. It has the solemn ratification of ten states. Shall it be said, sir, of the representatives of North Carolina that near three hundred of them, assembled for the express purpose of deliberating on it, refused to discuss it and discarded all reasoning as useless? I readily confess my present opinion is strongly in favour of the Constitution. But I have not come here resolved at all events to vote for its adoption. I have come here for information and to judge whether it really merits my attachment. I hope we shall imitate the laudable example of the other states and go into a committee of the whole house that the Constitution may be discussed clause by clause. I trust we shall not go home and tell our constituents we were afraid to enter into a discussion!"

Iredell's last sentence was delivered like a challenge. The word "afraid" seemed still resounding as he took his seat. The speech had obvious effect. There was an immediate outburst of whispering, and several delegates rose to confer with men near by. Adam saw Bloodworth make his way to where Wilie Jones was sitting. Jones did not turn his head as Bloodworth bent over his shoulder and spoke briefly. He seemed unaware that every member of the convention was waiting for his next word. He rose slowly and with great dignity. The man seated next to Adam, a Federalist from Carteret County whom he knew only slightly, tapped his arm. "There he is! The complete aristocrat, posing as the friend of the humble citizenry. He's like a spider sitting in the middle of a web."

Adam thought his neighbour had put it neatly. Certainly the Antifederalist leader was as sensitive as a spider to anything that touched a part of the web he had spun. He knew when to press the point and when to withdraw without retreating. His tone now was no less assured but more conciliatory.

"Mr. President," Jones was saying, "my reasons for proposing an immediate decision were that I was prepared to give my vote and believed that others were equally so. If gentlemen differ from me in the propriety of this motion, I will submit."

Person rose promptly to withdraw his seconding of the motion. Jones had properly judged the mood of the convention. There was an immediate relaxing of tension, obvious in the smiles of the delegates and their leisure in resuming business. Adam closed his mind to the polite speeches which were leading toward adjournment. The first fight was over, and the Federalists had won. He was as proud of Iredell's victory as he was resentful of Jones's arrogance. Yet if Jones had been successful, would Adam Rutledge have stood with his friend Jemmy Iredell? Only now Adam knew he had gone far toward a decision in that moment when it had seemed that he might have to vote without hearing further discussion. He could not have voted with Jemmy. If the question had been put directly, could he have voted to reject the Constitution? Thank God, he did not have to make that decision! There had to be a middle ground where he could stand with others who believed the Constitution fundamentally good but dangerous without full guarantees of liberty for all men. The questions for him—and surely for many here—were what guarantees were required and how their inclusion in the Constitution could best be ensured.

Johnston's voice, adjourning the convention for the day, interrupted Adam's thought. He had not even been conscious of the motions from the floor. He rose to go, relieved of indecision for the first time since he arrived and conscious now of purpose.

Stephen Cabarrus fell in step with Adam at the door of the church. Fragments of conversation came to them as they walked slowly down Cedar Lane on their way to the Star. Delegates were talking earnestly of the first day's proceedings. "Iredell was magnificent. He saved the convention from complete folly." . . . "Jones was right. He knew we had the votes. Why should we waste time and money here? I have crops in the fields. Must I

miss a harvest to hear Iredell speak?" . . . "I expected Spencer to speak out
for the Antifeds. But I don't wonder that he didn't try to answer
Iredell." . . .

Adam and Cabarrus walked slowly through the crowded streets. At the
Star they found their way blocked by a crowd standing on the terrace. One
red-faced man was talking loudly. "Say what you will, Wilie Jones is an
aristocrat. Look how he lives at the Grove. Any man who can keep up a
plantation like that won't be thinking much of us."

A slender man, dressed in butternut-dyed clothes, moved toward the
speaker. "You're talking about a patriot, Granger. He's the best leader we
could have."

"Leader, you say!" Granger held out his hands as if appealing to the other
men. "Dodds says Jones is a leader—Jones, with his horse-racin', huntin' and
and card-playin'! I say Tim Bloodworth is better than a dozen of him. Tim
is a true man of the people, he is. He knows how we live and what we
think. What if he was a blacksmith? Ain't that to his credit? General Greene
was a blacksmith, but it didn't keep him from beatin' Cornwallis at Guilford
Courthouse."

A man standing near Adam and Cabarrus spoke quietly. "I thought Cornwallis won that battle."

Granger was scornful. "I wouldn't say he won. His troops had to retreat
to Wilmington. I don't call that winnin'."

"Bloodworth is too extreme." A tall man in a green coat pushed his way
through the crowd. "I'm an Anti, but I don't hold with men like Bloodworth."

"Some say Jefferson is too extreme, and Patrick Henry. Do you hold with
men like them that fight for your rights?" Once again Granger made a
gesture of appeal to the crowd. "Better look to Bloodworth, not to Jones.
You know where Tim stands, but Jones is as crooked as a snake's back in
his thinking."

"You're a fool, Granger." Dodds stood directly before the taller man. "You
fellows from the back country don't understand clever politics in play
against play, thinking faster than the other side. That's Jones's way. All
you know is to use your fists or a rifle."

"You're right, Dodds. This'll prove it!" Granger struck Dodds a powerful
blow on the jaw, and the slender man fell, striking his head on the flagging
of the terrace. His friends quickly picked him up and began to help him
toward the Star.

Adam had started forward when the blow was struck. He spoke to the
two men who were standing by Granger. "You'd better get him out of here
before the little man's friends come back."

As the men led the protesting Granger away from the Star, Cabarrus
stepped to Adam's side. "You see, Adam, the Antis are divided. The western
men distrust Jones."

Adam shook his head. "Yes, and the eastern planters and merchants fear the western men and are hated by them. There's too much hate, Stephen. Our state could be destroyed by it." The men began moving toward the tap-room at the back of the inn.

"Where do you stand, Adam?" Cabarrus asked.

For a moment Adam hesitated. "I'm not sure I can make you understand. For almost two months I've been listening. From the Illinois country down to the Ohio, across the Kentucky lands to Virginia, I've heard men talking this problem out, fighting it out sometimes. That is a good sign, I think. We are not indifferent." He paused for a moment and looked down at the stones of the terrace. "Of one thing I am sure. We must have a Constitution. We must have a foundation on which to build. The foundation must be as strong as we can make it."

Stephen grasped his hand. "Then you do stand with us. Iredell will be happy. He thought you were much troubled about your decision. Last night he and Sam——"

Adam stopped him. "Wait. I have something else to tell you. I am convinced that the Constitution does not give full protection to human rights. It needs amendments, a bill of rights. I cannot vote for ratification until I feel sure the rights of every man are safe."

Cabarrus seemed scarcely to credit what he had heard. He looked at Adam in honest bewilderment. "But, Adam, if you believe in the Constitution, you can vote for it in good conscience. The way to amendments is open through Congress. Men in every state have felt as you do and have been willing to submit amendments to the action of the new Congress."

"I know, Cabarrus. I know the argument." Adam paused, remembering his talk with John Graham, who had voted against the Constitution because he put his trust in law and not in men. "But you saw what happened today. One man—Wilie Jones, who himself demands a bill of rights—would have violated the spirit of our laws and the rights of every man who differs from him. Except for Iredell, he might have been successful. Can we depend on it that Congress will not act as selfishly as Jones urged us to act today? Perhaps the method you and Jemmy urge is safe. Perhaps not. I know we must consider in this convention the question I've just asked." There was a long silence. Then Adam said, "Let's go into the tap-room. One of the Star's rarebits and a mug of ale would be good now."

Cabarrus shook his head. "I think I had better go back to Hooper's. They'll be expecting me there." He walked slowly away. Adam watched him until he turned toward Margaret Lane. He knew his declaration of belief had disturbed Cabarrus deeply. He would of course speak to Johnston and Iredell of what Adam had told him. They would all discuss Adam's position, and it would give them pain. What a pity it was that a man's political belief could interfere with his friendships! He had no illusions. There would be a change in the Edenton men's attitude toward him.

Adam went directly to his room. He was more settled in his mind, more at peace than at any time since he left Cahokia. He sat down in a chair near his window and gazed across the tree-tops toward the laurel-covered Occoneechee Mountains.

Details of his life in the Illinois country and of his journey east returned to him. He saw the figures of the men whom he had known since he first looked west: back-country men, men of the woods and forests, farmers hewing down great trees to clear a little patch of fertile earth. These were men to whom danger was a constant companion. They knew the fear of wild beasts, the fear of Indians, and always loneliness. Did they think of themselves as builders of a nation? He doubted it. They were too close to the perils and hardships of daily life to identify themselves as the advance guard of a movement by many into a country of new hope and promise.

Then there were the rivermen, the men he had known who fought the mighty force of the Ohio and Mississippi. There were these and, closest of all, his neighbours in the Illinois country: the prairie men who fought the heat and the insects that blighted crops, the prairie fires that blackened their fields and destroyed their homes. And with these he remembered the trappers and hunters who had led the way west.

These men and women who were part of the country he loved gave little thought to government. But government must give thought to them. Settlers in Tennessee had been victims of speculators who came with papers to prove that the land won by hard toil could be lost to trickery and dishonesty. They would need assurance that a central government would provide for their rights. And would the new Congress provide the bill of rights that could give this assurance? Unless debate convinced him of that, he would vote not to ratify until a bill of rights was sure.

Adam stood up and stretched. The sun had set. He was conscious of voices below. Men were coming and going from the tap-room. Some voices were merry, some angry. He heard a rap at the door. The knob turned and De' Medici entered. A flashing smile that showed even white teeth illumined his dark face.

"Adam, everywhere I have been searching for you. I have come across Mr. Collins in the tap-room. He says there is to be a supper out in the country at Tapley's ordinary. He extends an invitation and begs that you will join the company."

Adam did not feel inclined to join in a frolic, but De' Medici insisted. "I've already sent Herk ahead to mind our horses when we arrive. You need relaxation, my friend. All those months travelling the forests and down the wild rivers, meeting only uncultivated folk."

"The uncultivated folk are my friends." Adam spoke sharply.

De' Medici only smiled at Adam's answer. "No doubt. No doubt. You know I meant no offense. I think of the poor who laboured on my uncle's estates. They had a hard life, according to my standards. But they had one thing that I envied them. They had real communion with the land. They could not own it there. Here in this new America there is ample land. A man can possess what he loves here." Cosmo took off his coat and hung it on a peg. "Pardon me. I talk too much. I make what you call a lecture, but these things interest me. Love of the land—ah, that is a universal thing! France, Italy, Russia—everywhere it is the same. Give a man a little land to cultivate and you give him the world. You and I understand that, my friend, for we are land lovers."

Adam smiled at the enthusiasm the Italian displayed. "You are right. The great common denominator is land. But we must protect it, De' Medici. Ownership isn't enough."

De' Medici nodded. He had stripped off his small-clothes, his stockings, shoes and ruffled shirt. He poured the basin full of water from the brass ewer. "I sponge and take a small bathe. On a day so hot I would better like a plunge in some cool stream or the ocean, but one must be content. Come, let us dress and be on our way."

While Adam bathed and dressed, Cosmo talked amiably on a dozen subjects. Adam was amused in spite of himself. By the time they mounted Adam was better reconciled to an evening out.

It was an hour's ride on the northern trading-path to Tapley's ordinary. The night was clear. They avoided talk of the day's events. Cosmo talked of his Italy as they rode along the soft, shadowy path. Adam had visited Rome, Florence and Venice, and he followed his friend's reminiscence with understanding and sympathy. The air was fragrant from hedgerows of honeysuckle. Except for the whip-poor-will's call or the sudden screech of an owl in the forest the night was silent.

As they neared Tapley's Adam said, "I hope there are few guests. The night is too beautiful for hilarity and frolicking."

"Mr. Collins didn't say how many guests were invited. Perhaps only men from Chowan and Tyrrell. Perhaps others. Mr. Collins has friends everywhere. He does not allow friendship to be influenced by political beliefs."

Adam sighed. "I wish I could say as much for some of the others."

"My friend, you worry because you have said something that will be unpopular in your village. Don't. You show courage and character in your difference from your friends. It is easier always to accept and be silent. I know. I suffer sometimes because I broke with the traditions of my family."

Adam said nothing for a moment. He knew what might be ahead—criticism, blame, coldness. Mary. There was Mary with her strong loyalty to Edenton friends. He could not bear the thought that she might be hurt. He looked at Cosmo. "It must have been hard for you to break with the centuries and seek the new."

"Ah, yes. Difficult. Frightening. But the urge to seek new land, new living was so overpowering. . . ." He laughed softly. "We Italians bred Christopher Columbus, you know."

Adam did not ask his friend how he knew of his talk with Cabarrus. He realized the whole Chowan delegation and many of the other delegates would know what he had said. Adam Rutledge, for all his friendliness, was a reserved man. There was something saddening in the knowledge that his secret thoughts would be exposed to discussion, to derision certainly. Friendships so long cherished would be torn. There would be animosity. But he must not allow himself to dread the consequences of following his considered reasoning and his conscience.

They had arrived at their destination. The old inn was aglow with light. Candles were at every window, lanthorns were swinging in the galleries. A dozen or more horses were at the hitching-rack. Voices came from the inn dining-room mixed with loud laughter and snatches of song.

Herk came out of the shadows to take the horses to the stables. " 'Tis frolickin' dey are, master. Already some gen'lemen have been put to bed. Dey are shoutin' and hollerin' about dose politics, sar. Some has already been fisticuffin'."

Adam dismounted and tossed the reins to Herk. "All right, Herk, I don't intend to make myself drunk to-night. I'll keep my head."

"Yes, sar. You got a strong head for brandy, sar, but dis drink dey got is swamp stuff, might' green."

Adam laughed. To De' Medici he said, "Herk's been warning me that the liquor's potent."

Cosmo made a sound of disgust. "I'll stick to Madeira," he said. "If there's trouble, I want a clear head."

"Why should there be trouble?"

De' Medici shrugged. "You've heard Herk say there has been fighting. Some of the hot heads among the Federalists might feel that you have deserted them."

Adam laughed. "There'll be no trouble. A lot of talk, that's all." He walked swiftly down the path to the open door of Tapley's ordinary.

Interlude

16

THE innkeeper met Adam and Cosmo at the door and led them to an alcove off the common-room. Josiah Collins was waiting there to seat them with his other guests.

Two strangers were presented as Mr. Jenkins and Mr. Short, Virginia gentlemen whose interest in the convention had brought them to Hillsborough. Adam knew the other men. He was delighted to find the scholarly parson, David Caldwell, on his left, but not pleased to see John Hume across the table. He was the only delegate from Chowan for whom Adam lacked respect. It was typical of Collins that he should have put the ardent Federalist Hume beside so prominent an Anti as Thomas Person.

Within a few minutes the company was joined by Mr. MacFadden and Mr. Holden, both of whom Adam knew by reputation as leaders in the migration to the Tennessee country. They were an impressive pair. Holden was a squat man, broad-shouldered and powerfully built. MacFadden was tall and had the cold, steady eyes of the expert marksman.

Collins was a good host. He tried skilfully to keep the conversation away from controversy. But the Virginia men were Federalists, and several times they drew fire from Person. The Tennesseans were as hostile to the state government as to the Federal union.

"We want only our freedom," Holden said heatedly when Short asked for his views. "Land-grabbers and speculators have stolen our land. North Carolina and the Confederation strangled the independent state we formed. The new government is likely to give away our rights on the Mississippi. We stand alone, but, by God, we're not yet beaten!"

"The state you formed?" Short spoke tauntingly. "The glorious State of Franklin, eh? A republic of rabble. You're fortunate you weren't all hanged as rebels."

Holden smashed his fist against the table. Both he and MacFadden scrambled to their feet. Short glanced quickly toward Collins as if seeking protection. "Rabble, is it?" MacFadden roared. "You miserable, scrawny——"

"Gentlemen! You do our good host wrong." Adam tried to keep his voice calm in spite of the irritation he felt. He wanted a respite from politics. He thought Holden's views inaccurate and extreme. Yet he was sympathetic with the Tennessee men. Their hopes for a government beyond the mountains had twice been disappointed. And Short's goading was unendurable. He turned to the Virginian now.

"Mr. Short, you are misinformed. When North Carolina ceded her western lands to the Confederation the settlers there had every right to expect that they would become a new state. They created Franklin after North Carolina found it necessary to withdraw her offer. It was the act of men in whom the hope of independence would not die. We do not think of John Sevier and the Franklin men as rebels."

Short shrugged and filled his wine-glass. Obviously he was relieved by Adam's intervention and willing to let the matter drop. Holden looked at Adam as if uncertain whether he were friend or enemy. "The part about our freedom is right enough," he said. "But I don't hold with what you say about the state taking back the lands it had given. That was a shabby, greedy trick. And Governor Caswell didn't share your view about our not being rebels."

Adam admired the direct, unwavering loyalty of this sturdy Tennessean. He knew many Franklin men supported the Constitution in the hope that ratification would bring independence to their state. But Holden would accept no compromise with the facts as he saw them. His fiercely independent attitude was typical of most of the men who had founded their homes and hopes beyond the mountains. They were a breed apart, and there was the stuff of greatness in them.

Adam rose and put his hand on Holden's shoulder. "We will not entirely agree, sir," he said, "but we won't be enemies, you and I. I know and love your country. I have land even farther west, in the Illinois country. Yet I know this, too. North Carolina ceded her western lands in good faith. She gave away a great source of income to pay a part of her share of the war debts. It was not greed that made her repeal the act of cession, but the ungenerous attitude of Congress and other states. Governor Caswell had no choice under law but to insist that you men of Franklin submit to North Carolina's authority. Believe me, Holden, the future is yours. You will have your freedom."

Holden was silent. He glanced at MacFadden, and Adam knew that neither accepted all that he had said. But their belligerence was gone. Collins seized his opportunity to restore the company to good humour. He waved toward several slaves carrying huge trays to the table. "Our supper, gentlemen. Let's give over politics and turn to a much more pleasant business."

The food was excellent—roast duckling, ham, grits, snap beans, baked apples, hot biscuits, pickles, jam and half a dozen different kinds of jelly. A smiling slave set the ham before Collins. "Done baked to a turn," he said. "Yes, sar, and de beans is fresh out of de garden. Cook say save place for de pastries, dey sure is good."

Caldwell spoke quietly to Adam. "Allow me to say that I admired what you said to our earnest friends from Franklin. I know many such men. Their love of liberty is consuming. It will not be denied. Sometimes they are intractable children." The Scots parson paused and for a moment seemed hardly aware of Adam's presence. Then he spoke almost as if he were pronouncing a prayer. "But we must keep them close to us, these men who understand freedom. They are the true inheritors and guardians of our victory in the Revolution. I am very grateful that you understand that, Mr. Rutledge. You see, I know something of the sentiments you've expressed since you came to Hillsborough."

Adam sensed Caldwell's real understanding of his point of view, and he was eager to continue the conversation. But Cosmo interrupted from his seat across the table, where he had been in earnest conversation with Person. "Adam, I have just told Mr. Person about my purchase of a thousand acres of land near Bath. I've reminded him that when one plants one must have money. He agrees that it would not be unpatriotic for me to ask the legislature for my money."

"Indeed not, sir!" Like every one else who knew Cosmo, Person seemed to have surrendered to his charm. "You have fought our battles, De' Medici. We must not shirk our debt to you."

Adam smiled. Cosmo was winning friends. He would plant those acres at Bath. Adam was about to add a word to what Person had said when he heard a loud commotion in the common-room. There were sounds of chairs scraping and of men rising to their feet. Adam turned in his chair and looked out. Wille Jones was walking toward the alcove, smiling at the greeting but not pausing to talk to those who called out his name. He came directly to Collins' table.

"Please keep your seats, gentlemen. My apologies for disturbing your supper. Person and Caldwell, when you have quite finished your meal I hope I may see you upstairs. I'm sure Collins will not think you ungrateful guests."

Adam could not help being impressed by the cool authority of Jones's manner. For all his firmness he was not abrupt. Even his direct order to his friends had about it a certain elegance and grace. Jones bowed slightly to Josiah Collins and then walked to Adam's chair. He smiled warmly. "Ah, Rutledge. The news I had of you this evening delighted me. I think you will wish to see what amendments some of us propose. I'll have a draft of them sent to your room at the Star." Before Adam could answer, Jones turned away. "A pleasant evening, gentlemen. Pray continue your meal."

It was more than a minute before conversation at the table was resumed. Obviously the men felt constrained not to talk of Jones. Yet the impact of his brief appearance had been so great that any other topic seemed foolish. Adam was conscious that Hume was staring steadily at him, and he found this extremely annoying. He had never liked the man. Hume had come to Edenton after the war, and bought a lumber-mill on Rockahock Creek. Adam could not understand how he had managed to get himself elected a delegate.

Now as the other men began talking Hume leaned forward. "So you are now among Jones's friends, Rutledge. I suppose you know what kind of reception you'll get in Edenton if you vote against ratification."

Adam looked at Hume contemptuously. "If you speak for the town, then you should know that Edenton men are not accustomed to being told how to vote. It occurs to me that as a new-comer you would do better to attend to your own affairs."

Hume's face grew scarlet as Adam turned his shoulder and began to talk to Cosmo. For the rest of the evening he drank heavily but said nothing more to Adam. After the company had left the table he overtook Cosmo and Adam on the front gallery.

"No man alive can tell me to mind my own business. I'll give you a thrashing that will teach you manners." Hume moved toward Adam with drunken clumsiness, his fists raised. Before he could strike, his unsteady legs collapsed and he fell heavily to the floor. There were loud, derisive laughs from the men in the common-room, and Hume cursed as he struggled to regain his feet.

Adam and Cosmo walked to the hitching-rack where Herk stood by the horses. Cosmo put his hand on Adam's arm. "Give the fool no thought, my friend. He does not speak for Edenton. He does not speak for your friends."

Adam shook his head. "Men like Hume are quick to see where their advantage lies. The thought that I will be ostracized did not originate with him, you can be sure of that."

Adam leaned back in his seat and tried to find room to stretch his legs. The church was intolerably hot, and the proceedings of the second day of the convention had been drawn out interminably. It was now nearly time for the session to be adjourned, and it seemed to Adam that little had been accomplished. After the convention had been resolved into a committee of the whole house, the motion had been made and carried by a large majority to discuss the Constitution clause by clause. But thus far there had been no discussion. Adam was impatient with the tiresome detail of formal debate about minor matters of organization and procedure. He was relieved now to hear the clerk reading the preamble of the Constitution, and he listened with fresh excitement to the measured roll of the familiar words.

" 'We, the People of the United States, in Order to form a more perfect Union, establish Justice, insure domestic Tranquillity, provide for the common defence, promote the general Welfare, and secure the Blessings of Liberty to ourselves and our Posterity, do ordain and establish this Constitution for the United States of America.' "

In spite of his fatigue Adam felt a thrill of anticipation. This was the beginning, and this majestic passage the signal for meaningful debate.

It began with an attack on the first words. David Caldwell rose to state a fundamental objection for the Antifederalists. He spoke quietly, almost mildly, and yet his words had the commanding force of deep conviction— Adam thought of it as dedication.

"Mr. President, if they mean *We, the People*—the people at large—I conceive the expression is improper. Were not they who framed this Constitution the representatives of the legislatures of the different states? Did the people give them the power of using their name? This power was in the people. They did not give it up. It is the interest of every man who is a friend to liberty to oppose the assumption of power. This Constitution is a consolidation of all the states. Had it said *We, the States* there would have been federal intention in it. A dangerous assumption of power may be carried to more dangerous lengths in the actions of the new government.

We cannot expose ourselves to this power unless we secure our civil and political liberties."

Once again the Scots teacher and parson had come very close to stating Adam's own thought. As he listened he remembered what Caldwell had said of MacFadden and Holden the night before. He seemed to Adam to be speaking for them now and for all men like them, for Adam's friends in the Illinois country, for the men whose suspicions and doubts he had heard on the wilderness trail. If the rights of states were lost in the Federal union, would not the rights of these men be lost with them? For Adam the question could be more simply phrased. Would members of the new Congress from Massachusetts, New York and Pennsylvania consider the rights of Tennessee men as dear as their own and give equal consideration to the welfare of the settlers who would form new states in the West? Adam remembered the arrogant proposal of Gouverneur Morris to limit the political power of new states, the proposal that had aroused the first doubts in his mind.

But Archibald Maclaine was replying to Caldwell now, and Adam put aside his own thoughts to give him full attention. As usual, Maclaine was speaking as if anger were about to overmaster him. His voice was choked, and Adam heard him distinctly only when he turned to face the delegates after his address to the chair. ". . . I confess myself astounded to hear objections to the preamble. The Constitution is a mere proposal. Had it been binding on us, there might be a reason for objecting. I hope to hear no more complaints of this trifling nature and ask that we enter into the spirit of the subject at once."

Adam was impatient with Maclaine's peremptory and insulting manner. Certainly he had not really answered Caldwell's objection. A dozen delegates were on their feet bidding for recognition. It was apparent that order would not be restored for a few minutes. Adam stepped from his seat and walked outside. He was joined almost immediately by Iredell.

"I've only a moment, Adam. We can't content ourselves with Maclaine's reply." Iredell paused and smiled. "I found myself thinking of you while he was speaking. I'll wager you were not satisfied."

Adam felt a surge of affection for his friend. Jemmy's awareness of their political differences served only to make him more considerate. If all men were like this one . . . "Very far from satisfied, Jemmy," he said. "Perhaps there is no answer to Caldwell short of the amendments he wants."

"And the amendments you want, Adam?" Iredell didn't wait for a reply. "I'd like to have the talk with you we spoke of yesterday. I'll be engaged for half an hour after this session is adjourned. Can I find you at the Star when I am at liberty?" He glanced toward the door.

Adam laughed and took Iredell's arm. "It would be real cruelty to keep you from the debate a moment longer. Yes, Jemmy, I'll be waiting for you."

While Iredell read the amendments Wilie Jones had sent, Adam looked around the common-room of the Star. The place had been almost empty when Jemmy and he began their talk half an hour before. Now it was crowded with delegates. Men moved from table to table, pausing to confer with friends or to take part in arguments. The air was heavy with smoke. Calls for ale and wine added to the general loud confusion.

Iredell finished his study of the papers and handed them back to Adam. "There's little new here," he said. "As nearly as I can tell these amendments are those offered in the Virginia convention, with a few added. The declaration of rights is almost identical with that proposed by Mason and Henry. We anticipated that Jones would offer them here." He looked steadily at Adam. "Remembering our conversation before you left for the Illinois country, I can't believe that you subscribe to all these. Some of them have merit. We who want the Constitution ratified now do not insist that it is perfect. We have amendments to offer ourselves. With Jones, we believe that it should be stipulated that the states retain all powers not delegated to the Congress or to the various Federal departments. But, Adam, the amendments we want can best be secured when we have ratified and have our own delegates in the new Congress."

Adam spread the papers before him. "You're right, Jemmy. I do not question all that is questioned here. The Constitution still seems to me fundamentally sound. My first concern is for this resolution." He picked up one of the sheets and read aloud. " 'Resolved, That a declaration of rights, asserting and securing from encroachment the great principles of civil and religious liberty, and the unalienable rights of the people, ought to be laid before Congress, and the convention of states that may be called, for their consideration, previous to the ratification of the Constitution on the part of the state of North Carolina.' "

Adam let the paper fall to the table. "I believe in the necessity for a declaration of rights, Jemmy. I believe in the necessity to reassure those who have doubts. If they are not reassured, the Constitution cannot work in our state and there will be growing discontent in every state. I wish that I might make myself believe the people would accept a promise that Congress will consider a bill of rights. I fear a promise will not be enough. One by one, states that want amendments have ratified, content with this promise. Perhaps it is time for one state to take a stand, to make its absence from the union the conscience of Congress."

Iredell was silent. He looked down at the table, then raised his head slowly. "I will not attempt to change your conviction about a bill of rights. I understand your view, though I cannot share it. But we have common ground, Adam. Both of us love our state. Believe me, if she rejects the Constitution now, she may be left alone. The other states are not bound to accept us at a later date. There may be no second chance. I beg you not to make your decision final now. In the next few days——"

"Jemmy! Jemmy Iredell!" Adam looked up to see Richard Spaight walking toward their table. He nodded to Adam and went on talking to Jemmy. "Johnston and I need your advice about how to meet the attack on the clause preventing suppression of the slave trade. It's my view that we should point out that this is a compromise with Northern states. I can explain to the convention——"

"A moment, Spaight." Iredell spoke abruptly. He turned to Adam. "I'm sorry. I see Johnston is waiting over there, and I'm afraid I must go. I pray that you will reconsider, my friend."

Adam walked across the room with Iredell and Spaight to where Johnston was standing. The Governor ignored his greeting and immediately began talking with Iredell. Adam walked away, aware of the stricken look on Jemmy's face; Jemmy was not the man to approve of this attitude of Johnston's toward an old friend.

In his bedchamber Adam found Cosmo, booted and spurred, lying on his bed. He tossed to Adam a political broadside he had been reading. "It seems that the Antis fear the Southern states will be dominated by the Northern. What are your views on that?" Cosmo smiled broadly.

Adam crumpled the broadside and threw it into the corner. Then, seeing Cosmo's perplexed look, he said, "I'm sorry. I didn't mean to be rude. I've had enough of politics for the day, enough of bitterness. I've hurt and been hurt, and I want no more of it now. By God, Cosmo, why can't men differ without hating!"

Cosmo stood up. "Your friends from the village, eh?"

"My friends from the village!" Adam was stripping off his shirt. "I think only Iredell remains my friend. And yet I can't blame them. I've lived in a country so strange to them that they can't be expected to understand how it has changed me."

Cosmo smiled again. "Cultivate the light touch, Adam. Find amusement. Go to the ball to-night."

"I can't avoid that." Adam began to lay out his clothes. "But there have been balls I've attended with more heart."

The ball at which a group of Hillsborough citizens entertained a number of the delegates was held in the house once occupied by Isaac Edwards, secretary to Governor Tryon. For Adam the handsome rooms were filled with memories of the days before Alamance when Hillsborough had been Tryon's summer capital. As he watched the dancers he could almost imagine Tryon among them, moving ponderously through a minuet with his lady or, in a mood of gaiety, stepping a lively contra-dance with a Hillsborough belle.

Thinking of those troubled times, Adam reflected that the Orange farmers who called themselves Regulators had lighted the first small blaze of the Revolution. Governor Tryon's response to the challenge of Alamance had been regarded then as a justifiable if ill-considered means of suppressing a revolt against law and order. But it was now clear that in summarily hanging a demented old man Tryon had placed himself on the side of tyranny. And the farmers who battled for their beliefs at Alamance had embodied the same spirit that later won heroes' honours for the men of Lexington.

James Iredell's voice at his side interrupted his thought. "A cheering sight, Adam! In what capital in America could one find a gathering of more distinguished gentlemen or fairer ladies?"

"Nowhere, Jemmy, I'm sure," Adam said, smiling. "But the lady I seek is not in Hillsborough."

"Nor is my Hannah." Iredell sighed. "I wonder sometimes if I am foolish to follow public affairs and accept political offices. It means long weeks and months away from home and wife. And sometimes it means a painful difference with a friend. I deplore Johnston's attitude, Adam."

"Say no more of it, Jemmy. Let's put aside politics to-night. Wouldn't your charming niece enjoy the frivolity?"

"Ah, Nellie!" Iredell chuckled. "If she had heard of this party, she would have walked from Edenton to be present. Come, Adam, let us repair to the punch-bowl and pour out a libation in honour of our absent ladies. Here is William Davie. He'll join us, I'm certain."

The three men made their way along the edge of the dancing-floor to a doorway at the far side of the ball-room. In the smaller room they found a group of men standing near the punch-bowl, listening rather self-consciously to a little white-haired Negro who was addressing them earnestly.

"Why, it's old Harry!" Davie exclaimed. "I thought he . . ." He hurried toward the circle of men. "Harry, why are you still here? I told you I wouldn't need you again to-night."

Harry's audience seemed relieved at the interruption, Adam thought. He noticed that Governor Johnston, Spaight and General Nash's elder son were among those who had been giving the old slave their respectful attention.

As Davie approached old Harry straightened his bent shoulders and beamed proudly, seeming not to hear the mild reproof in his master's voice. "Yes, sar, Gen'ral," he said, "yes, sar!" He turned to young Nash. "This here's Gen'ral Davie," he said confidentially. "I been his man since you' daddy gone. Yes, sar, he a fine man, mos' as fine as the old gen'ral."

Davie smiled and laid his arm affectionately on the Negro's shoulders. "And Harry is a fine and loyal servant, gentlemen. He was with General Nash at Germantown, and when Nash was shot from his horse Harry carried him out of the path of frightened horses and advancing soldiers while Nash tried to reassure his troops. 'Never mind me!' Nash shouted. 'I've had a devil of a tumble. Rush forward, boys! Rush on the enemy!' . . . Isn't that the way it was, Harry?"

The old man's face had clouded, and he nodded sadly. "Yes, sar, dat de way. Dem hosses runnin' round in de fog, and de pore old gen'ral he a-shoutin' to he men. . . . Tell the gen'lemen what de gen'ral say at de las', sar."

"They were noble words, gentlemen," Davie said solemnly. "You know them, I'm sure, and it was Harry who heard and reported them. 'From the first dawn of the Revolution,' Nash said, 'I have ever been on the side of liberty and my country.'"

"Yes, sar. And den he die." There were tears in the old Negro's eyes. "And evvybody know what a good man he was. Gen'ral Washin'ton he know. He tole he officers to come to my gen'ral's funeral, 'cause he say . . ." He frowned and looked appealingly at young Nash.

"General Washington himself wrote out the order," Nash said. "His words were 'All officers where circumstance permit of it will attend and pay this respect to a brave man who died in defence of his country.'"

"'A brave man,'" Harry repeated. "Yes, sar, he surely was!" He rubbed his eyes with the back of his gnarled hand.

Adam and the others stood in silence as the music of the minuet sounded from the ball-room behind them. The moment was at once touching and awkward. The men were embarrassed, but none ventured to intrude on the old slave's grief for his lost master.

At last Governor Johnston cleared his throat. "When you came in, Mr. Davie," he said, "Harry was about to tell us a story. I believe he said it concerned a horse named Roundhead. I'm sure the others, like me, are anxious to hear it."

Harry's face cleared instantly. Adam felt he could almost see the old man's mind relinquish one memory and seize on another scrap out of the dimming past. "Yes, sar, Roundhead—dat de hoss's name, all right!" Harry was smiling now, although tears still clung to his cheeks. He embarked on his tale with a confidence that indicated he had told it many times before. "Old Jedge Moore he have a nice daughter, Miss Sally, what married of my Gen'ral Nash. And de jedge he know my master like good hoss-flesh, so he send all de way crost de ocean for a mare called Highland Mary. And he give she to my gen'ral. And dey mate dey mare with de jedge's Morayland Montrose and git a might' fine-lookin' bay colt. And dey call dat colt Roundhead."

Harry paused and looked craftily at his audience. "Well, gen'lemen, I never see de use of dat name. His head he wasn't round a-tall! He had a fine long head jes' like any other colt."

The men laughed politely, and Harry, satisfied, continued. "Now, gen'lemen, I know dat hoss like it was my own chile. I fotched he up, fed he, brushed he and put de first little saddle on he back. I was purely upset when I come back and find de Tories done raid our place and take dat colt. I coulda tole 'em dat hoss wouldn't bring 'em no luck. Dat Roundhead he wasn't raised to be no Tory hoss, no, sar!" He halted again to wait for murmurs of approval.

"Well, one day I was attendin' at another battle over by Guilford Co't-house, and right in de battle I see dat hoss! Yes, sar, it was Roundhead all right, and a gen'leman in a red coat was ridin' on he. And I shouted right out, 'Look yonder at dat redcoat ridin' our Roundhead!' And who do you s'pose dat redcoat turned out to be?" He paused dramatically and surveyed his listeners. "Well, sar, it was Gen'ral Co'nwallis, de head of de whole Tory army! And he done pick my Roundhead for he own hoss!"

Harry nodded happily, relishing the exclamations of astonishment with which the men greeted the climax of his tale.

"Harry is quite right," Davie said. "The horse was indeed Roundhead. He went to his death that very day, shot down under Cornwallis. Now, Harry, it's very late. You'd best go back to the inn and get to bed." He led the old Negro out of the room.

The talk turned to Cornwallis and his stay in Hillsborough. Adam knew that in a moment they would settle down to fight the Revolution over. He set his punch-glass down and walked away. His attendance at the ball had been long enough to satisfy the demands of courtesy. He slipped out a side door and made his way through the garden to the street.

Near the Star he overtook De' Medici and Cabarrus. Cosmo said, "You've missed a fight, Adam. While you were dancing and drinking punch, rowdies attacked some Federalist delegates. I offered help and had my coat ruined for my pains." He showed Adam a rent in his sleeve. "Otherwise I'm not hurt. They've arrested a man named O'Shaughnessy who seems to have started the trouble."

They had come to the inn. As they stood under the light of the gallery lanthorns Cabarrus looked challengingly at Adam. "You see the sort of villains whose side you take." He turned sharply and went down the path.

The town clock was striking midnight. "I'm going to bed," Adam said.

"And I to the tap-room," Cosmo said. "The evening is still very young."

Adam walked slowly to his room. He had never felt more alone.

A Convention Ends

17 THE convention had begun in the bright sun of a July morning with a splendour of pomp and ceremony. It was ending eleven days later on a day of lowering clouds and intermittent showers. The dim light in the old church gave the scene an unreal, almost spectral quality. The restless stir and murmur of the galleries seemed magnified and distorted by the oppressive atmosphere. The faces

of the delegates reflected the strain of passionate debate through long periods of the bitterest division.

It was ending, but it had not ended. The tension was greater at this moment than ever before. Adam knew, as all knew, that the burden of proof still rested with the Federalists. Wilie Jones had held the greater strength in delegates when the convention was called to order. He held it still. A report of the committee of the whole would be considered by the house today. The last hopes of the Federalists might well depend on the speech Iredell was making now. If he failed to turn the tide, they failed and North Carolina would not enter the union when the final vote was cast tomorrow. He had been on his feet for more than twenty minutes, speaking with the profound conviction and eloquent reason which had won the admiration, if not the vote, of every delegate.

Adam listened with intense concentration. Iredell was approaching the full development of his argument. His voice rang across the floor. "This is a very awful moment. Mr. Chairman, on a right decision of this question may possibly depend the peace and happiness of our state for ages.

"When the new Constitution was proposed, it was proposed to the thirteen states. It was desired that all should agree if possible. But if that agreement could not be obtained, they took care that nine states at least might save themselves from destruction. Each state undoubtedly has this right on the first proposition of the plan. In my opinion, when any state has once rejected the Constitution it cannot claim to come in afterward as a matter of right.

"If it does not, in plain terms, reject but refuses to accede for the present, I think other states may regard this as an absolute rejection and refuse to admit us afterward. I know the temper of the convention is to take the course of not acceding for the present. Be warned!

"Gentlemen wish amendments. I believe none will deny the propriety of proposing some. The question, then, is whether it is most prudent for us to enter the union now and propose amendments, or to stay out until our amendments be agreed on by other states. I beg leave to state the consequences of either resolution.

"By adopting we shall be in the union with our sister states, which is the only foundation of our security and prosperity. We shall avoid the danger of a separation which may occasion animosity between us and other states and so sever us for ever. If we refuse to adopt, we shall lose the benefit which must accrue to other states. Their trade will flourish; their commodities will rise in value. Their distresses brought on by war will be removed. Ours, for want of these advantages, will continue.

"We have been happy in our connection with the other states. Our freedom derives from that union we now threaten to end. If we are to be separated, let every gentleman consider well the ground he stands on before he votes for the separation. Let him not have to reproach himself hereafter that he voted without due consideration of a measure that proved the destruction of his state!"

Iredell's last words crashed out like cannon fire. He finished with his arm extended, his finger pointing here and here as if singling out each delegate in the house. There was a moment of absolute silence, then bedlam. Federalists were on their feet cheering. Arguments broke out instantly in every part of the auditorium. Delegates pushed their way into the aisles for conferences before debate resumed. Elisha Battle, who was sitting as chairman, roared for order.

Adam saw that the Chowan men were among those clustered around Iredell. Jemmy had been magnificent. The days of debate had taken their toll of him. He looked pale and very tired as he accepted the congratulations of his followers. Impulsively Adam rose to join the group, then stopped suddenly. He would not be welcome there. The barrier remained between him and the men who had called him friend.

For, impressive as it was, Iredell's speech had not persuaded Adam. In his mind the dangers of signing without a bill of rights still far outweighed the dangers of staying out of the union. Yet, Adam knew, Iredell had unquestionably won votes. The answer to his warning must be effective and prompt. And it should be simple, very simple—something like the homely illustrations with which he had so often amused Iredell during their discussions of the Constitution. Suddenly Adam realized that he could answer Jemmy perhaps more effectively than any of the Antifederalist leaders. He would be a new voice in the convention, doubly effective because he was the only Chowan delegate opposed to signing. Could he speak against Iredell? There was no other choice. He would speak for a principle, not against a man.

Mr. Battle had stopped trying to restore order and was sitting glumly in his pulpit chair. It would be minutes before debate was resumed. Adam walked back to his seat, his mind busy with what he would say. It seemed to him now that this moment had been inevitable from the first. His mind went back over the events of the convention.

The pattern of division and contest had been clear since the second day when David Caldwell challenged the right of the makers of the Constitution to speak for the people. He expressed the first of the two principal objections of the Antifederalists—the conviction that the Constitution proposed a consolidation of the states rather than a union in which each would remain free to serve the best interests of its people. With Jones directing the attack, Judge Spencer, Bloodworth, McDowell and Caldwell pointed out the dangers to state sovereignty they saw in clause after clause. They were alarmed by the power of Congress to levy direct taxes and by the threat of tyranny in having Federal officials not directly controlled by the people. They asked whether the liberties of the people would not be violated by the Federal courts. They stormed at the clause forbidding the states to issue paper money. They argued that the power of Congress to impeach could be directed against state officials. They feared that the Northern states would dominate the Southern.

The pointed criticisms and questions of the Antis left the burden of discussion on their opponents. Iredell, Spaight, Johnston and Maclaine all took up the challenge, with Iredell assuming the greatest responsibility. He spoke more frequently and at greater length than any other delegate. His object was to conciliate, and of this he never lost sight. He defended, he removed objections, he persuaded, he appealed to interest. In all he strove to bring to life a national pride and a faith in the Constitution as the supreme law of the land offering peace, security and prosperity.

As he listened Adam recognized that he stood on a middle ground. He believed in Iredell's conception of the plan for union. He did not share many of the objections of the Antifederalists. He knew that speculators who had profited greatly from paper money had fostered in honest, principled men the fear that no funds would be left for debts, taxes and commerce if the worthless currency were abolished. He understood well that debtors to English subjects inspired a part of the attack on the judiciary because they believed Federal courts might be used for collection of their debts.

Yet with every day his conviction had grown that men like the candid, wise and temperate Spencer were right in their expression of the second great Antifederalist objection the lack of a bill of rights. No answer from Iredell, Johnston or Maclaine reassured Adam. He followed with eager approval Spencer's argument that the Constitution should expressly declare that rights and powers not given up to the United States were retained for ever by the states. He cheered McDowell's demand that the right of trial by jury in civil cases be secured to the humblest citizen. In the bill of rights Wilie Jones would submit to this convention Adam found these provisions. He found, too, guarantees of the rights of a free press, free speech, peaceable assembly and freedom of religion.

Abruptly Adam brought his thought back to the present. The furor that had followed Iredell's speech was subsiding. Delegates were returning to their seats. He felt calm and confident. He knew what he would say.

Elisha Battle sat forward in his chair and peered sharply at the house, looking very much, Adam thought, as if he were about to read a stern sermon to his Baptist congregation at Edgecombe. "If the gentlemen have concluded their recess," he drawled, "we may proceed with the business of this convention. I will remind the gentlemen that they have obligations to the authority of this chair."

There was a ripple of laughter, and Adam rose instantly. This was a stroke of luck. The friendly amusement of the delegates was keyed exactly to what he wished to say. He waited for Battle's recognition and began.

"Mr. Chairman, I rise with some hesitation to reply to my good friend Mr. Iredell. As many of you know, I have the highest and most sincere regard for his great learning. I am no orator. If I speak somewhat less formally than he, as I shall certainly speak less impressively, I ask you to believe that I view the question before us with a seriousness equal to his.

"It seems to me more prudent to propose amendments before, rather than after ratification. Let us suppose that two men entered into a partnership and employed a scrivener to draw up articles in a particular form. If on reading them they found errors—and all gentlemen here find some error in the Constitution—do you suppose either of the prospective partners would say, 'Let us sign it first and we shall have it altered hereafter'?"

A wave of laughter rolled over the house. Adam glanced at the Chowan men seated near him. Cabarrus was scowling. Hume's face was contorted with anger. But Iredell—God bless his great heart!—was smiling. Adam went on. "For me the objection can be stated very simply. I can see no power that guards our rights. I have heard it said that no tyranny was intended by the makers of the Constitution. I am sure this is true, and every gentleman owes the tribute of this understanding to the wise men who served us in Philadelphia. But, sirs, this is not *declared* to be so in the document itself. We cannot for ever rely on good intentions and the continuation of wise men in high office. The Constitution confers great powers on government, and I have great hopes for the union it contemplates. But let those powers be confined to their proper boundaries. Let us make plain our intention to abstain until those boundaries are set for all time!"

The calm he had felt before speaking remained with Adam as he took his seat. He could judge that his speech had been effective by the response of the house. Federalists and Antifederalists were clamouring for the attention of the chair. He felt a hand on his shoulder and looked up to see Spencer smiling at him.

"Our gratitude, sir! Well done! You have set the stage. Now watch the climax of the action." Spencer waved his hand toward the front of the church where Wilie Jones stood waiting to speak.

As was his habit Jones waited for absolute silence before he began. He spoke almost softly, and his manner somehow implied that it was the obligation of every man to hear. "The delegate from Edenton has told you of dreadful consequences if we do not immediately enter the union. Be not in the least alarmed. We run no risk of being excluded when we think it proper to come in. There will be a majority of the states—the most respectable, important and extensive states—desirous also of amendments and favourable to our admission.

"Great names have been mentioned here in support of the Federalist view. I beg leave to mention the authority of Mr. Jefferson." Jones stopped and smiled slightly. "I think his great abilities are well known to you. When the convention sat in Virginia Mr. Madison received a letter from him in which he said he hoped nine states would adopt the Constitution, not because it deserved ratification but to preserve the union."

A murmur rose from the delegates. Jones allowed it to grow until it threatened order. Then he held up his hand and spoke in a suddenly sharp tone over the subsiding hum. "But he wished that the other four states would reject it in order that there might be a certainty of obtaining amendments!"

This time the Antifederalist leader made no attempt to stop the discussion. He turned his back on the house and walked to his place, where he accepted a sheaf of papers from Bloodworth. When the delegates were quiet again he returned slowly to where he had stood.

"Mr. Spaight has reminded you that ten states have ratified. Allow me to add that New York will very probably make the eleventh. For my part, I would rather be out of the union indefinitely than adopt the Constitution in its present defective form!"

Instantly Jones silenced the outburst from the house. "Gentlemen! Order, if you please, and your firm attention. I hold in my hand a resolution stipulating certain amendments to be made before this state adopts the Constitution. I hand it to the clerk to read, and I ask consideration for it as the report of the committee of the whole."

Adam expected an outburst. None came. The delegates talked in whispers, but there was no acclaim or protest. The clerk's voice began to drone out the resolution and amendments. Only then Adam realized why the house had remained so curiously silent. Most were hearing the articles for the first time.

Adam was only dimly conscious of the words. "That a declaration of rights . . . securing from encroachment . . . the unalienable rights of the people . . . be laid before Congress . . . previous to the ratification . . ." He had pored over the document since receiving it from Jones. How long had it been since Jemmy and he sat at the Star with the document between them? It had been between them today, and their friendship had bridged it.

The clerk was reading the amendments now. Adam shifted impatiently in his seat. It was over at last. There could be no doubt that Jones's well-disciplined forces would vote to adopt his resolution to-morrow. After that the vote taking North Carolina out of the union would be only a formality. Adam felt no sense of triumph. He had acted as his mind and heart dictated he must. But his state would not be part of the new nation, the nation whose way to freedom she had helped to open. He could take no pleasure in that fact.

The reading of the amendments was completed. The chair was entertaining a motion that the resolution lie on the table until to-morrow morning. Adam forced his way into the press of delegates leaving the church. He found Iredell waiting for him at the door, his hand extended.

Adam grasped it firmly. "Jemmy, it was a hard choice, I——"

"A choice you made in good conscience, Adam." Iredell looked at his friend soberly. "Perhaps I understand more than you think of what guided your reasoning. I do not know your Illinois country. But I remember when I first came to America from England. Its vastness and promise overwhelmed me. I wanted to realize all that promise, and I worked to that end with what talents I had. The Constitution seems to me to make all I desired secure. It does not seem so to you, but you have a different horizon now. Perhaps the Albemarle is your England. Good-bye, Adam, Godspeed!"

Adam was conscious of a constriction in his throat as Jemmy left. The church was almost deserted now. He looked briefly back into its gloom and then walked slowly through the doors. A fine mist was in the air, and Adam was grateful for its coolness on his face.

Stephen Cabarrus and John Hume were waiting for him in Margaret Lane. He halted as they advanced stiffly. Cabarrus was the spokesman. "I'll be brief, Rutledge. Unless the Chowan vote against Jones is unanimous, you will be ostracized. If you stand with Jones, you had far better remove permanently to the Illinois country that has so sadly corrupted you." Cabarrus' face was suddenly softer. "Adam, we beg it of you. Do not turn your back now——" He broke off and walked quickly away.

Hume remained. He strutted forward. "Cabarrus is too soft a man for this job. I'll say what's required. We have no use for traitors in Edenton. If you return, I'll give you reason to leave again—and promptly."

Adam's arm leaped out. He seized Hume's shoulder in a grip that almost lifted him from the ground. "Old friends have privileges you do not enjoy, Hume. Consider your threat again where you can remain cool." With a swift, powerful motion Adam spun the man away from him and sent him catapulting to the ground. Hume struck a muddy puddle hard enough to raise a shower of spray. He managed to crawl out of the water, but lay stunned and gasping for breath beside the road. Without a backward glance Adam strode swiftly toward the Star.

In their room he found Cosmo packing saddle-bags. "I'm leaving to-night," he announced as Adam came in. "Those acres at Bath call me, and after my talks here I can hope to hold and plant them."

Adam stripped off his coat and boots and flung himself on the bed. "I had hoped for your company in Edenton. Cosmo, I spoke against Jemmy Iredell today. Against him and for the measure the Albemarle planters think ruinous." Adam stood up and walked to the window. The rain and failing light made the mountains invisible. He tried to recall their serenity and beauty.

Cosmo stood behind him. "You will not be sorry. I know your heart. Trust in it."

They remained quiet at the window. Herk came in to take Cosmo's saddle-bags downstairs. His friend turned Adam about and clasped his hand. "We shall meet soon. Good fortune!" Adam heard the clatter of Cosmo's spurs on the stairs. The room seemed very empty. A blithe spirit, Cosmo, but a firm friend. Two men whom he admired had given him understanding today. He did not fear to-morrow.

The morning was fair, and the old church was crowded. Every one in Hillsborough who could gain admittance was there. Crowds lined the walk outside. The women's clothes made the balconies gay with colour. There were subdued whisperings, the shuffle of feet, the click of fans. The mood was formal. There would be no debate. This was an occasion of ceremony.

As Adam waited for the opening of the session he thought of the church as he had seen it before the Revolution. It was Church of England then. Now it was used by all denominations, most frequently by Presbyterians. The delegates were seated in pews once occupied by royal Governors and their ladies, by Lord Cornwallis and his officers. There was a sense of history here and also, Adam thought, of what endured through change. There had been bitterness and even hatred these days just past. But there had been hope and devout purpose, too. This morning the old church imposed its full and serene dignity on the convention.

The Reverend David Caldwell stepped forward and prayed for the blessing of God on the men seated here today. There was silence, then a brief stir in the galleries. Thomas Person rose. Samuel Johnston, who as president of the convention had again taken the chair, gave him recognition. The moment had come.

Person moved that Mr. Jones's resolution be accepted by the committee of the whole, and his motion was seconded by John Macon. Johnston put the question, and the clerk began slowly to call the roll. A murmur rose in the galleries with the mounting total of "ayes"—votes that declared North Carolina would stand firm for a declaration of rights. Adam heard in the rising sound a reaffirmation of the love of Carolinians for liberty. He heard it as an exalting music.

"Adam Rutledge." He thought he spoke normally. But his "aye" seemed a shout, resounding through the church.

It was swiftly over. Person's motion carried, 184 to 84, and the convention quickly concurred in the committee report. North Carolina had neither ratified nor rejected the Constitution. Alone among the states she had said, "Secure our rights!"

Adam left the church as the convention took up the business of fixing a permanent capital. It was generally agreed, he knew, that the site would be on or near the plantation of Isaac Hunter in Wake County. But the selection would hold the delegates another day or more, and Adam would not wait.

He left by a side door and made his way to the Star. Herk was waiting for him. His saddle-bags were packed. He had only to settle his account and mount his horse for the long ride eastward to Queen's Gift and Mary.

BOOK THREE

Queen's Gift

Ulysses' Return

18 IT WAS very late. Mary Rutledge was sitting in Duke Roger's study with Baron von Pollnitz's book *Love Life at the Saxon Court* on the small table in front of her. The Baron had presented it to her earlier in the evening when he and Lady Anne visited Queen's Gift and joined her at supper.

The night was more than usually cool for early August, and the air was very clear. The perfume of the garden came through an open window, and the smell of the pines was pungent and compelling. Instead of taking up the book Mary let her thoughts wander to the evening just past.

It was the first time this ill-assorted pair had visited her alone, the first time she had had the opportunity to talk with them together. Ill-assorted was an unpleasant term, but she felt it was accurate in the case of Lady Anne and the Baron.

He was reserved, Lady Anne the opposite. She had the mouth of a petulant woman. Her beauty was physical only—no warmth shone from her blue eyes. And she was patently bored by the Baron. Time after time during the evening she had interrupted him contemptuously. Mary thought he bore her sharp comments with good patience and more calm than was usual in a European.

Lady Anne had the studied rudeness of the fashionable circles in which she moved. During her previous visit and again this evening Mary had seen her examine appraisingly the furniture, ornaments and portraits in the drawing-room. But Lady Anne made no comment until they were seated at table. Then she remarked that the Lowestoft service was particularly pleasing.

The Baron said, "I understand china-ware very little, but I do recognize excellence in food. This ham is superior to our Westphalian. If I am not rude, may I ask you where you purchase such a delicacy?"

Mary laughed. "With those words you have endeared yourself to both my cook and my butler. Hams are their specialty. He oversees all the cooking. Perhaps one day you would like to see our smoke-house." She turned to Lady Anne, who was twirling her wine-glass in her slim white fingers. "We country housekeepers are very proud of our hams and bacon. We think them quite as fine as Cumberland hams."

Lady Anne's tone was indifferent. "I've always left such matters to my housekeeper and steward. I never thought much about food, although I must say Northumberland did. He was very much the country squire. Hunting, shooting, farming—those were his main interests."

Mary's eyes twinkled a little. "So I remember."

Lady Anne looked up quickly. "Oh, yes, I'd forgotten that you know my former husband. Of course, and your grandmother was Rhoda Chapman, who married Sir Nigel Carstairs. That accounts for all this."

"All what, my dear?" The Baron turned to her.

"Why, this house. The furnishings in the drawing-room, the hunting prints in the study, the elegant service. It's the house of a fashionable woman."

"We have no fashionable folk here in the county," Mary said. "We do have gentlewomen and gentlemen."

The Baron nodded. "I told you that, my dear Anne, but you've been too busy gambling with Montague to look about you."

"Well, Charles is on his way to New York. I shall have time now to look about. When do you hunt, Mrs. Rutledge?"

"Usually we begin in the latter part of September."

"Ah? I suppose you have hunters and a pack."

"My husband has his hounds from the Pitchley. Very good, we think them."

Lady Anne raised her brows. "Who is the M.F.H.?"

"My husband. He will be anxious to meet you both when the Hillsborough convention has completed its work." Mary rose from the table. To Ebon she said, "Serve brandy in Duke Roger's office, please."

"Yes, ma'am. I done took de decanter in dere."

Mary led her guests to the pine-panelled room. Lady Anne, glass in hand, stood for a long time before Duke Roger's portrait. "There," she said at last, "is a man. They don't rear them like that in our times." She lifted her glass and made a little bow. "Here's to you, my bold gentleman! Rest well, wherever you are."

Mary said nothing, but she felt irritation surging over her. Duke Roger, she felt certain, would not have been flattered by a tribute from this woman.

Lady Anne gazed a moment longer, then without a word she walked through the open door onto the gallery.

The Baron broke the silence. "I like it here so much, Mrs. Rutledge. Do you know of a plantation such as this which might be purchased?"

Mary was astonished. She'd had no idea these people contemplated settling in America. "I cannot think of a single plantation. You know, Baron, the people here don't sell land."

He smiled a little. "So I have found out. You seem surprised at my inquiry. Believe me, I am quite serious. I want to live in this new country."

"But—— Forgive me, but I wonder if your wife would be content here."

The Baron's mouth showed unaccustomed firmness. "Do not be astonished that many Europeans desire the blessings of liberty. From the year 1776 my chief wish was to be here. I arrange my affairs in Europe, but not until now do I have the pleasure to come."

He looked down on his interlocked fingers, silent. Mary said nothing. Suddenly he continued, "I was a chamberlain of the King of Prussia. I have letters from him, granting me my dismissal. I have no debts, and I am possessed of an ample fortune."

He turned his eyes toward the gallery. They could hear Lady Anne walking up and down, see the flutter of her skirts as she passed the door.

The Baron drew his chair closer to Mary's and lowered his voice. "My good fortune was strengthened by my marriage. I would not consider marriage until Anne consented to go to America. No compulsion, no thought of amelioration of future, but I say it boldly: the whole ambition to be a citizen of Columbia was my only motive." His eyes, looking earnestly into Mary's, were very blue and unwavering.

She had no words to answer the earnest man. He wanted no answer; this was an outpouring of his inner thoughts and dreams.

"I wish I had more flowing English to express my thoughts. I worship the exertions of spirit shown in the beginning of the Revolution. A grand idea! This Federal plan now adopted by a majority of your states leaves me no room to repent my choice." He rose from the hearth and filled his glass with brandy.

Mary said, "Baron, you rouse my admiration because you have recognized the goodness, the selfless courage of our leaders and our men."

"Ah, yes, courage, infinite courage! Now I must find land. I sometimes write little pamphlets on agriculture, Madam Rutledge. Some day I will send you my small contributions. You will like them better than the book on the Saxon Court."

Lady Anne came into the room in time to hear the last sentence. She smiled a cruel little smile. "You would think from the title that the Baron's mind runs to love. I assure you it does not. He thinks more of an acre of earth than the amours of Saxon princes."

The Baron flushed painfully. Lady Anne held out her hand. "The evening has been delightful. So pleasant for us, cooped up as we are in that stuffy tavern. I envy you your lovely, cool house. May we come again?"

"Oh, please come," Mary said politely. "I shall look forward to it. And I hope my husband will soon be here. He and the Baron will have much in common, for he too loves land."

"I hear he is very handsome," Lady Anne said. There was a sly, secret smile on her lips as she turned to leave.

Alone now in the study, Mary thought with sadness of the Baron's farewell. She had watched from the gallery as Lady Anne got into the carriage Mr. Horniblow had hired for her. Suddenly the Baron had turned and run up the steps. "Madam, I don't know what came over me to talk so much of my own affairs. Will you please pardon?" His smile was very boyish and engaging as he lifted her hand to his lips. "It must be because you have a heart that is kind; so very *simpatica.*"

Then he had abruptly run down the steps to the carriage. Lady Anne's comment had carried clearly to the gallery. "Whatever did you turn back for? You have talked unceasingly all evening. I am sure our hostess was frightfully bored."

Mary had watched the carriage move swiftly down the tree-lined avenue, its lights bobbing in the shadows. For a moment she had stood, listening to the night sounds. Down on the quarters line her people were singing in rhythmic harmony with the lapping water and the whip-poor-will's plaintive cry. Then she had returned to the study and the Baron's book.

It was too late to begin reading now, she decided. She went to her room. One of the housemaids got up from a pallet in front of her bedroom. Her personal maid slept in an adjoining room. House-boys patrolled the grounds all night. She was safe and secure, guarded by her people.

When she wakened the sun was at ten o'clock. She had overslept. She had planned to ride over to Mulberry Hill for breakfast with Anne Blount, but that was not feasible now. She threw a light robe about her and went to the window. A yardman was cutting the lawn with a small scythe. Little Negro boys were brushing off the walks with brooms made of rushes and broom corn.

Chaney came into the room, followed by a small boy carrying a tray. Chaney took the tray and deposited it on a small table. "Honey, here is you' breakfast. Eat every mouthful, and den I tell you somepin."

"What, Chaney? What's the secret? Why are the boys so busy with the lawn and the walks, digging up weeds between the bricks? I've been trying for weeks to get Cyph at that work."

"I tole him, Miss Mary. I tole dat Cyph a dozen times dis spring to putten salt on dey brick crack. He don' do hit. He's good for nothin', he is." She sat on a stool by the bed. "I've made little raisin tarts and a sponge-cake. We got six broilers ready and coolin' in de spring-house. Yesterday I cook a big ham. Felt it in my bones, somebody's comin'."

"Chaney, who is coming?" Mary tapped a tea-spoon on her cup. "Tell me at once!"

"Last night, Ebon he dream about he big hoss gallopin' up de pathway. He's nigh done dream about Master. This mornin' de old black hen done lay an egg wid a big double yolk. I break it. I cook it for you' breakfast. I say to myself, Bless de Lord! Master is comin' home dis very day."

Mary pushed the tray from her knees. She caught Chaney's fat shoulder. "Tell me instantly. Do you know he is coming? Has any one from Edenton seen him?"

"No'm. Not nobody come here dis mornin'. But he's comin' 'fore sun sets dis night. Ebon he know. I know. Yes'm, Master be here dis night. He bedchamber all made up wid fine new sheets, and everything ready."

Mary said, "Chaney, how could you get my hopes up with nothing but a dream to go on?"

"Two dreams, Miss Mary. Ebon's an' mine. He dream about dat big debbil stallion Master rides, an' I dreams about Master heself. Den dis mornin' de twin egg . . . dat's de both of you. 'Tain't right you don't believe." She gathered up the dishes and the breakfast tray and departed in a huff.

Mary was restless all morning, moving from room to room. She sat at her harpsichord a few minutes. She took up knitting and then put it down. The Baron's book could not hold her attention.

Chaney, in the dining-room, said to Ebon, "She's trompin' an' trompin' jes' like de old master. Maybe she believe what I say jes' a little."

She was interrupted by Mary: "Ebon, please send a boy for my mare. I'm going to ride."

She turned her horse into the Sound road and rode along the shore. When she arrived at Mulberry Hill she found Anne Blount had gone to Greenfield to visit the Creecys for the day. She turned her horse homeward. It was almost noon, and her bay mare was in a lather.

She pulled at the reins; the horse stopped and stepped directly on a cottonmouth. In an instant the snake was wrapped around the horse's leg. Mary tried to reach it with her crop, but couldn't. The mare was terrified. Her whole body trembled and quivered. Mary said, "Go on, you silly!" But the horse refused to budge.

Mary thought, I must make her run; then she will cast off the snake's body. She brought her crop down smartly on the mare's rump. The horse leaped forward, casting the snake clear. Mary leaned sideways so that the long writhing body missed her face, but it grazed her hand. Like the mare, she was quivering all over. She clapped her heel into the mare's side. The horse, released, flew like the wind for home.

Mary went directly upstairs and called for a bath. She scrubbed violently, trying to rid herself of the feeling of the snake's body against her hand.

Chaney put her head into the room. "Why fo' you scrub skin right off you' body?" Mary told her. Chaney's black face broke into a broad grin, showing her strong white teeth. "Dat what I say. Mr. Adam he come dis day. Snake he always bring good luck."

After dinner Marcy came to the office. He had just returned from Edenton. Nothing had been heard from Hillsborough, he reported, and no one had returned from the convention. He turned his broad straw hat in his hands nervously. "I don't know as I should tell you this, Mrs. Rutledge, but every black man and woman on this plantation *knows* that Mr. Adam is coming home today."

Mary said, "Yes, Marcy. Chaney and Ebon both had tales this morning. How do you think they got the idea?"

"God knows, miss. The longer I work among them, the less I understand.

It may be silly, but I've got the idea they *do* know things we don't know." He ran his hand through his curly sunburned hair, his honest red-brown eyes meeting hers squarely. "I believe Mr. Adam will be here before sunset. We are all ready for him. The tobacco harvest is completed. All the crops will be good."

Mary smiled a little. "I can't help believing he will come—perhaps because I want him home so desperately."

Adam Rutledge, followed by his body servant Hercules, rode up the long driveway just as the sun was dropping behind the green wall of trees on the Tyrrell shore.

Mary heard shouts of welcome from the Negro house servants. Slaves were pouring out of the cabins along the quarters line. The Negroes still in the fields threw down their hoes and ran along the rows. They gathered under the great tulip trees at the end of the garden. The women's bright turbans and calico dresses made the garden bloom in exotic splendour as they swayed rhythmically, clapping their hands to the incessant beat of drums. Over and over they chaunted their welcoming song:

> I am calling you loud, Lord of the Rivers.
> Rich Lord, I am calling you home.
> You have come home from a journey.
> Great Lord, let us rest awhile under the fig trees.
> We may leave our loads there.
> We are calling you, Great Lord of the Rivers.
> *Let the drums roll! Let the drums roll!*

As Adam ran up the steps toward her Mary murmured, "Dear Lord, I thank you."

Adam took his wife in his arms and bent his head so that his hungry lips might find hers. "How tall you are, my dear, how tall!" she murmured. "How tall, how strong and bronzed from the wind and the western sun!" She hid her face against his shoulder for a brief moment, then stepped back. Others were waiting—Marcy, the overlooker; the house servants, smiling, welcoming, bowing. Adam greeted each one in turn.

After a word to his wife he ran down the steps to the garden and stood before the field slaves, the women and the children. An old man, Puti, stepped forward and folded his arms across his chest. Bowing his head, he spoke the ancient words of greeting: *"Moni. Moni.* De master comes, our *bambo* comes, and we are made glad at his coming. He comes like de *kabrumbula,* de whirlwind. Suddenly he goes. Suddenly he returns. He goes from his people at de planting. He returns at de season of de dry grass. Welcome."

The crowd behind the old man shouted *"Cherezana! Cherezana!"*

Adam spoke to them in their language, which he had learned from Herk. "*Moni,* my people. I return. It is good to see your faces with smiles. Today you shall have extra rum. You may roast pigs. You may make feast, and for three days your burdens may be laid down. You may dance and take pleasure that your master returns from his long journey. *Weruka*—leave and go away. *Marisa*—it is finished."

Mary watched the delight in the faces of old and young as Adam spoke. When he dismissed them Puti gave the ceremonial salute, and they all trooped away toward the quarters, led by Puti and Herk. What wonders Herk will tell them! Adam thought.

Adam and Mary entered the house together. Adam looked about him. "How lovely you have made our home, my little Mary!" He put his arm about her waist. They walked slowly up the winding stair. The house was quiet now. The servants had gone; the throbbing drums and the singing were far away. Adam held his wife close. "It has been so long. So long, my little Mary. So very long."

Adam did not mention the convention until Marcy joined him in Duke Roger's office after supper. "The Antifeds won the first heat," he said then in answer to Marcy's question. "A clear-cut victory."

"You mean we are not to ratify?"

"Well, that's not exactly the right way to put it. A declaration of rights must be added to the Constitution before we will accept it." He went on to explain the debatable issues.

Marcy shook his head. "The Edenton Federals will be very gloomy," he remarked when Adam had finished. "They went away in the expectation that ratification was almost a foregone fact."

"They did not count on the West, Marcy."

Marcy said, "Mr. Wilie Jones was too much for them, eh? There is a smart, shrewd man, getting out among farmers to look at their crops or talking when they bring their brood mares to be bred to his fine stallions. I've seen him sitting on the top rail of the paddock fence, talking politics. You wouldn't expect that such an aristocratic gentleman could talk so easily with common folk."

"Jones is a persuasive man, certainly. His side won handily, a good strong majority." Adam followed Marcy's gaze and saw Mary standing in the doorway, a stricken look on her face.

"Adam, do you mean the Federals were defeated? Did the convention vote to stay outside the union?"

Adam repeated words he had heard at the convention. "North Carolina is now a sovereign republic."

Mary clasped her hands together. Her face was troubled. "I can't believe it. I can't. Jemmy Iredell said . . . He was so confident of success."

"So were Samuel Johnston and Stephen Cabarrus. I suppose Hugh

Williamson feels the same. He didn't come down from New York." Adam was watching Mary closely.

She sank into a chair by the table as though her knees refused to support her. "Poor Jemmy! He must feel dreadful. I didn't believe it possible that we could be defeated."

"Jemmy made a great fight. He and Davie carried the weight of the Federal cause."

"How could we lose, Adam? How could we?" Mary exclaimed. "It's so important that we stand by the union!"

"There are other considerations, Mary, equally as important as standing by the union," Adam said. He hesitated. "I'm afraid that you've heard only one side."

She spoke heatedly. "I wouldn't listen to Wilie Jones ever! What does he know about what is best for us?"

"I'm afraid the eastern and western sections of the state are of different opinions. But let's not talk about it now. I don't want you to be upset on my first evening at home. Besides, I've sat on hard church benches from the twenty-first of July to the second of August, listening to debates, wrangling, fighting, name-calling. By Gad, it's worse than fighting a battle! Let's have some music. You've no idea how often I've longed to hear you play. Come."

Marcy rose. "I'll be going along. It's good to have you home again, sir."

Adam walked the length of the gallery with him. "I voted with the Antifederalists, Marcy," he said. "I believe firmly that we must safeguard our liberties."

Marcy didn't speak for a few moments. Then he said, "Your vote for the Antifederalists won't be popular around here, sir."

"I realize that, but I couldn't do otherwise and live with my conscience. The only thing that worries me is my wife. I didn't realize she'd be so concerned."

"Mrs. Rutledge is mighty strong for Federalism. I reckon that's all she's heard in the neighbourhood."

"Yes."

"There're plenty of Antifeds here," Marcy said, "but not among your friends. Frazier the farrier is their leader." Adam said nothing. Marcy went on. "I've come to think there's something to the Antis' viewpoint, Mr. Rutledge. I've been reading Mr. Mason's bill and what they printed in the paper when Mr. Iredell answered, calling himself Marcus. He's a fair, fine lawyer, Mr. Iredell is, but he's not close to the common folk, no more than the Governor. . . . Good night, sir."

"Good night, Marcy. You have always been a strong right arm to me." Adam went into the drawing-room and sat down in a fireside chair. He watched Mary as she sat at her harpsichord. The candlelight was soft; shadows came and went on her small heart-shaped face and on her slim, straight body as she bent slightly to the keyboard. To-morrow he would tell her, but not now. To-night would be their own. Let it be untroubled by outside cares and worries. Let it be a night for a man and a woman who loved deeply.

Adam told his wife the following morning. They had been riding about the plantation while Mary explained what had been accomplished in his absence. The air was alive with the fragrance of pine forests, and from the small mill in the woods came the sharp, pleasant smell of freshly sawed wood. They rode down to the narrow beach and dismounted where the cypress trees stood deep in the water. It had long been a favourite spot of theirs. The bank was high, and they could see up the Albemarle Sound to where the waters of the Roanoke and the Chowan met at the fishery and mingled with the waters of the Sound. Avoca, the Indians had called the point—"the meeting of the waters." Downstream they could see for miles not quite so far as Roanoke Island, but it was easy to imagine that spot where the first English settlements had been made so many years ago.

They sat on a log. Mary said, "We should build a belvedere here with benches. Do you remember? It was here that we decided to make our home at Queen's Gift, since your house at Rutledge Riding had burned."

"I well remember," Adam said. "You were ambitious to make Queen's Gift the best plantation in the county. I think you have almost realized your ambition, my sweet. It is as nearly perfect as one can hope for with limited acreage."

She looked at him quickly. "Limited? I don't understand. We have almost the acreage that Samuel Johnston has."

"I mean really large acreage, where planters count in thousands, while we count in hundreds." Now I have done it, Adam thought. She will know I am thinking of the Illinois country. I hope she doesn't become alarmed. The subject wants a careful approach. But not now. This other thing comes first. I can wait no longer.

"Mary," he said, "I have to talk about the convention. There is something I must tell you."

She turned her face to him; her questioning eyes sought his. "What is it, Adam?"

He took her hand and held it in both of his. "Mary, I am bound to tell you before you hear it from any one else."

She interrupted, "You are going west again! I knew it. I felt it!"

"No, it is something else. Don't say anything, don't interrupt me until I've told you why I voted against ratification now. Along with the Anti-federalists, I want a declaration of rights added to the Constitution before North Carolina goes into the union."

His words brought Mary to her feet. She started to speak, but he laid his hand gently across her red lips. "Until last night I did not realize how strongly you felt." She tried to turn her face away, but he put both hands against her cheeks and kissed her, gently at first, then strongly. She did not withdraw; neither did her lips grow soft under his caress. Then he told her of the things he had seen in the West, of the people he had talked to, and their fears. Of the days at Hillsborough during which his conviction grew stronger, although he postponed his decision until he had heard the arguments of both sides.

Mary heard him through without comment. Before he finished he was pacing up and down the path in front of her. Her face, her eyes betrayed nothing. Adam watched her, anxiety rising in him.

"You did not tell me," she said, her voice low. "You wrote nothing that betrayed your thoughts."

"I could have written only of indecision. By the time I knew my mind it was too late. I knew I would see you as soon as a letter could reach Queen's Gift."

"Yes, then it was too late." Her voice was flat, lifeless. She stood motionless as the trees behind her.

He was aware, in the silence, of the movement of the water, the wind sighing softly through the tree-tops. Beauty surrounded them, quietude and an ecstasy of beauty. A loneliness came to him. Something had gone, some vague loveliness had passed him by. Was Mary thrusting him away from her? Was she closing her mind, her dear brave heart to him!

"Mary, you must think about this. Try to understand what is happening in the world about us. Do not close your mind to new ideas. Do not close your heart to me, my sweet, sweet girl. Have faith in me. See with my eyes, not the eyes of others. Look toward the mountains, love."

She turned away. He caught the faint words on her lips. "I will try, Adam. Do not press me now. I must think. I must think. Always you have seemed to me strong and wise, solid as a rock. Now . . ."

"I hope I am still strong, my girl . . . and perhaps wise. I want you to believe as I believe. But if you can't see my way . . . I cannot help it. There is no other way for me than the one I have chosen."

They rode home through the quiet of the forest. When they dismounted at Queen's Gift guests were awaiting them—Lady Anne Stuart, Sylvia Hay, young Dr. Moray.

Adam went forward to meet the strangers. There was a smile of welcome on his lips, but in his heart was profound sadness. Mary mentioned their names to her husband and excused herself. "I must change my habit. I'll be down in a moment."

Lady Anne turned to Adam. "Edenton is so hot and so dull. Every man in the village, I think, must have gone to this convention they are talking about. I don't understand conventions. What are they for?" She stood close, looking up into his eyes with round-eyed bewilderment.

Adam led his guests to the gallery. "We must make laws and a constitution," he said, smiling at her.

"But why a constitution? *We* don't have a constitution, do we?"

Sylvia Hay watched Lady Anne. She's trying the innocent act, she thought. She won't be happy until she has snared this magnificent male creature.

"You govern by acts of Parliament, as you well know." Adam's blue eyes twinkled a little.

Lady Anne smiled. "Well, perhaps I *did* know. I had a husband once who sat in the House of Lords and did something about laws. It's all very stupid, I think. Laws and more laws, all made to be broken. Else how would solicitors make a living?"

Dr. Moray turned to Sylvia. "Would you like to walk in the garden, Miss Hay?" Sylvia took his arm, and they wandered away together. Lady Anne settled her fluttering skirts into graceful folds. "Good! Now we can talk. I have heard nothing but Adam Rutledge since I came to the village." Her voice dropped to a lower, more intimate key. "I thought you would never come home, Adam Rutledge." She touched the sleeve of his coat with delicate fingers. "Now that I have seen you, I realize they didn't tell half the story."

Adam, standing at the rail, bowed slightly. "Praise from a beautiful woman is doubly dangerous."

"You are taunting me. I do declare I am quite, quite serious. You are so handsome with your bronzed skin and your yellow hair. So strong and bold-looking. Are you bold?"

"Perhaps. If occasion demands."

"I should like to see you in a bold mood."

"Again you flatter me. Beware—I might lose my head."

"Is it so remiss for a man to lose his head? I think it delightful, don't you?"

"Must I commit myself?"

Lady Anne clapped her hands. "This is delightful! Quite like a theatre conversation—a play by Mr. Sheridan or perhaps one of the Restoration comedies. They were bolder; even the men were bolder and took their pleasure where they found it."

Adam opened his snuff-box and took a pinch, touching his nostrils with a linen handkerchief. He drew a chair near hers. "You speak readily of boldness. What meaning do you give the word? Boldness may be brazen, it may be courageous, or again it may be mere brashness. Tell me your interpretation. Then I may answer."

She leaned forward, her lips half parted. The lace about her low-cut bodice fell away, showing her cream-white rounded breasts. She made a little *moue*. "You are teasing me, Mr. Adam Rutledge." She was taken aback that this strong vital man at her side was not awed by her condescension.

His answers to her quips were easy and assured. No country yokel he. She changed her tactics. "Let us have done with frivolities. You and I have something more serious to discuss."

"The tobacco crop or the price of pork?" His eyes were laughing now.

She tapped his shoulder with her little fan. "No, no. You sound like my husband the Baron. He is forever talking about land and crops and writing little dissertations on agriculture."

Adam showed interest. "I must meet the Baron."

Lady Anne gave him a long, level look in which there was exasperation and annoyance. Her comment was forestalled, for Mary came out onto the gallery. Adam drew up a chair for her, and she thanked him with a nod. "Where is the Baron?" she asked Lady Anne. "I am sure he and my husband have one thing in common."

Lady Anne said, "You mean farming, I presume. My husband went out to River Plantation to see the boys. He says he gets lonely for them. I confess I'm glad to have them away at a good school. I understand Mr. Earle is an excellent scholar."

"Yes, he is. And his daughter Ann is a wonderful teacher."

Lady Anne wrinkled her brow thoughtfully. "I'm not sure a woman teacher would be firm enough. However, it's the best arrangement we can make here, so it will have to do for the present."

"Believe me, Miss Earle will have discipline," Adam said. "I will do myself the honour of calling on the Baron when he returns."

"Please do. He has missed the company of cultivated men. I am longing for James Iredell to return." She walked to the rail and beckoned to Sylvia. "Come along, my dear. We must start back to the village."

Adam pressed them to stay for supper. He dreaded to be alone with Mary until she had had time to get accustomed to his changed political viewpoint. He talked for a moment with Sylvia Hay as they walked to the carriage, and he judged her a most attractive young woman.

He shook hands cordially with Dr. Angus Moray. The broad-shouldered Scot with the craggy face had an honest, straightforward look, Adam thought. "Come down early some evening," he said to Moray. "We'll sail over to Eden House. It's a pleasant sail, and the Eden House people are delightful."

The doctor promised. "I'm thinking of staying on in Edenton," he told Adam. "Dr. Armitage has made me rather a good offer to go in with him."

"Splendid!" Adam said. "The doctor has been overworked ever since the Revolution."

Marcy came up the steps as the guests were driving off. He had a lanthorn in his hand. "Sir, the little sorrel mare is due to drop her colt. Old Eph says she will be in difficulties. I thought you had better know about it. She's one you had bred to Mr. Wilie Jones's English stallion."

"I'll change my clothes and come right down to the stables. Don't wait for me, Marcy. I don't want anything to happen to her with her first colt. Perhaps we'd better send some one to town for the farrier. He's the best in stubborn bornings."

Marcy hesitated a moment. "Sir, I took the liberty of speaking to the young doctor this evening. He says he's experienced with animals as well as human beings."

"Good! Send a groom after Dr. Moray. He just left. Get Mel Frazier, too. I don't want anything to go wrong."

Adam found Mary in the office. She was standing at the window, looking out at the water. He went to her and put his arm about her shoulder. "Looking at the new moon, dear? Is it dry or wet?"

"It's a wet moon, Adam. I'm glad the tobacco is in," she answered.

Adam kissed her lightly on her smooth brow. "Don't wait up, my sweet. Brown Betty is going to have her colt."

"You expect trouble?"

"One never knows. Marcy has sent for Dr. Moray, who, it seems, knows about animal surgery. I'm going to change." He went upstairs, whistling as he took the steps two at a time. Mary thought, He is already settling down into plantation ways, unmindful of the change he has forced into my life.

He stopped on his way down. Putting his head inside the door, he called to her, "If I'm not back by supper-time, have Ebon bring me some journey bread and a jug of milk. If things are bad, I won't leave the stables."

Adam was not back when supper was announced, so Mary ate alone. Afterward she wandered about the house. She was restless, unable to settle down to read. The long twilight gave way to dusk and darkening shadows. The crescent moon moved across the heavens. Mary saw lanthorns bobbing about in the lot. She knew Adam was anxious to raise a colt by Wilie Jones's stallion Medley. She well remembered seeing that grey stallion at the Jones plantation, The Grove. A strong and active horse, at least sixteen hands high, of excellent breeding. His dam was by the great English jumper Aristotle and his grandam by old Jolly Roger, also a noted jumper. This should be a good colt.

Until midnight Mary sat in her chamber, reading. Then she rose and walked the length of the upper gallery. The crown of the tulip poplar shut off the view of the stables. The leaves rustled softly like faint voices. A branch brushed her head, ruffling her smooth hair. I must have the limbs cut, she thought again. But somehow the thought of whittling away, hacking at the great tree, hurt her deeply.

She touched a branch with her hand. A living, almost human thing, this tree had watched over three generations of her family. It had been part of her own childhood. She had spent dreamy days in its sheltering arms, hiding from her nurse, and in the evenings she had sat in its swaying branches to watch the stars come into view.

She went slowly to her room. The tree was near her there also. From her bed she could see the outline of its branching crown, hear it scraping softly against the house, as though it sang a lullaby to rock her to sleep.

In the stable Adam and Moray and the farrier Mel Frazier fought to save the life of a brown mare. Fought in vain. The first streak of false dawn against the horizon showed a long-legged awkward colt, trying to suckle its dying mother.

Daylight found the tired men, with sweating bodies and aching backs, looking at the body of the dead mare. An old Negro groom knelt beside the body, stroking the satin neck.

Angus Moray went to the horse trough to wash his hands. Mel Frazier leaned against the door of the stable, his eyes deep-ringed, his hands shaking.

Adam said, "I dread to tell my wife. She loved Brown Betty." He put his hand on the groom's shoulder. "Give her a decent burial down near the graveyard. She made a good fight, and so did you." He turned to Angus Moray. "A good fight."

Moray was rolling down his sleeves. He was white with fatigue. "But I lost her. By Gad, I'd have given anything to save her for you, sir. That little devil colt will have to be *good* to make up!"

Adam smiled as they watched the little colt struggling to get to its feet. He spoke to the groom. "You'll have to raise him by hand, Cato."

"Sar, yes. I'll make a little teat for he to suck on, right off."

Adam said to the farrier, "Come up to the house. Marcy's gone to see that breakfast is made ready."

Mel Frazier refused. "I must be getting back to town, Mr. Rutledge. . . . Before I go I'd like to say that there's lots of people in this county that's happy you voted like you did."

Adam's face expressed surprise. "You've heard already?"

"Aye, that we have, sir. All Edenton will soon know, but we had a rider in yesterday. Yes, sir, there'll be a few, some of your old friends, who won't understand. But the people are grateful. Don't forget that, Mr. Rutledge." The farrier went down the drive to his gig, limping painfully.

Adam turned to Angus Moray. "Come. I feel the need of hot food. I can offer that and a bathe in the Sound and a comfortable bed for a tired man."

"I am with you for all three," Moray said. "I am almost resigned to losing my first case in Chowan County."

Sylvia Hears About the Past

19 THE village buzzed with excited gossip after the return of the delegates from Hillsborough. Opinions were divided, and the resulting arguments were hot and acrimonious. Farmers from Rockahock and Yeopim and across the Sound, who came to Edenton to sell their crops, stood in groups on the Courthouse Green, sat on the coping in front of Cupola House, gathered at the docks and in Cheapside, arguing, making unrehearsed speeches, occasionally fighting.

At Horniblow's the arguments raged continually and sometimes in the evening reached such a fever heat that the innkeeper threw out all his customers, closed the doors of the tavern and refused to sell any liquor.

Much of the discussion centered around Adam Rutledge. In the Federalist view he was a traitor to his friends, his county and his class. "The West ruined him," they told one another. "He must have lost his mind. His standing in the community is for ever ruined."

The Antifederalists, on the other hand, lauded him as a man of courage, strength and unquestionable integrity, a man of foresight who looked into the future and cast his vote for the good of all the people rather than just the favoured few.

Soon the town was buzzing with a rumour that Adam and his wife were at odds over his decision. Mary was known to be a staunch Federalist. It was whispered that she and Adam no longer spoke to each other, or, at any rate, merely exchanged greetings in a coldly formal manner. Some people hinted that Adam planned to return to the Illinois country, where he had "taken a wife." And again the neighbourhood revived the old story of Adam's Arabian mistress and the child she had borne him—a son David, who now lived on Adam's holdings at Cahokia on the Mississippi.

But some of Adam's opponents refused to condemn him for this incident of the past. What if he did have a son by a mistress? his defenders asked. Alexander Hamilton was a love child. What of Henry McCulloh's son born out of wedlock, what of Nat Allen's, what of Harnett's? Many a man in the colonies had children by slave women. Why should a man's private life be dragged out and aired because of the way he chose to vote?

The common people—the men from plantations and farms, the tradesmen, the artisans and workers—made a hero of Adam Rutledge. They praised him, swore they would elect him as their delegate if there was another convention. "He will speak for us," shouted the impromptu speakers on the Green and the docks. "Rutledge will see that we are protected!"

Meanwhile Mary Rutledge went regularly to the village to visit the shops and see her friends. She gave no sign that anything was wrong, and the gossips did not dare to question her. She spoke with complete naturalness of her husband and made no reference to politics.

Only to James Iredell did she speak of her distress. "I don't know what to think, what to expect," she said despairingly. "That lawless Western country has got into his blood." Riding alone on her fine mare, she had encountered Iredell returning to town after a visit to Mulberry Hill, and they had reined in their horses at the roadside.

Iredell shook his head. "It isn't a matter of geography alone, Mary. Look at the national leaders. Alexander Hamilton thinks one way, Thomas Jefferson another; Patrick Henry opposes Madison and James Wilson. Yet we know all these men to be sincerely patriotic. Don't be critical of Adam. His deepest thought has gone into his decision. Mary, have you considered the struggle Adam went through before he made up his mind? He searched his soul, but he could not in honesty go against his conscience. I honour him for it. I regret that he is lost to our side, for he is liked and trusted by men throughout the county. But I do not change my opinion of him as a man."

"Oh, Jemmy, I don't need to be told that Adam is an honourable man!" Mary cried impatiently. "Of course he has taken the stand that seems right to him. But this new view-point of his is one that seems to threaten all I love best in the world." She paused, searching for words. "How often have I heard Sam Johnston say that the plantation life we lead in the Albemarle can be secure only under a strong and benevolent government guided by men who understand our sort of life and the problems we face! And that Madison's Constitution offers a sound basis for just such a government! And now Adam has rejected the Constitution, and I know in my heart that it means he is turning away from the Albemarle."

Iredell started to protest, but she forestalled him. "It's true, Jemmy! His dreams and ambitions centre in that wild Illinois country, and his sympathies are with the poeple he has known and worked with in the West. That is why he voted as he did. The Constitution must protect *them,* he says; the new government must be tailored to *their* needs. The Albemarle, his friends here, even Queen's Gift—these are of secondary importance to Adam now. But not to me, Jemmy!" There were tears in Mary's eyes. "Never to me! Queen's Gift is my home, the beloved home of my childhood, a legacy entrusted to me by my father and grandfather. The house, the land are a part of my being, and when Adam turns away from it he is turning away from me as well. That is why I cannot reconcile myself to what he has done or to what he believes!"

Iredell was startled by her vehemence, by the despair in her voice. He took her hand and said quietly, "Mary, forgive me, but I think your emotions have led you to exaggerate the situation. Has Adam ever said——?"

"Oh, of course he has not said that he plans to leave Queen's Gift. Adam knows how I feel about the plantation and that I fear the hold his Illinois lands have on him. Since he has been home he has avoided even mentioning Illinois so as not to alarm me, and I avoid it because I dread hearing him say what I know he feels. But doesn't his vote at Hillsborough show that I am right about him?"

Iredell evaded the question. "If you are right, Mary, you must eventually face a very painful decision of your own. You love your plantation. You love your husband. Which do you put first?"

"But it's not that simple!" Mary cried. "Queen's Gift is not a mere plot of ground. It's a charge, a trust! I would be disloyal to Duke Roger if I did not defend it and fight to preserve it."

"The decision is yours, Mary." Iredell's voice was gentle, but he spoke with deep earnestness. "I hope, however, that you will think long and carefully before you let family loyalty or sentimental attachment or political difference come between you and your husband. I am your friend and Adam's, and I ask you to think carefully."

Mary was silent for a time. When at last she spoke she did not look at Iredell. "Samuel Johnston will not speak to Adam. They are enemies now."

"Samuel is uncompromising. Dear Mary, I can only repeat what I have said. A man must act as his conscience dictates."

Mary turned her horse and moved away from him. "A woman has a conscience also," she said almost defiantly and rode off toward Queen's Gift.

Iredell looked after her with considerable concern, and his distress stayed with him as he rode on to town. He spoke of it to his wife that evening after supper while they strolled toward Horniblow's to call on Lady Anne Stuart. "I fear that Mary Rutledge is not showing her usual clear judgement in this attitude toward Adam. She is taking it very hard that he has turned Antifederalist."

Hannah said, "I'm not sure I blame her. Think who his associates will be!"

James's eyes twinkled. He pressed her arm against his side. "What would you do if I were to change my views, my dearest? Would you be in opposition to me?"

"Why, James! You never could do that. Why, you are the leader of the Federalists in all North Carolina. Oh, I know they say my brother Samuel is the leader, but you lead him, Jemmy."

"You haven't answered my question, my dear."

Hannah hesitated. "I suppose I should follow you, for I love you so dearly. But of course *you* wouldn't be an Antifederalist. You are much too wise."

He patted her hand. "Whither thou goest . . ."

"Yes, Jemmy, yes."

"I'm afraid Mary doesn't see it as you see it. Mary is an individualist. I'm thinking she is in for some unhappy days."

Hannah pressed closer. "Politics aren't really important, are they? Between husband and wife, I mean. A wife should believe as her husband believes. That is, if she is a loving wife—as I am, dear Jemmy."

At the inn they were received by Sylvia Hay, who told them that the Baron and Lady Anne had gone to Hertford for a fortnight to stay with the Laurence Bakers. But the Iredells, who had retained a pleasant impression of Sylvia from their meeting at Madam Barker's party, stayed to talk to her. James was delighted to have news of his cousin Margaret Macartney, and the three spent a pleasant hour talking of England and Edenton.

The next day Sylvia reported the visit in a long letter to Margaret:

Last evening your cousin James Iredell and his wife Hannah called. I had met them earlier, but this was my first opportunity to get to know them. Madam Iredell is a delicately lovely woman, reserved and soft-spoken—quite a contrast to her lively husband. He is all you said of him—a most delightful man. The people here say he is the outstanding legal mind of the state. Of that I am no judge, but certainly he has a pleasant address, a ready humour and a most elegant manner. He adores his wife, and she adores him, always aware of his high attainments. She seems a housewifely woman, quite content to remain in the background.

I wonder how it would be to live so completely for a man. She is the exact opposite of Lady Anne. But as Hannah Johnston she was in the large shadow of her brother Samuel, who is now the Governor of the state, so it is no new thing to Hannah to bow to the wishes of the men of her family.

She has very generously invited me to come to their home as a guest while Lady Anne and the Baron visit a near-by village for a fortnight. I shall go to the Iredells' in a day or so when Miss Nellie Blair, who lives with them, has recovered from a slight illness. It will be pleasant indeed to get away from this noisy tavern, where the men fight political battles from dawn until midnight. Quite like our election times. Yet I like Carolina. The people grow on one. They are kind, gracious in their hospitality. I sometimes feel I should not mind lingering on, living this lazy, indolent life.

Lady Anne talks of going to Philadelphia, but keeps putting off the journey. The Baron visits plantation after plantation, studying the methods they use in farming. I think Lady Anne is tarrying until her man of business, a Mr. Sayre, arrives from London early in the year. She talks much of him and his ability.

Now that I am acting as her secretary, she confides various business affairs to me. She has trouble collecting her allowance from Northumberland. That is a matter of discussion between her and the Baron from time to time.

My little charges are now at River Plantation, where Parson Daniel Earle has his classical school. They seem to like the country and are thriving. I have ridden out several times to see them. Lady Anne has never gone. The other day she surprised my by saying, "They are not my children." The idea had never occurred to me, for the younger boy especially seems so much like her. Perhaps it is just her influence. But it appears they are the children of an earlier wife, a French woman. I can better understand now Lady Anne's indifference to the boys.

My interesting friend Cosmo de' Medici has departed. The young Scot, Dr.

Angus Moray, is very taken up with his surgery. He has determined to stay here and set up a practice. I ride with him on occasions, but I think he is still enamoured of Lady Anne. Certainly I do not intend to be a second choice, or enter into rivalry with a woman of the world who is without scruple where a man is concerned.

I think there is little local news to interest you. All they can talk about here is signing the constitution. Very boring if one does not understand such matters.

Sylvia signed and sealed the letter, ready for the next ship to England.

It was not quite dusk when Sylvia finished writing, so she left the inn and walked to the end of the Green to watch the sunset. There she was overtaken by Angus Moray, who greeted her with his usual formality. He tucked his hat under his arm, and she saw that his dark wavy hair had been neatly dressed and tied with a black riband into a club. She wondered if he had just come from Mr. West the hairdresser. His dark blue coat looked new, and his vest of elegant dark brocade and the fine lace ruffles at his throat and wrists proclaimed that he had dressed carefully. Even his silver buckled shoes were freshly varnished. She smiled a little. If we were in Devon, she thought, the country-folk would say the lad had courtin' on his mind.

What she said was: "Lady Anne and the Baron are visiting in Hertford, Dr. Moray."

The smile left his lips. "If you are implying that I was on my way to call on Lady Anne, you are mistaken."

"Really? Isn't this the usual time for you to have tea with her Ladyship?" Her smile was provocative. She sat down on a bench at the edge of the water and pulled her skirts aside to make room for him. He brushed off the bench with his handkerchief and sat down.

Sylvia laughed aloud. "Always cautious, you Scots," she said. "But I don't blame you for protecting your fine new breeks from dust. You are indeed an elegant gentleman this evening."

"Dammit, ma'am, why do you always rouse my ire! I swear to myself that I won't allow you to put me in a tempery mood, but you manage."

Sylvia glanced at him out of the corner of her eye. Angus was staring gloomily out over the water, his features set in grim lines. She touched his arm with her fan. "Come, sir, it really isn't that bad, is it? You look as determined as Robert the Bruce gazing out from behind the spider-web."

He turned quickly and saw that her lips were smiling, her eyes merry. A little curl had escaped from the smooth bands of her auburn hair and clung damply to her forehead and cheek. He laid his hand over hers. "Sylvia, why do you take delight in perverseness? I come out this evening in a cheerful mood. The day has been good—I have helped some ailing people. I walk toward the inn to seek you, and what happens?"

"I at once put you in an angry mood—you have already told me that.

Why do I tease you?" she said archly. "It pleasures me. Perhaps I like to see you grow red from anger; perhaps I enjoy watching your jaw clamp down as though you were biting nails. . . . Why were you seeking me, Dr. Moray?"

"Dammit, ma'am, I've a notion not to give you the message at all."

"Oh, yes, please do. I promise not to tease."

"Well, it's from Dr. Armitage. He hopes you will come to supper at his house. Mrs. Rutledge and her husband will be there. May I call for you at eight?"

Sylvia rose quickly. "Please tell the doctor I shall be delighted to come."

"Where are you going?" Angus asked, blocking her way.

"Why, to dress—make myself attractive."

He took her hand and led her back to the bench. Sylvia hesitated a moment, then sat down beside him. "For me?" he asked, dropping his voice.

She lifted her head, looked at him from under her dark lashes. "For you?" she said. "No, Dr. Moray. I was thinking of Dr. Armitage, that dear man."

Angus stifled his irritation and sat quietly beside her, looking out across the Sound. The sun had lowered beyond the horizon, and the Tyrrell shore was slowly fading into the deep shadows of night. Behind them the town was silent, and when they turned away from the water they saw that candle-light now illuminated the houses facing the Green.

"What are you thinking that makes you so silent?" Moray asked at last.

"I was remembering what Mistress Horniblow told me of the Edenton Tea Party, which took place in that little house next Mr. Collins' place. Do you know that story?"

"I have heard it mentioned, I think," Moray answered.

"Mistress Horniblow grew quite excited as she described it. It is a proud memory among the Edenton ladies. Fifty-one of them met there and signed a pledge to drink no tea until the King removed the tax on it. It was Madam Barker's idea, and she carried it through, although many of the ladies were frightened at the prospect. Some feared the anger or ridicule of their husbands, others had visions of being sent to gaol.

"But Miss Hannah Johnston—she's Mrs. Iredell now, and such a gentle person—surprised every one by speaking up. 'What matter if they put us in gaol?' she said firmly. And Madam Barker said, 'We owe it to the men of our families to demonstrate that our courage is equal to theirs.' "

Sylvia paused. The story was very real to her; as she talked she felt almost as if she had been present at the Tea Party. "So one by one the ladies came forward and signed the paper," she continued. "For they did have courage, these ladies of Edenton—courage to defy the King of England!"

Angus had listened silently, his eyes fixed on Sylvia's mobile face, watching her changing expression. "Sylvia, there are tears in your eyes," he said wonderingly. "What happened? They weren't sent to gaol, were they?"

Sylvia rubbed her eyes angrily. "No, they didn't go to gaol. They just stayed at home and drank some terrible tea made from yapon leaves or dried raspberry. I'm silly to cry, but I think it's a thrilling story. To think of it makes me feel as I do when the Guards' band plays."

"Or when the Gordon Highlanders go marching past to the skirl of the pipes. I know the feeling." Angus patted her hand. "You're a grand lass, Sylvia."

She got to her feet. "I must run now, Dr. Moray. Run and make myself presentable."

He grinned. "For Dr. Armitage. . . . Wait, I'll step to the door with you."

But Sylvia was already hurrying across the Green toward Horniblow's. He watched her slender figure moving through the shadows. She's my own lass, he thought, though she doesn't know it yet.

After supper Dr. Armitage led his guests to the library on the second floor and Adam and the old doctor lighted pipes. From the window the Sound could be seen sparkling in the moonlight. "Why don't you young people go up into the cupola," the doctor said to Moray. "Miss Sylvia hasn't seen the view by moonlight."

Moray, who had been very quiet throughout supper, jumped to his feet and held the door open. He was smiling as Sylvia tilted her skirts to go through the doorway.

"Your suggestion was well received, Doctor," Mary said when they had gone.

"Yes, wasn't it? I couldn't bear to see my young assistant so morose. I fear he's love-sick."

Adam touched a taper to his pipe, which hadn't caught. "Do you think he has a chance?" he asked. "A charming young woman like Miss Hay must have many admirers."

"I've an idea she hasn't decided yet what she thinks of Moray. She rides with him occasionally, but I gather that she keeps him in doubt whether she enjoys his company."

"Nice fellow. Modest, but I fancy he's rather a stubborn breed. If he's settled his affections on Miss Hay, he won't give up easily. An earnest, straightforward young man, I'd call him."

The doctor grunted. "You should have seen him with Lady Anne. Now, she knows what she wants, if the girl doesn't." His eyes followed Mary, who had wandered to the far end of the room. She stopped to take a book from a falling-leaf table.

Adam drew deeply, puffed a cloud of smoke. He spoke casually, his eyes on Mary. "And what is it that her Ladyship wants?" he asked.

"As a man who has watched feminine tricks these many years, I would say she wanted a bedfellow."

Adam lifted his brows. "I thought she had a husband."

"You haven't met the Baron, have you? No? Well, he's much more interested in his agricultural pursuits than in pursuing his lady. Mind, I don't say he isn't a nice fellow. He is cultivated and all that, but the sort of man who stops wooing a woman when he's wed her."

"I see." A vague uneasiness came over Adam. Was the doctor using Baron von Pollnitz as a whipping-boy? Was he really commenting on Adam's differences with Mary?

Adam turned to look at Mary, who stood now at the window. He was aware that she continued remote, distant. They had not discussed the convention for these several weeks. He had been too busy on the plantation to give much thought to the whole affair. He'd assumed that Mary would eventually accept his altered political views and their estrangement would end. Now he wondered if he had taken too much for granted. The thought was disturbing.

The doctor called out, "Mary, please fetch me that letter on my desk—the one on thin paper. It came by post in a letter from Hugh Williamson. Perhaps you can help me answer the query it contains."

Mary brought the letter to him. The seal, bearing a crest, had been broken, she noticed.

"Read it please, my dear. I left my specs downstairs. Besides, your French is more active than mine. Wait a minute, here come the young folk. Perhaps they will be interested." He addressed Dr. Moray: "I always think you can better understand a village and the villagers if you know something of the past. This letter concerns something that is supposed to have happened in Edenton. Sit down, Miss Hay—perhaps it will interest you too, although I don't suppose you will be here long. Still . . ." He did not finish the sentence, but waved his long, thin hand as a signal for Mary to begin.

She pulled the candle closer to give a better light and looked at the signature. "It is from the French Embassy at Geneva. It is a memoir sent to Dr. Franklin by the Comte de Vergennes in Paris, at the instance of France's Ambassador to Switzerland, Comte de Polignac. It makes an inquiry relative to the death of one Jean Wallis of the Canton of Soleure, who died in Edenton, December 14, 1780, at the house of one F. La Fond of Bordeaux just on the eve of his departure to Europe by the ship *Vagington*." Mary handed the note to Dr. Armitage. "I can't remember any Jean who lived in Edenton except Jean Corbin. But I wasn't here at that time, remember?"

"Nor I. I was with the army," said the doctor. "It might have been some relative of the goldsmith Wallis who lived next door to Joseph Hewes for a time."

"It sounds quite international," Sylvia said. "Dr. Franklin—the French Ambassador in Switzerland—the Comte de Vergennes . . ."

Adam put down his pipe. "You should have been here during the Revolution when we had all our French visitors. From time to time we extend our borders to the great world of London or Paris or Rome, but then we draw back into our shells."

"What is wrong with that, Adam?" Mary asked quickly. "We meet emergencies when they arise."

No one spoke for a moment. Angus Moray broke the silence. "Doctor, you promised you would tell me something about this house and its history. Why not now? I'm sure Miss Hay and I will be eager listeners."

"Ring for brandy, Angus, before I begin." Armitage's old eyes twinkled when he looked at Adam and Mary. "You, my dear friends, will be obliged to listen. You know how I enjoy riding my hobby of history, but I won't bore you with too much detail."

A slave brought decanter and glasses. Adam unlimbered his long legs, poured and passed the brandy, apricot for the ladies.

The doctor turned to Angus. "We've always been a cantankerous people, we Carolinians," he began. "More than one King found that we couldn't be put upon. 'Way back in the days when we were governed by the Lords Proprietors we threw out governors we didn't like. In Charles II's time one William Drummond was appointed by Berkeley as Governor of Albemarle County in the newly created Colony of Carolina in 1668. William Drummond was a Scot, by the way, Moray. Something in the Carolina air inspired in him a distaste for tyranny, for after serving out his term he returned to Virginia and joined a rebellion against Berkeley, who had him executed. Then there was the Culpepper Rebellion right here in Albemarle. John Culpepper and George Durant led a party who arrested Governor Miller. They imprisoned him and two deputies of the Lords Proprietors and proceeded to establish a people's government. This was about 1677. Eastchurch, the co-Governor, who had lingered on the island of Nevis to do some courting, arrived only to find he had lost everything—the Governor's seat, the royal revenue, everything."

Dr. Armitage stopped to relight his pipe. He noted with amusement that Sylvia was following the tale with deep interest and that Angus was taking the opportunity to look his fill at her.

"Next the people were afflicted with one of the Lords Proprietors in person, Seth Sothel," the old doctor continued. "He was the most shameless reprobate ever seen as Governor in America. He left England in 1698, but on the way over he was captured by Algerian pirates. 'Twas a great pity they didn't keep him as a slave, for no sooner was he here than the people recognized him as a beastly and detestable monster. He took bribes, stole property, appropriated the Indian trade for his private purse. After five years the people could endure him no longer, and drove him down to South Carolina.

"When James II came to the throne he endeavoured to make the people

Catholic. Again they resisted. After several mediocre Governors had gone their ways John Archdale, a Quaker and a Lord Proprietor, ruled the Carolinas, from the Ashley and Cooper rivers to the Albemarle. He was wise and good, as were several of his successors. Then religious persecution against the Quakers, the Baptists and other denominations aroused the people to further protest.

"Queen Anne changed that. She gave her name to the creek and to this village, and all went well—until Cary's Rebellion and the Tuscarora War. For a time there were two Governors, William Glover and Thomas Cary. They fought each other until Queen Anne sent her cousin, Edward Hyde, to conciliate the two factions. Actually it was the Tuscarora War that united all the English after a horrible massacre in which two hundred whites were brutally killed. . . . Those early turbulent days set the pattern for our people. We have been turbulent and perverse ever since, standing strong and solid on our rights."

Dr. Armitage stood up and walked about, his hands in his coat-tail pockets. He glanced keenly at Mary as if to gauge the effect of his words. "Yes, they set the pattern," he said, glancing about the room.

"I'm not sure, but I like to think this house was planned by an ambitious Governor's wife, Madam Catha Hyde. Who but an ambitious person would insist on a cupola, the symbol of government? At any rate, we know from the records that Governor Eden owned Lot Number One and the houses thereon in 1713. He renamed the town after himself, but I swear I prefer the older name, Queen Anne's Town.

"He wasn't too bad a Governor, but he was suspected of taking a personal and profitable interest in the activities of Edward Teach, the pirate commonly called Blackbeard. People said that his country home across the Chowan River, Eden House, and his other house at Bath were built for use in his dealings with the pirates. But old Eden had his troubles. The people of Edenton would not sit quietly by while their Governor filled his pockets unlawfully. They hounded him constantly, and a group headed by Edward Moseley and Maurice Moore even broke into the government offices to search Eden's papers for evidence of his guilt. . . . Well, I've talked too long, children. Forgive a garrulous old man."

"But we are so interested!" Sylvia cried. "Pray tell us more."

The doctor took up the tale. "Eden died in this house, they say, and there was a great hue and cry over his will, with interminable lawsuits. Burrington was the next Governor, and his successor was Sir Richard Everard, whose authority Burrington fiercely challenged. They behaved outrageously, fighting in the streets, brawling drunkenly in this house. And then the Crown bought out the Lords Proprietors. We became a Crown Colony and were blessed with better Governors."

"But what of the date and initials that you pointed out to me on the finial above the gable?" Angus asked.

"Oh, those! Francis Corbin, land agent, set them in place. He was another bad one, taking fees, cheating." Armitage laughed. "The people got very weary of Corbin. One night they gathered together and came and dragged him from the house. Scared the poor fool almost to death. They warned him against further abuse of his office. He left not long after, or died—I forget which."

Adam got up. "All of which proves that we Carolinians are stubborn and want no infringement on our rights. A goodly heritage, I think, Doctor."

"Perhaps. If the protest is kept within bounds. If it is guided by suitable leaders."

Angus Moray said, "It all sounds familiar to me. The same spirit is to be found in Scotland."

Mary laughed. "There are many Scots here, you know. Perhaps that accounts for something. Thank you, Doctor, for a very pleasant evening. Adam and I have a long ride ahead of us and must get started."

She tied a linen dust-skirt over her summer frock and joined Adam at the block, where the horses were already waiting. She mounted quickly and led the way toward the eastern gate. They made the journey to Queen's Gift in a silence that persisted as they relinquished their horses to the groom and mounted the stairs to the house.

On the gallery Mary paused to listen to the mocking-bird singing a hymn to the beauty of the moonlit night.

Adam halted also and stood at the rail, his hands behind his back, his head uplifted. He was lost in thought. The moonlight played on his yellow hair and etched his fine profile against the dark background of the giant tree. The look on his face, Mary saw, was one of peace, of happiness. It hurt her deeply that he should be so serene, apparently undisturbed by the differences between them. What was he thinking about, standing silent and motionless in the pale light? She could reach out and touch him, she thought, feel the strength of his firm, strong hand. But she made no move. She felt remote from him as the moon was remote from the spreading earth that lay broad and open, drinking in her cool silver light. She tried to remember the times they had been together, when they had been one in spirit and in flesh. But the memories would not come; she could think only of the gulf that separated them now.

A splash broke the silence. Some forest creature was swimming out from the shore.

Without turning Adam said, "How blessed we are, Mary, living here, surrounded by such beauty!"

She moved toward him, a quick impulsive motion. But a step on the gallery made her hesitate.

Marcy's voice came through the dusk. "Mr. Adam, please may I speak with you? There is a little trouble down the line. Perhaps we should go down."

"What's wrong? That boy Cato been drinking rum again?" Adam turned to Mary. "Good night. Don't sit up for me." Then he disappeared into the shadows.

She went slowly to her room. The moment had passed.

Sylvia walked along the verge of the Green, Angus close beside her, matching his long stride to hers. "I feel close to these people to-night," he said. "Dr. Armitage has given me much to think about. How lovingly he spread out a panorama of events for us to interpret—an introduction to the thoughts and actions of the village! How jealously they guard their liberties! Actually the Revolution was only one of a long series of gallant protests against what seemed to them injustice. Through the years they have fought their battles, winning a little, losing a little, gradually advancing toward their goal."

Sylvia was silent. Angus' comments surprised her. He was not so simple and transparent as he seemed, this solemn black Scot. "Yes," she said, "but there was another implication in his story, didn't you think? One not intended for you and me, perhaps. Of course the doctor was enjoying himself thoroughly, but, although you asked him originally about the history of his own house, he talked instead about the independence of the colonists from the earliest times and their constant resistance to injustice and tyranny. And it seemed to me that he was directing his story to the Rutledges as if it should have a special meaning for them."

"You are very sensitive. Now that you speak of it, I believe you are right. But why?"

"I don't know, but I can't help feeling he was using history as a means of telling them something he hesitated to speak of directly." She turned from the shore to cross the Green. Angus detained her. "Let us walk a little along the shore. The night is too beautiful for us to go indoors."

Sylvia hesitated only for a moment. They moved slowly along the waterfront until they came to a narrow path that followed Queen Anne's Creek. Across the black water they saw tiny blinking lights moving along the road to Hayes, the Governor's house. Soon they were beyond the houses that faced the water, and only rice fields, silver in the moonlight, lay beyond them. The heavy heads of grain were swaying, rippled by the small breeze. A few birds chirped in nests balanced on the reeds that grew deep in the stream.

After a time Angus said, "It is like the night on the ship. You were fey that night, and very lovely." She felt his arm close about her as he pulled her to him. "You go to my head like strong wine," he whispered.

He pressed his lips against hers, a strong, deep kiss that left her trembling. It took all her will to push him away. But she too had memories of the last night on the ship.

"You must not. You must not," she whispered, struggling to keep her voice steady. "It's not I that you are kissing. My lips perhaps, but Lady Anne is in your heart." She regretted the words the instant she had spoken them.

He stepped back. "I am sorry," he said stiffly. "I did not know that I was so abhorrent to you." Then anger surged into his voice. "You are cruel, Miss Hay. You manage to spoil a perfect moment with bitter words. Come, I'll take you to the inn. The night is beautiful no longer."

He spoke not at all as they walked back, and at the inn door he acknowledged her good night with only a formal bow.

In her room Sylvia flung herself wearily onto the bed. Angus was right to be angry; he loved her and she had spoiled his perfect moment. Why did the memory of Lady Anne in his arms infuriate her so? Listlessly she undressed and lay again on the bed in the full light of the moon. "Let the moon enter and bring moon madness!" she said aloud.

After a time she slept, a restless, disturbed sleep. She dreamed of the downs and the circle of standing stones that had been set in place long before the Romans came to Britain. Strange shapes moved among the stones, carrying fire to sacrificial altars. In terror she watched the sacrifice, unable to move. But at last she felt the velvety nuzzling of the little moor pony she had had as a child, and she was released from immobility then. The sinister priestly figures vanished. The moonlight was serene and quiet, without menace.

The Cub Hunt

20 It was late September, a golden day. The sour-gum trees had turned from scarlet to maroon, the sycamores from yellow to brown. The oaks were still green, but a frost early in the week had coloured the edges of the leaves with gold and scarlet.

A rain crow sounded its morning cry. Adam Rutledge sat at breakfast on the gallery, watching the cotton-pickers go down the rows in the north field. A gay picture they made, the women's and children's clothes as bright as Joseph's coat of many colours. Men and women with bent backs plucked the white bolls with nimble fingers. Big tow sacks, tied about their necks, dragged the ground behind, some already half filled with puffs of cotton.

Children of eight or ten years followed their elders, each dragging his own sack.

Cotton-picking was an event in which whole families participated. They worked the rows in groups so that they could talk and laugh and gossip. At the far end of the field the overlooker sat beside a pair of large steel-yards, weighing in and recording in his book the poundage picked by each slave. A good picker could average three hundred pounds a day. At Queen's Gift the work was competitive. The workers with the best records at the end of each week received a prize—a length of calico for a woman, a shirt for a man. And at the end of every day, when the work had gone well, an extra drink was provided—corn whisky mixed with scuppernong wine.

Marcy, followed by a light coloured boy, came up to speak with Adam. "Little Mingo has something to tell you, sir."

The boy came forward bashfully, his bare feet making a swishing sound on the gallery floor. He twisted his broad straw hat in his hands. He opened his mouth once or twice, but no words came.

"Speak up, boy," Adam said.

"Sar, yes. 'Tis dat ole red fox dat foxed us las' year. I see him dodgin' along de cotton row toward Black Swamp. He jes' trottin' slow, makin' no mind about de black crows yakkin' overhead. He jes' don' care if de debil be in dose crows or not. No, sar. He ole dog fox, smart as you make 'em. My pappy say, 'Tell de master. 'Tis huntin' time for sure.' "

"Who is your father?" Adam asked.

"Sar, he's Mingo. He work de hounds. Master Marcy he know."

Marcy said, "The hounds are in Mingo's care. He's been trying out the young ones. We've a better pack than last year, I think."

Adam nodded to the boy. "Tell Mingo we will have a cub hunt this week."

The boy didn't move. He twisted his hat and tried to dig his bare toes into the floor-boards, forgetting that they were hard and not soft earth. "Mingo he say to-morrow'll be good. A little rain he come to-night, maybe. To-morrow de fox scent will lay close on de earth. Very good."

Adam laughed. "All right. To-morrow at sun-up we'll have a little run. Only the young hounds and a few couples to teach them." He turned to his superintendent. "Marcy, we'll have to get out the hound book and start the records and give them their new names. It takes time for them to forget their yard names."

The boy spoke eagerly. "Mingo he done named 'em hound names. Dey ain't got ary yard names a-tall. Mingo he tell you dey names so you can draw 'em in de big book."

"Good. Now run along, boy, and tell Mingo what I've said. To-morrow at sun-up. We'll hunt down by the boundary. I'll talk to Mr. Blount today about running his field if the fox takes off toward Mulberry Hill."

Little Mingo was showing his white teeth in delight. "Sar, dat ole red fox he don't know our land from his'n, dat he don't. He don't care if'n he racin' through Queen's Gift or Mulberry Hill, nor Sandy Point land. He ain't partic'lar whose chicken he eat if'n he can't catch nice fat wild turkey. Hé eat 'em and get away. He jes' push through dose prickly vines, and he get away and hide heself in he's nest in de toossock, where he's vixen hidden."

Marcy watched the boy as he ran down the line to impart the good news to his father. "I'm always amazed at their knowledge of nature, of the habits of wild animals and game," he said.

"And of the weather," Adam said. "I count on old Ebon and Chaney for my weather forecasts. They seldom fail me."

Mary appeared in the hall door and stood watching her husband. There was sadness in her eyes. They had made no progress toward resolving their differences of opinion. Both took care that politics and the Illinois country should not enter their conversation, and both made determined efforts to resume the pleasant life they had shared before Adam's westward trip. Outwardly they were successful. Adam was affectionate, considerate, and Mary was unreservedly glad to have him at Queen's Gift again. But both knew they were experiencing a waiting period and that eventually they must face again the issues that threatened to divide them.

"Adam," she said at last, "are you using the small sail-boat today? I'd like to go across the Chowan to Eden House. I heard in the village that Penelope Dawson is going up to New York this week."

"By all means take the ketch, Mary, and two boys to sail her for you."

"You know I'll sail her myself," she said, smiling.

Adam laid his hand on her shoulder and kissed her brow lightly. "Yes, but I want the boys along in case a wind should come up suddenly. You know how it is on the river."

Marcy said, "I'll have two of our best sailors get the boat ready, Mrs. Rutledge."

"In an hour or so, Marcy." To Adam she said, "I may stay the night."

"I've just planned to hunt in the morning. Mingo sent word the old red fox is running. But I could put it off a day."

Mary spoke quickly. "Oh, no, Adam, don't delay the hunt! I'll come home to-night and be with you for the hunt in the morning." After a moment she asked, "Will it be a full hunt? All the subscribers?"

"No. We want to try out some of the young hounds. I thought I'd send word to Blount and the Sandy Point people. We'll hunt in that direction."

"I'll be home. There'll be a full moon, so don't worry if I'm late. If there's wind I'll get home by midnight."

Chaney, the cook, came puffing up the steps from the garden. "I heered you, mistress. Dere be a wind soon as you reach de Sound, a right smart wind." She bustled importantly into the house.

Adam glanced meaningly at Marcy. "You see?"

Marcy nodded. "I'll look to the sail-boat," he said.

Adam put his arm about Mary's shoulders. "Don't take any risks. You know how dear you are to me. I'll come to the landing to see you off. I'm going down now to have a look at the hounds."

"Why don't you run Crossie with the young ones? She's a good teacher. And Nabob. And, Adam, I think that Druid, the black and white with touches of tan, has a nose. She's the one we got from Maryland last year. I was watching Mingo work her yesterday. Her bone structure indicates a hardy constitution. And speed, Adam—she's got real speed!"

Mary turned to leave. Over her shoulder she remarked, "You won't get 'Old Red Fox' with trial hounds, Adam. He has too many tricks."

"I know, but it's fun to try."

The morning was perfect for hunting. The early mists that lay on the ground, the miasma from the rotting vegetation in the pocosin, held the scent to the ground. The shy young hounds were bewildered by cross scents, but the older hounds were restless, eager to be away. They tugged and pulled at the leashes held by barefooted stableboys.

Six hunters rode up to Queen's Gift at cock's crow. Young Tom Blount brought two guests from South Carolina who were eager to see how Albemarle hunting differed from hunts in the Sand Hill country. Two Creecy boys came in from Greenfield and young Charleton and his sister from Sandy Point.

Old Ebon was ready for them, waiting on the gallery with hot toddy of considerable strength, for the morning was chilly. Soon Chaney and a pantry girl appeared, carrying trays of hot pone, split and buttered, with strips of bacon laid between. And there was foaming milk for riders who preferred it to the toddy.

When the first long fingers of light cut the eastern sky the hunters were all in the saddle. Mary thought they made a good show—fine upstanding men riding good hunters, their pink coats splotches of brilliant colour against the background of green trees. Margery Charleton's blue habit and her own Lincoln green toned in and gave variety. She was always glad when the hunt started from Queen's Gift. She liked the picture of horses, riders and hounds all restive, eager to be away at the blast of the horn and the cry of "Cast off!"

They moved slowly at the beginning, crossing the tobacco stalks and the corn stubble. At the first fence of tangled honeysuckle and trumpet-vine a ditch offered a nice jump to warm up the horses. After the riders came Negro grooms and stableboys, one riding a fast-walking grey mule. Adam always allowed this, if the hunt was small.

Mingo talked to the hounds in a kind of jargon he called "hound talk." "You, Nabob, keep off dat possum track! I know dey was a possum sittin' on dat log yesternight. Seen he myself. Crossie, don't wrassle wid de pups!

Leave be, leave be! Don't you know better dan to wear you'self plumb out startin'?"

In the brush that grew by the fence they flushed a covey of partridges. The young pups rushed this way and that, but the old ones kept going. The novices finally settled down.

They were thirty minutes out, running along the boundary fence at Mulberry Hill, when Mary heard the deep-throated baying of Nabob and Straggler, followed by yelps and whimpers from the young ones. She knew at once that the hounds were closing in. She was trailing the field and did not see the kill, for which she was thankful, but she came up in time to see Adam hand the brush to Margery.

The young girl's cheeks were flushed, her eyes wide, glistening with excitement. "Oh, Mrs. Rutledge, my first brush! My very first! I don't care if it is only a cub."

Then Straggler caught another scent and was off, followed by the pack.

Mingo came up beside Mary. "Dey doin' grand, mistress, now dey found de way to run. Dat Druid goin' to be a beauty. She sure is a smiller. Notice how she keep dat nose in 'zackly right place?"

The hunt crossed the river road and streamed into Blount's piney thicket. The woodsmen had been chopping trees, and the brush from stripping was piled high beside the narrow path. The pungent odor of fresh-cut pine hung heavy in the morning air. Jay-birds flew ahead, their ugly, raucous cries splitting the quiet of the forest.

Mingo shouted a warning. "De devil he ride ahead! Old Red Fox he take to de 'cosin. He'll wade right into de black water, and no one will see he dis mornin'."

"No matter," Mary said. "This is only a cub hunt."

The old Negro shook his head sadly. "I seen he early dis mornin' right down by quarters line. He got one of Chaney's roosters in he mouth, lopin' away."

They'd had an hour's run by sun-up. Adam had Mingo call in the fox hounds. "Too many cross scents," he told Blount, and the other men agreed. The hunt broke up, and the planters rode home. Not too bad, they told one another—one brush and a near for the first run of the season.

Adam and Mary returned to Queen's Gift by the river road, while the boys took the hounds back through the fields. Adam said, "I'm pleased with that young Druid. She settled down like an old hound, once she found out what was wanted. Mary, you've got a winner in that dog."

"Shall we try her in a real hunt? Do you think she is ready?"

"Yes, by all means."

"The man we got her from wanted to sell his pack," Mary said. "He was giving up hunting."

"How many?"

"Eight or nine couples. Pitchley-bred, I think, but the price seemed exorbitant. Three hundred and fifty guineas."

Adam laughed shortly. "Rather. Better to breed our own and school them ourselves. Mingo tells me we have ten couples and twenty youngsters. With Blount's pack, that would give us a really good hunt."

"Not if we had seventeen hundred riders, as they did in a meet my grandmother used to tell about. She said it was an unforgettable sight. Roads packed with riders. Scarlet and black intermingling with the white colours of Pitchley and the liveries of other hunts. A vast concourse of carriages following, and a mob of people on foot."

"That *must* have been a hunt! I expect your grandmother was in the thick of it."

"Oh, yes. She loved to talk about that hunt—the most thrilling she ever attended, she said. Brilliant sunshine and a bitter cold wind from the northeast—bad for the scent, but an exciting day for the riders. Empty saddles, horses running about riderless . . . At last the fox crossed the river, and the M. F. H. had the hounds whipped off because of darkness."

"Seventeen hundred riders!" Adam said. "Why, that would be every man, woman and child in Chowan County—aye, and part of Perquimans. I wish I might see such a hunt."

Mary said, "I like our little ones better, I think. This is pleasant country for hunting, but the rolling hills and the stone fences of the Quorn country remain vivid in my mind."

As she undressed and bathed she thought about her girlhood in England. A good life it had been, something to hold in one's mind always. But this morning had been good also. She felt alert and happier than she had been since Adam came home. He too had enjoyed the hunt this morning, and he was entering into the plantation's autumn activities with a zest that seemed genuine. There would be more work when all the crops were laid by. Fences must be repaired, wood cut for winter. Autumn wheat must be planted, and other fields made ready to lie fallow to the winter rains. And the crops must be sold.

Perhaps Queen's Gift will win his heart again, she thought. Perhaps we will never need to argue out the difference in our political opinion. But even while she tried to convince herself, she knew that Adam's new convictions were too strong, too compelling to be quietly laid aside.

After she dressed she went to Duke Roger's office. It was empty. Ebon told her that the master had gone to the village to see about shipping tobacco to Baltimore and pick up some Jamaica rum. "He ask me to give you de letter on de table."

Mary took up the letter. It was dated from St. Kitts and signed by Colonel de la Neuville. The name took her mind back to the days of the Revolution when he and the other young French officers had lingered in Edenton, waiting to join the American Army. She remembered their gaiety and pleasant manners and the ball they had given in the Panel Room of the Courthouse. She read a few paragraphs of the letter:

I was ordered to St. Christopher's, and in this place I shall be for some time. I confess ten years of American war would be less tedious to me than one single campaign here. Mr. Pemburn, of Edenton, has promised to take charge of some bottles of old rum which I desire you to accept. But until now I could not send them to him, as he is seven miles distant from this place. I hope he will sail for Edenton from Sandy Point so that I can entrust them to him for delivery to you.

Give me leave to present my respectful compliments to your family; to Mr. Iredell and Mrs. Blair and Stephen Cabarrus and the family at Pembroke. I well remember the exciting garden-party there.

What fine remembrance of your village we have! La Tour has returned to France. Pucheu was with Pulaski; where he is now I do not know. It would be of great interest to visit again your delightful Edenton; drop in at Horniblow's for a game of billiards with you or Iredell or Hardy. Or sit at one of the scarred old tables and talk with you and Dr Armitage and Charleton about this new-found liberty of yours over a brandy.

Mary put the letter back in Adam's desk among a mass of plantation papers, inventories, the latest *Gentleman's Magazine* and a volume of *Sir Charles Grandison*. On top of Fielding's *Journey from This World to the Next* lay a pamphlet on agriculture by Baron von Pollnitz.

Something like a sob rose in her throat as she noticed the gutted candles Ebon had not renewed. Adam must have sat up late the night before, reading *Sir Charles Grandison*. She remembered the pleasure she had found in reading Richardson's *Clarissa Harlowe* to him long ago. That Adam should now prefer to read in solitude indicated all too clearly how changed was their relationship.

Mechanically she removed the stubs of candles and threw them into the fire. The tallow caught instantly, making a bright blaze that flared for a moment, then died away. She swept the desk clean of tobacco, knocked the ashes from Adam's long clay pipe and put it in its place in the rack on the mantel.

A page of paper had fallen to the floor. She picked it up and saw it contained notes in Adam's writing. The heading was "Land."

We do not own the earth. It belongs to the rain and the wind and the sun. Land is a heritage, but it is ours only so long as we care for it. Nature waits to take it back. Jungles grow swiftly, lands untended revert to desert. We must give to the land, keep it as rich as we found it.

This thin layer of soil that covers the earth supports us, sustains all life. The land belongs to those who love it, the land and all the life it nurtures—the plants, the birds, the animals. The land confers freedom on those who work it, a God-given freedom which no man can abridge.

The cycle of the seasons is God's answer, plainly seen, to our questions concerning Eternal Life. Owen contends that the soil locks within its embrace the beginning of all life and receives at the last its discarded forms. It traces the progress of history and shelters its ignoble end. It is the imperishable storehouse of eternity.

Memo
Use the above in connection with the Rights of the People to Liberty and Freedom. Stress dependence on land.

Mary stared at the page. The ideas expressed were not strange to her, for Adam had often talked of man's obligation to the land that sustained him, and she knew too that her grandfather had held similar views. But now Adam was citing his familiar philosophy in support of his hateful new ideas! Mary felt angry and betrayed. To find these notes in Duke Roger's office, the heart of the plantation, made her feel that Adam was plotting against Queen's Gift, working from within to achieve its ruin. She recognized that her reaction was unreasonable, but Queen's Gift seemed suddenly less secure, more vulnerable than ever before.

Another memorandum on the littered desk caught her eye.

See Iredell about drawing up papers to set aside money for David's education at Princeton. Or send him to Cambridge? Owen Tewilliger is convinced David's abilities are extraordinary.

Resentment rose in Mary as she read the scrawled lines. Did Adam feel himself so far separated from her that he did not trust her to care for his son in case something happened to him? But then she realized that Adam's apprehensions were at least understandable. Never since his return had she mentioned David or asked after his welfare. She had known David as a child—had, indeed, helped to shield him from the resentment of Adam's first wife against the Arab slave girl who was the boy's mother. But since her marriage to Adam she had preferred to forget David, who lived now in Cahokia in the care of the schoolmaster Owen Tewilliger. Her effort to do so, she supposed, was a part of her fear of Adam's attachment to the West. David was an additional tie that drew Adam away from Carolina, and so she had rejected the fact of his existence and his importance to Adam.

And the same was true of Lavinia, widow of Adam's cousin Peyton Rutledge—beautiful, sad Lavinia who had been so unhappy with the irresponsible Peyton before his death at the early Revolutionary battle of Moore's Creek Bridge. Did Lavinia like life in Illinois and was she happy with her new husband Meredith Chapman? Mary had not asked. She was unwilling, she supposed, to concede that a fine-bred Carolinian could find contentment in that wilderness.

Mary was conscious of a great weariness, of spirit as well as body. She could no longer pretend to herself that she was without responsibility for the estrangement between herself and Adam. If it was true that he had turned his back on the plantation world she loved, it was likewise true that she had combated in small and petty ways his attempts to share with her his new visions. Queen's Gift could not satisfy her without Adam. Why was she unable to tell him so, tell him that she would follow him anywhere and lead any life he chose for her?

She was reminded suddenly of her grandmother. Rhoda Chapman could have been described only as a stubborn woman. She had always known quite well what she wanted at any given moment, and she had not been slow in making her wants known to those about her. Duke Roger, Mary had been told, had laughed at Rhoda's overbearing manner and had cheerfully given her her way most of the time. Apparently he had regarded wilfulness as a prerogative of a handsome woman. But Sir Nigel, Mary remembered, had found Rhoda's forcefulness less amusing than his predecessor. He had balked occasionally and had even won a concession or two after days or weeks of ominous silence. Their relationship had not offered a pattern for an ideal marriage, Mary reflected. Yet now she was allowing her own stubbornness, inherited perhaps from Rhoda, to create a breach between Adam and herself.

But was it stubbornness to love her home and to cling to a way of life that had satisfied Adam before and could again if only he——? Mary sighed and dropped the memorandum on the desk. The morning was passing, and she hadn't yet made her rounds of store-rooms, kitchen, weaving-house. And this was the day for the slaves to come to the dispensary for medicine.

At the dispensary a dozen slaves and half as many children were waiting. Ebon was, as usual, on hand to help her. He lanced boils and sores, sewed up small cuts and gashes, dug out chigoes.

A slave woman held her listless child up for Mary's inspection. "She blow hot and cold. She pukin' if I tries to feed she."

The child's skin was hot and dry to Mary's touch. She handed out medicine for chills and fever. "If she's not better by to-morrow, we'll put a blister on the back of her neck."

Mary called on her knowledge of curative plants as she listened to the complaints of the slaves. Sassafras tea was good for measles or colds, the leaves of benne for dysentery. The bark of dogwood made into a tea was used in reducing fever. Thoroughwort, which the Negroes called boneset, was a common remedy for seasonal fevers.

To one mother she said, "Give her a tea made from blackberry leaves if the running off is bad."

"You watch you'self, mistress," Ebon warned her. "Don' you take dat chile into you' lap, less she have lices in she head or bedbugs acreepin' in she's clothes."

"Can you make the tea yourself?" Mary asked, ignoring Ebon.

"Yes'm, I already gave she myrtle tea, but she don' have no checkin', so I tell she to chew a piece of holly root." The woman shuffled off, carrying the ailing child.

An old man with a cold came next. Mary gave him a tot of rum. And so it went until the plantation bell rang for the noon hour. The patients disappeared then. The bell meant food and the long rest until two, when the slaves again resumed their tasks.

Mary went to her room and washed her hands thoroughly with lye soap before changing clothes for dinner. The weariness she had felt earlier was now overpowering.

When Adam came to Mary's room at dinner-time he found her lying on the bed. She was sleeping restlessly, moaning a little. Her face was flushed. He laid his hand on her forehead. It was hot. Adam called the maid Pam and sent her for Chaney.

The old Negro woman came into the room and hurried to the bed. She touched Mary's cheek. "De fever done hit she hard. You go way, master. Pam and I'll get she in de bed. I tole she last week not to hold dose ailin' chillun at de sick-house. Now she done cotch hit herself."

Adam went downstairs and summoned Ebon. "Send a boy into town for Dr. Armitage. Tell him the mistress has the seasonal fever and we hope he can come out to see her." He paced back and forth in the library for ten minutes, then went upstairs. The two women had undressed Mary. She lay in the mahogany bed, her small body almost lost in its vast proportions. Chaney was bathing her forehead with a mixture of vinegar and water.

Adam said, "I'll do that. Go about your work, Chaney."

"Ain't got no work, 'scusin' doin' for she," the woman answered stubbornly.

Adam pulled a chair to the bedside.

Chaney gave way with reluctance. "Better I do for ma baby."

Adam took the china bowl from her hand. "Get me a linen napkin. I'll put a pad on her forehead."

"You got to change it 'bout as often as you take a breath, sar."

"I know." He smiled at the woman's insistence. "You sit in the dressing-room. I'll watch her until the doctor comes."

It was late when Dr. Armitage reached Queen's Gift. He shook his head when he came into the room. "If we could take September out of the calendar, we'd get along better. The town's overrun with fever. Sam Johnston came down with it last week. I sent him over to his plantation so his family could care for him. James Iredell's about again, and young Sylvia Hay is dragging around. She's staying with the Iredells, you know. I ordered her to bed, but she won't go. Says she's all right. Insists on taking over some of the household tasks from Hannah, who's expecting a baby next month, you know. Sylvia's a nice young woman."

He sat down on the bed and put his ear to Mary's chest. "I don't think it is serious," he said as he pulled the covers back in place.

Mary opened her eyes. They were bright with fever. She stared at the doctor a moment, then at Adam. Her long glossy brown hair lay like a stream on the pillow. There was no recognition in her blue eyes. Her slim fingers restlessly plucked at the covers.

Adam said, "This came on suddenly, Doctor. We hunted this morning."

The doctor nodded. "That's the way it comes sometimes. I'm going to give her a dose of Peru bark." He looked up at Adam. "Now don't get alarmed. Heaven knows fever is far from uncommon. People have it, and I give them medicine, and they recover, and that's that."

Adam got up and moved about the room.

"Sit yourself down, Adam, and be quiet." Armitage opened his leather case and fumbled among the bottles. "Here's what I want. You'd best get out of here, I think, and send her woman in. I'm going to give her medication and something to make her rest more comfortably."

It was more than an hour later when Dr. Armitage came downstairs. He found Adam in the library. Ebon had drawn the curtains and was lighting the candles with a lightwood splinter from the fire-place.

"Bring the doctor a hot drink, Ebon," Adam ordered, "and serve supper in here by the fire."

The doctor sat down, his long thin shanks to the blaze. "I'll stay to-night," he said. "I'll have to send for medicine. Better write a note to Moray to call on my patients." He got up out of his comfortable chair with obvious reluctance.

"That's mighty good of you, Doctor. There's paper and a quill on that table."

Adam met Ebon at the door and took the tray with glasses and decanter from him. "Have a boy and saddle horse at the door in five minutes. Instruct him that he's to go to Dr. Armitage's house and bring back a parcel of medicine. The doctor will give you a note for the boy to take."

Ebon said, "Yes, sar. At once." He turned anxious eyes to the doctor, who looked up from his letters. "I hope 'tain't nothin' bad with de mistress. She feel might' porely when she come to de dispensary, always puttin' she hand to she's head."

"A touch of fever. Nothing to worry about, Ebon," Dr. Armitage said.

The old man's face cleared. "Yes, sar. Thank you, sar."

When the note had been sent Adam poured the drinks. "Nothing like a good rum toddy when the weather's cool."

The doctor didn't reply. He sat deep in his chair, sipping his drink. "I've been telling that girl for weeks to quit driving herself. She's gone like a whirlwind for six months. I tell you, Adam, Mary's too high-strung."

"High-strung!" Adam exclaimed. "Why, Mary is always calm."

"That's a man for you. If a woman doesn't have hysterics or go into languors, you think she's calm and insensitive. It's the quiet, restrained women that want watching. The swooners and shriekers let off their emotions and are through with them. They slough off their burdens on some one else. Not your Marys; they let their troubles eat into them." He looked up from under his heavy white eyebrows. "Mary has been very worried lately, Adam. I hope it doesn't mean you have a woman out in that wilderness you're always going off to."

Adam laughed aloud. "Of course not! What makes you say such a thing?"

"One hears tales," the doctor muttered. "I'll tell you this, sir: if you make Mary unhappy, I swear I'll shoot you myself. Mary's like my own daughter. . . ." His voice trailed off, and he took a deep drink.

Adam stood by the mantel, looking down at the face of the old doctor, yellow as parchment and as deeply lined, but infinitely kind. "You may set your mind at rest, my old friend. Mary is my wife, and I'll have no other."

The doctor nodded, satisfied.

Dr. Armitage lighted a candle and went downstairs. The old case clock on the stairs chimed two as he made his way through the dark hall to the dining-room. Chaney had informed him that there was a "slight sketch of food on de table, in case you' stomach cry out in de night." He was seated at the table, cutting a slice of ham, when Adam came in.

"How is she?" he asked. "I looked into the room. Chaney was snoring in her chair, but Mary seems to be quiet."

"She has been resting quietly since midnight. She fought the sleeping-powder I gave her. I had to give a second dose. Some people are like that. The drug acts differently on different people. But I don't like the way the fever holds up. She should be sweating by now. These alternate chills and high fever are not reassuring."

Adam poured a glass of port for the doctor and sat down.

"You haven't been to bed at all," Armitage said. "Why don't you leave the doctoring to the doctor?"

"I couldn't sleep. I've been in the office, working on accounts. I thought she might call for me, and I wanted to be . . ." Adam hesitated a moment. "Is she seriously ill, Doctor?"

"It's always serious when fever is high as hers. I don't know yet whether this is just an acute case of ague and chills, swamp fever, or something more dangerous."

"You think it may be plague or pox?"

"I hope not, but there's plenty of smallpox up north. Letters from Philadelphia tell of a real epidemic. I'm not sure yet about Mary. Probably tomorrow I'll be able to tell you something more definite."

"Smallpox!" Adam said heavily. His eyes showed his anxiety.

"Mary's been scratched. Hugh Williamson inoculated her when he was here this spring. That's not always preventive, but it does prevent severe cases, I think. Don't worry, Adam. Go to bed. She'll sleep for several hours."

Adam got up and moved about the room restlessly.

He walks like a panther, the doctor thought. I've never seen a man of his height with finer co-ordination. Armitage liked Adam Rutledge and admired his integrity and generosity. He thought with impatience of the talk he'd heard in the village concerning Adam's vote at the Hillsborough convention.

Both men were silent. The house was filled with the strange, portentous silence of night. A soft wind fluttered the curtains at the windows. A mocking-bird in the tulip poplar practised a few experimental trills before beginning its song.

Armitage spoke suddenly. "The village is alive with disapproval, Adam. I suppose you know the hard things they say of you."

Adam nodded. "I know."

"But do you realize how difficult it's going to be to bear the criticism of all of your neighbours?"

"Tom Blount came here to hunt this morning, Doctor. Also young Charleton, and the Creecy boys."

"But not Lem Creecy, I take it? Nor James Blount? I thought not. There are a few who will respect your opinions or ignore them when a hunt is in prospect. But the majority of the landowners will neither forgive nor forget. They regard your action as the unforgivable sin, Adam—betrayal of your class. Mind you, I'm not one of your critics. I've always believed that a man is entitled to his own opinion, to do what he thinks best. A man has his rights."

"What of the rights of others? Hasn't a man some responsibility to look out for the folk less fortunate than he? As for deserting my class, as they call it, I am not alone. What about Wilie Jones?"

The doctor shrugged his thin shoulders. "Oh, Wilie! They consider him an eccentric. This is just another of his aberrations, they say, and he will soon tire of sponsoring the little farmers and the artisans and the lowly."

"If they say that about Wilie Jones, they are more stupid than I'd thought," Adam said heatedly. "This is no whim of Jones's or of mine any more than it is a fad of Thomas Jefferson or Patrick Henry or hundreds of our leaders from the North to the South. It's a fundamental thing. You may phrase it as you will—the voice of the people, the 'We, the People' of the preamble. I tell you, Armitage, there is still a division of our people. There is an awareness of danger to our liberties in every state. I am glad the dispute over the Constitution is not dying. Discussion makes for truth. A new nation is being formed. As sure as I sit here the nation will fail unless there are amendments to safeguard all the people. I am proud that North Carolina is one of the two states to stay outside the union. Her stand will help enforce on the new Congress the demand from people in all states for guarantees of their liberties. Only when those are sure can our state enter the union. Most of us who voted against ratification without a bill of rights deeply hope North Carolina can be one of the United States. But we can run no risk of sacrificing human rights."

The doctor drummed the table with his fingers. His face was grave, but he said nothing.

"I said I was working on accounts," Adam continued. "So I was for a time. The rest of the time since supper I've been reading again the pamphlets Jemmy Iredell wrote in answer to George Mason's objections to the Constitution. Jemmy has a better mind, a vaster legal knowledge than any other man in North Carolina. He ranks with the best in America. But with all that knowledge, with all his persuasive power, he will never convince the common people that they are protected by the Constitution as it stands. A bill of rights is not dangerous, as he says. The people see danger only in unrestricted power."

"You can't go around the country saying such revolutionary things, Adam."

Adam's fist came down on the table, a blow that made the dishes rattle and wine spill from his glass. "By God, I *can,* and I will!"

Unexpectedly Armitage cried, "Good for you, Adam! For a time I thought you had fallen under the spell of Wilie Jones, but now I see you are your own man. I should have known, but I've grown cynical of late. There are few real leaders and many who mouth their opinions without half understanding."

Adam was too startled to reply. He had been prepared for argument, not approbation.

Armitage leaned forward. "But you must have a care," he said. "They'll be after you like a pack of wolves."

"I'm not afraid of being unpopular, Armitage. Already I have felt the weight of the Governor's disapproval."

"How was that?"

"It was about tobacco. I heard he had called a meeting of his Council to discuss the disposal of the tobacco the state has acquired from the small farmers. I want to make up a large shipment next month, so a day or two ago I called on him to discuss buying some of the state's surplus. A message was sent out to me that the Governor was occupied, unable to see me. I was instructed to communicate in writing any business I had with him."

The doctor whistled. "Well, really, that *was* an affront!"

"I thought so. Especially when I heard later that at the time of my visit the Governor was going over the designs Mr. Hawks has drawn up for the new mansion at Hayes."

"Sam Johnston is set in his ways," the doctor said.

"Yes, I know that. I have always admired him for his integrity and forthright honesty. It is saddening to find that he has no regard for any opinion that differs from his own."

"What of James Iredell?"

"Ah, that is a different story. I had a talk with him at Hillsborough. He is sorry that I have cast my lot with the Antis, but he has no quarrel with my right to have an opinion. He agrees with Helvetius' stand: 'I disapprove of what you say, but I will defend to the death your right to say it.'"

"Aye, that's Iredell. Broad and fair."

Adam yawned. "Well, that's the way it stands, Armitage. The days ahead won't be pleasant."

The doctor wondered what Mary's feeling would be, for he knew she was a staunch Federalist. But he forbore to ask. "Go to bed, Adam. If you are needed, you will be called."

Adam lingered. "I'm surprised to find that you lean toward the Antis."

"I don't. I'm neither one nor the other. If God lets me be a good physician and keep my patients' bodies well and strong, I'll give way to the politicians to defend their rights." He yawned widely. "I'm for bed, my lad. Go thou and do likewise."

Adam slipped into Mary's room for a moment. She was sleeping, but her face was flushed, her fingers still busily plucking at the covers. He leaned over to kiss her forehead. It was burning-hot. She stirred a little, murmuring, "No, no, no!" and turned away from the touch of his lips.

The Tulip Poplar

21 For a fortnight Mary Rutledge hovered between life and death. When after seven days the fever had not broken, Dr. Armitage decided on violent measures. He would double the Peru-bark mixture and sweat her under blankets with hot sandbags at her feet and sides.

Armitage insisted on having another doctor present when he gave the heavy dose of Peru bark, so Angus Moray came with him. The two worked through one night and into the next day, but the hoped-for improvement did not occur.

On the tenth day Dr. Hugh Williamson arrived in Edenton to consult with Samuel Johnston and James Iredell about methods of convincing the stubborn Carolinians that they must ratify the Constitution. Armitage, returning to Queen's Gift after hurried calls on a few patients whom Moray was reluctant to treat alone, saw Williamson dismount from the Suffolk stage. He didn't allow Williamson even time to change clothes before he had him in a gig riding toward Queen's Gift. This timely arrival of the learned doctor who had had so much experience with bone-break fever as Chief Surgeon with General Greene's Southern Army seemed an act of Divine Providence.

"I can't place this fever," Armitage explained. "It isn't our seasonal sort. It isn't swamp-fever of the every-other-day variety. It's something different. The temperature stays abnormally high, and she passes black water."

Williamson shifted his huge frame so that he could face Armitage. Questions popped like bullets from his lips. "Eruptions?"

"A few only on the body. Definitely not pox."

"Her skin yellow?"

Armitage hesitated. "Yellowish, but no more than a trace."

"Black vomit?"

"No. Do you suspect plague?"

"I suspect everything until I've examined thoroughly."

Dr. Armitage touched his whip to the mare. After a time he said, "I've thought of dengue."

"Does she complain of bone ache?"

"She doesn't complain of anything. She's either delirious or lies absolutely still in what seems almost a coma. Sometimes her breath is heavy and harsh; sometimes one can scarcely discern any sound."

Dr. Williamson's large, homely face took on serious lines, which changed to impatience. "Hasn't that mare any more speed?"

Adam met them at the door, the lines of worry deep in his face. He grasped Hugh Williamson's hand in both of his, then led the way upstairs so swiftly that Williamson had to pause for breath. The doctor grasped the newel-post for support. "It's these blasted pounds around my belly," he said. Determinedly he mounted the remaining steps. "Where is she?"

In Mary's room old Chaney was kneeling beside the bed, stroking her mistress' thin hand and murmuring indistinguishable words. Angus Moray sat by the window, watching her.

Williamson strode to the bed and irritably thrust aside a length of mosquito net that had become unhooked. The buttons on his cuff caught in the stuff, and he swore mildly. "Get that thing back!"

Adam lifted the drapery and hooked it against the bed-post. Williamson leaned over Mary and listened to her breathing. His broad back stretched the seams of his blue coat. For all his quick movements, his touch on her forehead was gentle. He threw the blankets back and laid his ear to her chest. She moved, murmuring, "Water . . . water . . ." Her lips were cracked and dry, and there were fever sores at the corners of her mouth.

Williamson's hand encountered a hot sand-bag. "What's this?"

"We've been trying to get her into a sweat to break the fever."

Williamson jerked the sand-bag from Mary's side and flung it to the floor. He turned the blankets to the foot of the bed, leaving only the linen sheet to cover her body. To Chaney he said, "Get cool water. Cool, mind you, from the spring! A basin, linen towels, vinegar, two mustard plasters."

Dr. Armitage started to speak, but Williamson cut him short. "Weak as she is, I'm going to bleed her. I'm opposed to all this sweating when the body is burning with fever." Again he forestalled his colleague. "I know, I know. Sweating is the accepted thing, but you've tried it without success. When I studied in Utrecht with Doctors Hahn and Luchman we experimented when the usual medication failed. I'll wrap her first in sheets wrung out in cold water, then a blanket."

Williamson noticed Adam, who was waiting helplessly at the foot of the bed. "Adam, get out of here. Take a sleeping potion. Armitage, you look fit to drop. Go lie down. Where's that young Scot you've been telling me about?"

Angus Moray stepped forward. "Present, sir."

"Good! You and I and old Chaney will take over."

Adam opened his mouth to protest, but the doctor's calm assertion of authority was reassuring. He left the room, followed by Armitage, who was grey with fatigue. As he crossed the threshold Armitage stumbled and clutched Adam's shoulder to keep from falling. Adam was alarmed, but the old doctor spoke hastily. "No, no, it's nothing. Don't call Williamson. I'm not ill, just very tired."

"Can I help you to your room, Doctor?" Adam asked.

"Of course not," Armitage replied impatiently, "I can still walk unassisted. Go to your own room. We can both rest now. Mary is in the best possible hands. No one in America, not even Dr. Rush, is better equipped to care for her."

Adam shook his head. "You think I could sleep while she——?"

"You can and you must," Armitage said firmly. "You will be needed later. Conserve your strength. The time will come when she'll want your help."

In Mary's chamber the two doctors gazed at each other across the bed. Chaney had helped them wrap her mistress in a cool, damp sheet; across her brow they had placed a wet towel. Mary looked like a mummy swathed for the burial casket; her long braids lying beside her sunken cheeks and flowing over her shoulders appeared heavy and lifeless.

"It may be blackwater fever," Williamson said, "but, if so, why has her temperature stayed so high? And how in God's name did she contract it? Has there been anything like this in the village?"

The Scot shook his head. "Not that I know of. I've never seen a case of blackwater, although I've heard of it at the university."

"Edinburgh? I studied there, too." Williamson frowned and surveyed his patient. "I'm going to bleed her as soon as she's over the shock of this cold sheet. Try to get her to swallow cold water. Hold it to her mouth—a bit of cloth soaked in water might do. And for God's sake get some salve on those cracked lips of hers!" He put his hand on Chaney's shoulder and spoke kindly. "Take a rest, good old woman. Come back in two hours."

"Sar, what you goin' do wid she?"

"Get her well, old one. Get her well and on her feet."

After Chaney left the room Angus Moray said, "Doctor, I've just recalled something that may offer a clew to the source of this illness. Two slaves lately from the Indies died on this plantation a few weeks ago. I remember Dr. Armitage scolding Mrs. Rutledge when he heard she'd gone to their huts every day during their illness. Perhaps they had the blackwater."

"That could be it." Williamson sank into a chair, which creaked beneath his weight. He gasped and rubbed his eyes. "I'm dog-weary. The trip down from New York was hideous. Rough roads, and once the coach broke down and we had to continue in a springless waggon for miles." He pulled a turnip watch from his waistcoat pocket. "Well, I think we can begin to take blood. From her colour, she's full of bile. I didn't want old Chaney to be here when we use the lancet. The Negroes think you're up to murder." He got up slowly. "I'll wager you that old woman didn't go to take her rest. Right now she's consulting the witch doctor." He grinned at the horrified expression on Moray's face. "Oh, you'll get used to it if you stay around here. Many's the time I've had to combat 'conjuration' or burn up a spirit figure to show that I had more powerful magic."

Angus admired the deftness with which the old man opened a vein in Mary's wrist. She stirred a little. "She's insensible to pain," Williamson muttered. "What worries me is how much longer her strength will hold out."

Downstairs a stream of callers, neighbours and village folk had come to the house and been sent away by Ebon. "De doctor say she jes' de same," he repeated time after time. The jellies and broth they brought went to the kitchen, the flowers were put in water. "Look for ever like a funeral," Young Ben remarked as he carried a great bunch of Michaelmas daisies and asters to the pantry.

Ebon turned on him, his gnarled black hand clenched. "Don't you say dat word, you black rascal! Don't let it off you' tongue! Catch it back wid you' teeths and grind it up. Hear?"

"Yes, sar."

When Adam came downstairs near supper-time James and Hannah Iredell and Sylvia Hay were on the point of leaving. He greeted them quietly, and they stood in an awkward silence while the Iredells searched for words to express their sympathy. Hannah's sensitive mouth quivered, and her eyes filmed with tears as she grasped Adam's hand.

"Adam, we want to help," Iredell said. "What can we do?"

"Thanks, Jemmy, but for the present we can only wait and pray, Dr. Hugh says."

"Is Hugh Williamson here? I didn't know. Thank God for that!"

"Aye, thank God!" Adam turned to Sylvia. "It isn't that I haven't every confidence in Dr. Armitage and the young doctor, but Williamson has had so much experience with fevers and has written papers about them. For years he's been making studies to determine the cause of the terrible fevers we have in this part of the country."

"Can't I be of some use, Mr. Rutledge?" Sylvia asked. "I've had experience with illness. Really, I'm almost a nurse."

"That is kind of you. Suppose we ask Dr. Williamson when he comes down."

Hannah looked from her husband to Adam. "We had thought to leave. We don't want to disturb you."

Adam took her hand. "You could never disturb me, Hannah. Help me by staying to have supper. Waiting is difficult, and patience is something I have never learned. . . . Here is Dr. Moray." He rose quickly and went to the door.

Moray smiled encouragingly. "Dr. Williamson thinks there is a slight improvement. Your wife is resting quite easily. The doctor says he will come downstairs shortly. Dr. Armitage will stay with Mrs. Rutledge." He turned to the others. "Dr. Williamson hasn't left the sick-room even for a bite to eat since he arrived this morning."

Adam excused himself and hurried upstairs to Mary's room. But his eager steps slowed as he entered the chamber. He could detect no change in Mary's condition. She lay perfectly still, her head swathed in damp linen that partially concealed her face. He wished she would open her eyes. He wanted to assure himself of their blueness, that dear candid Irish blue. . . .

Williamson and Armitage stood near the window, talking in low voices. "I can't tell whether the hours have brought any significant improvement," Williamson was saying, "but she is quiet now and, I think, more comfortable. We got at least a quart of cool water down her by forcing a tube down her throat."

"Blackwater fever is rare here, as you know. I've no experience with it, nor have I had experience with the use of cold water. We always use hot, to sweat the body and break the fever," Armitage said worriedly.

Williamson spoke with some impatience. "I know that, but must we physicians be bound to old methods and superstitions? I want to get some strength into her. Broth next, even if we have to force it into her."

" 'Feed a cold and starve a fever,' " Armitage quoted.

"Damme if I believe in that old wives' saying! We'll feed her. She's got to have strength to combat this disease." Williamson looked up and saw Adam at the door. "I'm just coming. I'll welcome food and a drink."

"I'll stay here while you eat," Adam said. "James and Hannah Iredell are here, and a young woman who says she's 'almost a nurse.' "

"Good. We may want a nurse. Come along, Armitage. Let's eat a good supper, and then I'm going to send you home for the night." Armitage demurred, but Williamson took him by the elbow and pushed him out of the room. "Adam can sit here. I'll send your young Scot up as soon as he has eaten. I want to talk with Jemmy."

Adam sat down facing the great mahogany bed, but rose almost immediately to put a log on the fire as the evening chill began to penetrate the room. There would be a heavy frost to-night, he thought, perhaps a black frost. Autumn would soon be upon them in full force.

The afterglow faded, and the shadows in the room deepened. He forbore to light the candles; the firelight was sufficient. From time to time he changed the compress on Mary's head, dipping the linen into the basin of water, wringing it dry. It gratified him to be able to do even so small a thing for her.

A little wind came up, and the boughs of the great tree scraped against the window. The drying leaves rustled urgently, Adam thought, like a chorus of small voices trying to whisper a message to him. A message of hope or of sorrow? he wondered.

Angus Moray came to take over the vigil, and Adam went downstairs to his guests. Approaching the dining-room, he could hear Dr. Williamson holding forth. Food had indeed been what the learned doctor needed, Adam reflected, for his voice had regained its usual vigour. He paused to see which of his innumerable scientific hobbies held Williamson's attention currently.

"My records do not go beyond '76, but they cover the four previous years," he was saying. "During that time the westerly winds blew for around two hundred and nine days, easterly winds for a hundred and five—a ratio of almost two to one. Similarly, in Russia, according to a paper addressed by Dr. Gutherie to the Royal Society of Edinburgh, the days of westerly winds during the winter half of the year outnumber the easterly by two to one. Their coldest winds are from the south of west. Interesting, what? Well, to get back to our own country, it would appear from the findings of other men that the westerly winds no longer prevail as strongly as they did sixty years ago. Now why do you suppose that is?"

"Perhaps on account of cutting the forests?" Armitage ventured.

"I don't know," Williamson said shortly, and Adam, standing outside in the hall, smiled in amusement. Dr. Hugh was not accustomed to have his rhetorical questions answered. When he resumed he chose a different topic. "However, my consuming interest is still the search for the cause of fever. The facts thus far established are, alas, few. Fever is seasonal. It is worse in low country where there are swamps and stagnant water. When I have moved my patients from such regions they have improved visibly."

Dr. Armitage asked, "Do you think we should move Mary to higher country? To the Virginia Hot Springs?"

"Not yet. Just at present I wouldn't have her moved even from one room to another. Later perhaps. Catawba Springs might possibly——"

Iredell broke in. "Good Gad, not Catawba, Hugh! It was in that country that her first husband was caught and hanged."

"Of course! How could I have forgotten? We'll certainly not send her there." Williamson looked up and saw Adam in the doorway. "Ah, here you are. We are down to dessert. After your superb food we all are stronger. Is Mary resting quietly?"

"Yes. Stay where you are. Moray will call you if you are needed." Adam went to a sideboard and got out a bottle of brandy, which Ebon served in delicate liqueur glasses.

"We've been discussing climate and its effect on people in different parts of the world, Adam." Williamson raised his glass to the light to admire the colour of the old brandy. "Or perhaps discussion is scarcely the word. My friends have graciously allowed me to hold the floor almost exclusively." His deep laugh rumbled. "Come, eat that delicious supper Ebon has placed before you. You need it."

Sylvia smiled at the portly physician. "I think Dr. Williamson must have turned his mind to all the problems of the world."

"Now, young lady, you are poking fun. But to achieve wisdom one must first acquire facts. Perhaps I've been influenced by my friend Dr. Franklin, always a pursuer of knowledge."

"And of the ladies as well, I've heard," Sylvia said slyly. "My friends in London tell me that when he was there before the war he was constantly surrounded by a bevy of fashionable beauties."

Dr. Williamson's eyes twinkled. "Now don't tell me they still talk of the time he lost our diplomatic code just after a visit to a London belle."

"The story is that he dropped it right in the court-yard of St. James's Palace. So convenient for our diplomats to pick up the paper at their very door-step," Sylvia said demurely.

"Ah, you do know about that fiasco." Williamson chuckled. "I've always thought the code found its way into some lady's pocket."

James Iredell said to Hannah, "We must be going."

She rose at once. "You're right, Jemmy. Are you ready, Sylvia?"

"Miss Hay will be out to-morrow to assist us for a few days," Williamson told Adam. "I've questioned her, and I think she can be a real help. Dr. Moray will drive her out when he comes. I'll go up now and send him down."

As the party moved to the hall Armitage asked, "Are you sure you don't want Moray or me to stay?"

"No, not to-night. I don't expect any change of importance. Get your rest. And you must have other patients."

"I'm leaving them to Moray and Dr. Norcom, although I made some calls this morning. The fact is, I find it difficult to keep my mind on other cases. Mary Rutledge is more important to me than all the patients in the county."

Williamson patted Armitage's shoulder and called good night to Iredell. "If you are writing to Johnston, tell him I hope to call on him at The Hermitage in a few days. I've reports to give him and questions to ask before I go back. We've work ahead of us, Jemmy—work and more work."

Iredell glanced at Adam. Then he came back to Williamson and spoke briefly in a low voice. Making sure the doctor knows the sad truth about his host's politics, Adam thought. It was like Jemmy to want to save his friends from embarrassing misapprehensions.

When the two carriages had departed and Williamson had returned to his patient Adam walked to the bachelors' house to talk to Marcy.

On the way Herk overtook him. "Master, I'se been waitin'. Look lak I ain't seen you for a whole moon. All we folk worr'in' 'bout de lady mistress. Want I should get you' hoss? Look lak when you get debil ridin', you can get shed of Ole Satan ridin' you' hoss."

"Not to-night, thanks, Herk. Maybe to-morrow."

Marcy was reading by the light of a candle when Adam entered his room. He jumped to his feet. Adam noted that the book that had engrossed Marcy was a copy of Iredell's *Marcus* pamphlet. Adam did not sit down, but paced nervously about the room as the overseer answered his questions about the plantation.

"I've got the trash gang at work in the woods, cording what was cut last month and piling brush in the new ground. Twenty men are manuring the river field, making ready to sow grain, and as many more are pulling fodder."

"Good," Adam said absently.

Marcy opened an account book. "We averaged about twelve bushels of corn to the acre, and twenty bushels of wheat on that heavy land down by the pocosin."

"Good, very good. Marcy, I'm afraid I'll have to ask you to go over to the Tyrrell land to look after the turpentine. We should get the barrels off before the weather is too cold, and I haven't complete confidence in Flynn, who's in charge there. I hate to add to your work, but you'll understand I can't leave now."

Marcy's red-brown eyes expressed his sympathy. "Mr. Rutledge, you know I want to do everything I can to relieve you from worry."

"Thank you, Marcy, thank you. It will be a help to have you check the work across the Sound for me. The woods are about cleaned out. I've worked that acreage for ten years. Two years more are all I can hope for. I hate to see the long-leaf pines cleaned out, and I don't want to burn the trees for tar yet."

"I heard the Green Swamp people made a powerful lot of money from turpentine this year," Marcy said. "Five thousand pounds or so."

"No doubt. Their woods are heavy, and their distillery close by. Now, Marcy, I want you to find out how many boxes the hands are averaging. It should run above seventy or eighty boxes a day, four-fifty to five hundred a week. The young ones won't do more than fifty. We want to begin cutting boxes by the first of November at the latest so they will all be finished and ready when the dripping starts about the middle of March."

"Yes, sir. Don't give it another thought."

"Be sure Flynn understands about the boxes. Eight to fifteen inches long and smooth on the lower lip, so as to hold a quart of drip. Tell him to have his stakes cut and set up to square off the half-acres. The division ought to be wide enough to get a cart through easily."

"Yes, sir. Please don't worry. If you remember, that was my first work when you brought me to Rutledge Riding as an indentured man."

"So it was, Marcy. Much water has flowed to the Banks since then."

"Can you give me another minute, sir?" Marcy asked. "It's about the tobacco. Captain Emperor will be in next week. Have you spoken to Governor Johnston about buying enough tobacco to make up our Bideford order?"

"I didn't see him," Adam said shortly, and Marcy understood that he was not to pursue the subject. After a pause Adam said, "I understand Arthur Lee has written from New York, making inquiry relative to the sale of state tobacco and about its quantity, quality and price."

Marcy raised his eyebrows. "Ah, so we are to have a northern market opened up!"

"Can't say. Marcy, do you know where the state tobacco is stored? And how much there is?"

Marcy rummaged among his papers and pulled from the bottom of the pile a memorandum which he offered to Adam.

540	Hogsheads in	Wilmington, from Cross Creek
315	"	lying at the Mouth of Roanoke
250	"	at Lockhart's whse. near Edenton
150	"	at Ryan's, about two miles from Lockhart's
320	"	at John Gray Blount's whse.
1575	Hogsheads, total	

Adam studied the figures. "Do you have any record of the quality?"

"Most of it is good, especially the part inspected at Campbell's Town. I've no information about what's stored at the Mouth of the Roanoke, but there's a dismal account from Tarborough and Washington."

"What's wrong?" Adam asked.

"I was told it was originally good, but it lay for several weeks uncovered and was almost ruined by exposure. At least a third will have to be regraded when it's inspected again."

"All the farmers' labour lost because the warehousemen are negligent!" Adam exclaimed with disgust. "I'm glad we are in a position to handle our own and don't need the state to warehouse or sell for us. That's one advantage of living on the Sound."

"Sir, for a year there's been a lot of talk about this public tobacco, in the Assembly and among the planters." Marcy consulted a paper. "This says that our agents, Constable, Rucker and Company of New York, are sending a ship to Wilmington. They're raising some difficulty about redeeming the tobacco paper." Marcy searched out another paper. "And here's something that will interest you. The Minister of the United Netherlands 'has been sufficiently impressed with the upright views and friendly intentions of North Carolina' in this business for him to 'render any civilities in his power' to endeavour to establish an extensive Continental connection between the Netherlands and North Carolina."

"Marcy, that's good news. I must investigate. Perhaps we can do better dealing direct with Holland than through Constable, Rucker."

"It will bear looking into, Mr. Rutledge. You might read the report written by Mr. Benjamin Hawkins and William Blount on this matter. They are members of the tobacco committee appointed last year by the Governor."

Adam said, "This gives me much to think about. It was far-sighted of you to gather all this information."

Marcy ran his fingers through his curly red hair. "Mrs. Rutledge suggested it. She was eager that the plantation should make a fine record this year."

Adam looked at the sturdy body and strong, rugged face of the Irishman. He laid his hand affectionately on Marcy's shoulder. "It seems a long time since you came to me. I'm very grateful that you've chosen to stay with me all these years."

Marcy answered with ill-disguised emotion. "I've never thought of doing otherwise, Mr. Rutledge. I've not forgotten that you freed me before my indenture was up. And I can never thank you for giving me a home out in the West or for your kindness when my poor little wife died out there."

Adam's fingers tightened on Marcy's shoulder. "You did a noble thing when you took that sweet, sad girl and gave her happiness. . . . Aye, Marcy, we've fought some fights together." He went out.

Marcy watched him walking with bent shoulders toward the great house. Sure, good man, we've been side by side in many fights, the Irishman thought, but there's another looming on the horizon. When the mistress is about again you'll be feeling the weight of the wind on you, whirling and skirling about your shoulders—the sharp wind of disapproval and condemnation from those you thought your friends.

The following afternoon Angus Moray returned to Queen's Gift, bringing with him Sylvia Hay and also Miss Sarah Poor, the most experienced nurse the county afforded. Miss Sarah, who admitted to fifty years, was a tall, spare woman with white skin and a mass of golden freckles. Her light-red hair was alive with energy and stood out about her head like a fiery halo. Miss Sarah, however, deplored its frivolous appearance and customarily wore it in a tight knot at the nape of her neck, covered by a mob-cap. Her tongue was sharp, but patients found her irascibility concealed an instinctive kindness and sensitivity to their needs. "And she's tough as a pine-knot," Dr. Armitage always said of her. "I never heard Sarah admit fatigue."

Dr. Williamson greeted her with a roar of pleasure and a vigorous hug. "Sarah, my lass, you're as welcome as May apples. Wherever did you come from?"

Miss Sarah settled her mob-cap on her bright hair and gave her cape to Ebon. "Dr. Hugh, you are so impetuous! How can I go into a sick-chamber with my cap tilted and my hair in disarray? To answer your question, I came over from the Pettigrew plantation in Tyrrell. Dr. Armitage sent for me. Where's the patient?"

Adam stepped forward. "I'm so glad you're here, Miss Sarah. Follow me." He led the way up the broad stairs. Miss Sarah walked primly behind him, very erect, disdaining to touch the mahogany hand-rail.

"Perhaps I will only be in the way," Sylvia suggested to Williamson, "now that Miss Poor is here."

"Nonsense! I can use you both. Even Sarah must rest occasionally." To Angus he said, "There's no change. Chaney or I sat with Mary all the night. But she can't continue indefinitely as she is, and we must be ready for whatever happens. If you'll stay with her for a while, I'll catch a bathe and a sleep."

Adam said to Sylvia, "A maid is waiting to show you to your room. It is so kind of you to offer your services."

A young slave appeared to lead Sylvia to her bedchamber in the east wing. "Master he say, 'Not too far away from de sick-chamber, and quiet for resting.'" Sylvia changed to a light calico dress and had just bound her heavy auburn hair in a black net when the maid tapped at the door. "De doctor he say, please come."

Sylvia hastened down the side hall to the wide hallway that divided the house. Angus Moray was waiting for her. "Miss Poor has already given the patient a bath, and wants you to help roll her over while she changes the linen. Dr. Williamson was doubtful about the bath, but Miss Poor said, 'If Mrs. Rutledge is going to die, she may as well die clean.'" He smiled slightly. "Miss Poor reminds me of a Scotch woman in our village. She had as many sharp points as a thistle, but she was wholesome as oat-cake."

"I'd best hurry if she's waiting," Sylvia said.

The doctor put his hand on her arm. "I'm glad you came, Sylvia."

"Better be glad Miss Poor is here. I'll do what I can, you may be sure."
Sylvia found Miss Sarah on her knees by the bedside. "I'm almost ready
for you," the nurse said. "Just let me roll the clean sheet and secure it on
this side." With expert hands she tucked the linen sheet under the mattress,
made the corners tight and unrolled it to the middle of the bed until it
touched the still figure. "Now gently lift her head and shoulders, Chaney.
You take her feet, Miss Hay, while I lift her middle. We'll lay her on the
new sheet. . . . Good. Let her down easy. . . . That's it."

With a swift snap she pulled the old sheets off and threw them on the
floor in a heap. "Now we'll unroll the clean sheet, spread it out carefully
and square the corners so the linen's tight with nary a wrinkle. Now, you
see, she hasn't been disturbed at all."

Sylvia said, "I've never seen a sick-bed changed so easily."

"Learned it a long while ago," Miss Sarah said complacently. "A bathe
and clean, sweet linen will sometimes make a very ill patient feel like going
on living. That will be all now, Chaney. Go about your duties. Miss Hay,
I'll want you here from six until eight. I take my rest then. Tell that young
doctor he needn't stay in the room as long as he remains where I can call
him. I've had instructions from Dr. Hugh, and I don't need him here." She
sat down in a chair near the head of the bed where she could watch Mary's
face and change the cooling cloths on her forehead.

Sylvia went to deliver Miss Sarah's message. Angus was seated on a settee
at the end of the hall. He rose as Sylvia emerged from the sick-room. She
told him what the nurse had said, and they sat together on the settee.

"She's . . . she's terribly ill, isn't she?" Sylvia said hesitantly.

Angus nodded. "I think she might have been gone by now if Dr. Williamson hadn't changed the treatment. He's a fine surgeon, bold and free-think-
ing. He radiates confidence."

Sylvia said, "Isn't it providential that he came!"

"Yes, I suppose so, but perhaps it isn't her time to go yet. I'm inclined to
believe there comes a time in every man's life when no doctor can help him
because he is destined to die then."

"A gloomy belief, sir! Without hope."

"Nonsense. Of course there's hope, always. As a surgeon one fights all
one can, but . . ." He smiled. "You are thinking this is my Presbyterianism
talking. Maybe it is. I won't argue the point. I'd much rather sit here and
look at your lovely face, your strange eyes that seem like amber. Just now
they are filled with kindness. I would that they were always so when I——"

He broke off suddenly, and Sylvia looked up to see Miss Sarah standing
at the door of the sick-chamber, beckoning. Angus was on his feet in an
instant, and Sylvia hurried down the hall after him.

Miss Sarah said, "Will you wait here, Miss Hay? It's the doctor I need."
She led him inside and closed the door. "Come, look at her, Doctor. Your
eyes are better than mine. Hasn't she changed colour?"

Angus strode to the bed. The shadows of evening filled the room. "Light the candles," he said. "Yes, she's yellowing. A definite change of colour. I'll call Dr. Williamson at once," Angus said.

"It's a shame to disturb him, but I suppose we must," Miss Sarah said reluctantly. "I've worked with Dr. Hugh before, and I know exactly what treatment he'll want to try next. Couldn't you——?"

"I've never encountered this kind of fever," Angus said stiffly, "and I must consult the physician in charge before I undertake any new treatment."

"Very well, young man, very well," Miss Sarah said docilely. "Meanwhile I'll lay out the drugs Dr. Hugh will need. First he'll bleed her, and then . . . hippo, calomel, jalap, Dover powder, castor oil . . ." She turned toward the window in exasperation. "In heaven's name, why hasn't that tree been cut back from the house! It fair drives me nervy. Sounds like it's talking and talking!" She went to the window and pulled the curtains.

Moray left the room and returned in a few minutes with Dr. Williamson, who wore a nightshirt pushed into his small-clothes and a pair of list slippers on his bare feet. He took up the candle and leaned over the bed. "Light more candles. Fetch hot water and a bleeding basin. Moray, get my medicine satchel. We'll take a pint of blood from her first. After an hour an emetic of hippo. When the stomach's settled, ten grains of calomel and ten of jalap. Bowels opened, a routine of two grains of calomel and one of Dover powder every three hours until her gums are tender." He addressed the unhearing Mary. "I loathe to do this to you, my girl, but I know no alternative."

Miss Sarah flashed a significant glance at Angus and said quietly, "I have those drugs all ready for you, Doctor."

Williamson tied a bandage just above Mary's elbow and held the arm with his left hand, his thumb on the vein. Miss Sarah handed him the lancet. He touched the vein just below his thumb and pushed the instrument gently upward. Then he took away his thumb, and the blood gushed into the pewter basin.

"We could use leeches or a hot cup," Williamson said, "but this is quicker, and will leave no scar." He straightened up, handed the basin to Sarah Poor and bandaged Mary's arm. She stirred a little. Her lips moved but no sound came. "I've been keeping her under opium until I was sure how it was going to turn," he explained to Moray.

"You think now it's yellow fever?" Angus inquired.

"I wish I felt more certain, but I think we must treat it as yellow fever until we can identify it otherwise. What puzzles me is the unbroken high temperature. In yellow-fever cases the temperature is apt to drop sharply as early as the third day." He turned to Sarah Poor. "You have the medication ready? Good. We'll let her rest for an hour or so. Dr. Moray, tell Mr. Rutledge that no one is to leave this place or enter until I give the word. He is to post a slave at the gates and warn the people that a dangerous fever is sojourning here at Queen's Gift. We must avoid the spread of possible contagion."

He sat down in a chair and thrust his heavy legs out in front of him, sighing wearily. "I thought I might get away from pukes, purges, blood-letting and blistering. But Dr. Franklin's cold-air-and-water treatment does not cover severe cases, that's plain."

It was morning before Williamson left the sick-room. Outside the door he encountered Adam. "Don't go in for the moment. I want to talk to you." The two went to the end of the hall and sat down. "It seems quite possible that we've a case of yellow fever here. Any one who has been in the room may come down with it. Can you control your Negroes enough to keep them on the place?"

"Yes, I can do that." Adam tried to think calmly, but the words "yellow fever" kept echoing in his mind. "What about Miss Hay? She is worried because her employer may return next week and require her services."

"Damn her employer! Talk sense, man. I'm not going to be responsible for turning yellow fever loose in the county because little Miss Sylvia is afraid to risk her employer's displeasure. We all have obligations. Sarah Poor is due at Hannah Iredell's—Hannah is expecting next month, you know—but Sarah can't leave now. Hannah will have to get another midwife, old Granny Sills or some one." The doctor noticed how pale Adam was. He spoke more kindly. "See here, my lad, they tell me you've been spending all your time standing about by Mary's door. Go outside and get some air. Let us do the worrying."

Adam seized on the words. "Then you *are* worried!"

"Adam, you know as well as I that yellow fever is dangerous. You know, too, that people have recovered from it. More than that I can't tell you." He brushed his hand across his eyes wearily. "And we can't be certain even now that this is actually yellow fever. I'll go back now. I want to watch her myself for a while. Your business is to see that no one breaks the quarantine."

"I suppose it's all right to send Marcy for supplies. He hasn't been exposed."

"I suppose so. But what's become of the theory that every plantation is self-sufficient?"

"That's true only up to a certain point," Adam said. But Williamson had already started down the hall. For a large man he was surprisingly light on his feet.

For three days they fought for Mary Rutledge's life, Williamson, Angus Moray and the two women. Each time one of them left her room he wondered whether she would be alive when he returned. Adam stationed himself on the settee at the end of the hall, leaving it only to pace up and down outside Mary's door. Ebon served his meals there, standing by disconsolately when Adam refused anything but a glass of milk. The third day, Adam said, "Tell Chaney to leave the cooking to her helpers. I think her mistress would like to know Chaney was near by."

After that the old woman—nurse, cook and friend—sat in Mary's dressing-room, her gnarled hands busy with her knitting. Occasionally Adam sat there with her for a while, drawing a strange comfort from her stolid presence.

Once they heard Dr. Williamson say to Sarah Poor, "Can't you get any warm drink down her?"

"Not one thing," the nurse answered. "Her stomach refuses. I've tried everything—flaxseed, elderberry blossom, yapon. But always up it comes. I'm at my wits' end, Doctor."

Adam rose and stared helplessly at the bedroom door. Then he went into the hall and resumed his restless pacing.

When Marcy came in from the village that night he brought a packet of mail, most of it for Dr. Williamson—letters from New York, from Philadelphia and one from Samuel Johnston at The Hermitage. There was also a note for Sylvia Hay from Lady Anne, announcing that she expected to be in Edenton again the following week. "Be prepared to leave for Philadelphia," she wrote. "We may go there very soon unless the pox and the plague have taken over the city."

"I hmm, you'll leave here when I say so, and no sooner!" was Dr. Williamson's comment when she showed him the letter. His voice softened a little when he saw the troubled look on her face. "I know you are not afraid of the disease. You are a brave girl. Why are you afraid of this Lady Anne Stuart?"

"I'm not really, Doctor, but she is my employer—and she doesn't even know I'm here."

The doctor studied her. "Damme if I understand young Moray. If I were his age, I'd not let you out of my sight. Is it he you want to run from?"

Sylvia blushed and stared fixedly at the letter in her hand. Thank goodness Angus was in the sick-room, she thought. Who knew what this unpredictable man might say next?

But Williamson was breaking the seal of a letter. "Hmm," he said, "this is reassuring. I need not be back in New York for some weeks yet."

Marcy came up to where they stood on the gallery. "Dr. Armitage says there's no need of Dr. Moray coming back to town. He wouldn't be admitted to any one's home. The village is so frightened by the reports of Mrs. Rutledge's mysterious malady that every one who can is scurrying away. The Barkers are at Virginia Springs, the Blairs and Hardys in the Western mountains, the Joneses and Allens in Hillsborough. The Charles Johnsons are with Parson Earle at River Plantation. Even Madam Horniblow has gone to Norfolk."

Adam came onto the gallery and went with Marcy to the garden. "Is there no political talk going around?" he asked.

Marcy hesitated. He did not want to tell Adam that people were saying Mary's illness was a punishment from heaven for his conduct. "I saw Parson Pettigrew as he was ready to sail for Tyrrell County," he answered evasively. "He said he had read prayers at St. Paul's on Sunday and prayed for you in your affliction."

Adam made no comment. He signalled to Herk, who seemed always to be standing somewhere near by. "Bring out Diablo. I'll ride to the fishery."

"Nobody ride dat animal dese two weeks," Herk commented.

Adam spoke sharply. "Bring Diablo instantly!"

"Yes, sar. Instantly."

It was the dark of the moon. Stars shone brilliantly in the black sky. A strong wind was blowing up the Sound, lashing the water into small waves, bending the slender young pines that grew thickly along the shore. Adam guided his restive horse down the bank to the narrow strip of beach that followed the curving shore. The wind was rising, he noticed. Glancing over his shoulder, Adam saw that Herk was following. He pulled up Diablo. The horse plunged and threw his head back, almost striking Adam in the face. "Go on back," he shouted to Herk. "Go home."

But Herk continued to put his horse forward. "Master," he said as he came up, "Master, de debil ride to-night wid de wind. Better Herk stay wid Master. Herk got strong Mankwala agin de evil one."

Adam said no more. They rode swiftly, the water splashing against the horses' feet. At the verge of the pocosin Adam reined up and turned onto the Indian path.

They had been out for two hours when they reached Queen's Gift again. At the stable Adam threw Diablo's reins into Herk's hand and strode off toward the house. The silence of the night was somehow alarming. The moaning of the wind was the only sound, the moaning that always frightened the Negroes when some one was ill. Would Mary "go out on the wind," as the Negroes phrased it? He breathed heavily, his heart leaden within him.

As he approached the house a strange sight met his eyes. Beneath the giant tulip poplar he made out the figures of many slaves kneeling on the ground, illumined by a single lanthorn. Silent, motionless figures, waiting, waiting . . .

Then, still silently, at a signal not apparent to Adam, the Negroes bent down and rested their foreheads on the earth. He moved closer and saw that an idol had been set up on a low platform at the base of the mighty tree— a wooden image, crudely carved, with small head, long torso, short legs. The Negroes of Queen's Gift, skeptical as always of the power of white man's magic, had summoned the god of their ancestors to do battle for the life of their stricken mistress.

The wind bent the long branches of the tree, and dried leaves rustled to the ground. The sound startled Adam into action. He ran into the house and up the stairs to Mary's room. On the threshold he paused. A single candle burned at the bedside, outlining the massive figure of Dr. Williamson, who stood looking down at Mary.

Williamson turned to Chaney, who stood with Sarah Poor at the foot of the bed. His voice was quiet. "The tea you made has stayed down for more than an hour. She's beginning to sweat. You said it was tea, but . . . What did you give her that brought this blessed change, old woman?"

Chaney pointed a long black arm toward the window. A branch scraped against the pane, making a grating sound. "De great tree told me, sar. He say, 'Take my bark. Make her a cup of tea. I will give her strength and life.'"

Sarah Poor clutched the bed-post, her eyes wide.

"Dear God!" Williamson said reverently. "Dear God, a miracle has happened!"

Adam came into the room. He knelt at the side of the bed and pressed his face to Mary's limp hand. It was cool and moist against his cheek.

Pocosin at Night

22 THE first sound to pierce the consciousness of Mary Rutledge was the hunting horn. "Where is the hunt?" were her first words.

Adam, who was seated beside her bed, took her thin hand in his. "They are hunting from Mulberry Hill down the Indian path as far as Dr. Norcom's plantation."

She did not speak for some time. Her eyes, deeply sunken, surveyed the room. "The great tree has lost its leaves," she said wonderingly. She tried feebly to raise herself on the pillow. Adam quickly slipped his arm under her shoulders and lifted her gently to a half-sitting position.

"I have no strength," she whispered. "What is wrong with me?" Tears formed in her eyes and rolled down her cheeks.

"You have been very ill, my sweet. Do not exert yourself."

She closed her eyes. A moment later she was asleep, breathing easily and naturally. Adam laid his head on the bed and prayed silently, thanking God for His blessing.

He went to the dressing-room and beckoned exultantly to Miss Sarah. "She spoke to me! She asked where the hunt was."

Miss Sarah hurried to Mary's bedside. "Bless Thee, dear God!" Adam heard her whisper. When she looked around at him there were tears in her pale-blue eyes. "Go tell Dr. Hugh."

Williamson was in the dining-room, breakfasting with Angus Moray and Sylvia, and he was speaking, Adam noted, of the political subjects he avoided in Adam's presence. "Yes, we have problems, a great plenty. I've written a piece in the New York *Daily Advertiser* about the position of North Carolina. What disturbs me is that she won't be in at the beginnings of things. The new government is to originate next March, you know, and is delayed so long only because Virginia could not hold all her elections and still allow time for the Kentucky members to participate."

"Where will the new Congress meet, sir?" Angus asked.

"In New York, a choice I regret exceedingly. Eastern members will attend with too much ease. The location will give them an improper legislative advantage." He spread some wild strawberry jam. "Had North Carolina ratified with the rest, her five members in the House of Representatives could easily have turned the scale in favour of a more southern position."

"I understand North Carolina demands amendments to the Constitution —at least, I think that's what Mr. Iredell said," Sylvia remarked.

Williamson dropped his fork to his plate with a clatter. "My patience and temper have been tried to the utmost over this amendment business. A number of states want amendments. Some want as many as thirty-seven. There'll be plenty of time later for amending. I doubt now if we can call another convention before next year."

Adam broke into the conversation, his eyes alight, his mouth smiling. "Doctor, Mary was conscious! She spoke to me!"

"Was she rational?" the doctor asked as he pushed back his chair and rose to his feet.

"Perfectly! Evidently she had heard the hunting horn, for she asked where the hunt was. Then she noticed that the leaves were gone from the tulip poplar."

Dr. Williamson was half-way across the room. "I'll see her, Moray. Don't come up. You and Miss Sylvia were going for a gallop, remember?"

Adam said, "I'll have horses brought for you." He hesitated a moment. "You have all been so faithful. I can't thank you enough." He turned and left the room, lest they should see the depth of his emotion.

Angus said, "Do you suppose it was Chaney's bark tea that brought about the change? I can't make it out exactly."

"Perhaps the blacks Mr. Rutledge saw praying to their idol had something to do with it," Sylvia said lightly to cover a deeper feeling. "I'll go and change."

Angus lighted his pipe and went out into the garden to wait for her. He wondered how long it would be before Dr. Williamson raised the quarantine. A few days, perhaps. Only a few days more under the same roof with Sylvia.

Ben's boy brought the horses to the upping-block, and Sylvia appeared on the gallery wearing a holland splash skirt over her woollen frock. Her auburn hair was confined in a tight bun at her neck, its glorious colour dulled by a heavy black net. Angus advanced to the steps to meet her, longing to take her in his arms. He struggled to keep from showing in his face what he felt in his heart. Her studied casualness to him, the rebuffs she had given him had made him cautious. Sometimes he was sure she liked him, other times she seemed determined to show that she liked him not at all. He reminded himself constantly that a physician should not marry until he had an established practice, and his own position as Dr. Armitage's associate was not yet assured. All his work with Dr. Williamson had revealed to him what resources of professional knowledge and skill he had yet to master. But he found it difficult to remember all this when he was with Sylvia. Unconsciously he heaved a great sigh.

Sylvia looked down as he slipped the strap of her riding-skirt over the toe of her boot so that it would not flutter. "Why so deep a sigh, Sir Knight of the Woeful Countenance?" she said, laughing. "Surely there should be laughter on your lips instead. Has not your patient passed the crisis triumphantly? In a few days you will be back in the village, and soon the Baron and his wife will have returned from their visit."

Angus' heart sank like a stone. "Will you be so glad to be back at Horniblow's?" he asked as they trotted down the tree-lined drive.

"No, I don't look forward to it," she said seriously. "In spite of all our anxiety I have enjoyed my stay here. There's always satisfaction when one can be of service to one's friends, and I am very fond of Mrs. Rutledge. And knowing Dr. Williamson has been stimulating."

Angus said, "I can't for the life of me see why any one so eminent in his profession should give his valuable time to politics. I have never known a man more progressive in his thinking and no one so at home in so many fields of study. Dr. Armitage has shown me papers Dr. Hugh has contributed to the Holland Society of Sciences, the Learned Societies of Utrecht, the American Philosophical Society and God knows how many others. And now he has embarked on writing something he calls an introductory dis course on the history of North Carolina."

"And yet he's a comfortable person to be with," Sylvia said, "in spite of the startling things he says sometimes. I find myself chattering to him, even making little jokes."

Angus smiled at her. She seemed very young and appealing as she spoke of her awe of the scholarly doctor. "That is a part of his greatness, I think. He has studied the phenomena of the earth and the heavens without ever losing his interest in people and his affection for them."

Sylvia thought for a few moments. "I suppose that's the answer to your question, Angus. He represents North Carolina in the Congress because he knows and loves the people and feels an obligation to speak out in their behalf."

"Aye, and because of his intense love of this country and his ambition to see it grow to be the greatest nation on earth!" Angus spoke of the doctor with genuine feeling, but he had not failed to notice that Sylvia had used his given name. He felt a sudden elation. "Ah, we've come to the Indian trail. I'll race you along the straight road to the end of the woods!"

Dr. Williamson ordered Mary moved out of the room where she had lain so long. He and Adam carried her to a west-wing chamber without waking her. Afterward the two men returned to the sick-room. Under Chaney's direction the house servants were carrying away the basins of lime used to purify the air during the illness, and washing down the walls. Next, the doctor said, the room must be fumigated by the burning of sulphur.

Chaney protested violently when the doctor ordered all the bed linen and covers burned. "Dese sheets, dey's pure flax, woven right here in Queen's Gift. I don't dare to burn dey, less'n old Duke Roger come back and show heself."

"Would you rather every slave on the plantation got the same fever your mistress has had? Take them out, I say. Mind, no nonsense!"

"Yes, sar," Chaney said, subdued by the doctor's tone. "Yes, sar. I'll burn dey. I'll watch de fire an' see dey all burn." She turned to Adam. "But dese might' fine sheets, sar. Might' fine!"

Adam said, "Do as Dr. Williamson says, Chaney. We'll have new ones made this winter in the weaving-house."

"Yes, sar." Chaney stuffed the bedding into a large rattan basket and went away.

"Be sure you wash yourself with good lye soap, Auntie," Williamson called after her. "We don't want you as a carrier."

Chaney bristled. "I ain't no carrier, sar. Dat's field-hands' work. I's house servant, I is! I don' tote no load on my head!" She stomped out of the room.

Adam grinned at the doctor and followed Chaney. He wanted to look in on Mary again before taking up the day's work.

Mary was sleeping peacefully, watched over by Miss Sarah, who sat by the fire with her knitting. She looked up and put her finger to her lips as the old floor-boards creaked under Adam's heavy boots. He smiled at the nurse and withdrew, well content.

In the office Marcy was waiting for him with the latest news from the village. He had already heard of Mary's latest gain, and he congratulated Adam warmly. "Horniblow is complaining that his business is ruined," he said then. "Every one who has a touch of bone-break fever thinks it's Mrs. Rutledge's strange ailment. Dr. Armitage is rushed to death. He'll be glad

Pocosin at Night 251

to have his assistant back. And I've a message for Dr. Williamson. Governor Johnston wants to see him as soon as possible."

"So the Governor is at Hayes?"

"Yes, sir. He returned from The Hermitage yesterday, but his family remained. Oh, yes, Captain Emperor said he would be sailing week after next. He'll stop at our wharf about Friday fortnight to pick up our tobacco."

Adam looked out the window. "We'd best settle this matter of buying state tobacco, then. Will Emperor have room?"

"Plenty, sir. He's wanting ballast, and his sailing destination is Bideford."

"Good," Adam said. "I'll see what can be done. What about politics? Anything new?"

Marcy hesitated before replying. "I've brought you the *Gazette*. Mr. Iredell is in New Bern, they told me. Mr. Cabarrus is over in Hertford, visiting the Bakers with the Baron von Pollnitz and his Lady. Mr. Barker, as I told you before, is in Virginia. His lady is at the Springs, but he is visiting his daughter Mrs. Tunstall. Mr. Allen I saw, but he's so busy between his law practice and his mercantile business he says he isn't going to think of politics for a time."

What Marcy did not report was that he had talked with the farrier Mel Frazier. Frazier said the Antifederalists intended to keep quiet until after Christmas. Then they aimed to work hard on the county folk all around Albemarle Sound to throw their votes to the men who stood out for the declaration of rights. "We're goin' to put our faith in Mr. Rutledge as our delegate if the Federalists succeed in gettin' a new convention. We've figured it all out. We can outvote the Federals in this county, if we hang together."

To Marcy the Antifederalism in the county resembled a strong current. Like the Chowan River, its surface was smooth and its channel deep. He forbore to speak to Adam about Mel and his plans now. There would be time enough when the mistress was up and about again.

After Marcy had left Adam sat down at the desk and took up his quill. If Johnston would not see him, he must write.

Sir:

Being desirous of purchasing some two hundred hogsheads of public tobacco, you will oblige me by letting me know the terms on which it is to be sold.

I am informed that the wholesale price is to be paid in specie, and the money need be paid before the tobacco is delivered.

I beg to submit the condition on which I am ready to purchase.

1st. I will, in a week's time, pay the price of such tobacco as I may buy, in specie, to be passed to the credit of the state.

2nd. As some of the tobacco has been long in public warehouses at Edenton, and lost much of its original weight, I shall expect to have it weighed again.

3rd. I am willing to give three dollars per hundred pounds for tobacco of first quality.

4th. If the tobacco is not to be reweighed, I shall at least expect the liberty of taking tobacco that was inspected last season.

I am, sir, your obedient servant,

ADAM RUTLEDGE

To

H.E. Governor Samuel Johnston

Hayes, Edenton, North Carolina

Adam read the letter through, sanded it and folded the paper. He lighted a candle, prepared the seal and pressed his ring crest on the red wax. A very formal letter, he thought, but the Governor's actions had dictated its tone. He sighed and went out onto the gallery.

Marcy was coming toward the house from the lot. "The young colt is doing excellently," he said. "It's full of life and eating mash now. I think we've got ourselves a horse, sir."

"If he proves as good as his sire, that will satisfy me," Adam replied.

Marcy said, "We will train him early, let him run on the small track. Maybe you can race him with his sire if Mr. Wilie Jones is willing!"

The two men looked at each other and laughed. "Isn't it a little early for such plans?" Adam asked.

"Maybe it is, but one must look ahead. Doesn't a good farmer always plan for next year's crop and forget last year's losses?"

Adam handed Marcy his letter. "Will you send this note over to Hayes by young Ben? I want the governor to have it today. If we're going to buy tobacco, we must get it here and hogsheaded in time for Captain Emperor's sailing."

Marcy went toward the stables, and Adam stood at the gallery rail, noting with pleasure the familiar sights and sounds and smells of the plantation. During the weeks of Mary's illness he had been too preoccupied to look around him.

A small black boy came running up the path to the kitchen, carrying a basket of fresh eggs in his outstretched hand. He was too full of the importance of his mission to notice a rose-vine that had escaped from the trellis and lay across the path. He stumbled and fell to the ground, letting out a yell as the eggs rolled from the basket.

Chaney appeared at the kitchen door, her mob-cap awry, a fierce scowl on her face. "You, boy, you! You break my nice eggs! How am I goin' to make de Master he spoon bread eff'n you break all my eggs?"

The boy replaced the whole eggs in the basket, and Chaney snatched it from his hand. "Now you get a rake and sand over dat egg mess. I don't want no stink at my kitchen door, attrackin' dose hound-dogs."

Adam laughed aloud at the boy's crest-fallen expression, and he realized it had been weeks ago that he'd last heard the sound of his own laughter.

Now he could laugh again and take up the strenuous but peaceful routine of managing Queen's Gift.

When Adam returned to the house at dinner-time Sylvia Hay was waiting for him on the upper gallery. "Mr. Rutledge!" she called. "Please come up. Your wife is asking for you."

Adam mounted the steps two at a time.

"She awakened a little while ago," Sylvia told him. "Dr. Williamson said you may see her for five minutes. He instructed Miss Sarah that you must not stay longer."

"I might disregard Williamson's warning, but never Miss Sarah's," Adam said.

He found Mary sitting up in bed, propped against the long bolsters and two pillows. He caught his breath: she looked so small, so frail in the vast whiteness of the bed. Miss Sarah had braided her long red-brown hair in pigtails. Her skin was still very pale, but had lost its deathlike appearance.

Mary smiled as he knelt by the bed and kissed the palm of her hand. Her voice was weak and a little tired. "I've lost so many days, Adam. How shall I ever regain them?"

"Just get strong again, my sweet. What's the loss of a few days?"

"Miss Sarah won't tell me how many, nor will Dr. Hugh, but I know it is weeks. The leaves of the great tree are withered and almost gone."

Adam smoothed her hand gently without speaking.

"Dr. Hugh and Miss Sarah have been so kind," Mary continued. "They worked so hard. Sometimes I could hear them talking."

Adam was startled. "We thought you were unconscious," he said.

"It seemed to me once that I was floating above them, looking down at myself lying on the bed. And Dr. Hugh said, 'We must give her strength or she will slip away from us.' Chaney was there, and she kept saying, 'Let me make my baby some tea, Doctor.'"

Adam listened silently, conscious of a strange feeling of unreality.

Mary spoke dreamily. "Finally Dr. Hugh said, 'Go ahead, woman. Brew your witch's brew.' And, strangely, you were here also, Adam, although I could not see you as I saw the others. But I could feel your hand holding mine as I feel it now. And I could hear your voice calling my name over and over."

Adam's heart tightened as he remembered his thoughts during his wild ride along the beach and through the forest. Mary, do not leave me! he had cried in his heart. You must not leave me, Mary!

She sighed. "You were my strength, Adam—you and my great tree."

"Don't tire yourself, sweet. Rest."

"I want to tell you now, while it is still close, for I know it will grow dim and fade away like a dream one forgets in the morning." She paused. "I could hear voices in the tree, Adam. I seemed to be floating away, but the voices called me back, a rhythmic chorus bidding me stay. The tree is strong . . . like you . . . and it would not let me go. . . . And then Chaney was close by, feeding me as if I were a child—a warm, soothing liquid that ran down my throat. And that is all I remember. Is it not strange?"

Adam laid his face against her hand and remained there until he felt Miss Sarah's hand on his shoulder. He rose to his feet obediently and saw that already Mary's eyelids were closed.

"She hasn't much strength yet, sir, but she's improving by the hour," Miss Sarah whispered.

In the hall outside the closed door of Mary's room Adam halted, his mind bewildered by what she had told him. One could ascribe it to delirium, but how could she have known . . . No, it seemed clear that he and Mary had shared a profound experience. From the shadow of death her spirit had reached out to his and had found him. But the other events of that dark night, the black folk praying to their pagan god, the miraculous change in Mary's condition—these were beyond his comprehension.

After supper Dr. Williamson steered Adam to the drawing-room and sent Angus and Sylvia to relieve Sarah Poor's vigil in Mary's chamber. "Send her to bed," he ordered them. "She won't want to go, but she must have rest."

"She is afraid the fever will come back," Sylvia said. "She doesn't trust me or even Dr. Moray."

"Sarah is a stubborn woman certainly," Williamson conceded, "but you must be even more stubborn. Tell her I said the fever cannot come back. It's broken, gone, vanished, *whoosh!* Tell her anything, but get her to rest." He chuckled. "After all, your hair is red also, miss."

When Sylvia and Moray had gone Adam said anxiously, "Are you really so certain that Mary is out of danger, Dr. Hugh?"

Williamson seated himself comfortably in a chair near the fire-place. "Yes, Adam, I feel reasonably confident that the bad days are behind us. Mary has been improving steadily ever since the fever broke." He frowned. "I must confess the case has been a perplexing one for me. I cannot yet say that I know the disease which attacked her or precisely what started her toward recovery. I look forward to discussing the case with Dr. Rush. Meanwhile let us guard her strength and be grateful that she is still with us."

He put a taper to his pipe and puffed vigorously. "And now, my lad, I think we can settle down to a conversation I've been postponing because you were so worried about Mary. Tell me, boy, why in God's name did you let that rascal Wilie Jones talk you over to the Antis' side?"

Adam sat up in his chair. "Wilie Jones didn't talk me over." His voice had an edge. "You've known me long enough to know that I do my own thinking, sir."

"Tut-tut, don't get red in the wattles like a turkey-cock. But I can't see you as an Anti."

Adam said nothing. Williamson thought, He's a handsome man, this Rutledge. His straightforward look draws men to him . . . and the ladies, too. I must watch my tongue, lest I antagonize him instead of converting him.

"I wish you would tell me how you happened to vote with the Antifederals," he said quietly. "I was startled when I heard of it, and I've wondered about it a good deal."

Adam rested his blond head against the back of the red damask chair. "First of all," he said, "let us clear up this definition of Antifederal. If it means that I don't want North Carolina to ratify the Constitution, then I'm not an Anti." The doctor clucked his approval, but Adam said, "Wait. I'm not a Federal, either, if the term Federal means I think we should sign *now*, take the Constitution as it stands. My position is a middle one, I suppose. I want North Carolina a part of the union, but not until the rights of the people have more safeguards."

There was silence in Mary's yellow drawing-room. The fire crackled and blazed brightly. There was a pleasant odour from the lightwood Ebon had placed on the logs. But Adam's thought was, How empty the room without Mary! He crossed to her harpsichord, opened the lid, placed a few sheets of music on the rack.

Williamson watched him narrowly. There was no doubt that Adam was deeply in earnest about his new convictions. The doctor cleared his throat. "You've not told me yet what brought you to this middle ground."

Adam went over and stood near the fire. Once started, he talked easily. He told of his visits to the Illinois country, his talks with the people from the Mississippi River to the Virginia valley. He described his growing conviction, confirmed at Hillsborough, that protection must be guaranteed to all the people.

Dr. Williamson listened expressionlessly until Adam had finished. Then he sighed. "I can see it would be useless to argue with you, Adam Rutledge. I know you well enough to be sure your stand derives from principle, not from political expediency."

Adam looked at him, surprised. He had expected expostulation and strong arguments from Hugh Williamson. "Thank you," he said.

"I say I won't argue, but before I leave I hope we may consider together the points that trouble you. I admit that I myself am not satisfied with the section concerning the President. I fear a lesser man than George Washington might find ways of usurping power. But, by God, Adam, if you had seen Madison and James Wilson working on these problems and heard the committees in session, arguing, fighting, squabbling, you would realize how expertly the Constitution reconciles conflicting interests in a workable plan! Whatever its faults, it's the best plan of government man has yet devised."

"I will be glad to discuss it with you, Dr. Hugh, but my objections are based less on what is in the document than on what isn't."

Williamson shook his head ruefully. "You won't be swayed, will you?" The little French clock on the mantel struck nine. The doctor got up and laid his pipe on a table. "Perhaps you'll heed me more when I speak as a physician. I've been watching you as well as listening to you. You're restless as a cat, man! Standing up, sitting down, striding about! What you need is air and exercise." He walked to the window and peered out. "Your Chaney tells me it will rain to-night, but not for a while, I think. Get on your horse and ride. Clear the webs out of your brain."

"My brain's perfectly clear, Doctor."

Williamson laughed, a low rumble. "Dammit! Don't I know that?" He ambled off toward the stair. "Well, then, ride so that you can sleep to-night without dreams."

Adam called Herk and ordered his horse brought around. He changed to riding-clothes and a heavy cape and went outside. Herk arrived with the horses, and Adam mounted and led the way down the drive. The half-moon gave a pale light which made the landscape vague, shadowy, unfamiliar. The huge pines merged into towering masses of dense, secretive blackness.

Adam chose the Hertfort road. By day it was busy with yeomen driving to market in high-wheeled carts, drovers with bleating herds of sheep, elegantly dressed planters riding thoroughbred horses. But now it was silent and deserted. A chill wind struck them as they passed the long pocosin. In its depths a bull-frog opened and closed the great bellows in his throat, making a long hollow sound. He has strayed out of his season, Adam thought, a lost soul crying for companionship.

Carts passing since the previous day's rain had rutted the road. Mud clung to the horses' hoofs and made a sucking sound at each step. Adam called over his shoulder to Herk, "Have we lost the track? The ground seems swampy."

Herk rode up beside him. "Dis jes' de werry edge of de swamp-land, master. Soon we cross over." They passed the small neck and came to more solid ground. Herk said, "A big rain soon, master. Big, an' will come down like a sheet of water. Better we turn now."

Adam wheeled his horse, then halted. "I thought I heard a woman cry out."

Herk's voice had the tinge of fear. "Do not pause, master. May be woman of de swamp callin'. Dey draw men wid swamp-fire."

"Nonsense, Herk," Adam said. "It's a woman crying for help."

He turned his horse again and rode on, knowing Herk would follow out of fear of being left to the mercy of the swamp witches. Adam rode for a hundred yards before he heard the cry again. He raised his voice. "Where are you?"

"Don't speak to dey," Herk pleaded. He pointed ahead. "Look, sar, de swamp-fire!"

A woman's voice answered from the mass of shadows not far ahead. "Help, help! Here, at the side of the road!"

Adam advanced toward the voice. When he had crossed a crude wooden bridge he made out the dark mass of a carriage whose lamp gave the feeble light that had frightened Herk. Horses pulled and tugged under the direction of a Negro driver who alternately prayed and cursed. Beyond the vehicle a woman stepped out from the shadows of the trees, and for a moment Adam was ready to credit Herk's tale of swamp sirens. In the dim moonlight she was a misty, insubstantial figure with pale hair and long silvery garments. But when she spoke he laughed at his fancy, for he recognized the arrogant drawling voice of Lady Anne Stuart.

"Thank God you came, sir," she said. "This fool of a driver has got my coach deep in the mud, and he thinks the axle is broken. Can you help a lady in distress?"

Adam rode closer and dismounted, throwing the reins to Herk.

"There are two of you!" she continued. "What good fortune! I will pay you well if you help me. I must get to Edenton to-night."

Adam took off his tricorne and bowed. "I will try. But how do you happen to be here on this lonely road at such an hour? Don't you know that highwaymen travel these roads, Lady Anne?"

He moved into the light of the carriage lamp, and Lady Anne threw her arms about him with a cry of relief. "Ah, thank God! 'Tis the beautiful Adam Rutledge!" Her arrogance was forgotten for the moment. Her whole body trembled as she leaned against him. "Thank God," she said again, almost sobbing. "Ah, my dear rescuer, you can't imagine how terrified I've been, lost in this wild country, alone!" Her manner changed abruptly. "And for a driver I have an idiot who can't keep a coach on the road! The wretch! I'll have him whipped for this!"

Adam loosened her hold gently. "Let's have a look at your coach." He motioned to Herk to take one of the carriage lamps out of its socket. Two wheels of the vehicle, they saw, were mired deep and dangerously near the edge of a ditch that ran parallel to the road. Herk found a heavy pole left by the bridge-builders, and after considerable exertion he and Lady Anne's driver placed it under the back axle. With that leverage they raised the wheel a foot, only to find the axle was indeed broken. Herk pulled away the pole, and the wheel sank back into the mud.

"What will we do now?" Lady Anne cried despairingly. "We've been on the road since six o'clock. I'm exhausted."

Adam forbore to ask why she had started a journey at that hour. "I will ride back to Queen's Gift and send my carriage to take you to Edenton. I cannot ask you to our home, since the house is under strict quarantine."

Lady Anne would have none of that. "I won't stay here alone with that idiot of a driver!"

"Then you can ride pillion with me," Adam said patiently.

"And leave my boxes here with no guard but that fool? Never!"

Adam thought a moment. Clouds covered the moon and rain had begun to fall. The darkness was intense. He was reluctant to send Herk alone, knowing his fear of the swamp. His belief in creatures who roamed the pocosin at night was very real.

"Very well," he said. "I'll send my man and your driver for a carriage. I'll stay here. They should make it there and back in an hour or so."

This arrangement seemed to suit Lady Anne. She smiled and said nothing.

Herk shook his head when Adam ordered him to leave. "She a witch," he whispered. "Don't stay wid she, master."

Adam checked the rest of his protest. "Ride swiftly. Bring a crew with lanthorns, and some rigging to repair the axle. You'll need shovels and chains to drag the coach out of the mud." He spoke sharply to Lady Anne's driver. "Unhook one of the horses. You will ride back with my man."

He waited until he heard the clatter of hoofs on the wooden bridge. Then he turned to Lady Anne. She stood where he had left her by the door of the coach. The light from the lamp showed a pleased smile on her face.

"You must get inside the coach, Lady Anne," he said. "The rain will ruin your dress."

She entered the carriage and seated herself. "Are you not coming inside?" she asked.

"I must fix a lanthorn to the rear of the coach."

"Nonsense! No one will be riding this road so late and in a rainstorm."

Adam hitched his horse in the shelter of an oak tree and fastened a lamp to the postilion bench of the carriage. It was raining hard now, and he was glad to take shelter in the coach.

Lady Anne moved close to him as he sat down beside her.

"My cape is wet," he said.

"No matter. It will soon dry," she said. "I am most earnestly sorry, Mr. Rutledge, to put you to such trouble. How incredibly fortunate for me that you were riding this dreary road in the black of night! Am I keeping you from a rendezvous perhaps?"

"I was riding for exercise," Adam answered, "and was on the point of turning back when I heard you call. What is more to the point is how you happen to be here alone. Ladies do not travel these roads unescorted at night."

"It was foolish of me," she admitted, "but I was bored beyond endurance in Hertford. My husband, whose passion for information about agricultural processes seems uncontrollable these days, kept postponing our return to Edenton so that he might inspect more and more plantations. And my maid Dawkins, whom I brought from England, has apparently lost her senses after seeing all the absurd privileges you Americans grant your lower classes. She suddenly announced that she was leaving my service because she felt she had been mistreated! Can you imagine it, sir? As if I did not know how to behave toward a servant!" Lady Anne's voice was outraged at the memory. "I suspect the truth is she found a man who took her fancy —some half-savage brute from out of your wilderness, probably, who'll soon show her what it means to be mistreated."

She sighed pensively, and Adam found himself remembering Dr. Armitage's pungent comments on her ladyship's all too apparent dissatisfaction with her husband.

"At any rate," Lady Anne continued, "I was so unnerved by the incident that I felt I must get away at once. My hosts disapproved of my undertaking the journey alone, so I engaged this carriage and left without more ado. And here I am. Or, rather, here *we* are, Mr. Rutledge," she said, moving closer to him.

"I'm afraid I share your hosts' disapproval of your venture," Adam said firmly. "The roads are not safe for women travelling alone, and I hope you will remember that before you risk your life again in so foolhardy a manner."

Lady Anne laughed. "You are a masterful man, are you not, Adam Rutledge? I should not fear to travel any road if I could count on you to appear in my hour of need as you have done to-night. I cannot imagine a situation you could not cope with." She paused, then spoke in a deliberately provocative tone. "I *like* masterful men!"

Adam was amused. "And do you wreck them as handily as you wreck coaches, my Lady?"

"Ah, I had forgotten, sir, that you take pleasure in verbal duels. Well, and so do I! The Stuarts do not shy away from intellectual encounters. We find them stimulating."

"I seem to recall one Stuart who found his pleasure in encounters in which intellect played no part," Adam said dryly.

"You mean Charles the Magnificent, I suppose?" She laughed. "Do not belittle his intelligence, dear Mr. Rutledge. He was wise enough to know that life is short and that each moment of it must be lived to the full."

Adam felt her fingers touching his arm. Armitage had certainly been right about this woman, he thought with a smile. It would be wisest to guide the conversation to impersonal subjects. "Fortunately for us Carolinians, Charles spared a few moments for thoughts of others," he said. "He was responsible, you know, for the development of Carolina as a colony."

Lady Anne was non-committal. "Indeed?"

"Yes, King Charles gave this whole region, from Virginia's southern border to Georgia, to eight court favourites," Adam continued. "The Lords Proprietors of the Carolinas, they were called."

"Ah, how ignorant I am!" said Lady Anne indifferently. "I do not even know their names." Her fingers played idly with the sleeve of his coat.

"The Duke of Albemarle, for one," Adam began. "And Sir William Berkeley, the rascally Governor of Virginia, and his brother. Then there were Lords Shaftesbury, Craven and Clarendon, Sir John Colleton and Sir George Carteret," he finished glibly, disengaging his sleeve from her grasp.

Lady Anne yawned delicately. "His Majesty honoured you with a noble group," she commented.

"Perhaps. But, being noble, they stayed at home and left the task of governing to agents who wrung taxes from the colonists. Even so long ago they sowed the seeds of revolt that finally blossomed to confound your half-witted King George."

Lady Anne laughed delightedly and seized his hand in both her own. "You cannot make me angry with such talk, sir. I have heard my father apply the same term to him in the privacy of the family. If we must talk of history, tell me of the rascally Sir William Berkeley. I've known some engaging rascals in my time." With one finger she traced the lines in the palm of Adam's hand.

Adam withdrew his hand. "Your beloved King Charles made a choice comment on Sir William's career. 'That old fool has taken more lives, without offence, in that naked country,' he said, 'than I, in all England, for the murder of my father.' "

"Well, perhaps he was one of the less engaging rascals," Lady Anne remarked absently. She moved closer again and leaned heavily against him. Her fragrant hair brushed his cheek.

Adam, wedged into a corner, could retreat no farther. He wondered if Herk had reached Queen's Gift yet. He made his voice deliberately flat and dry. "Sir William himself made some remarks that the colonists found not at all engaging. On one occasion he publicly thanked God that there were no free schools or printing here and expressed the hope that there would be none for a hundred years."

"Free schools?" Lady Anne's voice was suddenly sharp. "Do you mean schools that any one who wanted to could attend? What an absurd notion!"

"And why absurd, Lady Anne?" Adam asked. At least, he thought with relief, she was paying attention now to what he was saying.

"You Americans have not had time yet to see what will happen as a result of all your ridiculous catering to the lower classes. If one attempts to be kind to them, they immediately become impudent and rebellious." Lady Anne spoke decisively. "This business of my maid Dawkins is a perfect example."

"I had not realized, Lady Anne, that it was kindness which drove your maid from you," Adam said deliberately.

Lady Anne sat up abruptly. "It was this American carelessness about keeping inferiors in their place that made Dawkins unfit to wait upon a lady of breeding," she said angrily. "She was a perfectly trained servant when she arrived on this barbarous shore, yet to-day she presumed to reprove me for the tone of voice I had used in speaking to her. She could stay no longer, she said, with an employer who denied her the respect due her as a person!" Lady Anne's voice trembled with rage at the recollection. "I was so dumbfounded I could scarcely speak!"

Adam grinned in the darkness. He felt confident that her Ladyship had found her voice and speeded the departing Dawkins with a few forceful remarks. "It was indeed a thoroughly American sentiment. Dawkins has learned rapidly. You must remember that rebellion against seeming injustice is an honoured tradition in this land, and as for impudence, I'm sure our Declaration of Independence must have impressed King George as very impudent indeed."

There was silence in the coach during which the downpour on the roof seemed louder than ever. Adam waited for Lady Anne's explosion, but she surprised him with a sudden peal of laughter.

"You are an amazing man, Adam Rutledge," she said. "Here we are, alone at midnight in a comfortable carriage, isolated from the world by miles of wilderness and a cloud-burst, and how do you choose to spend the time? Discoursing on history and lecturing me on how to treat a lady's maid!" She laughed again. "You sneer at Charles Stuart's intellect, but I'll wager he could have suggested to you a more diverting way of passing an hour with a personable woman."

Her garments rustled as she moved near to him again. "Or perhaps you do not find me attractive," she murmured. Her arms crept around his neck, and she pressed her body to his. Her lips were close to his, waiting for his kiss.

Adam's pulse was pounding. Damn the woman! he thought helplessly, and damn that fool of a Baron who was tramping about in some one's tobacco fields when he should have been keeping his wife out of mischief. "Lady Anne," he said weakly, "I . . ."

She stirred restlessly, and her voice in the darkness was cold and mocking. "Yes, Mr. Rutledge? Tell me more about America, Mr. Rutledge. Tell me about American men. Are they made of iron . . . or are they eunuchs?"

In a sudden burst of anger and desire Adam seized her in his arms and kissed her fiercely, a long, demanding kiss. Her response was ardent, greedy. When at last he drew away she clung to him, pressing her lips against his cheek. "Oh, Adam, Adam," she whispered, "never have I known a man so difficult to woo!"

A shout sounded through the noise of rain on the carriage roof. Then came hoofbeats and the rumble of a coach passing over the wooden bridge. Lady Anne drew back with an exclamation of anger, and Adam opened the door and stepped out into the rain.

Lights were bobbing up and down in the darkness beyond the mired coach. "Stop!" Adam shouted, running forward. "Don't come any closer! Turn the coach there by the bridge."

Marcy appeared out of the gloom carrying a lanthorn. Adam grasped his hand in welcome. "I thought you'd never get here," he said. "Let the boys transfer Lady Anne's boxes. Come on, we'll have to carry her across this slime."

The two men made a saddle of their clasped hands. "It will be easier, ma'am, if you place your arms about our shoulders," Marcy said as Lady Anne emerged from the coach.

"Of course," she said, her voice serene and pleasant. She laughed excitedly as her bearers sloshed through the mud and mire toward the Rutledge carriage. They deposited her on the high step, and she quickly stepped inside.

Marcy said, "As soon as they move the luggage, ma'am, I'll set the boys to work on the coach."

Lady Anne leaned forward. "Don't bother. Just see that the horses are taken care of. Let the coach stay there until the rain ceases." But Marcy was already returning to his crew.

When Lady Anne's boxes had been transferred Adam climbed into the coach and sat beside her. He opened the glass panel that separated them from the driver. "Drive to Edenton, Ben. And be careful of the low places. We don't want to have to pull this carriage out of the mud also."

"Please close the panel, Mr. Rutledge," Lady Anne said. "I feel a draught."

Reluctantly he pushed the panel into place.

"You have protection now, haven't you, my dear?" she said mockingly. "Were you relieved or disappointed when our rescuers arrived? Both, I suspect." She laughed. "Never mind. Our moment will come. This is not the end for you and me—only the beginning."

Adam cleared his throat. The woman was shameless, he thought angrily. There would be no more such moments. He would see to that. "You will find Edenton somewhat deserted, I fear, Lady Anne," he said formally. "We are just emerging from the fever season, and many of your acquaintances who took refuge on higher ground have not yet returned."

"So? Well, I shall have Miss Hay's company, and I dare say my husband will weary of counting tobacco plants eventually and come back to me."

"Unfortunately Miss Hay will not be available for a day or two. She has helped to nurse my wife through a serious illness, and the doctor will not permit any one to leave Queen's Gift until he feels certain the disease will not spread."

Lady Anne was incredulous. "Do you mean Sylvia is staying at your house?"

"Yes. She has been of invaluable assistance to the doctors. We are most grateful for her kindness."

"Well, I won't have it!" Her voice shook with anger, and Adam realized too late that he had unwittingly nominated a whipping-boy for her Lady-ship's irritation over the events of the night. "I left Miss Hay at Horniblow's to deal with my correspondence during my absence, not to go skipping about the country-side, imposing herself on strangers on the strength of my name! She is a servant in my employ, and I'll see that in future she remembers it!"

Adam wondered what he might say to soothe this choleric lady. It would be unfair to let Sylvia suffer for her generous actions, but any defence from him might anger Lady Anne further. "I am certain Miss Hay did not mean to go against your wishes, Lady Anne. She saw an opportunity to give help where help was needed. I can only repeat that my wife and I are most appreciative."

There was a brief silence. Then Lady Anne spoke contritely. "I am wrong to be angry, and you do well to reprove me. If Sylvia has been able to speed your charming wife's recovery, I am very glad. . . . You must for-give my outburst. This has been an unsettling day for me," she said with a hint of amusement in her voice. "Nothing—but nothing, Mr. Rutledge!—has gone according to plan."

Adam made no reply. They rode in silence to the inn.

Fire

23 WHEN Adam returned to the house after his morning round Dr. Williamson greeted him with a note from Gov-ernor Johnston which had been delivered by a slave from Hayes. "Johnston wrote to me also," the doctor reported. "He has asked some of the Federalist leaders to meet at his home, and he thinks I should be there. It's fortunate, isn't it, that I've decided to lift the quarantine?" Wil-liamson's eyes were twinkling. "Especially since you and Marcy and a half-dozen of your men were prowling about the country-side last night."

Adam ignored the jibe. "You really think there is no longer any danger of the disease spreading, Dr. Hugh?"

"I feel that, if there were to be more cases, we would have some evidence by this time. Sarah Poor will stay for a while to take care of Mary, and I recommend, Adam, that you keep her here for at least a month. Hannah

Iredell can find another midwife, and Mary's convalescence will probably be a slow one."

"Have you told Miss Hay and Dr. Moray that they are free to go?" Adam asked.

"Well—" Williamson was embarrassed—"I spoke to them but I said the quarantine would stay in effect until to-morrow. The fact is I've been hoping —old busybody that I am—that those two would make a match of it. Moray is a likeable young fellow, and Sylvia is a girl of rare spirit. I thought perhaps another evening here would give the boy a chance to speak his piece. I hope you don't object."

Adam grinned. "Of course not. I wish your little project every success, Doctor. I like them both."

"Good. We'll see what happens, then. Meanwhile, why don't you come upstairs and look in on Mary for a few minutes? She's probably awake, for Chaney took her a bite to eat not long ago."

"I want to see what Johnston has to say. Then I'll go up." The two men walked together into the hallway. "And when are we to have our private debate?" Adam asked. "I'm ready and waiting to point out the holes in your Constitution."

Williamson chuckled. "Suppose we set aside this evening for that. I'll be fresh from a consultation with the finest Federalist minds. I should be more than a match for a middle-of-the-road Anti!"

Alone in the office Adam broke the crested seal on Johnston's letter and scanned the few lines:

Sir:

I have your letter of yesterday before me. You may have two hundred hogs-heads of tobacco or more on your obtaining a credit in favour of this State.

If the tobacco is taken at the weights mentioned in Inspection notes, you may have it at three dollars. If it is reweighed, at three dollars and a third of a dollar. I believe the tobacco is of first quality.

Yours most sincerely,
SAMUEL JOHNSTON

He looked for an enclosure. There was none—no inquiry after Mary's health, nothing. "To the devil with him!" Adam said aloud.

He hurried upstairs and entered Mary's room. Her colour was a little better today, and she assured him she felt stronger. "I've eaten some calf's-foot jelly and a custard," she told him proudly, "and they tasted delicious."

Adam sat in a chair by the bed and talked quietly of plantation affairs— the extra tobacco he planned to buy, Marcy's ambitions for the new colt.

"Oh, I want to see it!" Mary cried. "When can I go out? Miss Sarah won't give me any satisfaction. And I can't bear to think I'm missing the hunting season. Have you had any good runs, Adam?"

"No, Mary, I've been too busy and too concerned about you." He did not want to tell her that he had not been notified of any meets, although he was titular M. F. H. of the Albemarle Hunt. He knew they were running the hounds down Greenfield way and—with a scratch pack—at the upper end of the county. The slight had hurt Adam, who was proud of his efforts to keep the sport alive in his state.

Mary's mind had wandered. "Adam, I've been trying to remember—did you tell me about David when you came home from the West?" There was a puzzled frown on her face. "It's strange, but there are things I can't remember—about the days before my illness, I mean."

"It's not at all strange, dear. Of course it will take a little time for everything to come clear again."

"I suppose so," Mary said worriedly. "But tell me about little David. Is he well and happy?"

"Yes." Adam smiled. "But he isn't little any more, you know. He's a fine, sturdy young man, almost as tall as I. Gwennie and Owen think he looks like me. Owen says he's ready to come east again and go to Princeton."

Mary sighed. "It's hard for me to think of David as grown up. What about Lavinia and Meredith Chapman? Is she still beautiful?"

"Very beautiful and very happy in the West. She and Meredith have built a house on a high bluff. From the gallery they can see the junction of the muddy Missouri River with the mighty Mississippi." He laughed. "Every one calls it that, but actually the Mississippi is scarcely wider than our own Chowan River at Parson Earle's plantation."

Mary was idly twirling her wedding ring, loose on her thin finger. "There is something else I have been trying to remember, Adam, something to do with my grandfather. But thinking tires me so," she said drowsily.

From the door Miss Sarah was signalling that it was time for Adam to leave. He kissed Mary's brow and said, "Don't worry. Everything will come back to you." But she was already asleep.

In the hall he spoke anxiously to Miss Sarah. "Does she always drop off so suddenly? Is it a good sign?"

"It's the best possible thing for her," Miss Sarah assured him. "Sleep is nature's great restorer, you know. She is growing stronger. All she needs now is rest and more rest."

Adam studied the nurse, suspicious of the kindly tone so at variance with her usual forceful manner. She had discarded her customary mob-cap to-day, and her red hair framed her face like a violent halo. He was reminded suddenly of a portrait of another indomitable woman, Queen Elizabeth of England. But there was no guile in Miss Sarah's honest eyes. It was true, then, that Mary was recovering, that eventually she would be well. Adam wondered what would happen if she remembered the controversy that had estranged them before her illness. Would the barriers rise again between them?

He wandered disconsolately down the stairs and into the drawing-room.

Sylvia Hay was reading by the fire, but she laid her book down as Adam entered.

"Dr. Hugh tells me we shall be free to leave to-morrow," she said, and then laughed at herself. "That sounds as if we were being released from prison, doesn't it? Actually," she added, looking away from him, "for me it will be more like going *into* prison."

Adam thought of Lady Anne's swift, unreasonable anger the night before. No, Sylvia could not be looking forward to a joyful reunion. "I saw your employer last night——" he began.

Sylvia caught her breath. "Is she back in Edenton? And I'm not there to do her bidding. Oh, she'll be furious!"

"I explained the situation to her, and she was most agreeable about it. She understood about the quarantine."

"Oh, thank you, Mr. Rutledge." Sylvia hesitated, clasping her hands together nervously. "You—you've no idea what she's like when she chooses not to be agreeable," she went on. "She can be charming when it suits her, so gracious when Madam Barker or Mrs. Iredell comes to call. But when they've gone she mocks them cruelly, sneers at their clothes and their manners. She despises Edenton—the whole country, in fact!" She turned to him apologetically. "I embarrass you by talking this way, and she is my employer, but—well, you and your friends have been kind to me. I've come to love this village and the people I've met here, and I admire the courage that led you to reject our stupid Hanoverian King. And it hurts me when she . . . Oh, what does it matter?" She stared into the fire so that he might not see the tears in her eyes.

"But why do you stay with Lady Anne if you are so unhappy?" Adam asked.

Sylvia sighed. "I have no choice. I signed a contract for the entire time of the Von Pollnitzes' stay in this country. And I could not do without the money they pay me. The Baron made a generous arrangement."

Adam was at a loss for an answer. "One may forgive a lady of fashion for being bored and impatient in a village like ours," he said, trying to sound convincing. "We have few elegant diversions to offer." He tried to lighten the conversation. "I must show you the epitaph on a tomb in St. Paul's Churchyard. It reads: 'Here lies a lady of London who died of the climate.' Not that Lady Anne is likely to follow suit. She's too vigorous a personality to succumb to Carolina weather."

Ebon came to tell Adam that two men were waiting to see him in the office. Adam rose at once, but he paused and spoke warmly and earnestly to Sylvia. "Miss Hay, even though you leave Queen's Gift to-morrow, I hope you will not desert us entirely. Come to us whenever you can for a meal or a ride or to stay the night. My wife must not exert herself for some weeks, and she will be delighted to have your company. And . . . if you should ever leave Lady Anne's employment, you will find a warm welcome here."

The expression in Sylvia's eyes told him she had understood his meaning: she could always take sanctuary from Lady Anne's temper at Queen's Gift.

Adam's visitors proved to be Jonas Brown and Tom Ingalls, both of whom farmed small acreages in the upper part of the county. They'd heard rumours, they said, that Adam was buying tobacco. They were tired of dealing with agents and offered him their crops. Adam promised to ride up their way in a few days to inspect the leaf.

The men seemed reluctant to go. After a brief hesitation Jonas Brown said, "To say the truth, Mr. Rutledge, we didn't come about the tobacco. Fact is, the farmers in our parts are bein' asked to put their names to a paper askin' for another convention to talk about the Constitution. Some of 'em are signin'. Seems they're frightened now we're out of the union. Those who ain't changed their minds want that you should come talk to a meetin'. We've got faith in your views. We want that you should explain things to them that's confused."

"Thank you, Brown." For a moment Adam did not trust himself to say more. In the months since Hillsborough he had been censured and even punished for his stand. This was reward, this trust of the plain men for whom he had spoken. He cleared his throat. "I'll talk to your meeting. Set a time and send me word."

When Brown and Ingalls had gone Adam remained at his desk. He had thought of what Brown had said as reward. It was also a challenge. The papers Marcy had brought home from the village made it abundantly clear that the Federalists were not abandoning their efforts to get the Constitution ratified without a bill of rights. The August elections for the Assembly had given them a small majority. Petitions were being circulated in all parts of the state asking the Assembly to set a date for another convention. The ratification by New York had been a heavy blow. Men were being persuaded by arguments that North Carolina's trade might be restricted by other states, that she would stand alone if attacked. Adam knew how real these dangers were. They were risks he had taken into account when he cast his vote at Hillsborough. His faith was unshaken in the rightness of the convention's decision. Freedom demanded sacrifice and risk. Fear must not weaken the first determined resolve of free men.

He stood and looked at the portrait of Duke Roger. His courage and strength had founded Queen's Gift. Adam sought the future in another land. He prayed that Mary would one day understand that his vision and hope were not different from Duke Roger's. Adam knew now that he must do what he could to defeat the new Federalist effort. Talking to the farmers near by would not be enough. There would be other meetings in other parts of the state, other hesitant and frightened men whose leaders had lost the hardihood to wait for a bill of rights. Adam walked to the window and looked out at the fields. In the weeks to come he must often ride away from

Queen's Gift. There was no other choice. God grant that he might one day
return to understanding and peace!

Dr. Williamson was bursting with good humour when he returned from
his Federalist meeting. After supper he sat in the office with Angus Moray
and Adam, relaying the latest happenings in the village. The fever scare had
abated, he said, and many of the refugees had come home, although the
Barkers still lingered at the Springs and Mrs. Johnston had taken her children for a visit with her father, Dr. Cathcart, at Cuffnels. She would remain several weeks, since Sam would be away from home most of the time
until Christmas.

"Sam is engrossed in plans for the new house at Hayes," he said. "He
showed me the drawings Mr. Hawks has made, and they are most impressive. The place will be a mansion. Sam is anxious to get it started, for
the family is crowded in the present house."

"I suspect Charles Johnson will have his house ready first," Adam said.

"Charles Johnson?" Williamson repeated. "I didn't know he was building."

"Yes. Parson Earle is turning River Plantation over to his daughter—
Charles's wife, you know—and Charles is planning some changes. I'm not
sure whether he means to enlarge the present house or build a new one."

Williamson emptied his glass, smacked his lips, and filled it again. "Sam
tells me the old Parson is getting feeble. He's relying more and more on
Pettigrew to preach for him. I'm amused at Sam's opinion of General Washington. Just before I left New York I had a letter from him." He searched
through his pockets, fishing out scraps of paper and letters which he piled
on Adam's desk. Finally he extracted a letter from his coat-tail and peered
at it closely. "Ah, this is the one. People are always telling me I carry too
much litter in my pockets. Don't see why a man shouldn't have about him
what he wants to refer to."

With some deliberation Williamson opened a shagreen case and took out
his spectacles. "Moray, I suppose you've heard that General Washington is
certain to be our first President? Doubtless you'd like to know much more
about him, but if I were your age and a pretty girl were waiting in the
garden, I think I'd manage to forego information about politics."

Moray jumped to his feet. "If you'll pardon me, sir, I'll take your advice."

Williamson smiled as Moray left the room. "You, Adam, have no escape.
Listen to this." He raised the letter and read. " 'You are well acquainted
with the public character of the proposed President. He is a man of great
moderation, firmness and integrity. Though not the possessor of the most
splendid talents or of literary knowledge, he has an excellent understanding
and has improved by experience in the course of long public service.' " The
doctor took off his glasses and chuckled. "Sam is always the judge. He
writes to an old friend of a man the whole country admires and he makes

his opinion sound as careful as if he were writing a letter of reference for a
clerk and addressing it to a complete stranger."

"I'm afraid Johnston is not so temperate in his opinion of me," Adam
said.

Williamson frowned. "Yes, yes. Too bad there should be that sort of
feeling in Edenton. Well, I won't say I think politics should estrange old
friends, but I will say that you Antis gave us a devil of a lot of trouble in
Congress when you threw our state out of the union and left us with the
large state of Rhode Island as our only associate. We had no voice in the
organization of the new government." He raised his hand as Adam started
to speak. "No, I don't intend to debate the Constitution with you after all.
We'd not change opinions, and we'd end bad friends. Let me pour you more
of your excellent brandy."

Angus descended the steps to the garden and peered along the shadowy
paths. "Sylvia?" he called softly.

"I'm here, Dr. Moray."

His heart pounding, he followed the sound of her voice and found her
standing alone near the centre of the formal garden, clutching a woollen
shawl about her as protection against the chill wind from the Sound.

"It's scarcely a night to be strolling in the garden," she said, "but I am
making my farewell to this beautiful place. I do not look forward to returning to Horniblow's in the morning." She sighed. "Did you ever wish
that a night would last for ever, that it were possible to make time stand
still?"

"Joshua tried it, I believe," Angus said, "but the sun continued to rise
and set at its accustomed time . . . and still does." He tried to keep his
voice natural and easy, but his words sounded harsh and flippant to his
own ears. "Let us walk," he said abruptly, angry at his awkwardness.

Sylvia fell into step beside him, and they moved toward the far end of
the garden. Angus found the silence oppressive, and he cast about for something to say. "Mr. Rutledge tells me Lady Anne Stuart is in Edenton again,"
he ventured at last.

Sylvia halted. "Yes," she said crisply. "So I shall be seeing you regularly
even after we leave Queen's Gift, shan't I, Dr. Moray?"

Angus groaned inwardly. How could he have been so stupid? "Sylvia
——" he began miserably.

"For of course you will resume your frequent calls on Lady Anne," she
continued coldly. "So wise of you, Doctor. Mr. Rutledge told me only today of the deleterious effect of this climate on fashionable ladies of London."

"Sylvia——"

"I trust her Ladyship is properly appreciative of your solicitude."

Angus seized her shoulders and turned her to face him. "Sylvia, I'll not let you go on like that," he said firmly. "You know it is you I want . . . and need!"

He drew her close to him. She was motionless in his arms, but her lips when he kissed her were warm and sweet. "Oh, Sylvia," he said at last, "I had not meant to speak now, for I cannot ask you yet to marry me. My position here is far from assured, and I must send what money I have to my mother in Scotland. I wish—I wish I might ask you to wait for me." He held her away from him and tried to find an answer in her eyes. "Sylvia, could I ask that of you?"

She broke away from his grasp and turned her back. A devastating fear came over him. "Is there some one in England?" he asked. "Some one you love?"

"No, Angus, it's not that," she said quickly. "But there is some one—a cousin—whom I am supposed to marry." There was resignation in her voice as she continued. "My father could not leave me his estate because of the entail, so he arranged that I should become the wife of the man who would inherit it. All this happened long ago when Donald and I were children. We have never been formally betrothed because Donald has been very ill. His physicians ordered him to Switzerland in the hope that the mountain air would help him. He has been there for some time."

Angus led her to a marble bench that stood against a background of dark pines. He sat beside her. "Sylvia, do you love this . . . Donald?" he asked gently.

She hesitated. "I'm very fond of him. He's a fine man. And, Angus, I could never reject him while he's so ill. You must see how cruel and unfeeling that would be."

"Then you don't love him!" Angus cried triumphantly. "Sylvia, is it me you love? You must tell me! Do you love me?"

She buried her face in his shoulder and sobbed despairingly. "Oh, Angus! Why couldn't we have met before it was too late?"

It took him a long time to quiet her. When at last her crying ceased he tried to raise her face to his, but she evaded his kiss and stood up. "No, Angus, it would be wrong of me!" She moved away. "I'll go in now. We must never speak of love again."

Angus rose, and they walked together toward the house. "It is wrong of you to think of marrying a man you do not love. I'll not force myself on you, my girl, but now that I know you love me I'll never let you go!"

Sylvia went directly to her room, and Angus wandered disconsolately into the office, where Adam and Dr. Williamson were talking idly over their brandy.

Williamson looked up expectantly as Angus appeared in the doorway. "Well, sir, is this an occasion for a congratulatory toast?"

"It is an occasion for brandy, certainly," Angus replied grimly, "but the congratulations must be deferred."

"Moray!" the doctor cried, disappointed. "She's not refused you?"

"It seems there is a cousin in Switzerland to whom she was promised as a child," Angus explained. "And, since I must care for my old mother before taking on other responsibilities, there's little to be done about it at present."

"Oh, well—" Williamson waved aside these obstacles—"you'll make money here, and these childhood matches sometimes come to nothing. In Switzerland, did you say? You should have no trouble eliminating him from her memory."

Angus shook his head gloomily. "She feels committed, sir, and she's not a girl to break her word lightly. Nor would I have her otherwise." He excused himself and went upstairs.

Williamson turned to Adam, who had made no comment on Moray's unhappy tale. "Poor children!" he said. "They've long years ahead of them for wishing they'd been less noble."

Adam poured himself another brandy and refilled the doctor's glass. "Right now they're convinced the world has never known a more poignant tragedy than theirs. And no one could persuade them that their marriage might bring deeper unhappiness than either has yet known."

Williamson, who knew the story of Adam's first marriage and had heard the village rumours about his estrangement from Mary, glanced at him sharply. But he said nothing.

It was two o'clock when the plantation bell rang out a piercing alarm—four sharp strokes followed by a continuous clangor. To every inhabitant of Queen's Gift the signal carried an instantaneous message: Fire!

Adam leaped from his bed and ran onto the gallery. There was a bright glow in the direction of the Sound. He dashed back to his room, pulled on breeches and a leather shirt, stepped into his shoes and raced downstairs.

As he emerged from the house, Negroes from the quarters line ran past on their way to the blaze. Marcy came to meet him. "It's the tobacco pontoon we loaded today," he shouted.

Ebon appeared, wearing a cotton night-dress. "I'll come help, sar!" he cried. "I sent Ben to de stables to get blankets!"

"Good man, Ebon!" Adam saw Dr. Williamson at the railing of the upper gallery. "Tell Mary not to worry!" he called, and ran with Marcy toward the Sound.

As they neared the wharf Adam saw that there was no hope of saving the blazing pontoon. Several slaves were still aboard, trying to roll hogsheads of tobacco over the side. A number of casks were bobbing about in the dark water.

"Get off the pontoon!" Adam shouted, running onto the wharf. "It's too late! Let it burn!"

Most of the Negroes were glad to obey, but Herk called back, "Yes, master; I get a few more!" With an iron bar he pried a hogshead loose from the load and rolled it toward the side. The flames were dangerously close to him as he worked.

"Damn it, Herk, get off!" Adam yelled again.

"Jes' one more, master!" Herk tugged at another hogshead, trying to slip his bar under it. Flames licked at the deck planking around him.

"Herk, come now or I'll drag you off!"

The pontoon listed suddenly, and the heavy cask swayed and toppled over, knocking Herk off balance. He fell to the deck. The hogshead rolled sluggishly toward the low side of the pontoon, striking Herk's foot.

Adam leaped aboard the burning scow and hesitated, seeking a path through the flames to where Herk lay. On the shore behind him he heard a shout: "Number One barn's afire!"

Adam turned to Marcy, who was about to follow him onto the pontoon. "Go to the barn! I'll get Herk!" Holding his arm over his mouth and nose, he crossed the blazing deck. A slave climbed onto the scow from the water side, and with his help Adam beat out the fire smouldering in Herk's shirt. Together they lifted the huge Negro over the side of the pontoon and lowered him into the grasp of a half-dozen slaves who waited below. Adam and his helper followed Herk into the icy water and assisted the others to haul him up the steep bank.

On the shore Angus Moray was waiting with a supply of salves and unguents. He caught a Negro by the arm. "Run to the house and tell Chaney to make gallons of tea. I want tea leaves to use on burns." He bent over Herk.

"Don't mind de burns, sar," Herk said. "Hit's de foot. He hurts."

Adam stooped beside the injured man. "The doctor will fix it for you, Herk."

"Yes, sar. Thank you, sar." Herk showed his teeth in a grin. "I got dat las' barrel over, sar!"

"That you did, Herk, and I thank you for it, but I'd rather you'd looked after yourself."

" 'Bacco might' valuable, sar. Costin' much moneys."

"But you are much more valuable to me."

Adam rose and ran toward the tobacco barns. He found that Marcy had mustered every man on the plantation and organized them into a team to fight the fire. A line of slaves stretched from the Sound to the burning barn, passing a continuous stream of dripping stable blankets to the men who were attempting to beat out the flames. Other slaves attacked grass fires with tow sacks or dug trenches to check the spread of the blaze.

A rising wind showered sparks and bits of burning tobacco on the other barns and out-buildings, and Adam turned his attention to this new danger. "Let Number One go," he told Marcy. "Put men on the roof of Number Two and send up wet blankets to cover the shingles."

Marcy pointed to a smaller building. "That's what worries me. Our turpentine and tar are stored there."

"Good God!" Adam cried. "Have men roll the barrels out toward the swamp. We'll lose the long warehouse if the turpentine catches." He started toward the shed, but Angus Moray stopped him.

"Let me see your hands, Mr. Rutledge." Angus inspected them. "As I thought. Come, plunge them into that tea solution Ebon has yonder, and then I'll bandage them."

But Adam shoved him aside. "Haven't time now, Doctor," he said, striding away after Marcy. For a moment Angus watched his tall, straight figure outlined against the chaos of rolling flames and billowing smoke. Then he turned away to care for an injured slave.

The sun had risen over Albemarle Sound when Adam decided the fire was under control. Number One barn and two smaller buildings had burned to the ground, but the other out-buildings were safe. He assembled the exhausted slaves and said, "Thank you, men. You have worked hard and well, and your mistress and I are grateful. Marcy will assign men to watch here until the fires are completely out. Any of you who have burns not yet cared for will report to Dr. Moray at the dispensary. The others may go to their rest. And Ebon is waiting at the warehouse to measure out a pannikin of rum for each man."

A resounding cheer went up as the men flocked toward the long warehouse.

Adam went wearily into the house and paused in the dining-room, where morning tea was ready on the hunt board. Dr. Williamson and Sylvia came in, already dressed and eager for details of the fire, but Adam went upstairs to tell Mary that the danger was past.

She was propped up against her pillows looking pale and thin, but seemed none the worse for the night's alarms. She was frightened at Adam's appearance—his smoke-blackened face and scorched clothes. He hastened to assure her that only his hands had been burned and Moray had already seen to them. "He had me plunge them into a tea solution, which drew out the pain at once."

"But, Adam, your eyebrows!" There was genuine distress as well as a tinge of amusement in her voice. "Your beautiful eyebrows—they're gone!"

Adam grinned. "They'll grow back. I'm much more concerned about your beautiful hogsheads of tobacco and your beautiful barn."

Mary was undisturbed by the financial loss. "Chaney says Herk was hurt."

"Dr. Moray says a bone is broken in his ankle. Some of the others were burned, but not seriously. I had Ebon dole out rum to all the men, so I suspect they're rather glad the fire happened. The whole incident could have been much more disastrous than it was." If Mary chose to regard his eyebrows as the night's most significant loss, he would not correct her.

As he bathed and donned fresh clothing in his own room he pondered the night's events. A pontoon, a barn, two smaller buildings and a fair share of the year's tobacco crop gone. Not pleasant facts to dwell on. Nor was he pleased by the realization that two simultaneous but widely separated fires involving the valuable tobacco could scarcely be regarded as spontaneous. The circumstances must be investigated, and Adam did not look forward to hearing the results. The threats Hume had made at Hillsborough passed through his mind.

When he went downstairs he found Sylvia, Dr. Williamson and young Moray waiting to bid him farewell before leaving for Edenton. Angus' manner this morning was morose, while Sylvia was determinedly vivacious. Williamson watched them both with a characteristic mingling of amusement, sympathy and exasperation.

"We've already made our manners to Mary," he told Adam. "I've warned her that I shall be back to see that she is obeying Sarah Poor's orders, and she has bidden Moray and Sylvia to call on her frequently, so you'll not be rid of us entirely."

After their departure Adam was suddenly aware of overpowering fatigue. Thanks to Lady Anne's misadventure in the pocosin and the tobacco fires he had had almost no sleep for two nights, and before that his concern about Mary had deprived him of rest.

Marcy, coming to report on the fire losses, was struck by his employer's obvious exhaustion. The overseer cited his statistics hurriedly. He had additional bad news. Some of the tobacco thrown from the burning pontoon was water-soaked and would probably disintegrate if heated again. When Adam raised the question of the fires' origin Marcy replied in guarded language. He promised an investigation, but he felt this was not the time to inform Adam that fires had been discovered in all the tobacco barns. The slave Ben, sent to check the other buildings after the alarm was raised, had found turpentine-saturated wads of cotton burning in barns Two, Three and Four. Ben and Marcy together had stamped and beaten out these small blazes before serious damage could result. Marcy had already sent for Yeoman Pierce to bring his sniffing hounds, but he doubted that the dogs would be able to separate the scent of the arsonist from the stench of turpentine. There was no point, Marcy decided, in adding to Adam's worries now.

Adam went upstairs, threw himself onto his bed and was immediately oblivious to the world. When he awakened the room was filled with evening shadows and two women were arguing outside his door.

"Chaney, you're talking nonsense!" Miss Sarah was saying briskly.

"Don't care what you say, Miss Sarah, dere's goin's-on!" Chaney's voice was stubborn. "First Miss Mary she get herself sick. Den Mr. Adam he done have dis big fire. Dere be one thing more a-comin', you wait an' see!"

"Chaney, you aren't to speak one word of this foolishness to your mistress! Do you hear me?"

"Yes'm, Miss Sarah, I hears. But Chaney she know. Some one makin'

Mankwala on us for sure!" Chaney's voice trailed off as she waddled down the hall. "Evil come in threes. . . ."

Adam heard Miss Sarah's snort of impatience. Then she rapped on his door and told him Mary was having her evening meal and hoped he could join her.

"Give me five minutes to change," he answered.

When he reached Mary's room she was resolutely downing a cup of broth, making a face at each spoonful. "I don't like it," she told him with a rueful smile, "but Miss Sarah says I must have it, and I daren't say no to Miss Sarah."

She put the empty cup aside. "Adam, I've been thinking about that nice girl Sylvia Hay. She seemed so unhappy this morning when she came in to say good-bye."

Adam told her of the impasse between Sylvia and Angus. "And she does not enjoy her life as Lady Anne's amanuensis," he added.

"I know," Mary said thoughtfully. "She needs to feel she has friends here and I'd like to show my appreciation for her kindness when I was ill. What would you say to giving her my emerald ring?"

Adam was startled. "It's a valuable stone. Wasn't it your grandmother's?"

Mary nodded. "I love it, but I want to give Sylvia something dear to me. And an emerald is just right for her colouring."

Adam kissed his wife gently. "It's a handsome gift, one she will treasure, I'm sure. I'll fetch your jewel-box from the strong-box to-morrow."

Dismissed from Mary's room by Miss Sarah, Adam went downstairs to a lonely supper in the big dining-room. The house seemed empty without Dr. Williamson's booming voice, without Sylvia's chatter punctuated by Angus Moray's monosyllabic replies. But it was pleasant to feel that the air of emergency had passed and Queen's Gift was left again to its own people. Except for Miss Sarah, of course. He thought of Chaney's conversation with her. Evil comes in threes, the old woman had maintained. The memory of the ominous certainty in her voice made him uncomfortable. What further catastrophe might lie ahead for Queen's Gift?

Chaney too was haunted by the uncompleted cycle of evil. When silence fell over the old house she made her way through the darkness to the quarters line.

Mifiti, the conjure woman, had been called from her hut by the pocosin to work healing magic for the slaves injured in fighting the fires. Angus Moray's bandages and medication had been cast aside, and the burned men flocked to an unused cabin at the end of the line which Mifiti had appropriated for the preparation of her own remedies.

When Chaney reached the cabin it was filled with awed Negroes, for the families of Mifiti's patients had come to watch the witch woman at her work. A murmur went through the crowd as Chaney entered, and there was triumph in Mifiti's eyes as she recognized the new arrival. For Chaney prided herself on her adoption of the white man's ways, and never before had she come to Mifiti for help.

The witch woman crouched before a small fire on the hearth. In a gourd she mixed bits of ram's horn with powdered charcoal and added unidentifiable substances from a deerhide bag she wore tied at her waist. Then she bent forward to the flames and with a bony finger traced Mankwala symbols in the ashes on the hearth. Her excited spectators followed each movement in a tense silence.

At last Mifiti announced that her medication was ready. The burned men went forward one by one, and Mifiti spread their wounds with the gritty paste from the gourd. Then she dismissed the crowd. Chaney and old Ebon, the butler, remained.

Ebon wanted only a charm for hunting. His old one—never too effective, he said accusingly—had worn thin and he wanted to be ready for a forthcoming deer drive in the swamp-land across the Sound. Chaney stood patiently while Ebon and Mifiti haggled over the price. Eventually Mifiti declared she would be content with the front quarter of the first deer Ebon shot, and she gave him a charm to hang on his gun. He eyed Chaney anxiously as he left the cabin, but she waited in stolid silence until he had gone. She wanted no witnesses to her interview with Mifiti.

Alone with the witch woman, Chaney regarded the sinister, emaciated figure with mixed hatred and fear. They were acknowledged enemies of long standing, each resenting the prestige of the other's position. Never for her own sake would Chaney have invoked Mifiti's power. Only when her master and mistress were in danger would she humble herself before her rival.

She spoke in her native tongue, rusty now from disuse. "I wish medicine Mankwala against fire and burning. Against the evil of sickness. Against the anger of the wind."

Mifiti rubbed her clawlike hands together. "The woman asks much. Strong medicine requires strong payment," she muttered, her blue lips flattened over toothless gums.

Chaney said, "I myself will pay. I want strong medicine, as powerful as that of the great chief Chibisa who stood firm in battle on his great ant-heap while his men fell all about him, shouting his war song."

"Chibisa fell of a sand bullet," Mifiti answered.

"Then a more potent charm. I do not want medicine to throw at an enemy, nor to bury under a tree to bring disease, but a strong charm to ward off evil. To protect and make safe!"

"Chaney will pay high for such charm."

"High enough, evil one, but I will not sell my soul."

After prolonged skirmishing Mifiti named her price—the body of the next child who died on the quarters line. But Chaney's wrath was so terrible that Mifiti hastily retracted her demand. At length the contract was made. The body of the next dog that died on the plantation was to go to Mifiti, also the heart of a goat the next time one was slaughtered. In addition Chaney would send her each week a fat hen and a dozen eggs.

When Chaney crept from the cabin she clutched in her hand the tip of a cow's horn filled with Mankwala medicine. And in her heart were pride and deep contentment. She had saved her master and mistress from a third disaster.

Next morning Marcy reported to Adam that the identity of the man who had ordered the Queen's Gift tobacco burned would probably never be known. At the verge of the swamp beyond Sandy Point an unknown Negro had been found dead, and tied around his waist under his shirt was a wad of cotton smelling strongly of turpentine. There were no marks of violence to indicate how the man had died, but Marcy suspected Ben had followed a trail from the burning barns and had administered black man's justice. And both Marcy and Adam knew that no questions could draw from Old Ben any account of what had happened.

Sylvia Takes a Stand

24 THE LATE afternoon was unseasonably warm. Only the bare branches of the sycamore reminded that the month was November. The autumn had been rainy, but now a delayed Indian summer held sway. Children played in the village gardens or on the Green. People strolled along Broad Street to finish their trading before candle-time closed the shops in Cheapside.

Angus Moray walked over to Horniblow's to join friends gathered for a game of darts or billiards. Often they would stay on through the evening, sitting at the battered tavern tables to talk of crops or politics, complain about the weather and heavy taxes or speculate on how they were going to sell their tobacco. Perhaps they'd discuss the question of compensation for the Tory landholders. Only last night Angus had heard that Samuel Johnston and James Iredell were representing Sir Nat Duckenfield and his mother Mrs. Pearson. The group would wonder whether Johnston and Iredell could get for Henry McCulloh compensation for a hundred thousand acres in the state—a grant that had come down from the Granvilles and other Lords Proprietors.

Friendly male voices and an occasional clink of glasses made a pleasant sound when Angus entered the tap-room. This evening the talk seemed closer home. He caught snatches about some feud between Robert Smith and Thomas Barker while he found a chair and ordered a mug of ale. Then some one mentioned poor Joseph Hewes's untimely death. Memories were green of the stirring days when Hewes had helped John Paul Jones get ships for the new Navy, a Navy that helped win the Revolution. One man recounted the story of the great Commodore's arrival in Edenton as a forlorn young seaman fleeing from a charge of murder in the West Indies.

At mention of John Paul Jones, Lawyer Hardy asked William Blair if he knew anything about a statue Robert Burton of Granville wanted to present to the state.

Blair said, "Yes, I saw the letter Burton wrote the Governor. He proposes to make a formal presentation of a bust of Chevalier Jones at the next Assembly. He made the offer to perpetuate the fame of a great man, who derived his appointment from this state."

Hardy asked what the Governor would do about it.

"Accept it, of course, with the gratitude of the people of North Carolina."

At that moment Dr. Armitage came in. "What will we accept with gratitude?" he asked as he motioned to a pot-boy to bring his pipe and a mug of ale.

"A bust of John Paul Jones. I don't know where it will be put," Hardy answered.

"Why, in the new Capitol building—where else?"

A laugh went up. Some one added derisively, "If it ever gets built! Where are we to find the money to build a Capitol when we can't take up our war debts?"

Blair said, "But we can't refuse the bust, now can we? It's supposed to be very fine, the work of a French sculptor named . . ." He scratched his head, searching for the name. "I disremember, but it's the fellow who did the bust of General Washington."

Angus was about to supply the name of Houdon, but he hesitated. These men suffered him to sit in on conversations and discussions, but he was still sensitive about putting himself forward, especially in a way that might show superior knowledge.

The talk drifted then, as it was apt to drift, to the Revolution and doings of the Tories. A visitor from Wilmington named Spooner spoke bitterly of a Major Craig. "His men rivalled Tarleton's for brutality. The massacre at Eight-Mile House in New Hanover was the greatest tragedy of our district."

"Hadn't heard of it," said one of the Edenton men. "You know how it was during the war—outside news was hard to come by."

The Wilmington man was not loath to add his bit to the conversation. "Twenty of our young men had repaired to a tavern on the South Road. They had planned a supper for some of the maidens of the neighbourhood. A damned Tory betrayed them. The young folks were dancing while an old Negro fiddled. Suddenly the blare of a bugle was heard. The boys tried to escape by door and window, but Craig's dragoons had surrounded the tavern and butchered them as they came out."

"Horrible!" the men chorused.

"To my thinking," Hardy said, "the Tory who informed on them was worse than Craig."

Moray looked about for a chance to get away. He felt a little uneasy about sitting through talk of battles and the experiences of Carolina during the Revolution. Fortunately the conversation was interrupted by Robert Jones and young Webb, who had finished their ale and said they must be getting home.

Jones stopped at Dr. Armitage's table. "Is Dr. Williamson still here? I'd like to talk with him about the Congress."

"No. He left last week by stage for Suffolk. From there I think he planned to go on to New York."

"Was he greatly disappointed when the Hillsborough convention failed to ratify?"

Armitage said, "He regrets that North Carolina will not be a part of the union when the country's first President is inaugurated."

"Isn't it a queer thing about Rutledge, Doctor? I mean his going over to the Antis? I've not heard that he's tried to defend his vote."

"Adam has had too much on his mind to think about politics lately. His wife has been very ill."

Webb broke in. "I heard he'd lost all his tobacco in a fire. Serves him right, I say."

Another man remarked, "Trouble goes in threes, you know. What comes next?"

Robert Jones cut him off. "Don't be a superstitious fool! But I say, Doctor, it *is* hard to understand. Rutledge going against his old friends. Something mighty strange about it. Have you asked him why he turned his coat?"

Armitage banged his mug on the table. "What sort of doctor do you think I am? I don't discuss a patient's affairs in a tavern. What Adam Rutledge thinks is his business. Come on, Moray. I promised to have you look in on a case down the street."

Outside the tavern he remarked, "Young idiots! I'd like to turn them over my knee. Not old enough to vote—and hear them talk!"

"Where are we going, Doctor?" Angus thought he had glimpsed Sylvia leaving the inn.

"Nowhere. I didn't like the climate in there, and by the look on your face I gathered you could do with a little fresh air, too." He began to chuckle. "Oh-ho! I see. I see. There's a young lady ahead of us taking a stroll. Better hurry or she'll get away."

Angus' face grew red. He stammered a hasty good-bye to the kindly old man. It took him only a few long strides to catch up with Sylvia, though she was walking quickly. She too had been eager to escape from Horniblow's.

"Lady Anne doesn't know I've gone," she said. "I had to get away for a while."

"Come on then. We'll walk down to the water. It seems a year since I've seen you!"

The autumn sunset was beautiful, and villagers were still abroad enjoying the balmy weather. They cast knowing glances at the young doctor who was looking so ardently at his pretty companion. Suddenly aware of the passers-by, Angus steered Sylvia toward three cannon which stood on the shore and asked if she knew they had been brought over for the defence of the town on the schooner *Holy Heart of Jesus.*

Sylvia seemed glad to have the conversation turn impersonal. "See there— three vessels lie at anchor beyond the Dram Tree."

"Yes," Angus said. "One is Captain Meredith's ship, brought from Wilmington to pick up a cargo of rice from Parson Pettigrew's Bonarva Plantation in Tyrrell County." He explained that he'd heard at Horniblow's the Parson was sending forty-one tierces of rice to Lisbon—a transaction arranged by Josiah Collins' vertical commission house as the Parson's factor. Captain Meredith was well pleased with this cargo, because in Lisbon he could fill his hold with wine for the return voyage.

Sylvia remarked that it was too bad Parson Pettigrew's interests as a planter kept him from giving Parson Earle more help. "It is disgraceful that the services at St. Paul's are not more regular. The people here do not go to church as they should. What is to become of them? In no time they will be heathens."

Angus said, "Dr. Armitage told me about a noted Methodist minister, a Dr. Thomas Coke, who once preached in the Courthouse. He said it was an elegant edifice, but there was nothing but wickedness in the tavern, and Edenton was a den of vice."

Sylvia did not laugh. It seemed to her a serious situation, when there was no one to instruct the young or minister to the spiritual wants of the people. "Old Parson Earle is too ill to hold services, Mrs. Iredell says. People won't donate enough money to pay a rector. The Society for the Propagation of the Gospel withdrew its support during the Revolution."

Angus found an unoccupied bench by the verge of the water. For the moment most of the strollers had moved away in the direction of the Rope Walk. "Why must we waste time talking about Captain Meredith's cargo and church parsons when this is the first time we've been together since you left Queen's Gift?"

Sylvia clasped and unclasped her slim hands nervously. "Lady Anne is determined I shall not see you alone. She says it is very improper. Perhaps it is. . . ." She looked at him earnestly. "Angus, I have thought and thought about us until my head whirls. We must not see each other alone any more—

not because Lady Anne orders it, but because it isn't right. I'm not free
. . . and you—you aren't either."

He put his hand over hers, but she drew away. "Don't touch me, please.
When I am so near you, I cannot think clearly. I can only feel. . . . And
we must think reasonably, you and I. If I were a different sort of woman, I
would throw caution to the winds. I would say, 'Take me, no matter what
the consequences.' . . . Or I might establish myself in a little house where
you could come to me at night and sneak away before the dawn, as some of
the men here do. But we are different. To me, love must be in all honour,
not something touched and tarnished by vulgar licence—no better than a
profession like the women's in the houses down the street."

"My dear," Angus murmured, "you must never speak such thoughts, nor
even think them."

"Let me go on while I have the courage. I have determined that I will not
see you alone—not because my heart tells me, but my reason."

"Damn reason!" Angus cried. "How can I be reasonable about you? I'm
not the man to love you silently and from afar. We're not like Dante and
Beatrice. Oh, do not force me to abandon hope! In a year or two I will be
established and can make a home. I'll never give you up. Say your feeling is
the same as mine. I must hear you say the words."

Sylvia stopped him. "I can't, Angus. I cannot say what you want me to
say. If I did, I would be saying in my heart, 'I hope Donald will die of his
illness.' Do you understand?"

Angus' lean strong jaw tightened. "I believe you love the fellow."

Sylvia's voice was sad. "I love no one as I love you. I never have. Something dies inside me when I think of living away from you. But I must face
what I have to face. Give me courage, Angus."

He sat silent, staring out on the darkening sky. Her shoulder touched
his for a moment. She drew away at the sound of voices. Strollers were
approaching. She got to her feet.

Angus rose also. "Of course you are right, my dearest. I cannot match you
in selflessness."

They walked slowly across the Green. Horniblow's was bright with light.
Sylvia saw a candle burning in the window of Lady Anne's sitting-room.
In her heart she said fiercely, But I won't let that woman have you. I swear
I won't!

The days that followed her return from Queen's Gift had been filled with
work. Lady Anne had dozens of disparaging letters to write to her sisters and
to her friends in London.

Sylvia found her pacing the floor restlessly. Lady Anne said, "Well, here
you are! I've had Dawkins searching for you for half an hour." She looked
closely at Sylvia. Her light-blue eyes were cold, her lips in a tight line.
"Miss Hay, you are employed by me to be here when I want you, at any

time, day or night. We have been away for three weeks or more. You have had a pleasant holiday, visiting the Iredells and Queen's Gift. Of course you do not expect to be paid for the time you were neglecting my work."

Sylvia had learned to curb her tongue. She wanted to say that Lady Anne had left no work for her, but she knew it would be useless.

Lady Anne went to her desk, drew a packet of letters from the pigeon-holes. She threw them on the table. "All these letters want answering. I understand two ships have sailed from Edenton while we were in Hertford. Through your negligence my letters will be a month or six weeks late in England."

"This is the first time I've seen these letters," Sylvia said.

Lady Anne whirled about. "Are you accusing *me* of lying?"

Sylvia's eyes met her employer's. Her voice was steady. "Certainly not. I am not accustomed to using the word liar, Lady Anne—not even to a servant."

"You are impertinent! You have been absorbing some of this American liberty of speech. Let me tell you, my girl, that I do not allow impertinence in my servants. Dawkins will tell you. She presumed to answer me impudently while we were at Hertford, and I left her there to shift for herself as best she could. Three days after I returned here she was back, begging to be reinstated. I took her back because I felt she had learned her lesson—that she is a servant and must remember to keep her place."

A red flush crept over Sylvia's face. Her hands were tightly clenched behind her back, but she spoke quietly. "I think you forget yourself, Baroness. I am not your servant. I am a woman in your employ."

Lady Anne took a step forward, her hand raised.

Sylvia did not give an inch. "I wouldn't do that if I were you, Baroness," she said.

Lady Anne screamed, "I'll do what I please and say what I please! You are getting beyond yourself, my girl. Who are *you* to tell me what to do or say? You, a nobody the Baron picked up in London!"

A slow smile came over Sylvia's lips. She did not raise her voice. "I may be a nobody, but my Devon ancestor faced King John at Runnymede. It was Devon men who put a Stuart King on the throne of England. Or have you perhaps forgotten?"

Lady Anne raved and stormed. Billingsgate poured from her tongue.

Sylvia took up the letters from the table. "I'll write the letters to-night, after your Ladyship has got control of your temper." She opened the door and almost stumbled over Dawkins. The maid's face grew red with confusion. To be caught with her ear to the keyhole!

Sylvia shut the door quietly. Dawkins followed her down the hall. "Oh, Miss Hay, you bested her, you did! She can't abide any one to stand up to her. You should have heard the way she carried on at Hertford when I told her I wouldn't stay on any longer. But I told her straight out what I thought of her, and I stood by my words. Then," she added bitterly, "my man ran off without me, and I had to come back to her—and glad she was to have me, too, to fix her hair and manage her fancy clothes. Next time I'll do better, and she'll never see me again. Meanwhile I know how to handle her. She wants that people cringe and show their fear. That's what I do when she shouts at me. It pleases her and don't hurt me one whit."

"You're a fool, Dawkins." Sylvia was annoyed at the woman for listening. She went into her room and closed the door. She was trembling; her knees were like water. Well, Sylvia told herself, let her discharge me without pay, if she likes. Though what I said about the Barons of Runnymede smacked of the theatrical, she may as well learn that I've Devon pride in me. She grinned a little, feeling better.

When she put the letters on the desk she saw a small square box addressed to her, and a little note tucked under the cord that bound it. She broke the red wax seal. It was from Mary Rutledge.

Dear Sylvia:
I have been waiting for you to come to visit us, but I presume you have been too busy. I am sending you under separate cover a memento which I hope you will wear as a constant reminder of the gratitude of
MARY AND ADAM RUTLEDGE

She took off the wrappings and opened the shagreen case. Her startled eyes beheld the emerald ring. She sat looking at it, not moving. After a time she slipped it on her finger, the third finger of her left hand, where it glowed in dark beauty. It was more than a beautiful ring. It was a symbol of generosity and friendship. Tears came to her eyes. She had controlled her emotions during the difficult hour with Angus. She had withstood the anger of Lady Anne. But this evidence of kindness was more than she could endure. She put her head on the desk and wept. . . .

At last she rose, bathed her face and washed away the traces of tears. She was tidying her disordered hair when Dawkins came to her room.

"Her Ladyship says please do not work on the letters to-night. She remembers that she had not made notations on how they were to be answered." The maid continued, "Her Ladyship says will you please join her at supper."

Sylvia looked up then and saw that Dawkins had several red marks on her cheek. She was careful not to show she had noticed them. "Thank you, Dawkins. Please tell the Baroness that I will be there presently."

Dawkins lingered at the door, her hand on the latch. There was the semblance of a smile on her lips. "She can't abide being called the Baroness."

Sylvia nodded. "Yes, I understand. You may say to the Baroness that I shall attend her presently. Can you remember the message?"

Dawkins answered, "Word for word, Miss Hay."

Lady Anne was dressed in a pale-yellow muslin negligee. Her ash-blond hair hung in long heavy braids to her slender waist. She smiled at Sylvia. "I have news that may interest you. I've had a note from James Iredell. His wife has presented him with a fine son."

"How is Mrs. Iredell?" Sylvia asked.

"Oh, well enough, I fancy." Lady Anne's voice showed her indifference to Hannah's condition. A little smile played on her curved lips. "The dear man, he is so happy! I must write at once to my sister Lady Macartney. I consider Jamie almost a relative. It's too bad he has no interest except silly politics." She paused suddenly, her eyes on Sylvia's hand.

An inn servant came with the supper, so nothing was said about the emerald. Nothing was said about their encounter, either. While they were eating Lady Anne talked of indifferent things. Sylvia noticed her eyes returning again and again to the ring.

After a time Lady Anne could stand it no longer. "Have I seen you wear that emerald before?"

Sylvia looked up from her plate and met inquisitive eyes. "I fancy not. I seldom wear jewelry." Something in her voice warned Lady Anne. She forbore to ask the question Sylvia knew was on her lips. Sylvia thought, She suspects some man has given it to me. Let her suspect!

Presently Lady Anne said, "It looks a very fine emerald. Emeralds can be worth a king's ransom."

Sylvia ignored the opening. She went on eating the gooseberry tart with relish. After a time she said, "Madam Horniblow told me she had put up more than a hundred quarts of gooseberries last summer."

The two women looked straight at each other. Lady Anne's eyes were the first to drop. Sylvia thought with some surprise, Why, I believe she's afraid of me! The idea gave her satisfaction, and now she was particularly glad she had not really let her tongue get out of control. She did not propose to give up the advantage she had gained. She doesn't want to let me go, she thought. She has some reason for keeping me on. I wish I knew what it is.

Things went along easily for the next few days. The Baron returned at the end of the week. He was in excellent spirits. He had stopped overnight at River Plantation to visit his boys. He was delighted at their progress. They were happy and had grown quite fond of the eight lads who were their fellow students. They were taken once a week to the marl bed and allowed to dig for Indian relics. They had a box of Indian arrow heads to take home to London.

The Baron was pleased. "I am content to leave them as soon as I have examined some properties on the Pee Dee in South Carolina," he told Lady Anne and Sylvia at supper.

Sylvia had asked to be excused from eating with them, but Lady Anne had insisted. Sylvia noticed that she preferred not to dine alone with the Baron. She either invited in James Iredell or Stephen Cabarrus, or insisted on Sylvia being with them.

To-night she said, "Let us drive out to Queen's Gift after supper."

The Baron made a mild objection and was immediately overruled. Sylvia got up to leave, but the Baron stopped her. "Come to the court-yard when you have your wraps. I'll order the carriage at once."

Lady Anne said, "Perhaps Miss Hay would prefer to remain here."

Sylvia took this as an order. Now it was the Baron who was reluctant not to have her with them. "You are working too hard. You look a little tired. Perhaps some change would be diverting," he said kindly.

Sylvia begged off. She was not out of the door when she heard Lady Anne's impatient voice. "So you are going to South Carolina! Another excuse to leave me stranded in this boring village. I warn you, Karl, I am going to be in New York in January, whether you go with me or not."

Sylvia went to her room and put on her bonnet and cape. She would run up to the Iredell house to inquire about Hannah and the little son.

At the door of the inn she met Mr. Horniblow. When she told him where she was going he sent for his Negro body servant.

"It's only a step," Sylvia said. "I'll run down the little street past the gaol."

"Indeed, miss, it's not good for a young woman to be out alone." He fetched a big sigh. "I don't know what the world is coming to. Every night I have to throw men out of my tap-room, drinking, arguing politics, fighting and disturbing decent folk. It's almost as bad as it was during the war with the Whigs and the Tories a-fighting. Why, I remember well when a crowd of roughs dragged Mr. Cullen Pollock out of his bed and threatened to tar and feather him! Mrs. Pollock came running and screaming up to the tavern in her night-rail, crying for help. Clem Hull had two hundred men with him. A fellow named Mercereau tried to break open the cellars to get at the wine.

"I asked Mr. Corry to go to disperse them while I went for the sheriff. My wife brought Mrs. Pollock, all barefoot, from in front of the Court-house. The mob burned Mr. Pollock's carriage right there on the Green. Some of those lads should have known better—Michael Payne and Joe Worth and Blackburn.

"Well, miss, I've talked too much, but it's just to show that even in this well-behaved village people will get out of hand when fair excited by elections and politics. Here's my man Sol. He'll walk you over to Mrs. Iredell's. I'll tell him to wait for you."

"I don't want to put you to so much trouble, Mr. Horniblow."

"No trouble for Sol. He'll be glad to visit with the Iredell cook."

Sol led the way down the lane, picking a good path across the low ground beyond the gaol.

Nellie Blair came to the door and invited her into the drawing-room. "I'll tell my uncle you are here."

Sylvia said she had come only to inquire about Mrs. Iredell's health and the new baby's.

"They are both wonderful, but Dr. Moray won't let any one see them for a day or two. Pray have a seat while I speak to my uncle." The young girl went swiftly from the room before Sylvia could protest.

In a moment James Iredell came in. He kissed her hand and invited her to the dining-room for a glass of port.

She found the Governor and Mr. Cabarrus at the table. She hesitated, but Nellie pulled her by the hand. "Please come, Miss Hay. They'll promise not to talk politics any longer. Aunt Hannah says Uncle Iredell gets too wrought up when he and Uncle Samuel get to blessin' out the Antis. Uncle Samuel is leaving in the morning for Fayetteville--the Assembly is meeting there—and he's been fightin' Wilie Jones all evening."

The men laughed. The Governor said, "You should be in bed, miss. Your Uncle Iredell is too indulgent."

"I know you think I am spoiled, Uncle Samuel, but I'm not really. I help my uncle all the time. I copy letters into his big letter-book. Long ones too, like the one to Lord Macartney explaining how he came to go over to the rebels."

Iredell tweaked her ear. "Secretaries don't tell tales out of school," he said.

The girl's lips trembled. "Oh! I didn't mean to say anything I shouldn't."

"There, there now! Don't burst into tears. Pass the little cakes to Miss Hay while I pour a glass of port."

Iredell pulled up a chair for Sylvia next to him. When she asked about his wife and the new baby his face took on a look of radiance. "My dear Hannah is improving every day. In a week she will be able to have visitors. She was speaking of you. Dr. Moray told her how wonderful you were, helping nurse Mrs. Rutledge."

At mention of the name Rutledge, Sylvia noticed that Samuel Johnston stirred impatiently and set his jaw. Evidently the name was anathema to him.

Stephen Cabarrus made this even more clear by changing the subject abruptly. He asked the Governor something about the harvest. "Are you finding it difficult to be a planter and a Governor at the same time?"

"Not too difficult. I have an excellent superintendent at Hayes. I've grown to be an industrious planter. I go to bed very early, and I'm always up before the sun. I use a great deal of exercise and avoid reading and thinking as much as possible."

Cabarrus laughed. "Imagine you not reading, Governor! And as for not thinking, that would be as hard for you as not breathing."

The Governor did not smile. What an austere man he is! thought Sylvia.

And so very remote. He has none of the warmth and sparkle of James Iredell.

Johnston went on. "I hope soon to arrive at that degree of stupidity and insensibility which, I begin to think, may be the only requisite of a happy life."

Iredell looked at his brother-in-law. "You're joking, Samuel."

"Indeed I'm not. I have long observed that the greatest fools have not only the most pleasure in life, but are as much respected as men of the best understanding, and have a greater share of good fortune."

Silence followed the Governor's words. Sylvia saw Cabarrus glance at James Iredell. She felt that what Mr. Johnston had been saying was the continuation of something said before she entered the room. She finished her wine, set the glass on the table and got to her feet.

"I must be going back to the inn," she said to her host. She bowed to the gentlemen.

Stephen Cabarrus said, "Allow me to offer you a seat in my carriage. I'm driving past Horniblow's on my way home to Pembroke."

Sylvia demurred. She said that Horniblow's boy Sol was waiting in the kitchen with a lanthorn to light her way to the tavern.

Iredell said, "Oh, no. You must ride with Mr. Cabarrus. I'll send Sol home."

So it was settled. The Governor rose when she left, and bowed. He had not once addressed a word to her.

On the way home Mr. Cabarrus said, "The Governor is bitter about Rutledge's defection. He won't get over it soon. I also had words with Rutledge at Hillsborough. It's not a thing I'm proud of now. I suppose a man's entitled to his opinion. But for Adam to——" He broke off. "Pardon me, Miss Hay, for such a frank expression. I'm troubled about Sam. Did you notice the cynicism in that comment of his about being a planter? That's not like him. I worry when I hear him voice such nonsense."

He changed the subject and talked of other things—of the Baron and his search for land, of Lady Anne. "I think it's quite wonderful that she should be content in our little village."

"But *you* are content, Mr. Cabarrus."

"Ah, that is quite different. I am a happily married man and my dear wife will soon be home from France. I have my plantation. And I flatter myself that I am a part of a great experiment in government. So I am indeed content. But here we are. The drive has been much too short. Will you give my respects to Lady Anne and the Baron?"

He assisted her from the coach. As she walked up the stairs to her room she thought of the contrast between him and the Governor. No doubt Mr. Johnston was a fine, upright man of ability and of known integrity, but severe and distant. Perhaps that was the way a Governor of a state should be.

She went to her room. The servant had been in. The bed was turned down. A candle had been lighted in the hurricane shade. On the table was a volume of Tillotson's sermons. She began to laugh. She had seen the book in Lady Anne's room. It was a subtle message to turn her mind to things spiritual—in other words, not to let angry passions rise, not to nurse a grudge. She realized, as she braided her long auburn hair, how weary she was. This had been a day filled with too many emotions. Shortly she fell asleep, the emerald ring pressed against her smooth cheek.

It was more than a month before Sam Johnston again had supper with the Iredells. During the meal he seemed even more reserved than usual. Hannah scolded him gently. "You've shown little interest in either the company or the food, Sam. I've begun to believe that you came only to see that your nephew was being cared for properly. Are you satisfied on that score?"

"Perfectly, Hannah." The Governor smiled at his sister. "You mustn't take my silence amiss. Your husband will tell you that there were trials and disappointments at Fayetteville."

Iredell rose and took the decanter of port from the table. "But there was a victory, too, Sam. We'll talk of that. Hannah will want to see to her son's comfort. Let's go to the fire."

Johnston appeared to relax when he was seated with a pipe in his hand and a glass of wine beside him. He leaned back in his chair and closed his eyes. There was no sound in the room except the crackle of flames biting into the logs.

Iredell did not disturb his brother-in-law. The man had earned rest. The session of the Assembly at Fayetteville had re-elected him Governor and called another convention to reconsider ratifying the Constitution. But it had also defeated his high hope that ratification could be accomplished speedily. Charles Johnson, who had returned from Fayetteville several days before Johnston, had told Iredell of Wilie Jones's adroitness in delaying the meeting of the second convention until November, almost a year from now.

Iredell shared Johnston's keen disappointment. Immediately after the adjournment at Hillsborough the tide had seemed to turn in favour of ratification. The annual elections for the Assembly had shown decided Federalist gains, even in the western counties. The changed temper of the people had become more evident as news about the formation of the new government reached all parts of the state. Presidential electors would be appointed in January and cast their ballots a month later. The new Congress would convene in March. Resentment grew that North Carolina would have no representation, though she still had to pay her share of debt for the war that had made the union possible. Effigies of Jones and Person were exhibited and reviled in previously Antifederal Edgecombe County. Federalist leaders had little difficulty in getting signatures on petitions for a new convention.

This was the situation Jones had faced at Fayetteville—and yet he had been able to defeat all moves for an early convention. Iredell got to his feet and walked across the room to replace his pipe in the rack. An incredible man, this Jones!

As he passed Johnston the Governor stirred, opened his eyes slowly and then came bolt upright. "I'm sorry, Jemmy. I seem to have gone promptly to sleep. Blame your own hospitality. You make me too comfortable in this house."

Iredell stood with his back to the fire. "You've earned comfort, Sam. You've given it to all of us in the certainty of a new chance to ratify."

"It's not enough!" Johnston spoke grimly. "Antifederalism dies hard among us. Jones puts his immediate hope in the possibility that there will be a new Federal convention to alter the Constitution. You should have seen the jubilation of the Antis when the news reached Fayetteville that Virginia and New York have asked for this. Why, sir——" Johnston could not go on for a moment. "North Carolina delegates were named for such a convention!"

Iredell laughed. "I know, Sam. But I very much doubt if you'll ever have to make out warrants for their expenses. Your digestion will be poor if we don't give over this discussion. Hannah will think you've lost your affection for young James if we don't go up to the nursery. It'll be a more congenial occupation to plan his future. Hannah says she hopes he will have no leaning toward politics and the law. She prefers that he be a nice comfortable planter."

Johnston did not smile. "I share Hannah's hope," he said, rising to his feet. "Shall we go?"

Mel Frazier seated himself heavily on a coil of rope and looked at the men who sat in a half-circle around him. "We're five now," he said. "One more's comin'. We'll wait." He bent and adjusted a brass ship's lanthorn at his feet. The light, illuminating the men's faces from below, gave them a strange, distorted appearance. Frazier glanced up and chuckled. "You look like a pack of rascals, right enough. But it won't do to have the light higher. It'd show through the shutters surely."

"Why shouldn't it?" Chase spoke sharply. "I'm not a conspirator. I'm an honest printer with Antifederalist convictions. Why should I have to hide? My rival printer Wills is frankly Federalist."

Frazier jerked a thumb at Andrews. "The tailor'll tell you that."

"I'm bound to be careful. My living depends on the gentlemen of the village. It wouldn't do for it to be known . . ." He paused. "Why, last spring I made four suits for Mr. Cabarrus and several waistcoats out of brocade material he had from London."

"Perhaps we all ought to wear masks," Chase said sarcastically.

"Andrews is right." The speaker was Timmons, a thin-faced joiner.

"Governor Johnston has bespoke me for the cabinet work in his new house. I'd not care to lose——" A sharp knock on the door interrupted him. Mel Frazier limped over to admit Marcy.

The men rose, suspicious and uncertain. The farmer Galloway spoke for them. "What's he doin' here? Ain't he the one you said was spyin' on us the day we had the meeting on the Green last summer?"

"Sit down!" Frazier roared. He put his hand on Marcy's shoulder. "This man comes from Adam Rutledge. I reckon that should be enough for you. As for his spyin' on us—there's others here has changed their minds. Seems I recollect another meetin' here when West spoke out against me. Eh, West?"

The little barber was not intimidated. "I said Chowan men should speak for Chowan men and not let men of other counties sway them. I say it still. I've read the convention debates Mr. Iredell had published. I stand by what Mr. Rutledge said. His speech was for men like us. But I surely hate to go against James Iredell, and I won't accept the word of men like Person and Bloodworth. I say let's——"

"You're wrong, West." Marcy stepped forward into the circle of light cast by the lanthorn. "We're fighting for a principle. Your own opinion of the men for or against it is not important now. And we need the help of men in other counties—men like you, who believe our state shouldn't join the union unless our liberties are secure." He stopped and looked slowly around the half-circle of men. "Isn't that right? We stand or fall by the vote of the state convention."

West nodded, but before he could speak Frazier assumed command. "Aye, he's right. Now sit down and listen to what he has to say."

Marcy remained standing while the men seated themselves on the floor. When he had their attention again he continued. "Mel has told you that there will be another convention. The Federalists are stronger. The danger to your rights is greater than at Hillsborough. We must plan now for the election of delegates in March."

"Ain't Mr. Rutledge going to stand?" Timmons asked. "We'll vote for him."

"He'll stand." Marcy spoke with new emphasis. "But it won't be easy to elect him this time. Remember, he was thought of as a Federalist before the last convention. The Federalists will be determined to beat him."

"It's what I've been tellin' 'em," Frazier growled. "If we want Rutledge, we've got to get our men to the polls."

"That's our task, Mel," Marcy said. "Between now and the election we've got to talk to every freeman in this district—men from Rockahock and Copper Neck, Yeopim and Hertford Road—every farmer, artisan and mechanic. These are the men who share our views. They can return Mr. Rutledge as a delegate from Chowan."

"Aye, they can and will." Frazier's voice boomed out. "And we've another man to elect. They'll need to know of that, Marcy."

"Mr. Rutledge has persuaded John Hamilton to stand for election as delegate from Edenton. He's a man respected by the whole county, and he stands firm for a bill of rights before we ratify. It's likely they'll be the only Antis standing. But each county will have only three delegates in this convention, and each borough town one. Elect Rutledge and Hamilton and you'll have as many delegates as the Feds. You men were selected to help build our strength. Begin now to get others to help you."

Timmons scrambled to his feet. "Why don't we get outsiders like last time to——"

"No!" Marcy cut him off firmly. "There will be no riots. We can win nothing by trying to frighten men. Talk to your friends. Have them talk to their friends. Mr. Rutledge will be travelling all over the state, winning votes in the convention for us. We must win his county for him!"

Chase rose and extended his hand to Marcy. "We're agreed," he said. "You'll find we'll do our part. The freemen of Chowan will stand by Mr. Rutledge."

Marcy took the printer's hand. This man would offer intelligent help. "One thing must be made clear. We are not fighting to keep North Carolina out of the union. Mr. Rutledge doesn't want that. No freeman in Chowan does. We fight for a bill of rights. Remember that. Make it plain to every one!"

"Plain it will be made." Frazier walked to the door and opened it. "I reckon every man has heard what he needs to hear. We've got real leaders now. You can go to your beds sure of that."

As he rode to Queen's Gift, Marcy wondered whether he had really been successful. Would these men and men like them take up their responsibility? Certainly Adam Rutledge never doubted it. Well, a start had been made. It would be three months before he had his answer.

It was long past midnight when Adam Rutledge finished the last of his work on the season's ledgers and opened his strong-box to put them with the other permanent records. As he rearranged the contents of the box he discovered a small package, which he drew out to examine. He recognized the crest imprinted on the seals as Duke Roger's. Puzzled, he turned the package over and found Meredith's note explaining how he had come by it in Antigua.

Adam took the package back to his desk and examined it more carefully. Obviously it had never been opened, yet Mary must have received it before he returned from the Illinois country. What was it she had said just after she regained consciousness? Yes, that she had forgotten something having to do with her grandfather. This must be it. But the mystery remained. Why had Mary not opened it immediately? He would take it to her to-morrow.

The case clock struck one. Adam replaced the package in the strong-box, snuffed the candles and walked to the door opening onto the gallery. The stars were brilliant in the clear, cold sky. In the morning he would hear Marcy's report. If the Chowan men would accept organization in the fight for their rights, then he could hope to persuade Antifederalist leaders in other parts of the Albemarle and all over the state to try the same simple plan. He could talk to groups of men with confidence that they would respond.

Adam stood for a time looking at the stars. These reaches of eternity made his concerns seem very small. Could they matter? Words he had read long ago returned to him. "Who marks with equal eye, as God of all, a hero perish or a sparrow fall."

Christmas Eve

25 MARY RUTLEDGE was having breakfast by the fire when Adam entered her room. Her dress was of warm maroon wool, for the November morning was cold. She no longer looked like an invalid, Adam thought gratefully. She was still quite thin, but her lips and cheeks had regained their normal colour.

Mary greeted him cheerfully and poured out a cup of tea for him. She was eager to talk of a subject Adam dreaded. "I have finally compelled Dr. Armitage to admit that I will be able to hunt in time for the Christmas meet," she announced.

Adam's heart sank. He understood only too well the doctor's reluctance. Armitage knew the Rutledges had not been invited to ride with the Albemarle Hunt this season.

Mary interpreted his silence as disapproval. "Don't look so worried. I shall ride by myself for a while each day to get accustomed to horses again. Even Miss Sarah concedes the exercise will be beneficial."

Adam raised his hands in a gesture of surrender. "Very well, my dear, I'll say no more. It will be good to see you on a horse again." He changed the subject quickly. "Mary, do you know there is an unopened package in the strong-box addressed to you?"

Mary's blue eyes opened wide. "Why, of course, the one from Antigua —Duke Roger's journal! That's what I've been trying to remember. Ring the bell, Adam, and have it brought up. We'll open it together."

"You forget, dear, that only you and I can open the strong-box. I'll fetch it myself."

Mary's hands trembled with excitement as Adam handed her the canvas-wrapped package. She struggled helplessly with the cords that held the wrapping in place until Adam found a paper-knife on her writing-table and cut away the cloth. Inside were a slim volume bound in vellum and a small leather box sealed with Duke Roger's crest.

Mary took up the book, whose cover bore the word *Journal* in decorated letters. She opened it and saw that the first leaves were covered with the spidery handwriting she had seen in the plantation's earliest ledgers—Duke Roger's hand. Instinctively she closed the book. She should be alone when she read her grandfather's words.

There remained the little leather box. She asked Adam to break the seal. Inside, on a lining of velours, was an oval locket of gold bearing an elaborate crest surrounded by a row of brilliants.

"What can it mean?" Mary picked up the locket and stared at it in bewilderment. "It's a beautiful piece, but I don't know the crest."

"Perhaps it is explained in the journal," Adam suggested. "Does the locket open?"

"I don't find a catch," Mary said, turning it over in her fingers. "It must be concealed. See if you can find it, Adam."

Almost at once Adam found that one of the small brilliants yielded to the pressure of his fingers. The locket fell open, revealing a delicate ivory miniature of a beautiful woman with pale gold hair and intensely blue eyes.

Mary and Adam gazed in silence at the portrait.

"Who can it be?" Mary said. "It isn't Grandmother Rhoda. 'To Roger,' the inscription reads. And . . . what is the other line?"

"It's French, I think. The letters are so small I can scarcely make them out."

"There's a magnifying glass in the desk." Mary studied the lettering. "It's Spanish, Adam, and it says, 'Heart of my soul . . . your Mary.' " She paused, then snapped the locket closed. "I feel as though I'm prying into a secret which I have no right to know."

Adam said nothing. He understood the thoughts that were racing through her mind. Mary's veneration for the grandfather she had never seen was intense and highly emotional. Anything that tended to undermine her faith in Duke Roger would be terribly upsetting to her.

Mary was staring at the vellum bound journal. "I think," she said slowly, "that I will not read this now. I . . . I can't get used to the idea that there was another woman in Duke Roger's life." She opened the locket again and studied the portrait. "She is beautiful, very beautiful. . . . Rhoda was not beautiful, but she was vivid and alive."

"Let me hang the locket about your neck, sweet," Adam suggested. "It will look well against your red gown."

"No!" Mary replaced the locket in its case. "I don't think I can. Not yet." She rose and put the box and the journal in a drawer of her desk. "Later

—some day soon—I'll read what he has written. . . . I'm very tired suddenly, Adam. Perhaps I can sleep for a while."

Adam nodded and left the room. Mary would have to work out her own adjustment to this new idea. He knew it would be painful for her, but he could not suppress a secret elation at the thought that Duke Roger might fall from his pedestal. Mary's unreasoning devotion to her grandfather and the plantation he had built was one of the barriers to the complete understanding Adam hoped he and Mary could some day achieve.

Later in the morning, with Chaney hovering close beside her to help if needed, Mary descended the stairs to the first floor of Queen's Gift for the first time since the mysterious fever had struck her down.

When they stood together in the wide entrance hall Mary's face was flushed with triumph. "You see, Chaney? I'm quite well now. I'll go onto the gallery to get my fill of fresh air. And this noon I'll have dinner with Mr. Rutledge in the dining-room."

"Bless de Lord, Miss Mary, dose de sweetest words I's heard dis many a day! I'll get you' cape. De wind he's might' sharp."

Mary went to the hall door and opened it. The November landscape was bleak, the air crisp and chill. Hunting weather! she thought. She walked to the far end of the gallery where the tulip poplar stood. It was bare of leaves, and the black and white of its bark stood out boldly. She stretched a hand toward the massive trunk. "My tree," she murmured. "My beautiful, life-giving tree!" The wind soughed softly in its branches. "What are you saying?" Mary asked, looking upward. "What are you trying to tell me?"

She jumped as Chaney spoke just behind her. "It don't do so well to talk wid de tree spirits, Miss Mary," the old woman said quietly. She laid a warm cape over her mistress' shoulders. "An' it ain't good to breathe too much mornin' air into you. Come set in Duke Roger's room, mistress. Ebon he got a roarin' fire of pine-knots all ready for you."

The office was warm and bright and smelled pleasantly of pitch and tobacco. On the table were a pile of newspapers from London and a copy of the latest *State Gazette*. She turned its pages idly until the name of James Boyce, the Perquimans planter, caught her eye. The article described the outcome of Boyce's trial for disturbing the peace. Mary read it with interest.

Boyce, it seemed, made a practice of declaring a holiday for his slaves on the completion of an important job of work, and on these occasions they were permitted to dance and sing. On one such occasion a patrol came to Boyce's plantation to protest that the noise could be heard three quarters of a mile away. The patrol burst open the door of Boyce's residence and began to tie up the Negroes. Boyce's son-in-law argued that they had the permission of their master to frolic, but the patrol whipped fourteen slaves and lodged a complaint against Boyce.

But the judge who heard the case exempted Boyce from paying a fine. The *Gazette* quoted his remarks at length.

It would really be a source of regret if, contrary to common custom, it be denied to slaves, in intervals between their toils, to indulge in mirthful pastimes, or if it were unlawful for the master to permit them among his slaves, or admit to the social enjoyment of slaves of others, by their consent.

The Keepers of the Law should expect a Negro dance to be accompanied by hearty and boisterous gladsomeness and loud laughs. Simple music and romping dances should be set down as an innocent and happy class.

Great amusement was afforded the court, the *Gazette* added, by the testimony of an old white-haired slave concerning the behaviour of another of the merrymakers: "He warn't doin' nothin' but stretchin' out he voice singin', 'I losted my shoe in an old canoe.'"

Mary smiled. If a patrol happened in on Queen's Gift on Christmas Eve they would surely hear frolicking and the noisy outpouring of glad hearts. She folded back the newspaper and laid it on the desk so Adam could not miss seeing the article.

Beneath the *Gazette* was a pamphlet entitled *To the People of the District of Edenton, by a Citizen and a Soldier.* Beneath the title Adam had written, "Whoever this man is, he is mad, quite mad!" Her curiosity aroused, Mary turned the pages, scanning fragments at random.

. . . outrageous proceedings of the late convention at Hillsborough. The hour fast approaches when the trumpet of calamity will reach you. The sun of North Carolina has already set. Clouds and thick tempests compass us. We are as the weary wanderers in midnight darkness.

Adam's comment in the wide margin was "Nonsense!" She turned a page and noted some underscored lines:

Your deputies must have given you an account of the Antifederal leaders, and the manner in which they conducted themself, with minds totally callous to conditions, with hearts bent upon the ruin of the people. Destitute of language or the tongue of expression, wicked, abandoned and depraved, they wilfully plunged you into so a forlorn state of human misery, that nothing but the most spirited exertions can possibly save you from destruction.

"He means Wilie Jones, Person and James Tate," Adam had written.

Can the Governor interfere to stop this mess of Judases? Could he, if an honest Federalist be condemned for treason against the State, grant a pardon?

The Governor now has no power to raise militia, to quell rebellion of Indians. We have no government; the Executive is civilly dead. We have no government abroad because the foundation stone has been taken away.

North Carolina is in a state of Nature, without law, without order or government. This is the melancholy truth. But this is what the Antifederals have done by not signing the Constitution for North Carolina.

Adam had indignantly marked out the entire last paragraph and written, "As errant a bit of untruth and lies as ever set to paper. No wonder the man refuses to sign his name. To the devil with such idiots!"

Mary dropped the pamphlet to the table. This, then, was the sort of dispute Adam had involved himself in! And doubtless in the next issue of the *Gazette* she would find that she was the wife of a heartless scoundrel, that Adam was depraved and wicked. Oh, it was too much! After years of warfare she had become Adam's wife and looked forward to a life of peace and contentment in the home she loved among the distinguished friends whose respect and affection Adam had earned. Instead she found herself shouldering the management of the plantation for long periods while her husband revelled in a crude frontier life hundreds of wilderness miles away from her. And when he came home it was to tell her that he had estranged her friends and imperilled her plantation, all for the sake of a handful of barbarous Westerners. Against the advice of all his friends, he had allied himself with a faction that instigated riots in quiet villages and aroused vulgar name-calling in public journals.

She turned, as she had so often in times of trouble, to the portrait of Duke Roger. His handsome face was smiling its eternal quizzical smile. Was he saying, *Foolish little Mary, don't try to judge a man by a woman's standards?* Or, she wondered suddenly, remembering the miniature upstairs in her desk, was it a smug smile, reflecting the satisfaction of a man who has betrayed his wife and succeeded in keeping the betrayal secret? No, Duke Roger could not have been that sort of man! . . . Perhaps I am losing Adam, she thought despairingly. Am I to lose Duke Roger as well?

She heard Adam's voice in the hall. "Where is Mrs. Rutledge, Ebon?" And the butler answered, "Sar, I think she in you' office."

Instantly she knew she could not argue out her differences with Adam to-night. Not yet. She needed his strength, his support. The question, once brought into the open, could not be laid aside again. She must have time to think.

When Adam entered the office she was seated by the fire studying the *Gazette.*

He came toward her eagerly, his arms outstretched. "Mary! This is a welcome surprise." He took her hands and raised her to her feet. "You should have warned me so that I could have dressed to suit the occasion. Ebon will announce dinner in a moment, and here I am in buckskins."

She tried to match his mood. "They become you. You look like a great stalwart back-mountain man." As they walked to the dining-room she deliberately turned the conversation to days past when their hopes and goals had been identical. "I remember how glad we were to see the mountaineers at Guilford Courthouse. They looked so purposeful, so confident."

"Guilford Courthouse!" Adam repeated. He seated Mary and went around the table to his own chair. "What a day that was! You were superb, Mary! I can still visualize you as I first saw you—running out to me from the dressing-station where you'd been helping Dr. Armitage with the wounded."

"You gave me a scare that day," Mary said. "I was so frightened when Herk came to tell me you'd been wounded. I had no idea whether I'd find you alive or dead."

Adam helped himself to a scone. "But I survived to see more battles."

"And Lord Cornwallis gave me his carriage," Mary went on. "He was sad that day. One would have thought he'd been defeated."

"Perhaps he realized what became clear to us later, that Guilford was actually a victory for General Greene," Adam said. "Cornwallis' troops were so depleted that . . . But here we are fighting the war over again. I suppose the truth is, such experiences can never be put entirely out of one's mind. It isn't easy to forget a tragic and bloody spectacle like Guilford Courthouse."

No, Mary added silently, and there are times when it is easier to relive even so tragic a spectacle than to face an uncertain and forbidding future. . . . She was relieved when Sarah Poor appeared in the dining-room door and ordered her upstairs.

"Did you have a pleasant visit at Mulberry Hill, Miss Sarah?" she asked.

"That I did, Mrs. Rutledge. All the Blount children were at home, and what a household it is! The boys had been coon-hunting last night—tramping through the swamp, wet to the knees, freezing their fingers. And they call it sport!" Miss Sarah glanced accusingly at Adam. "I suppose you enjoy coon-hunting, Mr. Rutledge."

"Indeed, Miss Sarah, if my dog trees a coon. There's something exciting about swamp-land at night the black water, the sinister cypress trees. I think sometimes that our pocosins offer a glimpse of what the world must have been like long ages ago."

"Nonsense!" Miss Sarah was contemptuous. "They're evil places, full of water moccasins and all sorts of poisonous vipers."

Adam laughed. "And 'scritch' owls and wild turkeys and perhaps deer and a brown bear or two."

Miss Sarah pounced on his words. "That's another thing I'll never understand—how a man can be so heartless as to shoot a deer with beautiful brown imploring eyes! And now, Mrs. Rutledge, you really must come upstairs and rest." She took Mary's elbow and shepherded her toward the stairs, confident that she had scored decisively in the skirmish.

Adam watched affectionately as the sturdy little nurse left the room. She had been complaining that she was no longer needed at Queen's Gift, but he hoped to induce her to remain at least until after Christmas. Mary was moody these days, and Miss Sarah's brisk manner and sound common sense were quite as valuable, Adam thought, as her medical care.

He left the table and went toward the stable where the fox-hounds were kept. Crossie, his best breeding bitch, had a swollen foot which was festering about the toes. He had ordered Mingo to apply a flaxseed poultice and was anxious to see if it had helped. Adam was fond of Crossie, a descendant of the memorable Crossie he had bought in England years before. All the pups of this line were fine, strong dogs with good noses—or, as Mingo said, good "sniffers"—and the current Crossie, already a veteran, was perhaps the finest of the lot.

As he emerged from the house, however, he saw young Tom Blount from Mulberry Hill riding up the drive. Adam went to meet him, but Tom refused to dismount. He was on his way to the village, he said, and hadn't much time. He merely wanted to speak about the Christmas Hunt. As soon as he had spoken the words he paused awkwardly and grew red with embarrassment.

Adam waited eagerly for the boy to continue. Had the planters relented and decided to include the Rutledges after all? But why would they send Tom? "Well, out with it, lad," he said at last.

"Damn it, I will. I don't know how to be diplomatic," Tom said. "You've noticed we haven't asked to hunt your pack or asked you to hunt. Well, a lot of people are bitter because of your vote at Hillsborough. They even call you a traitor, Mr. Rutledge." Tom paused, flushing again. "My father said I'd make a mess of it, and I guess I have. But what I want to tell you is that a lot of younger fellows like me don't agree with the others. We think you're right about the amendments. And when the Hunt held a meeting the other night to choose an M. F. H. to replace you I spoke out and said it was a sneaking thing to do. You'd done more than any one else except the old Parson, I said, to keep the Hunt alive, and I'd not vote to put you out."

Tom ducked his head sheepishly and indicated a purple streak under his left eye. "We had quite a dispute about it, I'm afraid. My father said he was ashamed of my behaviour, but afterward he clapped me on the back and said, why didn't some of us young fellows get together and form a hunt of our own? And that's what we did, Mr. Rutledge, and that's why I'm here now—to ask you to be our M. F. H." Tom sighed with relief at having finished his message.

Adam felt a warm glow of gratitude and pleasure. The county was not united in its disapproval of him. But what would Mary say to hunting with a group of youngsters while her friends rode with the Albemarle Hunt? "I thank you for the offer, Tom," he said slowly. "Exactly who is 'we'?"

"The neighbours along the Sound—the young fellows, I mean. Benbury and Vail and young Pierce and the Creecy boys. And there are some fine fellows along the Yeopim. They have their own mounts, and you'd be surprised at the hunters they're riding. We are about twenty, all told."

Adam hesitated, but he knew he could not reject this vote of confidence from Chowan's young men. "I'll be pleased to ride with you," he said firmly, and smiled in answer to Tom's elated grin. "What name have you chosen for the new hunt?"

"We've thought of several. Some fellows suggested Yeopim, but most of us thought Queen Anne's Hunt would sound elegant. After Queen Anne's Creek, you know. We thought we'd do a little hunting right off, but make the Christmas Hunt our first important meet."

"That sounds excellent, Tom. I hope," Adam said carefully, "that my wife will be able to join us that day."

"Good!" Tom said. "I'm sorry. I intended to ask after Mrs. Rutledge the first thing." He paused. "About the Christmas Hunt, sir—we could start from Mulberry Hill, but . . ."

"Of course the Christmas Hunt must start from Queen's Gift as it has always done," Adam said. "I suppose you would like to use my pack. I've fifty hounds ready to put in the fields and more young ones if you want them."

"Oh, Mr. Rutledge, that would be wonderful! I'm obliged to tell you I haven't enjoyed hunting with a scratch pack that stops to chase a rabbit or goes off on a possum scent."

Oh-ho! thought Adam. So that was it! Well, it was still a chance to hunt, and it meant, too, that the younger men were thinking for themselves. "Come over some evening soon, Tom, and we'll talk over the arrangements."

"Yes, Mr. Rutledge, I will. And would you mind if . . . well, a number of us would like to talk to you about the ratification question, sir. Mr. Mason's objections make sense to us, but all we hear from our families is the Federalist side. Could I bring my friends with me and ask you some questions?"

Adam's spirits rose. Here was an opportunity to reach the planters' sons who would be voting for the first time. "Name your evening, Tom, and bring anyone who's interested. I'll be glad to explain what I can."

He whistled cheerfully as he walked on toward the stables. But the tune ceased abruptly as he thought of breaking the news to Mary.

Mary knew from Adam's manner as he entered her room that he had news to impart and was apprehensive about her reaction. Her first thought was that he planned another trip to Illinois, but she rejected this idea at once. He would not leave her alone while she was still recovering from her illness.

She summoned her maid to take away her supper tray and waited for Adam to work around to the subject that preoccupied him. His face had changed in the months since his return, she thought sadly. The lines in his forehead were deeper, and in his expression there was a tautness, a seemingly deliberate immobility that suggested an inner tension and worry. He is no happier than I about our situation, she thought, and wondered whether she should be glad or sorry.

Rather to her surprise he turned the conversation to hunting, a subject he had avoided since her illness. He spoke of Crossie's injured foot, of the prime condition of the other hounds. Then he paused, and Mary knew he had come to the purpose of his visit.

He drew a deep breath and said evenly, "We shall not be riding with the Albemarle Hunt this winter, Mary. I've accepted an invitation to be M. F. H. of a new hunt, to be called Queen Anne's." He halted and waited for her reply.

Mary was too startled to speak at once. Her immediate reaction was anger. Was he so devoted to his new convictions that he would not ride to hounds with men who disagreed with him? And did he really intend to separate her from her old friends and force her to associate with Wilie Jones's rabble-rousing henchmen? Queen Anne's Hunt indeed!

But she checked the angry words on her lips as she noted the appeal in his eyes. He looked miserably unhappy, and his unhappiness, she realized, was not for himself but for her. There was something more that he did not want to tell her.

"But, Adam," she said carefully, "you're M. F. H. of the Albemarle Hunt. Are you resigning from it?"

"My successor is already chosen," he answered evasively.

"But what——?" She broke off as understanding began to come to her. Sam Johnston, she remembered, would no longer speak to Adam, and others of the Chowan Federalists must share his attitude. Edenton did not take its politics lightly; doubtless some of the planters were as outspoken in their denunciation of Adam as the author of the vicious tirade against Anti-federalism she had found in the office. While she had lain in her sick-room, receiving polite visitors who tactfully avoided political subjects, Adam must have been braving the displeasure of the whole community. Now—and this, of course, explained why Adam had not hunted since her illness—they had ousted him from his twenty-year tenure as Master of the Hunt.

She looked at her husband, who waited patiently for her comment. He had followed his conscience, and now he was concerned because she must suffer for his adoption of beliefs she did not approve. Beset with enemies on the outside, he faced opposition in his own home as well. He was Anti-federalist, but at this moment he was also a tired, harassed man who needed his wife's support. She smiled and offered him her hand. "Tell me about our new hunt."

Adam was having supper alone with Angus Moray one evening when Baron von Pollnitz and Lady Anne came to pay one of their frequent un-solicited visits to Queen's Gift. Adam received his guests with mixed emotions. He had developed a real affection and sympathy for the mild-mannered Baron, but never since their encounter in the pocosin had he been able to feel entirely comfortable in the presence of Lady Anne. She irritated him constantly by occasional oblique references and meaningful glances which indicated that she too remembered every detail of that incident and in retrospect found his behaviour very amusing indeed.

This evening she chose to be condescending and preoccupied in her greeting to him and demanded to be ushered at once into the presence of her dear friend Mrs. Rutledge. With relief Adam sent for Sarah Poor to lead her Ladyship to Mary's room and invited the gentlemen to sample his brandy in the office.

Upstairs, Lady Anne proclaimed her delight at the news that Mary now rode each morning and dined downstairs, although her nurse still insisted that she have supper in bed. "You'll soon be hunting, then, Mrs. Rutledge!"

"I'm determined to ride in the Christmas Hunt," Mary agreed. "That's why I submit to all Miss Sarah's restrictions."

"That's the twenty-sixth, is it not?" Lady Anne asked. "Two rather personable young men called at the inn and invited us to hunt that day. I told them I was not positive the Baron wouldn't have gone to South Carolina by then, but I would certainly join them if only I could secure a mount."

"Speak to my husband," Mary suggested. "I'm sure he can put a hunter at your disposal."

"Oh, I should be so grateful if he could!" Lady Anne cried. She abandoned her effusive manner and moved aimlessly about the room. On Mary's desk lay the golden locket that had accompanied her grandfather's journal. Lady Anne glanced at it, then took it from its open case and studied the design inside the circle of brilliants. "I declare, this is the Stuart crest! The Royal Stuart, I mean. And there is an initial M superimposed on it." She turned to Mary in surprise. "Surely it did not belong to Mary of Scotland!"

Mary laughed uneasily, hoping Lady Anne would not discover the catch which opened the locket. "Nothing so exciting, I'm afraid. It is merely a trinket which I . . . inherited from my family."

Lady Anne was interested. "Indeed! And is there a connection with——?"

"No, no. I really do not know its history." Mary was irritated by her persistence. She changed the subject. "Lady Anne, I hope you will ask Miss Hay to join us for the Christmas Hunt. She loves hunting, she tells me."

"Really?" Lady Anne returned the locket to its case. "I didn't know. I find her a strange girl—uncommunicative, almost secretive. She's betrothed, I fancy. At least, she has suddenly begun wearing a rather impressive emerald ring. But she's said not a word to me about it. . . ." Abruptly she resumed her former manner. "But I must be tiring you, my dear. I'll leave now. It's delightful to know you're improving so rapidly, and I'll look forward to seeing you on the twenty-sixth . . . if Mr. Rutledge can oblige me with a mount."

Miss Sarah entered as soon as Lady Anne had gone. The nurse fairly radiated disapproval. "There's a bold and arrogant lady," she said sourly. "I've seen her sort before. They're purely selfish and stop at nothing to get their own way!"

"Oh, Miss Sarah, you've scarcely seen Lady Anne," Mary said absently. "Hand me the locket in the leather case on my desk, will you?"

"One look at her kind is enough for me," Miss Sarah said authoritatively. "Every man in sight must have eyes only for her. Look at the way she treats poor little Miss Hay because the young doctor prefers her to her Ladyship!"

But Mary made no answer. She was staring abstractedly at the gold locket she held in her hand.

Lady Anne swept into the office and requested a glass of brandy. And her husband must give up his chair to her, for she liked to gaze at the portrait of Duke Roger. "A superb creature he must have been!" she said to Adam. "A fearless and gallant gentleman, I'll wager."

"Duke Roger was much liked and admired, I believe," Adam said formally.

"And are there more like him in America today?" she asked with a light insolence. "I've looked about me and seen not a one."

The Baron spoke nervously. "My dear, we were discussing Adam Smith's view of land as the basis of all wealth."

"And I interrupted you? Well, I'll withdraw at once and take Dr. Moray with me. I'm sure he must be bored to distraction by your talk of grubbing in the earth. When he turns to writing books he'll find livelier topics than trudging about after a plough."

Dr. Moray rose obediently and opened the door, anxious to end the embarrassing scene. But the Baron protested, "That is scarcely fair, my love. I've written on subjects other than agriculture."

Lady Anne's laugh was derisive. "*Love Life at the Saxon Court?* I've wondered sometimes if you actually wrote that treatise, Karl . . . or, indeed, if you have even read it!"

She walked swiftly into the hall and led Angus to the drawing-room. "The man drives me to cruelties by his eternal preoccupation," she muttered over her shoulder. "Come, close the door. I feel a draught." She sat on a yellow satin couch near the fire and arranged her voluminous green skirts about her. "Sit here on this stool at my feet, Angus. I should like to run my fingers through your hair."

But Moray chose a chair on the opposite side of the fire-place. "And ruin Mr. West's careful hairdressing?" he said coldly.

Lady Anne looked at him sharply. "You've changed since your arrival in America, Angus. I can remember a time when your *coiffure* was less important to you."

Angus made no reply.

"I wonder what has caused the change," she continued, watching him closely. "You've developed a taste for younger women, perhaps. The virginal type, although where you'll find an example I can't imagine. Virginity seems out of fashion. Why, even my young secretary——"

"Perhaps we should join our host," Angus interrupted.

Lady Anne ignored his words. "My secretary, Miss Hay—such a pretty girl!—has taken to flaunting a magnificent emerald ring as she goes about her duties. I pay my servants well, but I doubt that her wages would cover the cost of such a jewel. . . . I don't suppose, Doctor, that your interest in Miss Hay extends to covering her with priceless emeralds?"

"I've given no ring to any woman," Angus said shortly.

"I thought not." She regarded him sympathetically. "So our Sylvia has another admirer, and a wealthy one! I wonder . . . The handsome De' Medici seemed much taken with her. Or perhaps there is a lover awaiting her return to England. It's an interesting puzzle, is it not?"

Angus rose and strode from the room. Lady Anne's purpose, he knew, had been to annoy him, and—damn her!—she'd succeeded. Sylvia wearing emeralds! Did it mean that she had heard from Donald? That he was recovered and ready to claim his long-promised bride? He flung out of the house without taking leave of his host and went to the stable. Mounted, he sent his horse at a gallop along the deserted road to Edenton—a road as dark and lonely, he thought, as his own future if he lost Sylvia.

The weather turned cold and stormy, and there were two snow-falls. The Sound froze over—for the first time since 1728, the oldsters said. The Negroes hovered about their hearths and bundled themselves up in all the clothes they possessed. They wrapped tow sacks around their feet and legs, and laced them in place with deer-hide thongs, much in the fashion of Basque shepherds.

Despite the cold weather Tom Blount and his friends came every day or two to consult Adam about the Christmas Hunt. Could they hunt if there were more snow? Would the frozen ground hold the fox scent?

Finally Adam said, "We will hunt, come hell or high water! We'll have breakfast in the carriage-house, if the weather doesn't abate. Don't worry."

"Thank you, Mr. Rutledge. We do want this to be a good hunt, as fine as the Albemarle Hunt ever was."

Mary came out on the gallery in time to hear Tom's words. "Of course we'll hunt! Chaney is planning the finest barbecue ever held at Queen's Gift. There'll be a whole beef roasted and four pigs killed."

Tom's face took on a blissful expression. "James River!" he exclaimed. "Glory be! That will surprise them. Oh, thank you, Mrs. Rutledge. Thank you ever so kindly!"

Mary had other things on her mind besides the hunt breakfast. Christmas was always a big day for the slaves as well as for the masters. The kitchen was the scene of great activity long in advance. Plum puddings, and fruit-cakes rich with black walnuts, raisins, citron and candied ginger were made and set aside on swing shelves in the cellar. Though Chaney didn't hold with any cooking "coming from de North," she grudgingly prepared fillings for mince and spiced squash pies. A roast suckling with an apple in its mouth would grace the centre of the table on Christmas Eve.

Mary had her hands full arranging ropes of smilax and cedar. She was glad it was a good holly year; the trees were heavy with red berries amid spiked shiny leaves. Mistletoe had to be shot out of the highest oak trees that grew along the creek bank, and a kissing bell made to hang in the hall.

Adam came in one morning with a letter from Bath in his hand. Cosmo de' Medici would be up a few days before Christmas and stay over the holidays.

Mary's face was radiant. "How delightful! Cosmo loves to hunt. He'll enjoy every minute."

"Angus Moray has promised to be here for supper Christmas Eve when we bring in the Yule log," Adam said. "Couldn't we arrange to have Sylvia Hay come also?"

"We'll have to invite the Baron and Lady Anne as well, I'm afraid," Mary said, "and I can't quite picture Lady Anne entering into all our little Christmas rituals with great enthusiasm."

"She's an unpredictable woman," Adam said. "She might surprise you."

"Well, let's ask them then. And perhaps we should invite them all to stay until after the hunt. Christmas would be so forlorn for Sylvia at Horniblow's." She laughed. "We must be careful not to hint to her Ladyship that she is being invited because we want her secretary's company."

"No fear," Adam said, grinning. "The idea would never occur to her."

"And it will be pleasant to have guests in the house again. I should like to be very gay this Christmas. I have a horrid feeling that next year everything will be different." There was apprehension in her eyes.

"My silly little Mary, of course nothing will be different! Come, no sad looks! Remember, we must have the slaves' gifts ready for John Kuner's Day."

Mary laughed. "Don't let Chaney hear you call it 'Kuner's.' John Canoe is her version, and so she will have it. About the gifts—we have two clothes-baskets full of little gift cakes and sweetmeats for the children, calicoes for the women, and a new shirt for each man. My sewing girls have been busy for weeks. They worked all through my sickness. They've even stuffed miniature rag dolls for the girl babies. But you'll have to get the Christmas shillings—and a few dozen tin cups; most of last year's are rusted—and the tree, a great beautiful tree!"

Adam bowed deeply from the waist. "Madam, your orders are anticipated.

We have two trees tagged, one for the house—in the long hall—and one for the gallery where the slaves can see it."

"Splendid, Adam! We've never had two trees before."

With the changing moon a warm wind came from the south. The ice began to melt. The days grew balmy, with just enough tang in the air for proper Christmas weather.

On Christmas Eve the big trees were decorated. Festoons of holly and cedar were looped over mantels and mirrors. The clean smell of pine pervaded Queen's Gift. The east-wing bedrooms had been opened and aired, the beds dressed in lavender-scented sheets and cases. These rooms were for the single men—Cosmo, Angus Moray and Dr. Armitage.

"I was bound to come. Perhaps I'll not be here next Christmas," was the doctor's comment as he entered the drawing-room.

Mary shivered a little.

"What's de matter wid you?" Chaney asked her, looking up from the task of filling stockings. "Rabbit run over you' grave? You don't want to take luck dat-a-way. Paint de devil on de wall, and dere he stay."

Mary said, "Adam and Cosmo are in the office. I think I'd better go up to dress before any one else arrives."

"Your guests are on the way," Dr. Armitage said. "We passed Lady Anne's carriage at Queen Anne's Creek. Dr. Moray rode around to the stables. He wanted to look at Crossie's foot. I'll just go to my room, Mary, and catch me a nap before supper."

"Young Ben will show you the way. He'll be in your wing to valet you single men. Supper is at eight."

"Dressed to the nines?"

"To the nines, in honour of Chaney's little suckling pig and a baron of beef."

She went upstairs. Pam had laid her gown on the bed. It was not new. Mary had had no new party clothes since the war. This was her London dress of blue and silver brocade, made over a shell-pink satin petticoat, ruffled to the waist with Mechlin lace.

Pam brought out the bags and covers and went with Mary into the little powder room. Soon the air was filled with fine powder mist. Mary's brown locks were quickly transformed into high puffs white with powder and frosted with diamond dust.

The young mulatto girl had smudges of powder on her saddle-brown skin. She stood back, regarding the finished work with an artist's pride. Then she loosened the muslin sheet from Mary's neck and rolled it carefully from the bottom, so that all the flour remained within.

Mary stood up and shook the brocaded skirts, while Pam brushed her gown with a little white whisk. Mary applied two black patches, one at the corner of her right eye, the other at the corner of her mouth. Then her shoes, made of blue satin with flat soles, must be cross-ribboned and tied. Bracelets of square-cut lapis set in antique gold were the finishing touch.

Pam was delighted with the result. She made little clucking noises in her throat, turned her head this way and that, arranged a fold of Mary's skirt and adjusted the lace ruffles at her elbows. "Mistress needs a necklace," she said. "There is a bareness, with that square-cut bodice."

On sudden impulse Mary said, "Give me the locket in that case on my desk. And thread a black velvet riband into the chain."

Mary liked the effect. Pam stood behind her holding the end of the uncut riband. "How long do you think it should be hung, Pam?"

"Mistress, let it nestle in the little hollow that divides the breasts."

Mary turned a sharp eye on the girl. "Pam, you're growing up. How old are you?"

"Chaney says I'm sixteen." She smiled shyly. "I'm living with Young Ben. We tooken a cabin down the line."

"Pam, have you married Young Ben?"

"Well, not precisely. There ain't no parson to speak over us. My ma said if we jumped the broomstick it was just as good."

"The next time the parson comes you must have the words said over you. Hear?"

"Yes'm. The next time, yes'm. You was sick on the bed when we jumped. You surely looks beautiful. Won't be ary lady as pretty."

"Have the guests come?"

"Yes, ma'am. Ebon and Young Ben tote they boxes and show them they rooms. Ebon say supper be on time."

Mary looked at the clock. Half after seven. She must still make sure the table was properly set, check the seating arrangement. "Run along now and see if you can help Chaney."

"Yes'm. Young Ben and I are fixin' to help in the pantry when the dishes come out from the kitchen. Ebon he show Young Ben everything jes' right for the great folk." The girl left the room, moving swiftly to her rendezvous in the pantry with Young Ben.

Mary thought, I must speak to Adam about having our people properly married. I never liked these broomstick weddings.

After a last look in the mirror she caught up a little fur wrap and tapped at Miss Sarah's door. Miss Sarah had declined to dine with them. "If you please, I'll take a tray in my room," she had said, "and write Christmas notes for Ben to deliver in the morning. But I do want to see you when you are dressed."

Miss Sarah answered Mary's light tap. She had a woollen robe wrapped about her and wore a heavy net to confine her unruly hair. "You look just like a queen, Mary. Now go down to your guests and have a good evening."

"I wish you'd join us for supper. Adam and I would love to have you."

"No, thank you. I'm very content here. The little black girl has the warming-pan in my bed, and I'm going to get right in and read my books. I'm catching up on *Clarissa*. I found some old numbers I'd missed among your books."

Adam was waiting for Mary in the yellow drawing-room, walking up and down in front of the fire. He was wearing a plum-coloured satin coat and white breeches, and his waistcoat was of white and gold brocade. The ruffles on his sleeves, the stock at his throat were of fine lace. His hair was not powdered, but brushed into rolls over his ears, and the queue was tied with a black riband. The buckles on his shoes were silver, and his long stockings of white silk.

Mary thought, He moves like a leopard in a cage, but he looks like a gentleman of the Court. She said, "How handsome you are, Adam! That plum-coloured coat is perfect for this yellow room."

Adam turned at the sound of her voice. He crossed the room quickly. "Beautiful! You look more beautiful than ever to-night, my Mary." He raised her hand to his lips. "Come over to the fire-place. It is rather cool in here. I had Ebon fetch those brass braziers I got in Egypt when I made the Grand Tour and place them to warm the other end of the room. He has gone for the charcoal now. We'll soon have a nice glowing fire in them."

Mary shuddered to think what an open charcoal fire would do to the papered walls, but she smiled and thanked him.

Sylvia came in, wearing a simple emerald-green taffeta with lace outlining the square neck and her half-sleeves.

"What a lovely dress!" Mary exclaimed.

Sylvia's face brightened. "Do you really like it? I made it myself, with the aid of a little seamstress Mrs. Horniblow recommended." She held up her hand. The emerald ring shone darkly in the candle-light. "I was bound to have a gown to match my ring."

Mary said, "You should always wear emeralds. The emerald is your stone, and your colour—green and bronze, the russet brown of autumn."

The gentlemen came into the room then—Baron von Pollnitz, Captain de' Medici and Angus Moray. Dr. Armitage followed in a few minutes. The little French clock chimed eight. Ebon announced supper.

The Baron said, "My wife will be here at any moment. I can't think what detains her."

Sylvia thought, She's waiting to make an entrance.

And at that instant Lady Anne swept into the room. It *was* an entrance. She was gowned in white satin, over white ruffled lace petticoats. Her powdered hair was built up to a great height in puffs and curls. The only touch of colour was in her jewels—the rubies and pearls of necklace, bracelets and rings.

Adam led her to a sofa and De' Medici, bowing, brought a footstool.

The others watched her as she arranged her skirts and indicated to Cosmo the vacant seat beside her.

"The *signora* is as beautiful as a painting—the D'Este perhaps, or one of the Borgia ladies."

"Lucrezia, the poisoner, perchance?" There was laughter in Lady Anne's voice and eyes. She took a glass of sherry from the silver tray Ebon held out to her.

De' Medici touched his glass to hers. "I never believed the story that Lucrezia was a poisoner. Just a political accusation! Our Italian families, you know, despised the Spanish Pope and all his kin."

Lady Anne said, "Caesare was the magnificent Borgia—magnificent in his ruthlessness. I should adore to know a man like him."

Ebon collected the glasses, and Adam held out his arm to Lady Anne. Mary walked with Dr. Armitage and the Baron, leaving Sylvia to be escorted by Angus and Cosmo.

During supper Lady Anne directed all her bold sallies of wit and all her languorous glances at Cosmo beside her, but he managed very skilfully to lead the conversation into general channels.

The food was excellent, the wines were mellow. Rhoda's Chelsea dinner china and crystal glass gave a touch of elegance to the table, as traditional as the center-piece of holly and mistletoe and the glow of the sixteen candles.

Mary sat back in her chair and listened to her guests. All was well.

It was past ten when they left the table and went to the drawing-room. Then Ebon announced the Yule-log ceremony by bringing in a large tray heaped with sprigs of mistletoe. These he passed first to the guests and then to the house servants who had gathered in the hall and on the gallery. The guests took their places on either side of the fire-place as four boys led by Young Ben carried in the great Yule log. It was bark-covered cedar, decked with holly and mistletoe. The slaves wore the livery of the season—long red vests over ruffled white shirts, green knee-breeches, white stockings, stout shoes with wooden buckles.

They placed the log squarely on the brass andirons. Young Ben brought in a blazing piece of charred wood, a bit of last year's Yule log saved for the occasion.

A little slave girl, dressed as an angel in white with a halo sitting crookedly on her pigtails, poured wine over the log. Young Ben touched the log with the lightwood faggot. The wine blazed with blue and green light. The mistletoe and holly caught fire and sent flames roaring up the chimney. A small boy, with shield and wooden sword, walked toward the fire-place; on the shield of this miniature Saint George were holly berries in the form of a cross. Four slaves dressed as minstrels stood near the fire. They sang first of Saint George "who fought the fiery dragon" and then broke into Robert Herrick's Christmas ditty:

"Come, bring with a noise,
My merrie, merrie boyes,
The Christmas log to the firing;
While my good dame, she
Bids ye all be free,
And drink to your hearts' desiring."

Then, led by Mary and Adam, the guests formed in line and walked toward the fire-place. As each threw his sprig of mistletoe on the blazing Yule log, he would say, "I bring you my worries and cares of the year that is passing."

The guests moved aside and the house servants moved up, in their best dresses and brightest turbans, with their sprigs of mistletoe to cast into the flames. When they had gone Ebon and his helpers rolled in a table with a china bowl of egg-nog. All gathered round to drink toasts to Christmas, and Adam proposed a toast to each guest in turn. Cares and worries had vanished in the smoke of the burning mistletoe.

Lady Anne, Cosmo, Dr. Armitage and Adam made up a table of loo. The Baron and Mary started a game of cribbage. Angus led Sylvia to a little seat at the end of the room, near the great brass brazier.

Sylvia said, "How delightful that Christmas is celebrated in America as it is at home!"

"If I'd only had my pipes," Angus answered, "I could have played a highland fling for you."

Lady Anne said to Adam, "Do all the people here carry on the English traditions? I would have supposed they'd be banned after the great revolt."

"Queen's Gift has always celebrated Christmas this way. Mary sets great store by customs begun in Duke Roger's time."

Cosmo said, "How curious it is that people speak of Duke Roger as though they had known him personally!"

The doctor rattled his ivory fish counters. "That's the way of our village. The people who live here never die. Each new generation revives those who have passed on. Your play, Lady Anne."

Mary won the game of cribbage with ease. Baron von Pollnitz was an indifferent player. Obviously he had his mind on other things. He was enthralled by the prospect of his trip to South Carolina. Adam, he said, had increased his confidence. They had many interests in common. "I have been telling your husband that if he will look in *Fenno's Gazette* he will find many articles by 'Rusticus.' That is I—or should I say, That is me? This English language not only mystifies me, it confounds me."

Mary excused herself. She must go to the dining-room, where she was sure Chaney would be waiting to be praised for her supper and to get orders for breakfast.

The Baron went over to where Sylvia and Angus were seated and drew up a chair. "Is not this a charming evening? It is good that here in the New World they cherish the customs of the Old. Very good indeed to keep the best of European customs as a foundation to build on! I am more impressed every day with what I discern about these fine people."

He drew his gold and ivory snuff-box from his pocket. After offering it to Angus he took a small pinch between thumb and forefinger. He smothered a little sneeze with a fine cambric handkerchief.

The case clock in the hall began its slow, measured chiming as Mary came back into the room. "Midnight, and merry Christmas!" she cried.

They all moved to the punch-bowl. Cups in hand, they waited till the last stroke died. Then they drank their Christmas toast. Outside in the darkness the slaves were singing an old carol, "While shepherds watched their flocks by night"—voices of an alien, a pagan people praising the birth of the Christ child.

When they finished Mary said, "Perhaps we'd better retire. John Canoe's Day starts early, very early in the morning."

Lady Anne asked, "John Canoe's Day—what is that, pray?"

Mary smiled. "An old custom on the plantation brought by the slaves from the West Indies—or perhaps from Africa. No one knows. To-morrow you will see for yourself."

They trooped into the hall. Ebon was waiting at the foot of the stairs to pass out the bedside candles.

Sylvia, accompanied by Cosmo and Angus, went out on the gallery for a moment. A long line of flickering lights cut the darkness. The slaves were going home to their quarters, each with a blazing pine-knot in his hand. Now they were singing a wild pagan chaunt that had nothing to do with the advent of the Christ child.

John Canoe

26 EARLY in the morning the slaves of Queen's Gift were behind the great house, sitting in little groups where they could watch the bedroom windows. When the first blind was raised they began to call, "Christmas gif'! Christmas gif'!"

Sylvia went to her window. She saw Mary and Adam walk down the gallery steps and out to the carriage block. Herk, Ebon and the house-boys followed, carrying hampers filled with packages. Men and women ran and children skipped to meet them, all crying, "Christmas gif'! Christmas gif', mistress, master!"

Mary handed out the gifts for the women and little girls, Adam those

for the men and boys. Every face was smiling as the packages were un-
wrapped. Some of the men donned their new shirts over the old. Women
wrapped the kerchiefs about their heads and wound lengths of the brightly
coloured calico about their bodies.

Sylvia went out into the hall and onto the balcony, where she could
watch. She saw De' Medici and Angus on the gallery below.

The Baron joined her. "This is astonishing. Never have I seen anything
quite like it. . . . Barbaric colours . . . such happiness . . . and our hosts
are as happy to give as the pagan folk are to receive."

When the last of the packages had been distributed Mary and Adam
went into the house for breakfast. As soon as the meal was over the slaves
were back again. This time they came with great noise and hallooing.

Adam said to the guests, "You'll all want to see this. It's the John Canoe
celebration. Shall we step to the gallery?"

Sylvia stood at the rail beside Mary. She saw a procession forming down
near the quarters line. Horses with riders were placed first, gaily decked in
wreaths of pine, and with streamers of calico tied to their bridles. Then
came mules similarly caparisoned, and after them goats and sheep were
herded into line by small shepherds. The mass of black folk brought up the
rear. Some wore peacock feathers in their hair, or other fantastic head-gear.
Coloured streamers, with little jingling bells, flew from coats and skirts and
breeches.

The half-dozen mounted men wore horrible grinning masks made of goat-
skin, stripped thin and painted. The leather seemed moulded to their faces.
Some had cow horns tied to their heads. The masks had goat-hair beards,
staring eyes, cavernous mouths and huge noses. Those on foot also wore
masks and carried pipes and whistles, and strings of little horns hung from
their necks. Drummers pounded away lustily, and small boys ringing cow
bells and blowing on cow horns made hideous noises.

When the procession came to the circular drive the six riders dismounted.
The drummers formed a circle around the whole company. All began to
sing:

> "Hah, low, here we go!
> Hah, low, here we go!
> John Canoe come from Dohema,
> He come from Mombera. . . .
> He return to Dohema."

The women in the circle clapped their hands or beat little squares of
wood together in a steady rhythm and stamped their feet in unison. Two
men had Gimba boxes, wooden frames covered with tanned sheepskin,
which they shook violently or scraped with sticks.

At the foot of the steps Adam met Marcy. Herk rolled out a keg of rum.

Two men, not in John Canoe costume, came and stood in front of Adam. They sang to the clapping accompaniment:

"My massa am a white man—juba!
My missus am a white lady—juba!
De chillen am de honey-pods—juba!

Chris'mas come but once a year—juba!
Juba, juba, oh, ye juba!"

Adam poured small coins into a hat for distribution. A dozen boys passed tin cups around. Each man and each woman brought a cup to Herk for a measure of rum.

The singing and the clapping went on until every one had had a drink and a coin, presents from the master.

The drums now started a tantalizing tattoo. The six leaders divided into two facing lines and fell into an intricate dance.

Lady Anne joined the group on the gallery. She wore an elegant velvet robe, and her *coiffure* was held in place by a scarf of white lace. "This is bedlam. What in heaven's name are they doing?"

Mary said, "I warned you that John Canoe Day started early."

The tempo of the drums increased. The dancing grew more vigorous. The six men had spears in their hands now, passed to them from the crowd.

Mary beckoned to Herk. He approached her, tall and erect as a reed, moving with dignity. "Tell me what they dance and what they sing," she said.

"Dese not my people, mistress. De songs are strange to me, but de dance is de Lion Dance. See, dey creep forward in de elephant grass, spear in one hand, shield in de other. Dey see de lion . . . dey creep up on it. De first hunter t'row de spear, den de second. Now all de hunters have spears in de lion's body. Den dey draw near; dey dance around de dead lion. See, dey raise dey shields—de signal of victory. Now dey fall on de lion. De first man cuts out de lion's heart. Dey tear it apart and devour it."

"How frightful!" Lady Anne gasped.

Herk did not look at her. His eyes were on the dancers. "In Africa de man who eats heart of a lion partakes of de lion's bravery. A boy becomes a man when he eats heart of a lion. Now he is a warrior." Herk bowed his head in a grave salute and walked away.

Lady Anne said to Mary, "And you live here alone, amid these wild people. I would never have the courage."

Angus whispered to Sylvia, "Perhaps she should eat the heart of a lion."

The drums stopped suddenly in mid-beat. The dance ended. The procession moved away, down to the quarters. Two men were carrying the rum keg.

"Is that all?" the Baron asked.

Mary laughed. "Just the introduction. The dancing, the singing and the feasting go on all day and all night."

"And the drinking?" Cosmo put in.

"And the drinking, I'm sorry to say. But Adam has the rum cut to quarter strength, so it's not too bad."

"I must go make notes on this," said the Baron. "It's all so very strange, so African and so impressive."

Lady Anne called for a game of loo. Mary went about her duties. Miss Sarah left for the village to visit relatives.

Adam and Sylvia walked to the stables to see the horses. Adam said, "You'll find all the stables decorated with holly. Even the kennels have sprigs of pine nailed to the roof. . . . Christmas is really Christmas here. To-night the slaves will light great bonfires in the cleared fields. They will dance and caper. Some slave-owners object to this merry-making. As you see, we don't. We believe the Africans should have their holiday. If we pride ourselves on preserving English traditions, they are entitled to preserve theirs. During Christmas they enjoy comparative freedom. Some evil may come of the practice, but I'm sure it's trifling—a little extra drunkenness perhaps. It's all to be kept among themselves, so we shut our eyes unless they become obstreperous."

Christmas Day passed on. Some of the neighbours called—young people who had remained loyal to Adam. At one time ten horses were tied at the rack, besides several gigs. In the afternoon, Dr. Moray paid a visit to the quarters to look after minor casualties. He bound up a few heads in vinegar, took a stitch or two on cheek or arm where flesh had got in the way of a knife.

"I've done nothing but eat and sleep," Lady Anne said when they were gathered about the table that night to eat bread and cold meats and drink milk or ale.

"And won nothing at the loo table?" her husband asked.

Lady Anne patted her reticule with satisfaction. "I've a number of specie notes, a couple of English pound notes and some I.O.U.'s. I don't know what to do with this state money."

"Nor does any one else," Adam chaffed. "Perhaps I shall pay you my debt in tobacco. Let's see, my losings must come to five hands of tobacco at least."

Lady Anne smiled at him provocatively. "I may decide to declare a moratorium and cancel all debts." She yawned behind her slim white hand. "If we must get up at cock's crow for the hunt, I think I'll retire early."

Others followed her example. By ten o'clock every one was in bed.

Chaney limped to her cottage, escorted by Ebon. "Well," she said, "we fed about fifty head today, includin' de guests who jes' ate little cakes and ham and hot biscuits."

"I don't want to measure up. De rum and de whisky made a big hole in Master's cellar."

"What he care?" Chaney said. "Miss Mary was a-smilin' and a-laughin' all de while. After dinner she came out and said to me, 'Chaney, dat was de bestes' dinner you ever cook in dis world. Dose foreign folk like to busted deyselves eatin'.' I says, 'Dat's what we likes—to fill dey stomachs till dey 'most pop.' "

Ebon merely grunted; his legs were purely worn out, and cock's crow came early. "Lucky we don' have to giv'm nothin' but tea and little biscuits in de mo'nin', and a good stiff hot toddy for de cold."

Forty hunters gathered at Queen's Gift before sun-up. Tom Blount and his brothers from Mulberry Hill were early arrivals; so were the young men from Sandy Point, Drummond's Point, Long Branch and Norcom. The Creecy lads of Greenfield brought guests from Hertford. Four lads came from Bertie.

The planters wore red coats, white or buckskin breeks and visored caps. The farm boys from Mile Road were clad in butternut-dyed wool and buckskins.

Their jumpers matched the Queen's Gift horses. Adam was well pleased, though none of the old Albemarle Hunt members were present.

At the last minute, when Mingo and his helpers were fetching the pack from the stables, Charles Johnson trotted up. Close behind him was the old Parson and his gig with the side curtains up and a fur laprobe tucking him in. "Mary, child," he said in his hearty way, "do you think I'd miss a Christmas Hunt? No, my lass, no. Though Armitage forbade me to mount a nag, he didn't forbid my riding in a vehicle."

Mary squeezed his arm affectionately. "Oh, sir, I'm so glad you've come!" Tears gathered in her eyes.

"There, there! No wailing or gnashing of teeth! Here I am. I've made my plans. I'll ride down the Indian Trail a piece and see everything that goes on. Old Reynard's bound to come out in the open field somewhere."

Armitage joined them. "I told you to stay off your foot, Parson."

"Tut-tut. I'm off it."

"You'll catch a cold."

"With hot sand-bags surrounding me? And hot bricks at my feet? And a flask by my side?" He gave a good hearty laugh.

By this time the riders were all mounted.

Mary said, "Parson, will you bless the hunt? This is a *new* hunt. You'd make the boys happy."

Parson Earle grumbled a little. "It hardly seems proper to give the blessing standing up in a gig and without my clericals on, but I suppose for all that the Lord will hear good Saint Hubert's prayer."

He got unsteadily to his feet and raised his arms. The riders crowded forward about the gig. With bowed head they listened to the old Parson's blessing.

The dogs were brought up, pulling and tugging at the leashes. The small house-boys passed around cups of hot toddy.

Hunters and hounds then moved in the direction of the stables. By the tobacco barns the leashes were cast off. At the sound of the horn the Negroes shouted, "Offen wy!" Sylvia, who was near the pack, guessed that this meant, "Off and away!" And so they were—off on a long way. Shortly the excited yaps of the young hounds told the hunters that a scent had been picked up in the stubble field. Away the hounds went! The hunters took off down a narrow path. Some of them crossed a little creek that led to a sourwood thicket at the edge of the swamp. The old Parson, accompanied by Dr. Armitage, had already left. The station he had chosen for himself could be reached only by a more roundabout route.

Lady Anne and the Baron were now across the stream; so was Mary Rutledge. Sylvia's horse kept pace with Cosmo de' Medici's. Adam rode up to them and pointed with his crop. A fox was loping along the vine fence, his red brush straight out behind him.

"Reynard will make for the sourwood thicket, but he'll have to come into the open down by the swamp. Let's be off!"

The young lads had already passed them, riding hard, close behind the hounds. Adam said, "You've got to know the ways of an old red fox if you're going to outwit him. I know this fellow. He's got a hollow log up there a mile or so. He'll make for that by way of those briery ditches."

False dawn had given way to the red arrows of the rising sun. Near the Mulberry Hill boundary ditch the hounds lost scent. They padded this way and that, letting out mournful cries of defeat. Adam called to them. He had just caught a flash of red darting in and out of the heavy ditch briers and weeds.

Other riders also had seen Master Fox. Mingo and Young Ben on mules were waiting on a cross-path. Mingo cried out, "Hic-on-hi-yon! Yo-ho-hane!" and put his mule across a wooden bridge to shut off the fox's escape down the culvert. Now the wily fox was bound to take to the ploughed land.

A whipper-in moved along the far side of the field, closing down. The hounds tried to leap the ditch; some made it, some fell in. They were whimpering, eager to get at the prey. Along the Sandy Point lane farmers on horseback, in gigs or in Devon carts blocked every cross-path. Here the hunt was in full view, spread out over the fields of dead stems, to which bits of fluffy white unpicked cotton still clung.

Sylvia and Adam had outstripped Cosmo and were up close to the hounds. Now at the little stream by the sweet-gum spinney part of the pack lost scent a second time. Again they were travelling in circles, noses to the ground, crying mournfully.

A young lad who was standing up in a cart began to scream, "The fox! Look! Over there at the edge of the wood."

"Dammit," Adam cried. "Those green hounds! Why don't they follow Crossie?" Sylvia looked the way he pointed. The fox was running in a long easy lope. The length of the cotton patch was between him and the pack. Only Crossie, of all the hounds, was on the scent. The others milled around, catching cross scents.

Sylvia turned her horse and galloped down a cotton row alone. Ahead of the field, she saw the fox go over to a piece of land covered with low bushes. This shrubbery was so dense that for a moment she lost sight of him. Suddenly he reappeared, and Sylvia laughed aloud at his amazing cleverness. He had leaped up on the bushes and was running along the top of them—running, jumping and leaping with incredible lightness over this stretch of brush which seemed as thick-matted as a hedge, sinking in but plunging out again, never stopping, never touching the ground. Then Sylvia's heart palpitated with excitement as she sensed he was beginning a great circle that might perhaps bring him back toward the swamp-land, not very far from where she was.

She put her horse across a low ditch and pulled up on a path that she guessed the fox might cross, though she had now quite lost sight of him. Ahead were the old Parson and Dr. Armitage. She rode up beside them. They had let down the curtains of the gig and the Parson was standing, spyglass in hand. His cheeks were red with the thrill of the chase and his white hair blew loosely about his face.

"It's an old dog fox! Many a time we've chased his like."

Armitage asked, "How can you tell he's old?"

"It takes experience for such strategy. Devil take it, they've lost him for good!"

But of a sudden Crossie began to bay. She had the scent strong and clear. She knew Reynard's tricks. She circled the stretch of low bushes and picked up the trail.

The Parson looked disgustedly at the other dogs who were nosing along aimlessly past the crowd in the road, and, like Adam, cursed the green hounds. "Damme, why doesn't the whipper-in put them on Crossie?"

Sylvia turned in her saddle and viewed the colours of the scene—the hounds black and white, or liver and brown; the pink coats and light breeches of the horsemen; Lady Anne's bright-blue velveteen habit, Mary's hunter's green; the russet stubble of the field; the ring of pines rising against the morning sky; the red bricks of Mulberry Hill; and the shimmering water of the Sound beyond. "It is so fair a sight," she said.

"Aye, beautiful is the landscape on a clear, bright winter morning, but sweeter to me is the baying of the hounds." Parson Earle's eyes were shining.

"I love every voice—the eager cry when they first catch the scent, the deep lost barks of the confused ones, the sharp yelps when they follow hard, and the death bay. All, all are music to my ears."

"You *do* love hunting, sir!"

"Aye. Aye. But I'm ageing, young miss, ageing." He poked at Armitage with his spy-glass. "*He* says I won't hunt again."

"My uncle had to be strapped to his saddle in his last hunting days," Sylvia said. "Twice he'd broken the same leg, and he had no grip in that knee."

"Ah, that was a huntsman for ye. Where did he hunt, miss? In the Midlands?"

"No, sir. On Bodwin Moor, in the shadow of Brown Willie."

"Ah, yes! A wild country, where the Romans marched."

"And, before them, the Druids set up their pagan worshipping stones there. You know the country?"

"Yes, yes indeed—a country to hold a man's imagination. Damme, they've lost old Reynard again. Even Crossie's given up and joined the pack. Look! What have we now? They've picked up a fresh scent. They're off. Doctor, we'll ride down the Indian Trail."

"I don't see Crossie," Sylvia said, looking over the field.

"No, but I'd know her voice anywhere, her beautiful clear bay."

De' Medici and Angus came riding along. "Rutledge says follow the path to the Indian Trail." Sylvia galloped with them. They passed crowded mule carts and many people on foot, all moving to places of vantage for viewing the country-side.

Now once again it proved that Sylvia was ahead of the field. A path, flanked by pine forests, lay ahead of her and her companions. They jumped a log that lay athwart it. Not far beyond they saw the old dog fox crossing the path. He was tired and limping. His tongue lolled from his open mouth. His brush hung lower, a mass of cockleburs and stickers. He disappeared in the forest.

"I'm glad he escaped," Sylvia exclaimed, "the weary, weary creature!"

Cosmo laughed. "You women of sentiment! Think of the barnyard fowl he has eaten in his wicked career. I wager you, Maria's cook Chaney would not share your feelings."

They pushed on. Angus' mount was slower and began to drop behind. The hounds were in full cry now, heard at first off near the Sound shore, but drawing nearer. Sylvia and Cosmo jumped a ditch and a fence of tangled trumpet and honeysuckle vines. They went past a field where the pines had been recently cut and the smell of pitch was strong in the air. Then, at a small pocosin, the path made an abrupt turn. They had a glimpse of water in a dark bog. Streamers of light filtered through the sparse tree crowns and disclosed the weird twisted knees of cypress rising above the black water.

Abruptly Sylvia pointed. "Look! Look—on that fallen tree!"

A fox was making his careful way along the log—not old Reynard, a younger fox, now become the quarry. The horn blared not far away. The hounds had been coming fast but were stopped momentarily by the bit of swamp-land. Then Crossie, old at the game, skirted the swamp with Druid and Nabob at her heels. The pack followed.

Now it became a race among the hunters. Even Mingo was digging his heels into his mule. Adam and Lady Anne were getting close to the pack.

Sylvia saw a flash of green through the trees—Mary Rutledge's habit. Cosmo called to Sylvia, "Spur your horse!" Sylvia urged her mount to full gallop. She could hear the huntsman shouting at the top of his voice, "Wind him, Crossie! Wind him!" while the horn sounded "Gone away. Gone away."

The horses had caught the excitement. Sylvia let her mount take his head. She knew by the change in the tone of the hounds' cry that the kill was close.

They turned a curve in the path and were on the hounds before they knew it.

Mingo jumped off his running mule and pushed into the bellowing pack. Dogs were all around him, their jaws wide, their tongues hanging. He reached down, caught the fox in his bare hands and held him aloft. With the pack baying at his feet he jerked his hunting knife from his belt and cut the brush, as the fox, torn and bleeding, gasped its last breath.

Cosmo de' Medici caught the brush Mingo tossed to him. He moved swiftly to Sylvia's side. He lifted the brush and touched her face with it, leaving a spot of blood on either cheek. "In at the kill," he said softly. "I am glad." He was tucking the brush into the bridle of her mount just as Lady Anne and Adam joined them.

Lady Anne's face showed her chagrin. "I am always in at the kill," she cried to Adam. "Why didn't you give me a faster horse?" Her glance slid angrily past Sylvia to De' Medici, who was watching her with a quizzical look in his dark eyes.

He said, "Isn't it splendid Miss Hay secured the brush? So well deserved! She is a magnificent horsewoman."

Lady Anne made no answer.

The hunters arrived in groups of two and three. Mingo and his boys began to leash the hounds and load them into the carts that would take them back to Queen's Gift.

Sylvia saw Adam Rutledge squint at the sky. "We've been out two hours," he said. He gave a signal. The horn sounded a blast to call in any straying hounds.

Some of the hunters had already turned back, Mary first among them. She wanted to be at the plantation before the guests thronged in for breakfast. De' Medici galloped after her.

Sylvia found herself beside Angus. "Congratulations!" he cried. The wind carried his voice away. He pointed to the two little spots of blood on her cheeks. They had dried now almost black. They looked like love patches, enhancing the warm ivory of her skin.

The sun had brought warmth with it. By the time the hunters got to Queen's Gift the horses were in a lather; the men mopping their warm foreheads under their visored hunting-caps.

The tables, set on the lower gallery, were loaded with hearty plantation food. There was considerable confusion for a time as the returning hunters sought out wives or sweethearts and found places at the tables.

Baron von Pollnitz forced his way through the crowd to Sylvia. "Have you seen my wife, Miss Hay?" he asked anxiously. "She doesn't seem to be anywhere about."

"Is she perhaps in her room?" Sylvia suggested.

"I've just come from there." The Baron's eyes searched the gallery. "No one remembers to have seen her come back with the others. I am quite worried. Anne is reckless when she hunts." He wandered disconsolately into the house, dodging Ebon, who was bringing the toddy-bowl to the table.

In the doorway the Baron passed Mary on the arm of Cosmo de' Medici. Mary also seemed to be searching for some one. "I cannot imagine what is keeping Adam so long," Sylvia heard her say. "He knows he must propose the toast to the hunt, and it's time now."

"Can I officiate for him?" Cosmo asked. "Or must it be the host or hostess?"

"I suppose I had better do it," Mary said. "But I thank you, Cosmo. You are a comfort." She walked to her place at the head of the first table and waited until all the guests had been seated and served with toddy. Then she raised her glass and said, "My husband is delayed, so I shall have the pleasure of giving you . . . Queen Anne's Hunt!"

The young men responded with cheers, and all the guests raised their glasses high before drinking the toast. Then Tom Blount was on his feet to propose a toast to "Mary Rutledge, the gracious hostess of Queen's Gift" and another to the absent host.

The party settled down to their food, but almost at once some one called, "Here comes Mr. Rutledge! Look, he's riding pillion with the Baroness!"

Sylvia, whose back was to the railing, turned to see Adam's horse coming slowly up the drive with its double burden, Lady Anne sideways in the saddle, leaning heavily on Adam for support. Her blond hair hung loose in a rippling shower of gold against his shoulder.

"Fetch Dr. Moray!" Adam called. "Lady Anne is hurt!"

Angus rose from his place at the table. His eyes met Sylvia's for a moment as he crossed the gallery to the steps. The Baron and Tom Blount went with him to the upping-block, and together they lifted Lady Anne gently from the horse. She was limp in their arms, seeming barely conscious. "Careful, men," Adam warned. "Her ankle's injured. She can't bear to touch her foot to the ground." He dismounted and watched as they carried Lady Anne into the house. Then he hurried to Mary, who stood at the head of her table. "I'm sorry to be late. Lady Anne was thrown off when her horse failed to clear a ditch. The horse ran. I've sent Ben to find it."

"We've had the toasts," Mary said quietly. "If you'll be seated, Ebon will bring you some warm food. The rest of us have been back for an hour or more."

"I'm sorry, Mary," Adam said again. "You see, we——"

"Please sit down, Adam," Mary said. "Lady Anne is quite safe now. Perhaps you can spare some time for your other guests." She turned to Cosmo, who sat next to her, and began to talk vivaciously.

In the office, from which Lady Anne had banished her agitated husband and Tom Blount, Angus Moray was applying a hot bandage to her ankle. "Strange that is hasn't swelled," he commented.

"Yes, isn't it!" She lay back on the couch, watching his face. "I gave it a dreadful wrench when I fell. You see, I was pushing my hunter over a ditch, and the stupid horse didn't make it. Fortunately Mr. Rutledge was close by and came to my rescue." She sighed reminiscently. "Mr. Rutledge is so . . . resourceful. He carried me in his arms ever so far to a little farm cottage, but there was no one there. So he stayed with me until I felt able to make the trip back."

Angus made no comment, and his face was expressionless. Ebon came in with a basin of hot water. "Put your foot into the water, please, Lady Anne," Angus said crisply.

She complied silently. After a time she said, "Angus, I've wanted to ask you, have you talked to Sylvia about her ring? Do you know who gave it to her?"

"I've told you, Lady Anne, it's none of my concern!" Angus said sharply. But there was concern in his eyes and anger in his voice.

Lady Anne smiled contentedly. "Do you think, Angus, that you can put my ankle to rights by this evening? I should hate to miss the Blounts' ball at Mulberry Hill, and it would be so lonely here, since the Rutledges and their other guests are all going. Or perhaps I could persuade you to keep me company and care for my poor ankle."

"There is no reason why you should not lead every dance at the ball tonight and walk home if you care to," Angus said indifferently. "In any case, I am sure your husband would not leave you alone. He can do as much for your ankle as I."

Lady Anne's smile was frosty. "Dear Angus, you are so reassuring!"

"The Baron is waiting in the hall. He's very worried about you. I'll send him in."

Shortly Baron von Pollnitz entered, followed by Mary Rutledge. "Anne, my love, you have frightened me!" he exclaimed. "You were gone such a long time! I was certain you had had a fall, and, you see, I was right. You are so reckless. Perhaps you should not hunt again."

"Not hunt? What nonsense! The accident was the horse's fault. And Dr. Moray says my ankle will be all right." She smiled sweetly at Mary and added, "And I had an ideal rescuer. Your husband was wonderful, Mrs. Rutledge—so attentive and considerate, so very strong!"

Mary did not return the smile. "I am pleased you are not hurt seriously, Lady Anne," she said and left the room.

On the gallery the guests were waiting to thank their hostess. A trifle weary, she stood beside Adam at the top of the steps, acknowledging praise for the breakfast and responding to enthusiastic comments on the first important meet of Queen Anne's Hunt.

Tom Blount and his guests were the last to leave. "James River, that was a real run!" he said excitedly. "I wish we'd got the old dog fox himself, but at least we didn't draw a blank." He yawned and hastily covered his mouth with his hand. "I don't know what any one else is going to do, but I'm for bed. I'll sleep until the ball begins to-night."

The young people clattered down the steps to their horses.

Adam said to Mary, "I didn't see the old Parson at breakfast."

"Dr. Armitage ordered him home as soon as we arrived back at the house. Charles Johnson took him, and the doctor went along to see that the old man rested," Mary said.

"Was Charles in at the kill? I don't remember seeing him after the cast-off."

"He came back early and waited at the house for the Parson. His horse was lamed, he said."

Neither said what both were thinking. Even the Christmas season and the boisterous friendliness of a hunt had not broken down Charles's disapproval of Adam's politics. Charles had come under protest and had unobtrusively but firmly dissociated himself from this gathering of "renegades." Adam and Mary were gratified by the success of the new hunt, but they realized that to Charles Johnson and the members of the Albemarle Hunt today's meet meant that the Rutledges had recognized and accepted their banishment from their former circle of friends in the county.

At the end of the gallery Sylvia stood at the rail, watching Tom Blount's party ride off down the drive. When Angus Moray came up behind her she knew what he wanted to say, knew that he had been waiting all through their stay at Queen's Gift for a chance to ask about her ring. At their first meeting his eyes had gone to her left hand. Obviously he had been informed about it, and who could have told him? Certainly the Rutledges would not have boasted of their gift. Who, then, but Lady Anne? Sylvia could imagine the sort of explanation her Ladyship would have suggested to him.

She forestalled his questions with one of her own. "How is Lady Anne's foot?"

"A perfect foot," Angus answered. "Slender and aristocratic, shapely and . . . unblemished."

Sylvia turned to face him. "You don't mean that she was only pretending to suffer! That her 'accident' never happened!"

"I wouldn't know about that," Angus said. "My guess is that Lady Anne did fall and that for reasons of her own she chose to dramatize the incident. At any rate I feel confident that we shall see her dancing superbly at Mulberry Hill to-night."

Sylvia faced the rail again. "She is like a child sometimes. She is exasperated with me continually because I have not felt obliged to tell her who gave me this ring I am wearing." She displayed the emerald. "I have made it clear to her that I regard the ring as a personal matter, one that concerns only the giver and myself, and that I will not speak of it to any one. She finds this infuriating, but I think my attitude is quite logical, don't you?"

Angus was silent. She knew he understood that she did not want him to question her. She knew also that her words had hurt him. She could almost feel him struggling to find a way to break through the barrier she had raised. At last he mumbled something about having to see his patient and went into the house.

Oh, Angus! she thought unhappily. I don't want to make you more unhappy, but I must force you to see that there is no future for us. And if this ring will help me, then I must use it.

The old house was very quiet. The Rutledges and their guests were resting in anticipation of the ball at Mulberry Hill. Sylvia went to her room, but was unable to sleep. She wondered if Angus too was lying awake, tortured by his thoughts.

When the evening shadows began to invade her room she dressed and went downstairs. The first-floor rooms were deserted. All traces of the hunt breakfast had been cleared away.

In the office Cosmo de' Medici sat by the fire, smoking. As she entered he jumped to his feet and indicated the chair opposite his. "Miss Hay, I am delighted. Come, join me in pleasant contemplation of your triumph in the hunt this morning. You rode wonderfully well and deserved the brush." A look of mischief came into his dark eyes. "You will forgive me if I add that I was especially pleased to see you take the prize from your employer."

Sylvia tried to think of a suitably non-committal remark, but Cosmo continued without pause. "I think that beautiful lady likes always to be first in any contest, whether the object is a fox or a man's affections. Wait, Miss Hay." He smiled and raised a protesting hand. "You would say I should not speak to you thus of the lady who employs you, and I answer that you are undoubtedly correct but I shall do so anyway. We know her well, you and I. Why should we pretend we do not?"

"I had not realized that you were well acquainted with her Ladyship," Sylvia said formally.

"No? Then let me show you. I have observed her closely these past days, and I know many things. For instance, she likes to annoy you, and the reason is that she is envious of something you have—your youth possibly, your beauty certainly."

"She might well envy your imagination, Captain de' Medici."

"Ah, now you laugh at me," Cosmo said with a flashing smile. "But what I say is true, Miss Hay. I am not a stranger to women, and I find their little tricks and strategies amusing in the same way that playful clawing kittens are amusing. But it is well to be careful when the game becomes serious. The claws of a cat can dig deep."

"And do you find all women merely amusing?" Sylvia asked, smiling. "Do you never encounter one who inspires a deeper response?"

Cosmo shrugged. "I am content to be amused. I find them interesting always and sometimes exciting, and that is enough. I confess I do not understand the attitude of Northern men—so severe, so earnest, so gloomy. Life is to be lived, women are to be loved—that is the Latin way. We do not expect eternal faithfulness, so we are not deceived or disappointed."

"A thoroughly cynical attitude, *signor!*"

"To you it seems cynical, to me it seems merely sensible . . . and enjoyable. Latins know that an hour of love may last for ever in the memory."

"What you are saying," Sylvia said calmly, "is that you content yourself with the lesser goal rather than exert yourself to try for the greater."

Cosmo considered the statement. "Perhaps. . . . And now I wish to tell you, Miss Hay, that I have observed you carefully also. You are not happy, and I think you keep yourself from being happy. I do not understand why —just that there is misunderstanding between you and the young doctor. I would say to you, do not ask too much of a man. We are weak creatures, all of us. The Arabs understand this. They do not seek perfection in one another, for only Allah is perfect." His voice was gentle, his manner kind.

Sylvia fought to keep back her tears. How could she tell this frivolous but warm-hearted young man that she asked no more of life than the privilege of being Angus' wife but that it was denied her?

She was spared the necessity of answering, for Adam Rutledge entered the room from the gallery. He had been to the stables, he said, to see Lady Anne's horse, which Ben had found and brought back. The mare was badly lamed.

"Sit down and rest yourself, Adam," Cosmo said. "You look weary, and you will want to be at your best for the ball to-night."

"I wish we needn't go—Mary and I, I mean." Adam slumped into a chair. "I can't think it will be good for Mary, who is exhausted from the hunt, although she won't admit it. Probably she should not have ridden with us, but she was determined not to miss it."

"I have noticed that one is seldom exhausted by something one wants very much to do," said Cosmo. "Perhaps our good Maria's weariness has another cause. A disappointment, possibly."

"Disappointment? No, I think it's just that she hasn't regained her full strength yet. At any rate she's sleeping now, and I've told Pam not to waken her. You will find the ball just as merry without us. And I suppose Lady Anne will not be going either."

"Adam, I assure you she will be there, handsomely dressed and dancing every dance," Cosmo cried. "I would wager my new plantation on that. Now that her injury has served its purpose, she will discard it gracefully and swiftly."

Adam smiled uneasily and glanced at Sylvia before replying. "Let us be gentlemanly, Cosmo, and give the lady the benefit of the doubt."

"But there is not the slightest doubt, my friend," Cosmo persisted. "You will see."

Adam rose. "Very well, then. We shall see." He left the room.

Sylvia had listened to the exchange with some bewilderment. "You seem anxious to disparage Lady Anne to every one, Captain de' Medici," she said. "Has she injured you in some way?"

"Injured me? But not at all!" Cosmo laughed. "No, I find her Ladyship a delight to the eye and entertaining to watch as she goes about the business of getting her way. But she can be dangerous, and I should not enjoy to see her make trouble for my friends."

"Trouble for Mr. Rutledge, do you mean? But . . ."

"The good Adam is observant, even as I am," Cosmo explained. "He has observed that she is a ruthless and calculating woman. He has observed also—and I'm sure that she has given him every opportunity—that she is beautiful. Alas, he has not a temperament that would permit him to deal realistically with these facts. It seems best that Adam should keep in mind that she is calculating and leave the contemplation of her beauty to me."

"To you, *signor?*"

"Did you never see a partridge feign a broken wing to draw a hunter from her nest and her young?" Cosmo smiled broadly. "To-night I shall play papa to Adam and Maria and shall flap my wings with great vigour before Lady Anne Stuart."

The ball at Mulberry Hill was in full swing when the party from Queen's Gift arrived. Candles burned in every window of the three-story plantation house, and the sound of music and gay laughter greeted the Rutledges and their guests as they mounted the steps to the high stoop. Through the windows to the left of the door Sylvia could see a lively contra-dance in progress.

In the large entrance hall Madam Blount stood at the foot of the beautiful curving staircase. Lady Anne sailed forward to greet her, brushing past Mary Rutledge, who stepped politely aside. Mary looked tired this evening, Sylvia thought, but she had insisted on coming, in spite of her husband's protests. Sylvia suspected that to Mary her appearance here was an answer to the county's exclusion of the Rutledges from the Albemarle Hunt. Mary and Adam would present a united front to those who objected to Adam's political beliefs.

Madam Blount's greeting was cordial and displayed no hint of uneasiness at the knowledge that many of the guests already assembled would not be pleased to find themselves under the same roof with Adam. She led the party to the drawing-room, where Lady Anne appropriated a handsome sofa of crimson satin and seated herself with ceremonious care, talking gaily of her accident and her relief at not having to miss the ball. When her skirts were arranged to her satisfaction Lady Anne surveyed the dancers with an air of amiable condescension suitable, Sylvia thought, to a queen beholding a rustic frolic planned for her exclusive diversion. She indicated to Adam that he was to share her throne, but Sylvia noted with amusement that Cosmo de' Medici was there before him.

And Cosmo was a dazzling sight this evening, a fit partner for an Earl's daughter. He had arrayed himself in Court dress of white satin with a waistcoat brocaded in silver and gold and buttoned with brilliants. His shoe-buckles were of brilliants also, and he wore a short dress sword with a jewelled hilt. At his throat and wrist were ruffles of fine Venetian lace. He was a conspicuous figure even among the richly dressed planters, but he had the elegance to carry his finery, Sylvia conceded, and the white costume set off handsomely his olive complexion, dark waving hair and lustrous eyes.

Lady Anne eyed him appreciatively as he seated himself beside her. Sylvia, standing near by, heard her say, "I had not expected to see such splendour in this country, sir. You would do credit to any Court in Europe."

"If my costume has won your favourable attention, your Ladyship, it has served its purpose and I desire no further approbation from another sovereign," Cosmo replied suavely. His eyes, as they met Sylvia's, held a glint of secret laughter.

Lady Anne laughed. "You look a true Medici to-night—proud and handsome and compelling. I am sure all the stories I've heard of your ancestors are true. What they wanted, they took."

"All the world knows that some of the Medici were strong-willed," Cosmo said. "And there are family legends of ladies carried away to our castles for the delectation of my forebears. True stories? Who can say? One can only recognize a similar impulse in one's self and think sympathetic and envious thoughts of those other Medici more favoured by time and circumstance."

"But, *signor,*" Lady Anne cried in mock distress, "have the Medici fallen so low as to avow themselves slaves of time and circumstance?"

"Alas, one is compelled to admit that Edenton is not Florence, your Lady-ship, and that this infant country has yet to achieve that peak of civilization which makes it a simple matter to arrange the abduction of a beautiful lady," Cosmo said solemnly. "However," he continued more cheerfully, "these Americans are a young and vigorous people, and many Europeans have noted with interest the simple and direct methods they have evolved for attaining their goals. Some spirited ladies, for example, regard abduction as cumbersome and old-fashioned and do not wait to be taken forcibly where they wish to go."

"Indeed?" Lady Anne raised her eyebrows. "And you, *signor*—you do not find this procedure crude and barbarous and uncivilized?"

"On the contrary, Lady Anne, it seems to me a defiance of time and circumstance which, as a Medici, I find wholly admirable."

Lady Anne glanced about the room. "I have not previously heard Ameri-can customs interpreted by a cultivated European, sir. You must tell me more. But here comes Mr. Rutledge. I have promised to partner him in a minuet to assure him that my ankle is not seriously injured."

Cosmo rose and bowed. "Will you honour me by being my partner later, madam? I shall show all due consideration to your ankle."

She gave him her most dazzling smile. "I shall look forward to it, -sir." She moved away on Adam's arm.

Cosmo turned to Sylvia, who had rejected partners so as to hear the out-come of Cosmo's campaign. She took his arm, and they strolled to the far drawing-room. "I am making progress," he told her smugly.

"You are a bold and boastful man who takes pride in conquest," she answered reprovingly.

"But, Miss Hay, you know how noble are my motives," Cosmo protested. "No sacrifice is too great if it will benefit a dearly loved friend."

"Particularly if the sacrifice means sporting your most elaborate costume and ingratiating yourself with a beautiful woman?" Sylvia asked.

"In such cases," Cosmo admitted blandly, "my capacity for martyrdom knows no limit." He guided Sylvia into a position opposite Lady Anne and Adam in the dance. He smiled meaningfully as his eyes met Adam's, and with a slight nod he indicated Adam's partner. Adam flushed and looked away.

When the dance was concluded Lady Anne demanded some punch. Sylvia was uncomfortably aware of the way the group around the punch-bowl fell silent and moved away as the Queen's Gift party approached. Cosmo noticed it also, she was sure, but Lady Anne chattered gaily and unconcernedly.

Madam Blount came in from the hall and invited them to join her hus-band's grandfather at supper in the dining-room. "Mary is with him, and he is anxious to see you, Adam. He's always been so fond of you. And of course he will want to meet your guests."

In the dining-room the aged Captain Blount was describing the Queen's Gift Christmas celebrations in Duke Roger's day. Mary assured him that all the old rituals were still rigidly observed.

Captain Blount greeted Adam and Cosmo enthusiastically and examined Lady Anne and Sylvia approvingly when presented to them. Her Ladyship was amused by his old-fashioned gallantry and put herself out to be charming. But when the old Captain, who was proud of his memory, reverted to his usual topic of happenings in the Albemarle more than half a century before, she soon became bored.

She glanced past him to Mary Rutledge who sat, pale and tired-looking, on Captain Blount's right. "Mrs. Rutledge," she said suddenly, cutting into the old man's reminiscences, "I see you are wearing your fascinating locket. May I borrow it for a moment? I'd like to show it to Signor de' Medici. It bears the Royal Stuart crest," she told Cosmo, "and Mrs. Rutledge does not know its history."

Mary unfastened the locket—rather unwillingly, Sylvia thought—and handed it to Lady Anne without a word. Lady Anne turned to Cosmo. "You see, it bears the initial M, and I thought perhaps . . . " She paused in surprise, for she had unwittingly pressed the concealed spring and the locket had opened, revealing the miniature. "Why," she exclaimed, "surely this is the Duchess of Derwentwater! You did not show me this before. The locket grows more and more mysterious."

Captain Blount took her hand and held the miniature close to his eyes. "'Tis Lady Mary Tower," he announced decidedly. "Who could forget her? She lived for a time at Greenfield Plantation." He glanced around the table. "Of course none of you would remember. It must be seventy years or more since she left the Albemarle."

Lady Anne's eyes were fixed on the locket. "The picture is certainly the Duchess. I know the portrait from which . . . " She paused and looked at Mary. "This explains the crest, for she *was* a Stuart—the youngest daughter of Charles II, by some London singer, I believe. He made her legitimate and gave her the name Lady Mary Tudor. . . . I see the locket is inscribed 'To Roger,' " she added. "That would be your grandfather, I suppose? Interesting."

Captain Blount's eyes were bright with curiosity as he passed the locket back to Mary. "Your grandfather was much taken with her, Mary—as, indeed, were all our gentlemen. A great beauty, she was!"

Mary received the locket in silence, but Sylvia caught a flash of annoyance in her eyes as she glanced at Lady Anne. Almost at once Mary turned to her hostess and asked that the Queen's Gift party might be excused. "I find that I'm more tired than I thought, and I'm sure Lady Anne is feeling far from well. She had a fall on the hunting-field this morning, you know."

Lady Anne agreed with a glint of amusement in her eyes and even contrived to limp slightly as they went out to the waiting Queen's Gift carriages.

Cosmo ushered her into one coach with Dr. Moray and himself, leaving the other for Mary, Sylvia, Adam and the Baron.

There was little conversation in the second carriage. Mary leaned back against the cushions, her eyes closed. Sylvia said nothing, and the Baron, after receiving terse replies from Adam to a few mild queries, subsided. When they reached Queen's Gift the others had gone into the house. They entered in time to see Lady Anne going upstairs, leaning heavily on the arm of Cosmo de' Medici.

In the morning Mary sent her guests a message of regret at being unable to see them before their departure. Adam escorted Sylvia and the Von Pollnitzes to their coach. Dr. Moray had gone earlier on horseback, and Cosmo, who was staying on, had not yet come downstairs.

Lady Anne was radiant. She assured Adam that she had never had a more delightful holiday. The Baron also was in good spirits. On the journey he talked happily of the article he would write for *Fenno's* about the Queen's Gift Christmas celebration.

He patted his wife's hand. "You enjoyed yourself, I know, my dear. In spite of your unfortunate accident I have never seen you in better humour."

And why not? thought Sylvia grimly. Look at her accomplishments in these few days. She has met dozens of new people and charmed them all. She disrupted the hunt breakfast and drew the attention of every one to herself. She snubbed me constantly for three days and tormented Angus Moray about my ring. She managed to steal Adam Rutledge from his guests for more than an hour and thereafter encouraged his wife to think the worst about the incident. And last night she crept stealthily into Cosmo de' Medici's room. Yes, a delightful holiday indeed!

Conflict

27 WHEN she returned home after the ball at Mulberry Hill, Mary Rutledge fell into her bed and slept the dreamless sleep of physical exhaustion. She awakened in the morning feeling still too tired to dress and bid farewell to her guests—although she admitted to herself that she was influenced by a disinclination to face Lady Anne. She wondered why she resented so bitterly the fact that Lady Anne had been the one to penetrate the secret of the locket.

After she had had her breakfast Mary slept again. When she awoke it was late afternoon and there was a message from Adam saying that he had gone with Cosmo to Bertie County. From there they would go to New Bern and return to Queen's Gift early the following week.

She dressed and wandered restlessly through the empty rooms of the big house. Everything was in perfect order. In the months since the fever had struck her down, Miss Sarah, Ebon and Chaney had taken over the job of running the household, and Mary had not yet resumed control. To-morrow, she promised herself, she would go to the store-room with Chaney and check the supplies. To-morrow, not today.

She went into the office, chose a book at random from the shelves and read a few pages without being conscious of what she read. She raised her eyes to the portrait of the smiling Duke Roger. Soon she must force herself to read the journal, learn the truth about the serene golden-haired woman in the miniature. But not yet.

Why had Adam gone so suddenly to New Bern? she wondered. Or had the trip been planned earlier and kept secret from her? If it concerned his new politics, he would have been reluctant to talk to her about it. She thought of her promise to Charles Johnson that she would beg Adam to reconsider his Antifederalist stand. Charles had taken her to one side before the hunt left the house and spoken with honest emotion. "It's nonsense, Mary! Adam must realize he's working his own downfall and the downfall of all us planters. Queen's Gift cannot survive without profitable trade, and profitable trade will be impossible unless North Carolina is a member of the union. Tell him that, and tell him to forget Wilie Jones's wild talk."

She had agreed to talk to Adam, although it would mean destroying the tacit understanding that had carried them through the past months. When he returned she would broach the subject and let it carry them where it would.

Ebon came to tell her that supper was served, but she could not face the empty reaches of the dining-room. She asked him to bring a tray to her room. After she had eaten she undressed and got into bed, but sleep would not come. She thought with dread of the interview with Adam to which she was committed. But Queen's Gift impoverished, shabby, defeated—that was unthinkable! Surely he would not permit it to happen if she could only show him what the consequences of his folly would be. He loved the plantation—how devotedly he had applied himself to its care since his return! Or had he driven himself to work in order to avoid being confronted with evidences of his neighbours' anger and contempt? But very likely he disregarded their reactions, looking forward to the day when he would live in Illinois and the opinions of Albemarle planters could not affect him.

She tossed and twisted in her bed. Such conjectures were worse than useless, she told herself angrily. They would only frighten her so that she would be unable to speak calmly and logically when she tried to show Adam where he was wrong. She must think of other things, divert her mind from the dangers before her.

She slipped out of bed, lighted a candle and took her grandfather's journal from the desk drawer. She laid the little vellum-covered book on the desk and stared at it. So long she had delayed reading it, at first because she had wanted to share it with Adam and later—after discovering the locket—because she dreaded to learn that her grandfather was not all she had always thought him. But now she felt a sudden certainty that the book held words designed to bring her needed strength and courage.

She opened the cover and began to read. The book was not a journal, she discovered, but a letter to Duke Roger's only son—Hesketh, her father.

It seems unlikely, my dear son, that I shall ever see you again. At various times in my life—your mother can tell you of some of them—I have experienced exceptionally vivid and recurring dreams which have proved to be portents of the future. Sometimes they were so clear that I could act on them to protect myself or my loved ones from danger. The meaning of others has been veiled, and I have understood their significance only after the event to which they referred.

In recent weeks, while planning my voyage to the Leeward Islands and Cartagena, I have been visited several times by a dream whose meaning seems all too plain. Always I feel myself floundering in the ocean's green depths. I rise to the surface and strike out for a headland which is clearly visible not far off. But even as I do so I know that I cannot reach it. My strength fails me, and I slip down again into the green dimness of the bottomless sea.

Strangely, it is not an alarming dream. I am conscious of no desperation. Rather the ocean depths are friendly, welcoming, restful. The sea and I have been friends these many years, and if, as I suspect, I am not to return from this voyage, I shall not be sorry to find my last rest in the mighty ocean whose waters I have sailed so long. One thing is certain: I cannot stay ashore to evade the implications of my dream. Always I have gone forward to meet the challenge of my destiny, and I will not change the pattern of my life now.

I find that there is little to be done to prepare for my death. My business affairs are in order, and my agent in London will instruct you in their details before you leave your English school for the Albemarle. Instead of ships and cargoes, my thoughts in these hours turn to the place I love best in the world—Queen's Gift—and to the persons I love best—to my wife, to you, my son, and to one other. I feel a great yearning to see you, Hesketh, to say things I have never had time to say, to pass on to you the lessons that life has taught me. Failing of an opportunity, I have purchased this little volume and am devoting my last hours in port searching for words to say briefly some things I want you to know.

Another thing has happened which makes me feel that the cycle of my life has reached its completion. To make you understand it I must look back long years to the early days of my life in the Albemarle. Great days they were, Hesketh! Stirring days of high adventure and endless toil, of heart-warming triumphs and shattering defeats. We fought the Indians and won our place on the continent. We fought the forests and the climate and won sustenance for ourselves and our families. We fought one another when the remote hands of our English patrons divided us into supporters of traditional authority on the one hand and supporters of an ideal of justice on the other. And always we knew the joy of accomplishment because we were going forward—we were serving our country and bringing civilization to a raw and untamed land. That is why I have loved Queen's Gift!—because I created it. I bought land and made of it a plantation and a home. And now I relinquish it to you, my son, that you may love it and carry it forward and use it as the basis of your own creation.

To the Albemarle in those early days came an unusual woman, Lady Mary Tower, a cousin of the Royal Governor. She established herself at Greenfield Plantation with her niece and took no notice of the great curiosity of her neighbours. Every one admitted her rare beauty and great distinction, and almost every one had his own theory or rumour about her background. I cared not at all where she came from. I knew only that, of all women, she was the most beautiful and the dearest to my heart. She loved me also, and I tried to forget all else in the fulfilment of our love.

There were obstacles to our happiness. Mary was wed to a nobleman in England. I was betrothed to Rhoda Chapman, soon to come to America. But marriages can be broken, betrothals cancelled. More serious was a divergence in what we ourselves sought from life. Mary's world was England, the England of tradition and privilege and ceremony. My world was America, where any man was privileged to take what he could earn, own what he could build.

And so we loved and went our separate ways—Mary back to the security of England, I forward to meet the challenge of the New World. And at my side was Rhoda, your mother, who welcomed a chance to share in the great adventure.

Last month I came to Antigua on business and learned that my ship must await the arrival of another vessel whose cargo we were to take on to Cartagena. I accepted an invitation to spend some days at the cane plantation of a friend. His house is large and luxurious, and several guests were already in residence when I arrived.

Before the evening meal I strolled to the farthest reaches of the gardens at the very end of the island to watch the sun sink into the sea. Beyond a small grove of trees I found a secluded garden-house. Inside it, seated on a marble bench and watching the sunset, was the woman I had carried deep in my heart these twenty years and more.

She turned and saw me. We gazed at each other in a breathless silence. Not until she whispered my name could I believe it was really she.

Of the days that followed I cannot write. We moved through the house of our host as in a dream. Most of our days we spent alone in the garden-house by the sea. She told me of the life for which she had left me. The rumours we had heard in the Albemarle were true. She was the daughter of a King, and since our parting she had married a Duke of the realm. She was here only for a visit and would return to England on the ship that brought the cargo for which I waited.

One day we rode into St. Johns. She wished to visit a goldsmith, she said, and asked me to wait outside. When she rejoined me we rode back to the plantation together. In the garden-house where I had found her she took from her reticule a golden locket containing her portrait. She had had it inscribed to me. I can see her now as she was in that moment—cool and lovely in a muslin dress of pale green and a large flower-laden hat that shaded her blue eyes. And around us the flowers of a tropical garden, violet and red, purple and yellow.

It was there also that we said good-bye before she sailed out of my life for the second time. And soon I followed her to St. Johns to make ready for the voyage that may be my last.

I write you these things, my son, that you may understand what this unexpected meeting has taught me about myself and about the nature of men. For I found, when I met again this woman whom I have idolized through the years, that I could not honestly regret our separation so long ago. Deep as our love was, we were right to part. Mary could not understand or share my love for the Albemarle. She feared to cut herself off permanently from the life she had always known, and on that barrier our love must have foundered. Queen's Gift, my accomplishments there, my ambitions for it, were my life, and I should have been untrue to myself if I had turned back with Mary to a way of life that to me seemed dead and meaningless. Instead, I held true to my dreams and have had twenty-five good and fruitful and satisfying years. I have gone forward, and therein lies the true satisfaction and happiness.

You will understand now why I have told you this story, Hesketh. Your mother has wanted you educated in England, and I have agreed, for America needs the best Europe can offer in learning and culture. But do not forget that you are American-born. Bring your new knowledge back to us for the enrichment of this new land. Never stand still, my son. After your years in England, the Albemarle may seem strange and threatening to you. But never fear change. Move forward to find your destiny. These are the wisest words I have found to leave you.

I leave for you also the portrait of the woman who has lived so long in my heart. I need no picture to keep her face before me, and the locket is too beautiful to be lost to the world.

I pray that these words will reach you as a last evidence of my enduring love and confident hopes for you.

ROGER MAINWAIRING

Mary stared at the bold, sprawling signature. Here in these pages was the Duke Roger whose existence she had always sensed behind the tales she'd heard of the handsome, good-natured lord of the plantation who rode well and hunted enthusiastically, sailed his ships to the far corners of the earth, indulged his spirited wife and conducted his business affairs with audacity and ruthlessness. The author of the letter was the man whose personality she had felt lingering in the house he had built. Its atmosphere of peace and serenity was a reflection of the inner nature of a man who was true to his guiding principles and who came to terms with his sorrow.

Mary had known of Duke Roger's love for his plantation. It was revealed in every detail of the old house and in the setting he had chosen for it. It was echoed in each line of the ledgers in which he had recorded its development. But not until now had she known that for Queen's Gift he had given up the woman he loved.

Had Rhoda known the secret of her husband's heart? Mary wondered. Who could tell now? At any rate she had played the part Duke Roger had asked of her, never letting him know her enthusiasm for his great adventure was only an expression of her love for him. After his death she had gone home to the England that had drawn his Mary away from him. But Rhoda had sent her frail, bookish son to the Albemarle to carry forward the pattern Duke Roger had established for him.

Hesketh had been no adventurer. He had disposed of the shipping interests and lived out his brief and rather lonely life in faithful service to the heart of his father's empire—Queen's Gift. And at last he had relinquished his stewardship to the last Mainwairing, his daughter Mary.

And I will be faithful, too! Mary vowed silently as tears rolled down her cheeks. I will never abandon this plantation, never let it crumble away in neglect and poverty. Adam must understand. I am Duke Roger's granddaughter, his heir, and I must go forward with Queen's Gift!

It was sunset when Adam and Cosmo rode up the long drive. Mary saw them from her bedroom window. She sent for Chaney to revise the supper menu and told Pam to lay out one of her handsomest dresses.

At supper Cosmo talked entertainingly of Windsor and New Bern and the friends he had seen there. But neither he nor Adam mentioned the purpose of their trip, and Mary refrained from asking. She could not challenge Adam with Cosmo present.

After the meal they went together to the drawing-room, and Mary accompanied Cosmo at the harpsichord as he sang old Italian folk songs. Over the instrument she watched Adam, who sat by the fire. He looked tired and depressed. Should she postpone her talk of politics? But there would always be reasons for delaying it, she realized.

Cosmo laid aside the music, and he and Mary joined Adam by the fireplace. "I stopped to talk to Miss Hay as we came through Edenton," Cosmo said. "She tells me Lady Anne has decided to leave for New York on Friday."

Mary was surprised. "Has the Baron returned from South Carolina?"

"No, but her Ladyship refuses to delay her departure longer, Miss Hay says. Lady Anne's man of business has written that he will be in New York by the end of the month, and she seems eager to be there to greet him. The Baron will presumably join her later."

"Is Sylvia going with her?" Mary asked.

"Yes, and she asked me to tell you she hopes to ride out here to-morrow to say good bye."

Adam, who had been gazing into the fire, taking no part in the conversation, turned suddenly. "Mary, would you enjoy a visit to New York this spring? Penelope Dawson and others of your friends will be there, and I dare say we could persuade Miss Sarah to make the journey with you."

Mary was disconcerted. "Why . . . I had not even thought of going away. I . . . Why do you suggest it?" Adam hesitated, and she realized that his remark had not been prompted by impulse but by careful consideration.

"Well, I shall not be at Queen's Gift myself a great deal during these next months," he began, "and——"

"Adam, you are not going west again?" The words were spoken before she could stop herself.

Adam shifted uncomfortably in his chair. "Oh, no, but I shall have to make a number of trips to various places about the state. I . . . thought it might be lonely for you here by yourself."

"I see." It must be politics, she thought angrily. And of course the plantation did not matter to him. "Plantation business, do you mean?"

"No. You see, I——"

She interrupted him. "Or more trips like this one you have just made? Trips which you do not see fit to explain to me?" But this was wrong, she told herself. She must not be angry.

"I have tried to avoid discussing politics with you because you were so upset when I told you about Hillsborough. I did not want to disturb you further."

"Adam, I know you've tried to spare me, but your actions concern me also," she said carefully. "What will you do on these trips?"

"I plan to talk to men in various parts of the state who need encouragement before the election. Some of our Antifederalists have lost faith in our cause. They need to be reminded of the importance of amendments before we ratify the Constitution."

"And you are actually going out and make speeches against the Constitution?" Mary's exasperation made her voice tremble. "Adam, the whole county is up in arms against you already. All our friends, all the finest minds in the state support the Constitution. How can you be so confident that you are right and they are wrong?"

Cosmo leaned forward. "Perhaps I should withdraw to my room," he suggested. "I am weary after our journey."

Adam forestalled him. "No, Cosmo, please stay. You are our good friend, and you know better than any one how deeply I considered this question at Hillsborough before making my decision. I wish," he continued, turning to Mary, "that I could side with Iredell and Johnston and others whom I respect and admire. But on a question such as this a man must do his own thinking."

"Have you thought of Queen's Gift?" she asked. "You are fighting to keep North Carolina out of the union. Don't you realize what that will mean to the trading which supports this plantation?"

Adam was startled by her vehemence. But he answered quickly, "Would you have me place my own financial advantage before my responsibility to do what I can to safeguard *all* the people of this country?" He rose and stood with his back to the fire. "That sounds pompous, I suppose, but in all honesty I feel that my own experience has made me aware of dangers that Johnston and Iredell underestimate. I must do what seems to me right."

Mary stared up at his face. His calmness infuriated her. "What of your responsibility to me and to our home?" she demanded, her voice shaking.

"What of our responsibility to the people on this plantation who look to us for food and shelter and clothing? Will you sacrifice them to your noble ambitions to save the rest of the country?"

Adam was patient. "Mary, I have every hope that the Constitution will be amended to fill the gaps it now contains. And I work against ratification now in the hope that North Carolina's stand will stimulate the member states to initiate amendments. Meanwhile"— he paused and shook his head sadly—"meanwhile, my dear, I cannot persuade myself that our welfare is more important than the welfare of thousands more vulnerable than we."

Mary looked helplessly at Cosmo. He smiled sympathetically, sorrowfully. She burst into tears. "I can't understand, Adam. I've tried, but I cannot. To me all you are saying means only that Queen's Gift is in danger, and you are working against it. I . . ." She rose and ran, still sobbing, out of the room.

Adam started after her.

Cosmo caught him by the arm. "Wait! What are you going to say to her?"

Adam hesitated. "Why, I must explain what we . . ."

Cosmo shook his head. "No. Sit down, Adam. It is well that you asked me to stay."

"But——"

"Sit down and listen," Cosmo said firmly. "That's right. Now, promise me that you will talk no more politics to-night. Adam, your Maria is not a politician, she is your wife. Do you think she is really concerned because you are for or against the Constitution? Well, perhaps she is, but mostly she worries whether you are for or against her. You will not soothe her by talk of 'We, the People.' What she wants to hear is 'We, Adam and Maria.' Believe me, this is so."

"But, Cosmo," Adam protested, "Mary knows——"

Cosmo interrupted again. "Have you told her?" He smiled pityingly. "I thought not. Adam, you are old enough to have learned these things, which every Latin knows without being taught. Women, my friend, like to be told. Never assume that they know how we feel about them. Tell them. Tell them constantly."

"Mary's not like that," Adam said.

"Maria is a woman and should be treated as such. Consider what you have done. You go away for many months, then you come home and tell her you are a different man from the one who went away. Instantly she feels shut out. An important decision has been made in which she has held no part. Then for many months you tell her nothing of your inner thoughts —from the kindest motives, to be sure, but the effect is the same. When at last you speak it is to say you will be busy for some time, and perhaps she'd better get out of your way and go to New York or somewhere. Can you wonder that she is unhappy? If she were not gentle by nature, she would have hit you with a fire-iron."

Adam was bewildered. "But what can I do? I must carry out my plans."

Cosmo nodded calmly. "Of course. But now you must go to her and say, 'Maria, I love you.' That is your theme. No politics, no plantation, no Constitution. Just, 'Maria, I love you'—with such elaborations as may occur to you." He glanced at the French clock on the mantel. "She has had time to stop crying and begin to think with regret of the things she said. Now is the time for your entrance. Go!"

There was a faint smile on Cosmo's lips as he watched Adam hurry from the room. After a time he went to Mary's harpsichord and touched the keys, then sat down and began to play softly.

Adam opened the door of Mary's bedchamber. The room was in darkness except for a glow from the hearth. Mary sat by the window, her face turned away from him as she gazed into the blackness outside.

He halted on the threshold, feeling suddenly unsure of himself. Cosmo was so confident of his power to analyze all women. But there were things he did not know about the differences separating Adam from his wife. Mary felt that Adam had disregarded her opinions in choosing his course of political action, and how could he deny it? She believed that he dreamed of a future in which the Albemarle would play no part, in which he would create a new home for her in Illinois—and this was true. And unless she could concede that it was her husband's right and responsibility to determine the pattern of their life, how could they look forward to happiness together?

Mary turned her head and looked at him. In that instant a wave of affection and longing swept over him. Memories raced through his mind —the hopes shared, the joys of fulfilment. The grief of partings and the gladness of reunion. Long days in the Illinois country which had seemed incomplete because Mary was not there. There must be a way for them to find each other again.

He crossed the room and took her in his arms. "Mary . . ."

"Oh, Adam!" She clung to him. "I'm so frightened, Adam! I don't want to lose you. . . ."

"Trust me, Mary," he said. "Have faith in me. I love you with all my heart. We will find a way!"

Lady Anne stood in the centre of her bedchamber at Horniblow's, surveying excitedly the confusion that surrounded her. Most of her wardrobe was strewn over various pieces of furniture, and Dawkins scurried about resentfully, trying to keep up with her mistress' directions about packing.

"Brainless fool!" Lady Anne stormed. "Of course I shall want a ball dress in Philadelphia. Take the green brocade out of the New York box and pack it with the things that are to travel with me. And hurry, Dawkins! I want this room in order by half past one."

She turned and saw Sylvia in the doorway to the sitting-room. "Here you are at last, Miss Hay," she said coldly. "I've been waiting for you. There is much to be done. Your boxes for New York must be ready to send to-morrow. Dawkins will travel with them to see that nothing is lost. You and I leave for Suffolk on the diligence Friday morning and take coach there for Philadelphia."

She paused and considered, then turned to Dawkins. "Where have you put the yellow lutestring ball dress? It must go to Philadelphia with me!" She led Sylvia to the sitting-room. "We shall stay there four days to break our journey. I don't wish to arrive in New York looking like Tophet." She caught up a slip of paper from a table. "Now, you must write a note to each of these people—they've all entertained for me here and must be thanked. And these"— she handed Sylvia a sheaf of letters—"must be answered. I've made a note on the back of each one telling you what to say."

Sylvia took the letters to her own room and settled down to work. It saddened her to write farewell notes to the Edenton people who had been kind to her. After Friday she would probably not see them ever again. She began a letter to Dr. Armitage, but paused and laid down the pen. Thoughts of Angus Moray were too painful.

She picked up the London letters Lady Anne had given her and examined them. One had no notation on the back. She turned it over and glanced at the handwriting, which was unfamiliar.

I shall travel to New York by packet, arriving about the first of February. Cannot you plan to be there? I shall not have time for the long journey to Carolina, and there are matters of importance to discuss. I have seen Northumberland, and he has agreed to send your allowance to me henceforth instead of to the Baron. Your annuity will continue to be sixteen hundred pounds per annum, as settled in the Act of Divorce. But some of the debts he will not pay—those you contracted during the negotiation of the settlement. We shall see.

Try to come to New York. It is long since I have seen you, and London is so very dull without the light of the sun. . . .

The signature was "Stephen." So Lady Anne was "the light of the sun" to her man of business! Judging from the lady's frantic haste to get to New York, she was quite as anxious as he for a discussion of matters of importance, Sylvia reflected contemptuously. She wished she had not seen the letter, and she quickly decided Lady Anne would share her wish. She replaced it in the packet of London letters and returned to the note to Dr. Armitage.

In a few moments she heard quick footsteps in the corridor, followed by a light tap at the door. Lady Anne entered hurriedly. "Have you answered the letters from England?" she demanded.

"No, Baroness, I've scarcely begun the farewell notes to the local people."

Lady Anne sighed audibly. "I'll take them with me," she said, picking them up from the desk. "Perhaps I'll have time to answer a few myself. It will lighten your burden." She strolled to the window and glanced out. "You needn't write to the Iredells or Mr. Cabarrus. They're coming to supper to-morrow. And perhaps you'd like to carry my farewell to your friends the Rutledges. I won't need you this afternoon."

"Thank you, Baroness. I'll go after luncheon."

"Oh, didn't I tell you?" Lady Anne said casually. "I'm having a guest in for luncheon—Signor de' Medici. So you may go now if you like."

"But I have all these notes to write and packing to do," Sylvia protested mildly.

"Nonsense," Lady Anne said with a trace of irritation in her voice. "Dawkins can help you with your packing this evening, and I certainly don't care whether you get notes written to all these provincial nonentities. I insist that you take the rest of the day for yourself."

"Very well, Baroness, if you're sure it won't inconvenience you," Sylvia said demurely.

"Of course it won't, my dear," said Lady Anne in her kindest voice. "And as you go out please tell Horniblow I shall want luncheon for two served in my sitting-room at one-thirty."

At Queen's Gift Ebon ushered Sylvia into the drawing-room, where Sarah Poor sat close to the fire, an India shawl about her shoulders, her feet resting on a cricket. "Come in, Miss Hay, and shut the door, please," Miss Sarah said peremptorily. "Not that it will do much good—shutting the door, I mean. This cold wind blows right under every door in the house. I've put Mrs. Rutledge's sewing girls to work making sand-bags to lay at the thresholds for cutting out the cold."

"Where is Mrs. Rutledge, Miss Sarah?"

"The silly girl has gone for a walk," Miss Sarah said disapprovingly. "A ship tied up at the wharf this morning, and Mr. Rutledge is supervising the loading of some tobacco. Very likely she's down there, too."

"Thank you, Miss Sarah." Sylvia went into the hall and was immediately challenged by old Chaney, who was coming downstairs.

"Miss Hay, you ain't a-goin' out in de cold agin already, is you? You ain't had time to thaw out yet."

Sylvia laughed. "I'm not cold, really, Chaney."

"You an' Miss Mary is jes' alike. 'T's too warm,' she says. 'I wants a good brisk walk'—on a day like dis!" Chaney shook her head. "Miss Mary say you leavin', Miss Hay. We goin' to miss you might' sharp. You been might' good to Miss Mary."

Outside, Sylvia walked toward the wharf. Two mangy hounds belonging to some child in the quarters came loping around the house and ran sniffing at her skirt, but they fled when she snapped her fingers. The air was crisp and sparkling, and out on the Sound the east wind drove white-caps before it.

Mary came toward her, wearing a fur coat and a jaunty little fur cap.

She waved and quickened her pace when she recognized Sylvia. "I'm so glad you've come," she said when they met. "I'm quite deserted today. Cosmo had business in town, and Adam is too busy with the tobacco-loading to notice me. He's not even coming up to the house for dinner, so we can have a good gossip."

Then the smile left her face. "But I'm forgetting why you've come. Oh, Sylvia, I hate to think of your going away from us! It's difficult to realize that we've known you only a few months. I think of you as belonging to Edenton."

"Thank you, Mrs. Rutledge. Nothing you could have said would have pleased me more. I . . . I don't want to go."

"Then why should you?" Mary clasped Sylvia's arm, and they walked toward the house. "I know Ann Blount would be delighted to have you as governess to her brood."

"No," Sylvia said, "it's best that I leave Edenton now."

"You mean because of Angus Moray?" Mary smiled at Sylvia's surprise. "Of course we all know that Angus is in love with you, and we'd hoped you two would make a match of it. Why, Adam tells me that Dr. Hugh extended the quarantine at Queen's Gift for twenty-four hours just to give Angus a chance to propose."

"Oh, Mary!" The thought of gruff old Dr. Williamson playing matchmaker was too much for Sylvia. She began to weep softly.

"Come into the house," Mary said gently. "Why don't you go up to my room and bathe your eyes? I'll tell Ebon to bring us some luncheon there."

Sylvia could eat nothing. When at last she stopped crying she poured out to Mary the story of her love for Angus, the obstacles to their marriage and the misunderstanding over the emerald ring.

Mary said, "Do you love this Donald Hay?"

"I've never loved any one before I met Angus—I know that now. But I've known Donald all my life. He will be kind to me."

"Does he love you?"

Sylvia hesitated. "We've never spoken of love. We've known for years that we are to be wed, and we've just accepted it."

"But if he's kind and understanding, surely he'll release you when he knows you love another," Mary said.

"How could I write him such a thing when he's ill, Mary? You must see I couldn't do that. And Angus is not free either. He has no money, and what he earns must go to his mother." Sylvia shook her head. "No, there's no alternative. I must go to New York with Lady Anne and then to England to wait for Donald."

"Sylvia"— Mary spoke urgently—"promise me you won't dismiss Angus finally now. You are both young, and this situation may change completely in a few years or even months."

"I don't intend to see Angus again," Sylvia said.

340 *Queen's Gift*

"My dear, I've sent Ben to town to bring him here this afternoon. He's probably on his way here now." She raised a hand to halt Sylvia's protest. "No, don't say you can't bear it. You owe it to Angus to clear up this foolishness about the ring. If he is to be unhappy about you, let him at least know that you are worthy of his sorrow."

"I thought—I hoped it would make it easier for him to forget me."

"Sylvia, if he loves you as I think he does, he won't forget you ever," Mary said gently. "And how much better for both of you to remember that you faced a tragic situation and did bravely what your sense of honour told you must be done. See him, tell him good-bye. Let him draw strength from your courage."

Angus Moray rode up the drive to Queen's Gift at a fast gallop. Opposite the house he leaped from his horse, tossed the reins to a stableboy who ran to meet him, and hurried up the steps to the door.

"Where is your mistress, Ebon?" he demanded of the old butler. "What's wrong with her? Has the fever returned?"

Ebon was bewildered. "Miss Mary? Why, sar, she ain't ill. She bloomin' like a flower."

"Here I am, Dr. Moray!" Mary came into the hall from the office. "I'm perfectly well, but there is a young lady here who needs you very badly indeed. It's Sylvia," she explained. "She's to leave for New York in two days. I knew you would want to see her, and it would be awkward at Horniblow's. She's waiting for you in the office. And, for heaven's sake, Doctor, don't fret any more about her emerald ring. It was a present from Adam and me."

Angus raised her hand to his lips. "You are an angel," he said.

He opened the office door and went inside. Sylvia was standing by the fire-place. She gazed at him for a long moment, then came into his arms without a word.

After a time she drew away from him. "Angus, I've been foolish. I wanted you to doubt me, even to hate me. I thought——"

"Mrs. Rutledge told me," he said. "We'll not speak of it."

She looked into his eyes. "I love you, Angus. I said once that we should never have met, but I was wrong. I'm grateful to have known you, to have had a glimpse of what life could be and of the woman I could be with you at my side."

"No, Sylvia, no! It's not over. This is not the end for us," he said fiercely. "We were meant for each other."

"Angus, you know it's impossible," she answered gently. "I am not free, and you aren't either. There is no way for us."

"I'll never stop hoping. Never!" he said defiantly. "Every day, every hour, every moment, I'll be waiting for you to come back to me."

A warm peace stole around Sylvia's heart. There was unspeakable comfort in this stubborn devotion, hopeless as she felt their fate had made it.

The Election

28 MARY RUTLEDGE, accompanied by Miss Sarah, left for New York on St. Valentine's Day. The weather was warm and pleasant, and many of the trees were budding in the tender young green of spring.

As she rode down the avenue Mary turned for a last look. The house was serene and graceful in the bright air. The fields were freshly turned by the plough. Slaves moved down the rows in steady procession, giving the seed to the ground. According to an old custom this was the date for the planting of May pease. A new season of growing was beginning—and Mary was leaving Queen's Gift.

It was a strange leave-taking. She had not talked of politics with Adam since the night he had tried to explain his beliefs. Outwardly then life had been undisturbed. Last Sunday they had sailed across the Sound to the little chapel where Parson Pettigrew blessed the plough in the ceremony that always had held such meaning for both Adam and her. In other days they had found in the ritual a renewal of the ancient covenant with earth. This beginning had seemed a promise of the harvest they would win and share together.

Mary thought it had not been so Sunday. Adam had turned away from the home and fields in which their hope had been joined. He was often absent for long periods, winning other men to a course that threatened Queen's Gift. And she was leaving too. Adam had known the wiser course when he urged it. Being at Queen's Gift in this season would enlarge their differences. Those differences must not grow. Mary closed her eyes and clenched her hands. Dear God, they must not grow!

The carriage turned from the avenue into the road. Queen's Gift was no longer visible. Mary fixed her eyes ahead. Perhaps distance from home would help bring understanding. She remembered what Cosmo had said. "Maria, do not let a political difference stand between you and Adam. To-day a question of policy seems urgent. To-morrow it is not, and we turn to something else. But love, love is different. That must endure and bring understanding always. What are you doing to love, my little Maria?"·

Cosmo's question had haunted her. She knew the quality of his affection for Adam and her. He could not doubt that she loved Adam. Could he not understand how Adam's decision had frightened and hurt her? But no, he stood with Adam. She heard his words again: "This is the hope that brought me from Europe, this dream of liberty for all men. This, little Maria, is the beginning of a New World." She did not understand the dream. She knew only that it was attended by violence, hatred, the death of old friendship. She saw it only as a danger to all she loved. Was it selfish to cherish the familiar and the loved?

Miss Sarah poked Mary in the ribs with a sharp elbow. "You haven't said a word since we drove away. Wake up, we're off on a fine trip. Don't be so melancholy. Your husband will be here when you return. Where did he go this morning? I saw him leave before sunrise."

"He was going to Tyrrell, he said, and then on to Hyde County."

"Making more of those speeches, I'll be bound. Marcy told me about them. Well, a man like him can't live with himself unless he does what he thinks he must. I despise a man that won't stand on his own two feet and fight for what he believes."

The stage for Suffolk was standing in front of Horniblow's when Mary and Miss Sarah drove up. Marcy, who had ridden in before them, helped place their luggage in the boot. The driver sounded the horn, and the horses strained against the creaking harness. There were no other passengers. Before they had turned into the Sand Hill Road Miss Sarah was asleep. Mary looked out at the lovely country-side through which the coach was rolling and made a solitary farewell. New York seemed very far away and its attractions slight indeed.

Adam sank into the large chair in his office, stretched his legs out and tried to relax.

He had not realized until this moment how tired he was. A bathe, fresh clothing and Chaney's excellent supper had been compensation, but not enough. He had ended the last of the trips begun after Christmas. Yet without Mary there was no home-coming in this return. It was almost a month since he had seen her. His knowledge that it was too early to expect a letter from New York had not reduced his hope that it would be waiting for him, or his disappointment in not finding it. He had a sudden access of longing for his wife, and then with deliberate effort turned his mind away from her. Marcy and Mel Frazier would be returning from the village soon to review with him their plans for the election to-morrow. They must not find him disconsolate. They would expect a confident air and praise for their work.

Adam filled and lighted his pipe, letting his mind run back over all the events of the past months. In all honesty he could not think the prospect was hopeful. Federalist strength was growing. He saw again the angry faces in the crowds of men to whom he had talked, heard again the angry voices. *No ships in the harbours, no money in the treasury, and you want to bargain about amendments. . . . You Antis don't worry about the rights of man, you want to keep on paying your debts in worthless state currency. . . . What do we do if we're attacked—look to Rhode Island for help?*

Adam made no defence of the men who had hoped to profit by refusal to ratify. He did not deny the dangers of being out of the union or the advantages in joining it. He returned always to the principle that was for him more important than any other consideration. The security of property and trade must come second to the security of the rights of man. The courage of North Carolina to stand for freedom was challenged. He made his answer direct. He spoke out of the fervour of his own conviction to appeal to the love of liberty deep in the spiritual grain of every Carolinian. *Would you give up your right to speak out as you are speaking now? . . . Will you not keep safe the right to worship as you choose? . . . Don't you need the word of the Federal government that the rights of your state are for ever safe?*

If he found antagonism, he found support also. In the central counties, in Martin, Pitt, Edgecombe, Dobbs, Nash and Halifax, men took reassurance and new resolve from what he and other Antifederalist speakers were saying. Even in the solidly Federalist counties of the Albemarle—Perquimans, Pasquotank, Camden, Currituck and Tyrrell—men came forward to pledge their work and votes, men like those who had worked for Adam in Chowan. To these artisans, mechanics and farmers and to some of their leaders among the lawyers and merchants a bill of rights was a faith, commanding all devotion and any sacrifice. But there could be no doubt that Federalists now held the majority in all the counties he had visited.

Adam heard the sound of horses coming up the avenue to the house. Through the window he could see Marcy, Frazier and Chase dismounting. He rose to greet them at the door. One thing was certain: Whatever the odds, he would never abandon the hope that North Carolina would have the will to stand as the conscience of the new Congress. If to-morrow he was elected a delegate he would carry his fight to the floor of the convention at Fayetteville.

Frazier began his report as soon as he was seated in Adam's office. "We've been over the entire county, Mr. Rutledge, and we think you'll be elected sure. We've divided up the county, and three or four of our lads will be at every polling place. They'll make sure that every freeman has a chance to cast his ballot. And if any our men have talked to don't appear, they'll go after 'em."

"Excellent," Adam said. "But we've another responsibility. This has to be a sober, orderly election. Caution our men to do their part in keeping it so."

Frazier grinned. "Well, sir, one thing. I've got Horniblow and Barnes of the Red Lion Tavern out on Virginia Road to sell nothing stronger than spiced cider to-night and to-morrow. And I think the Sheriff will show more gumption than he showed last July. Mr. Hamilton, and, yes, Governor Johnston and Mr. Iredell have seen to that. That's mainly the situation, sir."

"That was the situation until a few days ago." Marcy got to his feet and stood before Adam and Frazier. "I think we'd better tell Mr. Rutledge all about this, Frazier." He faced Adam. "Last week a stranger came to town and moved into one of the cabins out on the Rockahock near Hume's mill. Name's O'Shaughnessy. He's been in Horniblow's every night, telling whoever'll listen that Rutledge and Hamilton want to make us a state of outlaws. He talks nonsense, but it's nonsense that might be believed. He's glib, sir, and he's dangerous."

"O'Shaughnessy!" Adam frowned, remembering Enos Dye's story at Hillsborough and Cosmo's knife-rent sleeve. "Yes, there was an agitator at the convention by that name. He spoke as an Anti there. If this is the same man, he's evidently for hire. Has he had any success?"

"I can answer that." Chase spoke for the first time. "We've reason to believe our people have paid little attention to him. But he has attracted a gang of bullies always ready for a brawl, worthless louts like Sanders and Logan. They've ridden with him out to Hume's mill. Those two have been showing more money than they'd be likely to have. If they're getting it from O'Shaughnessy, we've reason enough to worry."

Adam drove his fist into his palm. Hume again! There could be no doubt that it was his money that went to O'Shaughnessy and his hirelings. Iredell and Johnston would know nothing of this. The man must be stopped. He turned to Frazier. "Chase is quite right. We can't put much reliance in our Sheriff. But he might accept help. Can you find men who——"

"Beg pardon, sir." Frazier smiled grimly. "We ain't been asleep. We've twenty-eight stout men who served under you in the war. We've got mounts for all of them. Now, I can't say exactly what sort of mischief O'Shaughnessy's up to or where he plans to start it. But, by God, he'll find his hands full, him and Sanders and Logan and all the rest of 'em!"

Adam nodded gravely. "Good work, Frazier. It's likely he'll try to interfere with the vote at some of the county polling places where we'll be strongest." He felt his anger rising. He wanted to smash Hume's plan, to smash Hume. He paused until he had full control of his voice. Even a hint to these men of his feeling might be enough to make certain a fight to-morrow.

"If the Sheriff's men can't cope with trouble," he said quietly, "and a free, fair election is threatened, then we may have to act. Otherwise O'Shaughnessy's men must be left to do as they will. And we will act only if the Sheriff asks for our help. I want that understood." He laughed as he saw the disappointed expression on Frazier's face. "Don't worry, Mel. It was wise to organize and mount the men. We may yet have use for your militia."

Chase slapped Frazier on the shoulder. "Mel has never been able to separate politics from head-cracking. Ballots and barrel staves just go together for him. We've taken other precautions, Mr. Rutledge. To keep things peaceful to-night we've arranged entertainments in the county, singing and dancing. And it may be that we'll find opportunity to discuss the election with the crowds."

"Very good." Adam had come to have a real respect for the printer's talent and ingenuity. "Perhaps if you offered refreshment you'd be surer of holding the people."

Chase laughed. "The Feds thought of that immediately when they learned our plans. They've got more money to spend, and we could see our people leaving for the more ample Federalist food and drink. By luck I discovered an old law that stopped that."

"Law?" Adam asked. "What law is there against entertainment?"

"This, sir." Chase pulled a piece of paper from his pocket and read: " 'If any person or persons shall treat with meat or drink on the day of an election, or any day previous thereto, with the intent to influence the election, every person so offending shall forfeit and pay the sum of two hundred dollars.' "

"The Sheriff was a bit reluctant to enforce this," Marcy said, "until Chase read the last clause to him. I've never seen a man change his mind so fast."

Adam enjoyed the men's obvious satisfaction in their little victory over the Federalists. "What clause is that, Chase?"

The printer raised his paper and read with mock solemnity: " 'The Sheriff shall publish this law by advertising and reading under penalty of forty dollars fine.' That overcame his hesitancy promptly. As you ride to the village to-morrow you'll see notices posted everywhere." He looked from Marcy to Frazier with a broad smile on his face. "Fact is, I know exactly how many there are. Since I had reminded him of his neglect of duty, the Sheriff very wisely saw no objection to hiring me as the printer of the notices."

Adam joined in the laughter. "I'm sure the Sheriff could find no fault in my offering all of you a stirrup cup. Ebon has some hob and nob ready. We'll drink to success to-morrow."

"It's success you'll have," Frazier rumbled. "Good fortune sits beside you, I'm thinkin'."

"Beside *us*, Mel. It's our fortune together, good or bad. Yours and Marcy's and Chase's—the fortune of all men who have stood together in defence of their rights." Adam broke off as Ebon came in with the hot rum. When each man had a cup he continued: "Ours is an ancient brotherhood. You have served it honourably and well like so many Carolinians before you. I'm very proud of you—and grateful to you." He raised his cup. "Hob and nob, friends, and success!"

The men drank, and there was a moment's silence. Frazier cleared his throat noisily. "I'm for the village and my bed. Chase, you'll be comin' too?"

Marcy saw the men out and went to his quarters. Adam remained in the office. The fire had died to a few coals. The election seemed very distant. To-night he wanted a brief interval of peace, a respite from contests and quarrels. But there was no peace. The emptiness and loneliness of the house were oppressive. He picked up a book and forced himself to read until he was tired enough to sleep.

The morning was fair, with a warm gentle breeze stirring the branches of the trees. Adam and Marcy rode directly to the Courthouse when they arrived in Edenton. The village polling place where Adam would vote had been set up on the Green. Though the election would not open for nearly an hour, a crowd was waiting.

Adam found the Sheriff at the entrance to the Courthouse. Briefly and without mentioning Hume he explained his reasons for believing that there might be an organized attempt to disrupt the election. The Sheriff was more than glad to accept an offer of help. It was agreed that the men Frazier had recruited would remain at the smithy, to be dispatched by the Sheriff to any area where trouble threatened.

Frazier was waiting at the smithy when Adam and Marcy rode up. He was smiling broadly. "Good mornin', Mr. Rutledge. You come late. The lads who'll do our watchin' at the county polls have been gone more'n two hours. Every group's got a cart or gig to fetch people who'll vote our way. And out in back at the barn are the men who'll see to it we're not disturbed in our business. They're all your men, sir, and every one of 'em has fought with you before."

"We'll hope there'll be no fighting today," Adam said. "Come along, I've got a word to say to them."

He couldn't restrain a smile as he approached the barn. This looked like a bivouac of cavalry. Men were sprawled in the grass resting, horses were tethered in the orchard that adjoined Frazier's ground. He stopped and called out sharply, "You weren't so sleepy when I commanded you. I'm sorry to see you so far gone in sloth."

The men sprang to their feet and crowded around Adam. He went rapidly through the group, shaking each man's hand and calling him by name. Then he signalled for attention.

"Mel Frazier has told you that there may be trouble." He spoke slowly, keeping his voice calm. "It is the Sheriff's business to keep order. You will act under his orders. Remain here unless he sends for your help." Adam was aware of a murmur of protest. He raised his hand for silence. "I know your loyalty, and I'm deeply grateful. But we weaken our cause if we go outside the law. You understand that we can't have armed Antifederalists riding the streets. Fuller, you'll be in charge here. I'll rely on you to see that the order is obeyed."

Adam's old sergeant stepped forward. "Aye. I take your meaning, sir, and the lads here'll trust you, same as they always have. We'll bide here and be ready." Fuller turned smartly and began to talk to his men. Adam walked with Marcy and Frazier back to the horses.

The farrier was reluctant to miss the excitement of the voting on the Green. "It's a rare fine thing to watch the crowd," he said, "and pass a bit of talk with this 'un and that. But I reckon I'm bound to stay here. The men at the polls want me on hand. I'll get to cast my vote this afternoon. You'll be goin' now, I reckon."

Adam swung into the saddle. "Yes, Mel. This is a new kind of election, I think. Never before have the freemen of Chowan taken so deep an interest. It means something to me to see the voting begin."

The Sheriff was standing in the Courthouse door when Adam and Marcy got to the polling place. His voice thundered out over the crowd on the Green. "Oyez, oyez. Freemen of Chowan, a separate election duly advertised according to law twenty days in advance of this date is now open."

Adam and Marcy tethered their horses at the edge of the Green and walked toward the polling place. The line had already begun to move past the ballot box, with each man taking his ticket from an election official, marking it quickly and handing it back to be put into the box.

As Marcy took his place in line Adam felt a special satisfaction. His overseer, once an indentured servant, was now a freeman of the county who had paid public taxes and was qualified to vote.

The line moved slowly forward. Adam had turned to Marcy to remark on the orderly progress when there was a sudden jostling and pushing directly ahead. One of the men Mel Frazier had sent to work at the polls had identified a voter as a Tyrrell County man. The poll watchers, Federalist and Antifederalist, held the man at the ballot box while the Sheriff advanced across the Green at a ponderous trot to take him into custody.

Four men behind Adam slipped out of the line and ran toward Horni-blow's. Men and boys gave chase immediately, and there were shouts of "Tyrrell County men!" . . . "Head them off!" Quickly Chowan men spread across the Green to cut off escape. The Tyrrell fugitives fought desperately to win through. A huge farmer grabbed one and hurled him against a dodging companion. Both sprawled on the ground, showing no inclination to resist the farmer who stood over them with massive fists clenched. The others charged into a wall of defenders and lost their footing under a shower of blows.

Adam watched the Sheriff and an angry crowd lead the Tyrrell men off to jail. As order was restored and the line began to move again he said to Marcy, "Another of Hume's tricks, I'd guess. He must be really afraid of the strength we've mustered to try something so foolish. Surely he would know——"

He broke off. Marcy was staring steadily over Adam's shoulder, obviously unaware that he was speaking. "Look!" Marcy took Adam's arm and turned him about. "There, at the entrance to Horniblow's. That heavy, bearded man. That's Logan, the one who's been riding out to Hume's with O'Shaughnessy."

Adam followed as Marcy pointed. The man he had identified as Logan was engaged in a violent argument with a short, shabbily dressed fellow who cradled a large brownstone jug in his arms. Suddenly Logan slapped him across the face and shoved him against the wall of the inn. The man collapsed to the ground almost gently, still holding his jug. Logan hesitated, as if undecided whether to punish him further.

Adam broke out of line and raced toward Horniblow's. Marcy pounded along beside him. Adam gave orders as he ran. "Grab Logan. . . . Sheriff can hold him for this . . . maybe find out what O'Shaughnessy plans. . . ."

A crowd was collecting around Logan and the fallen man. Logan turned to face them and saw Adam and Marcy bearing down on him. He seemed to recognize his danger instantly. He broke quickly through the crowd to his horse, sprang into the saddle, wheeled and drove the mount into a gallop down King Street.

Adam pulled Marcy back as he started to swerve toward the place where their horses were tethered. "Talk to this man first. He may know something to help us."

The man Logan had struck lay as he had fallen, making no attempt to rise. As Adam and Marcy reached him he rubbed the side of his face absently, carefully uncorked his jug and drank deeply. Then he looked up and shook his head with a ludicrously mournful air.

"Logan's a cruel hard man," he mumbled. "Done his work afore . . . only wanted little money." His expression changed to a happy smile. "Someone'll bash 'im . . . that's it . . . he'll go ridin' out 'ginia Road . . . big fight an' he'll be bashed. . . ."

Adam gestured to Marcy, and they hauled the man to his feet. He pawed at them, trying clumsily to free himself. Adam showed him a handful of coins. "Who's going to fight Logan on the Virginia Road? Tell me that and you can put these in your pocket."

The drunken man bent and peered solemnly at the money. "Why, Antis, I reckon. . . . Antis'll bash Logan." The question seemed to amuse him. He chuckled and wagged his finger at Adam as if in reproach. "You don't know about fight. . . . I know about fight. . . . Logan 'n' Sanders . . . got thirty maybe fifty men . . . take votin' box out on 'ginia Road for man named . . ." He frowned and rubbed his forehead. "Man named . . . O'Shaughnessy. Now give me money."

Adam slipped the coins into the man's pocket and lowered him gently to the ground. Marcy was already pushing his way through the crowd. Adam forced his way to him. "It's what we expected. They plan to seize the ballot box at the polling place just beyond the Red Lion. Almost all the votes there will be ours. See the Sheriff and get authority to take the men waiting at Frazier's. I'm going after Logan."

Marcy broke for the Courthouse. Adam ran for Diablo, giving thanks that he had had the fastest horse in his stables saddled this morning. Once in the saddle, he threaded his way carefully through the crowd on King Street and along the first few hundred yards of Broad Street. Beyond Eden Alley the crowd thinned, and he let Diablo out, leaning low against his neck and feeling the tremendous power of his smooth stride. Logan had perhaps a three-minute start. If he could catch him, he might delay the raid on the ballot box and give the Sheriff and the men riding from Frazier's time to arrive.

Less than half a mile outside the village he brought Logan into sight. He was riding at a trot, obviously sure that there would be no pursuit. Not until Adam was within a hundred yards of him did he hear the pounding of Diablo's hoofs and look back. Adam could see his expression of alarm as he began to whip his horse into more speed.

It was too late. Diablo gained with every stride. As they swept into a curve of the road Adam had almost pulled abreast. Logan shouted an obscenity and yanked a pistol from his belt. He levelled his arm to fire. Adam suddenly swerved Diablo against Logan's horse. Both mounts stumbled. Logan's arm flew upward, and his pistol discharged harmlessly. Instantly Logan grasped the barrel and struck viciously at Adam's head. Adam ducked under the blow. He leaned far out of the saddle, reached down and caught Logan's ankle with his right hand. Bracing in his stirrups, he heaved upward. Logan gave a hoarse cry as he was unseated. His riderless horse spurted ahead of Diablo, and Adam glanced back to see Logan rolling in the dust of the road.

The Red Lion looked deserted as Adam drove Diablo by. The horse was lathered now and the action of his great, pounding stride less smooth. Adam dared not slacken the pace. Another half-mile . . .

A crowd of women and children huddled in the front yard of the small cottage opposite the polling place. They drew back as he reined in and jumped from the saddle. A small boy called out, "There's going to be trouble, mister. They're getting ready to fight over there."

Adam looked toward the polling place. A small group of men stood in a circle around the ballot box with Chase standing just outside the ring. Ranged along a fence some twenty yards distant from Chase was a line of perhaps thirty men, most of them dirty and ill-clad.

Chase came forward to meet Adam as he walked rapidly toward the ballot box. The printer's face was set and tense. "It's bad, Mr. Rutledge. O'Shaughnessy arrived about twenty minutes ago, and his men have been coming in a few at a time since. Appears you were right about them trying to stop the voting. That's O'Shaughnessy sitting on the fence. Sanders is standing beside him. I haven't seen Logan."

"Logan won't be here. I was able to change his mind about coming. But help is on the way." Briefly Adam reviewed for Chase what had happened in Edenton and on the road.

The printer shook his head. "I don't think O'Shaughnessy will wait much longer. His men are in an ugly mood. They've got guns, and they'll use them. One of our lads tried to get to the horses to ride for help. Sanders shot at him."

Adam studied the men along the fence. "Perhaps they're not so eager as you think, Chase. They're a shiftless, cowardly lot or they wouldn't be waiting for more men. I think I can delay them long enough." He started walking toward O'Shaughnessy.

Chase followed, protesting. "They'll kill you, Mr. Rutledge. We've got a chance if we stay in a circle around the box. You——" Seeing that he was accomplishing nothing, the printer broke off and fell in step beside Adam.

Adam stopped when he was about ten feet from O'Shaughnessy. The man was huge—a thick neck, enormously broad shoulders. He dropped to the ground with a grace surprising in a man so large and took a step toward Adam and Chase.

He turned to the men behind him and jerked his thumb at Adam. "Look who's come to our party. Adam Rutledge. An aristocrat with us common people. Ain't you afraid your fine clothes'll get soiled?"

Adam ignored O'Shaughnessy. He took a few steps toward the fence and then walked slowly along in front of the men. In a quiet, almost casual way he began talking to them, singling out by name the few he knew.

"We know what you're going to try. I wonder if you know what it will cost. Some of you are going to be hurt—those men over there will fight. All of you will go to gaol. Morris, you've got a large family. Who'll feed them while you're away? O'Shaughnessy can tell you about gaol, Russell. He was in the Hillsborough gaol for starting a riot. What has he given you, Andrews—a few coins? Some talk about how dangerous Antifederalists are? Perhaps you ought to know that he posed as an Antifederalist in Hillsborough. Are you really going to let him use you?"

Adam could tell that his words were having an effect. The men glanced at one another. There were whispers and a restless stir along the line. O'Shaughnessy had been unconcerned and confident when Adam started. Now he saw that he must act. He moved quickly to the end of the line and blocked Adam's way.

"Morris! Andrews!" he barked. "Suppose you show your friend he ain't scarin' you. Shut his mouth with a fist."

The men started uncertainly toward Adam. He spoke to them over his shoulder. "Don't be fools. I'll show you what kind of a leader you have." With a single fluid motion Adam stepped toward O'Shaughnessy and lashed out with his left hand. The blow smashed into the huge Irishman's face and staggered him, but he did not go down. Adam moved forward smoothly, set himself and drove his right hand to O'Shaughnessy's jaw. The blow spun the big man almost completely around and stretched him at Adam's feet.

But O'Shaughnessy was not through. He rose to one knee and wiped a hand across his bloody face. Slowly he drew a hunting knife from a sheath at his waist and crouched, poised for a rush.

Adam balanced on his toes, moving in a circle away from the long blade that flashed in O'Shaughnessy's right hand. The Irishman turned tightly in his crouch, waving the knife slowly up and down. Out of the corner of his eye Adam could see that Chase and Sanders were fighting. He was dimly aware that the men at the ballot box were running toward him and that some of O'Shaughnessy's men were moving out to meet them.

With a roar O'Shaughnessy charged. Adam side-stepped, and the knife thrust missed. Desperately he grabbed for O'Shaughnessy's wrist, but the huge Irishman was incredibly fast. He whirled off, crouched and moved in.

Adam danced away, O'Shaughnessy followed, a terrible smile on his face. Suddenly, sickeningly, Adam knew the reason for the smile. The fence was at his back. O'Shaughnessy leaped, and the knife flashed. Adam blocked the thrust, but not in time. The blade slashed into his shoulder. There was a moment when he felt nothing—and then everything was pain. He could see O'Shaughnessy dimly against a background of crimson, coming forward for one more thrust.

It did not come. Adam held to the fence and fought to straighten himself. He could no longer see O'Shaughnessy. As from a great distance he heard men shouting and the pounding of horses' hoofs. Then Marcy's voice was in his ears, and Marcy's arms were holding him up.

And then oblivion.

Returning

29 ADAM opened his eyes to a glare of light. He was in a bed in a large room, and it was all somehow familiar. Pain leaped in his shoulder, and he shut his eyes again. The darkness was better than the light. Yet now in the darkness he could see a knife flash and O'Shaughnessy coming forward. Then O'Shaughnessy was not there—only the blackness—and a long, rushing sound filled his ears.

A hand took his wrist, and the sound became a voice. "His pulse is better." And another voice. "The wound has stopped bleeding." Familiar voices. Whose voices? He forced his eyes open again.

The room swam dizzily and then was still. Dr. Armitage was bending over him. Angus Moray was standing at the foot of the bed. Adam struggled to sit up, but Armitage held him firmly. "It's Cupola House, Adam. You're in Cupola House. You've been unconscious more than twelve hours. You're going to be fine, but you must not move."

Adam tried to speak. His voice cracked, and for the first time he was aware of an overpowering thirst. Moray understood instantly. He came forward with a glass of water and held Adam's head up while he drank.

Now he could speak. "The men at the ballot box. Any hurt?"

Dr. Armitage smiled. "A few lumps and bruises. No one is seriously injured. Marcy is waiting here. He can tell you about the election to-night. Rest now, talk later. And don't move about. If you stir, your wound will bleed."

Angus Moray followed Dr. Armitage to the door. "Please do as he says. It was a near thing. Your shoulder and chest muscles are badly lacerated. Marcy saved your life by binding your shirt around your chest tight enough to stop the flow of blood. And he found a way to rig a litter between two horses to bring you here. Another few inches to the right and that knife would have struck your heart."

Adam had recovered enough to smile as Angus started to close the door. "It's a very restful thought you leave me with, Doctor Moray."

When he shut his eyes again it was without the sensation of plunging into an abyss. Sleep came quickly in spite of the constant throbbing pain in his shoulder. He woke several hours later with enough appetite to take a bowl of broth gratefully. By the time Marcy came in he was ready to talk, and to have some questions answered.

Marcy sat tensely on the edge of his chair. His expression was so grave that Adam laughed. "It's all right. It's all right, thanks to your action. Dr. Moray tells me I owe you my life. I add this to many other debts."

Marcy shook his head. "It wasn't me, sir. It was all the men. God, how they rode out that Virginia Road! It was Fuller who got O'Shaughnessy. I was riding beside him. You'd just fallen against the fence when O'Shaughnessy saw us coming at him. He jumped the fence and ran like a rabbit. Fuller took his horse over right after him and rode him down in the field. . . ."

Adam waited for Marcy to go on, to answer the question he was curiously reluctant to ask. But Marcy sat staring straight ahead as if seeing it all again, and Adam said quietly, "Dead?"

"No, not dead." Marcy's jaw was set. "He's not even hurt badly. But he's in gaol, and he'll stay there this time." His expression brightened. "But I'm not giving you the news. The returns have been counted, and we've won. You and Mr. Hamilton are delegates to Fayetteville. In a Federalist county you got almost as many votes as Governor Johnston and Charles Johnson. That is a victory!"

"Yes, Marcy, a victory." Adam closed his eyes. A victory which would mean more strife, more bitter debate, a further separation from friends. And Mary. . . . He turned his head toward Marcy. "Mrs. Rutledge is not to know about this stabbing."

Marcy frowned and looked at the floor. "I'm afraid I wrote her last night. The letter was on the stage today." When Adam said nothing he went on with a rush. "She *should* know, sir. It wouldn't be right to keep her——" He broke off and shrugged hopelessly.

Adam's momentary irritation passed. As usual Marcy had done the just and kind thing. "Forgive me, Marcy," he said. "I'm not angry. You could have done nothing else. The wound makes me an unreasonable man."

Marcy stood up, smiling again. "The wound makes it necessary for you to rest. I'll be going back to Queen's Gift now that I know you're all right. There was no sleep on the quarters line last night. Ebon and Chaney and all the rest kept their own vigil. They'll celebrate the news I have for them. Rest well, sir. I'll be back to-morrow."

It was two weeks before Adam left Cupola House to go home. For the first few days of his time in bed Dr. Armitage permitted no visitors except Marcy. Late one afternoon toward the end of the first week he announced that James Iredell was waiting.

Adam, who was being allowed to sit up for the first time, remarked on the doctor's broad smile. "You're looking very pleased with yourself, Doctor. I'll be delighted to see Jemmy too, but——"

"We all have reason to look pleased, Adam." Iredell came through the door and took a chair by Adam's bed. "You have been restored to us when we thought we might lose you, and—" he glanced at Dr. Armitage—"there has been another kind of restoration."

"Yes?" Adam looked from Jemmy to Dr. Armitage. "May I know of this restoration?"

"Indeed you may." Iredell leaned forward, suddenly more serious. "That exhibition of hate and terror out on the Virginia Road shocked your friends deeply." Adam started to speak, and Iredell held up his hand. "I know. Of course they had no part in it. But I think each of them feels a little guilt because each had shared a little in the kind of intolerance which in unprincipled men leads to violence. What I have to tell you is that you will find your friends are once more just that—friends."

Adam said nothing for a moment, and then only, "Thank you, Jemmy." He felt relieved of a great weight, but the best gift was that Mary would no longer suffer separation from the life she loved. For this he was profoundly thankful.

Dr. Armitage had gone to the foot of Adam's bed. The smile had left his face, and when he spoke his voice had an unfamiliar hard quality. "One other thing of which Jemmy doesn't know. There seems to be no legal proof, but few of us doubt that Hume was responsible for bringing O'Shaughnessy to Edenton. Hume seems to have been persuaded that he has no future here. I don't think he's in any real danger—I almost wish he were—but the man is terrified. He's selling his mill and leaving this part of the country." The doctor paused, his face set grimly. "It's an insufficient punishment, I think. But at least we're rid of him. Jemmy, you may stay for ten minutes more. That's all, and that's an order."

Adam hardly heard the doctor's injunction. He saw again the blazing pontoon and Herk's helpless figure. Hume's work, too? He was as certain of it as of the pain in his shoulder.

When the doctor had left Iredell brought Adam up to date about the results of the elections. Many of the men who had dominated the Hillsborough convention had been returned as delegates to Fayetteville. Davie and Steele would again represent the Federalists. Spencer, Reverend David Caldwell and Bloodworth were once more in the Anti ranks.

Jemmy paused in his discussion and smiled. "You know, Adam, it's been suggested that Wilie Jones refused to be a delegate to Fayetteville because he was ashamed of his followers at Hillsborough."

Adam laughed. "Entirely a Federalist interpretation, I'm sure. Is Jones's reason for not attending also yours, Jemmy?"

Iredell assumed an air of mock gravity. "I haven't considered my decision in that light. I will give the question my most earnest thought." His face grew serious. "It was a difficult decision to make. Because the convention will meet at the same time and place as the Assembly the pressure on me was great to serve in both bodies. I could not in conscience take the time from my other duties. But Hugh Williamson will represent Tyrrell. He will more than replace me."

"Much as I respect and admire Williamson, I doubt that." Adam selected his words carefully. "It means much to me not to have to stand against you on the floor, Jemmy. That made what I took to be my duty doubly burdensome."

Iredell rose. "I understand completely. The ten minutes Dr. Armitage allowed me have flown. Hannah and I will be coming to Queen's Gift to give you what solace we can in Mary's absence."

When he first returned to Queen's Gift Adam was able to spend only a few hours each day in his office. But his strength returned rapidly, and by the end of the second week at home he was riding out over the fields with Marcy to supervise the work of a new season.

He was grateful for the fatigue that hard work brought, for with it came surcease from his longing for Mary. There had been two letters since his return—delightful letters full of the diversion she found in a new scene. She described a ball, some teas, a party at the theatre to see Royall Tyler's play, *The Contrast*. There were paragraphs of sharp comment about Lady Anne, set down with all Mary's honesty and impatience with pretence. There were pages written out of an affectionate concern for Sylvia Hay's unhappy separation from Angus. There was everything in the letters but what he wanted most to find—the lost words of faith and understanding without which their love could not survive.

Within a few days of Mary's letter he had sent reassurance about his injury. He had asked her not to cut short her visit, but as loneliness and longing sharpened his hope grew that she would not obey.

He rehearsed the ways in which she would return. He would see her carriage coming up the avenue and race to meet it. Or he would see her standing on the upper gallery as he rode home across the fields. And in all this reunion he planned there was time for him to find the sure and magic words that would restore all that had been lacking.

When reunion came there was no time for words—and no need for them. He looked up as he came through the door one evening and she was standing in the hall. He dropped his hat and riding-crop on a chair. She was in his arms. His cheek was pressed against hers, and he was saying her name over and over.

Mary was crying and laughing at the same time. For a moment he heard only her voice, and then the words were plain and dear. ". . . your foolish letter. Oh, Adam, my dearest, did you think I wouldn't come?"

There was a clatter on the stairs behind them. Adam stood with his arm around Mary, watching Sarah Poor descend briskly. Ebon and Herk followed, loaded down with boxes and bundles.

Miss Sarah gestured to Ebon and Herk. "Just put those things outside. Marcy is bringing around the gig." She adjusted her hat with quick authority and looked sharply at Adam. "Well, Mr. Rutledge, she's back. She wanted to come five minutes after she got Marcy's letter. She had to wait five days until Dr. Williamson could get us passage on a packet to Norfolk. There was no living with her after your letter arrived. She *knew* you were dying."

Mary laughed. "Miss Sarah is leaving us, dear. She's been a perfect nurse and companion, but there are others who need her services more than I pretend to now. She says that any one who can survive the trip we had doesn't need a nurse and doesn't deserve a companion."

"A disagreeable and hideous passage of fourteen days." Miss Sarah shuddered. "And Dr. Williamson thought it might be easier than the overland trip! I can't think where he gets his reputation for wisdom."

Adam took her hands and, before she could avoid him, kissed her on the forehead. "Good-bye, Miss Sarah, and God bless you! Come back to Queen's Gift."

Miss Sarah struggled furiously with her hat. "Let me give you a bit of advice, Mr. Rutledge. Your wife fares badly away from you. See to it that she's not long absent again." She glanced at the open door, walked quickly to Mary and pressed her hand, then marched out to the waiting gig without a backward glance.

Adam put his arm around Mary's waist, and they walked slowly into the drawing-room to the little yellow sofa. She came again to his arms with unreserved warmth, and he held her close. When she looked up at him there were tears in her eyes. She put her hand gently against his shoulder. "Was it here?" He nodded, and she took his face between her hands. "And I might have lost you. I might have lost you while we were apart. How could I have doubted that our love was stronger than any difference between us?"

Adam began to speak, and she put her hand gently against his mouth. "Not now, dearest." She smiled. "It is I who have the speech to make. I'm going to dress for supper in my most beautiful gown. And when I have all your admiration I shall show you how I have gained in wisdom, too."

He was waiting for her as she came slowly down the stairs, looking more lovely than he had ever seen her before. The blue of her favourite gown made even more brilliant the blue of her eyes. Her face was luminous as she took his arm. She kept her head tight against his shoulder as they went into the dining-room.

At supper she talked gaily of the preparations for Washington's inauguration which had been going forward when she left New York. Lavish ceremonies had been planned along the President's route to the capital. The elegant salons of the city buzzed with excitement at the prospect of the brilliant social seasons to come.

Adam listened happily, rejoicing in Mary's high spirits. He was pleased when she described with real understanding and a lively interest the debate she had heard in the House of Representatives. Madison had been defending his proposed tax on imports against Fisher Ames's eloquent attack.

Then she was quiet, and Adam waited, knowing that she had come to the moment she had planned. When she spoke again there was a quiet urgency in her voice. "Adam, I told you I had gained in wisdom while I was in New York. I'm not sure I can make you see how. Perhaps only another woman in love would understand." She smiled at him. "New wisdom about my own heart began with the debate I told you about. Does that sound absurd?"

Adam met her smile. He moved quickly to a chair beside her and took her hand in his. "You say what you have to say, beloved. I'll understand."

She kept her eyes on his face as she talked. "There was a world I had never entered before. Each of these men spoke for thousands of other men who believe as he does. I had a sense of the burden each carries, the responsibility of defending conviction. And then I knew—forgive me, dearest, that I did not know before—that you carried a burden, too. I was proud of you, and deeply ashamed of myself for making your way harder."

"Mary! Mary!" Adam bent to kiss her, but she stopped him with a gentle motion of her hand.

"Let me go on, dearest. I was ashamed because I had been selfish. All you believed seemed to lead away from Queen's Gift. I was afraid. I denied you understanding because I was afraid." Her eyes filled with tears and her lips trembled. She sat very straight. "I'm still afraid, Adam. I do not want to lose Queen's Gift. But I know a greater fear now—the fear of losing you because I have not the courage to stand beside you. I want to be your wife again. Oh, Adam, Adam . . ."

He swept her into his arms and kissed her mouth. "Dearest, dearest, no more fear. Trust our love to guide us. Leave the future to itself. We have to-night, and we know for all the years ahead that we can never be apart. Here or in another place that is enough, and nothing else can matter."

In the small drawing-room of Dr. Williamson's house in New York, Sylvia Hay sat at a desk, preparing to write a letter, the happiest and most important letter she had ever written. And it was her own letter this time, she thought with satisfaction. Never again would she have to busy herself with Lady Anne Stuart's frivolous and insincere little notes.

She took up the pen and wrote, "My dearest Angus . . ." She paused. There was so much to tell, the fantastic happenings of the last few days. Or should she try to cover all that had happened since she had bidden him farewell at Queen's Gift? Should she describe her long, unhappy journey from Carolina, confined in a coach with the quick-tempered Lady Anne? And tell of her Ladyship's impatience, her constant demand for more speed, her abrupt decision to cancel the proposed stay in Philadelphia because of her eagerness to reach New York?

Sylvia thought back to the day they had arrived at their destination, a pretentious red-brick house in Battery Place which Mr. Sayre had engaged in Baron von Pollnitz's name. Dawkins was waiting to receive them, together with a complete staff of servants hired by the thoughtful Mr. Sayre. As Lady Anne and Sylvia entered the house a man emerged from one of the rooms opening off the entrance hall. He was tall and elegantly dressed in blue coat, buckskin knee-breeches, white stockings and silver-buckled shoes. His face was strikingly handsome—almost too formally handsome, Sylvia thought.

Lady Anne rushed toward him, crying, "Stephen, Stephen, it's been so long! I thought I should never get here!"

The gentleman evaded her embrace and adroitly manoeuvred her into the room he had just left. He followed her inside and closed the door, leaving Sylvia standing, open-mouthed, in the hall.

Dawkins, standing just behind her, said insinuatingly, "He's staying right here in the house, miss."

"Who is staying here?" Sylvia asked, turning to look at her.

"Why, him—Mr. Sayre, her Ladyship's man of business. He rented this house for her and moved in himself!" Dawkins' expression was almost a leer.

"A very sensible arrangement," Sylvia said coldly. "Doubtless they have much to discuss."

"Oh, doubtless, miss!" said Dawkins sarcastically. "I just hope the Baron comes soon to see what's going on." Apparently feeling she had gone far enough, she added meekly, "I'll show you to your room now, if you like. I think you'll find it comfortable."

Sylvia followed the maid upstairs, feeling that she was going to find her employer's new ménage even more distasteful than Horniblow's had been.

In the following weeks Stephen Sayre made persistent efforts to gain Sylvia's friendship. He talked to her of common acquaintances in England, showed an exaggerated interest in her reactions to New York and frequently invited her to accompany Lady Anne and him to theatres and musical entertainments. Lady Anne watched with complacence his attentions to Sylvia, who wondered if they had agreed between them that her approval was somehow important to them.

Sylvia, however, found Sayre's charm too calculated to be effective, and his good looks were spoiled for her by the fact that his eyes were set too close together. She answered his attempts at intimacy with a studied politeness that obviously baffled and irritated him.

The letters she was occasionally asked to copy out for Lady Anne made her increasingly uneasy about her position in this strange household. One was a last plea to the Duke of Northumberland to pay the debts Lady Anne had incurred before her divorce from him. Another, sent shortly afterward and obviously drafted by Sayre, was addressed to Joseph and Herman Bernes, London merchants, and suggested that they carry out their plan to arrest Baron von Pollnitz, who as Lady Anne's husband was now responsible for her debts.

When Mary Rutledge arrived in New York, Sylvia called on her at Dr. Williamson's house and discussed the situation. Mary advised firmly that Sylvia must dissociate herself from Lady Anne at once. Dr. Williamson offered her the hospitality of his house, and Sylvia agreed to discuss matters with Lady Anne at the first opportunity.

That same evening she waited in the library for Lady Anne and Sayre to return from a gala party. Lady Anne at last appeared, wearing sea-green satin and her diamond ornaments, and Sylvia requested a private interview.

Lady Anne glanced at Sayre and said calmly, "It's an extraordinary time to choose for a consultation, Miss Hay. Is it really essential? At any rate you may speak freely before Mr. Sayre, who manages all my business affairs."

"As you wish, Baroness," Sylvia said. "I want your permission to leave your employ to-morrow."

"Leave my employ?" Lady Anne's voice was guarded. "You surprise me. I had not realized you found your duties too strenuous."

"On the contrary," Sylvia said, "your correspondence is not sufficient to engage my time. You can easily find some one here in New York to deal with it."

Lady Anne smiled coldly. "I admire your conscientiousness, but I prefer to judge for myself the value of your work. Your duties are light, your wages are more than adequate. Consider yourself fortunate, Miss Hay, and say no more about leaving." She rose and started toward the door. "And now good night."

"I must ask you to hear me out, Baroness," Sylvia said sharply. Lady Anne halted and turned toward her with an elaborate air of boredom. "You have mentioned wages. I should like to point out that you have paid me none for several months."

"That is the Baron's responsibility," Lady Anne said indifferently.

"The Baron paid me until his sons were taken from my charge and placed in Parson Earle's school. Since then I have been doing your work, but you've paid me nothing from the time I spent at Queen's Gift while you were visiting in Hertford. You can scarcely expect me to continue as your secretary indefinitely without compensation."

Lady Anne's boredom had vanished. "Are you suggesting that you doubt my willingness to pay my employees?" she demanded angrily.

"Forgive me, Baroness, but the letters you have given me to write indicate that you are not invariably prompt in meeting your obligations," Sylvia said blandly. Lady Anne's rages could not harm her now; to-morrow she would say good-bye to the Baroness for ever. "The number of your creditors does not encourage me to expect immediate payment."

Lady Anne flushed and took a step forward, one hand raised as if to strike Sylvia. Instantly Sayre was at her side. He caught her wrist and said quietly, "Anne, control yourself."

She whirled on him. "Keep quiet, Stephen! Am I to suffer such insolence from my own household?"

His grasp on her wrist tightened. "You will do well to remember that you are in America, where your title and your father's influence mean nothing. I would not advise striking an employee. Nor would I recommend withholding earned moneys."

"Stephen!" Lady Anne glared at him. "Are you presuming to criticize me?"

"Don't be foolish, Anne. Sit down quietly and let me reason with Miss Hay." He released her arm and came over to Sylvia. "Now then, you want to leave Lady Anne because you aren't given enough work to do and because you wish to be paid regularly. Is that right?"

Sylvia was disconcerted by his directness. "Yes," she said hesitantly.

He smiled ingratiatingly. "Well, I can easily manage to give you some of my correspondence to cope with, and I feel sure Lady Anne will authorize me to get money from the strong-box this very night and pay you what she owes you. And then your problems will be solved."

Sylvia stared at him expressionlessly. She could not like this man. "Thank you, Mr. Sayre. I shall be glad to have what is due me, but I do not wish to stay on with Lady Anne."

Sayre's smile remained unchanged, but there was no warmth in his close-set eyes. Neither he nor Lady Anne liked her, Sylvia reflected, and her secretarial tasks were of small importance. Why were they so anxious to keep her here?

"Aren't you forgetting," Sayre asked suavely, "that you have signed a contract to remain with Lady Anne until her return to England?"

"I know of no such document," Sylvia said calmly. "I contracted with Baron von Pollnitz to serve as governess to his sons, and he has relieved me of that responsibility."

Sayre dismissed her remark with a careless gesture. "You don't understand these things. The contract required you to remain with the family. You cannot break it just because you've changed your mind."

"If you will examine the document carefully, Mr. Sayre," Sylvia said evenly, "you will find that Lady Anne is nowhere mentioned. My agreement was with the Baron, and he has broken it."

Sayre's smile vanished. "So you are a legal student, Miss Hay. May I ask just where you acquired your knowledge of these technicalities?"

"My father sat on the King's Bench. His name was Dougal Hay." Sylvia saw no reason to mention that she and Mary Rutledge had solicited Dr. Williamson's advice about the matter.

"I see," Sayre said bleakly. "But have you no pity for Lady Anne—alone and friendless in a strange city, with her husband far away?" He indicated the Baroness, who adopted a pathetic expression at his words; it did not become her, Sylvia thought maliciously.

Lady Anne rose and came forward. "Yes, Miss Hay," she said effusively, "you must stay. We have had our differences, it's true, but I depend so on your companionship. You can't desert me—at least not until the Baron arrives."

So that was it, Sylvia thought grimly. Lady Anne was afraid of scandal. Or, more probably, the prudent Mr. Sayre had pointed out to her the unpleasant possibility of being divorced a second time. And the mild-mannered, trustful Baron, still bedazzled by his glittering wife, was happily shopping for a plantation in South Carolina, knowing nothing of her intrigues. Well, if Lady Anne feared scandal, Sylvia knew how to protect her from it.

"Very well," she said amiably, "I will stay until Baron von Pollnitz arrives." She noted with amusement the triumphant glance that passed between them. "I will stay," she continued, "if you will agree to two conditions."

Sayre looked at her warily. "Conditions, Miss Hay?"

"Yes, Mr. Sayre. First, I am to be paid at once the moneys Lady Anne owes me. And, second, you, sir, are to leave this house and take up your abode elsewhere."

Lady Anne turned white with rage and unleashed the most expressive words of her vocabulary. But Sayre checked her outburst. "Stop it, Anne. Miss Hay is obviously not a girl to be intimidated."

He turned to Sylvia with a grudging respect. "Your conditions are accepted. Lady Anne will comply with the first and I with the second. Tomorrow I will move out, and you can resume your duties as governess—with Lady Anne as your charge."

Mary Rutledge was distressed when she heard of Sylvia's decision, but

Sylvia held to her resolve, although the weeks preceding the Baron's arrival were not pleasant. Mr. Sayre was pointedly polite to Sylvia when he came to the house each day, but Lady Anne wore a perpetual air of suppressed indignation and spoke to Sylvia only when she had letters to be written.

Mary, when she made her hurried arrangements to return to North Carolina, sent for Sylvia and begged her to come back to Edenton or else take ship for England at once. "I hate to go away, leaving you in that woman's clutches," Mary said.

"Please don't worry," Sylvia said. "At the moment Lady Anne is more in my clutches than I in hers. And Baron von Pollnitz has been most kind to me. I feel I rather owe him a favour in return. When he reaches New York I'll put Lady Anne in his keeping. What a relief! Then I'll withdraw to Dr. Hugh's house until I can book passage to England."

But the Baron had brought with him to New York a letter for Sylvia which had been delivered to Horniblow's in Edenton, and it had driven from her head any thought of returning to England. Indeed, for a time it drove out thought of any sort and left her thrilling with unspeakable joy. Margaret Macartney wrote excitedly that she scarcely knew whether to congratulate Sylvia or condole with her over the news of Donald Hay's sudden marriage to a young French girl who had been his nurse in Switzerland. Doubtless Sylvia had had a report of the marriage, Margaret added, but did she know that Donald was determined to settle on Sylvia a comfortable income from the estate he had inherited from her father? Margaret had talked to Donald's mother and could assure Sylvia that his family were much embarrassed by his casual disregard of his long-standing betrothal and were anxious to make amends.

Half laughing, half crying, Sylvia had told herself over and over how right Angus had been in refusing to accept the chains of circumstances. Now the chains were flinders. She wished she could hug that pretty French nurse who had smashed them so neatly and completely.

She had found it difficult to make any show of regret when she bade farewell to the kindly Baron and his haughty wife. Now, happily installed in the household of Dr. Williamson, who seemed as jubilant over the news as she herself, Sylvia stared at the beginning of her momentous letter to Angus Moray. "My dearest Angus . . ." How did one embark on a letter of such joyful tidings?

At last she took up the pen and began to write words that came from her heart. "Please come to New York as quick as you can and take me home with you to Edenton. . . ."

Mary and Adam, sitting in the office on an evening late in May, heard a horseman riding up the drive to Queen's Gift. In a few moments Angus Moray burst into the room, grinning broadly and waving a letter.

"It's from Sylvia!" he said.

"And good news, from the look of you!" Adam said, clapping him on the shoulder.

Adam and Mary scanned the pages together, but soon Mary looked away and dabbed at her eyes with a handkerchief. "Oh, Angus," she said, "I'm overjoyed for both of you!" She laughed. "This is not an occasion for tears, but I cannot help it."

Adam returned the letter to Angus. "And why are you dawdling here, young man?" he demanded. "Don't you know which is the road to New York?"

"I have a place on the first stage north—Friday's," Angus said, folding the letter and putting it carefully in his pocket. "I'll probably be running alongside half the way, urging the horses on."

"You must bring Sylvia straight to Queen's Gift," Mary said decisively. "I hope she'll want to have the wedding here. Shall you be married right away?"

"She says in the letter that she must hear from Donald himself before she'll feel free to wed," Angus replied. "You know how conscientious she is! But she does not doubt Miss Macartney's information."

"She shall stay with us," Mary said, her mind busy with plans. "The yellow drawing-room is a perfect setting for Sylvia, and I know exactly how I'll decorate it for the ceremony. I even have a bolt of satin for her dress."

Adam grinned. "I don't know why women are called sentimental creatures, Moray. Notice how quickly the tears of joy give way to practical planning for the wedding."

After Angus had gone Adam and Mary strolled together on the gallery. Near the old tulip poplar they stopped and stood at the rail, staring into the shadowy gardens.

"What are you thinking of now, Mary?" Adam asked. "The menu for Sylvia's wedding feast?"

"No." She sighed. "I was thinking that Sylvia and Angus are luckier than we were. We waited so long, Adam."

Arm in arm they walked into the house.

Ratification

30 ADAM looked about him with deep satisfaction. It had been a pleasant supper—as pleasant as any he could remember—with laughter among friends, good talk and the excellent food for which Queen's Gift was celebrated in Chowan County. Mary had outdone herself to make this last evening before he left for Fayetteville a warm and happy occasion.

As Ebon placed silver bowls filled with nuts and fruit on the gleaming cloth they were a relaxed and genial group. Hannah and Jemmy Iredell were always delightful guests. Sylvia Hay and Angus Moray were amusing and charming in their studied efforts to avoid appearing very young and very much in love.

Adam turned to his right and spoke to Hannah. "If I read the signs correctly, Jemmy is about to propose a toast. He's been twirling his wine-glass and looking hopefully around the table for the past five minutes."

Iredell laughed. "You're much too sharp an observer, Adam. No man likes to have it suggested that his little habits are so well known to his friends. But you're entirely right. I propose just that." He raised his voice slightly. "Friends, if you'll indulge a veteran speechmaker for a moment . . ."

There was quiet at the table. The light shed from the crystal candelabra caught and shattered brilliantly in Jemmy's glass as he raised it. "To this company," he said, "and the warmth of this household! To our gracious Mary, with grateful remembrance for the years of our friendship! To Miss Hay—Sylvia—and Angus, with the wish of all for long happiness together! To Adam—" he looked across the table to his friend—"Godspeed to Fayetteville, thanksgiving that his task is easier and a safe return to us! And finally to Hannah and to me for having passed a November evening so cheerfully!"

Mary smiled down the table at Adam as she picked up her glass. She kept her eyes on his as they drank. Then she reached out and put her hand on Iredell's arm. "That was very graceful, Jemmy, and I'm sure all of us thank you. But you're sadly mistaken if you intended it as a signal to dismiss the ladies. Adam is leaving early, and the evening must be short. Sylvia, Hannah and I refuse to make a proper retirement to the drawing-room. It's far too enjoyable here."

"Then you've disappointed my hopes, Mary." Iredell smiled and took her hand. "I wanted to give Adam the benefit of my sound advice about how to conduct himself at Fayetteville, and to counsel Angus about the problems of married life. However, if you are all three determined . . ."

Adam withdrew his thought from the conversation. One phrase in Jemmy's toast returned—"thanksgiving that his task is easier." There was reason for profound thanks and he had made them devoutly. He recalled the events of the past six months which had led to this gratifying evening.

The days following Mary's return from New York had been among the happiest in their life together. Joy in reunion had held in abeyance all thought of the distant future. They were content in the new strength of their love and in their common concern for the affairs of Queen's Gift— affairs which had prospered in the growing and harvest of a bountiful crop. To make reunion complete, old friends returned to their hospitality, and bitterness was gone. Sylvia took up residence at Queen's Gift after Angus brought her back from New York, and Mary found a real companion and friend in the beautiful English girl.

Adam had been reluctant even to think of politics. But politics intruded. The extreme Antis were jubilant that the new Congress had failed to consider a bill of rights in their early deliberations. Adam did not share their sense of triumph. He had prayed that North Carolina's stand might give an irresistible urgency to the demand general in all the states for firm safeguards to human liberty. If no bill of rights was forthcoming from Congress, he had no choice but to take the same stand he had taken at Hillsborough. He did not shrink from the prospect—he would never surrender his convictions to expediency—but he was bitterly disappointed.

Iredell had revived his hope. One morning in June he had ridden to Queen's Gift with the news that Madison had announced to the House of Representatives that in three weeks he would present a set of amendments to the Constitution.

Anxiety and hope alternated in the weeks following. Hugh Williamson, who remained in New York as an unofficial agent for the state, kept Jemmy and Adam advised of all rumour and speculation. Among other things he reported that Iredell was being considered for a position in the Federal judiciary, a position that would require his moving out of the state unless North Carolina ratified.

Hope had grown stronger late in June when Dr. Williamson sent the text of Madison's proposed amendments. Adam and Jemmy sat in the office at Queen's Gift poring over them. They agreed that the little Virginian had once again done an extraordinary piece of work. He had taken the one hundred twenty-four amendments proposed by the various state conventions and reduced them to a few propositions.

Adam had felt exultant as he held Williamson's letter. Here indeed was the realization of his dream—a strong bill of rights which placed beyond the reach of any governmental power freedom of speech, freedom of the press, freedom of religion, the security of all property, trial by jury, and—in general—every right of the people.

But acceptance had not been sure from the outset. The news of the proposed bill of rights did not content Antifederalist extremists in North Carolina, and the August elections for the Assembly were sharply and hotly contested. Adam spoke in Chowan for John Hamilton, who stood for election as Edenton's member in the Assembly, as he was to be the borough town's delegate to the convention. Hamilton agreed with Adam that their vote in the convention must depend on the passage of the bill of rights through Congress.

By early October Adam and Jemmy had the hopeful news for which they had waited so eagerly. The Senate and House had passed a bill of rights and submitted it to the states. No important changes had been made in the amendments originally proposed by Madison. Jemmy and Adam agreed that there could be no doubt that the amendments would be speedily ratified by the states. The sentiment in all the states for a bill of rights was too strong to permit any other outcome.

Adam's own struggle had ended there. His two hopes for his state—that the rights of her people be for ever secure and that she take her place in an enduring union—were no longer separate and opposed. And it soon became apparent that most of the men for whom he had spoken felt as he did. He talked with Frazier and Chase, who reported that his supporters felt the last barrier to ratification had been removed. Letters from other counties he had visited in the spring confirmed that the new faith of the freemen of Chowan was everywhere shared.

So it was over, and to-morrow he would ride to Fayetteville with his conflict resolved. He would ride with a high heart and high hope.

Adam was aware that Mary was speaking to him. Lost in his excursion to the past, he heard only the last of what she said: " . . . scarcely hospitable of you to go dreaming away. Remember it's to-morrow you go to Fayetteville. To-night we ask that you attend us."

"I ask your pardon." Adam looked around at the amused faces of his guests. "Now what were we talking of?"

"Nothing of consequence," Angus said. "But as a physician I must make note of your tendency to reverie. Perhaps it's in consequence of your wound. You know, sir, I'm the member of this party who has some licence to dream. You're assuming my privilege."

"Don't be disturbed, Adam." Hannah Iredell looked at him with real sympathy. "It's been a rare evening, but I think we should end it now. You have a long ride to start in the morning, and you will want some time with Mary to-night."

Over Adam's protest the Iredells prepared to leave. Sylvia and Angus retired to the drawing-room while Adam and Mary saw Jemmy and Hannah out the door.

Jemmy took Adam's hand firmly. "Last March we talked about who would fill my place at Fayetteville. Who else but you, my friend? You carry now the confidence of every one in Edenton and Chowan. Bring us the word we want to hear. Good fortune, and God bless you!"

When the Iredells had driven away, Adam and Mary went out into the garden and sat down on the bench under the arbour. Though it was November, there was no chill in the air.

Mary sat close to Adam, leaning her head against his shoulder. "Everything is perfect to-night, even the weather. But Chaney doesn't like this. She says it's too warm, and she predicts dread things."

"I will consider nothing dread to-night." He put his hand under Mary's chin and turned her face up to his. "I haven't thanked you, beloved. You understand the special nature of this leave-taking. You made me very happy."

Mary responded to Adam's kiss and then put her head against his chest. She was silent for a moment. "And will there be a final leave-taking from Queen's Gift, Adam?"

He pressed her tight, and all the faith he felt in his words was in his voice. "Not unless you wish it, my dear. Next spring I want to show you our Illinois country. I shall pray that you understand the magnificent promise I find there. But there will be no good-bye to Queen's Gift if you do not wish to say it. There will be no way we do not travel together. Trust our love to find the way."

It was enough. She said nothing, but he knew his faith was shared.

The days passed slowly for Mary until a letter arrived from Adam. Success seemed sure for all he believed in and had fought for. But she could not rid herself of concern—and she thought she had never been more lonely. She was in the office working on household accounts when Marcy knocked and entered, holding the letter proudly aloft. She took it eagerly. The seals seemed almost deliberately defiant, and then at last it was open and she was reading.

Fayetteville, 18th November '89

My beloved wife,

I shall set down first what I know you most want to hear. There can be no doubt now—North Carolina will ratify the Constitution!

Hugh Williamson made the motion to-day, and it has been referred to the committee of the whole. He confidently believes—and I share his conviction— that the entire action of the committee will take no more than a week.

Spencer, Lenoir and Person continue Antifederalist, and their influence will command the support of some delegations. But the temper of the convention is clear. The guarantees we wanted have been pledged. So now we will become part of the union.

Edenton men play a prominent function here. Governor Johnston has again been chosen president of the convention. Charles Johnson is vice-president and has thus far presided because of Johnston's illness.

Hugh Williamson has asked me to speak in support of his motion. I shall do so happily, and when the roll-call comes I shall shout my "aye" in a voice you will surely hear at Queen's Gift.

Do I need to say that I will leave here within minutes after the convention has adjourned? Until then, my Mary,

All my love,
ADAM

Mary called Marcy and sent him to Iredell, but with orders that he wait and bring the letter back with him. During the next few days she read it again and again, and with each reading she smiled to think how puzzled Adam would be at her devotion to what he would regard as a hurried note.

He returned just at dusk a week after the letter had come. She was sitting in the drawing-room sewing when Chaney rushed in. "Mr. Adam comin', Miss Mary! He comin'. Ebon say Herk and he jes' turn in."

She dropped her work and ran toward the hall. Adam met her at the door, his arms outspread. He was smiling. "It's over, Mary, North Carolina is one of the United States! We have ratified, but we have done so only after Congress took account of the demands we made. Both sides won!"

Mary kept her head tight against Adam's shoulder. "I understand, dearest, I understand."

"Think what it means, Mary! The amendments will safeguard the rights of all our people from the highest to the least. In the days to come it will be the everlasting glory of North Carolina that she would not ratify the Constitution until she was assured that the freedom of all her people would be protected. Mary, I shall always be proud that I was one of the men who stood for a declaration of rights." He held her away from him and looked down at her. "Tears now? This is a time for celebration. Have Chaney fix us supper while I change. And hurry, Mary. I'm certain no one else has beaten me to Edenton, and I want to carry the news to Jemmy to-night."

Mary had no clear memory of the supper and the carriage ride to the Iredells'. She knew only that she was supremely happy and that Adam was home, content and confident of the future.

But she would never forget how James Iredell received the news. He walked about the room, his hands clenched, finding it impossible to keep back tears of happiness.

Hannah put her arms around him and led him to a chair. "My dear, it is your victory. I thank God for it."

Adam found it difficult to speak. He walked to Jemmy's chair. "Charles Johnson asked that I put this letter in your hands. I know what he wrote, Jemmy. Please read it aloud for Mary and Hannah."

Jemmy took the letter and broke the seals with trembling hands. He glanced rapidly over the text and then read quickly and almost without expression.

"Fayetteville, 23rd November '89

"My dear Iredell,

"Permit me to congratulate you on the glorious event, which I know will give you the most singular satisfaction. Nobody had it more at heart than you; nor has any person contributed more to bring it about. I honour you, as we all do, for your patriotic devotion. I send you our heart-felt thanks which will be echoed in every part of the state. Your name and your faith will endure as an inspiration."

Iredell lowered the paper and sat looking into the fire. Hannah took the letter out of his hands. "For Young Jemmy," she said. "A part of his inheritance."

Adam and Mary Rutledge stood with Sylvia and Angus at the edge of the Green in Edenton on the outskirts of a crowd that included most of the population of the village. There were men and women from the country-side as well, and from the counties across the Sound. For this tenth day of December 1789 had been chosen for celebration of North Carolina's acceptance of the Federal Constitution.

On the steps of the Courthouse Samuel Johnston stood ready to read the first proclamation of the new Governor of the state. The Assembly had chosen Johnston to represent North Carolina in the Senate of the United States. He had resigned the Governorship to accept the post, and Alexander Martin had been named to succeed him. In spite of ill health and the pressure of official duties Johnston had come from Fayetteville to take part in the Edenton celebration.

Johnston made an imposing figure as he stood on the steps above the assemblage—tall, slim, dignified—and the people cheered him lustily in an enthusiastic expression of their vast good will toward him and toward one another. A spirit of rejoicing pervaded the Albemarle on this day and extended throughout North Carolina. The Federalists were elated that their state was to take its place in the union, and most of the Antifederalists now felt confident of the nation's adoption of the proposed bill of rights.

Johnston quieted the cheering and unrolled the scroll handed to him by James Iredell. Four buglers at the sides of the Courthouse steps sounded a fanfare, and the Clerk of the Court raised his voice: "Oyez! Oyez! A Proclamation by His Excellency the Governor of North Carolina, Alexander Martin!"

In a deep voice Johnston began to read the ponderous opening phrases of the proclamation, and a dense quiet fell over the people standing on the Green.

Mary Rutledge surveyed the crowd with interest. Near by stood the

Barkers with Hannah Iredell and Nellie Blair. Beyond were Marcy and Mel Frazier. Stephen Cabarrus, Josiah Collins and Nat Allen stood among a group of artisans who had supported Adam in the Antifederalist cause. Planters, yeomen, craftsmen, lawyers, doctors—all were here.

As Johnston's voice boomed on she studied their faces, impressed by the seriousness of their expressions. This was not, Mary realized, a crowd of unthinking holiday-makers welcoming a break in the routine of their lives. They understood what had happened and why they were here, and each had a definite idea of what North Carolina's new status would mean to him. And this, Mary thought with a sudden glow of pride, was in part due to Adam's efforts to take the facts to the people.

A comprehension of Adam's dream for the government of this new nation swept over her—a nation in which every man would make a thoughtful contribution to the formation of policies, in which the actions of the government would reflect the opinions of all factions. In such a government it would be supremely important that no one group should be able to enforce its wishes on the others, so of course Adam had had to brave the disapproval of his planter friends to safeguard the rights of his western comrades. "We, the People," he had quoted so often. It seemed to her suddenly a proud and significant and hopeful phrase.

"'. . . the adoption of the Federal Constitution by the convention of this state, a most perfect model of a free government under Heaven,'" Johnston read resoundingly.

Cheers broke the silence, and the people stirred restlessly, aware of the increasing unseasonable heat of the day. Men removed arm capes or jackets and women pushed back their colourful woollen hoods of green or scarlet. As Johnston resumed his reading many people, disturbed by the heavy stillness in the air, turned to cast uneasy glances at the bank of dark clouds on the horizon.

"'Let hereafter the Federal and Antifederal names no longer be heard as a reproof. Let our citizens again embrace their northern and southern brethren, determined to stand or fall together, a glorious band of brothers, united against all enemies!'"

Again cheers interrupted the speaker, but Johnston raised a hand for silence and pressed on to the reverent conclusion.

"'May the God of Virtue and of Liberty, who has so remarkably led these states to sovereignty and independence, not forsake them or suffer them to fall a prey to foreign or domestic tyranny, but preserve the states in His Holy Keeping.

"'Signed, Alexander Martin, Governor of the Sovereign State of North Carolina.'"

The cheering and applause were thunderous as Johnston rolled up the scroll and stepped back. The band at the foot of the steps began to play, and the Clerk of the Court, abandoning his dignity, ran forward and shouted,

"Three cheers for North Carolina's first Senator!" Only those nearest the Courthouse could hear him, but they responded lustily, and the rest of the crowd joined in with a will. The cannon at the verge of the Green thundered its salute. The people moved toward the Courthouse and formed into a line to shake hands with Senator Johnston.

Adam left Mary with Penelope Barker while he pressed forward with Marcy and Mel Frazier to a place near the front of the line. When he came opposite Johnston there was a brief pause while the two men looked into each other's eyes. Then Johnston grasped Adam's extended hand. "We have both won, Adam," he said warmly. "Now we can work side by side to build the new nation."

"You express my most earnest wish, Senator," Adam said. "I am pleased you are to represent our state, and I wish you good fortune."

James Iredell hailed Adam at the foot of the Courthouse steps. "I'm glad you went forward, Adam. I saw how gratified Sam was. Some of Sam's friends and the village officials are to have luncheon with him in the Council Room. Won't you join us?"

Adam declined because of the threatening weather. "It has been a great day, Jemmy—one we've waited long to see."

Iredell smiled. "Yes, a great day indeed. We can hope now to see the end of diverging loyalties among our people. Peace at last among ourselves—and long may it continue!" The two men shook hands warmly, and then Iredell went inside.

Adam joined Mary, Sylvia and Angus, and they strolled toward Horniblow's, where they had left their carriage. The court-yard was a press of laughing, shouting men and boys, for Horniblow was opening a keg of ale. "Free ale, gentlemen," the innkeeper called cordially, "for drinking the health of the new Senator. And there's the new nation to be toasted as well!"

Sylvia followed Mary into the carriage, then turned and extended her hand to Angus. Her eyes were shining. "It was exciting, wasn't it? I'm glad we are to live here."

Angus raised her hand to his lips. "We'll begin our marriage with a nation that's beginning also. I've high hopes for both, my dearest. *Au revoir.* I'll come to Queen's Gift to-morrow." He bowed to Mary, placed his cocked hat firmly on his head and went into the tap-room.

A dozen voices called out to him as he entered, inviting him to vacant places at various tables. A feeling of warmth, of belonging came over him. The people of the village knew him now and liked him; they had accepted him as one of themselves. Dr. Armitage placed such confidence in Angus that he had accepted Dr. Williamson's invitation to visit New York, leaving his practice and Cupola House in Angus' care. And, now that Sylvia had received verification from Donald Hay of his marriage and his intention to make a settlement on her, Angus could look forward to bringing Sylvia home to Cupola House in a few weeks as his bride.

He saw Cosmo de' Medici standing near the door, wearing riding-clothes and a long scarlet-lined cape slung carelessly from his shoulders. Angus hailed him, and Cosmo smiled and crossed the room to join him. They found a table and ordered brandy.

"I'm pausing only for a few moments to break my journey," Cosmo said. "I've been to my place in Granville County, and now I'm bound for Bath. I stopped in the hope Stephen Cabarrus could give me word of my petition to the Assembly."

"Cabarrus is in town. I saw him earlier on the Green."

"I think all the Albemarle is in Edenton today," Cosmo said. "I was about to add that I have seen Cabarrus, too, and he told me he succeeded in getting my petition granted." He acknowledged Angus' congratulations with a smile. "Thank you, my friend. I am doubly gratified. First, I am pleased to have the money, which, frankly, I need. But equally I am glad our state will honour its war debts." He finished his brandy. "I wish I could linger, but it's time I was on my way again."

"You'd best stay for the celebration," Angus said. "There's to be dancing in the Panel Room to-night and a bonfire on the Green."

"I wish that I could, my friend, and I wish I could take time to visit Adam and Maria. Tell them for me I hope to be with them at Christmas time."

"You'll be in time, then, for my wedding," Angus said.

Cosmo raised his eyebrows. "Ah, so? To Miss Hay? All my congratulations, my good Moray! Patience and virtue are at last to be rewarded, eh? Remember—" he grinned—"remember, my friend, the time when you feared I might take her from you? But I knew even then she was the girl for you. I am happy for you, Moray, sincerely happy. And now I must be off."

"But the storm, De' Medici," Angus protested. "The natives think we'll have heavy weather before evening. Come to Cupola House with me. I'll give you a bed, and you can start in the morning."

"Thank you, but I can cover several miles by sundown, and I can always take shelter at one of the plantations on my way." Cosmo rose and saluted Angus. "But I'll be at Queen's Gift at Christmas to dance at your wedding!"

Hurricane

31 THE STORM still held off. Late in the afternoon the sky had turned a greenish yellow. Sun-dogs, faint but definite, radiated along the eastern horizon.

Old Ebon went about the house, closing the strong wooden shutters in the unoccupied bedrooms. "Mistress, de storm come in de night, big wind maybe."

Mary said, "Nonsense, Ebon! This is December. The hurricane season is past."

The old slave shook his white head. "Ma'am, dat's what dey say, but Ebon he know. He smell a big storm comin'. Chaney smell it too."

Mary turned to Adam, who had just come in. "Ebon says we are going to have a heavy wind-storm. It's too late in the season for a hurricane, isn't it?"

"I'd think so, but I don't like the sky colour or the look of the Sound. I've been at the stables. Mingo has put up all the shutters on the east windows. He and young Ben are moving the hounds from the open kennels to the old warehouse. Every cabin on the quarters line is preparing for a blow. The only answer I can get from the old ones is 'namondwe,' big storm. The witch woman is making a little altar and setting up her idols." He looked at Mary with troubled eyes. "We may as well prepare for a storm. I've asked Marcy to turn the horses loose. If we are in for a blow, I think they are safer in the fields."

Chaney entered the living-room and stood beside Ebon. "Goin' to whirlwind, mistress, maybe today, maybe to-morrow, but like big *namondwe* when Old Master lived. Blew and blew for three days." The woman was frightened. "Bad times. Some one not put offerings to Mungula, de great, great dead."

Mary said, "Chaney, be quiet! You'll set every servant in the house by the ears."

Chaney shook her head stubbornly. "De storm is a storm of wind. It come from de south. . . . It raise up de sea and de water against us. . . ." She folded her fat arms over her ample chest and began to sway from side to side.

"Master, de dust will rise to de sky, and de trees will bend and snap dey branches." With Chaney, Ebon swayed and muttered some African incantation.

Adam said sharply, "Be quiet, both of you! Chaney, go to your kitchen. Can't you see you are disturbing your mistress?"

Chaney went reluctantly. Ebon was close at her heels. It was as though they drew strength from each other.

Mary opened the hall door and stepped out onto the gallery. The sky was darkening. The strange greenish yellow seemed to rise from the horizon and fill the dome of heaven. An ugly dark cloud-bank lay on the horizon's rim.

"It won't do any harm to be prepared," Adam repeated. "There's something unaccountable, something eerie, that precedes a big storm. The air is still and heavy. A sort of strange silence pervades nature. The animals sense the unusual—the fowls in the chicken yard, the sheep in the fold, the horses huddled together in the field. The horses turn their backs to the south before ever the wind rises."

By supper-time Sylvia had caught the feeling of apprehension. Now and then she went to the gallery with Mary and Adam and tried to look through the darkness. Adam would return from the gallery shaking his head.

At ten o'clock when he came into the office, where they were sitting, he said, "The glass is falling rapidly. I'm glad we ran the sloop into the cove where there's good shelter."

"There's nothing we can do but sit it out," Mary said. "We might have a game of piquet till bedtime." The women sat down to play. Adam went out and this time did not come back.

After an hour Mary said, "I'm sure he and Marcy are at the stables, seeing that nothing has been left undone." She laid her cards on the table and made still another trip to the gallery. It was black night. She could not see even the outline of her giant tree. She reached out and touched a branch. It was still under her hand, as though the tree had lost the power of motion. The silence bore in on her and weighed her down. She turned swiftly to go into the house. A branch caught her hair and jerked her backward. She felt as though it were holding her, pulling her toward the naked trunk. With difficulty she loosened her hair. A kind of terror swept down upon her. The tree which she had considered her strength and vital source had turned her enemy. She ran for the light.

Sylvia sprang to her feet when Mary rushed in. "You are white as a ghost. What is it?"

Mary sank into a chair. Her knees would no longer hold her up. "I don't know. Something out there terrified me. The tree . . ." She made an effort to compose herself. "Let's go on with the game."

After a while Sylvia said, "It's no use. I can't keep my mind on the cards. I'm sorry. I keep thinking of Dr. Williamson's letter about poor Baron von Pollnitz. Angus feels as I do—he's the most put-upon man in the world. That woman bedevilled him until she got her hands on his money and involved him to such a degree that he'll be obliged to pay all her debts. And all the time she was carrying on with Sayre. I keep wondering if I should have told the Baron what I knew about her when he came to New York. At the time I was reluctant to meddle, but perhaps I should have."

"Sylvia, you could not have protected the Baron for ever," Mary said. "That woman would have ruined him in spite of anything you could do."

Sylvia got up and walked about the room. Her eyes were bright with sympathy. "Dr. Williamson says the Baron would have lost everything if it hadn't been for Mr. Alexander Hamilton. He managed to preserve the brick house and twenty-one acres of land she'd persuaded the Baron to buy."

"Where is Lady Anne now?"

"She embarked for England secretly, by way of France. Mr. Sayre was seen putting her on a French packet for L'Orient." Sylvia pushed her auburn hair back from her forehead. The emerald flashed in the candlelight.

The office was silent for a while. Then Sylvia continued. "Through Mr. Hamilton's influence the Baron was able to lease the house to General Knox. I suppose he has gone to London by now, poor man!" Sylvia realized that Mary had not been attending. She was at the door, her head tilted as though she were listening for some sound that was not there.

Chaney came in, took a stool and sat down on the far side of the room. She drew wool from her capacious pocket and began to knit. Sylvia saw the look of worry deepen on Mary's expressive face. Chaney said, "He come soon now. Devil he whippin' up he storm riders."

"Be quiet, Chaney!" Sylvia had never heard Mary speak so sharply to the old woman. Chaney did not seem to mind, but her needles abruptly stopped clicking. She looked up at Duke Roger's portrait and began to mumble.

Now at last Adam returned. Marcy was with him, and Herk followed them, carrying a bucket of water. Herk went to the fire-place and began to scoop out the water in his cupped hands. It hissed and steamed as it hit the blaze.

Adam said, "We've doused every fire in the quarters and in the bedrooms. The slaves are gathering in the big barn, singing hymns and praying." He wiped his brow with a large silk handkerchief.

Marcy said, "Do you think I'd better go down and stay with them? They'll be terrified when the storm comes."

"No, stay here. Flynn is with the Negroes. I wish the storm would come, if it's really coming. Look outside again, please. Is the wind rising?"

As Marcy opened the door one of the lights in the candelabrum blew out. The wind was rising indeed. Adam called to Herk to light lanthorns.

"Ready, sar. Right in de back hall."

"Fetch them in. Bring wraps for the ladies. It may be cold with no fire."

Marcy re-entered. "Lightning along the eastern horizon—incessant flashes. The wind grows powerful."

No one spoke. Ebon brought Mary's cape and one for Sylvia. For long minutes they sat in silence. Then there was a loud knocking at the door opening onto the gallery. When Adam opened the door it flung him back against the wall. Angus Moray flew past him, as though propelled by the wind.

When Angus almost literally blew into the office Sylvia uttered a cry and threw herself into his arms. "I've been praying for you to come. Oh, Angus!"

The wind was pouring through the open door. Papers were blown from the table. A gust caught the portrait of Duke Roger and hurled it half-way across the room. It smashed down on the back of a chair. A round knob pierced the canvas and cut it almost in two. Mary cried out in dismay.

Adam was calling for help. Marcy and Herk sprang forward. It took the combined strength of the three men to get the door shut.

Angus said, "Herk, they're using the big drum. I heard it."

"No, master, not de drum. It's de storm coming up de Sound."

Mary cried, "Listen! One of the doors upstairs has blown open." She raced out into the hall.

Chaney, close behind her, shouted, "Let me do it, honey. I'll close it."

The house shivered as Mary ran up the stairs, followed by Chancy and Ebon, and there were sounds of twisting timbers. Reaching the second-floor hall, they saw that the door leading to the upper gallery was pinned back against the wall by the force of the wind. Mary caught at the door, but she stumbled and a whirl of wind threw her out onto the gallery. Chancy charged after her, calling frantically, "Miss Mary! Miss Mary!" Ebon, struggling to reach them, skidded beyond them. Suddenly rain descended in sheets of driving water. There was a blinding flash of lightning, a deafening thunder-clap.

Violent splintering filled the ears. The great tulip poplar swayed and bent. Adam appeared on the gallery and caught up Mary in his arms. He pulled her back into the hall just before the broken tree fell along the length of the house. Its huge limbs shattered the gallery, and Chancy and Ebon were dragged down with it.

Somehow Marcy and Angus got the gallery door fastened. The steps that had connected the upper and lower galleries at the far end were still standing. Herk, hoping to rescue his two fellow slaves, got to the steps through a window. Even with his great strength he could not stand erect. He slid down the steps on his hunkers.

Everywhere about, branches were crackling and falling, and trees were being uprooted. The noise was like a battery of guns on a battlefield. It *was* a battle, the earth against the mighty host of heaven. Every blast shook the house.

Adam, keeping one arm about his hysterical wife and holding a lanthorn in his other hand, led the way down the main staircase. As they entered the cross-hall leading to the office a shuddering crash behind them and clouds of dust welling up around them announced that the entire east wing of the house, weakened by the impact of the great tree against it, had collapsed. Mary screamed, and Adam wondered desperately if the west wing in which they stood would be dragged down before they could escape. But the walls about them stood firm. Angus brought Sylvia from the office, and the two women clung to each other in terror while Adam and Marcy took lanthorns and went toward the entrance hall to inspect the damage.

Adam came back alone to report that beyond the drawing-room doorway there was only a gaping blackness, open to the raging wind and rain. Soon Marcy returned with Herk, who had searched out the bodies of Chaney and Ebon among the wreckage of the galleries and the foliage of the tree. "Dey both dead," he said quietly. "I feel of dem. Dey holdin' each other for comfort."

Mary, her own fear forgotten, repeated his words sadly. "Holding each other for comfort. God rest them, my faithful people!"

Herk urged Adam to take the women to the seldom-used basement dining-room for safety. And Adam agreed that the rest of the battered house could probably not continue to defy the wind. Marcy led them downstairs, holding a lanthorn high to light the way. Adam supported the weeping Mary, and Angus followed with Sylvia. Herk came last, his arms full of carriage robes to protect them against the dankness of the basement.

The long room was cold, and rain beat fiercely against the small high windows, but the noise of the storm was somewhat blunted. Angus cast a professional eye on Mary, who was sobbing hopelessly, and sent Herk upstairs for wine and his leather bag of medicines. He selected a powder and mixed a draught, which Mary swallowed without protest. Then he prepared a pallet for her on the long dining-table and persuaded her to lie down.

Mary was already in a heavy drugged sleep when the heaviest blast of all rocked the house. A tremendous tearing followed.

Marcy looked questioningly at Adam. "The roof?"

Adam nodded grimly. They heard it crash to earth somewhere down the avenue.

After a time Sylvia lay down on the table beside Mary and fell into a fitful sleep. The men sat on the floor, praying for the wind to slacken. Every gust brought destruction nearer. Once a heavy falling of bricks shook the floor above. In all minds was one hope—that they would not be buried under debris. More than once Adam stood up and examined the great heart-pine beams, twelve inches by twelve, put together with mortise-and-tenon joints that were held by two-inch pegs. Everything depended on the strength of these timbers. Praise God, they were built for strength!

With the first glimmer of false dawn Adam and Herk tried the door that opened directly onto the yard. The wind was no longer at full force, but a fallen timber was wedged against the door. They took some time to open it wide enough to squeeze through.

Rain beat against Adam until he was ready to cry out with the pain of it on his body. When he could look about him his stomach rose against his throat. Nausea almost overcame him as he viewed the monstrous havoc.

The avenue of cedars and holly was gone. The tangled roof lay across the gateway, blocking the road. Moray's horse had wandered away from the shelter and was sprawled grotesquely in the road, feet up. Chaney's kitchen was flat; its timbers were in splinters. The grounds were covered with limbs of trees—pine, cedar and oak—from small twigs to giant boughs. The garden had been whipped to shreds.

The two men struggled to the tulip poplar. Herk had placed the bodies of the faithful servants, arms entwined, in a sort of shelter beneath the fallen foliage. There was no horror in their faces, only peace. Now Herk covered them with a blanket he had brought for the purpose. Then he followed Adam to the quarters.

By some curious twist of fate the quarters line was outside the main path of the storm; the cabins were almost undisturbed. And untouched were the big barn where the slaves had taken refuge and the old warehouse where they had put the hounds.

Dead fowl—ducks, chickens and geese—lay all about. Some had been lifted into the trees and caught on high branches. Dead birds were everywhere. Adam noted a white heron and a wild turkey.

The stock had fared better. The horses were huddled at the edge of a little pine plantation.

Walking the path to the stables in the driving rain, Adam heard a pitiful dog-whimper. He pushed aside some branches and found Crossie, with a limb pinning her down. He picked her up in his arms. That of all his dogs this favourite hound had not been sheltered! One leg hung limp, but she nuzzled his face.

Marcy caught up with them. "By some miracle the bachelors' house escaped. Shall we move over there?"

Adam thought the idea good. He told Herk to go to the people, tell them they could return to their houses. When the sun rose the wind would be spent.

Angus Moray set Crossie's leg. He made a little splint from a stalk of cane that had blown from the garden.

Adam said, "I don't know how my wife will stand this. . . . All gone, all of Queen's Gift. Only the office is left standing."

Angus found no answer to that. He wondered himself how much Mary could endure. He went outside and walked about. Never had he seen more thorough destruction. When the storm had turned off the Sound, Queen's Gift had stood directly in its course. The old house had fought back with a stout heart, fought and lost, but there was a certain grandeur in complete defeat. No patchwork destruction this; a finished task of melancholy ruin.

The rain had stopped and the wind died down before Mary wakened from her drugged sleep. The men had left the cellar room, but Sylvia sat by her side, looking at her sympathetically. Mary sat up suddenly as she recognized her surroundings and recalled the events of the night. She slipped off the table and ran out through the open door.

She stood in the ravaged garden, surveying the ruins of the old house and the devastation that surrounded it. Sylvia approached, watching Mary anxiously.

"Is Adam safe?" Mary asked. "And Angus and Marcy?"

"All safe," Sylvia said. "And Angus says no one from the quarters line was hurt. On the whole plantation only . . ."

"Only Ebon and Chaney," Mary said. "Probably they would have preferred it. Their whole lives were given up to caring for this house. It would have broken their hearts to see it like this."

Marcy approached them. "Mr. Rutledge is inspecting the warehouses, ma'am. I'll tell him you're awake."

"No, don't interrupt him," Mary said quickly. "I'm quite all right. Are those the plantation ledgers you have?"

"Yes, ma'am, I'm taking them to the bachelors' house. Mr. Rutledge thinks the office may collapse. We've rescued your grandfather's picture, and—" he shifted the ledgers to one arm and reached into his pocket—"and this, ma'am." He handed her the little journal in which her grandfather had written his farewell letter to his son. "I thought you would want to have it."

"Thank you, Marcy. I am very grateful. I was thinking of this book just now." She opened it and glanced at a page or two, then looked up. "Is the bachelors' house unharmed?"

"Yes, ma'am. The windows on the Sound side were broken, but nothing more serious. We are fitting up rooms for you there."

"Good. Let's go inside, Sylvia. I think there's going to be more rain, and I'd rather not see any more of the plantation just now." Mary slipped an arm about Sylvia's waist. "I'm sorry we can't have your wedding here, my dear. It will have to be St. Paul's, I suppose. I wonder what the storm did to the village."

When Adam came to the bachelors' house in search of Mary he found her sitting by the fire in Marcy's apartment with the vellum-bound journal open in her lap. She looked small and tired and defenceless, and his heart ached at the thought of the pain she must be feeling.

He crossed the room and knelt beside her chair. "Mary, this isn't the end of Queen's Gift," he said swiftly. "The house is gone, but the land remains. We can build a new house, plant more trees——" He broke off in surprise as he saw that she was smiling.

She put out her hand and smoothed a lock of hair back from his forehead. "Thank you, Adam. I shall always remember with gratitude what you have said. But we'll build no new house here." She picked up the book from her lap. "Look, Adam, this is the journal from the package Captain Meredith brought from Antigua. I never gave it to you to read, did I? I should have, for you would have seen at once what Duke Roger meant—the message that is his final gift to me."

She looked toward the window and the shell of her grandfather's house. "When I read it before I found only the words for which I was searching—'Love Queen's Gift and the Albemarle as I have loved them, never abandon them.' But this morning I find a different message, the true meaning of his words: 'Go forward with the husband you love and face bravely the life he chooses for you.' "

Adam was bewildered. "Duke Roger wrote this to you? But——"

She laughed at his confusion. "Read it and you will understand."

Adam sat on the arm of her chair, and together they read the words Duke Roger had penned so many years before. " 'Never fear change,' " Adam quoted aloud as they reached the end of the letter. " 'Move forward to find your destiny.' "

"Your destiny is in the Illinois country, as you've long known," Mary said. "And my destiny is to follow where you lead me. I have tried to cling to the Albemarle just as Roger's Mary clung to the security of England. She and I were both wrong, but I have found out in time."

"And you'll really come with me?" Adam asked. "You'll help me make a new home in Illinois?"

"I could never have let you leave me behind," she answered, looking up into his face. "I would have gone with you, Adam. But now I can go gladly, without looking backward, for with me I shall take Duke Roger's blessing."

After a time they left the bachelors' house. By the ruins of the big house Angus Moray and Sylvia stood watching the slaves searching the wreckage under Marcy's direction for objects which had survived and might find a place in a new house. As Adam and Mary watched, Angus put his arm about Sylvia's waist, and she looked up into his eyes.

Mary and Adam exchanged a smile. They turned and made their way toward the Sound, walking around the trunks of fallen trees, stepping over tangled vines and splintered branches. At last they reached the little cove where the sloop lay serenely at anchor. The unruffled waters of the Sound before them belied the havoc and disorder they had passed through.

Twice before, Mary thought, she and Adam had come to this spot at crises in their lives. After the battle of Yorktown they had stood here and planned their marriage, vowing to make Queen's Gift the most beautiful and most productive of the Albemarle plantations. And after Hillsborough she had sat here listening with anguish to the words that told her Adam had broken away from the life she cherished. Now the plantation lay in ruins behind them, but behind them also were the days of estrangement and misunderstanding.

Adam looked down at her. "You have loved this land a long time, Mary. Can you really turn away from it without sorrow?"

She smiled confidently. "I shall always love it, always remember the happiness I've known here. But there will be others who will find their destiny in the Albemarle, and they will love it and work for it as Duke Roger did and as we have done."

They sat in silence, watching the sun sink beyond the western horizon. A wedge of ducks flew past along the Sound, and a blue heron waded out from the bank and thrust his long neck into the water. From the forest came the scent of bracken and damp leaves, a rich dank odor redolent of the earth's fecundity and the distant promise of spring.

THE END

NOTES ON THE WORTHIES OF EDENTON
AND LADY ANNE STUART

JAMES IREDELL was appointed Associate Justice of the United States Supreme Court by President Washington. Born in England of a noble family, he became a lawyer and judge of great ability. The *Marcus* pamphlet, a brilliant reply to Mason's objections to the Constitution, was widely read and highly praised. In 1787 he was entrusted with the task of revising the laws of North Carolina. His son James became Governor of the state. The Iredell home, now a State Historical Shrine, is under the trusteeship of the Edenton Tea Party Chapter of the Daughters of the American Revolution.

JOSEPH HEWES, a signer of the Declaration of Independence, served in the Continental Congress and was chairman of the Committee of Maritime Affairs. He could not speak like Adams and Lee or write like Jefferson, but he knew where to get the sinews of war. As patron of John Paul Jones he found ships and advanced money to buy ships for the new Navy. He died in Philadelphia in 1779.

THOMAS BARKER was as generous as a man as he was able as a lawyer. He was one of four commissioners appointed to revise the statutes in 1746. He was an early friend and legal instructor of Governor Samuel Johnston.

ROBERT SMITH was an attorney, mercantile partner of Joseph Hewes and a lieutenant in Colonel Howe's regiment. He represented Edenton in the State Commons, 1780-1781.

CHARLES JOHNSON was a member of the State Senate, 1781-1784 and 1790-1792, a delegate to the Continental Congress in 1781 and vice-president of the Hillsborough and Fayetteville conventions. He also served as a United States Senator. He lived at Strawberry Hill, on the outskirts of Edenton. His wife was a daughter of Parson Daniel Earle of Bandon Plantation, and about 1800 he built the present house at Bandon on the site of an earlier house.

STEPHEN CABARRUS was a nephew of the Spanish banker Cabarrus of Paris. During 1783-1787 he was a member of the Commons from the Borough of Edenton and subsequently represented Chowan County in the same body, 1788-1793 and 1801-1804. His home, Pembroke Plantation on Pembroke Creek, is now owned by the United States Department of the Interior, Fishery Division.

SAMUEL JOHNSTON was twice elected Governor of North Carolina and was one of the first United States Senators from that state. He was a nephew of Royal Governor Gabriel Johnston, called the ablest of Colonial Governors for the Province of North Carolina. His seat, Hayes, was named after Hayes Barton, Sir Walter Raleigh's home in Devonshire.

DR. HUGH WILLIAMSON, statesman and scientist, was a signer of the Constitution for North Carolina, as shown in Howard Chandler Christy's painting of this historic event which hangs on a stair landing in the House of Representatives wing in the Capitol, Washington, D. C. As a delegate to the Fayetteville Convention he urged ratification of the Constitution and subsequently represented his state in the Congress of the United States.

LADY ANNE STUART and the Baron von Pollnitz actually came to Edenton a few years earlier than this story. The last we hear of that turbulent but beautiful lady is contained in a letter from the Baron to James Iredell, a portion of which reads:

Since This it is regulated that L Anne is nothing more to me in this world; Mr. Sayre sits for debts in King's Bench L Anne has voluntarily followed him to This Place, By ruining my fortune, the Duke is freed from what he Dreaded viz to account in Parliam^t for his Conduct of Deceiving the House, and as L Anne is now deserted by every one of her relations, The Duke has dropt her no longer useful ackwaintance.